GREEN DOLPHIN COUNTRY

Green Dolphin Country was written at
Providence Cottage, Westerland, in
Devonshire, and completed in 1944. It was
published both in England and in the
United States of America in the same year.
The American Literary Guild acknowledged
it the Book of the Year, and Metro-
Goldwyn-Mayer Pictures hailed it the best
novel. Well over half a million copies have
been sold.

Other books by the same author

The Scent of Water
A City of Bells
Gentian Hill
Island Magic
The White Witch
The Heart of the Family
The Dean's Watch
The Bird in the Tree
The Herb of Grace
The Castle on the Hill
The Rosemary Tree
A Book of Peace
The Middle Window

and available in Paperback

Green Dolphin Country

Elizabeth Goudge

CORONET BOOKS
Hodder Paperbacks Ltd., London

Copyright © 1944 Elizabeth Goudge
First Published, November 1944
Coronet edition, 1961
Second Impression, 1966
Third Impression, 1966
Fourth Impression, 1967
Fifth Impression, 1968
Sixth Impression 1972

Printed in Great Britain
for Coronet Books, Hodder Paperbacks Ltd.,
St. Paul's House, Warwick Lane, London, E.C.4,
by Richard Clay (The Chaucer Press), Ltd.,
Bungay, Suffolk.

ISBN 0 340 15105 6

NOTE

Though this book is fiction, and the characters not portraits, it is based on fact. That a man who had emigrated to the New World should after the lapse of years write home for a bride, and then get the wrong one because he had confused her name with that of her sister, may seem to the reader highly improbable; yet it happened. And in real life also the man held his tongue about his mistake and made a good job of his marriage.

The Convent of Notre Dame du Castel has no existence in actual fact, though it is true that monks from Mont Saint Michel crossed the sea in their frail little boats and founded a hermitage on the island of Guernsey. Le Creux des Fâïes exists today, and the footprints of the fairy Abbesses are still to be found imprinted on the rock, and Marie-Tape-Tout still guides fishermen home.

To all lovers of New Zealand it will be immediately obvious that the writer has never been there, and she most humbly asks their pardon for the many mistakes she must have made. She would also like to acknowledge her debt to "Old New Zealand" by F. E. Maning.

BOOK ONE
THE FIRST ISLAND

BOOK TWO
THE SECOND ISLAND

BOOK THREE
THE WORLD'S END

BOOK FOUR
THE COUNTRY OF
THE GREEN PASTURES

Three deep cravings of the self, three great expressions of man's restlessness, which only mystic truth can fully satisfy. The first is the craving which makes him a pilgrim and a wanderer. It is the longing to go out from his normal world in search of a lost home, a "better country"; an Eldorado, a Sarras, a Heavenly Syon. The next is the craving of heart for heart, of the soul for its perfect mate, which makes him a lover. The third is the craving for inward purity and perfection, which makes him an ascetic, and in the last resort a saint.—EVELYN UNDERHILL.

BOOK ONE
THE FIRST ISLAND

PART I

MARIANNE

Strangers and pilgrims on the earth . . . seek a country. And truly, if they had been mindful of that country from whence they came out, they might have had opportunity to have returned. But now they desire a better country, that is, an heavenly: wherefore God is not ashamed to be called their God: for he hath prepared for them a city.—EPISTLE TO THE HEBREWS.

CHAPTER ONE

1

Sophie Le Patourel was reading aloud to her two daughters from the Book of Ruth, as they lay prostrate upon their backboards, digesting their dinners and improving their deportment. This spending of the after-dinner hour upon their backboards instead of in the parlour was as a matter of fact a punishment for insubordination during the morning, but their Papa being from home Sophie was softening the punishment by reading aloud. She was an indulgent mother, adoring her children, anxious to keep them with her as long as possible, afraid of what might be done to them by the great world outside the schoolroom window, the great world that in this mid-nineteenth-century horrified her with its bustle and vulgarity and noise, George Stephenson's terrible steam engine hurtling people to destruction at twenty-five miles an hour, its dreadful balloons in which man in his profanity was daring the heavens in which it was never the intention of his Creator that he should disport himself, its restless young people with thoughts for ever straining towards new countries and new ways, and its insubordinate children like her daughter Marianne.

Not that Sophie had ever seen a steam engine or a balloon, for she lived in a remote island in the stormiest part of the English Channel, to which as yet, by the mercy of heaven, such modern horrors had not penetrated, but she had read about them and she experienced what might be called the backwash of modernity in the person of her eldest child Marianne, prostrate before her at this moment on her backboard, her hungry black eyes gazing out of the window at the wild tossing of the autumn sea, her lips set in a hard thin line and her mind somewhere far away, in the far place where her longings were; and where that was exactly neither she nor her mother knew.

"Et Horpa prit congé de sa belle-mère; mais Ruth demeura avec elle," read Sophie in her slow beautiful French. "Alors Naomi dit: Voici, ta belle-soeur s'en est retournée vers son peuple et vers ses dieux; retourne t'en après ta belle-soeur." Sensible Naomi! That was the advice she would have given herself, she thought. She liked people to stick to the old homes and the old ways, she didn't hold with all this dashing off to new countries; even though in Ruth's case it had turned out quite satisfactory. If only these restless young people could see it, all that they longed for was close beside them in the homes that had given them birth. But they couldn't see it. They were old before their eyes were opened. "Retournée vers son peuple et vers ses dieux," she repeated, savouring the words. She always read the Bible to the children in French even though she talked to them in English. In this bilingual Island, English by conquest but French in spirit, English was coming slowly to the fore as the medium of intercourse among the élite, but French had been the language of her own childhood and she turned back to it instinctively when she prayed or read God's word. "Mais Ruth répondit: Ne me prie point de te laisser, pour m'éloigner de toi; car j'irai où tu iras, et je demeurerai où tu demeureras; ton peuple sera mon peuple, et ton Dieu sera mon Dieu; je mourrai où tu mourras, et j'y serai ensevelie. Que l'Eternel me traite avec la dernière rigueur, si jamais rien te sépare de moi que la mort."

Marianne suddenly sat up and turned a transfigured face towards her mother. The hunger was gone from her eyes and her lips curved into the lovely smile that was seen so rarely. She was having what her family called one of her "moments". Something had touched and pleased her deeply, and for a brief second her hunger was satisfied. Her mother paused in her reading and smiled at her, trying with her sympathy to prolong Marianne's momentary joy in the stirring words. But it passed quickly, as it always did, and her eyes left her mother's face and went back to the sea.

"The mails are in," she said abruptly. "The packet is coming into harbour."

That was just like Marianne, thought her mother in exasperation. The moment one tried to sympathise with her she swerved away from one's sympathy like a shying horse. Never was there a girl who needed understanding so much, yet it was difficult to come close enough to her to achieve it. She shut herself up in a sort of box. Mon Dieu, but children are difficult, thought Sophie. And now Marguerite was sitting up too, the little monkey! Why could she never get her children in hand as other mothers did? Was she a weak mother, or were they unusually insubordinate children?

"I see the packet too!" shrilled Marguerite. "I can see the top of the mast and it's swaying about like anything. I wonder who's come on the packet? My, but they must have been sea-sick!"

"Lie down, children!" commanded Sophie. "Lie down at once! How many more times am I to tell you that you must not move during your hour upon the backboards? This perpetual popping up and down ruins your deportment. Lie down!"

But they continued to sit up, both of them gazing spellbound at the distant ship, as though the perfectly commonplace arrival of the packet were of immense importance to them.

"Children, if you do not lie down I shall be obliged to tell your Papa of your disobedience."

They lay down, Marianne looking like an obstinate mule and Marguerite like a naughty kitten. They were always like this when it was blowing up for a storm. The wind seemed to get into their blood. She had no doubt that they would be up to something really naughty before the day was over. She sighed as she recomposed herself and sought for the lost place upon the page.

"Naomi, voyant donc qu'elle était résolue d'aller avec elle, cessa de lui en parler." Naomi was as incapable of controlling Ruth, evidently, as she of managing her own daughters. As she read mechanically on her thoughts were tormentingly busy with Marianne. How this child could be the offspring of herself and Octavius she couldn't imagine. She herself was a fair-haired, blue-eyed, gently dignified, becomingly rounded creature, affectionate and conventionally minded, and her husband Octavius, handsome, worthy, affable, was in appearance and character exactly suited to the position in life to which it had pleased the Almighty to call him; he was the leading solicitor of the Island, the wholly trustworthy repository of its secrets, its best man of business, the most able speaker in its Parliament, the friend of the Bailiff and the Governor, one of its most devout Churchmen, highly respected both by himself and others.

Whence, then, Marianne?

There was nothing in her immediate ancestry to account for her. There was no explaining her except by the theory that some fierce spark of endeavour, lit by a forgotten pioneer ancestor, had lived on in the contented stuff of succeeding generations until the wind of a new age whipped it into a flame that was called Marianne Le Patourel. . . . Or by the theory propounded by the peasant nurse of her babyhood, who had vowed she was a changeling.

Her mother, as always, was almost painfully aware of Marianne as she sat very upright in her chair by the wood fire and read aloud from the Book of Ruth. She knew her Bible so well that though her beautifully modulated voice never failed to give appropriate expression to the lines she read her thoughts could be meanwhile entirely absent, fixed upon Marianne. And though her eyes were upon her book what they saw was not the printed page but the superimposed image of her elder child.

Marianne was an elfin creature of sixteen, totally without the beauty that distinguished her parents. She ought now to have been rounding out a little into the contours of womanhood, yet her body remained as thin and brown as it had always been, a boy's body without grace or softness, its angularities, pushing their way even through four cascading lace-trimmed petticoats, lace-trimmed pantaloons and a wide-skirted frock of stiff corded maroon silk. Her hair was dark and heavy and came out of curl upon the slightest provocation. There might have been beauty in her black eyes had they not been so needle sharp under the heavy black brows that so over-weighted her tiny sallow face, and so full of a hunger that disturbed one in the eyes of so young a girl. The small indomitable chin disturbed one too, and the lips folded in so mature a repression of her passionate temper, and the brain that was too quick and hard and brilliant for her years and sex.

Her parents were much exercised over this brain of Marianne's and were doing their best to repress it within lady-like proportions. But Marianne wouldn't be interested in sensible things like crewel work and watercolour painting and duet-playing on the pianoforte with her little sister Marguerite, even though she did all those things superlatively well. That was the trouble with Marianne, she did them too well, and her restless intellect reached out beyond them to things like mathematics and the politics of the Island Parliament, farming, fishing and sailing, knowledge that was neither attractive nor necessary in a woman and would add nothing whatever to her chances of attracting a suitable husband; chances that Sophie was already beginning to realise would need all the bolstering that could possibly be given to them by skilful presentation and attractive background if Marianne were not to die an old maid. But would Marianne ever allow herself to be skilfully presented? The chic, petite, vivacious brunette that her mother was perpetually striving to coax forth was perpetually shrugged off again by the tempers and sullen reservations of this appalling child, and the carefully spread background of wealth and gentility seemed to splinter into fragments every time Marianne lost her temper. There was no doing anything with so obstinate a creature. Whenever in the night watches Sophie considered her elder daughter's chances of happiness her pillow was wet with her tears. She had borne this child in rebellion to a man she did not love and had endured agonies at her premature and turbulent entry into this world on a night of wind and rain that was the farewell to the stormiest winter the Island had ever known, and like every mother she wanted her pain to be cancelled by the joy of her child; but the pain lived on in the realisation that Marianne's stormy highly-strung temperament would be impossible to train in the accustomed ways of joy. . . . And of the other ways her mother was ignorant.

She wept no tears over eleven-year-old Marguerite. That dimpled fragment of humanity had been the child of a woman reconciled, and had waited patiently for the correct date before making as modest and graceful an appearance as is possible in the circumstances of human birth. From the beginning she had given little trouble, for her naughtiness was only the normal naughtiness of a healthy child and she had always been more or less explainable. She had taken to herself her mother's fair beauty and as much and no more of her father's intelligence as it was desirable that a pretty child should have, and to them some good fairy had added something else, the best of all gifts, the power of enjoyment, not just animal enjoyment of good health and good spirits but that authentic love of life that sees good days. "He that would love life and see good days, let him refrain his tongue from evil and his lips that they speak no guile: let him eschew evil, and do good; let him seek peace and ensue it." Though she didn't know it that was the kind of person Marguerite had had the good fortune to be born. She had that transparent honesty and purity and serenity that like clear water flooding over the bed of a stream washes away uncleanness and makes fresh and divinely lovely all that is seen through its own transparency. We see the world through the medium of our own characters, and Marguerite saw and loved all things through her own bright clarity, and enjoyed them enormously. She had not got this clearness of happy sight from her mother, whose vision was always a little clouded by anxiety, nor from her father, whose sense of the importance of his activities kept his vision strictly limited to them. Perhaps it had come from the sheer happy loveliness of the Island spring and summer through whose months her mother had waited tranquilly for her birth. Wherever it had come from Sophie had only to cast one glance at her dimpled happy beauty to have all maternal worries instantly allayed. For just a moment, the face and form of her younger child taking the place of Marianne's upon the printed page, Sophie saw the little plump figure in voluminous rose-pink tarlatan stretched upon the backboard, the golden hair an aureole about the rosy face, the soft lips parted in eagerness, the shining blue eyes fixed upon her mother's face as the lovely history of Ruth and Boaz (so carefully edited by Sophie as she read that her children had no idea she was showing more delicacy in narration than the original historian) soaked into her through every pore. No, there was no need to worry about Marguerite. She was absolutely adorable, and throughout life she would be adored.

The clock struck. Sophie closed her book and the two girls shot up upon their backboards as though released by a spring.

"Please, Mamma, may we go out?" cried Marguerite eagerly. With the closing of the Bible the Book of Ruth had lost its grip upon her rapt attention and she was already enjoying in anticipation the buffeting of the autumn wind that swept to them across the Atlantic, tasting its salt on her lips and feeling the tug of it in her hair.

Sophie hesitated. It was Saturday, when she gave them more freedom than upon other days, the rain that had kept them in that morning and made them troublesome in consequence had ceased and fresh air would do them good before bed. Yet for some reason or other she felt loath to let them go out into the autumn gale, used as they were to tempestuous weather.

"Must you go out?" she asked.

"Please, please, darling Mamma!" cried Marguerite in her warm eager voice.

"I think it would be advisable, Mamma," said Marianne. "We need the exercise."

She spoke primly in her quiet, hard little voice, her clear brain leading her to make unerring attack upon the maternal sense of duty rather than the maternal affections, her mother being to her knowledge a deeply conscientious woman.

"Not beyond the garden, then," said Sophie, temporising. For what harm could come to them in the garden? Sheltered by its high walls they would not even feel that fierce exciting wind. "And put on your cloaks and bonnets, for it may turn chilly at the turn of the tide."

"Yes, Mamma. Come along, Marguerite." And the pit-pat of Marianne's small determined feet and of Marguerite's eager ones died away down the passage to the room that had once been the night nursery and was now their bedroom.

Sophie stayed at the window, looking down at the tossing world below her. Their house, a very old one that Octavius had bought at his marriage from an old sea-captain, was in Le Paradis, the most aristocratic street on the Island, built high up in the rock citadel of

Saint Pierre, the Island's only town, with the streets of the vulgar far down below it, as was only proper. All the élite lived in Le Paradis, and so of course it was the natural habitat of the Le Patourels. And it was a nice place to live. The houses faced each other across the narrow cobbled street, steep and twisting like a gully in the rock because Saint Pierre was built upon the sheer precipitous face of the granite cliff and partook of the nature of the rock to which it held. But their propinquity did not detract from the dignity and beauty of the tall old houses. The granite walls, built to stand as enduringly against the gales as the cliff itself, had been covered with pink stucco a century ago, and with the passing of the years the pink had weathered to every conceivable lovely shade of saffron, orange, yellow and old gold. Flights of shallow steps, scrubbed to a spotless white, flanked by fluted columns and beautiful iron railings and lantern holders, led up to handsome front doors with brass knockers beneath elegant fanlights, the windows were shuttered in the French style and the old tiled roofs had weathered to colours that equalled the stuccoed fronts in beauty. In front of the area railings, flanking the white steps and the fluted columns, grew the hydrangeas that were the glory of the Island, pink and blue, grown to amazing luxuriance in the sheltered sunny warmth of the lovely street, and seen through opening front doors on summer days, through a vista of shining oak-panelled passage leading to garden doors set wide to the scent and colour, were the old deep gardens with their velvety lawns, their roses and jessamines and great magnolia trees, their myrtle and veronica bushes and lavender hedges, and tangled vines upon the sheltering granite walls.

In the sunny sheltered street, or in the high-walled gardens, or downstairs in the snug panelled parlours, one could forget that one lived on a sea-girt island, for the roaring of the wind on stormy days was heard only as a distant rumour, but in the upstairs rooms that looked towards the harbour and the sea it was another matter, and it was at the window of such a room that Sophie was standing.

Below the sheltered garden, where the wax of the magnolia blossoms was still untarnished and the chrysanthemums and dahlias were like flames against the vivid green of the lawns, the narrow streets and the tumbled roofs of Saint Pierre fell steeply to the sea. From the aloof height of Le Paradis Saint Pierre looked not quite real, crushed to nothingness by the immensity of sea and sky around it. The narrow twisting cobbled lanes, the steep flights of steps, the old granite houses with their gables and protruding upper stories, the bow-windowed shops and the inns with their swinging signs, the tall church tower, the long sea wall guarded by the breakwaters and the grey mass of the fort, the masts of ships sheltering within the harbour, were dwarfed to the semblance of a dream town whose fragility caught at the heart. One feared for it in the violence of the forces that assailed it. Torn fragments of smoke whirled above it as though panic-stricken, the branches of trees that rose higher than the sheltering garden walls tossed as though in anguish, white waves dashed themselves against the breakwaters and showers of spray reached for the little town with clutching fingers; and round about as far as the eye could see white horses rode ceaselessly in over the grey labour and surge of the sea, and low grey clouds, mounting unendingly from below the horizon of the world, streamed overhead like the grey phantoms of terrible things that were yet to come upon the earth. . . . This was no world in which to let loose little children.

Sophie pulled herself up sharply. She was being ridiculously fanciful. The terror of natural forces was an illusory terror, for the spirit of man was always greater than they. For centuries the onslaught of the sea had not loosened the grip upon the rock of the small grey town that man had built; it had done nothing to it except immeasurably to increase its beauty by the buffetings. No shapes of doom, no torture, no fear, had chased man away yet from the tiny whirling star to which his spirit clung as tenaciously as did Saint Pierre to the rock. Why? Why? Why? thought Sophie suddenly. Why this obstinate refusal to be exterminated? Why such cheerful willingness to feed the flame of life with individual agony? One didn't know. One couldn't know. Only God knew, who had breathed human life into the void, and wondering whatever could have possessed Him to do such a thing only gave Sophie a headache. She didn't hold with metaphysical speculation, and always deliberately turned her thoughts when overtaken by it. Better not look at the wind and weather. Better look at the hackney coach toiling up the narrow street below her garden wall. Who was in it? That was the kind of curiosity that was really enjoyable, for one had some hope of satisfying it. So immersed in the coach was she that she paid no attention to the words that had slipped into her soul from somewhere or other and were tolling there like a deep-toned bell. "Be ye perfect. . . . Be ye perfect. . . . Be ye perfect."

Who *was* in that coach? Someone who had arrived on the packet no doubt. She too, though of course she hadn't let Marianne know it, had wondered who was on board the packet to-day. It sailed from England only twice a week, and these two voyages, and the weekly voyage of a French packet from Saint Malo, were the only contacts the Island had with the great world, so naturally it was a matter of burning interest, when the anchor rattled down and the sails were furled, to see what came up out of the hold and who walked across the gang-plank. There were no telegrams then. Knowledge of wars and revolutions, of royal weddings, of Stephenson's newly invented steam engine, of discoveries in far countries, news of the loves and deaths of friends and of new fashions in gowns and bonnets and cloaks, all came up out of the hold of the packet as out of Pandora's box of dreams. And the storm-buffeted figures who crossed the gang-plank were even more exciting. If they were old friends there would be the joy of reunion after long absence and danger, and if they were strangers then they might change the current of one's life for ever.

Who was in that hackney coach?

It stopped before the old empty house in Green Dolphin Street, just below the Le Patourels' garden wall. Why, of course! It would be Dr. Ozanne. Edmond Ozanne come home again after twenty-five years of exile. He had left the Island as a young man to study medicine in London, had married and settled there. Rumour had it that his wife had been exceedingly well born and genteel, but possessed of delicate health and an extreme sensibility that had caused her in the first place to cling to his medical knowledge and dote upon his good looks, but in the second place to be disillusioned by the efficacy of that knowledge when applied to her own symptoms, and to be much tried by his rough and ready manners. The latter she must have attributed to his upbringing on a remote and savage island, for she had steadfastly refused to visit the place responsible for them, or to permit him to visit it without her. They had not been very happy, it seemed, and had had only one child, born late in their married life. Now the poor lady was dead and he had come back to the Island again with his child to set up his plate in Green Dolphin Street. This information Sophie had gathered with difficulty, but perseverance, because when she had been eighteen and Edmond twenty, they had sometimes walked up and down beside the sea wall together, her hand in his, and looked out over the sea and talked of the great things he would do when he sailed away to England, and of how when he was a rich man he would come back to the Island and marry her. But he hadn't come back, and after some years of spinsterhood, because none of the aspirants for her hand seemed quite right somehow, she had married Octavius, and after a short period of misery had not regretted it. No one had known about those strolls beside the sea wall because the two families, Edmond's and hers, had not been socially known to each other. Edmond's parents had been respectable people, of an old Island family, but they had been In Trade; the Wine Trade, which of course holds a certain cachet, but still, Trade. The Ozannes and her own people, the du Putrons, had bowed to each other in the street, but no more. Well, it would be possible to know Edmond socially now, since he had become a doctor. Doctors ranked with solicitors and clergymen as People Whom One Knew. Their profession put the hall-mark of a gentleman upon them and one closed an eye to what their parents had been. One must close this eye at some period in man's social ascent, of course, otherwise, with the birthrate of the lower orders tending to be higher than that of the upper classes, gentlemen would die out. . . . But she must be very careful, before committing herself in any way, to find out what sort of man Edmond had turned into, and what his child was like, for she had her daughters to consider, and the child was a boy.

A cloaked figure stepped out of the hackney coach, clutching a large brass cage with a green parrot in it, but his hat was pulled so far down over his face that though she leaned swiftly forward, breathing childishly upon the window pane in her eagerness, it was impossible to see what he looked like, now. He was followed by a small boy, who gave a hop, skip and a jump as he left the coach, and carried a carpet bag. They went into the house, the coachman staggering after with their luggage, and the door banged behind them in a sudden gust of wind that rattled the schoolroom windows and roared furiously in the chimney. Sophie was suddenly scared again, and ashamed of the way she had breathed upon the window pane. She rubbed the mist off with her handkerchief and wished she had not said the girls might go out into the garden.

But here they were beside her in their cloaks and bonnets, bright-eyed with expectation. "Good-bye, Mamma!" they cried. "Good-bye!" And they had whirled off down the stairs before she could stop them.

2

There is something very thrilling about standing in a place of shelter while a gale roars by over your head. One tastes the excitement of violence without the fear. Standing beside the herbaceous border under the west wall the air was as still as on a summer's day. Not a petal moved, not a grass blade was stirred, while all about them the October flowers had a brilliance that summer had scarcely known. The massed michaelmas daisies and golden-rod, the dahlias and chrysanthemums, purple and scarlet and gold, seemed to burn with deeper and deeper passion as one looked at them, and the lawn after the morning's rain wore a green so vivid that one caught one's breath. A bonfire of dead leaves was burning in the corner of the garden and the acrid smell of its blue smoke, mingled with the smell of wet chrysanthemums and the west wind from the sea, was the authentic bitter-sweet smell of the turning of the year. There was something triumphant about the blaze of colour, something of fortitude in the determined quiet under the garden wall, that mocked at dissolution. The gale might roar as it chose but while that west wall of solid granite stood its ground the end was not yet for the garden. Life was not so easily extinguished and spring trod upon winter's heels. It flaunted its colours in the face of death and it laughed under its breath.

And Marguerite laughed too, extracting every drop of colour and scent and joy from the scene about her. Her face was rosy with pleasure in the depths of her brown beaver bonnet with its lining of quilted pink silk, and her brown caped cloak with its rosettes of rose-coloured ribbon could not hide the quivering excitement of her body. Her fair curls were already tossed and untidy and the bow of pink ribbon under her chin had come undone. She waved the folds of her cloak up and down like wings and swung laughing from her toes to her heels, back and forth, back and forth, like an intoxicated little bird rocking uproariously on a swaying branch. She did not want to go to any other place, or do anything except what she was doing, or be any other person. She was utterly contented in the place and the hour and the mere fact of her own existence. She lived. That was enough.

Marianne did not jig about like her little sister. She stood without movement on the garden path, waiting. She was dressed like Marguerite in a caped cloak with a beaver bonnet, only the rosettes on her cloak were brown, not pink, and the quilted lining of her bonnet was maroon like her dress. Sophie could not dress her in youthful colours for they made her look more sallow than ever. Her bonnet strings were precisely tied and her hands quite still under her cloak. She was always very tidy, which her mother thought odd in so passionate a creature, while Marguerite always had ribbons streaming and curls tossed in joyous disarray, but her tidiness was part of her intensity, part of the knitting together of body and mind and soul upon the one purpose.

Which at the moment was to get out of the garden into the exciting tempestuous world beyond the west wall. She waited until her mother, watching them from the parlour window, had turned away to write at her escritoire, and then she withdrew her right hand from her cloak and in it was the key of the door behind the magnolia bush, that led through the west wall to Green Dolphin Street, which she had taken from its hook in the hall as they came out.

"But Mamma said to stay in the garden," said Marguerite, wide-eyed, for her essential honesty was already a little prone to misgivings about the artifices to which Marianne was always prepared to stoop to get her way.

Marianne made no answer but dived behind the magnolia bush and unlocked the door. Marguerite followed her, silent at first, then with a gleeful chuckle at the adventurousness of the proceeding. For though she was a good child she was not abnormally good. No one ever felt any anxiety about her dying young, in spite of the angelic loveliness of her dimpled face.

The door nearly knocked them over as it swung back with the whole force of the wind behind it, and for a moment the storm, rushing through, invaded the serenity of the garden. The branches of the magnolia tree thrashed wildly, the great waxen blossoms buffeting their faces. The wind rushed up under their skirts, whipped their pantaloons about their ankles and swirled among their petticoats. It ripped Marguerite's bonnet off her golden curls and blew Marianne's cloak right up over her head. Laughing, they clutched each other to keep steady, Marianne, as the folds of her cloak fell down again over the two of them, found herself with her lips pressed against Marguerite's smooth cool cheek, Marguerite's laughter gurgling in her ear, her soft breath on her neck, the warm little body in her arms. She smelt delicious. Her clothes were scented with lavender, her skin with violet soap, and from her curls came the faint fresh scent that breathes from the hair of healthy children like perfume from a flower. Impulsively Marianne held her little sister pressed tightly against her thin chest and kissed her passionately, and as she did so there came to her another of her "moments", one of those flashes of heightened awareness, of vivid experience, that were the only sort of happiness she ever knew, moments that she awaited with such longing and when they came clutched with a greedy strength, warding off the sympathy or curiosity of others lest they smirch what was for her alone, what could only be savoured alone, only one day yield its secret to her if her soul was by itself. Her senses, full of passionate delight in the perfection of the human body she held in her arms, reached out through and beyond it and laid hold of the scent of the wet chrysanthemums, the flaming colours of the garden and the thrilling overtones of the storm, with an ecstasy that as far transcended Marguerite's steady love of life as a flash of lightning transcends the unwavering little candle burning merrily inside a lantern. But she could not hold her moment. For all her strength it had gone before she could know what it was for. It slipped from her just as a gust of wind seized the door and swung it shut upon the garden of their childhood. They leaped for safety down the flight of steps that led to Green Dolphin Street and fell in a tumbled heap of frills and flounces at the bottom of it, Marguerite submerged in laughter and Marianne in bitter weeping.

Marianne so seldom cried that Marguerite's laughter was abruptly checked by fright. She flung her arms round Marianne's neck and kissed her wet sallow face. "Where have you hurt yourself?" she demanded. "Where, Marianne? I'll kiss the place."

But Marianne, abruptly choking down the sudden storm of tears, shrugged impatiently away from the kisses that a moment ago had been so sweet to her. She forgot that it had been Marguerite who had given her her moment. She thought she would not have lost it if she had been alone. "Of course I haven't hurt myself," she snapped. "I never cry when I hurt myself. Only little girls like you do that."

"Then why are you crying?" asked Marguerite, wide-eyed. For herself, she cried when she had hurt her body and at no other time. She knew nothing yet about other sorts of hurts.

But Marianne did not answer. How could she say, "For a moment there was a key in my hand and then it was wrenched away"? Marguerite was too little and too happy to understand. She did not understand herself and the misery of her lack of understanding was almost as great as the misery of loss. "You look a sight," she said to Marguerite. "Your bonnet is hanging right down your back."

"And your cloak is twisted nearly back to front!" said Marguerite, and she began to laugh again, as she re-tied her bonnet strings and shook out her pink skirts, and then turned to face the excitement of Green Dolphin Street swept by a gale from the sea.

Marianne was facing it already but it was not giving her the thrill of excitement she had hoped for, when she had stolen the key from its hook in the hall. That thrill had come earlier than she had expected, had come during the moment before the garden door had banged shut behind them, pushing them out into the world as Adam and Eve had been pushed out of the Garden of Eden. Nevertheless it was good to stand braced against a wind like this, for it gave one no chance to feel anything but its own power. It swept one's mind clear of ecstasies that could not be retained and despairs that were unexplainable. Holding their ballooning skirts down with one hand and their bonnets on with the other they made their way through the swaying and dancing delight of Green Dolphin Street.

It was always a cheerful street, for the people who lived in it were the happiest sort of people, not too poor to have the joy of life ground out of them by poverty and not too rich to feel burdened by possessions, and the dead had left some of their happiness behind them in the homes they had made and the living were daily adding to it out of their own good cheer. Professional men who were not successful enough to aspire to Le Paradis lived in Green Dolphin Street, and nice maiden ladies who had seen better days but not better spirits, and retired seafaring men of every sort and kind who had laid by a little money. The population as well as the spirit of Green Dolphin Street was preponderantly of the sea. To-day it was feeling jollier than ever. The wet cobbles were glistening, the smoke that curled up from the crooked chimneys was dancing over the roofs, the window panes of the old bulging bow windows winked in the fitful gleams of watery sunshine, and the old sign of the Green Dolphin, hanging before Monsieur Tardif's inn, swung madly on its iron rod, its gyrations making it look as though it were really alive, rolling and tossing among the painted waves, grinning all over its face, whisking its tail in the white spray and winking its wicked blue eye. That dolphin was assuredly the genie of Green Dolphin Street. It expressed exactly the rollicking spirit of the place, its fun and good humour. And age did not weary it at all.

Down the whole length of itself Green Dolphin Street swayed and danced in glee. The packet was in harbour, safely gathered in out of the storm with no lives lost. A son of the island had come home again after long exile, and in the empty house beside the Green Dolphin Inn, that had been dark and shuttered for so long, the firelight was leaping on the walls and the kettle singing on the hob.

And the front door was wide open, so that when Marguerite let go of her bonnet, because her ballooning skirts were claiming both hands, it blew right off her head and down the dark passage inside. And Marguerite, of course, went impulsively after it, blown by the wind, and landed up at the end of the dark musty passage in the arms of Dr. Ozanne.

"God bless my soul!" he ejaculated, holding her with full masculine appreciation of her roundness and softness and warmth. "God bless my soul, here's a piece of luck! Hey, William, look at this!" And he carried her, giggling with delight, into the room from which the firelight streamed, and banged the door shut.

Marianne stood at the open front door a prey to conflicting emotions. For all her passion, and her unscrupulousness in pursuit of her desires, she was nevertheless a little prudish, and she was horrified at Marguerite's behaviour. If that wasn't just like Marguerite! To let her bonnet be blown into a strange house, to plunge in after it, to permit herself to be precipitated into the arms of a total stranger of the opposite sex and to be carried off by him with every appearance of enjoyment! Of course Marguerite was just a little girl, but she was quite old enough to know better. Indeed she *did* know better, but the fatal ease with which she enjoyed herself led her to enjoy things which no well-brought-up child should enjoy. . . . Heaven knows, thought Marianne in outrage, what she'll enjoy before she's done. . . . And then came a pang of jealousy. It was always like this, Marguerite was always running forward to enjoyment and leaving her behind. Arms were outstretched to Marguerite but not to her. When people had caught Marguerite to them they shut the door in Marianne's face. A little while ago, with Marguerite in her arms, she had most dearly loved her little sister, but now she quite desperately hated her. It was odd that one could hate and love the same person within so short a space of time. Yet one could. Time seemed to have nothing to do with what one felt; nor with living; for it was not the passing of time that made you realise that you were alive but those moments of intense feeling when you knew there was something in you that would not be extinguished though the whole of the universe crashed down upon your head. She was alive now, feeling the wind buffeting her, feeling the rough wood of the door frame under her hand, hating Marguerite. But it was a horrid aliveness, not like that ecstasy of living a little while ago. It was not a key that she had in her hand now but a sword that was thrusting not at Marguerite whom she hated but at that something in her whose pain was all the more intolerable because it could not die. . . . Yet she was glad to feel this hatred. She was glad of anything that made her feel alive.

She put one foot over the sill and then hesitated, trembling with outraged sensibility, and jealousy and pain. Should she go in and fetch out Marguerite herself or should she go back and tell Mamma, so that deserved retribution should fall upon the erring child? She was still hesitant when a peal of laughter sounded from within the room where the firelight was. It was not Marguerite's laughter, though she could hear that too as an undercurrent of rippling mirth below the clear ringing peal. Nor was it the laughter of the man into whose arms Marguerite had flown. It was a boy's laughter, and the joy of it called to the unhappy Marianne as nothing in her life had ever called to her before. She ran down the passage with an eagerness which outstripped Marguerite's, turned the handle of the closed door and went in.

He was standing on the hearthrug as a lord of creation should, his legs straddling arrogantly, his arms above his head as he stretched himself, his laughter caught up upon a prodigious yawn. He was broad-shouldered, strong, yet possessed of an elegance that was strangely mature, taller than she was but much younger. The last clear shining of the dying day and the leaping gleam of the fire, that had been newly lit from a smashed-up packing case, seemed to gather about his gay figure in a nimbus of light. The brilliance of it was entangled in the wildly untidy shock of red-gold curly hair and there seemed sparks in his tawny eyes. His face was round and ruddy, with freckles on the nose, but finely featured. He had full red lips and a deep cleft in his chin, and he showed a great deal of pink tongue as he yawned. His coat and waistcoat of vivid emerald green cloth were stained with seawater and torn linings protruded from the pockets. His white cravat was soiled, the straps that should have fastened his long peg-top trousers beneath his instep had snapped, so that they coiled round his legs like delirious green snakes, and his shoes needed a polish. Never was a male so much in need of female attention or so blissfully unaware of his need. He finished his yawn, dropped his arms and smiled at Marianne with lazy good humour. "Here's another of 'em," he said. "Come in, if you please, ma'am, and make yourself at home."

But Marianne could not. She stood with her back against the door, stiff and ungainly, staring at him with great dark eyes that seemed to devour his face with the intensity of her gaze, and she could not move or speak because her heart was beating so madly that it made her feel sick and faint. Her figure might have delayed to plump itself out into the womanly roundness proper to her age, but her heart did not delay to claim this male creature for her own. She was in love, in love at sixteen, desperately in love, as Juliet was, and with a boy who for all his height and strength and maturity was only a child of thirteen years. It was absurd. But then Marianne was never at any time in the least like other girls.

But she could not go to him, she could only gaze at him while he went to her, moving with a lazy animal grace like a leopard's, stifling a second yawn with the back of his hand. "It's a purple sort of one this time," he said, his eyes taking indolent stock of her. "The other one's pink, like a rose. Are there any more of you outside? A yellow one or a blue one?"

But at the sound of his voice Marianne came to herself. She was suddenly the huntress full of guile. She smiled at him and then lowered her eyes. Yet even with her eyes on the ground she was painfully aware of Marguerite in her pink frills perched upon the knee of the man who had captured her in the passage. . . . William had said Marguerite was like a rose but he had found no flower name for her. . . . It was Mamma's fault for dressing her in maroon. Why was she always dressed in these horrid drab colours? It was hateful of Mamma. Tears pricked behind her eyelids. But the change-over from intense experience to mere irritation had made her a child again, and it was as a gawky, prim, undersized yet somehow arresting little girl, with tears on the dark lashes that shaded the hungry intelligent eyes, that Dr. Ozanne saw her as she moved hesitantly forward into the light.

Something about her touched him to the quick. He had the experienced doctor's keen sight into human character, and he knew women only too well. Plain, clever, passionate, hungrily desirous of life, this one would not have an easy time. He plumped Marguerite down on the footstool by his chair (no need to worry over *that* one), jumped up and went to Marianne; for William, drugged with fresh air, was proving a rather sleepy and dilatory host.

"Come in, my dear," he boomed in his rich fruity voice, a little husky now after the sea voyage, and marred by a slight slurring of the consonants due to the whisky with which he had fortified himself against the inclemency of the weather. "Did I bang the door on you and not know you were in the passage? Holy Moses, that was a crime indeed, and you so small and dainty in that pretty gown, and the split image of the Queen, God bless her! God bless *you*, my dear. What's your name? Marianne? And this is Marguerite. Marianne and Marguerite. Two pretty names for two pretty ladies. I don't know that I ever heard two prettier names, did you, William?"

"Too much alike," said William on another yawn. "Damned confusing."

"Mind your language in the presence of the fair sex, William," cautioned his father. "Sit down, my dear. Take your cloak and bonnet off. William and I, we're just off the packet and about to have a dish of tea to make us forget it. Damned stormy weather for a man's home-coming. But if you will join us in the dish of tea, Marianne, then, bless my soul, it will be the sweetest welcome that ever a man had."

"You're talking to Marguerite. You've mixed them up," said William.

"No, he hasn't," piped up Marguerite. "She *is* Marianne. *I'm* Marguerite."

"Then it's you who are mixed up, my lad," triumphed his father. "And without a drop of anything stronger than salt water inside your stomach for the last twelve hours, either. You be careful, William, or weakness of memory and confusion of brain will land you in a nice mess one of these days. . . . Now, my dear, sit down."

His great hand enveloped hers, and his laughing brown eyes, that looked startlingly young above their heavy weary pouches, looked

down at her with all the warmth of his enormous kindness. Never
before had she had such a welcome. Never before had anyone
seemed to want her so much. She almost forgot William as she
looked up into the face of his father.

For most of his life people had forgotten other things when they
looked at Edmond Ozanne, but of late years, as his girth increased
and the great beauty that he had had in his youth began to crumble
into ruin, they had not been so forgetful and he had not been without a humorous chagrin at the change. So it was touching, as well as
comic, to have this changeling of a little creature gazing at him with
such whole-hearted admiration. And in the firelight, beaming with
kindliness, amused and touched, he was still worth looking at. He
was of a great height, though slightly bent now about the shoulders,
stalwart and strong like his son, but without William's elegance. He
had never had William's elegance, even in the days when he had
been as slim and straight as William, for that had come from his
mother. But his tawny eyes were William's, and his untidy shock of
greying hair had once been as bright and riotous as his son's, and in
his florid red-veined face one could still see something of William's
fine features. By drawing the line somewhere between William's
immaturity and Edmond's decay one could find again the glorious
young man with whom Sophie du Putron had strolled up and down
beside the harbour wall.

Edmond was as flamboyant and untidy in his style of dress as was
his son, though he kept to the style of some years back, with torn
white ruffles beneath the immense cravat that propped up his double
chin and a quantity of seals dangling from beneath his nankeen
waistcoat. His coat was of peacock blue, with padded sleeves that
increased his already considerable bulk, and long flowing tails. A
fine figure of a man was Edmond still, full of hospitality and bene-
volence and a pitiful kindness that knew no bounds, a coarse man, a
self-indulgent man, but a man capable of keeping the flag of his un-
conquerable good humour flying until the bitter end; it was only in
his rare moments of silence, when his face fell into repose and the
laughter died out of his eyes and his full lips drooped one upon the
other, that one observer in a thousand might have known him for a
man who dared not think. In those moments he looked like a mangy
sad old lion looking out upon the splendour of the grand old days
from behind the bars of his prison cell.

But there was no hint of anything remotely resembling lowness of
spirits of any sort or kind as the four sat enjoying an uproarious meal
before the fire. Everyone was uproarious in the company of William
and his father. It was impossible not to be. They were at all times

out to enjoy themselves, without scruple or fastidiousness, their rollicking pursuit of pleasure curbed by nothing but their kindliness of heart. Their enjoyment was not like Marguerite's, that was born of the love of the divine in life that is not far removed from holiness, it was an entirely pagan thing, partly animal high spirits, partly a defiant fire lit to frighten away the wolves in the dark. But they got no pleasure out of their fire if they sat at it alone. At their feastings beside it they invited the whole street in whenever possible, and the splendour of the subsequent rejoicings was unforgettable by those who experienced it.

There was even a splendour about this meal of strong tea and bread and treacle eaten in an untidy room with a storm beating at the window, William and Marianne sitting together on one packing-case and Dr. Ozanne overflowing the top of another with Marguerite still on her stool at his feet. If the glorious hospitality of the two hosts had permitted their guests to feel the influence of their surroundings they might have found them depressing, for Dr. Ozanne's furniture, that had arrived on a previous packet, was still stacked up around the walls all anyhow. Sheraton chairs with scratched unpolished legs lay helplessly upon their sides, and the green parrot in the brass cage, that Sophie Le Patourel had seen from the schoolroom window, reposed in a silent depression of spirits upon a carved prie-dieu turned upside down over a glass case full of wax flowers.

"Soon get it all ship-shape," boomed the doctor cheerfully, cutting a great hunk of bread for Marianne with his jack-knife. "We'll be getting some Island body to come in and do for us and then you won't know it, young ladies. No women like the Island women for keeping a house ship-shape. No women in any other part of the world to hold a candle to 'em. You remember that, William, my son, when your turn comes to wed. Pick her with beauty, William, and pick her strong, and with virtue if you like virtue, but above all, my son, pick her Island born." And smiling at Marianne and Marguerite, he plunged his hand into one of the enormous pockets of his coat, brought out a whisky bottle and poured a generous dram into his big blue china mug of hot strong tea. "Best thing possible after a sea voyage," he told the girls. "And a damned stormy voyage at that. William don't need any. William suffered no inconvenience, the rascal. Took to the water like a duck. I'll make a sailor of you, William, my lad. Pity to waste that fine steady stomach on a shore job."

"I wouldn't mind being a sailor, sir," said William thickly through an enormous slice of bread and treacle. "But I think it would be best

for me to keep a tavern, so's you can get your whisky cheap." And
he winked one glorious hazel eye at Marianne and the other at
Marguerite.

"You'll do nothing of the sort, you young rascal, you," boomed
his father in sudden jovial wrath. "Your mother was a lady if ever
there was one, poor soul, and she bred her son for a gentleman, and a
gentleman you'll be, though I have to take the cane to you. . . . My
poor wife's," he said to Marianne and Marguerite, indicating the
prie-dieu and the wax flowers with a flourish of his mug. "I keep 'em
in memory of her. She was a very religious woman, poor soul. And
artistic, too. She made those flowers with her own hands."

He spoke placidly. His grief for his wife did not seem very severe,
Marianne thought, only kindly and pitiful. Perhaps he had found
her too genteel. Perhaps she had patronised him and the patronage
had been painful. He was not, Marianne realised, quite what her
mother would have called a gentleman.

"After she died," went on the doctor, "William and I made up our
minds to come back to the Island. I'd never been happy away from
it, mind you, but my wife, poor soul, had no love for the sea. But I
have. If you're Island born you're not happy out of sight and sound
of it. You'll pine for the mewing of the gulls all your days, my dear,
and eat your heart out among the bricks and mortar."

"Was the parrot your wife's too?" asked Marguerite.

"That parrot Lydia's? Bless my soul, no! She'd never have that
parrot in the same room with her, his language being what it is. He
lived with me in my surgery. That parrot has seen life. One of my
patients, a seafaring man, gave it me in lieu of payment. He's silent
now, depressed by the voyage, poor fellow, but once get him going
with the nautical oaths he picked up from his first master, and the
medical terms he's picked up from me, and he's a treat. . . . William,
give Old Nick a drop of whisky to get him going."

"No, sir," said William firmly. "Old Nick's remarks are not suitable for young ladies."

Marianne looked at him with approval. It had not taken her long
to realise that William was much more of a gentleman than his
father. He was untidy, he was lazy, and she was quite sure that
Mamma would not approve of much of his behaviour and conversation, but his careless elegance and his intuitive knowledge of what
was suitable could have come only from good breeding. There must
be something of his mother in him. Yet what she loved best in him,
his looks and his overflowing kindliness, had come from his father.
Prim though she was she did not mind that Dr. Ozanne was without
the manners of a gentleman, that his clothes smelt of whisky, that he

handed her slices of bread on the point of a knife. She would never forget the perfection of his welcome when she had first come into the room. She did not wonder that Lydia his wife had descended from the heights of her gentility to marry him. Only if she had been Lydia she would not have kept him a prisoner in her country; however much she hated the sea she would have gone with him gladly to his. That was the way she would behave when she had married William. She would say to him as Ruth to Naomi, "Your country shall be my country". . . . And she would keep him from the whisky bottle and keep his clothes tidy. . . . Sitting beside him on the narrow packing-case, his body pressed against hers, she could feel the warmth of his young life in hers and she imagined, as do all children whose only experience of affection has been that of the parents whose devotion meets their own more than half way, that love is always mutual, and that what she felt for William he must feel for her. Secure in that conviction she thrilled with an ecstasy even deeper than that she had known when she held Marguerite in her arms. She saw the firelight leaping on the walls, and rain lashing at the window panes, and heard the roar of the wind over the roof, and was at one with them in the joy of her love. In that moment she gave herself to William. She had found in one moment her quarry and her mate, and as huntress and woman she was satisfied, tasting the sweets of the end of the way, unaware in her inexperience of the rigours of the journey that she was undertaking with so light a heart.

But to William the child her three years seniority turned her almost into the semblance of a maiden aunt. It was upon Marguerite, the other child, giggling with delight as she sat on the footstool at his father's feet and stuffed herself with bread and treacle, that his merry eyes were fixed in admiration. And her answering merriness met his half way. She dimpled at him, as she pursued with her pink tongue an errant drop of treacle that was rolling down her chin, and thought he was a nice boy.

An elegant figure in a grey bonnet and cloak, storm-buffeted, was vaguely seen by Dr. Ozanne to stop outside the bow window and look in, but the children were making so much noise that he did not hear the unanswered knock at the door, or the agitated footsteps in the passage, and was unaware of Sophie Le Patourel's entry until she actually stood in the doorway. Then he stumbled to his feet, fumbling to brush the tobacco ash off his stained waistcoat, painfully aware of the disorder of his person and his room. For he recognised Sophie and remembered their walks beside the sea wall. He guessed that she would be one of the great ladies of the Island now. He had meant to claim acquaintance with her, in the hope that she would have kindliness in her heart for his motherless boy. But it was not like this that he had hoped to encounter Sophie again; travel-stained, hopelessly at a disadvantage. This was a sorry beginning for the new start in life for which he had hoped so much, for himself as well as the boy. His look of a mangy sad old lion came over him and for once he had nothing to say, only a comical look of mingled dismay and pleading to give her as he held out his hand.

She took it, though her face was white with her horror at the change in him, and at the disorder and vulgarity of the scene in which she found her daughters ensconced with every appearance of comfort and delight. But though she smiled she could not for the moment speak. It was the parrot who spoke.

"My, what a fine craft!" shouted Old Nick, suddenly coming to from the comatose condition into which the journey had plunged him, and gazing at Sophie in admiration. "Come right in, my dear, and take a rhubarb pill."

Everyone behaved well, even William on his packing-case. With great presence of mind he buried his curly head in his right trouser leg in his efforts to choke his hoots of laughter.

Sophie was superb. For all the notice she took of Old Nick she might not have heard him; though the shock seemed to enable her to recover her power of speech. "Welcome home to the Island, Dr. Ozanne," she said gently. "I am come in search of my naughty girls. I was a careless mother and they played truant, and I am afraid they have intruded on you. I hope you will forgive us."

"No forgiveness required, ma'am," boomed Dr. Ozanne, clinging to her hand as to a lifeline. By gad, here was a woman for you! Putting him at his ease. Taking the blame upon herself. A fine figure of a woman too. She'd filled out grandly since her girlhood. No women like the Island women. Hadn't he said so? By gad, he had! "Your girls have given us a sweet home-coming. Had I known they were yours, ma'am—though surely I should have known, with all that charm and beauty before me, all that elegance—all that—split image of you, Sophie—charming girls, ma'am, charming——" He began to get a little confused and Sophie helped him out by an interruption.

"Is that your boy?" she asked.

"Stand up, William!" commanded his father.

William stood up, crimson-cheeked, moisture streaming from his eyes, but proud in the knowledge that not a sound of mirth had escaped him. Sophie went to him and touched his unruly hair with a gentle finger. "You are like your father when I first knew him," she said. She had intended, when she stood upon the threshold and

looked in at the uproarious tea-party, to see to it that for the girls'
sake there was no friendship between this house and her own, but
the sorrow that she felt at the tragic change in Edmond, and William's
untidiness and motherlessness, caused a complete reversal of her
previous intention. Unaware of what she was doing she pulled
William's cravat straight.

"You must come to Le Paradis and play with my girls," was the
remark that to her own intense dismay she heard issuing from her
lips.

And so on that stormy autumn evening Sophie Le Patourel took
the lives of William and Marianne and Marguerite and knotted them
together for ever. There was a little silence after she had spoken, and
looking up they saw that a watery sunset was illumining Green
Dolphin Street with a flood of gold.

CHAPTER TWO

1

William woke up and wondered why he was awake, for except for a
faint patch of grey in the direction of the window it was still night in
his little room under the eaves, and it was his habit to sleep without
fluttering an eyelid from the moment he fell into bed at night until
that moment in broad daylight when his father opened his bedroom
door and flung a book at his head. He lay and listened. Except for a
drip of water from the eaves and the distant surge of the sea there was
absolutely no sound.

That's why I've woken up, thought William. When he had gone to
sleep the wind had been blustering in the chimney, and shaking the
old timbers of the house so that they creaked and groaned in protest,
as it had been doing almost ever since they had landed on the Island
nearly three weeks ago. The sudden peace was startling.

A cock crowed, a raucous sound like a cracked trumpet being
blown by someone who was too excited to blow it properly, and the
grey square of the uncurtained window became a little clearer.
William, as excited as the cock, slid out of bed and put his boots on.
By the absence of snores next door, and even more by the feel of the
house, a secret conspiratorial sort of feel, he knew that his father had
been called out to a patient and he was alone in it. He liked being
alone in the house. He and the house were friends.

Whistling a cheery tune, stark naked except for his boots, for he
considered his nightshirt unnecessary and seldom bothered to put it
on, William felt about the room for the clothes he had scattered

broadcast the night before. He always put on his boots first of all because as they were the last things he took off before he got into bed they were always there handy. Socks he disdained. They were a nuisance, invariably in holes and never more than one of a pair to be found. And with peg-top trousers on no one knew if you had socks on or if you hadn't. His feet were as hard and tough as feet can be and never got blistered by the rubbing of the boots; he seldom washed them, so they did not suffer from the softening effects of hot water. As he rummaged for his clothes he hazily wondered where his father had gone. Some poor woman had had a baby, perhaps, or a drunken sailor had fallen out of a window, or there'd been a glorious bloody fight in one of the waterside taverns and his father had been fetched to stitch up the cuts. Though they had been on the Island three weeks only Dr. Ozanne already had quite a number of patients, though they were all poor people, not rich ones. How vexed Mamma would have been! It had always upset her so that Papa's patients were generally poor people who could not always pay their bills, and not rich people who could have even if they didn't. If a patient did not pay his bill William hadn't been able to see that it made any difference whether he was rich or poor. But Mamma had thought it made a lot of difference. She had cried sometimes when in London she had seen Papa's chariot waiting outside some poor hovel, but smiled when she had seen it outside a house with a polished brass knocker and scrubbed white steps. But she hadn't smiled very often. The fact was that Papa loved poor people who were very ill or dreadfully hurt, and they loved him, but he was not very fond of rich people who were not as ill as they thought they were and wasted his time telling him what they thought, and when he interrupted them to tell them that they thought wrong they weren't very fond of him either, and didn't call him in again. . . . And Mamma cried.

At least not now. She was dead. William, who had at last found his shirt, thrust his head up through it and looked at her portrait over his bed, faintly visible now in the growing light. She was very pretty with her golden ringlets, blue eyes, delicately pointed face and sloping shoulders, and he remembered her kisses with affection and her lovely scented clothes with an appreciative sniff, but he couldn't help feeling that life was a lot more comfortable now she was dead. She had cried such a lot, and scolded such a lot, and made Papa so unhappy. His loyalty had always been his father's. Even as a small child he had known that scolding and crying were not the way to make Papa stop doing the sort of things that Mamma did not like him doing. And if she hadn't liked the sort of person he was, why had she married him? Perhaps she had thought that she could change the sort of person that Papa was. Can one ever change a person? Mamma had apparently thought one could, but William himself was doubtful.

He never said these things to his father, only to himself, for he respected the feeling that had made his father hang his wife's portrait over her son's bed and keep her prie-dieu beside his own with his whisky bottle on it. She had been their wife and mother and she had done her best for them both; she had been beautiful and now she was dead, and it would not be chivalrous even to hint to each other that they were more comfortable without her. Indeed it was scarcely chivalrous even to think it, and William thrust the thought away as he put on his brilliant green coat and waistcoat and whistled "Blow the man down". Both William and his father were chivalrous to the very depth of their souls, their chivalry shot through with an amiable weakness that would make them easy game for the predatory until the end of their lives.

William poured an inch of ice-cold water into his basin, smeared his face and hands, rubbed the dirt off them with a towel, fished out a broken comb from beneath the bed and forced it through his tangled curls as far as it would go; he did not pursue the matter, however, for it hurt, and he never did things that hurt if he could possibly help it. Then he opened his window and thrust his tousled head out into the dawn.

Holy Moses, but this Island was a good place! The keen cold fresh air hit him like a blow in the face, stinging him into exultant life. The tumbled wet roofs of Green Dolphin Street gleamed like silver and over them the emptied rain clouds had thinned to a sheen of silver grey shot through with gold, with here and there a sort of lake of unclouded sky the colour of aquamarine. Far down to his left the night still lay over the sea, with one star bright like a lamp, and the boom and surge of the waves beyond the harbour bar came clearly to him now that the window was open. Up above him to his right his view was closed in by the roof of No. 3 Le Paradis, dark against a sky the colour of a rose, and from the hidden garden floated a scent of jessamine. Over the top of the wall drooped a branch of the great magnolia tree, heavy with rain, every leaf turned to silver in the dawn, one great blossom dropping its waxen petals one by one upon the cobbles of the street below. William watched each petal as it drifted slowly down, light as air, untarnished, lovely, until with a soft thud the whole flower fell and the branch above, relieved of its weight, sprang upward in delight and the raindrops showered down from it in a mist of silver spray. A clock struck somewhere far down in the town and then, quite suddenly as it seemed, the sun was up and the sea was a sheet of gold, and in the garden of No. 3 a bird was singing a mad wild paean of praise because the storm was over and the night was done. William suddenly dropped his curly head on his arms. The light was so brilliant now that it was hurting his eyes and there was a queer confused longing in him somewhere, because the loveliness of the world made him want to jump up and do something for somebody, and there was nothing he could do. There was not a soul within sight. . . . Yes, there was.

Something seemed to reach out and touch him, as though he had spoken and a voice had answered. He lifted his head from his arms and looked up. A dormer window high up in the roof of No. 3 Le Paradis had opened and a small figure in a white nightgown was leaning out as far as she could get, breathing in great breaths of the fresh air, her arms along the sill. Marguerite! No, damn, it wasn't, it was only Marianne.

He had seen Marianne and Marguerite twice since the day of that first riotous tea-party. He and his father had been to a Sunday family dinner at Le Paradis and he had also drunk a dish of tea with the girls in their schoolroom and played spillikins with them afterwards. But neither of these meetings had been very satisfactory. At the Sunday dinner he and his father had been ill at ease in their shabby clothes at the shining mahogany table, careful of their language, careful not to spill the wine, racking their brains to remember the good manners and the conversational gambits that Mamma had taught them but which had fallen into disuse since her death, horribly aware that they were a couple of uncouth heathens who had not been to church that morning. Sophie had been sweet to them, but the girls had been fettered by the obligation of being seen but not heard while partaking of nourishment in the presence of their elders, and the dignity of Octavius in a mulberry waistcoat, his chin propped up upon a stock at least six inches high, had been utterly shattering to super-sensitives like Edmond and William. They had wilted, and gone home early, and felt the worse for the dinner, and taken a glass of hot whisky and water and a rhubarb pill respectively, and gone to bed in much depression of spirits.

Drinking tea with the girls in the schoolroom had been much better because Octavius had not been there, but Sophie had been there, all the time, and her fair beauty and dignity had reminded him of Mamma, and thinking all the time of how Mamma would have had him speak, eat and move, had made him a dull dog. And Marianne's hungry black eyes had been fixed upon him all the time, and had made him feel most uncomfortable. They had seemed to be begging him for something, and to be mutely reproaching him for not being or doing what she wanted; and he hadn't known what it was that she wanted.

But little Marguerite had been the silver lining in the black cloud of both entertainments. He adored Marguerite. At dinner he had sat opposite to her and her merry blue eyes twinkling at him, her hearty appetite, the suspicion of a sympathetic wink that she tipped him when he spilt some gravy and blushed crimson with shame, and the irrepressible giggle that popped out when a wasp settled on her father's head, had made him her slave for ever. And at the little tea-party she had been even more adorable, dimpling and fat and friendly in the sort of utterly unselfconscious way that put one at one's ease, and enjoying everything so much, even the boring game of spillikins, that at last his natural powers of enjoyment had been restored to him and he had gone home happy, and had been busy for days carving a little wooden mouse for her, with pink sticking plaster for ears and string for a tail. This act of service had given him some outlet for his love, but prowl about the garden door of Le Paradis as he might he had as yet found no opportunity of presenting her with this touching token of his affectionate esteem.

And now it was Marianne up there at the bedroom window, not Marguerite, and he cursed his luck. Yet after the first pang of disappointment he found himself looking attentively at Marianne. She had not seen him. She was looking, as he had looked, at the swaying branch of the magnolia tree from which the silver raindrops were still falling, at the gleaming sea and the sky. Her small face, framed in the white frills of the nightcap tied so demurely beneath her chin, looked pure and lovely, transfigured, shining with the joy that had answered his like a touch, or a voice speaking. She too loved this place where for generations the men and women of her blood had lived and died. She too had had a moment of ecstasy when she had opened her window and seen it refreshed and shining after the storm; still there after the darkness of the night, still safe, still hers. Then she looked down and saw him and they smiled at each other.

"Come out with me, Marianne," he called. "Come down to the sea. It'll be grand down there after the storm."

She nodded happily, and then suddenly the lovely light went from her face and she blushed with shame, conscious of her nightcap and her nightgown. She withdrew quickly and closed the window. William also withdrew, very cross, for he knew why she had blushed and her silliness exasperated him, for surely she was dressed up enough in all those starched white frills. Girls *were* silly. Then he corrected himself. Only some girls. . . . Little Marguerite wouldn't have blushed. . . . And now he had committed himself to an early morning's outing with Marianne. Damn. Well, anyhow, she'd be ages dressing. He had time to go downstairs and light the fire and put the breakfast ready in case his father should come in cold and tired while he was still out, for Madame Métivier, who "did" for them, did not arrive until ten o'clock.

But he had done no more than lay the fire, and get soot all over his face, and start fumbling with the cups and saucers in the cupboard in the little dining parlour at the back of the house, when Marianne arrived. Her moment of embarrassment had disappeared as completely as her moment of luminous joy, and she looked trim and competent and self-possessed.

"Here, my goodness, give them to me!" she ejaculated, skilfully taking from William the top layer of the pyramid of crockery he was endeavouring to remove from the cupboard all at one blow, holding the apex against his chest with his chin. "Put the others down and go and wash your face. You're filthy."

William did as he was told, retreating to the kitchen that opened from the dining-parlour, and rubbing his face vigorously with the towel that hung behind the door and that always had a conveniently soggy patch on it that was as good as a sponge. Through the open door he surveyed Marianne. Her morning dress of striped dark green bombasine had a plain collar and cuffs of white lawn upon it and was severely belted at her tiny waist. Her shawl was green too, with a green silk fringe, and her green bonnet had ribbons like smooth seaweed tied beneath her chin. Her hair, newly released from curling papers, framed her face in a mass of dark ringlets that cast strange shadows on her sallow determined little face. For a moment she looked like some sort of a green fairy person who did not belong to his country, a changeling creature quite alien to his warm humanity, and William felt for a moment a little scared. Then, as she set out the cups and saucers, lit the fire with ease and put the untidy room to rights before one could say Jack Robinson, he felt a sense of rest in her efficiency. He strolled back into the dining-parlour, curled up in his father's chair and watched her with lazy pleasure. He was feeling a lord of creation now. It was nice to have a woman working for one. It gave one a good sort of feeling.

"I like watching you work, Marguerite," he said.

Marianne paused and looked at him, sitting there in his brilliant emerald green coat, the flames lighting up his fair curls, his tawny eyes and handsome smiling face.

"William, you're lazy," she chided sharply. "And I'm not Marguerite, I'm Marianne. Can't you even be bothered to remember my name properly?"

"I never remember names properly," said William. "Nor does Papa. It's in the family not to remember names. And I'm not lazy, Marianne. I'd have done the fire and everything for Papa if you hadn't come. I like doing things for people."

There was a note of childish pathos in his voice and Marianne's face softened. She came to him and stood looking intently down at him. He was an indolent untidy young rascal, but she guessed there was nothing he would not do for his father. Or for anyone else for that matter. She was not like that, and she knew it. Her conscious self had already given her a high opinion of Marianne Le Patourel, born of her subconscious unacknowledged knowledge that she would never be an attractive woman, and she was not of a mind to squander this valuable self upon all and sundry. For William only was she willing to give to the utmost. But William would always squander himself, giving back easily the affection and liking so easily given to him. "You're good, William," she cried impulsively. And for just one flashing moment, deep in her heart, she acknowledged his superiority. Then she pushed away the knowledge, thrust it away far down, not to be unearthed again until the end of her life. She was Marianne Le Patourel, the most important person in her world, and she had given to this beautiful young creature William Ozanne the inestimable treasure of her love. He was hers. She would make him. He was untidy, lazy, grubby, ill-brought-up, with a dangerous streak of weakness in him. But she would alter all that. She would make of him such a man as the world had never seen. And he would love her as she loved him; it was not possible that he should not when she loved him so terribly. He would die with her name on his lips.

"Take a little peppermint for wind!" cried Old Nick suddenly with great exasperation from beneath the red tablecloth that covered him by night. "Heave ho, my hearties, heave ho!"

"William, take the cloth off that horrid bird and come along down to the sea!" commanded Marianne, and there were tears of temper in her eyes. There was no one like a parrot for making one feel a perfect fool.

Chuckling, William obeyed her and followed her out into the gleaming glancing sunshine of Green Dolphin Street.

2

Almost at the bottom of the hill Green Dolphin Street was intersected by Fish Street running diagonally across it, and after this interruption it ceased to be Green Dolphin Street and became Pipet

Lane. Fish Street was very respectable and led by way of the Fish Market to the main shopping street of Saint Pierre, and then on to the harbour. Pipet Lane was not respectable and led straight into the sea through an archway in the harbour wall.

It was a filthy, noisy, smelly, beautiful, exciting place, very steep and very narrow, with the oldest and poorest and most tumbledown houses of Saint Pierre towering up to a great height on each side of it, and only kept from falling into it by the fact that their overhanging gables practically met overhead and propped each other up. Once wealthy people had lived in these houses. Through battered wide-open doorways with beautiful three-cornered carvings over their lintels one could see oak staircases, carved balustrades that had been torn away in places for firewood, and lovely moulded plaster ornamentation on damp-stained ceilings. In quiet moments it did not take much imagination to re-people Pipet Lane with lovely ladies in sedan chairs swinging along over the cobbles, or watching tearfully from the windows while gentlemen in cocked hats and powdered wigs came gaily out from the beautiful doorways, waved to them and went whistling down the lane to climb into the little rowing boats that waited beneath the archway. One did not need very quick ears to hear the click of the oars in the rowlocks as the little boats carried the adventurers to the sailing ships in the harbour that would bear them away to war upon the high seas or to trade with the new lands of the west. And one could fancy, at a quiet hour in Pipet Lane, that one heard the music of the harpsichord sounding from the old rooms, and women's voices singing, and the swish of silk skirts in the minuet.

Those great days were gone now and only the riff-raff of Saint Pierre lived in the stately old houses, and only the cows went down under the archway into the water, to have the mud washed off them before they went on to the market, or slatternly women with pails of refuse, or fishermen off for a night's fishing. And the only music nowadays was a drunken chorus roared out at midnight, or the twang of a banjo. Yet gaiety had not left Pipet Lane. To the casual glance everyone, drunk or sober, always seemed to be enjoying themselves there. The ragged barefoot children were always laughing and the slatternly women were stout and full of raucous conversation, and gay of a Sunday in their soiled scarlet petticoats, and the men in their striped jerseys had flashing dark eyes in their tanned faces, and gold rings in their ears, and were full of strange oaths and merry yarns. William simply adored the place. Marianne had never been allowed to go there.

Nor had she wanted to go there, for her fastidiousness hated noise and dirt and smells. "No, William!" she cried, as instead of turning to the left down Fish Street William bounded across to the entrance to Pipet Lane. "William! William!"

But William ignored the sharp admonition in her voice and pranced on, and she had perforce to follow him, or lose him altogether.

"It's all right," he said, when she had caught up with him. "It's quiet now, for they're all in bed still. It's too early to be rowdy. I wouldn't bring you here if it was rowdy, Marianne."

Quite suddenly Marianne began to thrill and tingle with excitement. The keen air and the sparkling sunshine, the scarcely comprehended influence of things past, yet alive for ever, and above all the being alone with William in an hour so fresh and enchanted that it might have been that first hour of the world that was without memory or fore-knowledge of evil, was like a draught of heady wine. She felt as light as air and mad as a hatter. These moods came upon her sometimes; some thought of adventure or memory of valour lit up suddenly like a flame in her mind and the whole of her exploded with excitement; and if she was in the house, stitching at her crewel-work under her mother's eye or bound upon her backboard without hope of release, she nearly went crazy trying to keep her body still and her thoughts and emotions within some sort of sane control, But there was no need to keep still now. Her tiny feet danced over the cobbles and her dark eyes sparkled. William looked at her over his shoulder, caught the infection of her mood, turned back and took her hand, and together they raced pell-mell down the rest of the lane, and stood with the dazzling water lapping at their feet, looking through the archway at the most perfect ship that either of them had ever seen.

"By gad!" ejaculated William. "Holy Moses!"

Marianne said nothing, but she neglected to reprove William for his language. Indeed she hadn't heard it. She was utterly enslaved by this lovely ship.

She had seen many ships in the harbour of Saint Pierre, apart from the mail packets and the fishing smacks; cutters, sloops, brigantines, coasters, frigates; but never before had she seen that culmination of the sailing ship, that glorious creature the clipper. This one must have been driven out of her course by the storm and had taken refuge in the harbour lest worse befall, otherwise she would never have so honoured Saint Pierre with her stately presence.

"What is she?" whispered William excitedly. He was a London boy and his world of ships and the sea was new to him; yet it was in his blood and his whole immature being unfolded at sight of that ship like a flower at the touch of the sun.

"A clipper," said Marianne. "I've read about them and seen pictures of them. She's one of the new clippers, the fastest kind of merchant ship. She's build for speed. Look at the lovely lines of her. Look at the length of them; she's five to six times the beam in length. She's built to sail with the wind; look at her bows. Look at the height of her masts."

"The sails are furled," mourned William. "What would she carry, when they're all set?"

Marianne considered, shading her eyes with her hand. "Foretop-mast, staysail, inner, outer or flying jib. Foresail and mainsail and mizzen, fitted with topsails, topgallant sails and royals. Then there's the spanker, look, there at the stern. It's her head and staysails and spanker that make her able to steal into the wind."

"How do you know all that, Marianne?" asked William in admiration.

"I told you, I've read about them," said Marianne. "I like to read about sailing ships and steam engines and adventure and discovery —and—and—things like that."

Her voice trailed off, breathlessly, for frustration had her by the throat.

"I didn't know girls ever did," said William.

"They don't," said Marianne, and the bitterness of her tone made William look at her in astonishment. He did not know what the trouble was, but he gripped her hand hard in sympathy.

"Look at her brass-work winking in the sun," he said, "and look, there's a figurehead carved at her bows. And, Marianne, what's that barrel thing up there at the mast head?"

"That's the crow's nest," said Marianne. "The lookout man sits there. He's so high, he can see for miles and miles. He sees dolphins and flying fish, and whales and icebergs, and new worlds rising up out of the sea."

"What's she got in her hold?" wondered William.

"Tea, perhaps," said Marianne, and then, dreamily, "or cedar-wood from Lebanon, perhaps, and gold to make twelve gold lions to stand about King Solomon's throne, and ivory and apes and pea-cocks."

William looked at her as though he thought she had gone mad.

"But the merchant navy of Tarshish wasn't any greater than ours," said Marianne. "There's never been a merchant navy like ours. William, if I were a man, I'd rather be in the Merchant Service than the Royal Navy. In the navy you just sail about fighting people, which you can do just as well on land, but merchantmen carry lovely things all over the world, and that's grand. . . . And then the captains of merchant ships can take their wives to sea with them if they wish, and in the navy they're not allowed to."

"I shouldn't want to take my wife to sea with me," said William. "A wife would be fearfully in the way."

Marianne gritted her teeth. Oh, to be a man, and not to be dependent upon the whim of a man to *live*!

"Look!" said William.

Under the archway was a small rowing boat moored by its painter to an iron ring in the wall. So close together were they, on this morning that was to be in both their lives the signpost outside Eden, that they did not have to speak to each other of the purpose that flashed simultaneously into their two minds. In a moment William had pulled off his boots and rolled up his trousers, waded out, pulled the boat as far up the cobbles as he could, laid a plank against it and helped Marianne to get in, and in another moment she had pushed them skilfully off, taken one heavy oar herself and given the other to William.

But how shamed now was William! His father had taught him to row a little on the river, but he had never yet struggled with one of the clumsy tubs of things they use on the sea, nor with an oar the size of this one. Their craft rocked with the violence of the crabs that William was catching.

"Take your time from me," said Marianne gently, with no hint of patronage. "Don't look at your oar. Keep your eyes on my back. You'll pick it up in a moment."

And in a moment William had picked it up, together with a respect for Marianne that surpassed anything he had ever felt for a woman before. Such a little bit of a thing she was, yet she seemed to have a man's strength. She had thrown aside her green shawl and under the striped green bombasine of her gown he could see the movement of her muscles as she bent to her oar. In and out went the blade, cleaving the ripples in perfect time, the wet drops showering off it with every skilful twist of her wrists. "One. Two. Three," she said. "One. Two. Three. Well done, William." And William glowed with pride. Now and then Marianne glanced over her shoulder, to see if they were keeping in the right direction, but William did not look. Like a child who will not open its Christmas stocking until the sun rises, he had made up his mind not to take even a peep until they were *There*.

But when he was easy with his oar he looked at Saint Pierre, and the sight of it under the early morning sun almost took his breath away. The tall houses rising above the wharfs and the long line of the harbour wall, up and up, one behind the other, climbing the

steep hillside, seemed to have absorbed the colours of the morning
into their very stone, so that Saint Pierre looked like a city built of
gold and mother-of-pearl. The windows flashed in the sun and there
was a flame of light burning in each ripple against the harbour wall.
The masts and spars of ships were etched as delicately as the tracery
of winter trees and there was no smoke as yet to mar the unearthly
clarity of the scene. Ramparts of golden cloud, built up behind and
around the furthest climbing roofs of the town, were like a second
city in the sky; one could hardly tell where the earthly one ended and
the heavenly began. But both of them were reflected in the water of
the harbour, and reality and reflection together made up a perfect
circle, a habitable globe in miniature, the city of man completely encircled by the city of God, the flawless shining thing of which God
dreamed when He made the world.

They stopped, rocking gently, and now that their oars were still in
the rowlocks they would hear the thunder of the sea outside the harbour bar and the mewing of the great gulls who were circling all
about them.

"It will never be the same again," said Marianne at last, when the
little immature vessels that were their spirits had taken their fill and
were brimming over because they could hold no more, and she spoke
bitterly because of the immensity of her thirst that could not be
slaked by that tiny draught. "We'll long to see it again, so as to see
it better, but we never shall. And we'll try to remember it just as it
was, and we shan't even do that."

"We'll remember something," said William stoutly. "I will, anyway. And I won't forget to-day, Marianne, though I live to be
eighty."

"And I won't either," said Marianne.

"Come on," said William.

Marianne roused herself and once more their oars dipped into the
water, and the bright drops dripped from the blades, and Marianne
glanced over her shoulder now and then and smiled a little, but William, bright-eyed and crimson-cheeked with excitement though he
was, did not look.

3

"Now!" said Marianne softly. And they ceased rowing and
William looked up.

They were right under her stern, beneath the Red Ensign of the
Merchant Service, and high above their heads there fluttered her
house flag of emerald green. The water, a little agitated by the wild

sea running high beyond the harbour, was slapping against her hull with that indescribable sound, not particularly beautiful but cool, vigorous, full of camaraderie, that together with the crying of the gulls, not particularly beautiful either, haunts lovers of ships and the sea until the day they die. That hull was a deep green in colour, barnacled, and the seas that had washed it had left upon it strange encrustations that were not of this sea. Their enthralled eyes followed the mighty sweep of it up to the taffrail with its shining brass-work, the poop, and then up and up to the dazzling intricacy of spars and towering masts. Slowly, oars resting on the water, they drifted the length of her until they were beneath her figurehead, and lo and behold it was a green dolphin, a boisterous light-hearted dolphin with a frisking tail, a wide laughing mouth and merry eyes like those of the dolphin on the signboard at the inn. Only this was an even grander dolphin. It was almost life-size, and so realistically carved that it seemed just about to roll merrily over and expose its flashing belly to the sun.

"The top o' the mornin' to you, an' what may you be doin'?" boomed out a great voice like a muffled foghorn.

William and Marianne removed their fascinated eyes from the dolphin and raised them to the figure leaning over the bulwarks, far up over their heads, so far up that they had to shield their eyes from the sun to see him clearly. They saw a large round red face, clean-shaven, with a bulbous nose, an enormous mouth without any teeth in it, and little snapping bright eyes nearly lost to sight beneath huge penthouses of bushy grey eyebrows, the whole surmounted by an old-fashioned periwig such as people did not wear nowadays, twisted sideways with the queue jutting out over the left ear. A dressing-gown of blinding cerise, with a pattern of yellow sunflowers on it, clothed the immense broad shoulders below the face, and two hands, mahogany coloured and the size of small hams, were laid upon the bulwarks over which the giant leaned. No answer being forth-coming from the two astonished faces turned up to his, he fumbled in the pocket of his dressing-gown, produced a huge set of white china teeth, fitted them in and spoke again, more clearly this time but with no less resonance.

"Bedad, an' what may you be doin', wakin' me out of the first sleep I was after havin' for a week, eh? Can ye tell me that now, eh?"

His "ehs" went off like gun shots and were most alarming, but Marianne nevertheless found her voice and answered him with considerable spirit.

"We can't have woken you up, sir," she said. "We haven't made a sound."

"Then what the divil did wake me, eh? Sittin' me up in me bunk as sudden as a jack-in-the-box."

"Perhaps the sun woke you, sir," suggested Marianne politely. "It's very bright this morning."

The giant straightened himself, shaded his eyes and looked at the flashing water of the harbour and the little town of Saint Pierre beyond it, built up so bright and fair against the golden city of the clouds behind, and he grunted softly. "Pretty little place," he conceded. "Nice little hole."

"It's one of the largest islands in the archipelago," flashed Marianne indignantly.

"An archipelago, is it?" enquired the giant genially, and hitching up his dressing-gown he turned himself about so that he could look out beyond the harbour bar to where other little islands could be faintly seen above the blown spume of the waves. "An archipelago!" he repeated with mock impressiveness. "Them little fleabites!"

"You have been glad to seek shelter from the storm here, sir," William reminded him.

The giant turned back to the children and grinned. "Faith, you're right," he said heartily. "Divil of a storm it was too. Drove me right off me course, an' me bound, would you believe it, for the port of Bristol. You two of the natives, eh? Frenchies? Hottentots?"

"Normans," said Marianne with dignity. "These islands belonged to William of Normandy. He conquered England. *We* conquered England. It belongs to us."

"Begod!" said the giant.

He leaned upon the bulwarks and contemplated the two. He liked young things. The girl, though a plain piece, had style about her, a regular little green enchantress she was, and the boy—begod, but that was a fine boy, with a fine head of carrots on him and a merry eye. He was in a genial mood. He had brought a valuable cargo safely from the other side of the world and was expecting much profit from the same, he had been in peril of death a score of times and had escaped; and not the least of his escapes had been the one at nightfall last evening, when he had got safely into harbour instead of wrecking himself on one of the hideous reefs of rocks that guarded these microscopic little islands. His luck had been in this voyage, and he liked this ending to it with two green-clad children from a golden town straight out of a fairy tale paddling about in the dawn over the bright waters of the neatest little harbour he'd ever set eyes on.

"Captain Luke O'Hara, at your service," he boomed at them suddenly. "Come aboard the Green Dolphin and have a bite of breakfast."

"Thank you, sir," said William. "As it happens, we come from Green Dolphin Street."

"Thank you, sir," said Marianne, and shipped her oar. She didn't wonder what Mamma would say. She had forgotten Mamma. She had forgotten Le Paradis. She had left her prudishness behind her when she entered Pipet Lane. She was in a new world. She was alive and happy.

"Nathaniel!" roared Captain O'Hara. "Nat! Come here, ye divil! Come here, ye son of—begorra, there ye are."

His roar subsided suddenly as a little man with the face of a wizened monkey, with gold rings in his ears and a bare chest tattooed all over with mermaids, hearts pierced through with arrows, anchors, a ship in full sail, and a good many other things that one would not have expected the human chest to have room for, popped up suddenly beside him, reaching little higher than his captain's elbow, and cocked an astonished eye; the other was made of round green glass, about as like an eye as the white china milestones in Captain O'Hara's mouth were like teeth, and from it a terrible red scar ran down one side of his face into his neck. Indeed the whole of that side of his face was dreadful to look at. The ear was gone and it looked as though the jaw upon that side had been smashed and had not mended very well.

"Get 'em aboard," said Captain O'Hara. "Put 'em in my cabin. Tell that lazy scoundrel of a cook to get the galley fire goin', an' look sharp with breakfast." And he rolled away to complete his toilet.

Nat flung them a rope to make the boat fast and lowered a rope ladder over the side. Marianne got on to it with skill and mounted with nimble ease, but William had more difficulty, owing to the way in which the Green Dolphin and the rowing boat decided to part company every time he endeavoured to transfer himself from one to the other. But he did it at last and Nat's great long hairy arm shot out as he mounted towards the bulwarks, gripped him in the small of the back and heaved him over as though he had been of no more weight than a puppy.

When one stood beside him one saw that Nat was immensely strong. It was only his face and his little short bow legs that were wizened; his chest and shoulders were broad and strong, and his arms and his huge hands were muscular and brawny. He wore a filthy scarlet night-cap on his bald head and his clothes were in rags after the voyage. His one eye was rheumy and sad and he had the most dreadful collection of rotting stumps of teeth in his gums that William had ever set eyes on, stained by the tobacco he was chewing. He did not speak at all, just chewed and spat, chewed and spat with

the regularity of a swinging pendulum. He was a horrid sight to
look at, and his person, as William rested against it in rolling over
the bulwarks, was most noisome. Yet with the first clutch of that
scrawny hand in the small of his back, the first glance of the sad little
eye into his own, William liked Nat.

Whether Nat liked William there was no knowing, but he set him
down upon the deck with surprising gentleness, spat an extra long
squirt of tobacco juice into the exact centre of a carefully chosen
ripple in the harbour, and led them along to the companion way. As
he walked it was noticeable that though he moved with speed he
dragged one leg painfully after him, like some sort of a grotesque
bird with a broken wing. What had been done to him, Marianne
wondered, that he had that eye gone, and that scar, and that dragging leg? Evidently life was not all joy in the Merchant Service. A
sudden cold breath blew from the sea, making her skirts balloon
about her, and she shivered as she pressed them back into place.

But glorious excitement gripped her again as they went down the
companion ladder to the Captain's cabin. "Sit ye down an' make
yourselves at home. Look alive with that breakfast, Nat," Captain
O'Hara bellowed from behind a ballooning curtain, where sounds as
of an elephant coming into collision with a hippopotamus in a restricted space suggested that his toilet was nearing completion.

Nat, with the gentle pressure of a hairy hand upon each of their
chests, sat them down upon a narrow bench running the length of a
bulkhead, spat through a scuttle and left them. They looked about
them entranced. It was a tiny place to be the cabin of so great a per-
sonage as the captain of a clipper, but then, as Marianne informed
William in a whisper, all available space had to be for the cargo.
Yet if tiny it was packed with an astonishing number of objects of
interest. The curtain that hid the captain's sleeping place was of
Chinese embroidery, richly encrusted with amazing golden dragons
with ribald faces and scarlet tongues. The heavy table of East Indian
teak before the bench where they sat had had initials carved all over
the top, and the great chair upon the other side of it was most richly
carved with sea creatures of every sort and kind, whales and sea-
serpents and mermaids and flying fish and dolphins and crabs all
mixed up together with such a glorious disregard of likelihood that
the very audacity of it made the foregathering seem quite probable.
But even this chair was outdone by the things that hung upon the
bulkheads. There was quite a collection of weapons; an old Aus-
trian wheel-lock, a tomahawk, a bow and arrows, muskets, pikes and
daggers. There was the jawbone of a shark, a stuffed baby crocodile,
the skin and awful tentacles of an octopus stretched across the ceiling,

and three strange brown objects, about the size of a man's head, with what looked like tattoo marks all over them, that were perhaps coconuts. These things covered every available inch of space so that the children, sitting on the bench, dared not move or lean back for fear the shark should bite them, the octopus reach down and wrap its terrible tentacles round them, or musket balls be discharged into their backs from behind. For none of the things in this cabin seemed inanimate. The ribald dragons, swaying backwards and forwards with the catastrophic heavings of Captain O'Hara behind them, seemed about to leap forward at any moment, and the reflection of the sun upon the water, passing in ripples of light over the bulkheads and ceiling, made everything upon them seem alive. . . . Especially those strange brown tattooed objects about the size of a man's head.

"But they *are* men's heads!" gasped Marianne in horror. "William, William, look! You can see the teeth, and the closed eyes—and —and—oh!"

She was interrupted by the simultaneous entry of Captain O'Hara from behind the dragons and Nat with a huge coffee-pot and an immense steaming dish of bacon and eggs.

"That's the style, my hearties," cried Captain O'Hara, flinging himself into the great chair opposite the children with no regard at all for the feelings of the mermaids who formed the seat of it. "Up with your knives and forks. More power to your elbow. Begod, bacon and eggs! Where did ye get them bacon and eggs, Nat?"

For the first time in the children's acquaintance with him Nat essayed to speak, but the strange stuttering noises that came from his mouth were incomprehensible to them. Captain O'Hara, however, seemed to understand. "Went ashore last night? Got 'em off the natives? It's meself that's proud of you, Nat. Good for the archipelago." He paused to place an entire egg within his capacious mouth. "Begod, it's good," he declared, munching with appreciation. "After all those months of that darned salt beef and rootie I tell you these eggs are darn good. Faith, Nat, what's the good of six eggs to the present company? Only a couple apiece. Look lively! Fetch 'em along!"

Nat dragged himself out of the cabin and as he went his mouth took on a painful sort of twist that was yet somehow recognizable as a human smile.

"Pleased to see me enjoyin' me vittles," explained Captain O'Hara. "Good old fellow, Nat. He an' me have been shipmates since boyhood. Where I go he goes. Keeps the young uns in order for me finely. Grand hand with a cat-o'-nine-tails."

Nat came and went with more eggs, more rashers, more milk and coffee and cream and sugar, and pieces of toast of the size and consistency of paving stones. He moved deftly, in spite of his dragging leg, and his great hairy hands never spilt anything. Marianne noticed that that parody of a smile twisted his lips several times as he watched his captain eat. And now and then he smiled at her and William, and both of them returned the smile. Marianne, as well as William, was beginning to like Nat. For some reason or other he made her feel extraordinarily gentle, a sensation to which she was not accustomed, but which she found pleasant.

"What has happened to him?" she asked Captain O'Hara, when the door seemed to have closed behind Nat for the last time.

"Happened to him? Happened to Nat?" asked Captain O'Hara in surprise, sitting back in his chair and investigating with a large forefinger some little maladjustment of his white china teeth. "A good deal happens to a man in a seafarin' life, me dear. Damn these teeth! I bought 'em off a Frenchman in Hong Kong. They're all the rage in Paris, so the fellow told me, but they're about as much use to me as a sick headache. No grip, if ye understand me, no grip at all."

"I mean, did he meet with an accident?" asked Marianne, pursuing the subject of Nat.

Captain O'Hara gave up the struggle, took out his teeth and pocketed them. "Several, me dear," he said, with decreased effectiveness of articulation. "Men do, who take to the sea. He smashed that leg of his fallin' out o' the riggin' in a gale off Cape Horn. Smashed his jaw too, an' I set it meself, and made none too good a job of it either, though you can make out what the old fellow's a jawin' of if you give your mind to it. As for the ruination of old Nat's beauty—well—I avenged that good an' proper." And Captain O'Hara jerked his thumb towards the three coconut things hanging on the bulkhead to his right.

The children gazed at him.

"Heads," said Captain O'Hara. "Tattooed cannibals' heads. The natives in New Zealand do a brisk export trade with 'em an' they fetch a pretty price all over Europe. Catch your enemy, ye know, tattoo his head, cut it off, eat the rest, sell the head to the white traders. A nice brisk little trade, bedad. But ye must be careful to tattoo the head while still livin' or the lines don't last, an' ye must be careful as the fellow don't make off into the woods with his own head while ye're lookin' about ye for the knife to cut it off with, or there'll be all your time an' trouble an' artistry wasted. I've bought a number of cannibals' heads an' got a good price for 'em. It's twenty pounds a piece, ye know, for a good head. But I ain't sellin' those three. No, begod. I had 'em in revenge for poor old Nat's eye an' ear, an' it warms the cockles of his heart to see 'em there, God bless him.''

The children continued to stare in fascinated horror. They had all three finished their breakfast now and Captain O'Hara inserted his teeth again, pulled out a great black pipe with a curved stem, filled it, lit it, puffed out clouds of blue smoke, and settled back in his chair to continue the story.

"It was six years back," he said, "an' I sailed for North Island from Australia for a cargo of timber that a fellow called Timothy Haslam an' his lumbermen were after fellin' in the forests. A great fellow, Timothy. There was nothin' he didn't know about a piece of wood. He could run his thumb over a bit of an old chair leg picked up in the gutter, tell you what wood it was, how old it was, just by the feel of the thing. An' there was nothin' he couldn't make out of a piece of wood. He made this chair I'm settin' on, carved it himself, begorra. An' he'd smell out good wood a thousand miles away an' sail straight for it. He'd smelled the New Zealand pines, the kauri trees, in a pub in Sydney, so he told me, an' I believed it, an' he sailed straight for 'em with his gang of lumbermen, ex-convicts, deserters an' the like, leavin' me to come after at a date fixed, an' fetch away the wood to Tilbury. A good price ye can get for New Zealand pine. There's no wood like it. Beautiful those forests are, with a grand scent to 'em under a hot sun an' a grand shade under 'em too, with the tops of the trees a swayin' in the wind a hundred and forty feet above your head, an' the ferns below 'em reachin' above your shoulders. Ah, they stretch for miles, those forests, over the plains an' over the hills, on an' on till they meet the great mountains with the snow on their crests, an' then a few o' them pine trees will go climbin' up into the snows an' stand with their heads in the clouds as pretty as you please. . . . Begorra, but it's a grand land, with always a wind blowin', the mountains that clear an' fresh lookin' you'd think almighty God had carved 'em out of jade an' amber only yesterday. A man can breathe there. A man can breathe."

He paused, smoking ruminatively, and looked out of the scuttle at the bright but restricted waters of the harbour, lost in a dream.

"You were going to tell us about poor Nat," said Marianne.

Captain O'Hara recalled himself to his story. "So I was, me dear. Well, I was captain of the Bluebell in those days, a tidy little craft but not the equal of this beauty, and Nat he was Bosun. Well, we anchored in the Bay of Plenty at the time appointed to wait for Timothy an' his men, an' they not bein' to time we went ashore, an' Nat an' the crew hobnobbed with the dirty whalers an' I hobnobbed with the missionary fellows. Not that I'm one for religion, me dear, but I

took off me hat to those fellows. Brave chaps, they were, riskin'
their lives night an' day to bring the heathen to see the error of their
ways. Well, as I was sayin', we waited for that timber, an' we waited,
an' still we waited, till, begod, I got that sick an' tired of waitin' that
I took Nat an' the first mate an' a store of provisions an' I went off
into the forest to see what they were after. Ah, but that was a grand
journey. The pohoutakawa trees were in bloom, ye see, all over
crimson flowers they were, an' the birds were singin' like a chime of
bells, an' the stars at night so big an' silver bright they might every
one of 'em have been a moon.''

Again he paused, his eyes on the bright sea beyond the scuttle, the
tobacco smoke curling in wreaths about his head. It was perhaps the
tone of his voice, even more than what he said, that painted for William and Marianne that far-away land of giant pine trees and snow-
capped mountains, birds who sang like chimes of bells and shining
silver stars as big as moons. Something very odd was happening to
William. His cheeks were on fire and his eyes were like lamps. He
was breathing the air of the spiritual country where he belonged, a
free and rollicking country where green dolphins sported in the clear
water and the great winds moved at will through the deep woods. He
had breathed that air when he first came to happy Green Dolphin
Street, though he had hardly known then what he did, but now, as
he listened to tales of that country where a man could breathe, he
knew he was at home. That country of his was not in one part of the
world more than another, it was wherever there were freedom and
laughter and good comradeship, wherever the doors were flung wide
in welcome to whoever cared to enter, and men lay down alone
among their enemies with no weapon in their hands, and slept well.

Marianne was in an odd mood too. Her hands were clenched on
her lap and her hungry eyes never left Captain O'Hara's face. The
world was so vast and beautiful and terrible, full of marvels and
adventures. If you were a man you could see and experience only a
little of it before you died, but you could hope to see and feel a little,
but if you were a woman you would have little chance of ever leaving
the tiny island where you had been born. . . . Unless with cunning
and contriving you spun the web of your own life to your own wish,
playing the part of good fairy to yourself. . . . Why not? It was no
good waiting on fortune. Her favour was inscrutable and uncertain.
What one wanted one must get for oneself. A man could use his will
like a sword but a woman had mostly to use hers like a shuttle.
Marianne's cheeks, too, were on fire and her eyes like lamps. Only
in those moments of vivid experience that made her come alive was
she at home in her own country. She was avid of experience, always

wanting to explore a little further, to see over the crest of the hill. And she *would* see. She would spin her web like an enchantress to get the colours that she wanted. She adored making things. Love, beauty, adventure, passion, danger, even agony, they were all fine colours and she would have them all.

"Well, we stopped one night at a clearin' beside a stream," said Captain O'Hara. "A pretty place it was, with poporo berries growin' about it as pretty as a picture, an' the stream so clear you could see every pebble at the bottom of it, red an' blue an' green like jewels. An' there were wooden huts in the clearin', with a palisade built round 'em, so we guessed we'd come to the lumbermen's camp. But there weren't no sign of Timothy, nor of his men, nor of the horses an' wagons he'd taken out to load the timber on, an' there was nothin' in the huts but an old tin mug an' a lot of bloodstains spattered on the walls, so we guessed the heathen had taken exception to the fellin' of the trees an' that Timothy an' all his men were in the pot."

"What did you do?" asked the spellbound William.

"Do? We slept there that night—leastways we lay down an' rested a bit, an' thought about them bloodstains an' poor Timothy—an' next day we followed the trail on into the forest, an' we found the timber stacked, masses of it, beautiful wood, but we didn't see the heathen, nor the wagons nor nothin', not so much as a bone, nor a bit of shoe leather that might have been tough eatin'—nothin' at all. So we lay down that night an' we slept beside the timber. An' we did sleep, too, for there were no bloodstains on that timber an' we felt more aisy in our minds."

"Yes?" asked Marianne breathlessly.

"Begod, me dear, I woke up sudden, all of a tremble, an' I lay listenin', but there was no sound at all, not a leaf stirrin', not a bird squawkin', nothin' but the great huge silence that ye get in them savage countries, where no man knows what's over the hill or round the bend of the stream. Yet somethin' must have wakened me surely, I thought, an' I lay listenin', an' then I heard it, just a tiny sharp sound, a twig snappin'. But still I lay an' listened, for I thought maybe it was just a wild beast stirrin'. Ignorant, I was. I didn't know that ye must never lay an' listen when a twig snaps in the forest—ye should be up an' doin' with your musket ready. Well, it seemed to happen all in a moment. One minute there'd been silence in the forest, an' the next there was yells an' curses an' scores o' dark men leapin' over the stacked timber, swingin' clubs over their heads, an' one with a knife it's my belief he'd pinched off Timothy. Well, I didn't have no time to think before the fellow with the knife was all but on me. All but, I say, for Nat got there first. But he lost his footin' someway an' fell on top of me, an' it was Nat got the knife, not me. Poor old Nat! He bled like a pig. There was his ear gone, an' his eye that injured it had to be took out later. He'd never been no beauty, Nat hadn't, but after that, begorra, he was enough to terrify the crows with, poor old fellow."

"How did you get away, sir?" asked William.

"Well, the first mate he was more slippy than what I had been. He upped with his musket an' fired, an' yelled like as he'd been twenty men an' not one, an' the heathen made off into the forest again. In those days they were terrified of firearms; I always say it takes a Christian to understand murderin' with a rifle. But three of 'em were left behind, kickin' on the ground, an' when we'd finished 'em off we cut off their heads an' carried 'em back to the Bay of Plenty an' had 'em properly seen to, so's they shouldn't rot, an' tattooed."

"And the timber, sir?" asked William eagerly. Manlike, he was less concerned with what had happened to Nat than what had happened to the timber that had been the purpose of it all.

"Oh, we fetched it," said Captain O'Hara. "We left Nat with the missionary fellows an' started off again with more wagons an' a gang of whalers an' ex-convicts who'd escaped from Australia. We thought maybe the convicts would murder us this time, but they thought better of it, an' we took the timber to Sydney an' delivered it to the timber merchant on the very day Timothy had promised it to him. An' then we sailed to China with a cargo of sealskins, an' I bought that curtain there with the dragons on it, an' then we sailed to the Old Country again with a cargo of tea."

"And what's your cargo now, please, sir?" asked William.

"I've a mixed cargo this time, son. Ginger in jars with blue flowers on 'em, an' bales of silk, an' spices of all sorts. I'm from the China seas again."

"An' you've never been back to New Zealand?" asked Marianne.

"No, me dear. But, begod, I'll be back one day. There's a country for you! A grand country, surely. A regular gold mine, with the timber, an' the flax, an' the whalin', an' the seal-fishin', an' grand pasture land between the forests. An' all undiscovered country, all virgin soil. An' it don't belong to no one. It's just a happy huntin' ground for runaway convicts, an' cannibals an' sealers an' missionaries an' such-like flotsam an' jetsam."

"It ought to belong to *Us*," said William, and his cheeks were still on fire.

"Give us time, son," said the old man. "Give us time an' we'll get the world, what God Almighty made for the Irish an' the English an' the Channel Islanders, an' not for dirty niggers that you couldn't get white however much you washed 'em. We're gettin' on. We're gulpin' away at India an' Australia now, an' throwin' up North America what we never digested proper from bein' in too much of a hurry to get it down." He twinkled at William. "In another ten years, son, when you're a man, it'll be time enough to take a good bite at New Zealand. We're nibblin' at it now, ye know, nibblin' away at the edges."

"Sir, may I sail with you to New Zealand in ten years' time?" asked William eagerly.

Captain O'Hara laughed. "We'll see, son. We'll see. But ye need to be tough for a seafarin' life, above all for the Merchant Service. Ay, ye need to be tough, damn tough, as tough as me an' Nat."

His keen, twinkling little eyes rested upon the beautiful boy on the other side of the table. There was tender, regretful affection in them, for he had never had a son, but there was also, perhaps, a shadow of doubt, and Marianne's spirit leaped up like a tigress in defence of her young.

"William's tough!" she cried. "All that you've done William will do, and more, when he's a man!"

Resolve flared up in her. William should succeed in life. He should be a strong successful man like Captain O'Hara. At whatever cost she would make a good job of William, or her name was not Marianne Le Patourel. It was not only for herself that she would be an enchantress spinning a web. Her face was suddenly soft and rosy, like that of a mother who is feeding her child. She thought she had discovered what she had been made for, and she was happy.

"An' now ye'd best be gettin' home," said Captain O'Hara. "Ye've respectable homes, I can see by the look of you, an' there'll be the divil an' all to pay if ye're not in 'em in an hour or so."

He walked to the curtain of golden dragons, pulled it back and disclosed his curtained bunk and an old battered sea chest. He lifted the lid of the chest, rummaged in it and took out two packages. Then he cleared the breakfast things on to the floor, laid the packages on top of the teak table and opened them. One was an exquisite little carved box containing a pair of beautifully shaped earrings of green stone, and the other was a knife with a carved handle and a carved wooden case to protect it. The carving on both box and knife was simple but lovely, with curves and arabesques beautifully interlaced.

"From New Zealand," said Captain O'Hara. "You wouldn't think murderin' heathen could do work like that, would you? But ye don't need virtue to be an artist, seemingly." He handed the box with the earrings to Marianne. "Take a look at 'em, me dear.

They're made of a stone called tangiwai. Green's your colour, I see. The Maoris use a knife like that, son, for cutting up fish and human flesh. You feel that edge. Men find a knife like that comes in handy."

They held the treasures on their hands and for a moment they were speechless. William felt the keen edge of the knife with a cautious forefinger while he held the handle in his other hand. The rough carved surface of it fitted well into the palm and helped one to get a good grip. Right on the other side of the world, thousands of miles away, the brown hand of a cannibal had held this knife. A thrill went through him, half pleasant, half horrible, as though the brown hand were holding his across the world, dragging at him, pulling, compelling.

Lying in the palm of her hand the beautiful green earrings lay and looked at Marianne. They were a clear, almost transparent green, with beautiful markings in them like ferns and fishes. Gazing at them Marianne though there would be nothing you could not see in them if you wanted to. You would be able to see visions in them, as fortune-tellers do in crystals. Yes, they were her favourite colour, elfin-green, the green of a curving wave on a grey day, undismayed though the sky is clouded, a brave colour; not the sort of exciting brave colour that scarlet is, flashing and flaming and soon burnt out, but cool and keen, quiet, the colour that even in mid-winter is never quite banished from the earth and that shows first through the melting snow, the best and most tenacious colour in the whole world. Her brown fingers closed over the treasures and her black eyes looked straight into Captain O'Hara's. "I'll have my ears pierced this morning," she said with finality.

The old man chuckled with appreciation. Not to-morrow, not next week, but this morning. It would hurt, but she wouldn't care. A plain piece, but plucky, and she knew her mind. That was a possessive, determined look she'd given him! Few women could meet a man's eyes with as direct a glance as that. Mostly they hid what they were after with veiled coquettish glances, as though they were ashamed of it. This girl would never be ashamed of going straight for what she wanted. She was after those earrings, and she'd said so with that look.

"But, sir, are these for us?" gasped William.

"If you want 'em, son."

"But you don't know us!" cried William.

"You're the first of me own sort I've set eyes on for many a long dreary week, son," explained Captain O'Hara. "An' it was a pretty sight ye were, surely, rockin' there on the waters of your harbour, with your pretty town in the sunshine behind ye, an' it was good rest an' shelter I had in this harbour of yours, this night that's past. It's grateful I am an' I'll not forget ye, an' you'll not forget me, for it's a grand yarn we've had together. Now here's me jack-knife. Sit ye down an' carve your initials on me old teak table. There's never a friend of mine but I have his initials on me table. Sit ye down now."

They did as he asked and it amused him mightily that Marianne needed no assistance but wielded his big jack-knife with a greater skill than William did.

"No, ye won't forget me, nor me you," Captain O'Hara announced in stentorian tones as they went up the companion ladder together. "There's much that goes to the makin' of a man or woman into somethin' better than a brute beast, but there's three things in chief, an' them three are the places where life sets us down, an' the folk life knocks us up against an'—what damn fool left this bucket here, right across the companion way, to trip me up like a drunken tinker on me own deck? Nat! Nathaniel! Nat, ye old divil, who put this bloody bucket——"

Nat popped up at his elbow and quickly removed it.

"What's the third thing, sir?" asked Marianne, to distract his wrathful attention. "The things we own?"

"Ah, you've an acquisitive nature, you have," chuckled Captain O'Hara. "No, me dear, not the things ye get but the things ye *don't* get. Ah, you'll learn, you'll learn!"

They were at the rope ladder now and Nat was waiting in the boat below to help them down. Captain O'Hara seized them like small puppies, first one and then the other, and swung them over the bulwarks. The powerful grip of his hands was the last experience they had of him, for when they were in their boat again, and looked up, he had gone. But Nat, after he had climbed back on deck, lingered a moment as they rowed away, and they saw his lips twisting as he essayed to smile.

"Good-bye, Nat!" they called. "Good-bye, Green Dolphin! Good-bye! Good-bye!"

As they rowed home their backs were to Saint Pierre and their faces to the clipper. To the last they could see the glorious shape of her, the long lovely lines, the masts and spars against the sky. Marianne caught her breath and then folded her lips on something that was rather like a sob. Oh, to be aboard her when she went to sea again! To feel the great lift of the ship as the sea took her and see the sails blossoming like flowers upon the masts.

"I shall be a sailor," said William suddenly from behind her. Though she could not see it his face was as soft and pink as hers had been when in Captain O'Hara's cabin she had discovered why she had been born. "Papa said it would be a pity to waste my steady stomach on a shore job. But I shan't take my wife to sea as some men do."

"She might make you take her," said Marianne darkly.

"Not if I was in the Royal Navy," said William.

"You're going into the Merchant Service," said Marianne, and her voice was as rasping and dry as a grasshopper's.

William, a peaceable creature, did not argue the point, especially as the keel of the boat was now grating upon the cobbles beneath the archway of Pipet Lane. He tied the painter to its iron ring, jumped out into the shallow water, seized Marianne in his arms and carried her, staggering and chuckling with glee, to dry land.

"That was a better way than the plank," he said. "You nearly fell off the plank. You're not a bit heavy, Marianne. I can carry you easily."

The tears suddenly rushed into Marianne's eyes as she looked at the beautiful flushed face so close to hers. At that moment she loved him neither as tool for her purpose nor as satisfaction for her longings, but simply because he was William.

"And what the devil are you two doing here?"

They looked round, and there was Dr. Ozanne coming out of one of the old tumbledown houses. Pipet Lane was not so attractive now. People were stirring. Raucous voices sounded from within the doors, hungry dogs were nosing about in some garbage. And Dr. Ozanne was not at his most attractive either. He had had an appalling night of it delivering a poor woman of a lusty man-child, and he was unshaven and haggard. Yet there was a certain light in his eyes that William recognised as a sign that life, not death, had been the outcome of his father's activities. It usually was with Dr. Ozanne. That was one reason why the poor loved him. He had continued the struggle last night when another doctor might have abandoned it, thinking the life of one waif more or less no great matter upon the teeming earth. But that was not Dr. Ozanne's way. Life was life, precious and divine, to be saved at all costs, and the saving of it was what he lived for.

But he was exhausted, and much irritated to find Marianne and William in such a place as Pipet Lane.

"I've a good mind to thrash you, William," he said angrily to his son. "What do you mean by bringing Marianne to a place like this? You know perfectly well that this is a bad quarter of the town. And you, Marianne, you're older than William, you know as well as I do that such junketings early in the morning are unseemly. By gad, you

both deserve a thrashing! Take my arm, Marianne, and try to behave like a lady. Look at your skirt! Sopped with sea water! Get
along with you, William. Pull your trousers down. You're not fit
to be seen. . . . And you'll be less of a beauty than ever when you've
had that thrashing that's coming to you."

But William was not abashed. His father's threats of thrashing
never materialised. He scurried along up Pipet Lane ahead of his
father and Marianne, hopping and jumping over the cobbles like the
child that he still was at heart. "I'm going to be a sailor!" he sang.
"I'm going to be a sailor and sail all round the world."

"In the Merchant Service," said Marianne.

But Dr. Ozanne unexpectedly sided with his son. "Merchant
Service be damned," he said angrily. "What would his poor mother
say? If it's a sailor he's to be his mother's son shall go in the Royal
Navy. . . . If I can afford it."

CHAPTER THREE

1

The next evening, after six o'clock dinner, Marianne in her maroon
dress stood at the schoolroom window twisting two little gold rings
round and round in her pierced ears. They must be kept continually
on the move, keeping the holes open, until the sore places had healed.
She made a wry face as she turned them, not because it hurt but because her memories of the last two days were not pleasant. It had
been late when she got home yesterday morning and she had had the
worst row with her parents that she had ever had. . . . And little
Marguerite had been stricken to the heart, and with reason, at having been left out of the morning's adventure. She should have been
awakened and taken too, she had said, and her reproachful sobs had
been harder to bear than the parents' scolding. . . . Altogether
yesterday had been a vile day, and as her request to be taken to the
jeweller's to have her ears pierced had been brusquely refused she
had had to pierce them herself with her mother's hatpin; a nasty,
messy business. Confronted with bleeding ears and a fait accompli
Sophie had relented sufficiently to produce the little gold rings, but
she had not spoken to her erring daughter, and though to-day things
had been pleasanter Marianne had nevertheless withdrawn into
solitude once dinner was over.

But the escapade had been a thousand times worth it, and from
the parlour window one could only see the garden, while from up
here one could see the harbour and the Green Dolphin. It was a

perfect autumn evening, blue and crisp and lovely. The gale had not risen again and the sea had moderated.

Suddenly her hands dropped from her ears, she gave a cry of delight, opened the window wide and leaned out. The Green Dolphin was moving. The wind was favourable and she was bound for the port of Bristol.

And Marianne's spirit was with her as she went. She hung out of the window and watched till her eyes ached, her pulses leaping as one sail after another blossomed like flowers on the masts. Ah, but she was lovely, that ship, the loveliest thing in all the world! And now she was running swiftly before the wind, a wake of white foam behind her. She was like a bird now, like a speeding gull, her wings alight in the sunlight, alive from prow to stern, in every fibre of her, a creature spun out of sun and air, free and indestructible, the spirit of the sea.

Marianne watched for a long while, yet it seemed but a moment. Now the clipper was hull down over the horizon, and now, like petals falling, her sails dropped one by one from sight. A mast-tip gleamed in the sunlight and then she was gone, a dream, an immortal memory, the loveliest that earth could give.

Marianne found that she was sobbing almost hysterically. She was tired after all the excitements and agitations of the last two days; and because she was a woman it might never be her lot to sail over the rim of the world in a sailing ship. William would. William was a man and was to be a sailor if his father could afford it.

Her sobs stopped abruptly. "If I can afford it." She could hear Dr. Ozanne's angry voice saying the words as he had said them yesterday in Pipet Lane. Unless his practice improved he would certainly not be able to afford it, and Marianne was shrewd enough to know that Dr. Ozanne's practice was not going to improve. She was also shrewd enough to know that he would never compromise with the Merchant Service for William. He had got the idea into his head that for his wife's son it must be the Navy or nothing, and with the obstinacy of his weakness he would cling to the idea like a limpet to its rock. And his laziness, combined with his pride, would prevent him from searching for some other man who would be able to do for William what he could not do himself. . . . Why, he had not even yet bestirred himself to send William to school, though there was a good boys' school on the Island. . . . And William was as bad. William, however much he longed for anything, would be far too indolent to set to work and encompass it for himself. No, it was she who must win his heart's desire for him, she who must make life for him and through him find life herself. And there was no time to

waste, either. If William was going into the Navy he must go now.
He was the right age. Later on he would be too old.

When Marianne decided to do anything she was in an agony unless
she could do it at that very moment. Luckily at this moment she was
free as air, free as a bird. She sped to her room, seized her green
cloak, flung it round her and ran down the stairs, through the garden
and down Green Dolphin Street to the Ozannes' door. It stood wide
open, and in the little waiting-room to the right of the passage, that
opened into the doctor's surgery, a row of patients still sat on the
hard bench. Evidently the evening surgery hour had stretched long
past its appointed limit and the doctor had not yet had his dinner.
Marianne hesitated, then slipped in and sat down quietly at the end
of the bench. After all, I've come on business, she thought, the most
important business in the whole world, William's future.

It was very quiet in the little room with its bare scrubbed floor and
whitewashed walls and gay check curtains of red and blue. The
evening light filled it and one could hear the sea. The waiting patients
spoke to each other in low murmurs. They were poor folk, heavy
with weariness at the end of a hard day, anxious, burdened with
their pain. There was a very old countrywoman bent almost double
with infirmity, with knotted hands that one would have thought
must be almost useless to her; yet the white frills inside her best
black poke bonnet were beautifully goffered, her apron was snow-
white, and the little scarlet cross-over shawl that she wore over the
bodice of her voluminous black dress was bright and gay. She had
a beautiful merry old face with unquenchable vitality in the dark
eyes. By her side sat a little pop-eyed granddaughter with a front
tooth missing, who held a basket with three brown eggs in it very
carefully upon her lap. It was a present for the doctor, Marianne
guessed, probably the only payment they would be able to give him.

Next to the pop-eyed little granddaughter was a girl with a shawl
slipping back from a small beautiful sleek gold head. She had a
drained white face with half-moons of darkness beneath her flower-
blue eyes, a child's face that looked oddly out of keeping above her
distorted swollen body. Marianne had never before seen a woman
quite so near her hour as this one, for Sophie had taken very good
care that she should not, and a flicker of fear went through her. So
one looked like that, did one? And just how much did it hurt to
have a baby? And how *did* one have a baby? Sophie belonged to a
generation that gave to its daughters no explanation whatever of the
very reason for their existence. Marianne was utterly ignorant, and
sullen and angry at her ignorance, shamed somehow by the dignity
of that girl and the proud carriage of her head. Though they were so

near to each other in age a whole world of experience lay between them. Yet when they looked at each other Marianne did not drop her eyes before the unconscious patronage that was in the other's glance. For she'd know too one day; she'd never acquiesce in ignorance of her own womanhood, in the lack of that pride and dignity, no, not whatever it cost, for there were things one was more afraid of being without with ease than possessing with pain. Another girl's fear would have undergone a change at this point but Marianne's died right out; for as yet her arrogance could entertain no doubts as to her ability to equal in experience a little girl out of the streets with a sleek gold head and flower-blue eyes. They smiled at each other, and suddenly there was neither patronage nor arrogance but a fusing of their youth and womanhood and a quick thrill of friendship.

Then their moment of intimacy was interrupted by the little boy with the swollen wrist who sat next to Marianne. He was a freckled dirty urchin of some seven years, afflicted with a running nose and no handkerchief and clothed in a tattered jersey that smelt strongly of fish, and he suddenly dissolved into tears. Normally Marianne would have taken no notice, for she was not fond of children as children, but the sight of the pregnant girl, and the quick thrill of friendship that she had felt for her, had quickened her own dormant maternity, and she put her arm round him and pulled him close to her, his fishy jersey pressed against her silk dress. "What is it?" she asked.

"He thinks he's broken his wrist," said the blue-eyed girl. "I say he's just sprained it. That's all it is. Une veine trésaillie. A sprain."

"I slipped getting into the boat," sobbed the small boy. "I slipped and fell down with my wrist underneath me."

They spoke in their Island patois, that Marianne found rather difficult to follow, but she gathered that the little boy, alone among the waiting patients, was afraid of what lay beyond the surgery door.

"Dr. Ozanne is kind," she said comfortingly. "And if it hurts you'll enjoy fighting not to let him see how much. Fighting can be fun, you know; any sort of fighting."

And then for a long time she sat silent, the small boy still held within her arm, while the old dame came out and went away and the young girl took her place in the surgery. Immense joy came to her from the small warm body pressed against hers. There seemed a hollow in her shoulder just made for his tousled dark head and the feel of his beating heart against her bare arm sent a tremor of delight through her body. . . . It suddenly came to her that she liked the poor. . . . When the blue-eyed girl came out of the surgery, bade her good-night and went her way into the sunset, she watched her go towards her travail almost with love.

"Now it's your turn," she said to the little boy. "I'll come with you. What's your name? Jean? Remember, Jean, that if it hurts it will be fun not to let the doctor know how much."

They went into the surgery together, Jean holding her hand.

"Hullo? Hullo?" said Dr. Ozanne. "This young man a protégé of yours, Marianne?"

"We have made friends in the waiting-room," said Marianne. "He comes first. He has hurt his wrist."

The surgery was a small room looking on the garden. It was wildly untidy and none too clean, and its atmosphere of whisky and anaesthetics and unwashed humanity was enough to knock you over. The shabby frock coat that Dr. Ozanne wore for work in the surgery was none too clean either, and there was a slight tremor about his hands, as he tried to bring a little order into the litter on his desk, that Marianne had not noticed before. . . . She had been right. His practice was not going to improve. He would never be a successful doctor.

Yet the moment he turned his attention to the boy she had to admit that there are two ways of being a successful doctor. As he took the child on his knee and pushed up the ragged sleeve to examine the wrist she lost all consciousness of the dirt and stuffiness of the room and was aware only of the huge warmth of this man's kindness. He was talking quickly and easily to the boy in the patois that he had learned in his youth, his whole attention centred upon him as though to have this child on his knee were the thing that he wanted most in the whole world. And the fear had gone out of the child's eyes and the dimples were showing in his cheeks. It was just so, Marianne remembered, that he had welcomed her when she had first come to Green Dolphin Street. . . . He had seemed to want her. . . . And he *had* wanted her, just as he wanted this child on his knee. Only in contact with humanity could the lover-like hunger of his kindness find satisfaction.

"There's a bone broken," said the doctor's voice, cutting across her thoughts. "Would you like to help me, Marianne?"

"Yes," she said with eagerness.

Bone-setting was a new experience for her, as had been the contact with humanity in the waiting-room, and her spirit leaped to meet it. She did what the doctor told her without fumbling or hesitation, as though she had been doing it all her life, eager and interested, giving the business her whole attention. Dr. Ozanne was not surprised. He knew her for a clever, capable girl, with just that touch of hardness that would keep her from being unnerved by pity. Yet she had feeling. Now and then she glanced at the child and smiled at him, and the boy smiled at her as though they had some secret understanding together. And when it was all over, and the doctor was hunting in one of the drawers of his desk for the toffee he kept for the consolation of the gallant among his smaller patients, she took the child on her knee with a mature tenderness he had not known she possessed. He was again touched and troubled by her personality, as he had been when he first saw her. If life gave her scope for her powers and emotions she would make a great success of life, but if it denied her the disaster might be equally as great. A nature as passionate as hers would never make a fine thing of frustration. It took a saint to do that, and Marianne was none of your saints.

"Well, my dear, do you want a salve for those sore ears?" he asked her jovially when the child had gone.

"No, thank you," said Marianne a little tartly. "I am perfectly capable of dealing with my own ears."

"So I see," chuckled the doctor. "You took a hat-pin to the job I gather. It's not so badly done either. You'd make a fine doctor, my dear, if you were a man. You've clever hands and a good nerve. You helped me well with that child."

Marianne swung round in her chair and faced him across his desk, her dark eyes blazing. "If I only *could* be a doctor!" she cried. "I believe it would be even better than being a sailor. Couldn't I be a doctor?"

"Certainly not!" said Dr. Ozanne with twinkling eyes. "You're a woman, my dear, and women are not doctors, and never will be, thank God. A woman's place is in the home, doing needlework and enjoying delicate health. What's the trouble this time? Palpitations? Sensibility? All-overness? Grippe? Migraine? Headache? Take your time. Delicate females have plenty of choice."

"There's nothing the matter with me, thank you," said Marianne. "There's never anything the matter with me. It's not about myself, I've come, it's about William."

"About William?" said the astonished doctor.

"Yes. I've come to tell you that Papa will pay for him to go into the Navy."

"What?" shouted the doctor, and the blood rushed to his forehead and his hands clenched themselves upon the litter on his desk. "What's that? What's that?"

Marianne repeated herself.

"The cheek!" growled Dr. Ozanne. "The damned cheek, by gad! Can't I pay for the education of my own son?"

"No," said Marianne. "You can't, and you know you can't, and it's not a bit of use getting in a temper like that. And why shouldn't you give Mamma and Papa the pleasure of helping William? They love helping people. They are the most generous couple on the Island."

She herself was very cool and precise now, sitting very upright in her chair, her hands folded quietly in her lap, her small elfin face very pale and cold within the shadows of her bonnet. Only the little pulse beating in her temple, that the doctor could not see, gave evidence that she was advancing now with hidden passion upon the warpath.

"And what the devil induced your father to send you along with such an outrageous proposition?" stormed the infuriated doctor. "The suggestion is infernal cheek in any case, but if it was to be made at all it should have been made by himself, not by you."

"Papa did not send me along," said Marianne sedately. "He'll be waiting upon you himself presently, after you've had your dinner, to make the suggestion in his own person; only I thought I'd better come and warn you beforehand in case you behaved to him as you're behaving to me now."

The doctor glared at her, tried to speak and failed.

"I think, sir, that you'd better give yourself a dose of something," Marianne continued. "I've never seen any one so red in the face as you are now. I'm afraid you'll have a seizure. You get angry much too easily. That's because you drink too much, you know, sir. I expect you've been told that before, but I'm telling you again. It's for your good I'm telling you. I'm very fond of you."

The mask of anger that had been clamped down upon Dr. Ozanne's face suddenly split into fragments, and he flung himself back in his chair and laughed till it seemed that the room shook. The solemnity and sedateness that had taken possession of the elfin creature in the chair opposite tickled him mightily. She was as variable in her moods as an April day, and had the same enchantment.

"You've shown great foresight, my dear," he said, wiping his eyes with a large spotted handkerchief. "Without your warning I'd certainly not have given your Papa the welcome his good intentions deserve. But there's no good purpose to be served by his waiting upon me. You run along home, my dear, and tell him to spare himself the trouble."

"I can't do that, sir, because he'd not be pleased if he knew I'd been to see you," said Marianne in the truthful tones of deep conviction.

"I daresay not," said the doctor.

"So don't tell him, please, sir, that I've been here," said Marianne. "And I think I'll sit with you for a minute or two longer, for it's been lonely at home all day. Papa and Mamma have not wanted to speak to me. They are angry that I went with William to see the clipper."

"So I should suppose," said the doctor drily.

"Well, it was worth it," said Marianne. "She was the loveliest ship I've ever seen. William loved her too. William was born for a sailor. I've never seen him look so happy as he did on board that clipper. He just seemed to belong there, as he belongs in happy Green Dolphin Street. Did he tell you the clipper was called the Green Dolphin? It seems more than a coincidence, doesn't it? More like destiny. William ought to sail on that ship."

"His mother's son shall never go in the Merchant Service," said Dr. Ozanne obstinately.

"He'd be just as happy in the Navy," said Marianne. "What matters is that he should go to sea. It's horrid not to be able to do what you want to do. It's horrid to be frustrated."

She got up and re-tied her bonnet strings, her eyes gazing sombrely out of the window, and the doctor's compassionate kindness, liberated by the cessation of his anger, flowed out to her again. "Horrid to have been born a woman when you would have liked to be a sailor or a doctor, eh?" he said.

"I was not thinking of myself just then," said Marianne. "I was thinking of William . . . and Mamma."

"Mamma?" ejaculated Dr. Ozanne in astonishment.

"She loves William," said Marianne. "She loves him very much. Mamma has always longed for a son, you know. When Papa waits upon you with his suggestion it will be partly because he himself wants William to be happy but even more because Mamma wants it. Mamma will be dreadfully distressed if you won't agree. I *hate* dear Mamma to be unhappy." Her sombre eyes came back from the window and fixed themselves upon the doctor's. "Sometimes I think that Mamma was very unhappy when she was very young. I think she wanted something very much and didn't get it. Perhaps she loved someone and he disappointed her."

For a moment more her eyes held the doctor's, then she walked slowly and demurely to the door. With her hand upon the handle she turned back to deliver her parting remarks in sad and dulcet tones.

"No, I can never be a doctor," she said. "It's horrid being a woman. One does not ever seem able to have what one wants unless a man gives it to one. Papa will never give his permission for me to study the subjects that interest me; engineering and things like that; he says they aren't ladylike subjects. That's his pride. He'd rather I was ladylike than happy. It's strange, isn't it, how often parents ruin their children's lives because of their pride? Good-bye."

And she was gone, closing the door tranquilly behind her.

But there was nothing tranquil about the mood in which she left the man upon the other side of it. He felt like the unfortunate Sebastian, stuck all over with arrows, each of them a sentence spoken very quietly by a demure elf in a green bonnet. "What matters is that he should go to sea. . . . It's horrid to be frustrated. . . . It's funny, isn't it, how often parents ruin their children's lives because of their pride? . . . Mamma has always longed for a son. . . . Mamma was very unhappy when she was young. . . . She loved someone and he disappointed her. . . . It's horrid to be frustrated. . . . It's horrid to be frustrated."

"Damn!" said Dr. Ozanne violently to no one in particular.

He had been saying to himself, before Marianne started shooting these arrows at him, that it takes a saint to make a fine thing of frustration, and here he sat convicted of frustrating through his pride three people who were not saints, and thereby courting disaster for them. William had set his heart on the sea, and Marianne had set her heart on William having what he wanted, and Sophie had set her heart on playing Mother to William. . . . Sophie who perhaps would have had a son of her own had her first love Edmond Ozanne not forgotten his tenderness for her in the proud excitement of a new life in a new land. . . . Dr. Ozanne was a sentimental as well as a credulous man. The strength of his sudden conviction that Sophie had loved him to distraction and that he had ruined her life by forgetting her was not shaken by any suspicion of guile in Marianne. No, the innocent child's thoughtless little remarks, dropped by a lucky chance just in the nick of time, had revealed him to himself as an unfeeling monster whose pride had caused him to trample alike upon the tenderest hopes of a loving woman and a trusting child. He was tired and befuddled after a long day of hard work and hard drinking, and the tears stood in his eyes. Beautiful Sophie! How adorable she had been in those days of their sweet youth when she had been as slim as Marianne, but much more graceful, and a featherweight upon his arm as they strolled up and down together beside the sea wall. If only he had known then how much she loved him! What a difference it would have made to both their lives. Darling Sophie. To think of her married to that pompous ass Octavius! He took out his large spotted handkerchief and blew a trumpet blast upon his nose. His mind was made up. Even though it meant humbling himself before that same pompous ass he must make what reparation he could.

2

Marianne was meanwhile speeding back up Green Dolphin Street to Le Paradis. Her mood of pensive sadness had abruptly left her and it would have astonished the doctor had he seen the fire in her eye, the set of her jaw, and her green cloak blown back from her shoulders by the wind of her going. She ran through the garden like a mad thing but in the hall she paused to take off her cloak and bonnet, smooth her hair and quiet her panting breath. Then she composed her features to a mask of penitence and slid like a shadow through the parlour door.

Marguerite had already gone to bed. Octavius, his monocle adjusted in his left eye, was reading "The Examiner" and Sophie was embroidering. They looked up for a moment, regarding her more in sorrow than in anger, and then continued their employments.

"I am sorry, Papa. I am sorry, Mamma," said Marianne, standing before them with downcast eyes and hands demurely folded. "My behaviour yesterday morning was most unladylike. I am sorry for it. I ask you to forgive me."

As a general rule it was not Marianne's habit to apologise after domestic disturbance, for it was her invariable conviction that whoever was to blame it was not herself, and this unwonted humility took her parents entirely by surprise. They gasped, and Octavius's monocle fell from his eye and Sophie's thimble rolled beneath the escritoire. Marianne retrieved them, kissed her parents, and sat down upon a very lowly stool.

"Dear child!" murmured Sophie, tears in her eyes. "Dear, dear child!"

"We'll say no more about it," said Octavius magnanimously, polishing his monocle. He had had several glasses of port after an excellent dinner and was in a mellow mood, tinged with sentimentality. "We'll say no more about it. The matter is closed."

"Not quite," said Marianne.

"Eh?" said Octavius.

"I mean not quite for poor William," said Marianne. "Dr. Ozanne has threatened to thrash him."

"Quite right," approved Octavius. "William is quite old enough to know that he should not take young gentlewomen upon the kind of escapade that he took my daughter yesterday."

"Oh, poor William!" cried Sophie pitifully. "He's only a child, Octavius. And motherless, poor lamb. His mother would have hated to see him running wild like a little hooligan in the way he does."

"Yes, it's a shame," agreed Marianne, "for he's clever. He'd like to go into the Royal Navy."

"Then why not send him into the Navy?" asked Octavius over the top of "The Examiner". "Excellent discipline."

"I believe Dr. Ozanne *is* thinking of sending William into the Navy," said Marianne. "He is looking forward to consulting you about it."

"Consulting *me*?" asked Octavius. "What on earth has it got to do with me?"

"I happened to tell him how fond Mamma is of William," said Marianne. And then, her eyes roving innocently from one startled parental countenance to the other, she asked sweetly, "Did I do wrong? I know how much you and Mamma love to help people. I've heard it said that you are the most generous couple on the Island."

Her eyes did not waver as they rested on her father's face, for she *had* heard it said. She'd just said it herself to Dr. Ozanne.

"And what do you mean by helping people?" asked Octavius. "Giving them the benefit of my advice?"

"Not only that, Papa," said his daughter, smiling at him. "Generous people give more than advice; and I said as much to Dr. Ozanne."

"What the devil *have* you said to Dr. Ozanne?" demanded her anxious parent.

"That I thought you would like to treat William like the son that dear Mamma has always longed for but has never had," said Marianne sweetly, "and pay for him to go into the Navy. After all, he is the living image of the son Mamma would have liked to have had, isn't he, Mamma?"

And Sophie, startled beyond measure, suddenly dropped her work on the floor and was a long time picking it up again. She was not only startled, she was touched to the quick that Marianne, who had always seemed so unsympathetic, should have divined this hidden longing.

"Darling Marianne!" she cried impulsively, and then her tear-filled eyes fixed themselves upon her husband's face. "Do what she wants, Octavius," they pleaded silently. "You can afford it. Don't shake her faith in you. Don't shame her before the doctor."

And because they had been married for so long Octavius knew exactly what her eyes were saying.

"When you go and see the doctor, Papa," said Marianne, "you won't tell him that we've talked like this, will you? I don't want him him to think that I've persuaded you to be so generous, when all the time it was your own idea."

And by this time Octavius, a little muddled as well as mellowed by his port, was beginning to think that it *was* his own idea. The glow of his generosity, as well as of his port, was warming him from top to toe, and having a markedly good effect upon his digestion, never very strong during the after-dinner hour. But he was nevertheless a little startled by the suddenness of his own nobility, and Marianne talked a little longer to give him time to adjust himself.

"Dr. Ozanne is very proud," she said. "You may have a little difficulty in making him see reason. But you've got such tact, Papa, you'll do it. Mention Mamma and her affection for William."

"I don't need to be told how to carry out my own ideas, thank you, Marianne," said her father, and there was just a hint of revolt in his tones, for his subconscious mind, not so fuddled by the fumes of his wine as his conscious one, was beginning to wonder whose was the initiative in this conversation. Marianne noticed the revolt and introduced a slightly dictatorial note into her next remark.

"Don't go this evening, Papa," she said. "To-morrow will do, or any time. Don't go to-night."

Octavius arose instantly from his chair. "I shall certainly go to-night," he said. "I shall go now. No time like the present."

As he passed his wife's chair she put up her hand and touched his cheek. "You are good, Octavius," she whispered. "I always knew you were good. . . . Take the doctor a bottle of our French brandy, my love. I'm sure it will be welcome."

"Certainly, dearest," said Octavius, and inflated his chest and went out.

The two women looked at each other in silence for a moment or two, and with increased respect. On Sophie's side the respect was a little startled, for it seemed to her that her daughter had grown from a child into an adroit and understanding woman all in the space of one half-hour, and on Marianne's side it was tinged with a new sympathy and understanding. . . . For when her mother had dropped her work on the floor she had known that her guess had been correct; Sophie had once loved Dr. Ozanne as she herself loved William.

"It was clever of you to think of the brandy, Mamma," said Marianne. "That will put them both in a good mood. It's the very best brandy, isn't it? The kind that we smuggle to England?"

For the second time the startled Sophie dropped her work on the floor. . . . She had had no idea that Marianne knew about the profitable smuggling trade in which so many respectable Islanders had a finger. . . . When she picked it up again her lovely face had flushed a rosy pink.

"How did you know I longed for a son, Marianne?" she whispered.

"By the way you look at William," said Marianne. "You'd like a son just like William. . . . And William is just like his father. . . . Did you love Dr. Ozanne very much, Mamma?"

Sophie gasped, and clutched her work just as it was about to slither off her silken lap for the third time.

"Don't worry, Mamma," said Marianne. "I won't tell Papa."

"Marianne," said Sophie, "I think you'd better go to bed. You seem to have grown up into a woman all of a sudden—but still—I think you had better go to bed before you or I say something we may regret later."

"Very well," said Marianne, getting up. "Good-night, Mamma," and she kissed her mother on her beautiful flushed cheek, whispering as she did so, "Mamma, how *could* you have married Papa?"

"Marianne! Marianne!" protested her mother. "Your father is very, very good."

"He's easily managed," conceded Marianne, and she curtseyed and left the room.

She mounted the stairs with a jaunty step. It had probably been quite sensible of Mamma to marry Papa, she decided on second thoughts. If you can't marry the man you love then the next best thing is to marry one who is easily managed. . . . But the best thing of all, of course, is to marry a man beloved as well as manageable, as she herself intended to do.

She undressed quickly, put on her frilly white nightgown and her white nightcap and slipped into the four-poster with the powder-blue curtains that she shared with Marguerite. She needed no candle, for the window was wide and uncurtained and the summer twilight still filled the room. Her little sister was already asleep, her face pearly white and innocent in its aureole of golden curls. Marianne kissed her softly before she lay down. She looked such a child and Marianne herself, now, was a woman.

She lay on her back, listening to the distant surge of the sea, and her womanhood seemed pulsing through her like the blood in her veins. She had learned so much about herself and what she wanted in the last two days. Maternity had been quickened in her, and love of the poor. And she knew that fighting can be fun up till the very end, and that she would never really be afraid, and that though a woman is hedged about with the restrictions of her sex she can get what she wants if she has sufficient of the enchantress in her to spin a clever web.

"And I spun my web cleverly to-night," thought Marianne. "I spun it very well. And I did not tell a single lie either. I did not say a word to Dr. Ozanne or Papa that was not the truth."

She sighed with contentment as the night gathered about her, and then began once more to twist the little gold rings round and round in her ears.

PART II

MARGUERITE

Call not thy wanderer home as yet
  Though it be late.
Now is his first assailing of
  The invisible gate.
Be still through that light knocking. The hour
  Is thronged with fate.

To that first tapping at the invisible door
  Fate answereth.
What shining image or voice, what sigh
  Or honied breath,
Comes forth, shall be the master of life
  Even to death.

GEORGE WILLIAM RUSSELL.

CHAPTER ONE

1

It was All Saints' Day and Marguerite's birthday, and the Le Patourels were enjoying an immense breakfast, a fine day, a whole holiday and the prospect of an outing. It was a family tradition that they should go for a picnic upon Marguerite's birthday and to-day they were to drive in the chariot to the other side of the island, to beautiful rocky La Baie des Saints, where the children would scramble about on the beach and their parents sit beneath Sophie's parasol and enjoy the view, while over them there brooded the great convent of Notre Dame du Castel, built upon its rock above the thundering Atlantic waves.

It was the habit of the Island, once it had put the storms of the autumn equinox behind it, to produce a spell of beautiful weather almost as warm and sunny as June, and in the heart of this weather All Saints' Day was caught up like perfume in a flower. Marianne and Marguerite could not remember a year when All Saints' Day had not been fine and lovely; as a festival it ranked only second in their minds with Christmas and Easter.

Religion was an integral part of the children's lives. All the

Islanders were devout, and had been since those days when their Island had been called l'Ile Sainte, l'Ile Bienheureuse, those days far back in the mists of time when monks from the great Abbey of Mont Saint Michel in Normandy had rowed across the stormy sea in their little boats, landed at La Baie des Saints and built themselves the monastery on the cliff top that had later become the Convent of Notre Dame du Castel. Many great saints at different times had visited the Island, not excluding St. Patrick himself, and there were several beautiful old churches built by those saints of old, and innumerable shrines and holy wells, all of them garlanded with legends that were as familiar to Marianne and Marguerite as Jack-and-the-Beanstalk and the Sleeping Beauty to English children.

At the Reformation the Islands had adopted the discipline of the reformed churches of Geneva and France, and the majority of the Islanders were not now Catholic, but the peasants remained always Catholic at heart, loving the old festivals and keeping the legends of the early saints fresh in their memories. Of the many religious communities that had once lived on the Island there remained now only two, the sisters of the convent school beside the Catholic Church of St. Raphael at St. Pierre and the nuns of Notre Dame du Castel.

The Le Patourels were not Catholics and had not been since the Reformation, but they were Islanders, and as they ate their breakfast on this festival morning their subconscious thoughts and memories, their deep and hidden instincts, were, unknown to themselves, distinctly unreformed.

Yet if their spirits moved through the shining paths of l'Ile Sainte et l'Ile Bienheureuse their bodies this morning were looking distinctly of this world, well-fed, well-clothed, shining with prosperity. The four of them were a pleasing sight. Octavius, pausing in the mastication of a slice of well-cooked ham to survey the scene before him, decided not for the first time that the Strength of the Empire was founded upon the Home, especially his home, with its beauty, wealth and culture, its lofty Christian sentiments and excellent cuisine. Octavius was a happy man. He was entirely contented with all that he possessed, including himself, and could see no room for improvement anywhere. He had not been born wealthy but the happy combination of an open guileless countenance with an astute and guileful brain in business matters had had its inevitable result, of which the beautiful room, the loaded table and the elegant females at whom he gazed with such benignity were the outward and visible sign.

The austere beauty of the outside of No. 3 Le Paradis was echoed within, where the simple furniture that had been good enough for

Octavius's parents was still good enough for him. Sheraton chairs stood about the mahogany table. There were a few family portraits hanging on the walls, but not enough to hide the beautiful panelling. The curtains were of pale gold brocade, the very colour of the sunshine that lay in pools upon the polished floor.

But there was nothing austere about the food. The Le Patourels were drinking fragrant coffee frothing with rich cream out of cups of exquisite French china, scarlet and blue and gold. There was a huge home-cured ham, "pâlette", upon the table, eggs, butter and preserves, dishes of fruit, crisp rolls and a home-made bread-cake called "galette", of a thick spongy consistency that was most satisfactorily filling. Sophie, who feared for the elegance of her figure, was toying with coffee and rolls in the French style, but Octavius and the girls were nourishing themselves with vigour and concentration.

Octavius, having demolished two boiled eggs and helped himself to a second plateful of pâlette, was about to admonish his wife to eat a little more when his eye fell upon her contours and he decided that her moderation was to be commended. He did not want her to lose her beauty. He was immensely proud of it. She looked particularly pleasing this morning in her gown of grey silk shot with fire colour, with its sleeves slightly puffed at the shoulders, then fitting snugly over her shapely arms, its long shining folds that reached the ground and hid her feet, and its delicate ruchings at neck and wrist. She did not favour the new fashion of extravagantly small waists, ankle-length ballooning skirts and sleeves extended on wires and stretched over bolsters on the shoulders, so that a woman looked less like a woman than an hour glass, and he was glad of it, for he was as conservatively minded as she was herself. He liked the graceful lines of her old-fashioned clothes, and the old-fashioned mob cap on her fair curls, as much as he liked the great gold locket enclosing a lock of his hair, and the huge brooch that held curls cut from the children's heads, tied with blue ribbon, confined beneath glass and framed in pinchbeck, and the heavy swinging gold earrings that had been his wedding gift. These were her invariable ornaments and were the symbol of her devotion to the family circle. She was a good wife. His only regret was that the brooch held only two little baby curls and not ten. But the limitation of her child-bearing was not his fault or hers, and before the inscrutable wisdom of Providence that had seen fit to deny him his quiverful he was content to bow his head; especially as a small family is less expensive to educate, and that now, by some process he had not been altogether able to follow, William Ozanne had become almost as a son to him.

And though small his family gave satisfaction to his eye. He did not agree with Sophie that Marianne was plain. Octavius was a wishful thinker. It was not within the bounds of possibility that any daughter of his should be plain, therefore she was not plain. Her new tartan frock of russet brown and deep green and dark red, with a full skirt long enough to hide the pantaloons that had never been becoming to her, gave fullness to her thin figure, and its colours became her dark hair (still in curl so early in the morning) and her dark eyes that for some reason or other had had a new light in them just lately. She was looking almost happy and she still had the colour in her cheeks that had bloomed there last night when she had insisted that William should make one of the picnic party, and Octavius had demurred because though he was about to pour out a mint of money upon him he did not really want William perpetually under foot, and Marianne had insisted and had got her way.

Marguerite of course always looked happy, but to-day being her birthday she was absolutely radiant with joy, her eyes as blue as her new blue dress with the gauze ribbons, and her plump legs in their clean white pantaloons (that still had to show several inches below the hem of her dress because she was still only little) swinging joyously backwards and forwards beneath the table with a soft swishing sound that it took Octavius a few moments of exploration to identify.

"Keep your legs still, Marguerite," he commanded. And she kept them still. She never made noises just to annoy, as so many children do. When she discovered that what she considered was a pleasant sound was not thought so by others she immediately desisted from making it.

"If you have finished, my dears, you may get down," said Sophie. "You have time for an hour's needlework before we start. As it is a birthday you may sit in the parlour while you sew."

They sat upon straight-backed chairs in a patch of sunshine in the parlour window, their feet upon small wooden footstools, and stitched at their needlework. Marianne had started a new and beautiful petit-point for a chair seat, representing a ship in full sail. She did needlework, as she did everything, with the maximum of competence and speed. Her fingers flew as she worked, and the room swayed and tumbled about her with the swaying of weeds beneath the water, the motion of the ship breasting the waves, the tumbling of the dolphins and the wheeling of the gulls. Her whole being was a loom where dim purples and pearly greys wove in and out of a stretched taut web of bright blue and gold; blue of the sea, gold of the sun, purple and grey of winds and waters, of veiled mornings, of evenings of silent rain and the dreams that come between sleeping and waking; with just here a flash of fire in the grey, seen and then not seen, a flash of exultation as though the key of a treasure house suddenly gleamed in one's fingers, yet when one turned to find the door one's hands were empty. . . .

Marguerite, sucking a pricked finger, looked at her with an envy untouched by bitterness. Marguerite, a clumsy needlewoman, was still labouring at that accursed sampler that darkened the light for Victorian childhood from the first stitch to the last. Marianne, starting her sampler at the age of six, had finished it in three years; Marguerite, beginning at five and a half, was still at it. Marianne's sampler, worked upon the finest of fine linen, measured four feet by three, contained thirty different examples of embroidery stitches, representations of twenty different flowers and fruits, exquisitely natural and graceful, interspersed with apocryphal birds and beasts, no two the same. In the centre were three verses from the forty-second psalm. "Comme le cerf soupire après l'eau des fontaines, ainsi mon âme soupire après toi, O Mon Dieu. Au bruit de tes torrents, un abîme appelait un autre abîme: tous tes flots, toutes tes vagues ont passé sur moi. Mon âme a soif de Dieu, du Dieu vivant: quand entéral-je me présenterai-je devant la face de Dieu?" Below this were her names, Marianne Véronique Le Patourel, and the dates, the whole enclosed in a beautiful border of green vine leaves. The finished work of art was now laid away in lavender and silver paper in the carved chest in Sophie's bedroom, far too beautiful to be put to any sort of use, or even to be looked at, lest usefulness cause a moulting of the feathers of the birds and the eye of the sun fade the colours of the flowers.

Marguerite's sampler was only two feet by three, for Sophie had realised that the acreage over which Marguerite must plod had better be small, lest she faint by the way. There were no flowers or birds on her sampler, but a geometrical border of gold stars round the edge, then rows of stiff little trees in pots, hung with golden balls. Marguerite's spirit had failed within her at the thought of embroidering a whole quotation from a psalm, as Marianne had done, but between the two rows of little trees she had worked in red the words without which no Island peasant ever began a new piece of work, whether it were the spring sowing, or the wearing of a new scarlet petticoat, or the building of a new boat—"Au nom de Dieu soit". And below it was a space for her names—Marguerite Félicité Le Patourel—and for the dates of commencement and conclusion of labour when at last the wretched thing should be done. She had quite finished the stiff little trees with the golden balls, but she was still very far from having finished the border. There were so many of the gold stars, and they all had to be filled up inside with minute cross-stitch, and it was so difficult to keep their points clear and bright. It had been her own choice to have a border of stars, but they were very, very difficult. Never mind, they would be finished one day, and the sampler would be folded up in silver paper and lavender, her childhood between the folds, and laid away in Sophie's chest, and then Marguerite Félicité Le Patourel would be a woman.

The samplers were typical. Marianne's was full of complexity, vivid imagination, and that fatal facility that left her longing for fresh worlds to conquer, and Marguerite's shining stars and trim little potted trees hung with happy fruit were typical of her own contentment that would be equally at home in the fields of heaven as in a walled garden. And the "Au Nom de Dieu soit" was of the essence of Marguerite. It had her simple clear directness. In the name of God she would lay hold of her being in two worlds, and her certainty that the hall-mark of happiness that she saw stamped on life was an authentic hall-mark would destroy all questioning about its worth.

But meanwhile she was only a little girl and the labour of sewing a sampler was tedious, and she rested from it. While she sucked the finger of one hand she caressed with the other something that she held nestled on her lap.

Marianne was suddenly aware of that something and emerged abruptly from the spinning of her dreams. "What have you got there?" she demanded.

Marguerite never hid anything from any one. She laughed and produced a wooden mouse from the folds of her soft blue dress. It had ears made of pink sticking plaster, attached to its head with large nails, and a string tail. "William gave it to me for a birthday present," she said.

"When?" asked Marianne sharply.

"This morning," said Marguerite. "He rang the bell before breakfast and asked to see me. And I came down and he gave me my mouse. He made it for me. Isn't he clever?"

Marianne gazed with venom at the mouse. Yes, it was well made. A good deal of acute observation and delight in living things had gone to the shaping of its body. Its bright pink pointed ears were gay, and whether by design or accident there was a ribald look on its painted face that was reminiscent of the dolphin on the inn signboard. No one who knew William could doubt that this was William's mouse, that had run to the folds of Marguerite's dress straight out of William's own country.

"Go on with your sampler," said Marianne harshly, and with her fat chuckling laugh Marguerite hid her mouse away again and picked up her needle. But Marianne's delight in her work was destroyed. Restlessness and intense dislike of Marguerite had hold of her again and she scarcely knew how to sit still in her chair until it was time to start for the picnic. But she did sit still. Marguerite had no notion, as she laboured at a golden star, that Marianne's flying fingers were driven by anything but love of petit-point.

2

It was a memorable picnic. All five of them remembered it for years but no one more vividly than Marguerite. Her birthdays were always important to her, for being a born lover of life she would always keep the day of her entrance into it as a very great festival indeed, but this one was more important than the others. In after years she looked back upon it as a signpost that showed her the way to her own especial country.

The others remembered that day chiefly because of Marguerite's outrageous behaviour; but also for its great beauty. Even Octavius, as he followed his family out of the front door and stood between the delicate pillars at the top of the steps in his dark blue caped driving coat and curly-brimmed top hat, drawing on his gloves, exclaimed at it. The storms of the equinox had swept the world clean and fresh as crystal. The blue of a happy day seemed not only in the sky but all about them, limpid and innocent, an atmosphere even more than a colour, and showers of silvery sunshine fell with blessing. It was cool beneath the warmth, but not cold. The houses of Le Paradis were bathed in the pure light that softened while it intensified the colouring of weathered wall and roof. From a tall tree between two houses golden leaves drifted quietly. There was no sound from a sea lying at rest far down at the foot of the hill, and over their heads a white gull drifted as quietly as the autumn leaves. Sophie beside him, in her cloak the colour of a dove's wing, was a motionless figure in a dream. There was not enough air to sway the small bue flower that was Marguerite, and Marianne's elfin face was pale and rapt within the deep green shade of her bonnet. By the curb the chariot rested, made of spun glass, and the dappled horses waited without movement. The whole universe was stilled as though listening for a voice. For the space of one heart-beat there was peace on earth. For one fraction of a moment there was no deed of violence wrought on the earth, no hatred, no fire, no whirlwind, no pain, no fear. Existence rested against the heart of God, then sighed and journeyed again.

One of the horses raised his head and shook his jingling harness.

William suddenly appeared among them in his bright green suit, and laughing and talking they moved down the steps to the chariot. But in each of them there was an infinitesimal change. A moment that comes perhaps once in a thousand years had touched them in passing and though the experience of perfection is feather-light it brands like fire.

Only Marguerite spoke of it because only Marguerite knew what had happened. "It all stopped making a noise," she said. "And God said something in a small voice."

Octavius hastened to restore things to normal. "Autumn weather can be very tricky," he announced. "Uncanny. Storms and then silences."

Then they all piled themselves into the Le Patourel chariot, which was one of the most admired upon the Island. It was pulled by two horses, Pierre the coachman riding the left-hand one. It held two inside and three in the dickey. There was space in front for a box when travelling, occupied now by the hampers of food. A second trunk could be stowed on the roof and behind was a bonnet box. It had four windows, two in front and one on each side, and was beautifully upholstered in a deep mulberry colour that looked very smart with the silvery coats of the dappled horses. Pierre's livery was mulberry, and he could drive like the wind. Sophie and Octavius looked very regal sitting inside, bowing right and left to acquaintances, and the three children in the dickey were gay and happy as three bright-plumaged birds.

They climbed up and up through the narrow twisted lanes of the old town until the houses ended and instead of walls on either side of them they had banks of turf and stones overgrown with brambles and bracken, and over their heads arched nut trees or stunted oaks or tall escallonia trees with clusters of pink blossom among the glossy leaves. The nut trees and bracken were pure gold, the oak trees tawny above their lichened trunks, and the brambles had red leaves that burned like fire. Sophie and Octavius, now that there were no more acquaintances to bow to, settled themselves to admire the landscape. It was the fashion just now to go for elegant driving picnics and admire the beauties of nature. In their youth they had taken the loveliness of their Island rather for granted, but now they studied it with deliberate self-consciousness, Octavius with his monocle screwed rather uncomfortably tight and Sophie with her eyes very wide open lest the drowsiness induced by a busy morning should cause her to miss anything that it was her duty to admire. . . . Perhaps they had really enjoyed the Island more when they had been the age of the children in the dickey.

Marianne and Marguerite sat one on each side of William, out in the air and sunshine, swaying to the motion of the chariot, sniffing the special Island scent made up of the smell of the sea and the sandy road, wet bracken and the delicious scent of the escallonia flowers that on this Island went on blooming well into the winter. William had seen escallonia growing in England, but only as stunted bushes; here in this blest isle it grew into great columns of scent and colour. He began to feel immensely excited. He had not driven this way before and as the chariot wound its way up through the coloured tunnels of the lanes he was gripped by the lust of finding out what is over the crest of the hill. This lust was fiercer and more enjoyable in carriage days than it is now in the days of speed. The anticipation lasted longer, the enfolding was more gradual and therefore more satisfactory, the beauty that came to meet the traveller over the crest of the hill had time to take him in its arms before it passed upon its way.

Marianne and Marguerite were excited too. Marianne had forgotten her jealousy and was lost in the joy of showing William the land of his inheritance, and Marguerite was excited because William was sharing her birthday with her. Though Marianne did not know it his right hand and her left hand were both together in the pocket of his coat, clutching the mouse.

"Now we're nearly at the top of the hill," said Marianne. "Look, William."

Up above them, framed in golden leaves, was a patch of blue sky the shape of an arched doorway. The hill was so steep that they mounted to it very slowly.

"When we get to the top you'll see nearly the whole of the Island," whispered Marguerite.

They passed through the blue door under the archway of golden leaves and stopped to rest the horses on the crest of the hill. Octavius thrust his head out of the charter window. "Stand up and look, William," he said.

But William was already standing up, Marguerite pulled up beside him because he was still holding her hand and the mouse inside his pocket. He did not speak as he looked at the little land of his fathers but his cheeks flamed and his eyes shone and his bare curly head looked like a flame under the sun. The group of islands was so small that it was like a handful of flowers thrown down upon the immensity of sea, with all the thousand scattered rocks floating about them like torn petals. William could see the other islands round about; shining through the autumn haze, each with its special shape and its special virtue; one a floating fair castle of fretted ivory, one squat and green with a bowed grey head, like an old man in an emerald cloak praising God, one distant and far away, coloured like an amethyst, shaped like some lovely bird just poised for flight, one near at hand, a gaunt pinnacle of blue-grey rock with seabirds sailing round it.

"That's Marie Tape-Tout, Marie Watch-All," Marguerite told him. "They say it is shaped like a woman standing with a child in her arms. When the fishing boats sail past it the fishermen lower their topsails in greeting to her."

"You'll see it better presently," said Marianne, "when we get to La Baie des Saints. It is just opposite the bay and the convent of La Dame du Castel. All those rocks have names, William. There is Le Petit Aiguillon, Le Gros Aiguillon and L'Aiguillon d'Andrelot."

But William, his eyes withdrawn now from what Marianne had called "the Archipelago", was examining his own Island. He could see very nearly the whole of it from the great granite cliffs of the southern end to Saint Pierre and the long level stretch of the sea marshes to the north, from the islands of the west to the belt of woodland that cut off his view to the east, and it amazed him that such a small space could hold so much. There were rocky bays and stretches of golden sand, old farms of grey granite braving the winds upon the cliffs or sheltering in the lea of stunted oak woods or green hills crowned with windmills. There were fishing hamlets where the cottages were thatched and whitewashed and fuchsia bushes and tamarisk grew about the doors, and inland villages where old church towers showed above the trees. There were holy wells embowered in ferns and old grey cromlechs upon windswept hillocks to tell of the length of life in this holy isle. There were fields where flowers were grown for the English market and others of bright green grass where small beautiful dun-coloured cattle were browsing, and bright fresh streams that ran swiftly through the water-lanes to the sea below. . . . It was surely Paradise.

"In spring," said Marianne, "you can hardly see the earth for flowers."

"Drive on now, Pierre," said Octavius.

As they drove along the winding sandy road, every fresh turn of it revealing fresh angles of loveliness, Marianne and Marguerite told William some of the Island tales. Every holy well, every village and cromlech, almost every patch of earth had its legend. Marianne showed him the cliffs where in the Napoleonic wars, when a French man-of-war menaced the Island, the peasant women in their scarlet petticoats and jackets gathered in a long line facing the enemy guns; and the enemy thought they were a regiment of soldiers and sailed away. And Marguerite told him about the sarregousets, the water fairies, who ride with the wind over the spume of the waves. And she told him how the seals love music, and how they will come and lie upon the rocks and listen to you if you stand on the shore and sing to them. . . . only you must sing perfectly in tune. . . . and how the mermaids come too sometimes, but not very often, and how they weep because they have no souls.

And Marianne told him how the Island peasants had always loved fine clothes, scarlet petticoats, ruffs fastened with golden hooks beneath the chin, muslin caps beneath black silk bonnets, blue coats with brass buttons and flowered waistcoats. She told him how the farmers would barter their corn with the Spanish merchants of Saint Malo for fur-bordered cloaks with Spanish hoods. And she told him of their festivals and merry-makings that flowered in the dun earth of their daily toil upon every possible occasion. "For the Island is like the Green Dolphin, it has always liked to laugh," she said, her great dark eyes upon him. "The Islanders like being gay, and making ordinary events like people being born and getting married, and sowing the corn and reaping the harvest, very unordinary and exciting with songs and processions and dances and feats. You're a proper Islander, William, and so is Marguerite. But I don't think I am, for I am not gay." She dropped her voice to a whisper. "My nurse told me once that I was a changeling, and changelings are never gay."

"Mon petit chou, you're *not* a changeling!" cried Marguerite in powerful indignation. "You don't laugh as much as I do because you're so clever, and the weight of all that's in your head makes you feel heavy. You have to feel light to laugh."

"Nonsense," scoffed Marianne. "Brains don't make you heavy."

"They do," said Marguerite. "Why, the Abbess of Notre Dame du Castel and the Abbess of Marie Tape Tout were so heavy with brains that when they stood and talked on Le Petit Aiguillon their feet sank right into the rock and you can see the footprints till this day. I'll show you, William, when we get to La Baie des Saints. The tide will be out and we can go across the sand to Le Petit Aiguillon."

"Who were those ladies?" asked William. He was not usually interested in Abbesses, but such very heavy Abbesses excited his curiosity.

"They were two very clever sisters," said Marguerite, "and they both loved the same man and as they couldn't both marry him they thought it would be best for neither of them to marry him, and so they took the veil and spent the rest of their lives praying for him instead of quarrelling over him."

"If I'd been the man I'd rather have had them quarrelling over me than praying for me," interrupted William.

"How very wrong of you, William," said Marianne severely. "Why?"

"I like to be let alone," said William with quite unnecessary heat. "I should hate to be made good by somebody's prayers when all the time I was wanting to be bad. One isn't happy being *made* to be good. Papa wasn't a bit happy when Mamma prayed that he shouldn't drink any more whisky, because it made him try not to drink whisky in case she should be disappointed in God if her prayer wasn't answered, and not drinking whisky made him very depressed."

"But it was good for him," said Marianne firmly. "It is very often necessary for women to depress men for their good."

"It isn't good for people not to be happy," said William obstinately.

"Oh yes it is," said Marianne.

"No, it isn't," said Marguerite. "And if I were a nun I'd pray all the time for people to be happy. I'd pray all day and all night for everyone, birds and animals and people and the whole world, just to be happy. Then they wouldn't want whisky. They'd be jolly without."

"Oh, that's too easy, Marguerite!" said Marianne impatiently. Marguerite's simplicity always annoyed her. Marguerite would never be aware, as she was, of the awful complexities of human existence. She would look always at the smooth surface of the water above the currents . . . or else right through to the stillness beneath them. . . . Marianne admitted that with people like Marguerite you could not quite tell which they did.

"Go on about the two sisters," said William.

"Just at the time when they decided to take the veil the monks of Mont Saint Michel left Notre Dame du Castel," said Marianne, "and so the two sisters went there and founded a nunnery. But they still went on quarrelling about the man because each wanted to be the one to help him most, and they used different methods of saying their prayers and couldn't decide which of them was the better. And so the elder sister left Notre Dame du Castel and went to Marie Tape-Tout, just a mile away across the sea, though you can walk from one to the other when the tide is out, and founded a second nunnery there, and she prayed *her* way on Marie Tape-Tout and the younger sister prayed *her* way at Notre Dame du Castel. And they prayed for years and years, until they were old ladies, and then the man died——"

"Good or bad?" interrupted William.

"Oh, good," said Marianne decisively. "Very, very good, very wealthy and respected, full of years and honour; though to start with he hadn't been any of those things."

"Well, go on," said William, disappointed in the man.

"And the two Abbesses decided that they would like to meet again, and kiss and be friends, and so when the tide was out the younger sister started walking across the sand from Notre Dame du Castel, and the elder from Marie Tape-Tout, and they met halfway at the low flat rock called Le Petit Aiguillon, and they put their arms round each other and kissed; and they were neither of them ever seen again."

"By gad!" ejaculated William. "What happened to them?"

"Nobody knows," said Marianne. "Some people say the tide came up suddenly, and being very old ladies they hadn't the strength to swim home, and were drowned. And other people say they were caught up to heaven. They left no trace except their footmarks on Le Petit Aiguillon. . . . Of course it's just a legend. . . . The nuns on Marie Tape-Tout left after their Abbess disappeared and went to Saint Pierre and founded the Convent of Saint Raphael that is still there. And the sea washed away the convent on Marie Tape-Tout. You can't see anything of it now except a little figure of the Virgin carved in the rock."

Octavius had again halted the chariot that he and Sophie might admire the beauty of La Baie des Saints from the top of the cliff, before descending and admiring it from below. He had his monocle screwed in again and was looking very self-conscious, and Sophie was leaning earnestly forward.

William gasped. They were at an immense height above the sea, gazing down at an amphitheatre of rock that took one's breath away. Pinnacles and bastions and towers of grey granite fell away below them, grand and terrible, though softened by the wheeling white wings of gulls and by patches of turf between the rocks where withered heather and bracken took on almost the colour of flame beneath the sun, and by grey veilings of old-man's-beard. Far down below in the bay a crescent of pale golden sand was slipping from beneath an almost transparent veil of blue water, like the moon from beneath a gauzy cloud. Sharp jagged rocks covered with seaweed were showing above the water, and the rocky island of Marie Tape-Tout, standing out to sea beyond the rocks, looked nearer than it was.

"The tide is going out," said Marianne.

To the right of the bay the great rocks withdrew a little and here was the little fishing village of Notre Dame, the whitewashed cottages sheltering within the crevasses of the cliff, their thatch kept secure against winter storms by netting and rope weighed down by stones. Smoke coiled up from their chimneys, and a few fishing boats, their hulls painted blue and green, lay peacefully upon the quiet water.

But to the left of the bay the rocks soared to a great height and crowning their summit was the Convent of Notre Dame du Castel. Built of grey granite like the rocks below it, weathered by centuries of sunshine and storm, it was now a part of the cliff. It was hard to remember that men had built it; even those almost legendary monks who so long ago had crossed the sea in their frail boats to bring the knowledge of the love of God to the Island savages. They had built well. Notre Dame du Castel reared itself above the Atlantic with a primeval power and strength that made it look more like a fortress than a convent. Marianne told the awestruck William that in the early days of its history the monks had kept a light always burning in the west window of the great tower of the church, so that by night as well as by day Notre Dame du Castel should be a beacon for mariners for miles across the sea. That tradition had never been allowed to die, and to-day the nuns still tended the light. Just below the window where it shone, within an alcove cut in the west wall of the tower, a life-size statue of the Madonna stood looking out to sea.

"There's not another convent like it anywhere," said Marianne. "It's famous, you know, all over the world."

It was she who was doing all the talking now. Marguerite sat silent, her hands in her lap, gazing at Notre Dame du Castel with an expression of fear and wonder on her round child's face. She had seen it may times before and probably she would see it many times again, but the sight of it never failed to lift her up into some other country, where the air was rarefied and hard to breathe, where it was very cold, and where the rivers ran so swiftly that there was always a singing in one's ears. Yet the snows of that country burned like fire and the light was so blinding that one walked with hooded eyes.

"How do you get there?" asked William.

Marguerite started and looked at him, but he was not talking about that other country but about the convent.

"There's a road cut through the rock from the landward side," said Marianne, "and round on the other side of the convent there's another little bay that you can't see from here, called La Baie des Petits Fleurs because of the lovely shells on the beach, and people say that from there you can climb to the convent up steps cut in the rock. But they say the steps are hard to find because the monks made them all those years ago to use when they went fishing, and now they are nearly worn away."

"'People say',", repeated William after her. "Haven't you been to La Baie des Petits Fleurs to see for yourself?"

"Papa has forbidden us to go by ourselves," said Marianne. "He's always saying he will take us but he always goes to sleep after a picnic lunch and so somehow he never does. It's dangerous. The tide comes in very quickly here, and rises very high in La Baie des Petits Fleurs, and if you are cut off there's no way of escape."

"Except by those steps the monks cut in the rock," said William.

"But they're difficult to find," said Marianne, "and they say that if you do find them they only bring you out in front of an old locked door in the tower, under the statue of the Madonna. It was the door that the monks used when they went fishing, but no one uses it now."

"There's a cave in La Baie des Petits Fleurs called Le Creux des Fâïes," said Marguerite. "The sarregousets feast there when the moon is at the full. There's a sort of chimney at the back of the cave, and when there is a bad storm the spray dashes right up through it and the peasants say, 'Look at the smoke from the sarregousets' fire!' Oh, I *wish* Papa would take us to La Baie des Petits Fleurs!"

"Drive on, Pierre," said Octavius, sticking his head out of the window. "And be careful going down. Hold on tight, children."

William discovered to his astonishment that a narrow sandy road, deeply sunk in a winding gully, led right down to the village of Notre Dame. It was so steep that the horses could only go very slowly, and obeying the instructions of Octavius everyone leaned as far back as they could to ease the weight. It was a strange sensation, after the wide view upon the cliff top, to find oneself enclosed in this rocky tunnel. A stream ran down one side of the sandy road and luxuriant ferns grew up the rock above it. The air was chill and damp but craning one's head back, gazing up, one could see the sunlit wings of the gulls sailing across the patch of bright blue sky over one's head.

The road widened fanwise and upon their right were the white-washed cottages of Notre Dame, each with its patch of garden with in front of it a low stone wall where fishing nets were spread to dry, while in front of them spread the dancing light of the sun upon sea and sand.

Upon the dry rocks above high-water-mark Pierre spread rugs and cushions and the hampers of food, plates, bottles and glasses, before withdrawing to visit a relative at Notre Dame. The high cliffs gave shelter from the wind and sitting full in the sun it was as warm as

June. Sophie had to put up her parasol to shield her complexion and Octavius discarded his greatcoat.

The birthday luncheon was excellent. It contained all Marguerite's favourite food, cold chicken and ham, gâche à corinthes, a delectable cake stuffed full of raisins and spice, anglicé currant cake iced in honour of the birthday, raspberry wine and something a little stronger for Octavius who, as he observed as he drank it, worked hard for his family, and "i' faut prendre une petite goutte pour arrousaï, ou bien j'n' airons pâs d'pânais". This was an Island saying which was translated to William as "One must take a sip to moisten the field or there will be no parsnips". William agreed and, being a male, was allowed to have a little too.

Marguerite was unusually silent as she ate. This silence during a picnic luncheon at La Baie des Saints was habitual with her and was put down by her family to her enjoyment of good food. It was true that she enjoyed her food, partaking of as much as she could conveniently hold with a thoroughness and almost religious concentration that caused her father to ejaculate, "Au Nom de Dieu soit!" when she started and, "Au Nom de Dieu c'est fini!" when she had done, but her silence was not only due to good appetite. It was due also to thwarted longing. Ever since she had been a tiny child and had first heard the tale of it she had longed to go to forbidden La Baie des Petits Fleurs. She wanted to see all the little shells. She wanted to see the cave where the sarregousets feasted and the chimney that carried away the smoke of their fire. She wanted to see the steps the monks had made that ended at the feet of the Madonna who had stood in her niche for nine centuries looking across the sea. They said the last person to use those steps had been the Abbess who went down them to kiss and forgive her sister on Le Petit Aiguillon, that very old Abbess who had gone down them to her death. La Baie des Petits Fleurs drew Marguerite with an attraction that it needed all her considerable strength to resist. It was only because she was so naturally obedient a child that she had not gone there long ago. . . . Perhaps, to-day, Papa would take them.

It took a long time to eat the beautiful birthday luncheon, and all the while the tide was going out.

"Let Petit Aiguillon is high and dry!" cried Marianne. 'Look, William, there! Mamma, we want to show William the footmarks. Papa, may we go?"

"They are a purely natural phenomenon," pronounced Octavius.

"Yes, sir, I know," said his daughter impatiently. "But may we go?"

They all shaded their eyes and looked at the low rock covered in green weed that lay midway on the shining uncovered sand between Notre Dame du Castel and Marie Tape-Tout. The sea had withdrawn very far away now; it was just a line of silver surrounding Marie Tape-Tout.

"Yes," said Octavius. "But watch the tide. Be careful."

"Come with us, Papa!" whispered Marguerite.

But Octavius only repeated upon a yawn. "Be careful!"

"Be *very* careful," said Sophie anxiously. She would have refused permission had she been applied to, which Marianne had known better than to do. "Marguerite, you'd better go behind that rock and take your pantalettes right off. You'll only get them soaked."

Marguerite obeyed, Marianne seized one of the empty baskets to collect limpets in, and then the three of them in their gay clothes went skimming away over the wet shining sand, looking more like birds than ever. To Sophie, watching them a little anxiously, it seemed that they flew westward straight into the sun, and that she lost them in the dazzling light. All adventurers, even the sun itself, fly westward, she thought; to the New World, to the Islands of the Blest, to the horizon like a rose. . . . She hated the west. . . . She averted her eyes from it and took out some tatting that she had brought with her in her reticule. Octavius reclined backwards upon the cushions, tipped his top hat over his eyes, folded his hands across his stomach and slept. . . . One day he would fulfil his promise of taking the children to La Baie des Petits Fleurs. But not to-day. It was too hot. He had eaten too much.

It took the children a long time to reach Le Petit Aiguillon because the rock pools that had been left uncovered by the tide were a world in themselves, to which William had not as yet been introduced. The brimming water in each pool was like a clear mirror through which one looked down at feathery seaweed like pale pink ostrich feathers or long streamers of dark red ribbon, the grass-like "plize" that made miniature fairy forests with shells entangled in the undergrowth, sea anemones of every lovely imaginable shape, some like smooth round crimson cushions, some like daisies, and others like velvet rosettes. Rock shrimps and tiny crabs darted about in the pools and limpets clung to the rocks. The gulls and flocks of red-legged cahouettes circled about them, but the cormorants with their snake-like black heads kept at a distance.

"When we've looked at the footprints we'll get some limpets for supper," said Marianne. "They're lovely cooked."

Marguerite sighed. She loathed prising the poor limpets off the rocks just to give relish to a meal for people who always over-eat themselves anyhow. Why should these harmless sea creatures be devoured by greedy humans? She was glad that there were cuttle fish and jelly fish about to retaliate a little. But it was no good remonstrating with Marianne because for her sister's practical nature enjoyment of a lovely view was greatly intensified if she could extract something for the larder out of its beauty.

And William was as bad. At the mention of the limpets his eyes sparkled with masculine lust for the chase. The happy Marguerite actually felt a little sad, for she did not like to feel differently from William.

But she forgot her momentary depression in the fun of climbing up the smooth slippery side of Le Petit Aiguillon. He was quite a big rock really, when one came close to him, and the two Abbesses must have been very agile in their old age to have chosen to kiss and forgive on his summit instead of down below on the sand. Yet there were their footprints on the summit of the rock, four fairylike prints as of two tiny creatures standing facing each other, nearly worn away by the washing of the waves but still discernible.

"They're just a natural phenomenon, like your Papa said," pronounced William. "They're too small for real footprints."

"Look!" said Marguerite. She had very tiny feet, almost too tiny for her plump little figure, and she slipped them quite easily into the prints of the Abbess who had come from Notre Dame du Castel. There she stood, looking westward, laughing, her arms held wide.

But it was William, not Marianne, who went into them. He gave her a great childish bear-hug that nearly knocked all the breath out of her. Her bonnet fell off backwards and her untidy curls tickled William's face so that he laughed and wrinkled his nose. They kissed, and tasted the salt of the sea on each other's lips. William had never kissed a girl before and he enjoyed it. Marguerite was delicious to hold, warm and soft and fragrant. She did not seem to have any bones but yet her softness was a quite substantial and satisfactory armful, and her plump arms about him felt strong. For both of them it was the first conscious experience of the happiness that can come from the mere fact of human contact. The human delusion that the arms of another are a sure shield against misfortunes and that hidden in the being of another there is safety, came to them in the form of conviction. . . . But only these arms; in this one being only. . . . Each took the shelter, and each gave it, and which was the greater happiness they could not tell; each was the complement of the other and created the fact of mutual love.

"The tide has turned," said Marianne. She was standing some paces away from them looking out to sea, and so deep was her wound that she was afraid, and her fear was discernible in her voice.

For just a moment she lost hold of her childhood's certainty that to give love is to receive it again in equal measure, and she wondered what it would be like to go through the whole of life giving more than one was given. . . . The hunger. . . . The dissatisfaction. . . .

Then Marguerite and William were one on each side of her, utterly mistaking the reason for her fear. "Silly!" said Marguerite. "Why, it hasn't even reached this rock yet."

"There's lots and lots of time," consoled William. "Time to get back to Mamma and Papa and get a basketful of limpets too."

Marianne smiled. Silly children! As if she didn't know the tides much better than they did. Of course there was time. Oceans of it. They were such children that her queer moment of panic was lost in a sense of her own superiority.

"That's the Atlantic, William," she said. "Over there are Australia and America, and Tasmania and New Zealand, and the other new lands."

She embraced them all in a vague but impressive gesture and he gazed awestruck across the smooth blue water. A sea mist was creeping up and the horizon was lost. The mist was like a mysterious curtain let down between the Island and the wonders that lay beyond. Nothing between them and those legendary lands. Nothing but sea. Marie Tape-Tout, nearer to the horizon than they were, seemed to be gazing too, a great column of rock shaped like a woman with a child in her arms; like one of those peasant women who so often in the cold dawns watched in patience on these shores for the return of a boat that had sailed into the sunshine for a night's fishing and had not returned. And behind them the carved Madonna of Notre Dame du Castel watched too. When they turned round they could see her far up in her niche above the locked west door of the convent, the great precipice of grey granite falling sheer away from her feet to the little hollow in the rocks that was La Baie des Petits Fleurs.

CHAPTER TWO

1

Marguerite was never quite sure what made her do it. Her parents said afterwards that it was just naughtiness; and certainly the temptation to go off on her own and explore the forbidden bay was not a temptation that she fought against very hard. But there was more to it than that. She did not want to see those poor limpets prised off their rocks to provide a relish for the supper of the overfed Le

Patourels. And she realised too that Marianne had felt very lonely when she and William kissed each other on top of Le Petit Aiguillon, much more lonely than she had felt when William's love of the chase had seemed a barrier between them, and that Marianne would like it very much if she and William were left quite alone to gather the limpets. However, those were no reasons for running off to La Baie des Petits Fleurs. She could perfectly well have gone back to Octavius and Sophie; and she did cast one glance towards the distant flame-coloured speck that was Sophie's parasol; but just at that moment a beautiful white gull sailed by over her head and drifted down into La Baie des Petits Fleurs. The sun touched his feathers to silver as he alighted there upon the little beach and he seemed to be beckoning to her. Marianne and William were absorbed in limpets. They did not see her pick up her blue skirts and skim away over the wet sand towards the forbidden spot.

The bay was further away than she had thought, and ran deeper into the cliff than she had expected. It was shaped like a horseshoe, and as she ran in between the great rocks that guarded it at the narrow end she understood why this little bay was dangerous, for the high tide watermark on them was well above her head. When she got inside, with the great cliffs towering above her, she felt as alone as though she were the only human being alive upon the island. But it was a pleasant kind of loneliness, not the sort when one has been pushed out by someone else, but when one has chosen oneself to be alone, the kind when one is less conscious of human creatures having gone away than of listening for the voices and the footsteps of faerie creatures trooping in.

Friendly faerie creatures. The bay was alive with peaceful friendliness. Yet at first she was too much awed by the beauty of this exquisite haunted place to move or to touch, she could only stand quite still and breathe it in as she looked about her. The bay was very small and the cliffs so high that it seemed their rocky crests must touch the sky, and the light that shone from the west through the narrow opening of the horse-shoe came as though flooding into a cavern. She had to tilt her head back before she could see the grey mass of the convent right up overhead, so high that it looked more as though it had been let down from heaven than built up from earth, with the Madonna in her niche, and below her the locked door opening upon a narrow sort of shelf in the cliff carpeted with green grass. Le Creux des Fâies, where it was said the fairies feasted round a flat rock at the full of the moon, was to the left of the bay, the narrow entrance half blocked by a big boulder covered with bright green weed. Most of the floor of the bay was covered with fine silver sand and beautiful small stones tinted like opals, with bigger rocks draped with deep purple-brown weed where the rock pools were full of the frilly kind of sea anemones. All the pebbles seemed to Marguerite to have fat smiling faces, and the anemones had mad bright eyes above their frills. At the far end of the bay the sand ran upwards into a hollow in the cliff, almost a second little bay to which the sea did not reach, and here it was carpeted with small coloured shells as a wood is carpeted with flowers in spring-time. And all the shells had mouths and all of them were singing, their myriad tiny voices making a music that one could hear and yet not hear, like the sound of bells that the wind is always catching away. There was not one of them that was bigger than the nail on a baby's finger, and some of them were no larger than a pin's head, but each was as intricately and perfectly fashioned as though it were a world all to itself. Some had the beautiful shape of wool upon the distaff, tapering to a fine point. Others were like rose petals delicately hollowed. Some were like the caps of elves, and others like drops of dew. And each cup or spiral had its own perfect veining of featherlight radiation, each line perfect in grace, drawn by a brush that had never faltered. And their pale flower-tints were as varied as their shapes; lemon flushed with salmon pink, dove grey lined with mother-of-pearl, pale amethyst powdered with green points of fire, saffron and turquoise and rose, and smoky-orange spotted with pale warm brown like the breast of a small bird. And there were no two of them just the same.

The seagull was sailing backwards and forwards all the time, seeming to gather all the light of the place with his shining wings and to trail it in long threads of silver after him as he flew this way and that, very high up between the rocks as though weaving a pattern in the air, filament by filament of light from cliff to cliff. Marguerite stood quite still and watched him, her hands behind her back. There was a legend on the Island that souls in prayer can take the form of a bird and hover over those they pray for, and she wondered if it were true. The silver pattern that he had woven in the air seemed suspended from cliff to cliff over her head like an invisible protection, like one of those canopies powdered with stars that one sees in old pictures held over the heads of Queens as they walk in procession.

It was this sense of protection that at last broke the spell of awe that had held her without movement for so long. With a cry of delight she ran and fell on her knees beside the little shells and picked them up one by one, holding them up towards the west so that the sun shone through them and lit their fragile shapes to dazzling fire.

Then she picked them up by handfuls, letting them fall again through her brown fingers, as children scoop up water in their hands to see the bright drops fall.

Then it was the turn of the rock pools, and her bright eyes peeped through the wild tangle of her curls at the mad bright eyes of the anemones that she imagined she saw glinting above the frilly ruffs about their necks; living frills made of slender crimson threads that swayed and coiled and groped in the water with a quietude and a velvet suppleness of movement that the most perfect grace in the world cannot achieve in the upper air. Marguerite had never seen anemones with eyes before. She was quite sure that they were not mere bubbles but mad eyes that saw strange things.

She went from mystery to mystery, with more and more courage. She was a long time playing with the shells, and longer still looking at the rock pools, exploring each miniature ocean from horizon to horizon, but at last she was ready for the fairies' cave. She did not feel at all afraid as she pushed past the green rock and went inside. Since she had run into this strange place through the horns of the horse-shoe she had felt no fear, only awe. She had discovered a new country, but it was her own country. In this place where one was alone that one might listen she felt at home as never before. In spite of its mystery it was so clean, so simple and so safe. Nothing befouled the air one breathed, the music that was heard but not yet heard, like the sound of bells caught away by the wind, was without confusion, cold and clear like crystal, and overhead the protecting canopy made by the beating wings was so transparently woven that one could see the sky through it.

The cave was a small one, spread with a clean white floor of shells ground to powder by the action of the waves. In the centre was the low flat stone where the sarregousets feasted when the moon was full, and right at the back of the cave was a fissure in the rock leading to the fairies' fireplace where they cooked their feast over a fire of vraic, a seaweed that when dried burns with as lovely a flame as apple wood. Above was the chimney up which the sea went dashing on stormy days to issue at the top in the white blown spray that the peasants called the fairies' smoke.

Marguerite tiptoed round the flat stone and then greatly daring she crept inside the chimney at the back and peeped up. It sloped inward and far up she could see a patch of daylight. The sides were smooth and slippery with the perpetual surging of the water, but feeling with her plump hands she found what felt like steps. The sarregousets must have made them, she thought, to run up and down when they swept the chimney, and a thrill of delicious awe

went through her as she put her fingers where they must put their
tiny pointed feet.

Then she withdrew her curly head and stepped delicately over the
fine white floor and sat down on the flat stone. There was mica in
the granite and it glittered in the dim pale green light with streaks of
gold. The only footprints to be seen on the sand were her own; she
could not see any fairy footprints because the sea swept into this
cave at every stormy high tide and the white floor was smoothed
out as by a broom. Marguerite shivered deliciously as she sat there
on the stone. The peasants had more stories to tell about this cave
than about any other haunted spot upon the Island, and though
Sophie and Octavius and Marianne declared their stories to be all
moonshine Marguerite was not so sure.

It suddenly occurred to her to wonder if she ought to go back to
Mamma. She seemed to have been here for only a few minutes, but
Mamma was an easily worried person and she might be getting in a
fuss. Marguerite jumped to her feet full of self-reproach, for she
realised that ever since she had run into the bay she had completely
forgotten Mamma's existence. Papa's too. They had just been
wiped out of her mind. Full of penitence she pushed her way past
the big green rock at the mouth of the cave, ran a few steps across
the sand and shingle, and found the world wrapped in mist, and sea
water lapping at her feet. Possessed by the magic of this place she
must have been oblivious of the passing of time and the tide had come
right in. From the place where she stood away into the mist the sea
stretched like soft grey silk. She looked towards the rocks where she
had entered the bay, the narrow part of the horseshoe, barely visible
now through the mist, and saw that the sea had reached the high
watermark that was above her head. She could not swim very well.
Marianne could swim like a fish but she was not very proficient yet.
She knew that she would not be able to swim through the November sea back to La Baie des Saints.

She stood very still, her hands tightly clasped, and watched the
beautiful half-moons of water that kept casting themselves at her feet
and then withdrawing again, sucking back the pebbles with them.
They wanted to pull her back too, she thought, and take her away
down to the caverns of the sea where she did not want to go. She
stood motionless, watching them, and just for a moment she was
very afraid. All colour had been drained away now from the bay.
All the world was grey.

Then suddenly the practical commonsense combined with the
mystical certainty of God's nearness that were her special heritage
returned to her, setting her free for action that did not admit of the

possibility of failure. "I must get out of this," she thought, and then, "the white gull was protecting me when he wove that pattern in the air." She looked upward and saw that he had flown away, but she did not doubt that the transparent silver canopy was still woven from cliff to cliff.

She must find those steps cut in the rock that the monks had used when they went fishing, and that the Abbess had used when she went to Le Petit Aiguillon. But she could not find them. The great granite cliffs rose sheer from the little bay and she could find no foothold in them anywhere. Then she remembered the fairies' chimney. She remembered her father saying that the legends of the old saints and the Island fairy stories were so inextricably mixed that one could not now disentangle one from the other. Perhaps it was not the fairies who had cut those steps in the chimney, but the monks.

She ran back to the cave, crept in the chimney and felt the steps again. Yes, they were real steps, and it would be possible, though very difficult, to climb them, and that chimney was quite wide enough for the passage of one small body at a time. The Norman monks had been little men, she had been told, dark little men, not so very unlike the fairies themselves.

She took her cloak and bonnet and shoes and stockings off and threw them away, for she knew that bare toes, though they may get scratched and bruised, cling best to bare rock, and then she began to climb.

"Thank God I took my pantalettes off," she thought devoutly, and then she banished irrelevant thought, for the climb needed every scrap of will and attention and courage that she had.

Clinging like a little ape with bare prehensile fingers and toes she crept up and up. Any one else might have turned sick with terror at the thought of the hideous fall that would be the result of just once missing her footing; but Marguerite knew that God would not let her fall. But plump as she was she got very out of breath, and her clothes were much too voluminous for comfort, and the sweat trickled down her back in the most uncomfortable way. Yet she giggled now and then, for now that her fear had left her she was finding the adventure fun. The pity of it was that William was not here to share it with her. Something hard pressed against her side. It was the wooden mouse in her pocket. She was glad William's mouse was here.

The patch of sky over her head grew wider, the grey light showered down and she lifted her face to it with joy. Just a few more steps, a last clinging of fingers and toes, a last panting effort, and her curly head came out of the top of the chimney like a fuzzy sweep's brush.

She gazed bewildered at the wilderness of toppling granite rocks shrouded in mist that was all she could see. She was still so far below the convent, and so close under it, that she could not even see it. Which way now? She climbed right out of the chimney and looked about her. She was standing on a ledge of rock like the flat top of a wide wall, with the precipice falling almost sheer beneath her to the sea, and upon the sides of the steep turrets of rock all about her, their summits lost in mist, there seemed no foothold.

Yet she explored patiently and without fear, for she knew the steps must be somewhere.

She found them again behind an outcrop of rock shaped like a sea lion couchant upon the wall, and they wound up and around one of the turrets, worn slippery steps that sometimes had a balustrade of rock to cling to upon the outer side and sometimes had not. But Marguerite tackled them without hesitation, not afraid at all but wishing very much that she was not so tired, and not so cold and shivery with the wet mist.

Afterwards it seemed to everyone an absolute miracle that she had survived that dangerous climb. It would have taxed the skill of an experienced climber and she was only a child. Her courage and strength were a nine days' wonder on the Island.

But it was a very weary, draggle-tailed child who finally reached the stretch of green turf before the convent door and fell in a wet heap upon it. She was so exhausted that she could scarcely breathe. Her body was ice-cold but her fingers and knees and toes were burning and painful from the scraping of the hard rock. Her pretty blue dress was torn and drenched with the mist, and her hair, that a sea mist always made curlier than ever, was a dank tangle of ringlets all round her white face. But oh, the blessed ease of lying still upon the wet green grass, the sweet smell of it, the joy of having finally accomplished something very difficult, a triumphant joy that almost banished pain. This was the first time in her short happy life that she had attempted and brought to a successful conclusion a supremely hard piece of work, and so it was the first time she had tasted this particular joy. It was about the best happiness she had ever known, equalled only by the joy of mutual giving and taking when she and William had hugged each other. And her faith had been vindicated too. It was the first time in her life that she had put her faith in God's protection to the test, and it had not failed her. Perhaps, after all, that was the best joy of the three.

She sat up and looked about her. She was completely enclosed by a wall of vapour. Mists came up very suddenly at this time of the year, turning the blue of a happy day to the grey of a sorrowful one

with alarming rapidity, but she had never known a mist come up
quite so quickly and thoroughly as this one had. She could not even
see the great convent towering up above her. She could see nothing
but a patch of green grass, a locked door in a stone wall, and above it
the statue of the Madonna. She and the Madonna were quite alone
together in a sort of little room hollowed out of the mist. It was
queer and very strange.

She got up and stood in her favourite attitude, hands clasped behind her, looking at the old door beneath its stone archway, with
four stone steps leading up to it, the treads worn down in the middle
by the passing of many feet centuries ago. For it must have been a
long while back that the courage to negotiate the climb to the beach
had deserted the inmates of Notre Dame du Castel. It looked as
though the door had not been opened for years. Ivy was growing
over it, and long thorny sprays of bramble set with crimson leaves.

The peasant nurse who had watched over the babyhood both of
Marianne and Marguerite, and who had declared Marianne to be a
changeling, had been a Catholic. Marguerite lying in her cot had
often watched her sitting before the nursery fire in her white mob
cap, her black quilted petticoat turned back over her knees, rocking
herself and praying. Looking up at the Madonna she could hear
again phrases of the murmured prayers. . . . Our Lady of the Castle.
Marie Watch-All. Hail, Mary, full of grace, the Lord is with thee.
O Virgo Virginum. Blessed art thou among women. For neither
before thee was any like thee, nor shall there be after. The thing
which you behold is a divine mystery. Hail, Mary, full of grace. . . .

And the mist descended a little lower and Marguerite could only
see the Madonna's feet.

This concentrated her attention upon the door. Somehow she
must get inside it. She went up the worn stone steps and hammered
upon it with her small fists. But she did not make much noise and
nothing happened. Then she looked up again and the mist had hidden even the feet of the Madonna, and for the second and last time
that day fear gripped her. Perhaps the nuns never went near the inside of the door. They would not hear her knocking. Was she going to be here all night? If she was she would perhaps die of the
cold. Papa, perhaps, would get a boat from the village and row
about and try to find her, but he would get lost in the mist; or perhaps he would find her bonnet floating on the sea and think she had
been drowned and go home again. She stood with her body
stretched against the door and hammered and hammered, and her
throat was constricted with her fear and her heart pounded so much
that she could scarcely hear the sound of her own hammering.

There was the beating of powerful wings overhead and some great creature came sweeping down out of the mist, and she shrank against the door in even greater fear. But it was a gull. His wing-tips touched her in passing and the wind of his flight lifted her hair. It was a seagull and she was not afraid any more. She could hear him crying somewhere far down in the mist. She was protected and it was all going to be quite all right. Her common sense returned. No good standing up and making herself more tired than she was already pounding away with her fists on the door; they did not make enough noise. She looked about her and saw a stone lying on the grass. She fetched it, sat down on top of the steps, made herself as comfortable as she could, and began to knock rhythmically and patiently at the door with the hard stone.

2

Mère Madeleine sat before the statue of the Holy Child in the convent chapel, alternately praying for the children of the world, as was her duty at this hour, and complaining volubly of her rheumatism. She both prayed and complained in a loud monotone, for she was deaf and had no idea what a row she was making. She was not more than seventy, but old for her age because the life of a religious is not an easy one for a delicately nurtured woman, and her wretched complaint had settled worst of all in her knees. She prayed sitting, by Reverend Mother's permission, her old black ebony stick beside her, for from November to April really she could not kneel at all, and she rubbed her knobbly old hands up and down over her knees and swayed her body backwards and forwards, and prayed and complained, and wished le Bon Dieu would take her away to Paradise before she had to face another winter in this ice-cold convent upon this wind-swept cliff-top at the world's end. She had been born in the south of France and loved warmth like a cat, but had not had it since she had taken the holy habit of religion. It was for the warmth of Paradise that she most chiefly longed, the warmth and not having rheumatism or being deaf and short-sighted.

"Ever blooming are the joys of heaven's high Paradise,
Cold age deafs not there our ears nor vapour dims our eyes;
Glory there the sun outshines; whose beams the Blessed only see:
O come quickly, glorious Lord, and raise my sprite to Thee!"

What in the world was she saying? Not what she ought to be saying. She was repeating the verse of some old Elizabethan poet whom she had read in the days when she had been a cultured young woman of

the world who had prided herself upon her cosmopolitan reading.
Yes, she had been young once, young and beautiful—and warm.
And now—.

> *"Never weather-beaten sail more willing bent to shore,*
> *Never tired pilgrim's limbs affected slumber more—"*

Mother of God, what was the matter with her now-a-days? After
almost a lifetime spent in prayer and contemplation she had believed
that at least she had her thoughts well disciplined, but as one got
older one's hard-won control slipped a little and one felt sometimes
as though spiritually one were back again in one's youth, with all the
battles to fight again. Mother of God, surely it was not so. Surely
the strength of the spirit, bought at such cost, was retained though
the mind and body weakened. It taught one humility, this weakness
of old age, and without humility one was a lost soul. It made one
again that little child who alone can enter the kingdom of heaven.
No doubt Reverend Mother had known what she was doing when
she commanded the oldest of her nuns to pray at this hour for the
children of the world. No doubt one prayed more effectively for the
weak if one were weak oneself. The faint light of dawn and twilight
are much the same. In both of them the stars of another world are
seen and the birds talk of something they do not mention when the
sun is up.

Mère Madeleine recollected and strengthened herself with all the
will and courage that she had. As a punishment for wandering
thoughts she dragged herself off her chair and knelt down, groaning
with the pain, to pray for all children in danger, her puckered colour-
less face framed in its white wimple lifted to the rosy smooth one of the
Holy Child within his niche in the massive old grey pillar. "Mother
of God, who heldest thy child safely in thine arms, hold safely all
children in danger. Mon Dieu, I wish it were not in my knees. I
should prefer it in the shoulders, which are not used in prayer. Holy
Jesu, who wept childish tears, comfort all children who fear or weep.
The rubbing did no good. I shall try the liniment. Holy Mother,
Marie Watch-all, hold out thine arms and gather all children to the
knowledge of thy love. I wish I were not deaf. I liked to hear the
birds. Little Jesu, save all children. Holy Mother, bless all children.
Holy angels, guard all children. . . . Never weather-beaten sail more
willing bent to shore. . . ."

So she murmured and prayed and rocked herself, until at last the
will triumphed, the soul shook herself free of the body's pain and
mounted like a bird into that clear air of contemplation where words
are caught away by the wind, where the soul listens, hovering with

spread wings, while through the silver feathers the light falls as sun through the rain, and men on earth look up and see the brightness and know that they are saved. Mère Madeleine rocked herself no more. Her lips were still, her hands quiet, her face an old cameo carved from ivory. Anyone entering the Chapel would have seen her only as a motionless shadow before the statue of the Holy Child, a rosy-cheeked urchin in a blue robe, his arms full of roses, candles burning at his feet and a golden halo behind his curly head.

The Chapel was very old, its windows mere slits in the huge thickness of the walls, and almost the only light came from those candles and from the sanctuary lamp. The stations of the cross hanging against the old grey walls, the gilded crucifix upon the altar, the statues of the saints within their niches on rood screen and pillar, were seen only dimly as patches of gold and azure and old rose glowing through the dusk. The air was heavy with the smell of incense that hung in cloudy wreaths beneath the darkness of the roof, and the scent of the festival lilies massed in white upon the altar. There was no sound in the chapel. To-day there was not even the sound of the surging of the waves. Mère Madeleine lost all count of time. She did not need to think of it, for at the time appointed another nun would come to take up her link in the chain of prayer that did not cease in the chapel day or night. She did not know how long she had been praying when the knocking disturbed her soul and brought her with folded wings to earth.

The statue of the Holy Child was right under the tower, close to the locked west door, or deaf old Mère Madeleine would not have heard the knocking. As it was she heard it so faintly that she thought it was a knocking within her, the Holy Child knocking at her heart. "I hear you," she said to the rosy-cheeked urchin. "The door is unlocked. I unlocked it half a century ago. You know that. What are you knocking for?"

But the knocking continued, and she turned her head sideways in vague bewilderment, as a bird does when it listens for some sound beneath the ground. Then she groped for her stick, got up, mumbling to herself, and shuffled over to the locked west door, where she put her head against the wood and listened. Yes, there it was, a rhythmic pounding; though to her deaf ears it sounded no louder than the light tapping of a bird's beak upon the bark of a tree. Yet her muddled old mind grasped the fact that to the Holy Child, or whoever it was out there, this door must be opened. She put her gnarled hands around the key and tried to turn it, but it was beyond her strength. She rubbed her nose with her forefinger and considered what she should do.

In a moment it occurred to her that this was the afternoon when Soeur Angelique scrubbed out the sacristy. Soeur Angelique was a lay sister, a peasant woman whose brawny arms were always at the service of the more spiritually-minded nuns whose strivings in the heavenly sphere led to a certain lack of muscle in the phsical.

"Comment?" she asked, looking up from the stone floor she was scrubbing at the frail figure of old Mère Madeleine leaning on her stick. "The Holy Child knocking at the west door? Holy Mother!"

She arose upon her large flat feet, pushing the soap-suds off her fingers into the bucket, and her little black eyes blinked with consternation in her foolish, good-humoured round red face. For some while now they had thought in the convent that old Mère Madeleine's wits were beginning to fail her. Well, now they *had* failed, and with a suddenness that alarmed Soeur Angelique. But she thought it would be best to humour the old lady and go along with her to the west door, and she began to unfasten the large black safety pins that pinned the skirt and sleeves of her habit up over her flannel petticoat and back from her arms for the scrubbing. She took a long time over this, as over everything she did, her capacious mouth slowly filling with safety pins as she laboured. She was a huge ponderous woman, immensely stupid and immensely kind. She had come to the convent after her husband and two young sons had been drowned at sea, and had learned at Reverend Mother's knee, word by word like a child, with great labour, the words of the prayers in which she prayed now for the repose of their souls in Paradise. For the rest she prayed with her scrubbing brush and broom, her dishcloth and polishing rags, and with her huge strength that carried the coals and shovelled away the snow and lifted the sick and dying as though they were of no more weight than a gossamer cobweb. . . . But she was slow.

"Hurry, dear Soeur Angelique!" implored Mère Madeleine.

Soeur Angelique took the safety pins one by one from her mouth and put them in her pocket. Then she shook out the skirts of her habit and waddled majestically, with earth-shaking tread, from the sacristy to the chapel, Mère Madeleine shuffling after on her stick. Their progress was held up for some while by Soeur Angelique's genuflection before the altar, which resembled the descent to earth and the getting up again of an elephant, and took as long, but finally they got going once more and reached the locked west door, where Soeur Angelique found to her awe and astonishment that Mère Madeleine was justified in her assertion that the Christ Child knocked.

"Mother of God! Mother of God!" she muttered in awe and fear, as her great hands closed over the key and the iron grated in the lock. It took the whole of her immense strength to get the door open, but at last it swung inward, bringing trails of bramble and ivy with it, and there, bright against the background of grey mist that was as mysterious as the background of a dream, was a golden-haired child in a blue robe.

The two old nuns gazed and ejaculated, crossed themselves and ejaculated again, and the mist streamed in to mingle with the heavy wreaths of the incense, and the smell of the sea with the scent of the lilies, and Mère Madeleine, all bemused, crying aloud endearments that she thought were whispered, dropped her stick and held out her arms and Marguerite stepped over the threshold and went with alacrity into them; while Soeur Angelique, clucking with the ecstatic pride and wonder of a hen who has just laid a silver egg with gold spots on it, shut the door to keep the wonder in, slumped heavily to her knees and praised God with a loud voice.

It was at this moment that Reverend Mother entered upon the scene. She did not usually come to the Chapel at this time; it was her hour for dealing with correspondence; but she had had a letter which troubled her and she had come to lay the problem it contained before her God. However, the problem of the racket going on at the west end of the chapel seemed to her at the moment the more urgent of the two, and she turned that way instead of towards the altar.

"What is this, Mère Madeleine?" she asked, raising her voice that she might be heard above the torrents of endearments and thanksgivings. "Soeur Angelique, need your prayers be quite so loud? And who is this dirty, wet little creature?"

The chill serenity of Reverend Mother's voice, as well as the solidity and dampness of the heavenly vision in her arms, brought Mère Madeleine back to earth. Her dim old eyes peered more closely at the child. It was a real child, a little girl! But what a sweet round smiling face, what long eyelashes! What a dimple! It was years since Mère Madeleine had set eyes on a child, though she had prayed for them so unceasingly. She croaked with laughter, hugged Marguerite closer than before, and kissed her, and Marguerite, always a responsive child, gave back the kisses with good measure and her merry answering laugh echoed in the chapel. . . . She was so happy to be safe inside the door at last, safe from that wet chill mist and that hungry sea.

"Mère Madeleine!" reproved Reverend Mother. "Soeur Angelique, get up at once. My child, come here to me and explain your presence here."

They all obeyed that voice that was like an incisive clean-cutting diamond. Mère Madeleine subdued her croaking laughter and reluctantly took her arms from the adorable body of the child, Soeur Angelique heaved and grunted herself to her feet and Marguerite went to Reverend Mother and stood looking fearlessly up into her face, her hands behind her back.

"I was cut off by the tide in La Baie des Petits Fleurs," she said in her clear voice, "and I did not want to be drowned, and so I climbed up the steps in the cliff and knocked at the door, and they let me in."

"You climbed up the cliff!" ejaculated Reverend Mother. "I did not know such a thing was possible."

"It was difficult," conceded Marguerite, "but God helped me."

Reverend Mother's face softened and she looked down intently into the childish face raised to hers. Very few people could meet Reverend Mother's eyes, but Marguerite could. She had never seen anyone quite like Reverend Mother and she was interested. She had seen lots of old ladies with wrinkled parchment faces like Mère Madeleine's, and many round red peasant faces such as Soeur Angelique's, but never a face like this one. Reverend Mother had a clear olive skin, without colour yet almost luminous in its purity, with a beautiful pencilling of fine clear lines about her grey eyes with their brilliant keen glance like the thrust of steel. Her eyebrows were dark and delicate, with one deep line of concentration strongly marked between them. But there were no lines of anxiety on her broad low forehead, and no laughter lines about her resolute tight-lipped mouth. But if her lips were resolute, they were also lovely, as perfectly modelled as the aquiline nose with the winged nostrils, and the strong and delicate chin. And the oval of her face was flawless in its framework of snow-white linen. A beautiful humourless face, cold with its clamp of iron control set upon its passion, yet alight with holiness; a powerful, brilliant, frightening face. Reverend Mother was tall and held herself superbly, and her habit became her long and supple limbs. It was impossible to tell how old she was. One would have guessed that many embattled years had gone to the making of a face like hers, yet her lovely hands, strangely indolent hands that she held loosely linked before her, were those of a woman still young.

So they stood, the nun and the child, each in characteristic attitude fearlessly, the one with linked hands before her, the other with her hands clasped behind her back, and they did not know why it was that their eyes so held each other and so questioned.

Then Reverend Mother moved, holding out her hand and smiling with frigid kindness. "Come with me, my child," she said. "You must get dry and have a hot drink. Soeur Angelique, your work in the sacristy waits for you. Mère Madeleine, I think it possible that this is the first time for a century that the chain of prayer has been broken in this place."

Bound by holy obedience Mère Madeleine turned away without a word, but the hunger in her face as she turned caused Reverend Mother to change her mind. "On second thoughts, Mère Madeleine, I need your help with the child," she said. "The situation in which we find ourselves is quite unprecedented. Soeur Angelique, leave your work in the sacristy and pray here instead of Mère Madeleine. Do not look so scared, my daughter. It will not be for long, and your bereaved soul should know beyond all other souls how to pray for children in danger. Kneel then before the Holy Child and add to your prayers for other children a thanksgiving for the safety of this one."

3

Marguerite sat in her petticoat on a little stool before the fire of vraic in Reverend Mother's study, drinking hot milk. Her wet blue dress had been taken to the kitchen to be dried by Soeur Cécile who did the laundry. Behind her sat Mère Madeleine combing the tangles out of her wet hair and murmuring sweet old-fashioned endearments that she had not had the chance of using for a lifetime. Slightly muddled though her brain might be she had not forgotten the little love-words of her youth. Her husky old voice never stopped at all, and the pretty words seemed to Reverend Mother to fill her bare study like a flock of butterflies. She herself sat very upright in a hard straight-backed chair of old oak, her hands folded in her lap, and gently questioned Marguerite as to her afternoon's adventures. Marguerite, stretching her bare feet towards the comfortable warmth of the fire and wriggling her toes with pleasure, gave clear straight-forward answers to clear straightforward questions, and Reverend Mother was soon in possession of all the relevant facts.

"Mère Madeleine, those tangles are quite straightened now," she said. "Find a lay sister and send her to the village with the news of the child's safety. Say that we will keep her here until she is fetched by her parents. Then leave me to talk with the child for a while. You shall see her again before she leaves us."

Reluctantly Mère Madeleine laid aside her comb and hobbled from the room. Reverend Mother and Marguerite were alone together, the nun observing the child and the child observing this strange room where she sat. The stone walls were white-washed, the scrubbed stone floor bare except for a strip of scarlet matting on the hearth and another before the big writing table. Through the two narrow windows in the thickness of the wall there was nothing to be seen but the mist-shrouded Atlantic. Besides the desk the room contained only a couple of beautiful old oak chairs, the stool, a bookshelf full of books, a little statue of the Virgin in a niche in the wall and a prie-dieu with a crucifix of ebony and ivory hung above it. The beautiful orange glow from the burning seaweed lit up the white walls and the white ivory figure on the black cross. It even gave a glow of warmth to Reverend Mother's white wimple and clear pale skin. In spite of its austerity the room was not cold. It was very beautiful in its simplicity and Marguerite within the flushed white walls felt as though she were inside a mother-of-pearl shell. She stored up every detail of it in her memory.

"I fear your Papa and Mamma will be very anxious," commented Reverend Mother a little drily, for it struck her that this little girl was giving excessive consideration to her surroundings and none at all to the no doubt lacerated feelings of her unfortunate parents.

Marguerite withdrew her eyes from the room and fixed them upon Reverend Mother's face. "Yes," she said. "I'm afraid they will. But it won't last long now. They'll soon have me back. But I'm sorry they've had to be frightened. It was wrong of me to go to La Baie des Petits Fleurs and I won't do it again."

Reverend Mother smiled, pleased by this matter-of-fact statement of the case. No, not a heartless child but one of those sensible people who do not agitate themselves when agitation can serve no useful purpose. Her whole heart had gone out to this child. She liked her courage, her honesty, her good sense, and some quality that she felt was best described by the word clarity. The sensitive nun felt this quality as the child's particular atmosphere. It seemed to beautify what she looked on not merely for herself but for others. Because of the presence of the child Reverend Mother found herself delighting afresh in the orange glow of firelight upon her austere white walls, and noting as though she had not seen it before the beauty of the old Spanish Crucifix that had companioned her through all her years of prayer. Such a gift of kindling awareness in others spoke of a spiritual strength unusual in so young a child. And she was so simple, so happy. "Une vraie religieuse," said Reverend Mother to herself, and then, aloud, "Are you a Catholic, my child?"

"No," said Marguerite decidedly.

The answer was so uncompromising that Reverend Mother found herself unable to pursue the subject.

"But I like it here," added Marguerite courteously, conscious that her monosyllable had been perhaps a little abrupt. "It is like La Baie des Petits Fleurs."

"And what is that like?" asked Reverend Mother, who could see no connection whatever between the two.

"It's difficult to explain," said Marguerite. "There are fairies and things there that you don't see, and things you don't understand, but yet being alive there is not so confusing as being alive at home."

". . . as being alive in the world," corrected Reverend Mother. "You don't mean 'at home'. Our home, our special country, is for all of us the place where we find liberation; a very difficult word, child, that tries to describe something that can't be described but is the only thing worth having."

"I've finished my milk," said Marguerite. "Where shall I put the glass down?" The conversation had shot abruptly to a point far above her head and she saw no use in wasting her time trying to get to a place that she was not tall enough to reach.

"On my writing table," said Reverend Mother.

"You've been writing letters," said Marguerite in surprise, as she obeyed. "I thought you only prayed."

"Even in a convent there is always a certain amount of business to be seen to," said Reverend Mother. "It was because of a problem in one of my letters that I went down to the chapel to pray, and so found you."

"Could I help you with it?" asked Marguerite sweetly.

"Not just now, I think," smiled Reverend Mother.

"But perhaps I shall never see you again," said Marguerite.

"I should be sorry not to see you again," said Reverend Mother, and she got up and came to stand beside the child at her desk. She opened a drawer and took out a little book that she had had in her youth and gave it to Marguerite. "Your mother, if she is Island born, will not object to my giving it to you," she said. "The Island born are all Catholic at heart."

"No, Mamma will not mind," said Marguerite. "Thank you."

There was a discreet knocking at the door.

"Don't forget me," said Reverend Mother. "For I am your friend. And don't forget Notre Dame du Castel, or where it is that we find our special country."

"No, I won't forget," said Marguerite, and she stood with her head lifted, her hands behind her back, looking up into the face of the tall nun. They did not kiss each other, for Reverend Mother had no use for kisses, but their eyes met with the unflinching look of those who face a parting with full determination to meet again if possible.

Then Reverend Mother withdrew her keen glance. "Entrez," she said, and Mère Madeleine came in with Soeur Cécile carrying the now dry blue frock, and the information that the Papa of the little cabbage—much agitated—was already at the convent door.

"Good-bye, my child," said Reverend Mother. "Kiss Mère Madeleine, put on your dress and go with Soeur Cécile."

Marguerite did as she was told, and Reverend Mother was left alone with Mère Madeleine rocking herself upon the stool in a sudden tempest of sobs.

"It is for the love of God that we deny ourselves children and grandchildren, ma Mère," she sobbed. "It is for the love of God that we take the holy habit of religion. . . . For the love of God. . . . For the love of God."

Reverend Mother, who disliked tears, swung abruptly away from them and looked out of the window at the shrouded sea. "Or man," she muttered.

PART III

WILLIAM

O my luve's like a red, red rose
  That's newly sprung in June;
O my luve's like the melodie
  That's sweetly played in tune!

As fair art thou, my bonnie lass,
  So deep in luve am I:
And I will luve thee still, my dear,
  Till a' the seas gang dry:

Till a' the seas gang dry, my dear,
  And the rocks melt wi' the sun;
I will luve thee still, my dear,
  While the sands of life shall run.

And fare thee weel, my only Luve
  And fare thee weel a while!
And I will come again, my Luve,
  Tho' it were ten thousand mile.

ROBERT BURNS.

CHAPTER ONE

1

There were few things that seventeen-year-old Marguerite enjoyed more than waking up in the mornings in the four-poster bed with the blue curtains that she still shared with Marianne. Life was so wonderful a thing to her that the return to it was sheer joy. She savoured every minute of it, and made her awakening last as long as possible.

And this morning she knew she had some extra reason for being even happier than usual. Two extra reasons. Three. Four. A whole host of reasons. It was Midsummer Day and there was to be a Review of the Militia, and she had a new dress for the Review, white muslin with blue gauze ribbons. It was Midsummer Day and several battleships of the Fleet were visiting the islands. The Orion was

among them, and William was on board. She was seventeen and
William was nineteen and they loved each other. William did not
know it yet but she knew it. She believed she had known it ever since
that day six years ago when the little girl that she had been then had
stood on Le Petit Aiguillon and held out her arms, and William had
gone into them. She had known then that William's being was her
natural refuge, and her being his, but she had been too little to think
more about it, and William, if he also had understood, had soon forgotten. But deep within her she had not forgotten, and for six years
she had gradually become increasingly aware that there was a bond
between her and William that could never be broken. Whenever she
saw William now she felt that bond tighten and hold. There was no
need to strain or worry. If William was not aware of it yet he soon
would be. This oneness with each other seemed to her such a vital
thing that she could not think of anything in heaven or earth that
could possibly come between them.

It was still very early and Marianne was not awake yet. Gently,
so as not to disturb her, Marguerite turned over on her back,
stretching her long limbs luxuriously beneath the bedclothes, delighting in the strength and youth of her body, and let her thoughts
slip back over the past six happy years in which her love for William
had grown, and put forth shoots, and strengthened itself in the sun
and air of their health and happiness, until at last it had reached
this perfect flowering that was surely the loveliest thing that would
ever happen to her.

What fun it had been getting William into the Navy! The struggle
to make a success of the indolent William had fused both house-
holds, the doctor's in Green Dolphin Street and theirs in Le Paradis,
into one ardent whole. They had all become one family, focussed
upon William, all doing their part to stir up his laziness and fire his
ambition. And how hard they had worked! Skilfully handled by
Marianne, Octavius had put hand to pocket again and again to pay
for William's training and outfit, and had thought from start to
finish that he did so of his own volition. And Dr. Ozanne, goaded
by Marianne, had entered into a heated but successful correspondence with his wife's relations, which had led to wires being pulled
on William's behalf and the attention of exalted naval personages
being favourably directed to his person. And for six years Sophie
had never failed to react as desired to Marianne's suggestions about
the despatch of new linen to William, and books, and tuckboxes full
of the kind of delicacies that make a boy popular with his associates.
Marianne had been magnificent. If it had not been for her William
might never have passed a single examination or acquired any

knowledge whatsoever. Any subject that he had had to study she had studied first, and mastered from A to Z. Then, she had coached him in it, brilliantly, remorselessly, standing no nonsense, making such use of her sarcastic tongue when he was slack or stupid that he had sweated like a nigger lest worse befall. She had driven him so hard that it was a wonder to Marguerite that he had not come to hate her. But he never had. He admired her energy and her competence more than words could say, and he never forgot all that he owed to her. He might be indolent, and easy-going to the point of weakness, but he was just enough to acknowledge gratitude where it was due and big enough not to dislike his benefactors. There was no hatred in William as yet. Loving kindness to every human creature filled his nature to the brim.

And Marguerite, what had she done for William all these years? Not very much, she said to herself. She wrote to him when he was away but she was not very good at letter-writing, she did not know how to express herself with a pen in her hand, her letters were stilted and dull, not like Marianne's brilliant and sparkling epistles. And when he was at home she helped her mother with his darning, though she was not very good at needlework either. Apart from that, she thought, she had done nothing but love him. Once she had said to him laughingly. "What have *I* done, William?" and he had replied with answering laughter, "You've just been Marguerite."

And neither of them had known what he meant by that. They had not known that by being Marguerite she had satisfied in turn each craving of his developing nature so easily and unconsciously that neither of them had been aware either of the need or its satisfaction. At first she had been the little sister who comforted his boyish sorrows and told him the Island fairy tales that both of them loved. Then a little later she had been the confidante to whom he told the stories of his prowess. Her admiration had been the mirror in which he saw his own strength and comeliness, and gained a needed self-confidence that Marianne's sarcasm might have kept him from acquiring. But she had been more than this. It was because of her clear truthfulness that he loved things that were simple and clean, because of her delicate kindness and courtesy that his own kindness and goodwill were now very little tainted by his father's vulgarity. She was his criterion in all things. All that he met in daily life he unconsciously measured against the fact of her and found it desirable or found it odious according as it stood the test.

But he did not know this, for the things that he owed to her were not so obvious as the things that he owed to Marianne. He took her as much for granted as the sunshine and the flowers. Just as it takes death to awaken us to the full stature of someone loved, so it took the deep cleavage between his life and hers that waited in the future to awaken William Ozanne to the knowledge that though he might owe all his material possessions to Marianne he owed the spiritual ones to Marguerite.

The sunlight of a perfect summer's day was growing beyond the blue curtains of the bed and Marguerite pushed them aside and slipped out, for it was not possible to lie any longer in idleness; especially on this day of all days.

For the day on which the Lieutenant Governor reviewed the Militia was one of the great days on the Island. The Islanders were enormously proud of their Militia. It had been formed on the pattern of the "Garde Nationale" of France and had been in existence for generations. Every able-bodied man on the Island between the ages of sixteen and sixty, gentleman or peasant, was in the Militia, knew how to fire a heavy musket and wear his shako with an air. For situated as they were between those old enemies England and France the islands had had a stormy history. In the old days pirates or invasion had always been upon the doorstep, and they had had to know how to protect themselves.

But now were the days of peace and the Review had become not so much a rehearsal for war as a great social occasion and a whole holiday. It was over by noon and the rest of the day was given over to merry-making, with bunting hung in the streets and flowery garlands decorating the houses, and when night fell illuminations in the harbour and bonfires and fireworks upon the hilltops.

One dressed in one's best the moment one got up on Midsummer Day, for after a hurried early breakfast it was time to start. Marguerite, as she slipped out of bed, heard her parents' door open and her father's feet on the stairs. He was a Colonel of Militia and on Review day he had to get up early. She flung her pale blue wrapper round her and ran to the window that looked out on the street, and saw him come out of the front door in his brilliant scarlet uniform with the gold braid, his shako with the cock's feathers set at an angle upon his handsome head. Pierre their coachman was holding his black horse Trumpeter, and he mounted and sat waiting to be joined by his neighbours, Trumpeter pawing the ground in his impatience.

From every door in Le Paradis the men were coming out in their gay uniforms, laughing and calling to each other. The sun was pouring down out of a cloudless blue sky and the air was full of the scent of flowers. Down in the town the bells were pealing and from far away came the thunder of guns as the Fleet greeted the great day with a salvo. William on board the Orion must even now be getting into his uniform, for the officers of the Fleet would be the guests of the Lieutenant Governor to-day and appear at the Review in all their glory. Marguerite leaned as far out of the window as she could get, her nightcap falling back from her golden head and her blue wrapper with its white lace frills fluttering in the breeze, and called to her father and blew a kiss to him, and another to Monsieur Sebillot, just issuing from the front door of No. 5, and another to Monsieur Corbet, who was coming out of No. 10 across the way. And then all the men in the street were looking up and waving to the radiant vision at the window, and she was waving back and laughing.

"Marguerite! Marguerite!" Marianne had awakened and her shocked voice drew Marguerite back into the room. "What in the world are you doing?"

"Waving to the Militia," said Marguerite.

"With nothing on!" said Marianne in horror.

"I've heaps on," said Marguerite. "There's yards of material in my nightgown and even more yards in my wrapper, and they are both of them much higher in the neck than any of my day dresses. I'm as respectable as a woman can be." And she swung round to look at herself in the long mirror.

It always gave her quite a shock to see herself in the glass nowadays, for during the last year she had grown quite suddenly to look a woman. Gone now was the round fat little Marguerite of the past. She had grown tall and slender, one of those naturally graceful women whose every movement cannot help being one of beauty. Her small head was proudly poised on her long neck, her clear skin flushed with health and tanned by the sun, her hair a riotous mop of natural curls, her eyes even bluer than they had been in her childhood. Her complete naturalness and her unselfconscious delight in life shone from her like sunshine. "Why!" she ejaculated in astonishment, "I do believe I'm beautiful!"

"Very conceited of you to say so," said Marianne tartly, thrusting a dainty little foot out of bed.

"Why?" asked Marguerite. "It's not to my credit if I'm beautiful. The credit is God's, and I like to give credit where it is due."

"Now you're being irreverent," said Marianne, feeling for her bedroom slippers.

"Not at all," said Marguerite. "I'm being grateful. Thank you, God, for making me beautiful. I give a lot of pleasure." And she pirouetted round the room like a mad creature, a whirling pillar of blue and white and gold.

Marianne stood up and looked at her. Yes, she did give a lot of pleasure. She had had three proposals of marriage already from

charming and impecunious young men, though she was only seventeen, while Marianne at twenty-two had had only one offer; from a
widower. "For goodness sake stop whirling about like that!" she
cried in exasperation. "You make my head ache."

"I can't stop!" cried Marguerite, whirling faster than ever. "I'm
too happy to stay still. Too happy! Too happy!"

"Then go and dress in the schoolroom," said Marianne. "How
can I attend to my toilette with you making my head ache behaving
like a lunatic?"

Marguerite seized her festival clothes, already laid ready over a
chair, and her brush and comb from the dressing-table, and whirled
from the room. With a sigh of relief Marianne shut and locked the
door behind her. Marguerite's toilette required no concentration,
for every garment she put on fell into graceful folds about her long
limbs, and hair like hers did itself, but Marianne's needed a great
deal. And not only concentration; it needed time and brains and
money and artifice if Marianne Le Patourel was to keep up her
reputation for being the best-dressed woman on the Island.

For Marianne had become now the chic, petite, vivacious brunette
that in her youth her mother had been striving after. Sophie's strivings had had no effect whatever, but as the years passed Marianne
had seen for herself that she must study her looks and curb her temper and cultivate feminine graces if she was to achieve any sort of
social popularity and importance, and what Marianne saw for herself that she must do that she did with competence and success.

She was in demand everywhere; in far greater demand than was
Marguerite. Hostesses delighted in the brilliance of the conversation at their dinner-tables if Marianne was present, and men of distinction liked to be seen with her smartly dressed little figure strut-
ting beside them. No important social function seemed quite right
if she was not there.

But she was not loved. Hostesses invited her to their parties because she was of use to them, not because they liked her, and the men
who thronged about her, delighting in her wit, were the older married men, not the young ones. Young men were frightened of her
brilliance, and girls of her own age were repelled by the scorn for
their stupidity that try as she would she could never quite hide. But
her conscious mind had as yet refused to face the fact that she was
not loved. . . . She was as certain of William as Marguerite was. . . .
Yet perhaps not quite as certain, for Marguerite spread no net to
ensnare the man whom she believed to be already a part of her being, while Marianne the huntress spread all the nets she had. Her
conscious mind admitted no uncertainty; yet she spread the nets.

Her love for William had increased, not slackened, with the years. Now that she was fully a woman, old for her age and immensely vital, it had become an unsatisfied passion that was almost wholly pain. She knew that if it were not satisfied it would wreck her life. But she did not yet doubt that it would be. She did not yet doubt her power to get what she wanted.

When she was dressed she stood for a long time before the long mirror, turning herself this way and that, and she did not, like Marguerite, suffer from astonishment at the radiance of her own reflection. For she had expected to look like that. The credit was not God's, but her own, after an hour of hard labour. She was not beautiful, she knew, but she was immensely chic.

Her tiny figure, encased in stays of iron, was so upright and so dignified that one was scarcely aware of her lack of height, and her waist, reduced to wasp-like proportions by dint of hooking her stay laces to the bed-post and then pulling, was the smallest on the Island, and accentuated by the scarlet ribbon that she wore twisted around it. With her sallow skin she did not look her best in the white muslins that were the vogue for unmarried young women, and so her dress was of her favourite green, a deep rich silk, very full in the skirt, with a low boat-shaped neck, and beneath the skirt she wore one of the new hoops that were now all the rage in London. The boat-shaped neck in the day time, and the new kind of hoop, were daring innovations, and she hoped they would be the first of their kind to be seen on the Island. She had a lace scarf for her neck, and a huge green poke bonnet and a green parasol to match. She wore no jewels except the earrings of mysterious green stone that Captain O'Hara had given her six years ago, but the rosebud craze being now at its height she wore scarlet rosebuds round her face inside her bonnet, against her stiff artificial dark ringlets, and a posy of them on her tight bodice and another tucked in at her waistband. Make-up was not fashionable at this period but Marianne always rubbed geranium petals on her sallow cheeks to give them colour, and kept a pot of scarlet geraniums on her window-sill for this purpose. She no longer used lavender to scent her clothes. Her perfume was a highly provocative one from Paris. . . . Altogether the vision that looked back at her from her mirror was arresting. There was no youthful charm about it but there was colour and animation and a rather disturbing challenge. Her brilliance seemed daring fate to thwart her, yet her eyes when she was not laughing or talking were still the sombre hungry ones of her unhappy girlhood, and her mouth had a tight look, as though she held it in its smiling curves by sheer force of will.

She took her gloves and scented handkerchief from her drawer, pulled on the gloves and went out of her room and down the beautiful old twisting staircase to the hall, her high-heeled little scarlet shoes going tap-tap on the bare polished boards, her silks rustling, her earrings swinging and the very air about her electrified by her vitality.

Sophie and Marguerite, standing in the hall, looked up at her as she came down the stairs, one tiny gloved hand laid on the bannister, the other holding her green parasol. Marianne, now that she was twenty-two, permitted no interference in the choice of her clothes, and neither of them had seen the outfit in which she was now arrayed. . . . They gasped.

"The neckline!" cried Sophie in distress. "It is much too low for the day time, Marianne! It is scarcely modest!"

"It is the mode," said Marianne briefly.

"Isn't Marianne odd?" said Marguerite. "She is shocked because I lean out of the window in a nightgown that buttons right up to my chin, yet she goes out in full daylight so décolleté that if it wasn't for the scarf she'd catch her death of cold. But I like it, Marianne. And I like the hoop. As usual all the women will be mad with envy when they see you and the men will be round you like a swarm of bees."

Marguerite was not jealous, for elaborate clothes only bothered her. She was perfectly contented in her crisp white muslin with the blue ribbons, and her white chip bonnet with the pink rosebuds framing her face.

"I don't know what your Papa will say when he sees you, Marianne," sighed Sophie, but she knew it was no good arguing and she led the way out to the chariot with resignation. She herself in dove grey silk, with white ostrich plumes in her bonnet, was as beautiful as ever, though six years had added considerably both to her weight and her dignity.

"I should say we were all three dignified women," said Marguerite meditatively, as they drove off up the hill. "I because I'm so tall, Mamma because she is plump and Marianne because of her stays. Your waist is small to-day, Marianne. No wonder you didn't want any breakfast. Your inside must be squeezed out of existence. What will you do about lunch?"

"For heaven's sake, Marguerite!" cried Sophie in anguish. "Do be careful with your conversation. I live in perpetual dread as to what you will say next."

"I'm always careful before gentlemen, Mamma," Marguerite consoled her. "But I really am worried about Marianne's lunch. It's such an extra good one, and it will spoil it all if she can't have any. There are lobster sandwiches. I made them while Marianne was getting dressed. William is so fond of lobster."

The eyes of the two girls met but there was no animosity in their glance. Though each knew that the other loved William each felt so secure of him that she felt only compassion for her sister. And they loved each other. Marianne had never forgotten that moment when she had held her little sister in her arms and experienced through her beauty one of the best moments of her life, and Marguerite never ceased being sorry for Marianne because she had not been born enjoying life. Her sister's surface animation never deceived Marguerite for a single moment. She knew that the real Marianne was revealed by the sombre eyes and the mouth that had to be held by willpower in its smiling curves.

Through every twisting street of Saint Pierre chariots and phaetons and britschkas full of gaily dressed women and children were climbing up towards the cliff top of Les Tuzes above the town, where the Review was to be held, and through the lanes from the villages wound the farm carts decorated with garlands and piled high with peasants in their festival clothes. The very poor came on foot, but no matter how poor they were each woman had a scarlet petticoat to wear and each child carried a posy.

There were few open spaces on the rocky Island, but Les Tuzes was one of the few, a wide flat stretch of turf and heather upon the cliff top high above the sea. From it one could look down on the town of Saint Pierre below, with the harbour and the fort, and far away across the sea was the coast of France. To-day the scene was as gay as it could be. The sky and the sea were a peerless blue and the air so clear that one could see the sun glinting on the guns of the warships, the white ensigns stirring in the breeze, and the host of brightly-coloured little fishing craft anchored within the harbour. The Militia in their scarlet and gold, drawn up in long lines on the green grass, were a goodly sight, the flower of the Island's manhood, descendants of courageous forbears and fathers of fighting generations yet to be. As the officers spurred their horses up and down the long lines, as the bugles sounded and the guns thundered again from the fort, the watching crowds behind the barriers had hearts that beat high with pride and pulses throbbing with excitement. These gaily clad men were merely their husbands and lovers and brothers and friends, mundane creatures who would be scolded and humoured and liked and disliked as usual when to-morrow morning they were back again in their familiar clothes, busy at their familiar tasks. But to-day in their scarlet and gold they were heroes.

A sharp word of command rang out and a burst of cheering came from the spectators, for His Excellency the Lieutenant Governor had arrived. The Island occupied the same proud position in regard to England as was to be held in a later age by the great Dominions. She had her own parliament, the Court of Saint Michael, and managed her own affairs, but a Lieutenant Governor from England held a watching brief for the Crown. He lived in style in one of the finest houses on the Island, he was permitted to attend the sessions at the Court House, though not to speak there, and with the Bailiff, an Islander whose position was analogous to that of Prime Minister in the Court of Saint Michael, he was the centre of the Island's social life. His Excellency was invariably a fine figure of a man, chosen for his ability to occupy a somewhat ambiguous position with grace and diplomacy, yet perhaps the limelight beat less fiercely upon him than upon his wife; for it was Her Excellency's business to reveal to Island society the latest trend of fashion in the great world in all matters relating to dress, hospitality, furnishing, cooking and manners. His Excellency held his appointment for a year only, so that a whole succession of Her Excellencies were perpetually arriving on the Island with the latest mode. The Island, of course, might disapprove of it, and frequently did, in which case it blandly ignored Her Excellency's way of doing things and continued with its own, but it was Her Excellency's duty to be the mirror of London fashion, and were she to be by evil fortune a Frump or a Puritan her husband's mission was doomed to failure from the start.

But Their Excellencies at this date played their part to perfection, especially on this sunlit morning of the Midsummer Day Review. As their carriage, drawn by its fine bay horses, swept down the course, Their Excellencies bowing superbly to right and left, the cheering rose to a roar. His Excellency looked magnificent in a grey chimney-pot top hat and a frogged grey frockcoat with a pink rose in the buttonhole. The ends of his moustache were turned up and waxed to admiration and his curly iron-grey hair, as dictated by the latest fashion, was worn long enough to cover the ears. Her Excellency was a vision of beauty in sky-blue satin sprinkled all over with rosebuds, almost more rosebud than satin, with the new boat-shaped neck and the new hoop. She and Marianne were the only women present to display the new neckline and the new hoop. . . . But Marianne's neckline was a shade lower and her hoop a trifle larger than Her Excellency's, a fact which caused Octavius, who from some distance away had taken in every detail of his elder daughter's appearance with extreme annoyance, to have his irritability somewhat allayed.

With Their Excellencies were the two senior captains of the visiting battleships, resplendent in gold epaulettes and cocked hats, and behind the leading carriage came six others filled with Their Excellencies' guests and other naval officers. These last, however, did not drive down the course, but took their place with the spectators.

Marianne and Marguerite instantly lost any interest whatever in the Review, for there was William standing up in one of the carriages with a clinging minx in pink, reported to be Their Excellencies' niece and an heiress into the bargain, supported affectionately upon his arm.

It was the opinion of Marianne and Marguerite that not a single man in all that colourful crowd could hold a candle to William. Since he had been in the Navy, where his slow brain and sunny good nature and amiable weaknesses had won him instant and lasting popularity, he had developed with amazing swiftness. He looked much older than his nineteen years. He stood six foot in his stocking feet and was correspondingly broad and muscular, yet he held himself so well that he appeared always not quite so large as he was, and the look of breeding and elegance that he had inherited from his mother had been accentuated by the years. His red-gold hair was as curly as ever and his tawny eyes as merry. His freckled face with its fine bones and full generous mouth was clear-skinned and ruddy with abounding health, and when he laughed it was like an amiable lion roaring. Those who had only known Dr. Ozanne in these later days of his decline found it hard to believe that this magnificent young man was his son, but those, such as Sophie, who had known Edmond Ozanne in his youth declared that except for the air of elegance William with all his beauty was yet not a patch on his father at his age.

While chattering agreeably to the clinging minx in pink William yet had a roving eye beneath his gold-braided cocked hat, and presently it found the Le Patourels' carriage. Thereafter it was an education in manners to watch with what grace he slowly but surely detached himself from his new friends to seek the company of the old ones to whom his faithful heart inclined him. His progress towards them was of necessity slow, for everyone he greeted wanted to detain him, and Marianne and Marguerite watched in an agony of impatience. In Marianne this impatience was scarcely discernible. She seemed entirely occupied in flirting with the men who as usual had crowded about her, and only a slight tightening of her small gloved hands on the stick of her parasol betrayed her. But Marguerite watched William's approach with the frank absorption of a child, her lips a little parted in her eagerness and her blue eyes shining.

At last he arrived and joined the group of men standing by one of the opened doors of the chariot. Marianne gave him one quick appraising possessive glance and continued her conversation with the man nearest her, but Marguerite held out her hand, took William's and squeezed it happily. "There are lobster sandwiches, William," she whispered.

"That's why I came," he whispered back. "I could smell them from Their Excellencies' carriage."

It was twelve o'clock. The guns boomed again from the fort and the long scarlet lines broke into happy disorder as each man slung his musket over his shoulder, doffed his shako and made tracks for his family and food.

"Why, the Review is over!" cried Marguerite. "And I never even looked at it!"

They all laughed at her, but she did not care. William had neglected to let go of her hand again and she knew that it was not really because of the lobster sandwiches that he had come; he could not possibly have smelt them all that way away because they were so very fresh. They had only boiled the lobster yesterday and it had been alive and kicking when they put it in the pot.

The picnic parties were now scattered all over the cliff, the well-to-do eating in their carriages, the poorer folk sitting on the grass. When they could all eat no more they strolled about in laughing groups, appraising each other's clothes and hair and jewellery, laughing at the peasant children as they chased each other in and out of the gorse bushes, watching the ships in the harbour and the white gulls circling overhead.

"What do they all do now?" asked a charming middle-aged Irishman, a guest of the Lieutenant Governor who had been introduced by William. To her hidden fury he had monopolised Marianne and was walking with her at the edge of the cliff. Had William not been there to-day she would have been delighted, for he was a man of obvious distinction and had singled her out for attention very markedly, but with William present it taxed her to the uttermost to keep her attention upon the worthless person and to reply adequately to the futile conversation of another man. In every fibre of her body she was aware of William and Marguerite walking quickly away together. . . . Where were they going? What were they going to do? . . . Mamma should not permit them to go about together in the way they did; especially with their best clothes on. They were grown-up now and it was not seemly. She must speak to Mamma about it.

"I gather that this is a whole holiday upon the Island?" continued the Irishman.

Marianne pulled herself together. "It's the most riotous day in the year," she told him. "Down in Saint Pierre there will be crowds in the streets all day, and the taverns will be full, and everyone will be gloriously merry by night-fall. And in the country each village will be busy with all the old Midsummer customs. In every cottage the jonquière, a sort of couch where the women sit to do their knitting, will be spread with fresh fern and decorated with flowers, and when they have decided which jonquière in the village is the best decorated they will make some pretty girl sit on it like a queen and call her 'La Môme' and do her homage; and if she has a lover he will be allowed to kiss her. And then they will dance out of doors until it is time to light the bonfires on the cliffs. We call these bonfires 'les feux de la Saint Jean'."

"And in Ireland we call them 'Beltain'," said the Irishman. "They are a relic of sun-worship. And this homage of 'La Môme' enthroned upon the jonquière, that must be a relic of heathen worship too. Who is she, this girl? Persephone? Demeter? Both, I think. Persephone the girl become Demeter the woman. April grown to June and ready for her lover's kiss." He paused and looked at Marianne. "I would dearly love a drive round the Island and a glimpse of these same festivities. I have a curricle here. Will you do me the honour of accompanying me?"

Marianne hated him. She did not wish to spend her afternoon in the company of a middle-aged Irishman, no matter how charming and distinguished, she wanted to spend it with William.

"I shall have to obtain Mamma's permission," she said stiffly.

Her companion immediately led the way to Mamma and made the request himself, standing beside the Le Patourel chariot with Marianne upon his arm, her lips smiling but her dark eyes fixed upon her mother with that fixed and steely regard that Sophie recognised only too well; it was a command of some sort or another that must not be disregarded if there was to be domestic peace. But upon this occasion she misunderstood Marianne's wishes. "I will be happy to trust my daughter to you for a short drive, sir," she said sweetly. It was not perhaps quite comme il faut, but she had been hearing excellent reports of this Sir Charles Maloney, and he was not a young man, and Marianne was twenty-two and old for her age and impossible to live with if she did not get her own way. "It's a lovely day for a drive," she concluded sweetly, and smiling upon the distinguished stranger she failed to notice the sudden anger in her daughter's eyes.

2

William and Marguerite only walked until they were out of sight of the crowd upon the cliff top; then they ran. It was really too hot to run but the instinct of escape was strong in them. They had not been alone together since William had come home.

"Here, I can't run in a sword," said William suddenly, and he took it off and hid it with his cocked hat behind a clump of ferns.

They were in one of the narrow waterlanes for which the Island was famous. It was not more than a few feet wide and was paved with smooth stones, and down one side of it ran a small and merry stream. The steep banks upon either side were covered with ferns and trees arched overhead, their branches intertwined to make of the place a small cool green tunnel. The sunlight pushing its fingers through the green leaves made a checkered pattern of delight all over Marguerite's white dress, and William's tawny eyes were just the colour of the brown stream that tinkled over the stones. As they went down the lane the physical contact of their feet with the earth and their linked hands with each other seemed to make the three of them one entity, and they were as happy as two mortals can be.

"I haven't been on this jolly, kind little Island very much really," said William, "yet I'm happier here than anywhere else in the world,"

"You feel at home," said Marguerite simply.

"We don't understand what we mean when we talk about feeling at home," said William. "It's not just being in the place where your ancestors lived, or being with the people you love best, it's more than that because one feels at home sometimes in strange places and with strange people; if the places are kind and jolly and the people are good fun. . . . I don't know what it is."

"Someone once said to me," said Marguerite, "that our home, our special country, is where we find liberation. I suppose she meant that it is where our souls find it easiest to escape from self, and it seems to me it is that way with us when what is about us echoes the best that we are. You feel at home in places that are kind and with people who are good fun because you're kind and amusing yourself."

"What's your home like, Marguerite?" asked William.

"I can't describe it exactly," said Marguerite. "But when I am living in a particular sort of way I say to myself that now I am in my own country. It is when I am living very simply, and rather hardly, and the light is clear and the wind cold and there aren't any lies or subterfuges. When I am there I have a feeling that a door opens out of it into yet another country where my soul has always lived, and that one day I shall find out how to unlock the door."

"You *are* a queer girl," said William. "One minute you're a child and the next you're being wiser than Marianne."

"I could never be wiser than Marianne," said Marguerite with awe.

"She's deuced clever," agreed William. "She frightens me to death. She frightens all the men to death. She'll never get a husband."

"Won't she?" asked Marguerite, with something of dismay in her tone. "She's very chic and fashionable. Surely a man who was cleverer than she is would not be frightened of her?"

"A man cleverer than she is never appears in this archipelago," said William solemnly. "My word, Marguerite, but those lobster sandwiches were good. I'm glad we both like lobster."

And then they laughed, and their conversation sank abruptly to the level of sheer frivolity. They always had great fun together. They liked the same sort of jokes and took the same sort of simple pleasure in all the good things of life.

The water-lane ran out of its tunnel of green leaves and became the main street of the village of Saint Pierre-du-Bois, a small hamlet at the edge of a wood. A more modern road skirted the village upon the other side of the wood but the paved lane with the stream running beside it was the original village street, and a small stone bridge spanned the stream before each arched cottage doorway. The cottages were built of white-washed grey granite, with thatched roofs and small diamond-paned windows. On most days in the year Saint-Pierre-du-Bois would have looked empty and deserted, for the men would have been working in the fields or away fishing and the women busy indoors, but to-day chattering groups of men and women and children, bright as butterflies in scarlet petticoats, chintz gowns, blue coats with brass buttons and jean trousers, the men carrying bunches of flowers, were going from house to house in laughing excitement, trying to decide which cottage had the prettiest jonquière. Unseen, William and Marguerite stood for a little and watched the pretty scene. They had watched it many times before upon Midsummer Day but it was a sight of which one could not tire, for it was like a scene in a fairy story. The gay beautiful clothes, many of them of a great age, handed down from father to son and from mother to daughter and treasured between festivals in the old carved chest that each bride brought to her home with her bridal linen, the centuries-old cottages of white and gold with their little bridges across the singing stream, the sunshine and the flowers, the bright blue sky overhead and near at hand the cool green whispering wood, all had a bright and fragile beauty that was like the beauty of a rainbow soap bubble. William and Marguerite felt that it had drifted to their feet from another age, and they dared not move lest their clumsy feet smash it to pieces.

Then the laughing crowd drifted into a pool of colour that spread itself before the arched doorway of a house a little larger than the others, more of a farmhouse than a cottage, and from inside came a burst of cheering whose robustness was certainly of to-day. The spell was broken. William seized Marguerite's hand and pulled her forward. "They've chosen!" he cried.

They ran across the little bridge and joined the group that was surging in through the opened half-door, the "hecq". Inside was a typical Island kitchen, cool and dim, the earth floor covered with clean sand, with a low oak ceiling crossed by a huge oak beam, the "poûtre" from which hung a rack where the bacon was kept, and the grease for the "soupe à la graisse". There was a huge chimney beautifully carved. Inside its enclosure were stone seats, a large bread oven built in the thickness of the wall, and the crâset lamp hanging from its hook. The furniture of the room, the long table and forms, the spinning-wheel and the oak chest, had been pushed against the furthest wall to keep a clear space before the jonquière, which stood in its recess between the hearth and the window.

It was raised about eighteen inches from the ground and thickly strewn with fresh fern, and in the fern brilliant flowers, marigolds and veronica, camomile daisies and tamarisk, roses and passion flowers, pansies and mignonette, had been arranged in a formal pattern to make a tapestry of flower petals lovelier than any that had ever been woven from silk and wool. Over the jonquière was a canopy decorated with the pink and white trumpet-shaped Island lilies, and upon the fresh sand before the jonquière had been scattered the plucked petals of the gorse that the Islanders call the fairies' gold. No queen could ever have had a lovelier seat. It was so perfect that after the first burst of cheering there was silence, for the love of flowers was a passion with the Islanders, and the sight of them never failed to move both men and women to an emotion almost akin to worship.

Then, that their worship might have expression, the men looked about them for the prettiest girl to play the part of La Môme. The method of choosing was for each man to fling a flower at the girl he thought the prettiest, and she who caught the greatest number was La Môme, and it was for this purpose that each man carried a bunch of flowers. Yet the moment was one of some delicacy, for all the girls were pretty and each man thought the one he loved the prettiest of all, and there had been occasions in the past when hot-blooded youths had refused to abide by the decision of the flowers, and the ceremony had ended with a bloody battle in the village street. Great tact was required, and if the maid was of such outstanding beauty that there could be no question as to her superiority, then everyone was heartily thankful. But among the village girls such was not the case to-day and there was a certain atmosphere of strain in the room.

A tall young fisherman with a white rose in his hand stepped first into the centre of the floor and looked about him. He had been chosen to throw the first flower because the girl he loved had died two months ago and so he could be trusted to show no favouritism. His dark eyes were sombre as they passed from one pretty face to another that meant nothing to him, and at that moment a white summer cloud that had been obscuring the face of the sun drifted away and a beam of light shone straight through the window beside the jonquière and lit like a pointing finger upon Marguerite where she stood beside William at the door, watching the scene, with a grave face and steady eyes. She had no part in this ceremony, she thought, and her lovely serenity was unruffled by any desire. She had taken off her bonnet and her hair was lit to a mop of gold by the sun. And she, among all the girls, was the only one who was dressed in white. She looked like a visitant from another world, a happy spirit come back from the fields of Paradise to see how it fared with those she had loved on earth. The young man caught his breath and flung the white rose to Marguerite.

She did not understand at first and she let it fall at her feet, but when the flowers came at her thick and fast she understood that she was La Môme and she gathered them up with delight. For it was fun, oh it was fun! She had never expected that she would be La Môme in an Island village! And catching the infection of her pleasure everyone else was soon laughing too; and the girls as well as the men pelted her with flowers, for the choice of a stranger for La Môme, and a fine lady too, did away with all jealousy and spite.

When her arms could hold no more they picked her up and carried her to the jonquière, and sat her down on the tapestry of flowers with her feet upon the petals of the gorse. And then, as the master of the house came forward with a chaplet of white lilies, a sudden silence fell, a strange silence that reached back into the primeval age where this ceremony had had its birth. In silence he crowned her and bent the knee to her, and in silence each man and woman and child came and knelt before her and laid caressing hands upon her feet. She sat still and straight beneath her canopy of flowers and her eyes were like stars. She was not herself only at this moment, William thought, as he watched her wonderingly from the door. Something possessed her, something divine that men would always worship, the selflessness of woman who gives her body to man to ensure his immortality on the earth, divine Demeter, who bares her bosom to the sun and rain that the seed within it may have life. William's heart constricted painfully as he looked at the transfigured girl on the jonquière, and his throat felt tight and his eyes hot as the flame of desire surged for the first time through his body. Then, brushing his hand across his eyes, he came to himself again and found that all the men were looking at him. This was the moment for the accepted lover of La Môme to go to her and give her the kiss that should both set the seal upon her womanhood and bring her back again as a mortal girl into the world of mortals. Though he had taken no part in the proceedings so far William did not hesitate now. He went to Marguerite, lifted her to her feet and kissed her beneath the canopy of the pink and white lilies. He too was something more than himself at this moment, and with his own small personality lost in something larger he had no sense of embarrassment that so many eyes should be watching as he gave Marguerite the first kiss of his manhood. They had kissed only once before, years ago on the rock of Le Petit Aiguillon, but that had been only the kiss of childhood, giving the sense of security that children crave. This kiss neither promised nor gave security, it was rather a dedication of themselves in comradeship to the danger and pain of living. And living is another word for creation; they knew that as for one short moment they clung to each other; creation by body and mind and soul for a future of humanity whose nature cannot even be guessed at. "I love you," whispered the man to the woman. "For ever and ever and ever." But he was speaking as man, not as William, and afterwards he did not remember what he had said.

Marguerite burst into a sudden peal of laughter and pushed him away. Her queer exaltation had fallen from her and she was Marguerite again, and Marguerite Le Patourel always saw the funny side of things. And it *was* funny that she and William should be kissing solemnly like this before all these peasants. And William laughed too, like an amiable lion roaring, and an answering roar of delighted laughter swept through the whole room.

But there was one who did not laugh, a woman in a smart green gown who with her companion had entered from the sunshine outside some minutes before William took Marguerite in his arms. She stood now erect in the doorway, her cold still little face giving no sign of the rage and despair that seemed to herself to be tearing her to pieces.

"Marianne!" cried Marguerite in delight when she saw her sister, and she ran to her and kissed her impulsively, because she was looking so odd and so cold. "They chose me for La Môme! Isn't it fun? I'm La Môme! Whatever will Mamma and Papa say?"

"I cannot imagine," said Marianne with icy disapproval. "I think it would be better not to tell them what has happened to-day."

"Oh, don't be such a prude!" flashed Marguerite in sudden exasperation. "Don't be such a disapproving old maid. It was only fun. Can't one have a little fun sometimes!"

William looked at her with astonishment, for never before had he heard Marguerite speak with such sharpness. He could not know how Marianne's sudden burning hatred for her sister had seared across Marguerite's sensitive soul and caused the inevitable flashback of anger, for which she was no more responsible than a dog is responsible for the snarl that follows a blow.

And then the sudden painful tension snapped, for they had been carried by the happy crowd out into the village street and away towards the clearing in the wood where an old fiddler already sat on a fallen tree trunk tuning his "chifournie".

The Irishman, who had left the curricle tied to a gate upon the other side of the wood where the main road ran, and had persuaded Marianne to walk with him through the wood to the village, was delighted with the success of his afternoon's adventure. He would never forget the lovely ceremony of the crowning of La Môme. He would never forget the picture that Marguerite had made as she sat in her bower of flowers, or the look on her face when young William had lifted her in his arms and kissed her. He had lost all interest in Marianne now. Her brilliance had attracted him for the moment, but it could not compare with her sister's natural grace and gift of laughter. He could not take his eyes off Marguerite as she went swaying round the circle of men and girls in the lovely old country dance of Mon Beau Laurier, arms akimbo, sunlight and shade flickering over her white gown, her feet making no sound on the soft earth. Charles Maloney was infatuated and made haste to claim her as his partner when Mon Beau Laurier ended and the dancers swung two by two to the tune of an ancient roundelay.

William acquiesced good-humouredly in the loss of Marguerite and put a willing arm round Marianne's tiny waist. He considered her a damn good dancer, but in any case he would have wanted to dance with her because his instinct told him that she was vexed about something and his kindness longed to apply what balm he could. He was deuced fond of her, even though her brilliance did terrify him into the middle of next week. He had reason to be, he told himself.

When he thought of what he owed to her he was more or less deprived of breath.

"You're an angel, Marianne," he said. "Anyone would think you liked having a clumsy ass treading on your feet."

"I do," she whispered softly, looking up at him with a smiling gentleness that was the achievement of nothing less than a genius for deception. For gentle was the very last thing she felt. Her dream world had tumbled into fragments about her and the reaction of her strong temperament was neither sorrow nor self-pity but a boiling fury that was being slowly tempered by resolve. Marianne had something of her father in her and was capable of deluding herself as well as others, but it was self-deception with a difference. Octavius's conviction that his affairs could not turn out in any way contrary to his desires was rooted in his conceit, that expected all things to work together for good for such a high-minded creature as himself, but Marianne's was rooted in her faith in her own strong will. Up till now she had got all that she wanted and she had not believed that what she wanted most of all, William, she would not be able to get too. She had spun all her dreams about the love that she would win from him and had seen them as reality. And now she saw them for the fantasies that they were. When she had seen William and Marguerite together just now she had no longer been able to deceive herself; it had been obvious to the dullest sight that their love was the authentic mutual fairytale love between man and woman that was breathed into the world as the germ of its life; and Marianne's sight was not dull.

But now, as she danced smilingly with William, the fury that had been tearing her to pieces was giving way before cold calculation and a fresh determination. "Don't be such a disapproving old maid!" Marguerite had cried out to her in exasperation. "An old maid." Was that how they saw her, these boys and girls who were younger than she was? With all her brilliance and popularity was it as a probable old maid that perhaps the whole Island regarded her? If that was how they thought of her then she was going to prove them all wrong. Her resolve was spreading right through her now, seeming to stiffen her limbs as she danced. She was going to marry. And she was not going to be fobbed off with a second best and be contented with it, like her mother, she was not going to marry one of the elderly men who were so invariably attracted by her and have the Island see her marriage as a mere compromise. She was going to marry the young man she loved, William, even though at present he loved Marguerite. She was going to fight his love for Marguerite, and win.

She had no compunction about this fight, for she considered that it would be a fair and equal one. On her side she had her wit and brilliance and the great debt of gratitude that William owed to her, but Marguerite had her youth and beauty, and William already loved her, and after that embrace in La Môme's bower of flowers he was probably a great deal nearer to realising it than he had been. All her life she had had moments of hating Marguerite, but they had only been moments, below them was a constant love for her sister. Even if the inconceivable happened, and Marguerite won, she thought that she would still not really hate her. . . . But Marguerite was not going to win.

"Only another week," said William's voice regretfully. "Only another week of the Island, and then we leave for the China seas."

Yes, only another week. The utmost she could hope for in this week was that by playing her cards with all the skill that she had she might prevent William from proposing to Marguerite before he left.

She looked up at him and smiled. "I've been reading about these new paddle steamers," she said. "You know, William, it won't be for very much longer that the Navy moves under sail."

William's eyes, that had been watching Marguerite over the top of her head, came back to her, and they were flashing with indignation. "Those damned steamers!" he snorted angrily. "They're all very well for river traffic but they're no earthly use for the sea. It's sail, and sail only, for the sea. You waste your time reading about those filthy steamers, Marianne. I tell you they're no damn use."

"They will very soon be a great deal of use," said Marianne quietly. "And I don't waste my time reading about them. I move with the times, William, and so should you, if you mean to get on in your profession. As a sailor you should study steam. When the change-over comes do you want to be one of those old reactionaries who are left high and dry because their minds are too rusty to take in new ideas, or do you want to be one of the men who will lead the vanguard in the revolution?"

"What revolution?" asked William angrily.

"The revolution in the art of war at sea," said Marianne. "Sea warfare will be a new thing altogether when a battleship is no longer dependent on wind and tide."

"I tell you steam will never be any use for fighting ships," said William, and the arm that held Marianne was trembling with his rage. "Except under sail a ship has no power of manoeuvre. Look at that old Comet of Henry Bell's; it's so unmanageable even on a river that it does nothing but bump into the bank."

"The Comet type of steamer was out of date years ago!" said Marianne impatiently. "Don't you ever read a *thing* about steam? There's an article in this week's 'Examiner'—I've got it at home—describing this new engine——"

"No sort of new engine will make the thing any easier to handle," interrupted the infuriated William. "I tell you that in war easiness of manoeuvre is what matters, and with sail——"

"You're treading on my feet," said Marianne tartly, and gave his shoulder a sharp pinch.

"Oh for God's sake let's sit down," snapped William. "One can't talk and dance at the same time." And taking her by the arm he pulled her roughly towards a fallen tree trunk in a secluded spot, where they could fight in peace and quiet.

This argument about steam versus sail was one of perennial interest to William and Marianne, and one of the few that William found completely engrossing, so there was a little smile of triumph on Marianne's face as with apparent unwillingness she permitted herself to be dragged to the tree trunk. For with luck she could keep William at the boiling point of enjoyable rage, shouting at her and drawing diagrams on the backs of envelopes, for days to come. That was where she had the advantage over Marguerite—in her wits that enabled her to argue with a man until he forgot that she was not a man too. She knew that it was in these times of easy comradeship that William liked her best.

CHAPTER TWO

1

Fortune favoured Marianne. The steam versus sail controversy kept William's mind occupied for a couple of days, and after that the doctor was not well. He had not felt like himself on the day of the Review and had not attended it, and now he sat hunched up in his armchair in the parlour looking more like a moulting old lion than ever, and complaining of "les côtais bas". Old Nick the parrot sat in his cage beside him in much depression of spirits, swearing horribly. William, who as life went on increasingly loved his father, fell into a paroxysm of fuss and anxiety. "Keep your hair on," said Old Nick, but William took no notice and dashed up to Le Paradis for reassurance and assistance. Sophie was out but Marianne snatched up her bonnet and went at once with William to Green Dolphin Street. . . . But Marguerite did not go. She wasn't much good when people were ill, for illness both frightened and repulsed her. And Dr.

Ozanne, nowadays, rather repulsed her too. She had never loved him as Marianne did and her fastidiousness shrank from his alcoholic kisses and broad jokes and the general untidiness of his house and person. The happy-go-lucky atmosphere of Green Dolphin Street, that had charmed her as well as Marianne six years ago, had with the passing of the years and William's absences become a sort of looseness that she hated, for it was in direct contradiction to the austere clear atmosphere of her own especial country. . . . But afterwards she reproached herself that she had not gone with William to his father. If she had it might have altered the whole course of her life and his. She was a coward that day, and cowardice more than any other failing demands a ruthless paying of the price from those who give it hospitality.

So it was Marianne who gave William courage as they stood together before the old lion hunched up in his chair. "Les côtais bas?" she said gently, one of her slim hands gripping the doctor's and the other giving William a comforting clasp. "Why, that's nothing. Lots of your patients have that and you get them right in no time. I know what you give them, too." And she went briskly away into the surgery, her high heels tapping on the floor with a confident note, William following her greatly reassured.

"It's a white peppermint drink he gives," she said to William, her eye running along the bottles on the shelves. "I remember years ago sitting in the waiting room and seeing an old fisherman come out with it."

"You don't think there's anything seriously the matter with him?" asked the anxious William.

"Of course not," said Marianne with the certainty of complete ignorance. "Just digestive trouble. Self-indulgence is bound to lead to bad health in the end, you know."

"It's nothing to do with self-indulgence," said William, in swift defence of his adored father. "He's worn out. He didn't get home till two o'clock last night. He was sitting up with old André Perot."

"Are you sure?" asked Marianne. "I think you mean André Torode."

"Oh, what does it matter!" exclaimed William irritably. "The point is that he exhausts himself looking after these selfish old peasants who never pay him a single cent."

"It *does* matter that you should be so inaccurate," said Marianne. "Your habit of confusing people's names is a bad habit, William. It's a weakness and——"

"Here's what you want," interrupted William, taking a bottle of whitish fluid from the shelf. "It's got 'Digestive Mixture' on the label." But as he led the way back to the parlour he was not as exasperated by Marianne's prim admonitions as he usually was. He was so grateful to her for her strength and her decisiveness.

"Pour the filthy stuff down the sink and get me a tot of whisky," said Dr. Ozanne when he saw the white mixture.

"But it's what you give your patients," protested Marianne.

"It may be what I give my patients but it's not what I give myself," said Dr. Ozanne. "Take it away."

"It's a nice soothing mixture," said Marianne, pouring it out, "and it can't do anybody a scrap of harm, or you wouldn't give it to your patients, so you can just drink it to please me."

Dr. Ozanne looked up at her trim little figure and small determined face, and his dulled eyes lit up with a twinkle. "Give it here then," he said. "I'll drink it to please you. And tell William to take himself off. Madame Métivier will be here soon and he was due back on board half an hour ago."

"I'll not leave you alone, sir," said William stoutly.

"I'll stay till Madame Métivier comes," said Marianne, "and Mamma or I will come down again later. Go on, William. Do you want to be court-martialled for dereliction of duty before the ball tomorrow?"

"Be off with you," said Dr. Ozanne to his son. "What more efficient nurse could I have than Marianne?" He set down his glass with a wry face. "No other woman in the world could have forced this filthy mixture down my throat."

William laughed, and dropping his hand on his father's shoulder he gave it an affectionate squeeze. Marianne smiled and her sharp features softened. She loved to see father and son together. Though he had never said so she knew that Dr. Ozanne loved her and was her ally in all things. Therefore the mutual affection of father and son could bring her nothing but good, for his father's championship of her would be bound to increase her worth in William's eyes. It had done so already. It was with a look of very real affection that he left her to take care of his father.

When he had gone she fetched paper and wood and lit a fire in the grate, for it was a cool rainy day and she saw that the doctor had suddenly begun to shiver.

"Chilled to the bone by that peppermint filth," he complained. "The worst thing you could have given me. Damned cold on the stomach."

Marianne fetched another rug and tucked it round him. "You shall have some hot milk presently," she promised him.

"Milk?" said the doctor. "Milk? Not if I know it!" And he snorted in disgust.

Marianne laughed and sitting down beside him she took his cold hand in her two warm ones and began to rub it gently. The loving physical contact comforted him and in spite of the peppermint drink he felt a little better, and less afraid of the abyss that he knew was opening at his feet. His strained face relaxed and he shut his eyes.

Now that neither he nor William were looking at her the confident smile left her face and she looked at the doctor anxiously. He had aged incredibly in the last six years, and now that his face was drained of its usual high colour she did not like the grey look about his mouth and the increased heaviness of the pouches beneath his eyes. Looking at him she believed that William was right and that though he was not yet an old man he had yet come to the end of his strength. Day by day he had spent himself to the last ounce in the service of the suffering humanity he loved, and day by day he had renewed himself for that purpose by the worst means possible. As a doctor he must have known better than most men that an abused body never fails to take its revenge. She supposed that nothing had ever really mattered to him except that daily renewal that made his service possible, that he had deliberately counted the cost and accepted the penalty. In that case there had been a flash of greatness in his weakness and she loved him more than ever. She could imagine William doing the same thing. She could imagine William deliberately doing what he knew might wreck his life simply to be kind.

In a few moments Dr. Ozanne opened his eyes. "You can get me that hot milk," he said. "But if you don't put a lacing of brandy in it, my girl, I'll wring your neck."

She did as he asked, and after the milk he slept a little, and she sat beside him, his hand in hers, and waited. Madame Métivier, the doctor's housekeeper, was very late this morning and she was glad. She felt very near to the man who once in this room had been so kind to her unhappy adolescence and she did not want this time of union to be interrupted.

Presently he woke up, and with a flicker of renewed energy. "What was that ball you spoke of?" he asked.

"There is to be a ball on board the Orion to-morrow night," said Marianne. "A good-bye ball before the Fleet leaves."

"Is the Fleet leaving? Is William going?" asked Dr. Ozanne, and there was painful distress in his tone.

"They sail for the China seas on Friday," said Marianne.

"You are going to this ball?" he asked.

"Yes," said Marianne. "Marguerite and I are both going."

She made her answers quietly, but there was panic in her heart. For yesterday Dr. Ozanne had known all about the ball and William's departure. He and William had dined at Le Paradis and Marianne and Marguerite had shown him their ball dresses.

"Did you say that William sails on Friday?" repeated the doctor stupidly.

"Yes, on Friday," said Marianne. "But the time will soon pass. He'll soon be back again."

"Not soon enough," said the doctor, and his hand moved restlessly in Marianne's.

Her strong warm clasp did not falter but her panic grew. An abyss seemed opening at her feet too, as for the first time in her life she realised the meaning of death. However strong religious faith may be death remains an abyss that swallows the familiar companion of everyday as though he had never been. It is the most awful fact of human life, and at the moment Marianne knew it not only with her mind but for the first time with her panic-stricken soul as well. . . . What if William died out there in the China seas?

There was the frou-frou of silk petticoats, a familiar fragrance, and she looked up to see Sophie standing by her. "Mamma," she whispered, and for the first time in her life seized her mother's hand as though for protection.

But Sophie was for once oblivious of her own child. Though she left her hand in Marianne's her whole being was focussed upon Edmond Ozanne and behind the smile and the cheery words she gave him her daughter could sense her anguish. Marianne in her heightened awareness could almost fancy she could hear the unspoken words of it lamenting with many voices, the voices of all the women who have ever loved with constant hearts. . . . You were young once, and strong and comely as a man can be. Now you are old and the evil days are upon you and your beauty is destroyed as though it never had been. You were young once and I loved you. I love you still, even though you forgot me as the years went by. Love's not time's fool, my dearest, love's not time's fool. . . .

Marianne found herself out in Green Dolphin Street, drawing great breaths of the damp salt air, and intensely grateful for it after the stuffiness of the doctor's room. She was standing outside the inn, she found, underneath the sign of the Green Dolphin, for the same instinct that had driven her out into the street had made her move quickly away from the parlour window, lest she should find herself in the position of one of those who spy upon the mystery of things at a moment when the door should be shut in the street and the window darkened.

The fresh cool air revived her and in a moment she was herself again. As she went back to Le Paradis her momentary panic had entirely vanished. What was death, after all? Only one more thing to be fought and conquered. And Dr. Ozanne was not dying at this moment, and nor was William. The fight upon which she was engaged just now was the fight for William, and her present enemy was Marguerite. The hours of her danger, she knew, would be the hours of the ball, for with Marguerite in his arms again William could not fail to remember that moment at the crowning of La Môme. Yet perhaps even at the ball Dr. Ozanne would in some way be her ally, as he had been this morning when his weakness drew her nearer to William. She thought of him with love as she crossed the garden, and it did not occur to her to hate herself because she was using a sick man to further her own purposes.

CHAPTER THREE

1

The weather was not upon her side, Marianne thought, when upon the night of the ball she waited at the harbour, with Marguerite and her father and mother, for the picket boat that was to take them out to the Orion. For it was a night made for love.

> "... In such a night as this,
>   When the sweet wind did gently kiss the trees
>   And they did make no noise ... in such a night
>   Did young Lorenzo swear he loved her well."

The words slipped into her mind with a sense of doom. Yes, it was that sort of night. The kind of unearthly night that is made for the fairytale love that is not of the earth either, the seed of it carried upon that wind that blows where it listeth and you cannot tell whence it comes or whither it goes, or why it should scatter the seed in those two hearts and not in others, or why the flowering of the seed should be so perfect a thing that man and woman are ready to fling away all that they have to enjoy it for only a day and a night.

A day and a night, said Marianne bitterly to herself. She told herself that it did not last for much more than that, this fairytale love that was yet the authentic seed of life, while the kind of comradeship that she would have with William if he chose her, rooted in the need of his weakness for her strength and her need of his manhood that

she might be a woman, would be a comradeship that would endure
as long as their mutual need endured; and that would be for as long
as they were themselves in this world. Yet this fairy love, as
ephemeral as it was unexplainable, was preferred above the other.

Marianne found that Marguerite was beside her, pulling at her
cloak. "What's the matter with you, Marianne? Look, here comes
William!"

He had promised to fetch them himself if they would wait at the
top of a certain flight of steps at the harbour, and now here he was
running up the steps from the picket boat, exhilarated and happy.
Dr. Ozanne was much better, though not well enough to come to the
ball, and William had cast all care aside and abandoned himself to
enjoyment as only he could do. Neither past nor future existed for
him now, but only the exquisite fun of the moment. It was impossible
to stand against such a mood. The little group who had been so
silently waiting for him were suddenly caught into mirth as a heap of
fallen leaves is blown into life by a rollicking breeze. Laughter tossed
upward into the blue air and the music that had sounded so far away
was suddenly all about them.

"You ladies can't walk down those steps, they're covered with
weed," said William, and he picked up Sophie with supreme disregard of her weight and handed her down to a burly impassive seaman who stood at the bottom to receive her. Then it was Marianne's
turn, and for a moment she remembered the day when he had lifted
her out of the boat under the archway at Pipet Lane. Then he had
been a child, and had staggered beneath her weight, now he was a
man and lifted her little figure as though it were a featherweight.
"Remember the Green Dolphin?" he whispered laughingly, as he
handed her to the impassive seaman. "Always," she answered.

He said nothing to Marguerite as he lifted her down, and when
they looked at each other they did not even smile. They had not
been smiling, Marianne remembered, when they stood in each
other's arms before the bower of La Môme. It seemed it was not
altogether a laughing matter, this love. "Wilt thou be gone? It is
not yet near dawn," Juliet had cried in anguish. And Romeo's
answer had been, "Night's candles are burnt out. . . ."

Then the boat pushed off and Marianne's queer retrospective
mood vanished completely in the excitement of the moment. Several
other girls whom they knew, with their Mammas and Papas, had also
embarked in this same picket boat, and their billowing silks and
laces filled it to overflowing. And every youthful female eye in the
boat was fixed upon the tall figure of William at the tiller. And
William's eyes made answer, and his gay talk kept the boatload in a

gale of mirth. He could flirt as buoyantly and easily as a cock robin, and so harmlessly that he could do it in front of Papas and Mammas with complete impunity. For it was not admiration that he wanted, or power over others, but just that everyone should be as happy as he was himself. He flirted, too, with a bland impartiality that was almost godlike. For he liked women as women, whether they were pretty or plain. If they were pretty he enjoyed their prettiness, and if they were plain he was sorry for them and flirted with them all the more that they should forget it.

But he never flirted with Marianne and Marguerite. Marianne seemed to him more like a man than a woman, and Marguerite was the other half of himself.

The music grew louder over the water and the moons of light and the festoons of little stars that had seemed from the shore to be shining in another world were suddenly blazing all about them. And then the Orion was looming overhead and an awed silence fell.

Yet looking up at the great ship, with her masts towering to the evening sky and her great hull pierced by the muzzles of the guns, Marianne did not feel quite the same thrill of delight that had been hers when she had looked up at the Green Dolphin. The same thrill never comes twice, she thought, and only once in one's life can one board a great ship for the first time. And that first time there had been no undercurrent of anxiety to mar her joy, for the day had not come when she must put her certainty that William was her own to the touchstone of actual fact. It was not easy, this translation of personal conviction into fact. It required the co-operation of other people, and that was a thing that the strongest will in the world could not always command.

Yet once upon the ballroom floor of the quarterdeck Marianne had a moment of experience that was new and strange, and greedily she gathered it to her. Never before had she danced to the fiddle music of bronzed seamen with the sea about her and the night sky overhead. The scene was bright and gay but it seemed very tiny in the surrounding immensity of space, and brittle and dangerous, as though this handful of laughing men and women were clinging together on a star that was hurtling through space to destruction, or on a small desert island beleaguered by the darkness that was flowing in now from every side. This sensation of danger, born perhaps of her knowledge that her personal happiness hung in the balance to-night, or of the sight of the great guns masked with flowers, stayed with her through the whole evening and gave by contrast a clear-cut sharp brilliance to the beauty of the scene.

Lanterns were swinging overhead and as one danced one looked up between them and saw the stars, and starlight and lantern-light mingled bathed the scene in a magic light that made pretty girls appear beautiful and handsome men as gods. All the men wore uniform, and the blue and gold of the Navy and the scarlet and gold of the Island Militia, with the gleam of medals and the clink of swords, were a challenge that the finery of the women could scarcely meet.

But fortunately the year eighteen-forty was not a year of female dowdiness. Hair was smoothly parted to fall into bunches of curls over the ears. White shoulders gleamed above low-cut gowns with tight bodices and tiny waists, and full skirts swaying over stiffened ballooning petticoats. The older women wore colours, with heavy gold bracelets, lockets and earrings, but the unmarried girls wore white, with wreaths of flowers in their hair and posies tucked into their waist-bands and carried in their hands, and their dancing-shoes were bound about their ankles with satin ribbon. Marguerite wore white with yellow rosebuds and stood out among the other girls only because of her height and beauty, but Marianne challenged as much attention as ever in a gown of cherry red. She did not wear rosebuds to-night but green gauze ribbon twisted in her dark hair and round her waist, and at her breast was a bunch of exotic orchids. She wore, as she nearly always did, the bizarre green earrings that Sophie had hated with undying hatred ever since that day when Marianne had brought them back from a morning of adventure in which her mother had had no share. Somehow those earrings seemed a symbol to Sophie of something that she dreaded, the pull of the outer world that sooner or later takes all adventurous children away from their homes, and of something too in Marianne herself that she disliked, something scheming and bold that she described to herself as "not quite nice".

Sophie was not happy to-night. Even though he had rallied, she was not happy about Edmond. And she was not happy about either of her daughters. Marianne was attracting a great deal of attention, as usual, but it was not the right sort of attention. And Marguerite, dancing with William, seemed not quite her usual self. She was not talking fifteen to the dozen as she usually did when she was enjoying herself, she was silent and a little withdrawn. She had been like that since yesterday, Sophie remembered, since they had been so anxious about Dr. Ozanne. She had noticed William's reliance upon Marianne and had quietly effaced herself. "Don't do it!" Sophie cried voicelessly to her younger child, and did not know why she said it. But in a minute she knew. The figure of the dance brought William and Marguerite together again and she lifted her face and smiled at him as a girl smiles at the only man in the world.

Sophie was dismayed. She had not known it was like that with Marguerite. Time had passed so quickly that she had scarcely realised that Marguerite and William were no longer a couple of children who were like brother and sister to each other but full-grown man and woman free to love and marry. She turned her eyes away from the two of them, but wherever she looked she saw again her daughter's smile, and she was more and more dismayed. For self-effacement and patient waiting were not the virtues to win an Ozanne. Sophie knew they were not, for she had practised them herself with Edmond, and she had lost him and condemned him to an unhappy marriage. The Ozanne men were too lazy, even in love, to get what they wanted without vigorous assistance. "Fight for him to-night, Marguerite!" whispered Sophie under her breath. "Fight hard!" But even as she whispered the words she knew it was no good. Truth was of the essence of Marguerite and not even to save her life would she be able to take action not in accordance with her nature.

Sophie watched anxiously. When the dance ended Marianne's partner, no less a person than Captain Hartley of the Orion himself, returned her elder daughter to her as in duty bound, handing her to her seat beside her mother with much ceremony and standing beside the two ladies to chat of this and that with a cultured charm that drove them both to the verge of hysteria. For it was hard to keep up a show of flattered attention when their whole souls were rivetted upon the erring William and Marguerite, who had not returned to Mamma but were standing by the bulwark on the opposite side of the quarterdeck looking out to sea. They stood in the shadow, their two tall forms very close together, the lantern light gleaming only fitfully upon their two bright heads, upon Marguerite's white dress and William's blue and gold. There was something utterly absorbed in their attitude, as though they were oblivious of the light and laughter and movement behind them, aware of nothing but each other and the sea. Even so had Edmond and Sophie once leaned upon the harbour wall. In her passionate sympathy for her daughter Sophie could feel the pressure of William's body against her own, and the trembling of her nerves made answer. She was her daughter at this moment. Her hand stole down beside her as though to feel for William's and her desperate happiness seemed wrapping itself about her body like a flame.

Then Captain Hartley turned to answer a banality of Octavius's and Marianne turned to her mother. "Mamma!" she whispered fiercely. "Look at William and Marguerite! They are disgracing us before everyone worth while upon the Island."

"I don't think so, dear," said Sophie peaceably. "I don't think any one has noticed them over there in the shadow."

"You're too lax, Mamma," said Marianne, one foot beating a maddening little tattoo upon the deck. "You should send Papa to bring them back."

"Well, that *would* be to draw attention to them, and no mistake!" said Sophie. "No, my dear, we'll leave them alone. They only have another five days."

Marianne looked sharply at Sophie. So Mamma had noticed this love that was between those two. Had other people noticed it? Had the whole Island noticed it? Was it, perhaps, a thing of stronger growth than she had realised? It took all the self-control that she possessed to wait quietly until Captain Hartley had turned back to her mother again before she rose and laid her hand on her father's arm. "Papa, stroll round the deck with me. I like to be seen with you. You're much the handsomest man on board."

Octavius, though he agreed with her, was none the less flattered. "And you're the smartest woman," he whispered to her as they strolled away. "I don't say I like the colour of that gown but it certainly takes the eye."

Sophie watched them go, first with sorrow that Marguerite's moment of bliss must be sacrificed upon the altar of her sister's sense of propriety, and then, suddenly, with a sense of revulsion and horror. Was Marianne jealous of her sister? Was she deliberately trying to wreck her happiness? Oh, I must be mad, thought poor Sophie. It's not possible that Marianne loves William too; she's so much older than he is. It's not possible. But she could not convince herself that it was not possible, for Marianne was a strange creature whose passionate fancy moved with an unpredictable waywardness. She and Octavius were moving now only very slowly, stopping as they went to talk to acquaintances, but Sophie could find little comfort in that, for their progress though socially correct was dexterous and inexorable, and they would get there in Marianne's good time. "Oh, be quick!" cried poor Sophie in her heart to William and Marguerite. "Be quick! Be quick!"

But William and Marguerite quite naturally did not hear the cry of her heart, for their own were much occupied. They had no very clear idea what they were talking about as they stood in the shadows looking out over the darkening sea. Anyway it didn't matter. What mattered was the slight trembling of Marguerite's hand in William's, the warmth of his reassuring clasp, the strange luminous light that seemed shining from her face when she lifted it to answer him, the soul in the eyes that each recognised as though it were a tried friend known centuries ago. The soft lap of the quiet water against the ship's hull far below them was a voice to which they had listened when the world was young, and they knew from ages past that harp-thrumming of the breeze in the rigging. Over their heads the floor of heaven was thick inlaid with patines of bright gold, as it had always been, and presently they would turn to each other, as they had always done, and find again that perfect comfort of each other's arms. They would be one flesh, one mind, one soul then, a unity that nothing could divide.

But there seemed no hurry, because just now there was no time. On such a night one moved beyond the confines of it. On such a night a moment was eternity and eternity a moment.

Yet presently in William's slow brain there began to grow a sense of urgency. Though the part of him that lived beyond time was already locked in union with the essential being of this immortal woman yet there was another part of him that had taken on mortality, and to that belonged the trembling of her hand and the touch of her hair and the sound of her voice making trivial answer to his trivial whisperings; and to her mortality there belonged the reassurance of his clasp and the strength of his body and the thoughts of his slow and stupid mind; each had a right to those things in the other but between their mortal rights and their possession of them there could come a cleavage. Time was the enemy of these things and time must be forestalled before he struck. William's mind suddenly knew that. There was something he must say, quickly, while there was time. His trivial whisperings must become the decisive word that would ensure to each of them their mortal rights.

"Marguerite," he whispered, gripping her hand tighter. "Marguerite——"

"Grand night!" boomed Octavius's jovial voice suddenly, and his hand fell on William's shoulder. "Taking a look at the Islands, William? Well, you'll be far enough away by this day fortnight."

"Aren't you cold, dearest?" whispered Marianne tenderly to her sister. "I've brought your scarf. They're just tuning up for the next dance."

"Thank you," said Marguerite, as her tiny sister stood on tiptoe to put the scarf round her shoulders. Her voice was only a toneless whisper, flat with exhaustion. Was she in time, wondered Marianne in an agony? She looked from one to the other with her bright bird-like glance, her lips held in that tense controlled smile that would not let them droop. She had taken a chance when she moved so slowly round the deck, she had gambled with her happiness that she might keep up the appearances that a weaker woman would have thrown to the winds. Yet one quick glance told her that as usual courage had won. The bewilderment in William's face and the despair in Marguerite's told her that she was in time, and she hoped that for to-night at any rate the danger of a declaration was averted. The perfect moment, once lost, is not easily found again.

Yet as the evening wore on it was obvious to Marianne that William meant to look for it. He was gay as ever as he danced with her and with the other girls to whom he had engaged himself, but fits of abstraction would seize him and he would gaze over his partner's head with the expression of a lost dog, searching for the tall swaying figure of Marguerite. When he had found her his tense face would relax a little, but the answers that he gave to his partner's conversation were wildly wide of the mark.

Never had there been so gay a ball, never so lovely a night. To most of the dancers the hours sped by on wings but to Marianne they were leaden-footed. She got so tired that at last, during a dance when for once she had no partner, she went away by herself, with her green cloak wrapped about her, and found a shadowed corner where she could sit and rest on a coil of rope in the comfortable dark, looking out over the taffrail towards Saint Pierre, where in many of the homely little houses lamps still shone behind the drawn red curtains. She felt herself suspended now between two worlds, the magic world of the dancers and the world of the lighted town across the sea. Don't I belong to either of them, she asked herself, neither to the fairyland where men and women love each other nor to that homely place where they put a light in the window at night and kindle a flame on the hearth? The one should lead to the other, she thought, as she sat there between them. From the fairyland of love there should be a door leading out into the homely place of the fire on the hearth. Yet even though she won William as her husband the key to those two worlds would not be in her hand unless she could learn how to win his love. Passion upon her side only would not be enough, there had to be that mysterious mutual something between a man and a woman before the key was forged. She remembered suddenly how in all her precious moments of vivid experience she always felt that a key had been put in her hand, but she did not know what it was or how to use it. She wondered if it was a particular sort of love that she did not understand, that admitted one to a state of being of which she could have no comprehension because she did not understand the key. A mood, not only of misery but of a most unwonted humility, possessed her. Perhaps I shall never know, she thought, perhaps I am not capable of knowing. Perhaps I shall be an outcast all the days of my life, a changeling who can never find the way home.

She sat there frozen by her unhappiness, head bent, and for the first time in her life she had taken her hand off the tiller and was waiting patiently for something beyond herself to take her in charge. She was like a little child lost in the dark, just sitting there waiting and weeping. It was a strange experience, peaceful in spite of its sorrow, and one that for the rest of her life she would know only briefly and at rare intervals; until at the very end it would possess her utterly.

The sound of oars moving rhythmically but urgently made her lift her head. A rowing boat had come out from the harbour and was gliding swiftly towards the Orion's ladder. Marianne had the sense that it was for this that she had been waiting. She jumped up and ran along the deck and leaned over the bulwarks beside the ladder, looking down into the face of some poor peasant woman who was standing up in the boat, holding the ladder and looking anxiously upwards. The lantern-light gleamed on her strong bare arms, as strong as a man's, that had rowed the heavy boat out from the shore so quickly and easily, on her lined rugged face and heavy figure, both coarsened and unlovely from too much toil and too frequent child-bearing. Yet instinct told Marianne that this woman was still young. She wore the scarlet festival petticoat, shabby and patched but gay, with a bright shawl thrown over her shoulders. Her head was bare and there was something familiar to Marianne in the proud poise of it, and in the smooth gold hair drawn back and knotted in the nape of the neck.

"Yes?" asked Marianne, and her heart was beating painfully against the hard rail on which she leaned.

"Is Dr. Ozanne's son on board, m'selle?" asked the woman.

"Yes," said Marianne.

"Then tell him to come quickly, m'selle. The doctor is at my house in Pipet Lane and I think that he is dying."

Marianne found William and Marguerite talking to the Lieu-tenant Governor in a green forest of palms in the stern of the ship. She had a fleeting moment of wonder as to whether they had dis-turbed his solitude or he theirs, and then she delivered her message and ran to find her father and mother. So quick and skilful was she that she had the five of them down the ladder and in the boat in just a few moments, with no one aware of their trouble except the Governor, who helped get the ladies down the ladder and then leaned sympathetically over the rail, watching the boat slip away into the darkness. All that he had heard of Dr. Ozanne had not been particularly favourable, but he was sorry all the same, for though death was a common occurrence he always found it a damned depressing one. A man never knew when it would strike at him once he'd got himself the wrong side of sixty.

"How came my father to be at your house?" asked William of the peasant woman who had fetched them, as he and she bent to the oars. "What happened?"

"There was trouble at my home, m'sieur, and I fetched the doctor."

"But he was not fit to go out," said William, his voice sharp and impatient with his grief. "He was ill himself."

"I could not know that, m'sieur," said the woman simply. "For six years, ever since my eldest son was born, the doctor has been my best friend. It is always to him that I go. And not only in sickness. In all my troubles."

"What was your trouble to-night?" asked Sophie gently.

"My husband was not himself, m'dame. He hit our son and the child fell down the steps and cut his head open. Had it not been for the doctor I think he would have bled to death, but the doctor saved him."

"And then?" asked Sophie.

"When it was all over he had a seizure of the heart, m'dame. It was bad for a short while and I could not leave him. But now he is not conscious so I came to fetch you. There is another doctor there now, whom my husband fetched, and he thinks it will not be long. It was only this last autumn, m'dame, that I noticed an apple tree in the doctor's garden with flowers and fruit growing on it together. I trembled then, m'dame, for I knew that in a year there would be a death."

There was a silence in the boat. Marianne, sitting beside Sophie, found she was holding her hand. Her heart ached for her mother as well as for William and herself. It was they three who would mourn for Edmond Ozanne; the other two who had not loved him would remain uninjured by his death.

But Marguerite was very white as she sat within the shelter of her father's arm, and William, who sat facing her, observed her anxiously.

"You must not come, Marguerite," he said. "It will not be the sort of place where you should come."

"But I want to come," said Marguerite, her eyes looking steadily into his. She was determined, this time, that she would be brave for William's sake. Where he went she would go, for her being was his refuge as his was hers. "I want to be with you, William."

Her voice came clearly, and Marianne, not yet beyond the influence of that moment of humility on the Orion, heard the quiet words as the declaration of a love that was as strong as her own but of an infinitely finer quality. Had fate been kinder perhaps William would have heard them as a declaration of love too; a declaration that he would have made himself had the Governor not been first in that quiet place among the palms. But just then the boat grated on the cobbles under the archway of Pipet Lane, and they were getting out as quickly as they could, and Octavius was subjecting them all to as much fuss and argument as possible in the process.

"It will be no place and no scene for ladies at all," he declared. "Sophie, take the girls home."

"You must take them home," said Sophie. "I am going to Edmond."

There was no gainsaying that. Sophie was an obedient wife but just now and then, in some question that affected a part of her that he had never possessed, she would oppose her husband with every ounce of strength that she had, and experience had taught him that on these occasions he must yield at once if he wished to retain his dignity.

But his instinctive jealousy of Edmond Ozanne led him to keep a firm hold of Marguerite, who in looks was now so like her mother at her age that there were times when Octavius could imagine that she was the same beautiful girl with whom he had fallen so madly in love twenty-three years ago, and who had given him her affection and faithful obedience but never her inmost soul. "Come, my love," he said, his arm about her.

But Marguerite resisted him gently. "I want to go with William, Papa," she said.

"You will do no such thing," said Octavius obstinately; but it was not really Marguerite, but her mother, whom he held so possessively against him.

"Please, Papa," she said.

And the obtuse William, anxious to shield her, backed up Octavius. "It would be best for you to go home, Marguerite," he said.

"No," said Marguerite.

"Don't be silly," said Marianne tartly. "I'm going with Mamma and William. There's no need for both of us to be there."

Marguerite looked appealingly towards her mother, but Sophie was already moving quickly away with the peasant woman. She had forgotten all about Marguerite and William. Neither of them had been born when she had first known Edmond.

Marguerite thought it would be sheer selfishness to argue further, and she yielded. She looked once more towards William as her father took her away, trying to give him something of herself to strengthen him, but he was already following her mother, his arm through Marianne's.

Marianne held William's hand, that he had slipped within her arm, tightly against her side as they went up a flight of stone steps to the doorway of one of Pipet Lane's most beautiful old houses, partly to comfort him, partly to give herself the reassurance of his warm flesh and blood. For she had a frightening sense of dreamlike unreality, as though not only a life she loved, but the whole world, were receding from her, as though she herself were dying, and looking at the familiar world of streets and houses, moonlight and starlight and the murmuring sea, said to herself, "They are going now. They are not real any longer. They are a dream. When the dream passes there will be only the darkness." She had a moment of terror, and wondered if it was a faint echo of a fear that had visited Dr. Ozanne during that time that the woman had described when she said, "It was terrible for a short while."

They went up an oak staircase and into a lofty beautifully proportioned room that had once been a lady's parlour but now, divided into two by a curtain, was living-room and bedroom for a man and his wife and five little children. Marianne never forgot that room and its poverty, lit by the faint light of the two tallow candles stuck into bottles on the old Adam mantelpiece with its lovely broken carving. He was no good, that drunken brute of a fisherman who sat on a stool hushing a wailing baby in his arms. He had been momentarily sobered by what had happened, but he could be no good or he would not in six years have reduced the girl with the flower-blue eyes whom Marianne had first seen in the doctor's waiting room to this toil-worn unlovely woman. The mark of his brutality was upon everything in the room; it was visible in his wife's coarsened body and the faces of his children, bone-thin beneath their tan, and in the battered condition of the few poor scraps of furniture and remnants of china that had not yet been swallowed by the pawnshop. The woman's bridal chest had gone, Marianne noticed, and her spinning wheel, and the carved cradle that her mother would have given her when her first child was born. She had nothing left now but her pride. It was that remembered proud poise of the head that had caused Marianne to recognise her.

Beyond the curtain were an old battered fourposter and a little truckle bed. On the small bed lay a white-faced boy with a bandaged head, muttering and moaning under the tattered coverlet that covered him, and on the other lay a figure utterly quiet and unstirring. It did not need the fact that the doctor who had been fetched had turned now from the large bed to the small one to tell them that they were too late. The sudden sense of impotence that caught at their hearts, that bitter hopelessness of being able to do no more and go no further, told them what had happened. Edmond Ozanne was dead.

The other doctor turned and straightened himself. "I am sorry," he said. "There was nothing I could do."

"Will the boy live?" asked Marianne urgently. That was what mattered, she thought. Dr. Ozanne had given his life for this child and she did not want it to have been given in vain.

"He's in no danger now," said the doctor. "They're tough, these children, and he's been skilfully treated. But he'll need care."

"He shall have it," said Marianne. It was a vow, and she made it standing at the foot of the four-poster looking at the dead man lying before her. He had been dead long enough now for the amazing dignity of death to take possession of his mortal body. There was strength in his rigidity, an assurance of purging in the sharpened lines of the white face, peace in the stillness, and a sudden throb of triumph in Marianne's soul; for this, in spite of all, had been a man who had left the world the richer for his passing through it, and even if immortality were an empty dream that were sufficient justification for the fact of life. He had lived for the poor and the outcast, he had served them up to the moment of his death, and she in whatever ways she could find would serve them too. This moment linked up with that other moment in the doctor's waiting room six years ago, when the poor had taught her something of the meaning of courage. She would try to serve them as the doctor had, and maybe they would teach her one day what love meant too. "Good-bye," she said to her friend. "Good-bye."

Then her practical nature turned immediately to the problem of the living, and she turned towards her mother and William standing together beside the bed. It surprised her that the tender-hearted Sophie was not weeping, and it surprised her even more to see the look of happiness, almost of relief, that shone upon her mother's face. She was too young yet to realise how those who know life can, in that moment before the selfishness of their own grief claims them, rejoice in the passing of someone loved. . . . Safe. Past all further corroding by the sin of the world. Past all danger and all pain. Safe. . . . Oblivious of those about her Sophie gently kissed the cheek of her love and then knelt down to pray.

But William had been visited by neither triumph nor relief, for he had lost his father. His face was buried in his hands and he was sobbing like a child.

The doctor touched Marianne on the shoulder. "Your mother and I will see to things here," he said. "Take this young man home."

Marianne took William's arm and led him away. "I will see you again," she said to the woman who waited beyond the curtain. "What is your name?"

"Charlotte Marquand," said the woman, and their eyes met again in friendship, as they had done in their girlhood. Then Marianne and William went down the stairs, William so blinded by his tears that he would have fallen had she not guided him. It amazed her that he, the man, should be weeping so while she and her mother were dry-eyed. He was nothing but a child, she thought. He would never be anything but a big, sentimental, warm-hearted child; a child whom she adored. "Don't cry, darling," she said, as she would have said to the little boy with the cut head on the bed upstairs.

They went out into the clear moonlight and turned homeward, but when she would have taken William to Le Paradis he resisted. "I'd rather go home," he said. He had never liked Le Paradis; since his boyhood its elegance had always made him feel a clumsy ass. In his bewilderment he forgot that Marguerite would be at Le Paradis. He wanted to go to his own place, like a fox to its earth.

Marianne understood and yielded at once. Dr. Ozanne had left the lamp burning low, and the cushions in his armchair were still hollowed to the shape of his body, and there was a whisky bottle on the small table with an open book beside it. Old Nick sat in his cage with hooded eyes, drooping and silent. These things hurt her as had nothing yet, but William dropped into his father's armchair so abandoned to his grief that she did not think he noticed the hollowed cushions, and she quickly picked up the book and the whisky bottle and carried them with her into the kitchen where she went to brew hot coffee. It amazed her, as she heated it, that Marguerite did not come. She, in Marguerite's place, would have been watching from the window of the old schoolroom, and now she would have been in the parlour with William in her arms.

But Marguerite did not come and it was she who after she had made him drink the coffee sat on the arm of his chair and comforted him. Though she was not a naturally tender woman the right words came easily and he clung with a sort of desperation to the fact that she too had loved his father, realising dimly that every human heart that loves the dead keeps something of them still living upon this earth. "You liked him," he kept saying. "You understood him. You sat here with him yesterday morning when he was not well." And Marianne replied patiently again and again, "Yes, William, I loved him. He was kind to me and I loved him. He was kind to many people. He was kind."

Kind Green Dolphin Street. She looked about her at the shabby room that she knew so well. Strangers would live here soon, and she might not enter it again. But she would often see it. Its walls would be about her whenever a door swung wide in greeting and a warm hand gripped hers.

And suddenly, most surprisingly, it was she who was weeping, sitting on William's knee with his arms about her, and he who was comforting her.

2

The next five days, until the Orion sailed, passed like a sort of nightmare, for there was so much to do, so much to decide before William left for the other side of the world, and so little time to do it in. The ritual of an Island funeral was in itself so complicated a matter that until it was brought to a successful conclusion no one could spare a thought for private grief or love. Every thought was centred upon the number of yards of black crape that would be required for trimming for the complicated mourning garments that must be tried on by the hour together if there were to be any hope of their fitting, and upon the choice of bearers to carry the coffin, six bearers who must be of high standing in Island society and must carry the dead man to church by the way he had taken in his lifetime. And then there was the preparation of immense supplies of food for the funeral feast, with especial care taken over the funeral ham; for on the Island "màngier la tchesse à quiqu'un" was the proverbial way of saying that you attended his funeral; the ham was very important. Then invitations to the funeral must be written out on black-edged notepaper and carried around to all the friends of the deceased by a rider on a black horse, and those who had loved the doctor must be given the opportunity of seeing him in his coffin and touching the forehead once in blessing. And then when it was all over there was the ritual of the reading of the will, leaving all that the doctor died possessed of to his son William; only it was found that the doctor died possessed of nothing but debts which with luck would only just be covered by the sale of the house and furniture.

When the day of departure came William had not slept for nights and had scarcely eaten. Through the mist of grief and bewilderment he had been only dimly conscious of his surroundings. He had been vaguely aware that the Le Patourels had been amazingly good to him, but he had scarcely distinguished Octavius's exasperating but highly competent fuss from Sophie's motherly advice or Marguerite's loving and self-effacing care. The only thing he was really clear about was that Marianne had loved his father and had been with him that morning when he had not been well. . . . Though he had died without any of them being with him, his only son having left him for a ball, at least Marianne had been with him on that morning. . . . In all the misery of self-reproach for all the times he had failed his father, from his boyhood until that night when he had left him to die alone that he might go to a ball, the only comfort was in the thought that Marianne had been there that morning. He clung to that, and to Marianne herself, as to a lifeline.

"Write to us, William," she commanded, as the five of them stood on the harbour wall on the blustery morning of William's departure, surrounded by his baggage, waiting for the picket boat that was coming to fetch him. Marguerite, clinging to her father's arm, said nothing. The chill wind whipped her long skirts about her ankles and her face within the shadows of her bonnet was white, with ugly blotches beneath the eyes. She had cried all night, it was easy to see, and now there was no more strength left in her. They were all listless and tired after the strain of the last few days, and drained of emotion. The picket boat was late and the bleak embarrassment of a delayed departure had them all in its grip. They had said all there was to say before they left Le Paradis and now they were only longing for the pain of parting to be over. It would have been easier if the sun had been shining and they had all been looking their best; there might have been happier last memories, then, to keep and carry away; but it was a cold and ugly morning, with rain in the wind, and they were all looking their very worst. Sophie was shivering in a black cloak that did not become her at all, Octavius had cut himself while shaving, William had a streaming cold and Marianne looked forty if a day.

"Here's the picket boat," said Octavius with a sigh of relief.

It was speeding towards them across the harbour and it was time for the last embraces. Sophie got up and folded William, cold in the head and all, to her motherly bosom, brokenly murmuring the old Island blessing, "Allez en paix; vivez en paix, et que le Dieu du Paix vous bénisse," and Octavius gripped him by the hand. Marguerite kissed him without a single word, for her misery was so great that she could scarcely breathe, let alone speak, and her lips against his cheek were cold. A day and a night. She had been so happy, but it had been so soon over, and William had said no word of love.

Marianne had turned away when the others said good-bye to William, but she went down the steps with him and at the bottom she flung her arms passionately round him. "Don't forget me," she pleaded with a desperation that after Marguerite's coldness was like a warm and living flame.

"As if I could ever forget you!" exclaimed William. "And I'll never forget what you were to my father."

It was at her that he looked last as the picket boat slid away, and his eyes were shining with his gratitude. . . . But he had said no word of love.

Marianne climbed back up the steps with dragging feet and stood with the others waving her handkerchief. William stood up in the picket boat waving his hat for as long as he could see them. As the boat slid out of the harbour a pale gleam of watery sunshine lit up his tall figure and his bright hair, and then he was gone.

"China is so far away," sobbed Sophie. "He's never been so far away from us before."

"Soon be home again," said Octavius a little querulously. "Time passes. Nothing to cry about. Now for God's sake let's get home and have a hot drink." And he offered his arm to his wife and hurried her away.

Marianne and Marguerite followed more slowly, queerly aware through their desolation of that love for each other that nothing seemed able to destroy.

"You're an odd girl, Marguerite," said Marianne wonderingly. "It seemed so strange to me that you were not watching for William to come home on the night his father died."

"But I was," said Marguerite. "I was watching from the schoolroom window. It was bright moonlight. I saw you bring him home."

"Then why—why——" gasped Marianne.

"Why did I not come down? Because you were already there," said Marguerite. "I knew that if you two were alone together you might be able to comfort him, but if I had been there too your jealousy of me would have spoiled what you were trying to do for him."

"You did yourself great harm," said Marianne.

"I was just thinking of William," said Marguerite simply.

Marianne let out a great sigh; something between exasperation, wonder and relief.

"You are a saint, Marguerite," she said. "But you are also a fool."

BOOK TWO

THE SECOND ISLAND

THE SAILOR

They that go down to the sea in ships and occupy their business in great waters;

These men see the works of the Lord and his wonders in the deep.

For at his word the stormy wind ariseth which lifteth up the waves thereof.

They are carried up to the heaven, and down again to the deep; their soul melteth away because of the trouble.

They reel to and fro, and stagger like a drunken man and are at their wits' end.

So when they cry into the Lord in their trouble he delivereth them out of their distress.

For he maketh the storm to cease so that the waves thereof are still.

Then are they glad, because they are at rest; and so he bringeth them unto the haven where they would be.

PSALM 107.

CHAPTER ONE

1

William, hand in pockets, wandered through the strange streets as through the labyrinthine ways of some fantastic dream. He felt as though he were in a dream, and not only because of the queerness of this eastern city, but even more because of the queerness of his own mental state. As in dreams, shapes and colours and perfumes drifted past him with an utter unexpectedness that left him baffled. They seemed to have nothing to do with reality and his mind could get no grip of them. And he also seemed to himself not quite real. His thoughts drifted in the same sort of way that the scene about him drifted; he could get no grip of them. His body seemed drifting too. He just followed where his feet led and what was directing his feet he had no idea.

He would have been much astonished had he been told that he was utterly exhausted, and that not only physically but emotionally as well. The voyage from home had seemed to take an eternity, and

had included his first experience of what the Atlantic Ocean can do
at its worst. Yet, after all, storms are all in the day's work for a
sailor, and William's exuberance would have remained unaffected
had he been able, after his usual habit, to fall asleep the moment he
rolled into his bunk. But he hadn't. For the first time in his life he
had been afflicted with sleeplessness. For hour after hour he had
lain pitching and tossing in the stuffy darkness below hatches,
wrapped about in the greater darkness of his grief for his father.

His grief bewildered him. He couldn't understand it. After all,
he had said to himself, as he lay in his bunk, his father had been
getting on in years and everybody had to die. And, after all, it wasn't
as though he saw a great deal of his father; if one was a sailor one
didn't see much of home. And, if what people said was true and
souls lived on beyond death, why make this fuss about it? But
reason didn't help at all. In the first glimpse of dawn, that had always brought him such uplifting of the heart because life renewed
itself once more, came the thought, he's dead, he'll not see the dawn
again. In the middle of clamping one's great teeth enjoyably into a
huge slab of ship's biscuit and salt beef, in the middle of gulping a
glorious drink of fiery grog, came the thought, he's dead, and the
food was dust in one's mouth and the drink gall. One could forget
for a few minutes, but always the grief came back, and the pain of it
made one feel very muddled in one's head.

And there was another thing that was confusing him, and that was
a new and desperate longing for Marguerite. In the past, whenever
he had left Marguerite, he had always missed her for a while and
then been completely comforted in the thought of her secure and
content in her island, counting away the happy days that should
bring them together again. But it wasn't like that now. His first
experience of death had struck all sense of security from under him,
and it had not been a happy girl whom he had left standing buffeted
by the wind on the sea-wall at Saint Pierre. Always he seemed to see
her standing there, bent to the wind, bewildered, sorrowful, denied,
while he like an ass had been more taken up with Marianne because
she had been good to his father. That was it—denied. They were in
love, and fate or his stupidity had kept him from saying what he
should have said to bring them together. He wanted to go straight
back home and save her from the sorrow in which he had left her;
and the width of the world was between them. "I'll write," he had
said to himself, as he lay in his bunk in the roaring stuffy darkness.
"I'll write and tell her I love her, and we'll be married when I go
home."

But he hadn't written yet, and the decision to do so had not very much eased him, for in his restless longing there was something more than just the longing for Marguerite, something huge and primeval and thirsty that had come alive in him when he had held a La Môme in his arms, and which he did not in the least understand. It was in him even in this dreamlike exhausted state when all things drifted by like petals on the wind and his will did not answer to the helm.

For even in dreams the wraith that we are thirsts for the drifting beauty, and on awakening weeps for it, and sometimes through long years remembers it. So did William long vaguely for the beauty all about him to take concrete form and come alive as something that he could take in his arms and save from sorrow, as he would have saved Marguerite if she had been here. And so to the end of his life was he to remember this eastern city, recalling its beauty correctly, when the horrible thing that had happened in it was so blurred by time and distance that it was as though it had never been.

It looked as though it had been carved out of a flower. The beautiful high-arched stone bridges, forming with their reflection in smooth water a perfect circle, the pagodas with their curly roofs and projecting eaves, even the curve of the streets and the shapes of common things like the lintels of doors, or the steps leading to water that flowed beneath the bridges like uncoiling lengths of silk, had a beauty that William could not reconcile with the clumsy hands of men. The lines of this city sprang and flowed and radiated like the veinings of a flower, and the colours of it, bright and haphazard though they were, struck no discordant note. The blue roof-tiles, the sedan chairs of scarlet and green, the bright trappings of the donkeys, the gay garments of the people and the smouldering colours within the shadows of the shops were a shifting kaleidoscope of brilliance that was never still long enough for any one colour to clash with another, or for any shape of beauty to eclipse another. And surely each colour had its perfume, thought William, trying to attach the drifting scent of flowers from a hidden garden to a swaying scarlet chair, and the smell of incense to a dim blue roof. Surely the scent of cedar wood came from the umber shadows of the doorways and that faint illusive perfume of jessamine from the swinging folds of a sea-green coat. A flock of wild geese passed overhead, their wings beating white and grey against the blue, and the bells on the donkeys' collars tinkled as they trotted by. A minstrel leaning in the shadows of a doorway fingered a guitar, and the cries of alien voices rose and fell and rose again. Strange—it was all strange—and William felt more utterly alone than ever before in the whole of his life. He did not feel at home in this strange city, as he had so often felt in other foreign cities. It was not his sort of country. The narrow slits of eyes that gleamed at him out of olive faces seemed not to belong to the same sort of human being that he was himself. They never seemed to laugh aloud, these people. They sang, they murmured, they smiled their secret smiles, they cried aloud their wares with strange high cries, but they never laughed aloud.

"I was a fool to come alone," said William suddenly to himself.

The Orion was anchored in the wide estuary, a tall, aloof, self-conscious presence among the lemon-sailed craft of the fishermen, and a party of young officers had come ashore with strict injunctions to be back by sunset, for at dawn they would sail again. Willaim had kept with the others for a little while, and then had slipped away by himself. Solitude was not a thing that he usually craved, but he wanted to buy pretty things for Sophie and Marianne and Marguerite and he did not want to do it to a running commentary of jokes and laughter that would completely upset his aesthetic judgment, weak at the best of times, and destroyed altogether if his sense of humour got the upper hand. If he was quite alone in a shop he could sometimes tell the false from the true by the instinct of his own sound decency, helped by the strain of fine breeding that was in him, but if people were cracking jokes all round him he got confused, and his purchases were of the type that are subsequently regretted and given to the deserving poor.

"Yet I was a fool to come alone," he repeated to himself. He was hopelessly lost in this strange city. And he had not bought anything yet, so lazy and drained of energy was his mood. And he must have been drifting about in this aimless, idiotic sort of way for longer than he realised, for there was already a slight haze of rose colour in the sky. And he was suddenly afraid; not of physical violence, for the right hand that he had thrust into the pocket of his monkey jacket held his gun, and in his left trouser pocket was the Maori knife that Captain O'Hara had given him long ago, and his huge physical frame always stood him in good stead in street brawls; but of something more subtle, something intangible that he was aware of beneath the surface of things as one is aware of some corruption hidden under a pile of sweet-smelling flowers.

And then in his weariness and distress he was aware again of the scent of jessamine and of the slow swinging of a sea-green coat, and he was abruptly back again in the Island. He was leaning out of his bedroom window in Green Dolphin Street in the early morning, sniffing the scent of the jessamine in the Le Paradis garden and watching rain-drenched magnolia petals fall one by one through the golden air. A great wave of longing surged up in him. Who was it who had thus transported him to the place where beyond all others he was happy?

He looked, and suddenly he had his wish and the beauty that was all about him took concrete form in the person of a slip of a girl, seeming scarcely more than a child as she swayed along in front of him. Her green coat was worn over long green trousers, and he saw to his surprise that she was not a tottering lily-foot girl but walked with easy grace upon unbound feet shod in little peach-coloured shoes with golden heels. Her small head was dark and sleek, the hair braided into a pigtail that hung to her knees, and behind each ear she wore a bunch of jessamine blossoms. The skin of her neck was white, not olive-tinted, and flawless as the flowers she wore. She looked back over her shoulder and her eyes met William's; not narrow slanting eyes but wide and innocently opened, full of child-like wonder and sorrow, not black but a deep, soft pansy brown with curling fan-like lashes. The eyes smiled through their sadness, though the demurely folded and poignant lips did not move, and then she looked away again. For how long had she been drifting along like this in front of him? Was this the first time that she had looked back over her shoulder with that pathetic childlike glance? He could not be certain, for it still all seemed like a dream. It was in a dream that he saw her pause on the threshold of a doorway, looking back once more over her shoulder; and this time her lips as well as her eyes were smiling. It was in a dream that she drifted away into the shadows and in a dream he followed her.

He found himself in just the sort of shop he had been looking for. Beautiful things were all about him; boxes of carved rosewood, little figurines of clear green jade, strips of silk embroidered with flowers and butterflies, exquisite china bowls, tasselled necklaces and shoes of coloured brocades. The shop was shadowed and fragrant, with sticks of incense burning before a shrine, and he saw the beautiful things in it only dimly. But the girl, standing facing him in the shaft of yellow sunlight that struck through the open door, he suddenly saw so clearly that he might have been the first man ever created, gazing in stupid astonishment at the first woman God ever made.

She must have known she was quite perfect or she would not have dared to stand like that in the full glory of the sunset light. Her small white face was heart-shaped, tapering to a rounded chin like a baby's. Her poignant mouth was coral-coloured, and the dark hair was drawn behind her ears to show their delicate shell-like curves beneath the jessamine flowers. Her green coat, he saw, was of silk, embroidered with magnolia blossoms. She held her hands demurely linked in front of her and behind their sadness her pansy eyes were sparkling.

"Yes?" she said. "Yes, you English sailorman, what do you wish to buy?"

Her voice was sweet and light and she spoke not pidgin-English but the authentic language of his country, with an inflection that made of it something that was very nearly music.

"You speak English?" gasped William.

She nodded at him. "My father was English," she said. "My father was an English sailor, like you, and he gave me my brown eyes and my white skin and taught me to speak English. But my mother was Chinese and she gave me my little hands and feet and taught me to swing my pigtail and wear my trousers with an air."

"Was it because I am English that you smiled at me like that?" asked William.

"Yes," she said. "I always smile at the English."

He stared at her like an astonished ox, his mouth slightly ajar, and it was not until a peal of rather mocking laughter broke from her that he remembered what he was here for. "I want to buy something," he said, looking about him and scratching his head in perplexity.

"For a lady," she said.

"For three ladies," said William lugubriously.

She pursed her coral mouth and looked at him wickedly.

"*Three* ladies?" she mocked. "Then you want three somethings. What are they like, these ladies?"

William found it difficult to remember. When he tried to visualise Sophie and Marianne, and even his adored Marguerite, this other girl's flawless face seemed to get in the way. She was standing very close to him now and he felt half stupefied by the scent of the jessamine. "They are a mother and two daughters," he got out at last. "The mother is fair and beautiful, with blue eyes, and her elder daughter is little and dark and smart, and the younger daughter— she's a little like her mother," he ended lamely.

The girl did not hesitate. "This for Mamma," she said, and lifted from the wall a strip of pearly satin sprinkled with pale pink blossoms and butterflies of blue and gold. "And for the daughter who is small and dark, these little red shoes—when we have tiny feet we like to go brightly shod, you know, to draw attention to them. And for the other daughter, whom you could not describe to me——" She stopped and laughed. "For her you shall have this necklace of carved beads. The bottom bead is fashioned like Lung-mu who protects sailormen, and she will pray to it for you when the wind blows."

And standing on tiptoe she slipped it over his head. He lifted it and looked at it, for it was one of the loveliest things he had ever seen. The beads were large, made from some fragrant wood, and each one, while keeping its cylindrical shape, was exquisitely carved into the shape of some bird or beast, insect or flower or sacred figure of a god. There were strange little monkeys, with hands covering eyes or ears or mouths that they might see or hear or speak no evil, lotus flowers and chrysanthemums and apricot-blossoms, swallows and robins and bees and goldfish, there was Buddha with his little dog in his arms, and swinging at the bottom, in the place where the cross would have hung on a rosary, was the figure of the dragon goddess who keeps mortals safe when they pass to and fro in boats upon the water. It was a perfect thing. William gasped and then scarcely knowing what he did thrust it away for secrecy beneath his coat. Then he stood staring dumbly again while the girl wrapped up the embroidery and the shoes and set them aside. She was laughing all the time now, laughter like a peal of bells that intoxicated him. She had a dimple in one cheek and the tip of an absurd pink tongue showed between her teeth.

"There!" she said. "And now, sir, do you understand Chinese money? Do you know the value of the tael? If not, then show me your purse and I will take from it what you owe me." It was something of a command and though he understood the Chinese currency he was too bewildered and infatuated to deny her what she wanted. He gave her his purse and she denuded it of half its coins with swift darting fingers that seemed not to belong to the demure hands she had held linked before her when first he had entered the shop. Those quick fingers woke in him some vague distaste, some shadow of the fear he had felt out in the street, but he failed to connect his sensations with the person of this lovely child with the innocent face and the flowers behind the ears.

"They grow like that at home," he said, and touched the blossoms with his finger.

She came close to him and laid her hands on his great chest and looked up into his face. "You are homesick?" she whispered, and then, without waiting for his answer, "You poor boy! So am I. I am homesick for the house where I lived before my father and mother died. I weep at night for my father's courtyards and my mother's arms."

The sadness that had been momentarily banished by her laughter had come back. Her eyes were swimming with tears and her mouth drooped at the corners. She was so tiny that the top of her head did not reach his shoulder. She had lost not only her father, thought

William, but her mother too, and his stupid heart ached to bursting for her. And then somehow she was in his arms so that he could comfort her better, a little bit of a thing who seemed to have no bones, an armful of soft silk and perfume and flower petals. Her skin was so cool and satin-smooth that he was not quite sure if he was kissing her cheek or the jessamine flowers. And then her warm rosy mouth was on his, and it was as though he had been for a long time parched and tormented with thirst and heat, and now had flung himself into a cool deep river of delight. It flowed through the dream swift and strong, and he gave himself up to it with a sigh of relief. Just lately, for the first time, he had been finding life a painful business, and he knew now with what passion men will turn to anything at all that causes the waters of forgetfulness to close above their heads.

"This way," said the girl, and he found that with her hand in his she was leading him down a narrow passage. It led out of an alcove at the back of the shop and in this alcove there stood a Chinaman, his hands folded in his robe of dark blue silk, his head bent and his eyes cast down. Had he been there all the time, wondered William, watching what went on in the shop? He took no notice of the girl as she passed him, nor she of him, but as they went down the passage William heard the rustle of stiff silk, as though the man had passed out into the shop. The slight sound vaguely scared him, as though it were the rustle of a reptile in dead leaves.

And then he forgot his fear in delight at the beauty of the little courtyard to which the girl had brought him. It was very small, with a lily pond in the centre of it, planted with flowers and sweet-smelling bushes and blossom-bearing trees, surrounded by a pillared verandah protected by a curly blue-tiled roof, from which led rooms closed in with exquisite carved screens. Near the pond was a stone seat, with low stone table before it and beside it a little dwarf pine tree growing in a pot. Over the courtyard the sky was pure gold and a sudden cool breeze ruffled the surface of the lily-pond. It came from the Estuary perhaps. In any case it blew a tiny breath of common sense into Willian's cobwebbed brain, for he suddenly remembered the tall Orion rocking at anchor among the lemon-coloured fishing smacks, and he caught his breath sharply.

But the girl, reading his stupefied mind like an open book, gave the cobwebs no chance to blow away. "There is time," she whispered. "There is plenty of time. We will drink a little rice-wine together, and talk a little of England, and you will comfort me in my homesickness, and then you shall go away." And she drew him down upon the seat beside the dwarf pine tree and sat down beside him with her hand in his.

William was not sure if it was the same Chinaman, or a different one, who almost immediately stood before them with a small tray in his hands, for he kept his eyes cast down as he set it on the table, and was gone again almost immediately, with no sound but the rustle of his robe. The tray had candied red apples on it, and sweetmeats, and bowls of warm rice wine. They ate up all the sweet things, laughing like children, and they drank the wine, and William felt sleepy but amazingly at peace. The scent of the flowers seemed to flow through his body with every breath he took, and mind and soul he was steeped in the golden light. And the girl who sat beside him, in the shelter of his arm, was a part of the beauty and the peace, warm and friendly and comforting. Vaguely he remembered that he wanted to comfort her, too, and save her from sorrow. Only he was too sleepy to think of the words. The dream seemed deepening all the time, and nothing was quite real.

2

"Damn fool," groaned William, sitting with his head in his hands, his back against the cool stone of the bridge. He sat beside it, the great arch soaring above him, reflected as a perfect circle in the water that flowed beneath it like a lazily uncoiling length of pearl-grey silk. "Damn fool," he repeated, for cursing himself seemed at present the only comfort. "Bloody fool." Then he groaned again. He had not known it was possible to be so continuously sick as he had been, to have such a ghastly pain in his head, or to have every limb so turned to lead that movement seemed impossible. Yet move he must, round to the other side of the bridge where there was shadow, for crouching here in the sun was only increasing his misery. He clawed himself upright with the help of the bridge, staggered across it and round to the other side, crawled down to the water and bathed his head and face, crawled back to the shadows and lay down. No one took any notice of him. He was nothing to this city carved out of a flower; only one speck more of the corruption that hid beneath the sheen and flutter of its myriad petals.

After what seemed to William an eternity of pain and misery and self-loathing, it occurred to him that he had not been sick for quite a while. He pressed himself and sighed lugubriously at the deflation. But he was better. He was empty as a burst bladder and weak as a kitten, but his memory was functioning again and a few vague ideas were assembling themselves in his aching head. His immense physical strength began to assert itself through the weakness and presently there was taking place in his mind that undirected haphazard activity which he was accustomed to describe to himself inaccurately as "thought". He ceased his mechanical cursing of himself and tried to get a little order into its confusion. He was a truthful person and one by one, out of the welter of detested images that thronged his consciousness, he picked out the blistering facts and had a look at them.

He had been bewitched by a pretty wanton, and that as easily as though he had been a mere child with neither knowledge, will, nor the rudiments of sense and decency. He had slept with that wicked little witch and been drugged and robbed by her. He did not say to himself that other men got into these scrapes and thought nothing of it, for he had never been taught to take shelter behind the common backslidings. And he was not other men. He was himself. He was the son of a father who, whatever his weaknesses, had as a doctor regarded this particular kind of scrape as sheer idiocy, and had taught his son to do the same. And his moral standards had been set for him by Sophie with her sweetening, wholesome fastidiousness, and by the clean austerity of Marguerite. When he thought of Marguerite he was seared with shame; odd that a spiritual thing like shame should hurt so much that one caught one's breath and one's body twisted over as though the lash of a whip had caught it.

Well, that was the worst of it just now—the shame. But there was the other side, a purely material side, to this disaster, and that was bad enough. Heaven knew what had been in the sweet rice wine of which he had drunk so much, for with the girl in his arms he had very soon slept, a horrible drugged sleep from which he had only awakened out here in the street in the full light of early morning, stripped of all the valuables that he possessed. His money had gone, his watch and gold chain, his gold compass, his gun, his uniform coat and waistcoat. He had nothing left but his shirt and trousers and—yes—the Maori knife in its sheath in his trouser pocket and the carved wooden necklace that was still hanging round his neck. He took the necklace off and looked with puzzled bewilderment at the beautiful carved images of birds and beasts and flowers, with the figure of Lung-mu, who protects sailormen, hanging at the bottom. What had induced them to leave him his knife and Lung-Mu? Had the little witch felt some tenderness for him after all? Had she been not entirely false? Or was it simply that the knife was a thing of no value and the necklace had been hanging about for years unsold in the shop and so they had not bothered to remove them? Though the second reason was probably the correct one there was balm in in the thought of the first; for she had been so exquisitely pretty; he could feel even now the touch of her hand on his cheek when he lay in her arms, and the softness of her mouth.

He staggered to his feet. He must get on quickly and forget the images that filled his mind. He must get down to the harbour before the Orion sailed. If he followed this river flowing at his feet like uncoiling grey silk, then he would come to it.

But in his ridiculous weakness he found it a long and toilsome way, and when he tried to hail an empty chair the bearers glanced sideways out of their slits of eyes at his disreputable figure, smiled inscrutable smiles and took no notice. And the sun rose higher and beat down on his bare head, so that he would have been sick again had he not been so completely empty. And there was a maddening sentence beating with hammer strokes in his head, each stroke a throb of blinding pain, the last words he had heard on board yesterday before he went ashore. It set itself to some equally maddening tune whose origin he could not remember. "H.M.S. Orion sails at dawn. H.M.S. Orion sails at dawn." What *was* the damned tune? Somehow, as he stumbled on, it seemed all-important that he should be able to put a name to it. He was a fool about names. Always forgot them, or got them mixed up. Marianne was always nagging at him about it. She was a bit of a nagger, Marianne, always trying to make people and events conform to her own chosen pattern for them. Not like Marguerite, who took people as they were, loved them and let them alone. "H.M.S. Orion sails at dawn." Now he had it! It was the tune of "Mon Beau Laurier". Marguerite had danced to it in the woods at home. He could see her now, swaying alone in the centre of the circle. Men had come, swung her round, and then she had been alone again. Now there was just one word beating in his head. . . . Alone. . . . He had a vague idea that he had done something, he could not now remember what, that had condemned her to perpetual loneliness; Marguerite, who had always seemed like the other half of himself.

It was the harbour at last, crowded with the shipping of all nations, junks, merchantmen, sloops, cutters, barquentines, ships of the Levant, of Scandinavia, of Asia, but not, as far as he could see at the moment, of the British Isles. He looked out towards the Estuary, where the sea birds were wheeling round the lemon sails of the fishing smacks, but the raking masts of the Orion were no longer towering there. Too late. H.M.S. Orion had sailed at dawn.

He stumbled into a corner and sat down, his head in his hands again. The Orion did not wait for drunkards, for laggards who forgot the time. The Navy has no concern with what men do with their shore leave; it is when they forget the time that they are damned.

What was the time now? A chime sounded over the water. Eight bells and the forenoon watch, that would have been William's watch had he been on board. The Orion was well out to sea now, and the bells were ringing out the doom of a damned soul.

He must do something. From what ship had those eight bells sounded? He had heard them, he thought, away to the left. Evidently her crew was on board and she was getting ready to put to sea. But it might be that they were a hand short, that some besotted fool had fallen out even as he had done, that even at the very last moment they would take him on. That was what he must do—try to get to sea again. He was not going to stay here in this detested city. He hoped never to set eyes on the place again.

He made his way round the harbour, scrutinising the ships as he passed them, but none that he saw looked ready to put to sea, and none called to him with a voice that awoke any answer. Yet still he stumbled on, increasingly convinced that he had heard those eight bells ringing, increasingly certain that on the ship where they had rung there was an empty hammock where he could sleep and a job to be done that he could do. Somewhere to sleep and something to do. Shelter and work. If one had those one could carry on.

Her masts and rigging were delicate yet strong against the sky and her brass work was winking in the sun. And, Holy Moses, the wonder and style of her, lofty and thin, raked to the nines and built for speed! Mad excitement gripped him. He fell over something, picked himself up and stumbled on again until he could see what flag she flew at her stern. It was the Red Ensign, and above the sky-sail fluttered her house flag of emerald green. She was an English clipper. And just below the Ensign he read her name. The Green Dolphin. Was he mad? He must be. Things did not happen this way in real life. He was standing beside her now, at the foot of the gang plank, but he could not see her very clearly because the world seemed pitching and tossing about him and there was a film across his eyes. He rubbed them and looked again. The Green Dolphin. No, he was not mad. And where else in the world was there a ship with lines as exquisite as that? And just such qualities of courage and aristocracy, qualities that set one's heart beating and one's pulses throbbing? The men were busy about her decks and the whole ship was humming with activity. It seemed that she herself was humming, singing to herself because soon she would be aslant in the wind, the sails blossoming upon her masts and the water rippling back from the curve of her prow. The world was pitching about him again, yet somehow he managed to get up the gang plank and leap upon the deck. "Here, you, what now? Get out of that, you dirty swine." The great hairy hand of an old shellback hit him in the chest, spinning him round, and then a huge boot assisted him expertly towards the plank again. But he clung grimly to the bulwarks. "Captain O'Hara's orders," he gasped, winded from the blow. "Let me be, damn you. You're a hand short, aren't you?"

"You a new apprentice?" ejaculated the man. "Then get forward, you fool, and find the Mate."

But William, body and mind still sick and confused from the poison of the drug he had been given, was back again on a summer morning of his childhood. He did not look for the Mate. Instead he went down the companion ladder to the Captain's cabin, and stood there clinging to the teak table where years ago he had carved his initials, and looked about him. It was all just the same. There was the old chair, richly carved with sea creatures, the weapons hanging on the bulkheads, the tattooed heads of cannibals. And there was the beautiful curtain with the golden dragons that hung before the captain's bunk. Only to-day it was drawn back, showing the bunk with its pillow and neat blue coverlet. William let go of the table, staggered to the bunk and lay down. The pillow was exquisitely cool to his madly throbbing head. The water shadows flickered gently over the bulkheads and the ceiling. It was infinitely peaceful. It was like coming home. He shut his eyes and listened to the familiar ship sounds that were a part of his life, the creak of cordage, the shouting of orders, the gurgle of water against the ship's side. Then came the scrape of a fiddle, voices singing, the rattle of the hawser and the steady tramp of feet as the men manned the capstan. Then they were moving. He could picture the smooth waters of the estuary slipping away between the green fertile banks, the wind filling the sails as the ship gathered way. Faster and faster, and now there was a sound of humming overhead and the wind whistled in the rigging and the shrouds. They were drawing near to the mouth of the estuary, and then, suddenly, the scream of a gull, the great buffet of a wave, the glorious lift of the ship as the sea took her. . . . William sighed, turned over and went to sleep.

3

He was awakened by a volley of vigorous oaths and a great hand clawing at his shoulder, and found himself looking up into an enormous scarlet full-moon of a face with a roaring mouth in the centre of it full of immense china teeth. William was a powerful man but Captain O'Hara was even stronger. With one great wrench he had William out of his bunk and prostrate on the floor. But even as he fell he was joyfully conscious of the rolling of the ship, and his instinct told him that they were well out to sea. . . . Captain O'Hara would surely never turn about now to return him from whence he came.

"Who the devil are ye? Eh? Eh?" roared Captain O'Hara, stirring the prostrate William with his foot. And then, raising his voice to a bellow, "Nat! Nat!"

And, suddenly, there was Nat, with his filthy scarlet nightcap, his wizened mutilated monkey face, his tattooed chest and his glass eye—just the same. They had scarcely changed at all, these two, for when William first met them they had been at that time of life when to that of which a man is capable he has already attained and life has little more of his story to write upon his face. It was William who had changed, William who had grown from a boy to a young man to whom all things were yet possible.

"Nat! Nat!" said William softly, and swaying in the chair he felt again in memory the clutch of Nat's scrawny hand in the small of his back, as he had felt it years ago when Nat had helped him scramble over the bulwarks. And he knew again that he liked this noisome, hideous little man. And in Nat's one eye, as he stood back staring at William and rubbing the bristles of his ill-shaven jaw with a horny finger, there was a faint puzzled glimmer of recognition.

"What the devil?" enquired Captain O'Hara, and pushed up his old-fashioned wig to scratch his bald head.

"You said you'd never forget me, sir," said William, and putting his hand in his pocket he tossed the Maori knife on the table.

Captain O'Hara was still puzzled, but Nat let out a sudden hoot of laughter and croaked out a few of those almost unintelligible sounds that passed with him for speech, while he pointed to the initials W.O. on the table.

"*That* boy?" shouted Captain O'Hara. And he too roared with laughter and slapped his great thigh with his hand. "Begorra! That boy from that tight little Island! Remember that little harbour, Nat, and the town on the hill? Bedad, it seems like yesterday." And then suddenly his laughter ceased. He had never forgotten the beautiful boy that William had been, or the affection he had felt for him. He looked at him with concern. "What's up, son?" he asked. "What's the trouble? Eh? Eh?"

The mention of the Island had been unfortunate. William's head suddenly went down on his arms and he sobbed like the great baby that he was.

"Empty stomach," diagnosed Captain O'Hara, and speeded Nat with a jerk of the head towards the door. "Now then, son," he con-

tinued, "we'll have a meal together, like we did before in that little
Island of yours, and when you've some vittles in your belly ye can
tell me what you think you're doin' as a stowaway upon my ship."

Then he spat reflectively through the scuttle, filled his pipe and left
William to sob himself quiet until Nat reappeared with crusty dough-
nut twists, pigeons' eggs, fresh fruit and fragrant China tea.

"The last shore meal we'll have, son," said Captain O'Hara, knocking out his pipe and adjusting his teeth. "Do it justice."

They ate hugely, William's resilient stomach rising to the occasion
with an ease that was astonishing considering what it had recently
gone through, and then Captain O'Hara reached for his pipe again
and raised one eyebrow.

"I've nothing much to say, sir," said William wretchedly, for his
momentary happiness had left him now and he was back again in the
depths of his shame. "I'm a seaman. I had shore leave and got into
trouble. When I got back to the harbour my ship had gone, and I
thought I'd better find another. I saw the Green Dolphin and came
on board."

"Damned cheek, surely, to chuck yourself down in me bunk without a with-your-leave or a by-your-leave?" enquired Captain
O'Hara.

"Yes," said William. "I'm sorry, sir, I don't think I knew quite
what I was doing."

Captain O'Hara raised the other eyebrow. "Women an' dope?"
he enquired.

"Yes, sir," said William.

"Damn fool," said Captain O'Hara equably.

"Yes, sir," said William.

"So you're a seaman, are ye?" said Captain O'Hara. "In the
Merchant Service I don't doubt by the look of ye. Grandest service
in the world. What was your ship, eh?"

William flushed scarlet to the roots of his hair, choked a little and
did not answer, for it seemed to him now that even to mention either
the Orion or the Royal Navy in connection with himself would be to
tarnish the fair fame of them both.

"Never mind, son," said Captain O'Hara. "I'll not be troublin' ye
with questions. The past is the past. The future's the thing. What
of it?"

"You're an apprentice short, aren't you, sir?" asked William
humbly.

"Aye, a little fool of an apprentice got himself washed overboard
off Madagascar," said Captain O'Hara. "You can take his place.
But you'll have to sleep in the apprentice half deck and swab the

decks with the rest. How'll ye like that? Eh? You've been an officer this year or so past, I don't doubt. It'll be puttin' the clock back, eh?"

"Serve me right," said William stoutly.

"That's the spirit," said the old man with approval. "Start again. An' mind ye, son, if ye can take a fall, an' then start to climb the blasted ladder all over again with a good heart, you're a seaman. If you can't you're nothin' but a bloody landsman. Now ye can get out. I've me work to do."

"For where are we bound, sir?" asked William, getting up.

"For New Zealand with a cargo of tea," said Captain O'Hara briefly.

CHAPTER TWO

1

William took up his abode in the apprentice half deck, an apartment six foot by twelve, in which the five other apprentices, young boys of half William's size, received him with something of dismay, for he entirely blocked the whole place. And he did not know his work either. As an officer in Her Majesty's Navy he was inexperienced in the holystoning of decks and the cleaning out of hen-coops and had to be instructed in these things. The rest of the crew viewed him with strong suspicion; for what was a grown man doing masquerading as an apprentice? He was a gentleman, too, and yet possessed not even a coat to his back. They had to fit him out with clothes and bedding, and resented it, even though he gave them his pay in exchange. They took it out of him in every way they could think of, and they knew a good many ways of tormenting the body and soul of a man. Captain O'Hara took not the slightest notice of him, apart from cursing him volubly for his stupidity whenever he set eyes on him. He knew better, of course. Any sign of favouritism on the part of the Old Man, and the crew would have taken it out of William more than ever. Only Nat of all the crew was kindlily disposed, though he dared show it in no way except an occasional gleam of the eye and an abstention from active persecution. And they ran into dirty weather almost as soon as they left China, and dirty weather for an apprentice on a merchantman was a blacker kind of misery than that endured by a sub-lieutenant on a man-of-war. It was sheer hell to mount to the heights of the topsail yard in a storm and cling there a hundred feet above the hissing fury of the sea, clawing with bleeding hands at the cracking ballooning canvas, feeling with benumbed feet for the one-inch foot-rope, aware always that one false movement meant a sickening fall, with death or fatal injury at the end of it. William was used to periods of being always wet, always cold, always in danger when on duty, but on the Orion he had at least had a comfortable dry bunk, some small measure of privacy, the respect of the crew and the friendliness of brother officers. But here there was no relief from pain. On deck there was the perpetual nervous misery of a weakened and overdriven body, the smarting of torn hands with salt in the wounds, the endless drenching of the great seas that swept the decks. And when he had crawled into a hammock far too small for him, and soaked with the wet that leaked through the roof, in the fetid atmosphere of overcrowded quarters, there was no hope of sleep with the misery of cramp and hot-ache, no space to dry wet clothes, very little possibility of being clean or decent in his person. And always there was the mental misery of persecution, the searing of his soul with shame and loneliness. He had not known it was possible to suffer so much. And like all those in acute misery he could visualise no ending to it. Pain seemed to have fastened its teeth into him with so bitter a clench that surely it would hold on now till the end of life. He understood in these days why men sometimes killed themselves; it was because of this quality of eternity that seems to dwell in pain. Yet he did not himself contemplate that way out. There was doggedness in him, and with the eyes of a suffering dog he endured. Captain O'Hara, observing him acutely even while he cursed him, said to himself that if the strain upon the boy went on too long he must intervene. But he did not want to do that. Always better to let relief come quietly and naturally in its own time, as hard winter earth softens at the touch of the sun and the spring light comes stronger day by day.

And so it was. William himself would have found it hard to say when it was that he began to gain the liking of the crew. It came slowly, won by the fact that whatever they did to him he never lost his patient good humour. And he never shirked, never boasted, never refused any demand made on his generosity. And yet within the limits set by his decency and kindliness he always gave as good as he got. If he was struck he struck back, with a smile and above the belt, but with most effective accuracy. And tired though he was he was still as strong as an ox, and physical strength was to them a worshipful thing. It was perhaps when he picked up the two largest apprentices, one in each hand, carried them the length of the ship and deposited them side by side upon the spanker boom, that they really began to love him. The change took place so slowly, yet by the time the Philippines had been left behind, with Mindanao a blue smudge

on the horizon, William was once more in the position to which he was accustomed, securely enthroned as the most popular member of the community. He did not know that he was, he had never known it, but he felt again the familiar happy atmosphere of good fellowship that was the atmosphere of his own country, and he was a little comforted. But only a little, for his shame was still with him. "Young fool," thought Captain O'Hara, watching him. "A sensitive conscience is like a dead hen hangin' round a dog's neck. A man can't go through life with his past stinkin' on his chest day an' night. No, begorra. A man should chew the string through an' be quit of 'em, an' there's a weakness in a man if he can't do it. Yes, there's a softness in the boy, for all the fine muscle he has on him, an' for all that he's as good a man with his fists as any I set eyes on; an' for all I love the lad as though he were my own."

So thought Captain O'Hara, smoking a pipe in his cabin in the peace of the evening, his teeth removed for comfort and his wig hung over the back of his chair.

For the storms were behind them now, and so was the suffocating heat of the Equator, with the endless days of sweating labour, pulling the yards round to catch every breath of vagrant baffling wind. And the grim dangers of the Great Barrier Reef had faded away too. The ship was gracefully bowing now to a favourable breeze, her fair-weather sails all set, dipping through water so clear that one could lean on the bulwarks and see the fungi and coral of the ocean bed scintillating with every colour imaginable, and the exquisite little rainbow fish who would be phosphorescent when the darkness came. This was the weather that the seamen loved, when they could wash their shirts and hang them to dry in the sun, and tell yarns beneath the blaze of the tropic stars, and catch the silvery flying fish and fry them for their supper. Upon this ship they were not allowed to catch dolphins, and it seemed the dolphins knew it, for they followed their namesake in perpetual delight, rolling and tumbling mirthfully about her, every roll a shout of unheard laughter, every tumble a silent yet roystering oath that life is good. This was the true Green Dolphin weather; joyful, comradely, serene.

But somewhere up on deck there was a young fellow who had his life before him and who, Captain O'Hara considered, was lacking in that touch of hardness that makes for success. If he was to be as prosperous at the end of his days as Captain O'Hara then that worthy considered that he'd need a bit of gingering, a deal of plain speaking, a kindly kick in the pants now and again, to assist him in the right direction. No time like the present. Captain O'Hara knocked out his pipe, adjusted his teeth and his wig and went on deck.

The port watch was lazing in the bows. Among the group of men William was conspicuous by reason of his fair curly head and the immense difficulty he was encountering in sewing a patch on a pair of trousers.

"Hey!" bellowed Captain O'Hara. "You there! Ozanne! I'll have a word with ye on the subject of the deckhouse skylight. Come below, damn ye, an' look sharp."

Then he stumped down to his cabin again, and William, amid the jeers of the port watch, followed in a condition of abject humility. In cleaning the skylight that morning he had contrived to smash it. He had a great gift for injuring inanimate objects, towards which his intentions were always wholly good. He was, he told himself, the most blundering ass who ever lived.

Yet when the delinquent stood before him Captain O'Hara's tone was surprisingly gentle. "I've watched ye for weeks, me lad," he said, "an' you've about as much idea how to holystone a deck as how to put a neat patch upon a pair of trousers or clean a skylight. You've done well, son, this voyage, you've done your damned best and I've been proud of ye, begorra, but you've done it in a hard school of which ye had no previous knowledge. It was not in the Merchant Service, son, that ye learned to be a seaman."

They were standing facing each other, the old teak table between them. The old man's tone was questioning and kindly, but it was only the dumb pain in William's eyes that gave him answer.

"Ye held a commission in Her Majesty's Navy, son," he stated gently. "I thought as much, watchin' the blunderin' fool that ye are with a swab an' a bucket of water. It's all been gold braid, an' dinin' with the Admiral, an' makin' eyes at the ladies with you, son; not the sweat an' blood an' curses that are the merchant seaman's probation to the sea."

William flushed crimson, but he let the gibe at the Navy go by. They were approaching the crux of the conversation and his throat and chest felt so tight with apprehension that he could not speak.

"If I'd known, son, when I found ye sleepin' in me bunk, that ye were a naval officer, I'd 'ave turned right round an' taken ye back to China," said Captain O'Hara. "There'd 'ave been time then; it's too late now. Why didn't ye tell me, ye young fool?"

William swallowed hard. "It would have been to tarnish the reputation of the service, sir," he said at last.

"Fiddlesticks!" said Captain O'Hara. "It takes a darn sight more than unpunctuality on the part of her junior officers to tarnish the reputation of Her Majesty's Navy. You take yourself too seriously, me lad. You know the damn fool thing you've done, don't ye? If you'd gone straight to Her Majesty's Consul at the port an' made a clean breast of it you'd 'ave been sent back to England, reprimanded and reinstated. Instead of that you chose to desert an' join another ship. If you go back to England now, or to that little island of yours, you'll be nabbed an' court-martialled. A fine mess you've made of things, son—a fine mess entirely."

It had been put into words. That terrible bit of knowledge, that had been gradually eating into William's mind throughout the voyage, was now brought out into the open. He had thought that that was how it was, but he had not been quite sure. Now he knew. There was a certain relief in knowing for certain.

Captain O'Hara looked at his blanched and stricken face with compassion. The boy had no idea what to do with himself, he realised; not the faintest ghost of a notion. "Sit down," he said. "Sit down an' we'll talk it over."

They sat down, Captain O'Hara in the teak chair and William on the bench.

"Maybe ye don't remember, son," said the old man, "that when we sat like this seven years ago, one on each side of this very table, I told ye a yarn or two about New Zealand."

"Yes," said William.

"Ye thought then, hearin' me yarns, that it must be a grand land, surely. Ye said it ought to belong to old England."

"Yes," said William dully, but as out of a far-off dream he remembered how he had thrilled at the thought of the beautiful land.

"Maybe ye were too busy, son, dinin' with the Admiral, to take note of the fact that on January twenty-ninth of this year of Our Lord eighteen hundred and forty a representative of the British Government landed at the Bay of Islands an' took possession of the country for the Queen. An' ye may have lacked opportunity, son, while makin' eyes at the ladies, to gain information as to the foundin' of the New Zealand Company, an' the grand job it is doin' establishin' white settlers on New Zealand shores. The Company has purchased nearly a third of New Zealand, son. There's been no stealing from the bloody natives, mind ye, but a fair price given. Two hundred muskets has the Company paid down, begorra, three hundred red blankets, a ton of baccy, seventy-two writin' slates, four hundred an' eight pocket handkerchiefs, twenty-four combs an' no less than one hundred and forty-four Jew's harps. What do you think of that for a fair price, eh? An' the settlers purchase their land from the Company at one pound an acre. If that's not dirt cheap I don't know what is, bedad. At a rough computation, son, there must be between two an' three thousand Britishers in New Zealand now.

It is to take 'em their tea that the Green Dolphin is sailin' through the tropics at this very moment."

He leaned back in his chair, his eyes holding William's. There was a faint sparkle of interest, he noted, in the boy's face.

"Who are those settlers?" asked William. "Whalers and escaped convicts?"

"Faith, no! These new fellows are as different from the old settlers as chalk from cheese. There's every sort an' kind of fellow among 'em, but all good fellows. There's crofters an' squires an' parsons, an' Free Kirkers an' Trade Unionists, with wives an' children complete, most of 'em wantin' to get away from somethin' they calls injustice to somethin' they calls freedom, an' all of 'em, for this reason or that, wantin' to make a fresh start, an' with the guts to make it an' not just set thinkin' about it. I take off me hat to 'em, son, though it seems many of 'em ain't got the sense they were born with; which it ain't to be expected that they should have, an' they most of 'em with their poor cracked heads full of new religions an' new social an' educational systems what's to build Utopia overnight. It ain't that I object to ideals, son; let them as enjoys 'em have 'em, say I; live an' let live; but if your head's too full of ideals it don't leave much room for horse sense. An' horse sense was not what those settlers showed, son, when they landed in a cannibal country in crinolines an' silk shawls, frock coats, beaver top hats an' tall canes with tassels on 'em. That's no sort of costume in which to leg it when there's a Maori after ye with his club an' knife." He paused and puffed at his pipe, smiling. "Begorra, but they've got the right stuff in 'em. They've got the guts. More power to their elbow, say I. I'm told they've tucked up their skirts, rolled up their shirt sleeves, put their ideals an' beavers away in their hat boxes for use on Sundays only, an' got goin' finely buildin' their houses, tillin' the ground, raisin' the crops, settlin' the livestock. It'll be a hard fight for years to come, a damn hard fight, but if there's a thing better worth doin' in this world than goin' straight to earth an' sun an' water for salvation of body an' soul, then, bedad, I've yet to be told of it. That's what pioneerin' is, son, an' seafarin' too. You've nothin'. Ye stand on bare earth, or set sail on the deep, an' ye wrestle with 'em as Jacob wrestled with his God, for your very life. That's worth doin', son, that is. I don't give a damn for most men's religion but I do give a damn for standin' face to face with the Almighty an' wrestlin' with Him for me life at His hands."

Captain O'Hara's ideas of God were peculiar to himself. His God spoke with the voice of winds and waters, sat enthroned among the snows, crowned with the stars, His sword the lightning and His shield the sun. His garment was the green of upland forests, and kneeling among the bladed wheat, among the flowers and grass, one touched the hem of it. And with this God one fought for physical existence, and was lamed and scarred by the fight even as Jacob, and with the pain of the fighting, though Captain O'Hara could not have explained to you how, one somehow bought one's soul. It was a stern creed, with no place in it for the God who suffers, or for Marie Watch-All who gave him birth that he might mark where the sparrows fall, but it was exhilarating. It put one on one's mettle. William's eyes kindled as he said shyly, "Do you think one of those pioneers would let me work for him just for my keep? And, then, maybe, one day I could have a bit of land of my own."

Captain O'Hara eyed William's proportions. "I should say that biceps like yours, goin' dirt cheap too, would be at a premium in any pioneerin' country, son. An' you're a friendly fellow, too, an' good company when you aren't payin' too much attention to your damn conscience."

"It'll be hard to leave the sea," said William slowly.

"You'll be near it, son, for all the settlements cling to the coast as yet. You'll hear its voice, an' there'll be the tradin' ships comin' an' goin'."

"What about the Maoris?" asked William.

"Bound to cause a deal of trouble sooner or later," boomed Captain O'Hara cheerfully. "They've signed a treaty with us, cedin' to Her Majesty all powers of sovereignty, and in return we've guaranteed 'em full possession of their own lands. But they'll not see the white folk encroachin' further an' further into their country without showin' fight. It's not to be expected that they should. Faith, no. They're a grand people, the Maoris. They'll give ye some fun, me lad. If your head don't adorn some native Pa one of these fine days the natives'll not have the sense I give 'em credit for. Fine lot of meat on ye."

With this dreadful prognostication Captain O'Hara brought the interview to a close and William went on deck. The tropic night had come. The wheeling stars were like great suns and the fiery fishes streaked the sea with flame.

2

The Green Dolphin was standing in towards the coast. William, leaning over the bulwarks, felt his heart beat high with excitement. This was New Zealand, this was Aotearoa, the Long White Cloud. They were approaching Cook Straits and he could see both the islands. He was glad there were two of them, not one. It was more homelike, somehow. Wellington Harbour was not likely to bear much resemblance to Saint Pierre, yet it would be a little like. All harbours have the same welcoming arms for the wanderer, promise the same shelter, have the same small ripples slapping musically against the hulls of quiet ships. Always the bells seem ringing on the land and the air is all movement with the wings of gulls.

Slowly, with sails reduced, they glided nearer. It was very early and sea and sky alike were tinctured with rose and amethyst upon the blue. It was a strange primordial landscape that William looked upon. The strong outlines and the cool colours of a clear dawn seemed inherent in it. The harbour was ringed round with mountains, the nearer saffron-coloured, streaked with the colours of morning, shining here and there with patches of pure gold where the sun lit the gorse, the great peaks behind them a clear translucent green reaching up to the wonder of the snow. The lower slopes of the hills were clothed with bright green grass, contrasting with red earth and golden sand and the darker green of trees, and here where the belt of vivid colour linked the colder, paler colours of mountain and sea there was a settlement of mud and daub or wooden houses, smoke curling up from their chimneys, the wooden steeple of a little church, a jetty running out into the water, a few ships rocking at anchor. So clear was the air that one could see cattle moving far up on the green slopes, the streams that watered their pasture, the weathercock upon the steeple and the tiny figures running out from their toy houses to watch the glorious ship glide into her anchorage. A chill air blew down from the mountains and so deep was the silence that one could hear the chime of birdsong; not the warm melody of bustling English coppices but music as unearthly and remote as the mountains, true dawn music, beautiful, lonely and cold.

"Back the mainyard!" came the order, and then, in Captain O'Hara's most deep and cheerful boom, "Let go the anchor!"

And suddenly all was joyful noise; the rattling of the hawser, the trampling of feet, shouts and laughter, the rush of wings overhead. The toy-like figures that had come out of the houses were life-size now, and running quickly down the jetty to welcome them in, the women with their skirts bunched up in their hands, the children leaping and scampering with joyful cries, the men cheering. A bell rang joyfully out from the wooden steeple and the rising sun lit the weathercock upon its summit to a fiery gold.

CHAPTER THREE

1

The idealism of the new settlers submerged William almost at once in the persons of Samuel Kelly and his wife Susanna, who with warm-hearted generosity flung open their hospitable door to him for as long as he liked to remain; which would not be for long, William decided almost at once, for the passionate all-pervading piety of the Kelly household was a little oppressive to his easy-going temperament. He was inclined to resent the fact that Captain O'Hara immediately upon landing dumped him upon a parson. It was treating him like a child, he thought, a naughty child who must be forcibly kept upon the path of virtue.

"Who else am I to impose ye upon but a parson? Can ye tell me that now?" Captain O'Hara demanded, when he noted this slight resentment in William's eyes. "Ye must be imposed upon some poor besotted fool, ye can't sleep in the open. An' 'tis always good policy, son, if ye have inordinate demands to make, to make 'em of a parson. He can't refuse ye a kindness, ye see, without shamin' his God. He mayn't like sharin' his vittles and his fireside with young vagabond seamen from God knows where, but if he don't do it his Christ won't know him at the day of judgment, as expressly stated in Matthew twenty-five. So ye can always impose on a parson, son, an' get your vittles dirt cheap."

But there was no shadow of unwillingness upon Samuel Kelly's eager face when William was commended to his fraternal care. His sallow features lit up as though a light had been kindled behind thin alabaster, his deep, dark eyes blazed fiercely, the grip of his delicate hand all but made William yelp. This was pioneering Evangelical piety, white-hot in its passion for souls. William had not met it before and hoped he would not meet it again, for that hot firm grip upon his hand felt to him almost like a grip upon his spirit, that he wished to be possessed by no one but himself and Marguerite. Later in his life he was to revise his opinion of Samuel Kelly, was to revere him as he revered no one except Marguerite, but at this first meeting he did not feel at home with him. This was not his sort of man. Nothing easy-going about Samuel, nothing of the rollicking Green Dolphin about him, and nothing either of that serenity and love of life that softened Marguerite's austerity and made her such an adorable companion.

For Samuel, so he told William and Captain O'Hara when three days later they sat with him in the glow of the evening light in the bare little living-room of his parsonage, had never in his youth had any reason to love life. He had been one of twelve children, born of poor parents in the industrial north, in those bitter days when half-naked women dragged coal in the mines, and little children worked in the weaving sheds for such long hours that in winter they did not know what it was to see the sun. Samuel had been one of them. He had grown up with a shrunken sickly body, eyes that had looked upon little beauty but yet had a questioning look in them, as though they knew they had been created for some purpose other than to be dimmed by semi-darkness and foul air, a precocious and brilliant mind that had sucked up knowledge of every kind from God knew where, and because of that mind a soul embittered and infuriated by social injustice and the apparent hopelessness of pain. The battle of reform fought by organised labour had had no more bitter fighter in its ranks than he, Cobden no more ardent disciple. It was not for himself only that he had fought, for from the very beginning his thirst for souls had been an integral part of him, it had been for the dumb and suffering poor, for his unborn children and his country's soul. For though he had seen few of her beauties he loved England. There was good yeoman stock in him and somehow, somewhere, through some gleam of rare sunlight or some broken snatch of birdsong in the heavens, she had stretched out a finger and touched his heart, and he could have wept that the England who had won Waterloo could be guilty of Peterloo. He had been present when that orderly concourse of working men and women, assembled at St. Peter's Fields, Manchester, to demand parliamentary reform, had been shot down by a charge of yeomanry. He had been one among the hundreds of seriously injured and for weeks had lain in the garret of a friend's house suffering the tortures of the damned, and likely to have lost his reason had it not been for the visits of a little old parson, in a shabby black coat and an old-fashioned white wig, who climbed up the rickety attic stairs again and again to sit beside him and discourse upon the cross of Christ. The little man had been exceedingly obstinate. The rain that dripped through the roof had disconcerted him not at all, nor the stench of the neglected sickroom, nor the indifference, and sometimes the curses, of the wretched man in the bed. His had been the white-hot fanaticism of Evangelicalism at that time, that surging re-birth of faith that had swept England in reaction from the formalism of the eighteenth century. He had believed with all his heart and soul, with no shadow of doubt anywhere, that in what he had to say lay the salvation not only of this man but of the whole human race. Faith such as his moves more than mountains, it moves even the hardened hearts of embittered men. It had moved, at last, even Samuel Kelly's heart. Obsessed as he had been by the apparent uselessness of pain, this notion of a suffering God, ransoming human souls through the slow dropping of His blood, of a fraternity of His followers who as His mystical suffering body continue to bleed and to redeem, had won him utterly. Somehow, somewhere, England had touched his heart to give himself to suffer for her sake, but in the midnight darkness of his little attic, as out of the depths of his own pain he had looked with awe upon the pain of God, Christ had broken his heart and then healed it again to beat for ever for His sake. When he had crawled out of bed at last, lamed for life by his injuries, without material help or prospects of any sort, it had been to look out at a world suddenly irradiated with glory, utterly transformed by the fact that for him now, at last, pain had meaning.

Incapable as he had been of physical labour he had gone to live with the old parson and had become his secretary. He had read voraciously, his fine mind fulfilling itself most gloriously; he had studied for the ministry and became a priest, he had married Susanna, the old parson's housekeeper, a mousy-quiet, grey-eyed, soft-voiced woman whose devotion to the gospel of Christ expressed itself in unceasing service to the men who preached it. Susanna had never been at any time a woman whom anybody noticed very much, but she could work her fingers to the bone with more to show for it and less to say about it than any woman living.

But in the new loyalty to Christ and the new fight under the banner of His cross Samuel had not forgotten the old loyalty to England and the old fight for her suffering people. He had remained a disciple of Cobden and an ardent Trade Unionist. But Peterloo had destroyed something more in him than the proper functioning of his left leg; it had destroyed also his belief that social justice could ever be established on the soil of England while the bulk of the people remained so utterly blind to the vision that seemed to light the eyes of the minority only. His thoughts, like the thoughts of many of his kind, had turned westward to the new lands. If, out there, one could build the perfect community, then, perhaps, beloved England would see, take heed and do likewise. When a number of his Manchester Trade Unionist friends had decided to emigrate to the new colony of New Zealand the call had come to him to offer to go with them. The old parson was dead now and he had no ties in England. His offer had been accepted and he and Susanna had been among the crinolined, top-hatted company who had landed at the Bay of Islands on January the twenty-ninth, eighteen hundred and forty.

This was the story that he told to William and Captain O'Hara. Captain O'Hara was not staying at the Parsonage—not he—but he had strolled up to say a last good-bye to William, for to-night he would go on board the Green Dolphin, and very early to-morrow he would sail for Auckland to pick up a cargo of sealskins for China, and to his own intense surprise he had remained smoking his pipe in Susanna's neat little parlour, entirely captivated by Samuel Kelly. He thought him a poor fool, of course, but he was enslaved by his sincerity. And he thought, too, that if William could succeed in being similarly enslaved the little parson's friendship might keep him from the women and the drink. For every time the old sailor looked at William, so full of sociability and weakness and good nature, he remembered that other, older element of pioneering life that had been merely overlaid by this new tincture of idealism, that raffish element still so vigorously alive in the bush and in the lonely settlements along the coast. A lot of good in it, magnificent good, but full of danger too for a boy like William. So he encouraged Samuel to talk, drew him out with deep grunts and gurgles of sympathy, tried to show William that he respected this daft little man.

But William sat silent, watching them, but held aloof by his sense of desolation. To-morrow he would be left alone in this strange land, in this bare cold house, with this austere fanatical man whose creed of saving pain awoke no response in a heart that wanted neither to suffer nor redeem, but to have and hold and enjoy. He looked about him and shivered. The evening was drawing in with a wind that seemed to blow right through the frail walls of the hastily constructed little house, that was the bleakest thing in the way of a house that he had ever encountered. The furniture of the parlour was plain and hideous. Susanna, who had finished washing up the dishes used in a supper so meagre that it had done no more than whet the edge of William's colossal appetite, had glided silently into the room and sat darning by the window, straining her eyes in the fading light, but determined, for reasons of economy, not to light the lamp until she was obliged. William liked her, and had been courteous and kind to her as he was to all women, but it is to his discredit that though he returned the smile that lit up her worn plain face whenever their eyes met, he was without the imagination to realise that he was eating her out of house and home. Susanna would have given him their last crust, and still smiled, but he would not have known that it cost her more than all Sophie's rounds of roast beef put together. He longed for Sophie and the luxury of Le Paradis. He longed for his father and the shabby comfort of Green Dolphin Street. He longed above all for Marguerite. And he would never see them again. He could not now write that letter to Marguerite asking her to marry him. He felt that he could not even send her the carved wooden necklace that hung round his neck, for it had come from a place that could not even be thought of in connection with Marguerite. He had written a letter to Sophie telling her the bare facts of what had happened. It was spotted all over with the stupid great tears he had shed when he wrote it. It was in his pocket, and presently he would walk down to the jetty with Captain O'Hara and give it to the skipper of a schooner that was setting sail for England in the morning. They would set sail together on the ebb tide, Captain O'Hara for China and his letter for England, his last two links with home, and when they had both gone he would be utterly alone. His wretchedness surged over him again and he clenched his hands so hard that the nails bit into the skin. Samuel Kelly's eyes were on him, full of pity, burning with the lust to help and save him. But he would not meet them. He resented their possessiveness. He hated the pain that was tormenting him and he wanted nothing whatever, not even salvation, if the way to it was through a continuance of pain. He hated this suffering God of Samuel's. He saw in His suffering no excuse for the fact that He had created man to suffer also. It was a criminal thing to have created a world in which such appalling consequences could follow a moment's sin or folly. He preferred Captain O'Hara's God, the God of great winds and waters, a force without ruth, without excuses, with whom one wrestled in titanic conflict for one's daily bread. It would be easier when he had started that conflict. It would be easier to forget. And he must forget, or he would go mad. He moved restlessly, kicked the cat entirely by accident, felt he could bear the gaze of Samuel's eyes no longer, got up, knocked over Susanna's workbasket and went out.

2

The spring wind caught him as he left the fragile little house, that New Zealand wind, speaking with its multitude of voices, that was to be his companion for so many years and come in the end to feel like a living and godlike immanence of power. The perpetual sweep of its wings seemed to burnish the stars to a greater brilliance, and on the earth the tread of its feet passed like a cleansing fire. The house stood high and he could look down on a jumble of wooden roofs to the ruffled waters of the harbour with the mountains rising beyond. So clear was the air from the sweeping of the wind that the mountains looked as though carved out of crystal, and very near. He could have put out his hand and touched them. Suddenly he seemed to hear Marguerite's voice describing her own country. "The light is clear and the wind cold and there aren't any lies or subterfuges."

Was this her God, this pentecostal wind with its piercing cleanliness, its comfort of light and fire? Man conceives of God as Three in One, he remembered, and perhaps in that tiny beam of reflected light that each soul catches from the eternal shining there is in one soul a revelation of one aspect of the Godhead and in others of another and another. Creator Father, Saviour Son and cleansing comforting Spirit. Do we reveal Him to each other, reach Him through each other, conversely find union with each other through Him? If that is so, thought William blunderingly, perhaps whenever this wind blew the stars to flame he would feel close to Marguerite, and when he wrestled with the good earth for his daily bread he would be near to Captain O'Hara, who had been like a father to him. But for the other God, Samuel's suffering God, he had no use at present. Like Simon of Cyrenae he would bear the cross under compulsion only.

Moving restlessly, as though to escape from it, he paced up and down until Captain O'Hara joined him, then silently they made their way down through the swaying shadows and the dappled moonlight to the harbour where the ships rocked at anchor with the wind singing in their shrouds. Two dinghies lay beside the jetty, one loaded with stores for the schooner that would sail for England, the other waiting for Captain O'Hara. William delivered his letter to the man in the schooner's dinghy and then turned dumbly to the man at his side.

"Well, keep a good heart, son," said Captain O'Hara, his great hand descending like a sledge-hammer upon William's shoulder. "I'm not much of a hand with a pen, unless I've taken a drop, but I'll make shift to drop ye a line now an' again. An' as trade develops maybe the Green Dolphin will be often back an' forth between the old country an' the new, an' I'll be able to keep an eye on ye. But remember, son, that there's always as good fish in the sea as ever came out of it. It's hard to part with the old friends but the new ones are jolly good fellows who'll be needin' ye as you'll be needin' them. There's stuff in that little parson, son. Touched in the head he may be, poor chap, but it takes all sorts to make a world, an' there's always stuff in a fellow who lives for some purpose outside himself. I've never been one for religion, son, but yet I've never been what ye could call an unbeliever. What I say is, nothin' don't seem impossible once you've clapped eyes on a whale. Well, God bless ye, son. Don't fret over past mistakes. Better keep away from the bottle to-day than waste time countin' yesterday's empties."

Captain O'Hara exhaled the last breath of his homily with relief, crushed William's shoulder almost to pulp, and climbed into the dinghy. The two men in her, one of whom was Nat, looked at

William kindly, but he stood with head bent, hearing the soft dip of
the oars in the water, the creak of the rowlocks, the sound of the
wind, but not able to watch the going from him of all that was left of
the past, or to look out over the harbour to where the raking masts
of the Green Dolphin were etched against the background of the
crystal mountains. Even when minutes had passed he could not
bear to look at her, or at Captain O'Hara climbing aboard her. He
looked once, listlessly, at the schooner that was to carry his letter, a
poor little craft that did not look very sea-worthy, and then he turned
and stumbled away into the cold wind that blew down the alley-ways
between the houses.

It was a desire for warmth more than anything else that made him
pause outside the half-open doorway of Hobson's Saloon. There
was a fire inside. He could hear the crackle of the flames and a bar
of light lay across his path as though to stop him from going further.
Then he heard a great roar of laughter from inside, and smelt a most
appetising smell. His empty heart, longing for comfortable companionship, and his empty stomach, completely unsatisfied by
Susanna's dainty supper, then rose up and took charge. He pushed
the door wide and went in.

Instantly he felt at home. In spite of the heat, the noise, the
atmosphere that could be cut with a knife, this was his sort of place.
The wood fire on the hearth sent clouds of smoke into the room with
every gust of wind, but it gave forth a glorious heat, and a kettle hung
over its flames was whistling cheerfully and belching forth clouds of
jolly steam. The lamp hanging from the blackened rafters was smoking a little, but it burned brightly enough to illumine the rough
wooden counter at the far end of the long room with its rows of
bottles and twinkling well-polished glasses. Two trestle tables ran
the length of the room and sitting round them on long benches were
some twenty men, eating, drinking, smoking, playing cards, talking,
laughing, cursing, quarrelling, with Hobson with his broken nose
and merry eyes and wooden leg stumping about them ministering
to their needs. Mrs. Hobson, red-faced, jolly, broader than she was
long, bustled back and forth from the kitchen with plates of steaming
stew and hunks of bread and cheese. Before he knew what had happened to him William was seated at the extreme end of one of the
tables devouring stew, a glass of hot toddy beside him, gazing with
delight through a blue haze of tobacco smoke at the men about him
and returning their rough jests with vigour and good humour. They
accepted him instantly, without question, swallowing him as the sea
swallows a small rivulet flowing to it from the hills. With no abate-
ment of its cheerful gusto the noise flowed over his head, sucked him

down, absorbed him into its primeval depths of darkness and of laughter.

For instinct told William at once that that was what this gathering was—primeval. These were not the new pioneers, but the old, and not of this country but of the earth itself. These were the sons of the men who had first ploughed the earth and fished the seas for food, and fought the wild beasts for their skins for warmth and learned to make fire with flint and tinder, who had begotten children with animal simplicity and lived to satisfy the hunger of their bodies only. They had lived on into a new age, when men set a greater value upon the victories of the mind and spirit than those of the body and had become arrogant warriors who aimed at being not conquerors of the earth only but of heaven too, but they had lived on in no spirit of subservience but rather of a laughing and tolerant contempt. They knew that the new activities were built upon the old. . . . No food, no thought, no power to pray to God. . . . The old activities might be regarded now only as means to an end but they were an indispensable means, while the end could be foregone and still the world would wag upon its way. They knew this and they laughed.

And asked no questions. That, William soon found, was the chief point of etiquette in this society. The convict settlements of Australia were not far away, and the daring could find means to break away from them, and mutinies at sea were of common occurrence, and sometimes it was necessary to swim for it or die. In this society you did not ask a man where he had come from, and he did not ask you. You shared your last crust with him if you liked him, stabbed him in the back if you did not, but whichever you did you observed this courteous reticence until the end. And as with your past so with your soul. Primeval man laid no possessive hands upon your soul; naturally, since he did not believe that you had one. Such a belief might be sterile but to William at this moment it was refreshing. He leaned back in his chair, relaxed and laughed, and was comforted.

Yet there was one man who seemed to be not quite of this company, though utterly at home in it. He sat opposite William, looking at him with interest. He was silent, yet without movement or speech he dominated the whole room. He was tall and thin, with bent shoulders. Hard labour and the passing of the years had contorted and hardened his limbs to queer crooked shapes, but he gave no impression of deformity, as Nat did. So of the earth was he that he looked more like a tree than a man, one of those tough old pine trees that nothing in the way of weather except a thunderbolt will ever get the better of. He was immensely strong and vigorous. His eyes were dark and sombre but as full of vitality as the curly grizzled hair at his temples. His skin was the colour of old oak, so roughened and seamed by exposure to weather that the scar of an old wound that cut across his head and ran down one side of his face was scarcely noticeable. He wore a pair of homespun trousers girt about his lean middle with a leather belt, and an old coat tinted every conceivable colour by sun and rain. He wore neither cravat nor waistcoat and his shirt was open at the neck showing a strong column of a throat with veins like whipcord, and an immensely powerful chest from which issued a rough deep voice with a sad and thrilling quality about it, an echoing quality, as though from the great sounds of nature it had caught the mourning and the angry resignation of the trumpet notes but missed the murmuring undertones of hope. No, there was no hope about him, only a sombre endurance and an iron pride. He ate nothing, but absorbed hot rum and water equably, relentlessly, without cessation, like the parched earth sucking in the rain. Yet it seemed to have no effect on him. The hand that held his glass remained as steady as a rock, and the hand that lay on the table, the crooked fingers curved about his gun, looked as though carved out of dark stone; until with a disconcerting suddenness he stretched it across the table and reached for William's throat, when those dark talons of fingers looked more alarmingly alive than anything that William had ever seen.

But he intended no harm. William's shirt also was open at the throat and he had seen the carved necklace that William was wearing round his neck; for the stupid, sentimental, childish reason that Lung-mu reminded him of Marie Tape-Tout at home. He lifted it over William's head, moved his gun and glass to stand within the protecting circle of his arms laid upon the table, and took the necklace into his two hands. William, dumbfounded, watched his hands. They held the necklace as though they loved it, the fingers curved questioningly, the balls of the thumbs moving lightly over the exquisite little carvings; just so had William seen Nat holding the spokes when he stood his trick at the wheel. His grim mouth relaxed with a slight smile and his eyes softened. Then he tossed the necklace back to William and re-possessed himself of his drink and his gun.

But a quick flash of liking had sprung up between the two of them. William had finished his drink and found that with the jerk of an eyebrow and the flash of a coin his new friend had stood him another.

"You know a good bit of work when you see it, boy," said the deep rough voice. "New to the country?"

"I've just landed, sir," said William. The respect in his voice was sincere and spontaneous, drawn from him by the quality of this stranger, and it gave obvious pleasure. The man smiled again and leaned across the table.

"Got work to do?" he asked.

"No, sir," said William.

"Fond of wood?"

It was a strange question, and William pondered it. "Not that I know of," he said at last. "I've been a sailor."

"Good enough," said the man. "The wind in the kauri trees sounds like the sea, you know. I'm a lumberman. You can join me if you like."

"You know nothing about me, sir," gasped William.

"All I need to know. You've a fine physique and will not make a nuisance of yourself by falling sick. You've respect for an older man and will do what you're told; if you don't I'll tan the hide off you. I've lost one of my best men—knifed by the Maoris—and I'm in Wellington to find another. My shack's some way from here, going north along the coast. There's a settlement of perhaps forty souls, all in the timber or salt-pork trade, natives and white men—the old pioneering stock—not these new fellows who plough up the land with a bible in one hand and a dictionary in the other—and no women, thank God, except the Maori women. I'll work you like hell, but there's plenty of drink to wet your whistle. You must be ready for any sort of trouble, for there'll be war between the natives and the white men before we're all much older, but if you're a friend of mine you'll never lift a hand against the Maori. I've lived among the Maoris, as a Maori, for years. I like 'em. They call me Tai Haruru—Sounding Sea."

"I'll come," said William.

"Then be here at eight to-morrow morning. I can get you a horse and a gun if you don't possess 'em."

"I have nothing in the world," said William, "except a few garments, a string of carved beads and a knife. The last coin I had paid for the stew I've just eaten."

Tai Haruru laughed. "There's many a man has started life here with less," he said. "I've known of fellows, stowaways or mutineers, who've swum ashore and landed on the rocks stark naked. Nothing like utter loss for a fresh start. It puts you on your mettle. Good-night, boy. If you're late to-morrow morning I'll not wait for you."

He supplied William with another drink and then turned from him. While they talked his strong will had seemed to hold the two of them locked together, quiet and absorbed in the midst of the tumult about them, but now it relegated William also to the outer darkness and confusion. Withdrawn into the citadel of his endurance and his pride Tai Haruru brooded, and absorbed rum and water as the earth the rain.

William sat for a while laughing and talking with the other men, and then found himself out in the wind again, thanking heaven for Tai Haruru and hot toddy. He was warm and comforted, and hummed a little song under his breath as he walked around in circles looking for the Parsonage; which he was unlikely to have lighted upon had not a slight, halting figure appeared out of the shadows and seized his arm. The iron grip of Samuel Kelly's hand was once more astonishingly painful, and William swore angrily and tried to extricate himself.

But to extricate oneself from Samuel Kelly, once he had decided to keep a firm hold, was not an easy task. The resolution of the martyrs was in the little man, the power of God and the obstinacy of the devil. With these three he prevailed over the hulking young giant in his grip, and William was haled home to the Parsonage, held over Susanna's washtub, doused with cold water and put to bed.

He awoke drenched with sunshine. With one agonised bound he was out of bed. Heaven help him, what was the time? Had he done it again? Tai Haruru, like the Orion, did not wait for drunkards. In the name of heaven, what was the time?

A cheap clock from Manchester ticked upon the window-sill of the bare little attic room that Samuel and Susanna had put at his disposal. Seven o'clock. This time he was lucky, but such luck was more than he deserved. It was with the utmost humility that he washed himself in the tin basin on the rickety table beside his bed, and rolled up into a bundle the few disreputable garments that he had bought on board the Green Dolphin with his pay. Susanna had washed and mended them, he noticed suddenly, and his heart smote him that he had not noticed it before.

Then, his bundle under his arm, he went downstairs. Samuel and Susanna had been up and doing for a good hour; the parlour was neat and tidy and breakfast ready on the table. Susanna was already sitting behind the big brown teapot and Samuel was cutting the bread. Standing just inside the doorway, his great bulk seeming to fill the little room, his face as red as fire with shame and embarrassment, William blurted out an account of his meeting with Tai Haruru, asked pardon for last night, thanked them stumblingly for their kindness and bade them farewell.

But he was not to escape as easily as that from the grip of Samuel Kelly.

"Sit down," said the little man sternly, pointing out a chair with the bread knife, that he held as imposingly as a prophet's staff. "And come to your senses before it is too late."

But William did not sit down. He stood mulishly where he was.

"I have not the acquaintance of this man they call Sounding Sea," said Samuel, "but from all I've heard of him he's not a man whose company should be sought after by an educated Christian gentleman such as yourself."

William flushed redder than ever. "He's one of the finest men I've ever met," he said, his voice tending to rise to a belligerent bellow. "And what's more, I believe he's a gentleman too."

"No doubt," Samuel agreed, his voice also tending to rise towards those thundering trumpet notes that were his when once launched upon one of his fine resounding sermons. "That type of gentleman is quite thick upon the ground here, but Lucifer fallen from heaven is not more hopelessly cast out from the life that once he lived than is a civilised man who has reverted again to barbarism. The law of gravitation is not only a material law, it holds good in matters of behaviour also. Nothing can overcome it but the power of God, which men such as you desire to live with neither acknowledge nor invoke. You may think you can keep yourself civilised in the midst of uncivilised surroundings, but I tell you that a young man such as yourself, well-meaning, but, if I may say so, excessively undisciplined, is powerless against the weight of the common mind. If you desire to remain what you are you will remain here in the company of those who live their lives on the same level as that to which you yourself are accustomed, but to which, judging by your condition last night, you cling with an extremely precarious hold."

Samuel had got well away. His eyes flashed and he brought his fist down on the table with a crash that set all the crockery leaping, and put poor Susanna all of a tremble. "You will remain here, young man," he shouted, "and save your soul. You will remain here, or go to hell."

"What should I do here?" demanded William.

"I have a suggestion to make, which I should have made last night had you been in a condition to receive it," said Samuel. "I ask you to remain here under my roof as assistant master in the school we are founding for the children. You are a man of education and should use it for the good of others. I ask you to stay here with me, and give yourself body and soul to the service of God."

"Teach children?" asked William incredulously. "Me teach children? Good God, whatever should I teach them?"

"Their catechism," said Samuel. "Reading, writing and arithmetic. The use of the globe."

William groaned. "Not my sort of work at all," he said. "I should be bored to death."

"At first, no doubt you would," said Samuel. "Would that matter if with your initial boredom you bought your soul and theirs?"

William stared.

"Fling it down," said Samuel with loud ardour. "Trample on it, together with all those emotions that are tinctured and stained with self. Do you know what salvation is? It is the flinging away of self that the soul set free of it may be abandoned to the saving knowledge of the love of God. He who loses his life shall save it, together with the lives of those for whom he suffers. Salvation is the right use of pain. Salvation is——"

But William, unimpressed, was rolling an apprehensive eye upon another cheap little clock from Manchester that was ticking on the parlour mantelpiece. "I thank you for your kindness, sir," he interrupted, "I thank you with all my heart. But now I must say good-bye."

"Stay with us," pleaded Susanna gently, raising her meek grey eyes to William's. "All that we have we will share with you. Throw in your lot with us and be our son."

So spoke Susanna, lovingly, though knowing full well that William's appetite would be to her the last straw that broke the camel's back. But she was a humble woman at all times, most matter-of-factly prepared for any sort of martyrdom. She was saved, perhaps, for she had long ago passed the point where she thought her own feelings of the slightest consequence. She did not win William's company but she won his love by that speech. He went to her and took her hand. "I can't stay, but I'll often come to see you," he said thickly. "Thank you for mending my clothes. I'll be your friend always."

And then he went, no more deflected from his purpose by her gentle pleading than by Samuel's thunder. Sighing bitterly Samuel cast aside the knife and speared a piece of bread upon the toasting fork. He knew it was useless to pursue William with further arguments. Not the strongest soul that ever lived can drive a weak one along a path for which it is not yet ready. "He has far to go, yet, wife," he said sadly. "He has very far to go." And then he groaned, and took the bread off the fork again and could not eat, because William had gone from him and he feared for his soul.

But Susanna poured her tea and buttered her bread with good appetite. She was less apprehensive than was her husband. William had been unfailingly and gallantly courteous to her all the time he had been in her house, and that though she had now neither youth nor comeliness. He was kind, and women drew out the best that was in him. It was her opinion that the gates to salvation are many, and she guessed that it would be not for the sake of a creed but for the sake of a woman that he would one day choose to give himself up to a purpose outside himself, with eyes wide open to the fact that he was irrevocably bound over to a lifetime of endurance.

"Maybe our way was not the way for him, Samuel," she said. "Our sort of life is not his sort, perhaps. It is out of one's own sort of life that the gate of salvation opens."

3

They had been riding for days, mostly in silence, and now it was evening and still they rode. The sky was lit with such a depth of limitless light that when one looked up into it one was afraid. Yet if one looked from the sky to the mighty flanks of the hills the blond grass that clothed them was illumined too, and the headlands running out into the sea were all on fire. The forests were without this terrifying light, but the depth of their primeval darkness was also not without its fear. The sea was cold and clear and green. The wind had dropped and in the silence the rhythm of its slow boom and surge upon the rocks was the rhythm of life itself. This is an awful country, thought William. It may be free and clean and beautiful but it's stark and terrible too. Anything might happen in it. Anything. I wish Tai Haruru would say something.

And as if in answer to his thought Tai Haruru drew rein on the crest of a hill and dismounted. "We'll sit down here," he said. "Have a rest and smoke a pipe. New Zealand sunsets are worth watching. I've watched 'em for twenty years and still they search my soul."

The horses cropped the grass, and it was as though they sucked up light. William stretched his cramped limbs beside Tai Haruru and watched his brown hands curving about the bowl of his pipe; it was curiously carved in the likeness of a bird in flight, and the flame that sprang up from the flint and tinder shone through Tai Haruru's fingers as though it were the living light of their own vitality. It was pleasant to watch them, and to take one's aching eyes from the terrible splendour of the world.

But Tai Haruru was not in the mood to allow him the comfort of small things. "Do you see that creek?" he said, pointing to a silver streak far down in the darkening valley, to which their flaming hilltop fell precipitately. "The settlement clings to its banks. You can see it there. That's where you'll live, boy, perhaps for years to come, perhaps for a short while only. Who knows? For this is a country of storms and earthquakes, cannibal country, pioneer country. You have to be on the alert always to preserve your life. For remember, boy, we're of value only while the clay that we are holds together; after that, nothingness."

William eyed Tai Haruru with a certain apprehension. It struck him that in this country the men, as well as the landscape, ran to extremes. Samuel, now, was almost tedious in his insistence upon the fact of the immortal soul; Tai Haruru on the contrary seemed likely to harp unnecessarily upon its absence. Somewhere between the two of them was what he considered the happy medium, that free friendly place, Green Dolphin country. When as a boy he had thought of the landscape of New Zealand as the landscape of this country he had not imagined that it would arouse in him this awe and fear. His adolescent mind, that had still regarded his own being as the centre of the universe, had dared to tinge a whole great territory with his own especial colours. That had been farcical. There was room here for the countries of many men, and the great stage was finely set for many other dramas besides his own. What had Marguerite said about one's special country? "Where we find liberation . . . where our souls find it easiest to escape from self . . . where what is about us echoes the best that we are." Perhaps it was to find just those very conditions that some two thousand white folk had within this last year come to this country. It would not fail them, thought William. The very best that was in the very finest man that ever lived would not fail to find resounding echo in the perfection of the beauty of this land.

In the clear cold light he could easily see the creek and the village of small houses beside it, set about with a patchwork of harvest fields. The tiny settlement looked alarmingly fragile, held there between the sea and the forest, like a toy between the two hands of some mighty giant. It looked as though it might be crushed to pieces at any moment. Of the two inimical forces it was the forest that struck William as the more threatening of the two.

"We fell the kauri trees only upon its fringes," said Tai Haruru, reading his thought. "Only the fringes are ours. The interior of the forest is a Maori stronghold—a country within a country. It has its entrances and its frontiers that a white man dare not pass—yet I lived in that country for perhaps ten years—maybe longer—I don't know—I lost all count of time."

He puffed silently for a moment or two at his curiously carved pipe. When he spoke again it was jerkily, unwillingly, as though he dragged forgotten lumber from some hated room.

"Though we don't ask questions in this country, yet you'd better know a bit about the chap you're to work for. If I don't tell you the truth about myself another chap will tell you lies. They all tell tales about me—God knows why. I was born in Cumberland, of fine stock, in a grand old house. My family have always been staunch Catholics—ancestors of mine have been martyred for the faith—but though as a boy I was dragged to hear mass every Sunday in an old grey church among the hills it never took hold of me at all—I always knew the whole thing was a fairy tale. But I loved those hills, and my home, and a woman there whom I'd known as child and girl. I'd have lived a life like other men, the good life, had I not had wild blood in me, and a foul temper. One day I struck a man in fury, and he died. I struck him because he ill-treated a wild thing up in the woods, but I did not mean to kill. I never kill if I can help it. They brought it in as manslaughter. I served my sentence, and when I came out my woman had married another fellow and my people were ashamed of me. So I went to Australia. I never stay in any place where I'm treated as my people treated me. Nothing living should ever be treated with contempt. Whatever it is that lives, a man, a tree or a bird, should be touched gently, because the time is short."

William understood now why Tai Haruru's hands were not as the hands of other men. They touched gently.

"No need to expatiate on my first few years in Australia," said Tai Haruru. "It would have been easier to reconcile oneself to an eternity of hell, I used to think in those days, if one had not been flung into it by a flash of madness that had lasted only for a moment. Such a stupid action, so hastily done. That was the worst of it." William shivered suddenly, and not with the chill of the twilight. Tai Haruru looked at him kindly but asked no questions. The moment he had set eyes on the lad he had felt between them the union of a common experience. "But in this world, lad, you're not really damned if you can make something, save something, burnish up something. From a boy I'd always loved wood—there were woods about my home—and I'd always been good with my hands. In Australia I became a cabinet maker and wood carver and I was happy for a while. I did some good work. The best thing I did, I remember, was a chair carved with sea creatures—the captain of a clipper bought it off me. But there were not many in a pioneering community who could afford to give the price he did just for a bit of carving. I couldn't make a living that way, so I turned lumberman as well. I came to New Zealand to fell kauri trees, and the Maoris got me."

"Is your name Timothy Haslam?" asked William quietly.

"It was," said Tai Haruru.

"Captain O'Hara still has your chair," said William. "It's in his cabin on board the Green Dolphin. It was the Green Dolphin who brought me to New Zealand. It was just a chance that you did not see Captain O'Hara in Wellington two days ago, before he set sail again for China."

"We were friends once," said Tai Haruru. "But he'd not know me now if he passed me in the street. A white man can't live alone among natives for years and be the same man he was before. No, O'Hara would not have known me if he'd passed me in the street two days ago."

The coincidence had surprised neither of them. This was not a country in which anything could surprise.

"He thinks you are dead," said William. "He found your deserted huts, with bloodstains on the walls."

"I was as near dead as makes no difference," said Tai Haruru. "All my men were killed and I got this head wound whose scar you can see, and they battered my body nearly to pulp with their clubs. We'd gone too far, you see. Travelling from the north from the Bay of Plenty, making south-west through the forest, we'd passed without knowing it beyond the frontiers of the Maori kingdom. We were cutting down trees in their sacred stronghold, which is forbidden. They surprised us by night and carried our bodies away with them, to eat the flesh and stick the heads on stakes to decorate their Pa. But when they found the life was still in me they kept me alive. God knows why. They liked the look of me, perhaps. They take strong likes and dislikes, as children do. Later they found me useful, for I've power in my hands; there's nothing I can't make and I can heal pain with the touch of them. I lived with them for years, as I told you. I had been badly injured. I was a sick man and lacked the energy to escape. Also I liked them. They have great courage and a fine courtesy. The only thing I had against them was their lust to kill and mutilate. Even the women, mourning the dead, will cut themselves up with sharp stones, so that a whole lovely young body becomes a pillar of dripping blood. Their belief in the fairytale of immortality leads them to outdo the most horrible of religious mystics in their disregard of the exquisite beauty of the living clay. This disregard did violence to the best that is in me. In the end I couldn't stand it. I left them, crossed their frontier by night, travelling westward, and came back to what passes for civilization in this primordial land. Civilization, boy, according to my interpretation of it, is another word for respect for life. One can't have too much respect for a loveliness that's brittle as spun glass."

Samuel would have put that the other way round, William thought; you can't have too much respect for a thing whose tough fibre is the stuff of immortality. Though he felt far nearer in spirit to Tai Haruru than he did to the little parson, he yet preferred Samuel's more invigorating faith. Tai Haruru laughed suddenly and clapped him on the shoulder. "Cheer up, boy. I'm not the only man who lives yonder. You'll find men after your own heart down there to laugh and drink with. Eat, drink and be merry is their motto, and it's only Tai Haruru who remembers that to-morrow we die."

Two men was running up the hill to meet them. Their beautiful half-naked bodies were light brown, their hair auburn; both skin and hair seeming to absorb the last of the sunset light and to give it out in a warm glow of welcome. They had bright feathers stuck in their hair that burned like tongues of flame, and they ran both fast and fearlessly.

"Jacky Poto and Kapua Manga the Black Cloud," said Tai Haruru. "They are my friends and will be yours if you always speak courteously, always keep your word and never show fear before them. If you can do that then your 'mana' will always be high with them. Mana is an untranslatable word. Prestige is the nearest one can get to it. But it's an important word in this country. When you lose your mana there's no hope for you."

"Maoris?" gasped William. "I thought they would be black!"

"The Maori rangatira, the true gentleman, is no more black than you are," laughed Tai Haruru. "He comes of the same racial stock as yourself and you will feel at home with him. He's not an alien creature, like the Chink or the Jap. Haere mai, Jacky Poto! Haere mai, Kapua Manga!"

It was very nearly dark now, and the stars burned in the green sky. The bodies of the runners no longer held the light but their answering cry of welcome came clear and strong out of the shadows. "Haere mai! Haere mai!"

That was all right, thought William. That was the genuine cry of his own country.

PART II

THE GREEN DOLPHIN

Whither, O splendid ship, thy white sails crowding,
Leaning across the bosom of the urgent West,
That fearest nor sea rising, nor sky clouding,
Whither away, fair rover, and what thy quest?
ROBERT BRIDGES.

CHAPTER ONE

1

The April wind flung a shower of bright raindrops against the window. The sun was hidden and then gleamed again; there must be a rainbow somewhere, though Marguerite could not see it from her bedroom window, where she sat darning her best petticoat with meticulous care. She was now twenty-seven years old and she had become a less clumsy darner than she had been in her youth. She enjoyed sewing now, for the reason that it gave her the opportunity and the excuse for being alone in her room. She and Marianne no longer shared the same room; she had their old bedroom looking on the street, and Marianne the schoolroom looking towards the sea. Marianne had made this arrangement. To look out upon the sea was to her what solitude was to Marguerite; a way of escape, a relaxation that she considered she deserved and Marguerite did not.

For Marianne, ceaselessly busy from morning till night with good works and social duties, gave it as her opinion that Marguerite was frivolous-minded, selfish and abominably lazy. It was true that she visited the poor occasionally, but according to Marianne her visits were entirely useless because she never could find anything of an improving nature to say, and her rare attendances at dinner parties were rendered equally futile by her apparent inability to make any attempt whatever to be an uplifting intellectual influence in Island society. She seemed to her sister to be devoid of any sense of the duties incumbent upon her owing to her superior advantages of breeding and education. She seemed unaware, even, of the basic fact of her superiority. When she visited an Island cottage with Marianne her laughter as she sat on the floor and played with the children, or returned with gusto the unrefined winks of some old bedridden grandfather whose thoughts should have been upon his latter end and not upon pretty young women, completely distracted the attention of the whole family from the earnest remonstrances and good advice doled out by Marianne. And in society it was the same. Though her beauty gave her great power over the susceptible hearts of young men her conversation with them at the dinner table seemed generally to be upon the subject of crabs and bait rather than upon general reading or Lord Palmerston's latest oration in Parliament. And at home, too, Marianne considered that Marguerite was light-minded and idle. Certainly she was her mother's unfailingly loving companion in those boring and entirely unnecessary domestic activities to which Sophie with increasing age was tending to attach more and more importance, such as the washing of china that was already perfectly clean and the re-tidying of boxes of lace that were already perfectly tidy, a method of wasting time that Marianne considered should by no means be encouraged. Also she would read the sporting news aloud by the hour together to Octavius, whose sight was failing and his temper with it, a daughterly duty that Marianne herself felt incapable of undertaking, so insulted was her intellect by Octavius's low taste in literature. But these services once performed Marguerite made no attempt to do anything useful; she went selfishly to her room and lazed.

Was she really as useless as Marianne thought her, wondered Marguerite this morning? She thought that she was not. She knew that in the eyes of the world her life must seem a very trivial thing, just a passing of the time somehow by a woman whose first youth had passed away without her having been able to lay hands upon the blessed employment that the care of husband and children would have given her, but she knew also that what the world sees of the life of any human creature is not the real life; that life is lived in secret, a reality that moves behind the façade of appearance, like wind behind a painted curtain; only an occasional ripple of the surface, a smile, a sudden light or shadow passing on a face, surprising by its unexpectedness, gives news of something quite other than what is seen. And Marguerite believed that her real life was of value, besides being an immense joy to herself. She assured herself that the practice of the presence of God, that she had learned with such self-discipline of thought and will, was not a selfish thing but something absolutely essential if one's soul was ever to be of the slightest use in this world or the next. This faith had come to her from the book Reverend Mother had given her on that far away day of her childhood, that she had picked up and for the first time read

with attention soon after William had left the Island, a book written
in French and containing the letters written by a barefoot Carmelite
brother nearly two centuries ago. It was a very short book, but that
was perhaps an advantage, for its brevity had enabled Marguerite
to get it by heart. When she was alone she did not laze as Marianne
imagined, she did not even gossip with herself about this, that or the
other, for like Brother Lawrence she had learned by bitter experience that "useless thoughts spoil all", and that nothing so
thoroughly ousts the sense of the presence of God as talking to oneself. Through years of hard mental discipline, carried on with
homely unseen heroism, she had learned to silence the chatter of
self, to focus her mind in meditation, until the beauty dwelt upon
became not a picture but an opening door, and then with sealed lips
but open ears to go away through it by her secret stair to God.
From that place she came away again with power and laughter in
her soul, and with her natural clarity so burnished that she could
radiate them through its clear transparency. She knew that she did
that, and the knowledge delighted her. Wherever she went with her
gift of laughter she saw light spring up in the eyes into which she
looked. During the hours that she spent with her mother, washing
clean china and sorting tidy lace, she could feel the strength ebb from
her to Sophie, who was frightened now because Octavius was going
blind, and she herself had a sharp and alarming pain in her chest
after eating roast beef, and because her life had reached the crest of
the hill and now was going down and old age and death did not
strike her as things she could possibly face; unless she happened to
be sitting with Marguerite, in whose presence, for some reason or
other, all fears seemed to melt away. And it was the same with
Octavius, even more unhappy than Sophie upon the shadowed side
of the hill because he had always believed himself invulnerable to
disaster, and if blindness could happen to Octavius Le Patourel, the
best fellow who ever lived, then either he was not the fellow he had
thought he was, or else the deity was not the discerning creature in
whom he had believed. He was between the Scylla and Charybdis
of humiliation or apostasy, tipping this way and that between them,
and most uncomfortably dizzy; except when Marguerite was reading
the sporting news to him and from the very tones of her voice he
caught a queer unexplainable sense of balance. She steadied him
against that inevitable moment when the scales must fall finally one
way or the other. She knew that she did, and rejoiced in her power.
It seemed that she had been formed as an instrument of comfort, as
Marianne had been formed as a tool for making things. She liked
her sort of person best. She thought it was grand to be her sort of

person. At the bottom of her heart she was not really surprised that everybody loved her.

There were times when she felt the comforter in her cross the barriers of time and space and reach even to William. She would pray for him then, as she prayed for all whom she loved, on and on with determined persistence, until words died in her and she felt her soul lift itself up in speechless adoration, and then she would say to herself with gleeful satisfaction that her prayer was answered. She alone of those who loved him upon the Island believed him to be still alive. No letter had ever come from him. The last they knew of him had been his disappearance in China, and it was natural that everyone should think him dead. But she knew that he was still in this world, and still thought of her. That bond that had always been between them still held. Whenever she felt the pull of it she gave herself to the thought of him with all the strength that she had, and it was for fear of breaking this union that she had chosen to remain unmarried; tenuous though it might be she knew it was more valuable to her than the bodily satisfaction and protection of marriage that she did at times most desperately long for. She never forgot the moment in William's arms on the rock of Le Petit Aiguillon, or the other moment standing beside him on board the Orion when her soul had seemed to recognise him as a tried friend known centuries ago: In his arms only would she find her earthly riches and her shelter; or go poor and storm-beaten all the days of her life. If her body could not companion through life the body of the man whose soul was eternally her friend, then it would walk alone. There was no question about it. That was how it was with her.

But with Marianne, she realised, it was not so. Marianne believed William to be dead, and now that the period of her bitter grief had ended she could pose to herself and the world as a woman who had been separated from the man she loved by death, not by his indifference, and so could turn without diminution of her pride to the second best she had hitherto scorned, but that her passionate nature demanded now for the salvation of her thwarted womanhood. Only the second best was now forthcoming. She had aged and hardened once she had made up her mind that William was dead. There was nothing that Marguerite would not have done for her sister, but it was not in her power to preserve her youth, or to hand on to her her own rejected lovers.

2

Marianne closed her bedroom door with a sigh of relief. She would have a good half hour of quiet before it was time to dress for

dinner. She would be able to lie down and rest her head, that
always ached if she was argued with, as she had been argued with
to-day by those tiresome women at the meeting who had dared to
disagree with her upon the subject of Adult Education for the
Lower Orders, a subject upon which she was the only woman of
good family on the Island entitled to express an opinion, the rest of
the females present either having no education worth speaking of, or
being incapable of handing it on to the Lower Orders if they had it.
Knowledge and the ability to impart it are not always concurrent,
and Marianne knew no woman upon the Island in whom they were
so happily allied as in herself.

She removed her cloak and bonnet, her gown, her three petticoats
and her crinoline, loosened the agonising tightness of her corsets,
wrapped herself in a green silk wrapper and lay down upon her bed
to contemplate the achievements of those same ten years. The contemplation of her achievements always did her headache good, for
they had been remarkable, and had both astounded and infuriated
the Island. She had become not only a leader of fashion but a social
reformer into the bargain, and her name was as well known as that
of the Governor himself. Every task that she attempted she accomplished with a shattering success that did not endear her to those who
had attempted the same thing and failed, and her ruthless exposure
of corruption that had lain comfortably hidden for years beneath
the pleasant surface of Island life was most unpopular. Why rake
up these leaky roofs and lice-infected walls, asked the Island, and
search out these houses of ill-repute, and gambling saloons and
smuggling dens and what and all? These things always existed in the
slums of towns, especially harbour towns, and it was a pity but could
not be helped, and one was much more comfortable not thinking
about them. It was, of course, an age of reform. The underworld of
London was being strenuously coped with, and about time too from
all one heard, but there was really no need to go in for that sort of
thing here. Saint Pierre was such a small town that its little bit of sin
and degradation could quite well be ignored; it was really too microscopic to matter. And anyway it was not seemly that an unmarried
woman should pry into those things; especially it was not seemly
that she should pry into details of the smuggling trade, in which
most of the best families, including her own, had all been heavily
involved at one time or another. These same best families continued
to invite Marianne to their parties, because with every year that
passed her taste and brilliance became more marked and could not
be dispensed with at social functions, but they increasingly disliked
her. And the poor for whom she laboured so indefatigably were not

very fond of her either. They tried to be grateful for what she did for their bodies, but her pride that took gratitude and admiration so completely for granted was a source of acerbity to their souls.

For Marianne had never with deliberate intent sought to enter the valley of humiliation. Moments of humility came to her sometimes, as on that night aboard the Orion, but they came without her wish and she thrust them from her instantly. If she gave in to them, she thought, she would be so weakened that she would not be able to live. In the year of grace eighteen hundred and fifty it was not easy for an unmarried woman of thirty-two either to win or to maintain a position of importance. It was marriage and motherhood that won authority for a woman, not efficiency. It needed all Marianne's fighting ability to hold her own among young matrons of her own age; and to hold her own, and if possible to outstrip her contemporaries, was, she thought, as necessary for her well-being as light and air. Her position in the world was all she had, the only thing that made life worth living; except the strange love that was growing up in her, the hungry, mystical love of the poor whose seed had been sown when as a child she had waited in the doctor's waiting room, and had been brought to birth by her promise to him.

She did not understand it. Lying on her bed she marvelled that the simple fulfilment of a vow made long ago to a dead man could have had such astounding results in her own soul. She had not known, when she first gritted her teeth and set herself to face depravity and dirt and pain for Dr. Ozanne's sake, that after long years the healing of diseased bodies and the sweetening of evil conditions would become such a passion with her that she could even welcome the vileness that enabled her to give it satisfaction. If she stopped to think she was a little horrified by the eagerness of her approach to sordid things. It was partly due, she knew, to her passion for experience, her longing to build beauty where had been ugliness, her love of stamping her personality upon her surroundings, her love of danger and her love of guiding others for their good, as she would have guided William if he had not died, William who had been so weak and faulty and so in need of her strength and her protection. But in her love of the poor there was something more than all this, and she did not know what it was. She did not realise that they stood to her for something necessary to salvation, that great principle of childlikeness that she sensed as a presence standing by her, for ever demanding something of her and for ever unsatisfied with what she gave; even as she was unsatisfied by the hungry aching of her heart that was all the return she seemed to get for the magnificence of her service. She thought that she loved when she tried to mould what she cared for to her own fine pattern, but she was far yet from the child-like abandoned cry of love, "ton peuple sera mon peuple, et ton Dieu sera mon Dieu." Love was in her, its tentacles wound about her will and pride, but they were tiny as the fingers of a little child and had no strength.

From where she lay on the bed she could see the sea and the harbour, and hear the spring voices of wind and rain and bird song sounding about the house. There was a rainbow arched over the sea beyond the harbour and in its perfect half-circle there appeared, seen dimly through the veil of a power, the phantom of a white-sailed ship. Tears gathered and made stiff tracks from the corners of her eyes to her ears before they trickled to the pillow. She rubbed them away angrily with her handkerchief, for weeping was always unbecoming to her, and she indulged in no weakness that would cause her fading charms to recede even quicker than they were doing anyhow. It was absurd to be for ever stabbed by the sight of a sailing ship. Both William and the Green Dolphin had sailed out of her life so long ago that it was useless to think of them any more. Perhaps it was really rather silly of her to have chosen this room that looked out upon the sea. She picked up her cut glass scent bottle, breathed in its scent of frangipani, and resolutely closed her eyes.

She was disturbed by Marguerite.

"The packet is in!" cried Marguerite. "I saw it from the passage window. Marianne, the packet is in!"

"What of it?" asked Marianne dampingly, without opening her eyes.

Marguerite, standing in the window, laughed and refused to be damped. "The packet coming in always excites me," she said. "One never knows what it will bring."

"What could it bring?" asked Marianne.

"Once it brought William and his father," said Marguerite.

Marianne sat up suddenly. "How dare you!" she whispered, trembling with almost hysterical anger. "How dare you! You ought to know that I cannot bear to speak of them. All the understanding and love I ever had they gave me. When they went out of my life there was nothing left . . . except the poor . . . except the poor."

Marguerite came to the foot of the four-poster and stood looking down at her sister with love and compunction. Unerring though she was in most of her human contacts she was somehow always a blundering idiot with Marianne. She ought to have remembered that though to her way of thinking, that tinged all things with that quality of eternity that she had discovered as the ground of existence, no past happiness can ever be cancelled out by later misfortune, to

Marianne's way of thinking the experience of the moment was the only thing that mattered. She could not see her life as a complete and timeless thing, and roam back and forth at will through the spaces of it and rest herself where there were wells of cool water and green shade; to her it was a series of isolated footprints in the sand, with nothingness ahead, and the sea of time rolling in behind to obliterate them one by one.

"Why must you come bursting into my room without even knocking?" demanded Marianne. "You behave like a schoolgirl still. An undisciplined, impetuous schoolgirl. It's ridiculous at your age."

Marguerite laughed, quite unruffled by the tirade. It was one of the most exasperating things about her, Marianne thought, that she seemed nowadays impervious to annoyance. If she would have cancelled out temper with temper sometimes, as she had done in her girlhood, they would have got on better, for it is very hard not to dislike those who are the cause of the accusing of one's conscience. And yet she never quite ceased to love Marguerite. She was her little sister and they had both of them lost William.

"I came to see if your head was bad and if you'd like to go to bed before dinner," said Marguerite.

"My head's splitting," snapped Marianne. "But what would be the good of going to bed? I'd have Mamma knocking at the door every five minutes, and Papa perpetually bellowing up the stairs to know how I was. Never, never, can they leave us alone."

"They made us and they want us to be happy," explained Marguerite. "When things go wrong they are perpetually at work upon us, like someone unpicking a crooked piece of needlework to get it right again."

"Most annoying," snapped Marianne. "So I shall get up. Give me a dose of camphor julep and find me my magenta tarlatan."

She took the restorative and lay back on her pillows, watching her sister. Marguerite had already changed her gown and her crinoline was covered by a frothing mass of primrose-coloured flounces that set off her fair beauty to perfection. She had a little bunch of the first primroses, her favourite flower, pinned into the front of it. She was very lovely still "Because she feels nothing," thought Marianne. "She is colder than any ice."

Marguerite set out the magenta gown and searched in the trinket box for the heavy gold bracelets and locket that went with it. "Why, here are your green earrings," she said. "You've not worn them for years." She was looking at them as they lay in the palm of her left hand and failed to notice that Marianne was sitting bolt upright again, that once more she had said the wrong thing. "The markings in the stone are so lovely," she murmured. "Like ferns and fishes. One ought to be able to see things in this stone, as fortune tellers do in crystals. Marianne, I can see a little house by a river, with huge ferns all about it, and behind it are great woods."

"Give them to me," commanded Marianne, and Marguerite gave them. Holding her aching head with one hand she looked at them and for just a moment, wrought upon by the power of suggestion, she thought she saw the little house. Then it was gone. "Nonsense," she said, but she hung the earrings in her ears for the first time for years. Marguerite should not touch them again. That little house, whatever it was, was hers, not Marguerite's.

Then she got off the bed, and Marguerite, while she held herself braced to the bedpost, laced her corsets tight again, helped her on with her crinoline and petticoats and put the magenta tarlatan over her head. It was a magnificent garment, twenty yards of material having gone to the making of it, not counting the frills. As Marguerite hooked it up silence fell between them, and a sense of awe, as though they were preparing for some great moment in their lives. Marguerite took the little bunch of primroses from her own dress and pinned it into Marianne's. "For luck," she said. The packet was at anchor in the harbour now, her masts bare, and the spring voices of wind and rain and birdsong sounded about the house.

3

Every evening after dinner the four of them played piquette for the amusement of Octavius, who could still just manage to see the cards. But he played fumblingly and his slowness drove Marianne almost to desperation, as did Sophie's gentle sighs and Marguerite's smiling inexhaustible patience. And she hated the parlour too, that had been the setting for so much deadly boredom for so many years; especially did she hate it when as to-night the dusk was closing in with a storm of sudden heavy rain, the shadows were gathering in the corners of the room and the lighted candles on the card table lit up their aging faces with a gleam of mockery.

Her usually steady nerves were clamorous to-night. She could have screamed when a log fell in the fire, and a sudden rat-tat at the front door, sounding loudly through the wind, made her drop her cards and press her clenched hands against her aching temples.

"Marianne!" expostulated her mother.

"It's only the post," said Marguerite. "Charlotte will bring it in."

A tall, fair-haired woman entered with letters on a silver salver, and handed them to Octavius. She was Charlotte Marquand, whose little boy's life Edmond Ozanne's timely surgery and Marianne's after-care had saved to be a thing of boisterous and happy health. Three years ago Charlotte's good-for-nothing husband had been drowned at sea, and Marianne had immediately announced her intention of bringing the whole family to Le Paradis. Octavius and Sophie had expostulated frantically, for not only was the family young and boisterous but Charlotte was a devout Catholic, and they feared not only for the tympanums of their own ears but for their daughters' religious convictions as well. But their expostulations had not been attended to by Marianne. She had got her own way as usual, and Charlotte and her family had been installed at Le Paradis. And Octavius and Sophie had now repented of their expostulations, for Charlotte had developed into an excellent house-keeper, had trained her children very carefully to be both invisible and dumb when Monsieur and Madame were in the house, and had kept her religious convictions to herself. Marianne had no more loyal friend in the whole world than Charlotte, yet as she turned to leave the room and her eyes moved from one sister to the other, they rested upon Marguerite with adoration. They did this very often and when she saw it Marianne would say in her heart, "Et tu, Brute".

All the cards were laid down now as Octavius lifted his magnifying glass to peer at the envelopes. His letters had to be read aloud to him, but he liked to study the envelopes for himself first before he handed them over to Sophie or Marguerite; the action a little alleviated the bitterness of his dependence. Usually the three ladies waited without speaking until he had done, but to-day Marguerite's voice, very quiet and gentle, slid into the silence, parting it, shearing away the smooth continuity of life that lay behind them from the troubled parted years that were to come.

"There is a letter there in William's handwriting."

On the other side of the chasm, stunned as they were, silence held them again for just a moment, and in that moment Marguerite was suddenly vividly conscious of the familiar little scene about her that unlike Marianne she had always loved and found more full of beauty than of boredom. . . . The shadowed room, the tall silver candlesticks holding the petals of light that were reflected in the dark polished wood of the table, the beautiful colours of the women's gowns, magenta, primrose and blue, Octavius's handsome grey bent head. . . . She knew, as the little scene suddenly burned up before her eyes like a flame, that it was the last time she would see it so, and that she would remember it until she died.

Then Marianne, the strong-minded vigorous Marianne, screamed and fell sideways in a dead faint into her mother's arms.

Thereafter, for a few minutes, all was bustle. She was laid upon the sofa, her gown was unhooked and her corsets unlaced. Marguerite ran for the camphor julep and her sister's smelling bottle while Octavius smacked the hands of his firstborn and Sophie held burnt feathers beneath her nose.

She recovered quickly and with determination, sat up and swung her feet to the floor. "Give me the letter," she commanded.

"It is addressed to me," said Octavius obstinately. "And Marguerite shall read it."

It was a long letter, crossed and re-crossed. Marguerite carried it to the table, sat down and spread out the sheets where the candle-light fell upon them. As her hand lay on the pages she knew with absolute conviction that William had penned them with a heart full of love for her, and she had no doubt that what he had to say was something that would bring them together even in this world. Her face was shining with her love and joy, so that Sophie thought she had never seen her look so beautiful, but her heart was aching for Marianne. "She will have to know now that it is me William loves," she thought. "What can I do? There is nothing I can do now except read the letter right through in a very steady voice. I must not show what I feel. Whatever the letter says I must read it in a very steady voice." And she pulled one of the candles a little nearer, and from beginning to end she read the letter in a very steady voice.

William began by saying that since leaving the Navy and emigrating to New Zealand ten years ago he had written to them twice, but had received no answers to his letters. The first he had written soon after his landing, and when he had received no answer to it he had thought that perhaps it had been lost at sea, but his enquiries had brought him no information as to the fate of the schooner that had carried it. The second he had written after the outbreak of the Maori War to tell them, in case they had received his first letter and knew of his whereabouts, not to be anxious because he knew in his heart that he would not die in the conflict. When he had received no answer to that letter either, though of course he knew that in the confusion of the times that also was only too likely to have gone astray, he had nevertheless grown afraid for the Le Patourels themselves. Then he went on to say that only a few weeks before the penning of this present letter, by one of those strange chances that seem like the miraculous intervention of God himself, a Channel Islander had landed in New Zealand and come to see him. This man was unknown to the Le Patourels but knew of them, and had given him news of them and their circumstances, and he had been happy to know them in good health. Then he wrote briefly of his experiences during the ten years since had left them. Three years of desperate back-breaking work, employed as a lumberman by an Englishman, one Timothy Haslam, who went by the name of Tai Haruru, had ended with the outbreak of a war that was the result of endless land disputes with the Maoris, with whom, William confessed, he had been from first to last in complete sympathy. "They love their native soil as I love the Island," he wrote. "It was agony to have it wrested from them by the white man. 'The parent who maintains us is the land,' they say. 'Die for the land! Die for the land!' I do not know what you will think of me, but I went into the bush with my friend Tai Haruru and I lived with the Maoris, and I helped him to care for their wounded and their sick. I did not fight against my own countrymen, of course, but I did not fight for them. I did not fight at all. It was a strange and terrible war, for there were a few white men who sided with the Maoris as I did, and there were Maoris who fought for the white man. At first things went well for the Maoris, for they outnumbered the settlers, but when troops were sent from Australia equipped with more modern weapons than the Maoris had, that was the end of it, for courage is no use against guns, or singleness of mind against a bullet. The weakest in equipment, thought not in greatness of heart, went to the wall, and five years ago there was peace upon the surface of things, and Tai Haruru and I went back to the lumber trade.

"We have prospered since then, for the peace has been maintained and we have a great governor, Sir George Grey, whose 'mana' is the best guarantee of it that we could ask for. With increasing confidence the number of settlers is also increasing. That means new houses and a greater demand for wood here in New Zealand than there has ever been. The export trade is also steadily increasing, as shipping facilities improve and labour is more easily come by. Now I am in partnership with Tai Haruru, my worst years of struggle are behind me and I am a fairly successful business man. I live in the same settlement, beside a creek that takes one very quickly to the sea, to which Tai Haruru first brought me, but I have bought land to make a garden and I am building a house of my own. Indeed I have everything a man can wish for, except a wife.

"And now, sir, I come to the purpose of this letter. My Island friend told me, to my great astonishment, that your daughter Marianne is still unmarried. I have loved her all my life. No other woman has ever taken her place in my heart. The thought of her has through many years of trouble and conflict kept me sane. Is it possible that you could permit her, and that she would be willing, to come out to New Zealand and be my wife? I cannot offer her an easy life. My home is several days' journey from Wellington, and though I am what is termed a well-to-do man in these parts the life is lonely and rough for a gentlewoman. Moreover there is danger in it. Though most people are confident that peace has come to stay I do not myself think it impossible that 'the fire in the fern', as we called the Maori War, is merely smouldering and may break out again in years to come. These are the disadvantages, and I feel it only right to set them before you. But on the credit side I can offer your daughter a free and active existence in a country of great beauty. I know she loves winds, and wide spaces, and austerity and truth, and these she will find in pioneer life in this land. The voyage out is, I know, lengthy and arduous, and owing to the unfortunate fact that I left the Service in rather regrettable circumstances, I am unable to return to my native land to fetch her. But since the happy dawning of the days of peace I have once more made the acquaintance of my old benefactor Captain O'Hara, whose clipper the Green Dolphin is now engaged in the wool trade between England and New Zealand. He is racing home to England with a cargo and will carry this letter with him, remaining at the West India Docks for some weeks for refitting. If your daughter can find it in her heart to make me the happiest man on earth Captain O'Hara will deem it an honour to bring her out to New Zealand on his ship, and will take the most paternal care of her, and it is probable that there will be some other passengers also to provide the female companionship that Madame Le Patourel will no doubt deem necessary for her daughter upon so long a voyage. The Green Dolphin is an old ship now, but seaworthy, and still one of the finest clippers flying the Red Ensign. Meanwhile Captain O'Hara has information that a sister ship, the Good Hope, will be leaving the docks a couple of weeks after his own arrival. A letter sent care of her skipper Charles Martin, whose address in England I append at the end of this letter, with that of Captain O'Hara, will reach New Zealand some weeks before the Green Dolphin, and will tell me whether or not I may look forward to the exquisite felicity of welcoming your daughter as my wife. I enclose a short note for your daughter, and I send my humble duty to yourself and Madame Le Patourel, and I sign myself with trembling hope and deepest, most grateful affection, your unworthy yet devoted son, William Ozanne."

Marianne was on her feet, her cheeks on fire and her eyes blazing. "The note!" she cried. "The note he wrote for me myself. Where is it?"

"I must have left it behind in the envelope," said Marguerite, and her hands groped upon the table as though she, as well as Octavius, were going blind. It was Sophie who picked up the envelope, shook out the little cocked hat of a note inside, and handed it to Marianne, who clutched it as though it were all the treasure of the world, turned away from her family with a passionate frou-frou of silken petticoats, carried it to the window and read it by the last light of the dying day.

Meanwhile Sophie gently pulled William's letter towards her and turned back the sheets to the place, the only place, where the name of the lady whom William desired to marry had been set down in black and white. "Marianne." Yes, it was Marianne. William's boyish handwriting was unmistakably clear. She laid the sheet down again and looked at Marguerite, who sat with her head held high and a smile on her lips and a face the colour of ashes. Sophie did not even dare to touch her hand beneath the table. She saw that for the moment she must be left alone. If she was touched she would break.

"The young blackguard!" said Octavius angrily. " 'Left the Navy in regrettable circumstances.' That means he deserted. After all the money I spent on him, he deserted. The blackguard!"

Marianne, her high heels tapping, left the window and came back into the light. She stood there looking for the first time in her life utterly beautiful. Her mouth was passionate and trembling, her eyes hungry and bright. She was oblivious of the tears on her face or of the fact that both hands were clasping her letter on her breast; until they lifted it that she might kiss it before she pushed it away inside her dress. She did not know what she did. She was unselfconscious and lovely, transfigured and made anew.

"The damned cheek of it!" raged Octavius, who could see the face of neither daughter clearly. "The overweening, outrageous conceit of the man. That he should imagine that a daughter of mine, delicately nurtured, well-trained in all the Christian virtues, could for one single moment consent to ally herself with such a man as he is, a deserter and a common lumberman, the companion of thieves and murderers and worse in a savage country fit only for convicts to live in, brands the man as a fool as well as a knave. Marguerite, fetch pen and ink and take a letter down at my dictation. There is no time to waste, for the packet leaves in the morning and I run no risk of the Good Hope sailing for New Zealand without a letter aboard bearing to William Ozanne my exact opinion of his arrogant presumption."

A slight trembling took Marguerite's body. Her father's bitterness, crashing down in its angry turmoil upon the loving humility on William's letter, was to her the measure of the misery of his soul.

Such injustice was never the outcome of anything but unaccepted, resented pain, visited with sadistic relief upon some innocent victim coming opportunely to hand. It horrified her, even as the abandon of Marianne's rapture, beautiful though it was, horrified her by the nakedness of its revelation of primeval fire. So we're like that under the skin, she thought, we're like that. Savages. Nothing can save us but the grace of God. She turned to Sophie and saw that her mother, aware that one child had been bitterly hurt and that the other was to be wrested from her, was sobbing softly into her lace-trimmed pocket handkerchief. She stretched out her hand and touched her mother's hair. It was a relief to find herself aware again of those about her. For a moment or two, after the dagger had struck, she had been like a dead woman, numbed to all sensation, and only a will resolved before she took up the letter had enabled her to read on mechanically until the end. Now she was herself again, glad of the demands made upon her by her father's bitterness, by Marianne's rapture and her mother's grief. While she answered them she need not face the knowledge of what had happened in her own soul.

"What an absurd to-do about nothing, Papa," said Marianne gaily, but with something of her old hardness showing again in the timbre of her voice. "You speak as though I had been insulted, whereas I have had the honour of a proposal of marriage from a very fine gentleman. It was courteous of William to write to you, Papa, for as I am of age there was really no necessity."

Octavius glared at her. "No daughter of mine shall marry a deserter, a common lumberman, a fellow no better than a convict," he announced.

"I am sorry, Papa, but that is exactly what your daughter intends to do," said Marianne.

And now she was angry too. Standing there in her magenta frock, ablaze with her joy and rage, she was like a vivid flame in the room. One could have warmed one's hands at her, Marguerite thought, and her own soul seemed to catch alight and blaze up too, so that for the moment it was almost easy to say the proper things.

"Well done, Marianne," she cried. "You're brave and you'll be happy. Papa, why should you be angry? And you are unjust to William. He has written you a fine and straightforward letter. However foolish he may have been in the past he has paid for it, and now he is a man of means and quality, a fit husband even for Marianne. We must be glad for them, Papa. And you too, Mamma. A pioneering life won't hurt Marianne. Look at the terrible things she sees, the dreadful places she goes into, when she is working for the poor.

She likes adventure, you know. She likes new experiences. We must all be glad for her."

"Glad for her?" ejaculated Octavius, responding as he never failed to respond to his younger daughter's clear vision and good sense, but still slightly acerbated in temper. "Glad for my daughter to go down on her knees and scrub floors, and cook the dinner, as though she were the wife of a common working man?"

"And the children?" sobbed Sophie. "She'll have babies with perhaps no doctor and no nurse, and her mother not able to be with her!"

Marianne's head went up. "I'm not afraid," she said.

"You don't know what you're talking about!" wept poor Sophie, brandishing her tear-soaked handkerchief. "I've had two and I know. Even with all the doctors for miles round gathered about one's bed one wishes one had never been born!"

"Marianne won't," said Marguerite. "She won't mind about the scrubbing or the cooking or the babies or anything. She will live to the full and be glad."

"Isn't she living to the full now?" demanded the outraged Octavius. "Look at all her good works. She's never at home."

"Yes, Marianne," cried Sophie, clutching at a straw of hope. "How will you bear to leave your poor and the 'Gentlewomen's Mutual Improvement Society'? However will all your charities get on without you? And Charlotte and her children?"

Marianne's rage and long-pent-up resentment suddenly boiled over like an erupting volcano. The room seemed to tremble and grow hot with it.

"My charities!" she stormed. "What good are they? What good have I ever done with them? Because I have a better brain than most women, because I don't let myself be hampered by the stupid conventions that won't let women be useful in the world, because I go where I like and say what I like, I am hated by everyone. If I build up a good piece of work those who dislike me see to it that no one lifts a finger to hold it in its place and it falls to the ground again. I've had to work alone. I've had to carry the whole world on my shoulders, like Atlas, because people hated me too much to help me. One can do no good that way. Unless you are loved the good that you try to do is cancelled out. Even the poor don't love me, though I've worked my fingers to the bone for them. Even Charlotte doesn't love me as much as she loves Marguerite. And yet I *am* love-worthy, I *am*, I *am*! All my life I've been misunderstood, except by William and his father. And so now I'm going to William, who understands me, and to a pioneer country where convention won't hamper me at every turn, and I shall be loved and respected and some real use in the world at last!"

The fingers of one hand closed convulsively over William's love letter, that she had thrust into the bodice of her dress, and the crackle of the paper set her mind leaping fiercely upon another track. "William's letter must be answered, Papa, and now! Now at once! The packet leaves in the morning and the letter must be on it. Pierre must go down to the harbour with it to-night, for the Green Dolphin may have been delayed, and the Good Hope sailing perhaps this week. Write *now*, Papa. Dictate the letter to Mamma. No, *not* Marguerite, *Mamma*. He must recognise the handwriting of one of my parents. The ink, Marguerite, the paper and the wax. Quickly! Quickly!"

Deafened and bewildered, Sophie and Octavius gave themselves into the hands of their daughters. The cards were swept from the table, ink and wax and paper spread out instead. It was, in the end, Marguerite who dictated the letter, for Octavius's wits seemed to have deserted him. It was a kindly, courteous letter, calculated to rejoice the heart of any prospective son-in-law. The only odd thing about it was that from first to last the Christian name of the lady was not mentioned. She was referred to throughout as "my daughter". For Marguerite had not yet absolutely grasped the truth of what had happened. When a blow falls suddenly the human mind quickly wraps itself in protective layers of unbelief lest the shock prove more than can be borne. They peel off one by one and it was the last one left that kept Marguerite, although unconsciously, from giving the name "Marianne" to William's bride.

Sophie finished writing the letter, Octavius signed it, and Marguerite sprinkled the sand to dry the ink. "Will you not write him a little note?" she asked Marianne.

It seemed that Marianne in her exaltation had not thought of this, and was quite incapable of composition. All she could do, when Marguerite pushed a piece of paper towards her, was write the three words "I love you" in a shaky unrecognizable handwriting. Then she took the little bunch of primroses that Marguerite had given her from her dress, kissed them, and folded them within the sheet. At that, with a wholly unprotected mind, Marguerite knew. Her primroses were going to William but she herself might never see him again.

4

At last she was alone in her room and, her common sense still reigning supreme, taking off her corsets. Never weep in corsets.

Hearts break with less pain if there is no restricting band of whale-bone clamped upon the top of them. It is also wiser, if you are about to fall into an abyss of misery, to get into bed first, for once you have fallen it will not be easy to get up and clean your teeth and brush your hair and tie on your nightcap. Marguerite was wise, and she did all these things with punctilious care before she locked her door, blew out the candles, crept within the shadows of her blue-curtained bed, lay down and knew that she had believed a lie. It wasn't true that William loved her. Either he had never loved her, and she had deceived herself from the very beginning, or else he had once loved her a little and then her cowardice when Dr. Ozanne had been taken ill, that shrinking from illness that she had since learned to overcome, had come between them and turned him to Marianne, who had been so brave and had helped him so wonderfully through those last days. She remembered now how William had clung to Marianne at that time, and how his last look had been for her. In either case that perfect union in which she had believed had never existed. It was a lie and she had been the most conceited idiot ever born to imagine that she had it in her to inspire it. Why should any man love her in that way? Why? She saw now that there was nothing in her to merit such a love. She was nothing, a nonentity with a pretty face, a weak, conceited, self-deceiving fool; and what she had believed had been a lie.

And if that was a lie, was there any truth anywhere in her life? Her union with the earthly love had stood to her as a sort of symbol of another union. If she had deceived herself in the matter of this earthly union had she not also deceived herself in the matter of the heavenly one? Was it really true that she had rested in the presence of God, and come from it to strengthen and comfort, or had she merely imagined it? "I've imagined it," she said, and fell immediately into a pit of darkness so terrible that she thought she would go mad. "Why should I think that I could be so used by God?" she kept asking herself. "Why should I be? What is there in me to use? I am nothing—nothing—nothing."

The hours of her humiliation passed slowly and leadenly in the darkness. Once she heard her mother come to her door and knock softly, and for some moments she lay trying to force herself to get up and admit the companionship she did not want, but just as she was lifting herself up Sophie went away again and she thanked her mother in her heart for her understanding. I am nothing—nothing—nothing. She was clinging to that, she found, as to a sort of anchor, because it kept her from having to face the terrible possibility that God Himself was not, and the realisation of God's nothingness would be the final horror that could not be borne. Yet as time passed she knew that that possibility, too, must be faced. She must let go of the very last thing left her, the knowledge of her own nothingness, and face it. And she let go, and looked around for God and did not find Him; and then there was nothing, except the dark night.

But there *was* the dark night. Very slowly she became conscious of it, and then she found that she was hugging it to her, wrapping herself in it as though it were a cloak to hide her in this hour of her humiliation. For a long while the night was all that she had, and then suddenly, like a sword stabbing the darkness, came a trill of music. It was a bird welcoming the dawn. That, too, was added. She drew back one of the curtains of her bed and saw a patch of grey light where the window was. That also. During the hours of the night she had been completely stripped, and now one by one a few things were being handed to her for the clothing of her naked, shivering, humiliated soul. For a few things one must have to make one decent if one was to step forth again upon the highway. For that, obviously, impossible though the task seemed to her at this moment, was what she had to do as soon as the full day came, because there wasn't anything else that she could do. She had to go on living and serving, with the living and serving stripped of all pleasure now that she could no longer enjoy the delight of knowing herself the bringer of God's gifts. But there would be something. There would be darkness and light, night and day, both sweet things, and music linking them together. The full glory of the dawn chorus seemed all about her as she dragged herself out of bed and set to work with slow laborious movements to wash and dress herself. In her exhaustion she was so long over her toilet that it was full day by the time she pulled back the muslin curtains that covered her window and flung it wide and leaned out, the scent of the spring earth rushing up to meet her. That also was given back. . . . By whom?

CHAPTER TWO

Marianne sat bolt upright in the hackney coach, jogging through the cobbled streets of London towards the West India Docks. Incredible though it might seem, she, who had never left the Island in her life, had performed the whole amazing, stupendous journey to London entirely by herself. Her family, Sophie and Octavius and Marguerite, had implored her to let them come with her and see her on board the Green Dolphin, but she had curtly refused. From the moment when the packet left the harbour of Saint Pierre she had wanted to perform alone this epic journey to the man she loved.

"My darling," had run his little cocked hat note to her, "have you the courage to leave your little island and come out to me quite alone? It will be a great undertaking for you, and I know it. Indeed it amazes me that I can even ask such a thing of you; only I know that you and I are one, that we always have been and always will be. I have known that increasingly through all these years of parting. There have been times when you have felt so near that I could have put out my hand and touched you. And so I know that though it must be alone and through much danger, yet you will come. William."

The hackney coach gave a great jolt over a heap of garbage and with one hand she held tightly to Old Nick in his cage on the seat beside her, while with the other she clutched her reticule. It held her money and her jewels, and she had scarcely let go of it day or night since she left the Island. When she was in bed she hugged it to her breast, and when she ate she sat on it. It was a pretty reticule, made of bottle-green velvet with a very strong clasp. It matched her new green merino travelling dress trimmed with bands of velvet, with a matching cloak lined with orange satin, and her green velvet bonnet with an orange feather in it, and a thick green curtain veil whose green silk cord had a little gold bobble on the end. She had a green umbrella, too, with a golden ring at the top that fitted over her arm, and of course she wore her green earrings. Altogether it was the most fetching costume she had ever had, and she intended to put it on when she landed in New Zealand, with her green umbrella hung on her arm, Nick in his cage in one hand and her reticule in the other.

Nick, of course, was a dreadful nuisance, but she had not for one moment contemplated leaving him behind. He had been a part of William's childhood, and beloved of Dr. Ozanne, and she was sure that William would be pleased to see him. Evidently Old Nick thought so too, for he had spruced up in an amazing manner since they set sail from the Island and had made nothing at all of the toils of the journey. He had, indeed, been all impatience. "Up aloft, lad," he now adjured the driver. "Get for'ard, you tripe hound! What the blue, blazing hell——"

Marianne pulled over his cage the covering of dark green plush, shaped like a bell, that Marguerite had made for occasions like this, and he was silent. It was a handsome covering, worked with the parrot's initials—O.N.O.—in scarlet crewel work. It had been Marguerite's own idea to make it, knowing how embarrassing Old Nick

Ozanne's outspoken comments could prove. Marguerite had been full of these merry jokes during those hurried weeks of preparation on the Island. Marianne wondered what she would have done without her, for Sophie and Octavius, feeling that they would never see their elder daughter again, had been plunged in gloom, and friends and neighbours had done little to hide their dumbfounded astonishment that any man in possession of his senses could plead across hundreds of miles of sea, after an absence of ten years, for Marianne Le Patourel to come to him as the companion of his bed and board. But Marguerite had resolutely kept before the minds of them all that weddings are occasions for joy and festivity. The trousseau, the good-bye parties, even the final farewells, had been lifted out of the doldrums by her gift of laughter. Marianne would never forget how good she had been, even though she hadn't looked at all well during those weeks. Had Marianne not been so self-absorbed she would have been full of consternation at the exhaustion that every now and then had seemed to submerge Marguerite's gaiety. But as it was she had just thought it natural that Marguerite should look tired, when they were working day and night at the trousseau, and she had thanked God that her sister had outgrown that childish infatuation for William. Dear Marguerite! Never had she felt so full of love for her as when, the victor in the fight for William, she had stood upon the deck of the moving packet and waved to her where she stood in the spring sunshine by the harbour wall. Marguerite had seen her off alone, for Sophie and Octavius had been too upset to leave Le Paradis. That was Marianne's last memory of the Island—her tall sister standing in her blue cloak in the sunshine against the background of the tumbled roofs of Saint Pierre, waving her lace handkerchief gaily over her head.

From Saint Pierre to this jolting hackney coach—what a journey it had been! She had left the Island in fine weather, with a fair wind, and the long day's voyage to England had been sheer joy. She had sat enthroned upon the pyramid of her trunks upon the deck, keeping her eye upon them, Old Nick beside her, her umbrella in one hand and her reticule in the other, her food for the day in a neat parcel upon her lap, and looked out exultingly upon the sparkling sea. At last! The years of her frustration were behind her, she had thought, and she was setting sail for adventure, for love, for battle, for pain, for that full measure of experience of which she was capable.

Weymouth! Fashionable, salubrious Weymouth, beloved of the Aristocracy, patronised by Royalty, she had read of it often and at last her eyes had beheld it. As a Crusader looking upon the Holy

Places so had she looked upon the bathing machines of Weymouth. Hundreds of them, and all so brightly painted! Down those steps Crowned and Coroneted Heads had stepped with courage and determination, and dipped up and down in the brine. And the fashionable folk—thousands of them, so it had seemed to Marianne —strolling up and down on the esplanade, and the chariots and phaetons and britschkas rolling by in their millions on the road behind them, and the grey houses with their windows and door-knockers winking in the sun stretching on and on apparently for ever, as though this magical town had got no end. It had been almost too much for Marianne. Like the Queen of Sheba, the half had not been told her. So overwhelmed had she been that it had been a matter for thanksgiving that when the packet had glided to its anchorage, and she sought for a hackney coach, she had been taken possession of by a fatherly driver who had daughters of his own at home and conveyed her and her baggage to the Temperance Hotel beside the station without taking any further advantage of her exalted condition than charging her double for the fare.

Sophie did not know much about foreign travel; in fact the one and only thing she did know about it was that young females must always stay at Temperance Hotels if they do not want to be molested by the male. But when Sophie had insisted that Marianne stay always at Temperance Hotels she had not known that those virtuous places are generally situated next to railway stations. She had not known that for the rest of Marianne's life the two words Temperance Hotel would be a pseudonym for the condition known as ecstasy.

For her bedroom window at Weymouth had framed a view of the station. Steam Engines! Marianne had read about them. She knew, perhaps, more about their internal affairs than any woman living, but never until the night at Weymouth had her eyes beheld them. She was thirty-two years old and never before had she seen a Steam Engine. She had knelt at the bedroom window, her precious reticule clasped only mechanically to her bosom, and worship had filled her soul. She had not been able to tear herself from her window even to go down to the coffee room and have some supper. She had been kneeling by the window when the chambermaid brought her hot water at bed-time, and she had been in the same position when she was called next morning in time to catch the train that would carry her to London. Whether she had ever gone to bed at all the chambermaid had no idea.

She never forgot the subsequent marvellous journey. She had sat entranced, wearing an old grey cloak and bonnet and well shrouded in veils against the streaming smoke and soot, the happiest woman in the world, as the great and mighty engine pulled them by the miraculous principle of internal combustion, and at the breath-taking speed of some forty-five miles an hour, through the loveliness of the English spring.

The journey had ended in the amazement and confusion of London itself. There she had stayed for three days with a friend of Sophie's childhood, a woman who had left the Island as a girl and had married a wealthy London solicitor. She was a brilliant and polished woman of the world and had been fully prepared to patronise the middle-aged, plain, travel-stained and exhausted little woman who had been set down with a parrot and a pyramid of boxes upon the snowy steps of her Park Lane mansion. And so had the butler, the footmen and the lady's-maid. And for the period of that one evening Marianne had submitted to patronage, so over-whelmed had she been by the hugeness, the magnificence, the crowds, the noise and the squalor of this city. Weymouth had been positively eclipsed. She had not known that so many people could live all together in any one city, or dwell in such a multitude of houses, or reach such extremes of poverty and grandeur, to make so much noise and dirt, and for just a few hours her spirit had quailed and sunk beneath the immense impact of the fact of London.

But the next morning she had sailed down to ten o'clock breakfast in her very smartest trousseau gown, nipped her hostess's patronage in the bud with finality but no discourtesy, flattered her host, put the servants in their places by the very carriage of her head and the quality of her smile, and even got London itself into focus as a mere town that derived its present importance from the fact that Mari-anne Le Patourel was now the central point of its activity.

For the rest of the period of her stay, though inwardly astonished to the point of stupefaction, she had maintained the most perfect out-ward nonchalance. And the only moment when she had failed in the slightest degree to behave as a gentlewoman should was when she had flatly refused the customary attendance of a servant in her drive to the docks. She had even refused the loan of her host's carriage; she had chosen to make the journey alone in a hackney coach from Park Lane to the Green Dolphin. "I'll not be spied on," she had said to herself. "If, when I see the Green Dolphin, I behave like a little girl of six arriving at her first party, there shan't be a soul to see."

Fortunately her driver knew the way to the docks even when in liquor. They rocked and jolted on over the cobbles, and then they rocked to a standstill, and Marianne jumped out like a little girl arriving at her first party and jerked her veil aside. Yes, there she

was, the lovely Green Dolphin, incomparable as ever. She might be
old now, but she was no whit less beautiful; indeed like all fine
characters she seemed to have grown in dignity and grace with the
passing of the years. Hastily paying the driver and leaving her
luggage to look after itself, clutching only her reticule, umbrella and
parrot, she made her way up the gangplank with rustling skirts and
swinging crinoline, and like William at the Chinese port ran straight
to Captain O'Hara's cabin.

He was there, standing by the teak table with a letter in his hand.
"Captain O'Hara! Captain O'Hara!" she cried, dropped Old Nick
and ran straight into his arms. It was an outrageous thing for the
prim, elegant, self-controlled Mademoiselle Le Patourel to do, but
she was no longer Mademoiselle Le Patourel, she was a little girl at a
party. She would have kissed him if she could have reached up as
far as his round, red, astonished countenance. As it was she stood
on tiptoe with her arms round his neck and laughed up into his
face.

He held her with appreciation, for she was a smart little woman in
her orange and green, exquisitely perfumed, tiny and dainty as a
Dresden figure, and with the light in her eyes and the colour in her
cheeks she was almost pretty, but he had no idea who she was until
suddenly he saw the greenstone earrings swinging in her ears. Then
he roared with laughter, picked her up and kissed her with great
smacking kisses one upon each cheek.

"So it's you, me dear!" he shouted. "Begorra, if it isn't the little
green enchantress after all!"

"Who did you think it was?" she asked him.

"Your husband to be, me dear, that great stupid fellow William
Ozanne, had not the time to tell me much about ye before I left New
Zealand. His horse fell lame on the road to Wellington an' when he
reached the harbour he'd only time to fling me the letter for ye, an'
shout out a few instructions before I sailed. 'Is it the little green
enchantress?' I shouted to him as he went off down the gang-
plank. 'No,' he shouted back. 'The more fool you,' said I. 'You've
not the sense ye were born with.' But here ye are after all, me
dear."

"He'd not have known whom you meant by the green enchantress," laughed Marianne. "But I'm the girl to whom you gave the
earrings, Captain O'Hara. Who else could be William's wife? You
and I and William and the Green Dolphin—we're all bound up
together. And Nat. Where's Nat?"

"Aboard," said Captain O'Hara. "Polishin' your cabin for the
nine hundredth and ninetieth time, bedad. 'Tisn't every day of the

week the Green Dolphin has a lady passenger. There's a second one, too, a Mrs. Dunbar who's to be your chaperon, God help you. The crew's as nervous as a pack of cats."

They were sitting one on each side of the teak table now, appraising each other. Old Nick, in spite of his muffling cover, poured out a volley of nautical oaths from his position on the floor, and squawked and fluttered in a frenzy of delight. For he knew quite well that this was not a frail craft like the packet that had brought him to England, but a real ship, a deep sea ship, that would sail on and on for week after week. He was a real old shellback, no landsman, and like Marianne he was only himself when he could smell the sea.

Captain O'Hara was now an old man, Marianne noticed with something of outrage, for it struck her as preposterous that old age should dare to lay its hand upon anything so superbly vigorous as the man she had first seen twenty years ago in the harbour of Saint Pierre. His face was as round and red as ever, but covered with a network of fine wrinkles like the markings on a shrivelled apple. His great china teeth did not fit as well as they did and were apt to fall out suddenly. His huge old-fashioned wig, a little too big for him now, fell sideways when he laughed, and there was in his eyes a look of bewilderment, as though the slight failing of his tremendous strength had taken him by surprise and he did not quite know what one did about it. Marianne put out a small hand impulsively and laid it on his, and wished with all her heart and soul that old age would be merciful to him.

Captain O'Hara took her hand and considered her with kindness but considerable gravity. Her little-girl mood had died away now and he saw her for what she was, a prim little middle-aged spinster, elegant but deucedly plain, not at all the sort of woman whom he could imagine a young man like William fancying as a wife. For he could see that she had developed a very considerable will of her own, and something of a temper, and a sharp hard brilliance that might be smart but would be damnably uncomfortable to live with. No, not at all the sort of woman whom he would have expected the easy-going William to fancy as a wife. He could only come to the conclusion that either this woman had changed immeasurably since William last saw her, or else that the boy had far more good horse sense than he had given him credit for. For there was no denying, thought Captain O'Hara, that this woman with her wiry little body and her resolute will was just the type to endure without breaking the hard life that lay before her, and just the type to keep that fellow William with nose to the grindstone and unwilling feet glued firmly to the path of virtue. But he was sorry for William, God help him, he

was sorry for Marianne too, who as she talked to him of her bridegroom seemed to have entirely forgotten, or never to have realised,
that between the boy she had last seen and the man she was to marry
there stretched ten years of pioneer existence. She had no conception of what that was, of course. He looked at her exquisite but
most unsuitable clothes, and her smooth little hands unscarred by
any toil, and he said very soberly, because in spite of her sharpness
he liked the little woman, "God bless ye, me dear. It's meself that's
proud to have you on the Green Dolphin."

CHAPTER THREE

1

He liked her increasingly as the days went by, and so did the crew.
Fastidious in her dress and person though she was, and primly correct in her behaviour, she was yet entirely without squeamishness.
She took the rough with the smooth, made no complaints, and
adjusted herself to rough speech and rough ways with grace and
tact. The presence of Nat, who did not become more handsome as
the years went by, seemed in no way repulsive to her; indeed she
welcomed his dog-like devotion and let him potter about her cabin
in the capacity of lady's-maid to his faithful heart's content. Almost
she seemed to love the little man. "You see," she said to Captain
O'Hara, when he told her to kick out Nat as soon as she could stand
him no longer, "I have always loved the poor, but this is the first
time they have loved me."

"The poor?" ejaculated Captain O'Hara. "Begorra, I have it to
me certain knowledge that Nat has as tidy a fortune stowed away in
an old stocking as any miser could wish for. He don't squander it on
his person. Hasn't bought himself a stitch of clothin' for a hundred
years. Had that nightcap in his cradle, bedad."

"I did not mean that quite literally," said Marianne, with slow
consideration. "When I say I love the poor I mean—at least I think
I mean—that I love that which can take what I have to give, and be
made by it, and in return let me see myself stamped upon it as a king
sees his own head upon the little bit of metal that he has commanded
shall be a coin of the realm."

"Ay," said Captain O'Hara reflectively. "That's what we love,
me dear. Take meself, now. Fightin' a storm takes every ounce that
I am, an' when I'm victor, when the sea takes me imprint, then I
love it. Faith, you might say it is God to me, surely."

A month of the four or five months' voyage was now behind them and they were sailing through halcyon seas, the Atlantic in the friendliest possible mood, giving Marianne no hint at all of what it could do to her if it felt so inclined. The past month had been almost the happiest of her life. The rough seas of the Channel and the Bay had not upset her at all, for she was an excellent sailor and she scarcely knew what physical fear meant. She had sat below undismayed by the sliding, tilting floor of her cabin, the eerie creaks and groans of the woodwork, the gurgling and chuckling of bilge water and the roar of wind and waves. Nat, when he had brought her her meals, had always found her sitting quietly at her embroidery with a little smile on her lips, as though the voices all about her were friendly voices that she loved. And so they had been. During those days and nights she had seemed to herself to be sheltering within the arms of the old Green Dolphin, feeling the throbs of her heart, listening to her good-humoured grumblings and gurglings as a child listens to the complaints of a loving but querulous old nurse who rocks it on her knee. "You'll keep me safe, you old Green Dolphin," she had said. "You'll see to it that I come safe to William."

She had been allowed on deck again just in time to enjoy a moment of experience that was one of the most thrilling of her life—the departing from her of the coast of Europe. It had been at sunset, and wrapping her cloak about her she had crawled up the ladder from her cabin, and up the sloping deck until she had reached the bulwarks, and had clung there gazing like some green ant of a creature, submerged for long in semi-darkness, who has crawled up a swaying blade of grass and holds there perilously at the top, dumbfounded at the wonder of the upper air.

The wind had dropped and the rain had ceased but the racing grey seas had still gone by with snow on their crests, and the Green Dolphin had still muttered and groaned as she climbed upwards with patient dogged weariness, and then chuckled and slithered, and then gurgled and climbed again. The glorious freshness of the air, enveloping her so suddenly and startlingly as she emerged from the stuffiness below, had struck Marianne's soul to a leaping awareness that had answered flame to flame the leaping lights on the horizon. That light had swung away the dark clouds overhead on lifted spears and poured over the sea in a steadily advancing arc of gold, and in the perfect circle thus hollowed out of the darkness there had appeared a vision of blue hills, a white-walled town, a froth of silver foam on the rocks; a vision out of a picture book, a fairytale vision of childhood like that vision of Saint Pierre in the dawn. "Spain," had said Captain O'Hara's voice behind her. "Your last sight of the Europe that cradled ye. Look long, me dear." She had looked long, her pulses throbbing. . . . Europe, mother of her race. Europe, old and lovely, good-bye, good-bye. Paradise of childhood, good-bye. I'll not see you again till life comes round full circle and the gate that a child came out of will be the gate where an old woman enters in. . . . The golden spears had fallen, a sweeping rainstorm had blotted out the vision, and she had turned away to slide once more down the tilted deck and the swaying ladder to her cabin and the shelter of the Green Dolphin's arms. All night she had lain there between sleeping and waking, conscious that now at last she was fully launched on her adventure, that nothing whatever could pluck her back.

And now the Green Dolphin sailed on and on over the halcyon sea, and perhaps when she next caught sight of land it would be Africa. Africa! She laughed and rocked herself. Would she see immense forests rising up out of the water, and towers and pinnacles of pink and white coral, and elephants with ivory tusks disporting themselves in the white surf?

"You're livin' in a fairytale," chuckled Captain O'Hara, watching her face. "You don't know what the sea is yet, my girl, you've not a notion, God help you. You thought it was a hurricane we met a couple of weeks back—it was just a good fresh steady breeze."

"I know there's worse to come," said Marianne imperturbably. "But I'm not afraid. I know the Green Dolphin will bring me safe to William."

Captain O'Hara left her and strolled off to talk to his other two passengers, a dour elderly Scotsman from Leith and his even dourer wife. They were bound for South Island, New Zealand, where the Scottish colony was rapidly growing, and illness had kept them from joining the last colonists' ship that had sailed from the Firth of Forth and condemned them to the chaperonage of Marianne upon the Green Dolphin. But to Captain O'Hara's amusement Marianne and the Dunbars made no further contact with each other than that demanded by civility. The elderly couple disapproved of Marianne with her smart gay clothes, her blasphemous parrot, her friendliness with the crew and her flirtations with the Captain. And she, deeply conscious of her own rectitude, resented their disapproval. Moreover there was between them that great gulf fixed that separates good sailors from bad sailors. Marianne's imperturbable health was a source of outrage to the suffering Dunbars, and their unfortunate prostration, continued even in fine weather when the ship's roll was no more than the soothing rock of a cradle, struck Marianne as very distressing evidence of an infirmity of will that she could by no means approve.

And so the days and weeks went by, rounded and perfect like pearls upon a chain, with so little to differentiate one from another that it seemed they must continue so for always. Marianne rocked and lazed and watched the crew busy upon fine-weather tasks, patching sails, polishing brasswork, spinning rope yarn, cheery and contented as the rolling porpoises and the fishes she could see when she leaned upon the taffrail and looked down into the limpid depths of tranquil water. The fine-weather tasks were little tasks, seeming all the smaller and busier because over and around them there brooded the blue vastness of the sky, the limitless stretch of the slow-breathing, slow-moving, entranced, entrancing ocean. There were days when Marianne knew that this sense of secure continuance was nothing but a spell cast by the sea upon their senses, and that their little activities were a sort of defiance in the face of danger, a beating of the drums before the fight. The sea was just waiting. Captain O'Hara laughed when one night he found Marianne standing stock-still in the moonlight, before she went to bed, turned a little sideways to the sea, one hand to her throat, listening.

"Not yet," he told her. "But you'll come on deck one morning an' see grey skies, an' a grey sea that'll ruffle suddenly, like a bird's wing, yet there won't be no cause for the ruffle, that ye can set eyes on. An' then, maybe, in an hour or two, maybe longer, you'll see white horses gallopin' astern. Good-night."

But it did not happen quite like that, for what Marianne first noticed was what she thought was the dim shape of a range of mountains, so far away that it was no more than a blue smudge on the horizon. It was Sunday morning and crew and passengers were gathered before Captain O'Hara on the poop, listening to his terrific voice issuing his orders to his God in prayer and psalm. "O eternal Lord God, Who alone spreadest out the heavens and rulest the raging sea . . . receive into Thy Almighty protection the person of us Thy servants, and the ship in which we sail. Amen."

The words were humble yet the tone in which he addressed the Almighty was, she thought, more dictatorial than usual, if that were possible, and the tail of his eye was on that mountain range.

It was astern of them, yet oddly enough as the day went on it seemed to draw nearer and by evening the blue smudge was grape coloured, serrated with strange peaks lit with gold. She had not the slightest idea where they were on the wide ocean, and she wondered vaguely if it was Africa or South America. "What country is that?" she asked Nat, who was coming behind her in his capacity of faithful retainer, carrying her book and workbox. She could understand, now, the strange noises that passed with him for speech. The actual words she could not always distinguish but their significance was always clear to her mind.

" 'Tain't no country, ma'am," Nat signified. " 'Tis cloud. A blow, maybe, before mornin'." And then he expectorated gloomily and crawled crabwise after her down to her cabin. She had noticed that his mis-shapen body always took a sort of sideways twist when menaced with discomfort, as though it no longer desired to move straight forward but sought upon one hand or the other for some hole in which to hide itself. Down in her cabin his one sad eye peered adoringly at her out of his monkey face, and he scratched himself and sighed.

"You're tired of blows by this time, Nat?" she asked.

He shook his head, for his body's search for shelter was merely automatic and was without the consent of his mind, but she thought he left her as an old dog does who has been turned from a warm fireside into the night. He, too, must be old now. She wished suddenly that she might take him with her to that wooden house beside the creek where she would live with William. She knew she would not weary of caring for him because for some reason or other he touched something in her that had never been touched before, and the springing up of tenderness refreshed her almost beyond her own believing. Those other poor folk for whom she had laboured on the Island had not been able to release this spring, and so they had not loved her. "Nat is unique," she said, with one of her rare flashes of understanding. "He was born humbled, and so if he suffers it is without sense of outrage. But he'd never leave Captain O'Hara to go with me. He's like a dog. He'll never follow a new master if the old one is still with him."

She awoke in the first light of dawn, aware that the ship was rolling heavily, and lay as she always did listening for the busy hum of awakening life upon the ship. But this morning its tempo was quickened and changed. Instead of the chink of buckets, the scrubbing of decks, the cluck-cluck of the hens and the whistling of contented seamen, there came a thundering and a booming and a walloping, and a shouting of urgent orders. She got up, dressed quickly, and climbed the ladder. Captain O'Hara was on the poop, bellowing orders through a speaking trumpet, and men were in the rigging, lying out on the yards, calling out with quick high cries, like birds up there in their black oilskins, clawing and slashing fiercely in a mad race against time. Flying kites and stay sails came down with a great clatter, and the ship's bell beat clang, clang, clang, with a warning note that was echoed by a queer sort of moaning in the air. The world was all grey and a cold breath of wind touched her neck with clammy fingers that made her suddenly afraid. "Get below, ma'am!" Captain O'Hara roared at her in a rage, and she turned obediently, but not before she had seen the grey sea ruffling like a bird's wing, and far away on the horizon mad white horses galloping with the fast and furious speed of unleashed demons.

"All snugged down, ma'am," Nat assured her when he brought her breakfast. "She's drivin' with nothin' but a reefed foresail, a spanker an' a jib."

And suddenly Nat and the breakfast tray seemed to disappear, and Marianne found herself cascading in a smother of crinoline and petticoats down the side of an apparently vertical wall. The ship seemed diving, her stern kicked clear out of the water. Old Nick hanging in his cage from the cabin ceiling cursed loudly. Screams rang out from the Dunbar's cabin, and the sound of smashing crockery, and then, crashing down on them, the most devilish and appalling noise, a shrieking and moaning and neighing as those pursuing white horses caught up with the Green Dolphin, leaped at her, poured over her, fastened upon her and dragged her down. Lying amid the welter of smashed whalebone and torn frills that was the ruin of her gown, with her hands over her ears, half-stunned, Marianne could yet hear the pounding of their hoofs and see their white manes flying, and knew as though she had looked into their hearts their devilish delight that they had got their quarry. Well, this was the end. Her confidence in the Green Dolphin had been mistaken. One jolly old Green Dolphin was no match for the devil's own herd of white horses.

But apparently it was not the end. Slowly the Green Dolphin nosed her way up out of the pit into which she had fallen. The vertical wall became level for a moment, and then became vertical the other way on. "The Skipper, 'e ran it a bit fine," Nat's noises signified imperturbably from somewhere or other. "All but caught in 'er ball dress. But the Skipper's always lucky, an' the Green Dolphin she's a lucky ship."

Marianne found that Nat's long strong arms were lifting her up and putting her into her bunk. She was not frightened or hurt at all, but she was bewildered by her fall, by the noise, by the frantic pitching and tossing of the ship. She shut her eyes and lay still while Nat, keeping his footing in some miraculous way, cleared up the debris and fetched her fresh tea. He stood by her while she drank it, swaying to to the motion of the ship. "Just a blow, ma'am," he assured her. "Just a good strong blow, ma'am," and put one great hand upon her left ankle. It was as though a dog had stretched out a paw and laid it caressingly upon her, and she laughed. "I'm not afraid,

Nat," she said. "You can take the cup and leave me, for I'm not in the least afraid."

And reassured as to the trustworthiness of the Green Dolphin she remained unafraid, though very soon the gale rose to something in the nature of a hurricane. She managed to extricate herself from the smashed cage of her crinoline, put on her wrapper, and crawl to Mrs. Dunbar's cabin, but that poor lady had given herself up for lost and was beyond the reach of aid from a woman she disliked, so Marianne crawled back again and spent what seemed an eternity of days and nights in her bunk. On the whole, in spite of the noise and darkness and perpetual motion, she welcomed the experience, even though its refusal of one moment's respite gave to it a quality of never-endingness that bore hardly on the mind. Her head ached madly and it was not possible to sleep, but she would not weep or grumble, for that would be to let the enemy put its mark upon her, to align herself with him against the Green Dolphin. Yet through it all she did not hate the enemy, though she desired to beat him; she loved him and agreed with Captain O'Hara that it was grand fun to put one's imprint on the sea.

Nat came to her often, and grinned, and laid his hand upon her left ankle, and just once, when it seemed to her that things were at their worst, Captain O'Hara came. How could she ever have thought he was getting an old man? His immense bulk seemed to fill her tiny cabin, and his laughter rolled about it like genial thunder.

"Past the worst," he roared at her through the tumult of the gale.

"Past the worst?" she ejaculated, clinging to the side of her bunk as once again the Green Dolphin dived madly downwards. "Why, these are the worst seas we've had yet."

"A seaman always knows, me dear. Granted there's no perceptible difference in the ragin' of wind an' water, yet somethin' tells you that, glory be, you've won."

He inflated his chest and grinned at her.

"Don't you be too sure," she snapped at him, as a huge wave struck them and the ship heeled sickeningly over on to her side. "You're too confident. You take too many risks. One of these days you'll take a chance once too often."

It was not like her to deprecate recklessness in the courage of another, for there was plenty of it in her own, but the long days and nights of tumult were at last beginning to take their toll of her strength. The Green Dolphin's will to carry her safely to William might be as firm as ever, but just for a moment now and then she was afraid lest the fallible humans who directed it might fail or blunder.

"Risks, is it?" bellowed Captain O'Hara in a sudden glorious rage, for adverse criticism was a thing he could not tolerate at all. "An' who may you be to talk to Denis O'Hara of risks, an' you skippin' half across the world to marry a man you've not clapped eyes on for ten years? Risks, begorra! As soon as this wind moderates, my girl, I clap on all the sail I can, risks or no risks, or lose me reputation as a punctual seaman, an' you'll set an' watch me, an' hold your tongue, for you've as much need to make the port of Wellington in double quick time as I have, my girl. Ten years! If young William waits for you much longer, sitting on the jetty at Wellington an' kickin' his heels, it's likely he'll get tired o' waitin' an' go off with the barmaid, God help him. Too many risks, is it? I'll not be called to account for me own actions, on me own ship, by a mere slip of a woman no larger than me little finger. Bedad, I will not! Good evenin' to ye, ma'am. Rest aisy."

He swore under his breath and departed, banging the door. They must have shipped a big sea this time, Marianne thought, for her cabin was more deeply awash than ever before, and the chuckling of the scupper holes rose to a ribald laughter. How dared Captain O'Hara! The outrageous old man! Yet she found that she was echoing the Green Dolphin's mirth. On the Island she would not have laughed even at Captain O'Hara, if he had addressed her with such vulgarity, but aboard the Green Dolphin laughter was the ground one trod on and the air one breathed. It might not be one's own ground, but for the period of the voyage one shared it with the Green Dolphin.

A few hours later she realised that Captain O'Hara had been right and the worst was over. There was less savagery in the shriek of the wind and the buffetings of the great seas were the buffetings of a spent giant. And the ship still sailed. Once more Captain O'Hara had successfully set his imprint upon his God.

2

The weeks went by once more with a peaceful rhythm, but not without their dangers and excitements, and moments of experience that would be unforgettable while life lasted. One morning Marianne came on deck to find that they were among icebergs. Sea and sky were a cold blue-green and the crystal ramparts of ice scintillated with every colour of the rainbow, gashed here and there with yawning caverns of intense blue. For an hour she leaned on the bulwarks, oblivious of danger, as the Green Dolphin pursued her way with slow caution. No recklessness now. Captain O'Hara had more respect for these mighty floating castles than for any wind that ever blew. Even the sea itself seemed awed. The waves crawled up the precipitous crystal walls only very slowly, and then fell back, and they did not venture near the blue mouths of those dreadful caverns. Some of these ice castles were half a mile long, towering to pinnacles that cut the sky two hundred feet above the water. The glorious Green Dolphin seemed to shrink to a mere cringing speck upon the sea as she crept past them, her sails dirty and buff coloured against their peerless white. They would have crushed her to powder had she come too near.

They sighted Wellington at ten o'clock on a perfect New Zealand winter's day. For a wonder there was no wind and the air was crisp and still like that of an English October, when the first tang of frost is in the air. The mountains rose up opal-tinted out of the crystal sea against a sky veiled yet translucent, and seen from a distance in the clear cool light it seemed to Marianne that the houses were built of pearl and roofed with amethyst. That was her first impression of this country—that it had been cut with sharp precision from precious stones—and all the wind and dirt and heat that she subsequently endured were never to expunge it from her mind. Her first impression was much the same as William's, but while he had been struck chiefly by its primordial quality she was almost wounded by its sharpness. Like all young things it would strike hard and not care how much it hurt. Well, she was sharp too, she flattered herself, with something of the same jewel-like brilliance. They would be a match for each other.

From the moment when New Zealand had first been sighted she had been seated on her pyramid of boxes, in her green gown and green cloak, and the green bonnet with the orange feather, clasping the umbrella and reticule, Old Nick in his cage beside her. Now, as the Green Dolphin entered the harbour, she walked to the bulwarks and stood there waiting, erect and still, showing no outward sign of agitation; but her face was dead white and her heart was beating so madly that she was almost suffocated. For a moment or two, as they glided towards the long quay, backed by a row of shops and offices, that had taken the place of the old wooden jetty, she could not see, then with a great effort of will she controlled herself and gathered up mind and soul and body for the supreme moment of her life.

She saw William a full five minutes before he saw her, for her gay little figure was almost submerged by the sudden irruption of Mrs. Dunbar's immense grey crinoline beside her, while he stood head and shoulders above the men about him. Yes, there he was, pushing through the crowd on the quay like some great animal trampling down the undergrowth, oblivious of the fate of what got in his way, fighting his way towards the ship with a wild mad eagerness that tore at her heart. He was wearing a sky-blue coat with brass buttons and carried his hat in his hand, and his hair was the same tossed untidy red-gold mop.

Then he came nearer and with a suddening sickening sense of shock she saw that ten years of pioneer life had changed him almost out of recognition. Little of his great beauty remained with him, and his elegance and look of breeding had entirely vanished. He looked ten years older than his actual age. His figure had thickened and his face had coarsened. She shut her eyes and a trembling shook her. She was not an inexperienced woman and she knew in that moment exactly what her life with this man was going to be. She was, in modern parlance, up against it, and her task was not going to be made any easier by the fact, evident in the letter he had written to her father, that he had no idea to what an extent he had changed.

Then once again she controlled herself. She loved this man. She remembered his old comeliness, kindness and courtesy. These things were not yet dead in him. He was only twenty-nine. He could be saved and she would save him. Her generation was not troubled by the fear of priggishness, or by an overdeveloped sense of its own limitations. It could found a thing called "A Mutual Improvement Society" without a smile. It saw life in strong contrasts of black and white, and was aware of neither presumption nor absurdity in the spectacle of what it called a good woman solemnly dedicating herself to the reformation of what it called a bad man. In sentiment, if not in intellect, Marianne was of her generation. "I'll be a perfect wife to him," she whispered passionately. "I'll make a fine man of him. I will. I will. So help me God." And if the last words were a mere platitude, and not inspired by any awareness of her own frailty, the tone of them gathered up all that she was, all that she ever could be, into one white-hot flame of genuine and dedicated courage.

He had come to her before she was aware of it. She opened her eyes and saw him standing there, his face dead white, as though he had just passed through some moment of almost unbearable emotion, his figure set and still. "William! William!" she whispered, looking up at him with devouring eyes, the tears streaming down her face, her arms moving with a helpless childish gesture of frustration, because they were impeded by reticule and umbrella and could not embrace him. It was the still muteness of his emotion that touched her to such a tempest of tears, bearing witness as it did to the intensity and depth of his feeling. "William! My darling! Together again after all these years! At last!"

He could no longer stand there like a stuck image. Very gently, reticule and umbrella and all, he took her in his arms and kissed her. It was not the embrace that she had expected but the immense tenderness of it was very sweet, and more suited to a public place than passion. For a long moment they clung together and then he picked up the parrot and led the way down the gangplank. At the bottom he stopped and turned round, smiled at her, set down the cage, picked her up in his arms and lifted her on to the quay, as a man lifts his bride over the threshold of her home. Then leaving her there with Old Nick he went back to see about her luggage. He had not said a single word, but she did not mind, for the smile that he had given her was the old smile of the boy William whom she had known ten years ago, the old cheerful grin full of the old comradeship and kindness with added to it a man's resolved goodwill. She was happy as she stood there waiting for him. She had the conviction that whatever the struggle and pain that lay before them, yet they would somehow win.

PART III

THE WIFE

For better for worse, for richer for poorer, in sickness and in health, to love and to cherish, till death us do part.—THE MARRIAGE SERVICE.

CHAPTER ONE

1

The thud of axes and the rasping of the great saws were the only sounds. Then, at a shout from William, echoing back and back into the forest from man to man, they gradually ceased, and the huge primordial stillness fell like a blow.

The golden sunset poured down into the clearing and the little circle of human activity shone and glowed against the dark forest background. There were the two huts, thatched with reeds, the orderly rows of felled trees, the raised platform for the sawing of the planks, all the littered paraphernalia of the lumberman's trade, saws and axes, planks and ropes. And there were the lumbermen themselves, foremost among them Jacky Poto and Kapua-Manga, the Black Cloud, and Bob Scant and Isaac, hardbitten old scoundrels who had come from no-one-knew-where and had been William's good friends and cronies for many years, and William himself in charge of them. They were all stripped to the waist, glistening with sweat, their sunbrowned bodies taut and hard yet with muscles quivering under the skin after the long hard day of labour. In the fiery glow every note of colour seemed intensified, while in the background the forest gloomed and darkened and drew a little nearer.

William put on his coat and contrary to his custom left his men to round off the day's labour without him while he turned homeward. Samuel and Susanna had arrived a week ago for a brief holiday. He and Marianne had been married for eighteen months but this was the first visit the hard-worked Kellys had paid them, and it had to be made a happy visit, for the Kellys' hospitable door was always thrown wide for them when they went to Wellington and they had much kindness to repay. To-night Marianne would cook a special meal, and Tai Haruru would dine with them, and they would have a little festivity. It was a damned shame that Marianne would never invite Scant and Isaac to dinner, for they had been gentlemen once, but however hard he begged her she would not do it. She liked and admired Samuel and Susanna, from whose house they had been married, and all the brave company of pioneering gentlefolk who had come to New Zealand since its inception as a British colony, but for the old pioneering stock, tough foul-mouthed hard-drinking old fighters like Scant and Isaac, she had no use whatever. And she took no trouble to conceal her dislike either. William ground his teeth together in fury as he walked along the winding forest path between the glorious shoulder-high green ferns, remembering the biting sarcasm that reduced dear old Scant and Isaac to speechless misery, the cold silence that greeted the visits of Tai Haruru, to whom as her husband's partner she could not refuse hospitality. Then he smiled, suddenly, bitterly. Tai Haruru was a match for her and silence was her best refuge against him. On the rare occasions when he was able to inveigle her into argument he invariably managed to get the best of it. . . . She was paid back then for her cruelty to poor old Scant and Isaac.

Suddenly William stopped dead on the path, swore, and slashed at the great ferns with his stick. Oh God, this cursed hatred, his for Marianne and hers for his friends, this devilish desire to hurt that which one hated. Yes, it was devilish, not human, an alien thing trying to destroy that which was made in the image of God. He remembered dreadful faces that he had seen, faces distorted by cruelty; it had been their inhumanity that had made one shrink and avert one's eyes. Humanity. Humanism. Those were good words, used always to connote the very antithesis of hate. He threw away his stick, and his hand was shaking. His hatred of his wife horrified him. It was the first hatred of his life, it was growing in bitterness and intensity day by day, and he had no idea what to do about it. Another man would have left her, but it never even occurred to William to do that. When he had taken her into his arms on the Green Dolphin he had taken her for better for worse, and he was no quitter. Tai Haruru, breaking him in to a pioneer's life, had taught him not to quit. But there was something that Tai Haruru had not taught him, and that was how to cleave to a hated bargain without hatred. It did not occur to him that such a paradox was possible and at present he was cleaving to the wife of his bosom much as a bulldog clings to the throat of its victim, letting go just now and then to refresh himself for a new grip in ways that judged by the standards he had accepted for years past were normal enough, but which filled Marianne with rage and repulsion.

He tramped on again, quickly, lest he be late. They must keep up appearances to-night for the Kellys' sake, for the Kellys had been good to them. That was what he must do to-night; keep up appearances.

He found it difficult now, after the long dragged-out unhappiness of the last eighteen months, to remember with exactitude the extraordinary emotions of his wedding day and night; but he tried to do it as he blundered along through the fern. He had scarcely been sane, of course. The shock of seeing Marianne upon the deck of the Green Dolphin, when he had expected Marguerite, had first knocked him silly and then set his brain racing at a white-hot feverish speed that had driven his body into immediate and demented action. He had realised at once how it was that he had made that hideous mistake. He had written that letter to Octavius in a maze of love, with the whisky bottle beside him to aid composition, and what with the drink and the love his stupefied mind had played its silly old trick upon him and he had confused the two names that from boyhood he had always vowed were much too much alike. A series of hateful coincidences had done the rest; the omission of the bride's name both in Octavius' answering letter and in her own little note scrawled in unrecognizable handwriting, and the inclusion of the little bunch of primroses, Marguerite's favourite flowers. He had seen it all in a blinding flash as his great body lumbered mechanically up the gangplank, without the slightest idea of what it was going to do when it got to the top. Then he had seen Marianne standing there by the pile of luggage and the bird-cage, alone now because the Dunbars had moved away. The microscopic size of the brilliant figure, the slightly scared way in which she had been clutching reticule and umbrella, the look of rapt ecstasy on her small white face, with the eyes childishly closed, as though she were a little girl at a party who when she opened them expected to see a lighted Christmas tree, had struck from his sentimental easy-going nature a sudden rush of almost unbearable tenderness. She had always loved him. All through his boyhood she had worked for him unceasingly. All the happiness and prosperity of his young manhood he had owed to her. She had stood by him and his father in the days of adversity. She had journeyed all alone from one world to another, through danger and discomfort, dragging that cursed parrot with her, simply to answer the cry of his heart for home and mate. Could he go to her and say that he did not love her or want her, that she must turn round and go home again? Could he ask her to face once more the danger and hardship of a long voyage just because he had made a stupid mistake? Above all, could he ask her proud spirit to face the contempt and derision of friends at home when she was returned like damaged goods, thrown away by a fool of a fellow who had been too tipsy even to recall correctly the name of the woman he loved? Another man might have done those things in the name of truth and common-sense, but he had lacked both the strength and the cruelty. Instead he had gone to her and taken her in his arms and kissed her. Holy Moses, but he'd been a fool! He had married for pity, exactly as his father had done. He had vowed as a boy that he would never do that, and he had done it. Holy Moses, but he'd been a fool!

He had moved through the rest of that day in a condition so dazed that he could remember nothing at all about it now except his excruciating longing for the strong drink that had not been provided by Samuel and Susanna, who had staged his wedding. He and Marianne had been married that afternoon in Samuel's wooden steepled Church, and he had subsequently gathered that the bride had been so magnificently arrayed that half Wellington and almost the entire crew of the Green Dolphin had gathered to see her walk from the Parsonage to the Church on Captain O'Hara's arm; Captain O'Hara being also a sight for sore eyes in a bottle green coat, a flowered waistcoat and a stock so high that his round red face had been permanently tipped backwards for the rest of the afternoon. The enthusiastic crowd had waited patiently at the Church porch all through the ceremony, and had cheered themselves hoarse when the dainty little bride had appeared again, radiantly happy, her hand on her husband's arm, the bells pealing out over her head. Of the ceremony itself William had now not the faintest recollection, but he supposed that he and Marianne had stood before Samuel, Captain O'Hara on the other side of Marianne, the first mate of the Green Dolphin beside him as his groomsman, Susanna and dear old Nat and a few others looking on, and that in the presence of these witnesses he had spoken those appalling words, "I, William Edmond, take thee, Marianne Véronique, to be my wedded wife, to have and to hold from this day forward, for better for worse, for richer for poorer, in sickness and in health, to love and to cherish, till death us do part."

Well, there it was. Those had been the words. One could not get away from words like those without being a quitter.

2

Their relationship as man and wife had been poisoned from the outset by his inability to satisfy her ardour. His reluctance put her in an odious position; it wounded not only her love but her woman's pride.

At the evening of their wedding day his memory started function-

ing again with a hateful clarity. After supper she had gone up to the
guest-room that the Kellys had put at their disposal, accompanied by
Susanna carrying the candle, and something in the way in which she
had left the room, with silk skirts importantly and possessively
rustling, had stung him out of his dazed condition into sudden
appalling awareness of just exactly what he had done. And Samuel,
tactless blundering ass of a fellow, had suddenly at this moment
started quoting from the wedding psalms: "O well is thee, and happy
shalt thou be. Thy wife shall be as the fruitful vine upon the walls
of thine house, thy children like the olive branches round about thy
table. Lo, thus shall the man be blessed that feareth the Lord——"

"Hold your tongue, Samuel!" William had bellowed suddenly at
the well-meaning little man, and had dragged himself to his feet and
lumbered out of the room and out into the night, where the burnished
stars were shining and the wind rising, and walked up and down in
an agony, remembering how once he had likened this austere wind
to Marguerite. Marguerite! Marguerite! Through so many years
he had remembered and adored her, as a suppliant a saint. In pesti-
lence and earthquake, in war and tumult, in pain, fear, defeat,
frustration, loneliness, he had stayed himself upon the thought of
her. When the better days had come, and with them the news that
she was still unmarried, it had been as though the gates of heaven
had opened, so glorious had been his hope. . . . No, not hope, certainty. . . . From the moment of the writing of his letter he had been
perfectly certain that she would come, so certain that from that
moment on he had set himself to become the sort of fellow that Marguerite's husband should be. But in spite of much well-meaning
effort he had not succeeded very well, and his lack of success had
opened his eyes a very little to the slow unconscious approximation
of his standards to those of the men about him, a ten years' process
that had completely changed the boy that he had been to the man
that he was. He had been a bit scared then, but not badly. Marguerite had never been a prude. She would neither condemn nor
scold, she would simply see clearly, understand thoroughly, forgive
completely, and then they would start again.

Marguerite! Marguerite! But as he had paced up and down in
the cool lovely wind he had said to himself that he was not married
to Marguerite. It was not Marguerite's forgiving love that waited
for him in that attic room. It had all been for nothing, that grim
battle to recapture some of the integrity that he had lost. It had
been for nothing . . . nothing . . . and how in the name of all that
was fantastic could the man whom he had tried to make anew for
Marguerite become the husband of that sallow-faced, passionate,

possessive little woman for whom at this moment he felt nothing but dislike? Scarcely aware of what he was doing he had swung down the hill to Hobson's saloon and spent the night there.

He guessed that Hobson and Mrs. Hobson had been hard put to it next morning to get him into sufficiently good shape to present himself at the Parsonage, together with the wagon that was to convey himself and his bride and her luggage to her new home. But they had managed it, and he had been there, hat in hand, shamefaced, miserable, obviously the worse for wear, but completely sobered and deadly polite as he stood in the parlour and bowed to his wife and wished her good morning. Samuel and Susanna, retreating from a situation which completely bewildered them, had seen to it that the two were alone together.

Marianne's face had been dead white, with dark smudges beneath the sleepless eyes, but she had held herself stiffly erect and drawn on her gloves with nonchalance. "Good morning," she had whispered, and then gasped and said no more. It was her nature to turn in fury on those who injured her, but the pain of this wound that William had dealt her had been so great that it had struck her speechless.

She had turned aside from his offered arm and swept before him out of the room and down the steps, and settled herself without his assistance in the wagon, the parrot on one side of her, her husband on the other, and her luggage piled up behind. It had been the light farm wagon belonging to the settlement, and Victoria the great roan mare who pulled the plough had been between the shafts. Susanna had had the forethought to put a cushion on the hard plank seat for the bride, and stow rugs and a basket of provisions behind the trunks, and she had tied white ribbons on the whip and on Victoria's harness.

It had been the sight of those white ribbons that had enabled both William and Marianne to thrust their misery out of sight and don the smiling faces suitable for the occasion. They had remembered suddenly that they were bride and bridegroom and had reacted automatically to the remembrance. Samuel and Susanna, coming out to wave good-bye to them, had thought that perhaps nothing was wrong after all except William's habitual lack of sobriety, of which it was earnestly to be hoped that his good wife would soon cure him.

The journey, slow and rough going with the laden wagon bumping over roads that were never more than a cart track, and often a great deal less, and involving several cold nights spent in the open, had most unexpectedly proved almost happy. It had brought out all that was best in Marianne; her courage, her love of adventure, her passionate delight in new experience, her joy in beauty. And William, observing the fortitude with which this elegant fashionable little woman endured the first rigours of a life for which little in her previous existence had prepared her, had been seized with compunction. He had not sufficiently realised, he had told himself, great hulking strong fellow that he was, how hard this life would be for a woman, and his huge natural kindness had welled up through his bitterness and enveloped Marianne in the old tenderness. The thing was done now, he had said to himself. Nothing for it now, so far as he could see, but to make the best of a bad job. And so when driving was easy he had driven with his arm round his wife, to ease the jolting, and each evening he had made her a little tent with the rugs under the wagon, and built a fire to warm her, and had cooked her delicious pioneer meals in the open and laughed and joked and told her stories of this land to which she listened with the delight of a child listening to fairy tales, a delight that touched him to renewed tenderness. . . . If only they could have gone on for ever like this, he had thought, not living but just playing at it, then it would not be so bad. Travelling is always like a children's game, he had thought, with its picnic meals and makeshift sleeping places, its sense of having escaped alike from past and future; it is the childishness of it that one enjoys. But games don't last. Presently it is reality again, with past and future barbing the easy jests and rendering the idle actions consequential.

One night, as he had sat by the fire preparing their evening meal while Marianne lay with her weary aching limbs stretched upon the rugs beneath the shelter of the wagon, he had forced himself to speak of Marguerite. It had been torture to speak of her to this other woman, but he had felt that he must know whether the mistake that he had made had caused her suffering.

"Marguerite is—well?" he had asked.

"Well, but a good deal changed from the girl that you remember," Marianne had replied.

"How—changed?" he had asked.

"Like so many beautiful women she has become lazy. It is always the way; when a woman has a pretty face too much attention is paid her and she thinks of herself as a queen with nothing to do but sit still and smile and receive homage."

William had sat silent, for he had not been able to reconcile this picture with the Marguerite whom he had known.

"She is assiduous in attentions to Mamma and Papa," Marianne had continued. "She is affectionate, and they are the immediate entourage; that is the explanation, I imagine, for I do not think that she ever feels very deeply. She has not married, you know, though she has had many offers. It appears that she has not been able to summon the emotion that would have enabled her to overcome her natural reluctance for exertion."

"Marriage is certainly full of exertion," William had said drily. The exertion of being Marianne's husband was, he had felt, going to wear him out completely before he was much older. "Did she feel the parting from you?" he had asked again, painfully and tentatively.

"If she did she gave no sign of it. She made the goodbyes easy with her laughter, for she still has that happy gift of enjoying everything enormously. She enjoyed getting my trousseau ready, and she was laughing when she waved good-bye to me. I expect she was glad that I was leaving her to rule with undisputed sway at home."

Though these obviously prejudiced statements had told him little yet William had extracted two crumbs of comfort from them; whatever her emotions might be Marguerite was still the mistress of them, and though by his stupidity he had deprived himself of her adorable companionship he was not guilty of having taken it away from Sophie and Octavius. No life seemed wrecked except his own.

And so, once again in the sunset light, they had come to the hilltop from which one looked down on the settlement and the creek. This was the moment that he had looked forward to almost beyond all others; pausing at the top of the hill and showing Marguerite the home that he had made for her beside the creek. But with Marianne beside him he had not stopped, he had driven straight on down the hill. "That is our house, the one with the flower garden running down towards the water," he had said, and when Marianne had cried out aloud in delight he had forced himself to smile and meet her eyes, but he had not been able to say any more.

Marianne, rightly attributing his silence to excess of emotion, had forgotten her weariness in ecstatic happiness as the beautiful scene unfolded below her. The settlement was still lonely and small but had grown since William had first seen it. The houses of the white men, built of kauri wood, thatched with reed, the barns and stables made of the intertwining elastic stems of the raupo plant padded with green flax, had looked that evening an integral and beautiful part of the landscape about them. The gardens of the kauri houses had been gay with flowers that glowed in the sunset, and beyond the gardens the fields and farm buildings had looked peaceful and home-like. The crowing of cocks had come up to them in the still air, the lowing of cattle and the sound of the creek flowing over the stones in its bed as it made its eager way down to the sea. It might almost have been an Island village, Marianne had said, had it not been for the immense height and luxuriance of the ferns that edged the creek, and

washed like a green sea right up against the wooden palisade that
protected the settlement against the encroaching forest. But the
extraordinary clarity of the atmosphere, the depth and darkness of
the forest and the majesty of the mountains that rose beyond it, had
struck no note of earthly familiarity; rather it had brought to remembrance the landscape of dreams, "thoughts from the visions of the
night, when deep sleep falleth on men, and fear and trembling, and a
spirit passes. . . ." Marianne had suddenly seemed glad to fasten
her gaze within the palisade that man had built, and to cry out again
in pleasure as the colours shone and sparkled in the light that
streamed through that great gash in the western mountains towards
which the creek unrolled itself like a ribbon of gold through the fern.

The wagon had rumbled over the wooden bridge that crossed the
creek and jolted up the rough cart track beyond towards the roomy
house with the wide verandah that William had built for Marguerite,
choosing a southerly aspect that would have given her, as she sat
sewing in her rocking chair at the top of the verandah steps, a view
so breath-takingly lovely that she would have had to sing out loud
as she rocked and sewed. Through all the long months during which
he had laboured at the house he had heard her singing, and heard the
swish of her blue skirts and the creak of the rocker, and sometimes
he had spoken out loud to her. "I am putting a shelf for your books,
Marguerite, beside the bed, and a hook for your bonnet behind the
door. Your bedroom window looks west towards the sea, but the
parlour has a window that looks east to the forest, and you'll sit there
and watch for me at evening when I come home."

He had pulled up at the garden gate, jumped down, and thrown
the reins over the hitching post. Then he had lifted Marianne to the
ground, offered her his arm and laughed, and the man who stood
waiting for them in the shadows of the verandah had lifted his head,
startled, as though the laughter was one of the most unpleasant
sounds he had ever heard. But Marianne, walking up the garden
path on her husband's arm, had been intent upon the flowers, growing in this sub-tropical climate in a glory and profusion that outdid
even the Island. "William! William!" she had cried. "Did you
plant all these for me?" And she had turned on the garden path and
flung her arms impulsively round his neck.

"We are not alone, you know," he had said coldly, for if she had
kissed him at that moment he would surely have struck her.

She had swung round again and seen Tai Haruru coming down
the steps, dark, contorted, full of sombre power. She had caught her
breath as she looked up into the dark eyes that had flashed suddenly
as though they had recognised her, then darkened again as he gave

her the formal greeting of a stranger. "Welcome, Ma'am," he had said, and William had felt her tremble on his arm as if the rough deep echoing voice had plucked at her nerves as though they were harp-strings that must vibrate to his will. He had taken her small gloved hand very gently, yet once his fingers had tightened about hers she had seemed powerless to withdraw her hand. William had realised that with a sudden panic of fear, a stab of hatred, she had known that this man was stronger, more subtle, than she was, that his power over her husband was infinitely greater than her own, and that she was going to be intolerably jealous of him. She had given him her most accomplished smile, she had met his glance unflinchingly, and she had left her hand confidingly in his since it was not in her power to withdraw it. But William knew that she had not deceived Tai Haruru. He had released her with a smile that had recognised her worth as an antagonist but yet had not been troubled as to the final outcome. Then, having bowed and wished her happiness, he had gone away to his own home further down the creek.

The house that William had built was perfect. Tai Haruru and the lumbermen had made for it beautiful simple wooden furniture, and gay rugs of native weaving were on the floor. Susanna had seen to it that the crockery and pots and pans were all they should be, and she had bought the dimity curtains of cool green and white that hung in the windows, and the dainty flowered hangings for the big four-poster bed. A glorious log fire had roared on the hearth, with a kettle singing over it, and the table had been spread with a white cloth, decorated with a bowl of beautifully arranged flowers, and a dainty meal had been set ready; Tai Haruru had done all that he could to make William's woman welcome. In the light of the glori-ous afterglow they had eaten their meal, and when the stars had shone out, those silver stars as big as moons of which Captain O'Hara had told them so long ago, they had lit the candles and sat before the fire and talked together of the future. At least Marianne had talked, full of ambition, while William had smiled and held her hand with all the gentleness that he could muster. Yet behind the talk and the smiles, the candlelight and the glowing warmth of the fire, she must have been aware all the time of something wrong, for suddenly she had seemed to find that she was talking for the sake of talking, and that William's mechanical stroking of her hand was merely madden-ing. She had pulled it away, and bitten her lip upon impatient words, and sat listening in silence to the sound of the rising wind as it swept up the creek from the sea. He loved the New Zealand wind, but already it had seemed that she hated it. Sitting silently beside her he had known her thoughts. . . . She was thinking that this wind had

none of the friendliness of the Island winds, a
was combining with her husband's strange
the passion in her breast. But no voice, no
do that, she had thought. Her love would
expected that she would hug it to her on
quisite joy, and now it was a thorn that th
there was no power in the whole wide worl
. . . Half lost in the big chair her little body
over, and he had jumped up and lifted her
tired out," he had said gently. "I was a selfish
long. Come to your bed, my dear."

He had taken her to her room, lit her candles, help
what she needed and waited upon her with great kin
clumsiness that must have strained her taut nerves al
ing point. Then he had taken her in his arms and once
board the Green Dolphin, he had kissed her. "Sleep w
anne," he had said, and then he had left her. He did not know
she had slept that night. Sitting slumped before the dying fire in the
next room he had listened fearfully for the sound of weeping, but if
she had made any sound the wind had folded it within its own
lamenting, for he had heard nothing.

3

The great trees thinned out, and the ocean of green fern flung itself
frustrated against the palisade that protected the vegetable garden.
William unlatched the gate and went in. It had no lock, for everyone,
Maori and white man alike, was William's friend. He went slowly
along the winding paths between the English vegetables that grew
here with such amazing luxuriance. There was a riot of runner
beans, the flowers like scarlet tongues of flame in the golden sunset
light, a sea of purple and white potato flowers, raspberry canes,
strawberry beds, pumpkins of an enormous size, thyme and mint and
marjoram. In the flower garden New Zealand and English flowers
ran riot together, the white feathery raupo jostling the tall holly-
hocks, and a Scotch rose blooming at the foot of a great pohoutakawa tree covered with crimson blooms.

Marianne had worked wonders in the garden as well as in the
house. Her whirlwind energy called forth William's astounded
admiration even while it exhausted him almost to the point of hysteria. Her adaptability also amazed him. She arose at dawn and
cooked, scrubbed, washed, ironed, sewed, dug and planted as though
she had been doing these things all her life. Her home-made bread

er preserves melted in the mouth. Never had
l or so well and daintily cared for . . . and
erable. If he let himself go in enjoyment of
s well out, jaws champing in the unrefined
tyle that he had unconsciously picked up,
l exquisite manners of his prim little wife
or his coarse greediness. However much he
at he always seemed to leave tracks on the
oved he seemed knock something over. And
o clear up the wreckage of his own disasters, it
opinion (well-founded on experience) that he in-
onfusion worse confounded. Tight-lipped, she
out of the way and herself mop up the spilt milk or
e broken china. She never let him help her in the house
h she was often utterly exhausted at the end of the day,
by the heat and the unaccustomed labour. Her fastidious-
could not endure that anything should be done otherwise than
just-so in her house, and William's domestic labours were more remarkable for goodwill than accuracy. There was no way in which
she would let him serve her, and the milk of his human kindness had
turned to a sour bitterness and his tenderness to the first hatred of
his life. To forget it, and to get his clumsy person out of Marianne's
way, he would go off at evening to the Maori village in the forest, or
spend a night with Tai Haruru or Scant and Isaac, and gamble and
lose a good bit of money, and get most gloriously drunk. . . . And
the next day drop things worse than ever, and have to listen to Marianne's bitter probing questions about the Maori women at the village,
or her angry tirades against the friends who were making a wastrel of
him, and hate her worse than ever because she hated them. How he
loathed this hatred, and hated Marianne the more because she was
the cause of it. Slowly and heavily he made his way through the
vegetable garden, dreading, as always, those thoughts of the might-
have-been that always came rushing in upon him when he came home
in the evening to confront the what-was. He turned into the flower
garden that he and Tai Haruru had made for Marguerite, and they
were all about him like a flock of birds. . . . Marguerite sitting sewing in the parlour window watching for him, her wave and her smile
when she saw him coming. Marguerite, less efficient than Marianne,
finding her feet in a new way of life slowly, amusingly, making mistakes, letting him help her. Marguerite tired at the end of the day,
letting him carry her to bed, letting him finish the washing up, only
laughing at him if he did it wrong. Marguerite with her clear sight
and quick sympathy friendly to his friends, understanding that the

suffering and hardship that had made of them hard-drinking, hard-swearing, gross-grained old blackguards would have deprived lesser men of reason or life or both. Marguerite in his arms at night, a part of himself, his true mate, their love equal and serene, asking no more than could be given with ease, yet getting all there was to get because for either to have given less than all to the other would not have been possible. Marguerite bearing him the child that he longed for. Yes, Marguerite would have had a child. She was no hater, with body and soul so hardened that life could not germinate within the iron earth. . . . He straightened his sagging shoulders and went resolutely up the steps to the empty verandah. Somehow or other they must get through this evening creditably. They owed it to the kind Kellys.

Susanna was laying the table in the parlour when he went in, and she smiled at him gently. She was allowed to help Marianne, for she also was an excellent housewife, and she was humble, nimble and obedient. Marianne, though patronising her as her social inferior in a manner that made William squirm, nevertheless almost loved her, and her voice, issuing her orders through the open kitchen door, was less harsh than usual.

But the harshness came back as she called out, "Is that you, William?"

"Yes," said William heavily.

She left her labours for a moment and came into the parlour, squeezing her crinoline through the narrow doorway, sending Susanna away out of earshot to her own room with the cold flicker of a "go away" glance. The cooking of an elaborate meal at the end of a hard hot day had tired her; there were dark lines under her eyes and the droop at the corners of her mouth was more pronounced than usual. Yet beneath the big apron that she wore she was exquisitely dressed, and the smells that accompanied her through the kitchen door were delicious. She might hate Tai Haruru but it was not in her to offer any guest less than the very best that she could do. There was not a single lazy bone in her body or a slatternly thought in her mind. Her striving for perfection in all things, while it exasperated him, yet stirred William's admiration. For himself, for many years now, he had not bothered overmuch about the little niceties of living.

"Why are you so late?" demanded Marianne. "Supper will be ready in five minutes, and look at you! I've been slaving to prepare a dainty supper for your friends and you can't even pay me the compliment of being ready for it."

She held herself a little aloof from him, distastefully, and he blushed crimson, horribly aware of grimy hands and sweat-drenched clothes and the aroma of whisky on his breath. It was quite impossible to fell trees all day long in this heat without wetting one's whistle now and again, but she could never understand that. She said no word about the whisky but she gave him the look she always gave him when he had been drinking; a hurt, desperate look that acknowledged the fact that though she had been fighting his weaknesses for eighteen months yet he was now in worse shape than when she had married him. What more could she do, her look demanded? If only he would love her . . . love her . . . love her.

He swore and turned away, barging like a great elephant through the kitchen sending a plate crashing to the floor as he did so, and went out to the pump outside the back door to wash. As he sluiced he heard her voice, with an exhausted edge to it, scolding shrilly. "William, how dared you swear at me like that? Haven't I enough to endure, with your drinking, and your frightful friends, and your abominable laziness——"

William straightened himself in sudden indignation. "Laziness?" he interrupted. "Good God, Marianne, if ever a man worked, I do! I sweat in that damn forest till I'm ready to drop."

"You swing your axe hard enough," said Marianne contemptuously. "But any idiot can do that. Do you ever use your mind? Never. Neither you nor Mr. Haslam. You're both bone lazy. You'll never get anywhere. You could be the leading timber merchants of the country if you wanted to be—between you you've the knowledge and the brains. But all he cares for is carving owls on pieces of stick, and the drink, and all you care for is gambling, and Maori women—and the drink."

William pumped again with violence, gritting his teeth. It was hell to have an ambitious wife. He could not understand her longing for wealth and position. Materially speaking, what more did they want than they had? They had enough to eat, enough to wear, a sound roof over their heads, a garden, incomparable beauty spread all about them. If they were to gain all that she longed for she would still be unsatisfied, her eyes always beseeching him to love her, love her, love her, when he could not. He went to their bedroom by way of the garden, and climbed in through the window, so as not to have to pass through the kitchen and meet her eyes again.

4

Fifteen minutes later a strangely exotic little piece of festivity, called into being by the genius of Marianne, unfolded its petals in her parlour. Blooming here in the wilderness, thousands of miles from the ancient civilization that through centuries had shaped its form and content, it reminded Tai Haruru of a cactus flower blossoming strangely amid the arid contortions of the surrounding stalks and spikes. He leaned back in his chair, his thin brown fingers caressing the stem of one of the beautiful wine glasses that she had brought with her from England, and smiled at his hostess, the smile broadening as he met her glance of politely veiled but most intense dislike. Her hatred amused him and disturbed him not at all. In fact he enjoyed it, as he enjoyed all manifestations of vitality. He liked the little woman. An artist himself, he understood and reverenced her passionate creativeness, expending itself so uselessly upon human material and so finely upon the trappings of life. Witness the mess she was making of her husband and the success she was making of this party. He wished that she would understand herself, would realise that the artists of this world make things, not people, cease her disastrous efforts to save William and give herself into his hands that he save her. Creators. Saviours. Comforters. It would save a lot of trouble, he thought, if every man and woman could realise at the outset which leaf of the triune clover claimed their allegiance, accept the limitation with humility and not try to behave as though they had it in them to be the whole damn plant. But humility was not Mrs. William's strong suit. Poor Mrs. William! He raised his glass and bowed to her.

"Your health, Ma'am," he said.

"Thank you, Mr. Haslam," she replied stiffly. She would never call him Tai Haruru, the Sounding Sea, nor allow him to call William by the Maori name of Maui-Potiki with which the Maoris had honoured him, calling him after the Hercules of their legends because he was so strong. She thought it ridiculous affectation for Englishmen to adopt these fancy names. And by doing so they put themselves on a level with the Maoris, as though the brown men were their equals. Englishmen were Englishmen, members of a superior race, and should not forget the fact. It was that they should not forget it that she made for them these little civilised feasts here in the wilderness.

And Tai Haruru appreciated them and for that she was grateful to him. "A Flemish interior," he said now, looking about him. "Jordaens or Van Dyck. The colour and composition are quite perfect."

She smiled coldly. Though she regarded him as half a savage yet at the same time she had to acknowledge that whenever she had created one of her "interiors" he was always quite unconsciously the central figure in it, his careless aristocracy giving a distinction to her masterpiece that she would have been sorry to be without. She withdrew herself a little now and looked objectively at this present picture. The window that opened towards the forest was uncurtained, the door to the verandah open, as all doors were always open for fear of earthquake, and beyond them the illimitable blue of the deepening twilight, the voice of the wild crying out distantly yet insistently in wind and water, the brooding loneliness of this new world, made a setting that intensified by its contrast the intimate brilliance of the scene within. It increased, too, the sophistication of the lighted dinner table with its silver and glass and elaborately cooked dishes, and the group of men and women from the old world seated about it erect and mannered, voicing the soft sentiments consonant with the occasion, and wearing the glowing fastidious garments proper to the hour, with the ease of such long custom that their artificiality was not noticeable except to the suddenly sharpened perceptions of those whose souls for a moment or two stood back and watched. How absurd but yet how beautiful were the voluminous skirts of herself and Susanna, spreading over their crinolines in waves of heather-purple and delphinium-blue, how ridiculous yet how pretty their tiny waists, their great bell sleeves, their trinkets of gold and cornelian glowing like fire in the light of the candles. And how absurd was the cut of William's mulberry coat and Samuel's black one, and how unnecessary the great white stocks that propped their chins. The human form was as completely disguised by these trappings of tradition as their emotions were hidden by their cultured talk. Was it the final achievement, or the final absurdity, of civilization, that she could smile so politely upon Tai Haruru while her heart swelled with dislike for him, that she could love her husband to the point of agony and yet sit there apparently oblivious of his presence, that Samuel and Susanna could discuss animatedly with William agricultural subjects that interested them not at all, and that all of them could endure the agonies of boned and padded garments on a hot night just so that their bodies should look a different shape from that intended by Almighty God? This type of question, that had never occurred to Marianne in the old world, occurred to her constantly in the new, where the natives went half naked and the voices of wind and water spoke only of what was true, and it confused her. At every turn the new life was continually testing the values of the old. She had always taken everything about her at its current valuation, and herself at her own, with absolute certainty, and she had looked forward with passionate eagerness to stamping her valuations upon the malleable material of the new life and the new land. But was she doing it? Her reforming zeal had had about as much effect upon William as this little civilised picture that she had created had made upon the vastness of the wilds beyond this lighted room; which was simply none at all. Was she not every bit as frustrated now as she had been on the Island? A momentary silence fell and she looked at Tai Haruru touching the flower petals with the finger tips of one hand as though they were holy things. He turned and smiled at her.

"It's not what you expected?" he asked softly and mockingly. "Freedom? Scope? Satisfaction of love and ambition? You thought that here you'd have 'em all, eh? Life's much the same, my dear, wherever you live it."

There were times when his disillusionment touched her sympathy so sharply that for a moment or two she failed to resent his subtle reading of her less reputable thoughts. . . . For she was very near to a disillusionment as great as his own. . . . She looked at him attentively, seeking knowledge of him from his looks. Disillusioned though he was, yet in some way that she could not define he had found a peace that she had not found, and she envied his peace. There was no artificiality about Tai Haruru. The old olive green coat that he kept for these festive occasions, shrunken to a tight fit by much washing, did not disguise the bony structure of his strong body, and his vigorous speech was always the perfect vehicle of his thought. Yet he was not out of the picture; he was the centre of it, an aristocrat to his finger tips; but an aristocrat not of one particular mode of life but of life itself.

A slight sound made them all turn their heads towards the door opening upon the verandah and that deep blue twilight, where now a few stars were shining as the sky lifted up and up to the depth of night. Dark figures, shaped out of the darkness of the night, were padding silently upon bare feet up the steps from the garden. Then they seemed to disappear, the shadows of the verandah absorbing them as they squatted down. Then both within and without the house there was a deep listening silence, broken only by the murmuring of trees and water. It was broken quite suddenly by a voice rising up into the night with sudden passionate lament.

> "*It is well with thee, O moon! You return from death,*
> *Spreading your light on the little waves. Men say,*
> *Behold, the moon reappears;*
> *But the dead of this world return no more.*
> *Grief and pain spring up in my heart as from a fountain.*
> *I hasten to death for relief.*"

It was the lament for a great chief killed in the Maori war, and the Maoris sang it at this time all over the island.

"They do not forget," whispered William.

And Tai Haruru lifted his thrilling rough deep voice and cried back in the native language, "Farewell, Hauraki! Go, taking with you your kindness and hospitality, your generosity and valour, and leave none behind you who can fill your place. Your death was noble. Your life was short; but so it is with heroes. Farewell."

The meal was nearly finished, but in any case it was not possible to continue the old-world festivity, for the new world had broken in; the new world so-called, because it was new to the white man, but in reality hoary with legend, lit with primeval fires. They got up, blew out the candles and went out onto the verandah, lit now by the first radiance of the rising moon.

"Waipiro? Waipiro?" came a chorus of insistent voices. "Rum? Rum? Tobacco?"

"Tobacco, but not rum," whispered Marianne fiercely. "Do you hear me, William? And you, Mr. Haslam? No rum. It is enough that you white men should be sodden with the drink. There is no necessity to pollute these children too."

Her whisper was low and passionate. To William's great surprise, though she hated Scant and Isaac, she liked the Maoris. They were to her "the poor". She had no sense of fear when they came out of the forest at night and squatted on her verandah. If she had not disliked him so much she would have asked Tai Haruru to let her help him in the little surgery that was attached to his house, where he toiled evening after evening, the power that was in his hands at the service of any native man, woman or child who liked to ask for it. She admired him for that service; and for the fact that when they were settled in their chairs, and the tobacco jars and dishes of sweetmeats were going the round, he, like William, had heeded her word and had no glass beside him. . . . Though of what it cost him to sit still of an evening, and not absorb rum and water as the thirsty earth absorbs the rain, she had not the slightest idea, nor did she guess that his obedience to her wish was the measure of his liking for her.

The moon rose higher and a soft light flooded the garden, seeming to draw up the scent of the flowers like incense. One by one small flames blossomed around her, and she saw dark fingers curving about the bowls of strange carved pipes. Then the scent of tobacco rose to mingle with the scent of the flowers and there was a deep contented silence. She lay back in her chair, letting the loveliness of the scene soak through to her weariness and ease it, looking from face to face and adoring the beauty that the magic of the hour had lent to each, even the plainest. Susanna, her work-worn hands folded quietly in her lap, was so at rest that her thin ageing face had softened into a sort of fluid loveliness, like a blossom that trembles under the moon. Samuel was leaning forward, his hands clasped tightly between his knees. No relaxation ever softened Samuel's face, the lines of it were as taut as his spirit that was ever as a bent bow in the service of his God. Yet in the moonlight his tense face shone as though it were made not of flesh and blood but of some exquisite, tempered, white-hot metal that· time would never touch. His eyes were burning as they passed from one Maori face to another, and his thin lips moved. She knew that he was praying for these children of God, his soul thirsting to gather them into the fold. Tai Haruru, puffing at his long pipe shaped like a bird, was looking at Samuel with a deep and thoughtful attention. His face, too, was beautiful, eagle-keen, carved out of dark wood, his eyes gentle as she had never seen them. . . . Reverence. . . . There was something in Samuel that he reverenced. His thought, whatever it was, must have been as the brushing of delicate wing-tips upon the other man's soul, for Samuel stirred, withdrew his eyes from the Maoris, looked at Tai Haruru and smiled. The comradeship of their meeting glances astonished Marianne, for surely Samuel with his passionate belief in God, and Tai Haruru who denied God and worshipped only life, could have little in common. And William? She could not see his face, for he sat slumped in his chair, his head bent, as though he sat there bowed down by heavy sorrow. She felt a slight stirring of resentment (for what in the world had William to be sorrowful about?) but it was quickly lost in her wonderment at the sense of power, mighty to save, that his heavy figure gave her. For William was a weak man. Yet the power was there, and it was not only physical; what the moonlight was bringing out was a spiritual quality. Yes, they were all beautiful in this unearthly moonlight, folded in this silence. She could not see herself, but her ballooning purple skirt made a glorious pool of colour about her, and her folded hands were at peace.

And then there were the children, the Maoris. A few of them she knew well; Jacky Poto and Kapua-Manga the Black Cloud, William's faithful friends and lumbermen, and Wi Rapa and Ngati-Pou, each of the four a rangitira with the light brown skin, the long head, aquiline nose and white-soled feet of perfect breeding, princes wherever they went, chivalrous and brave, kindly souls who had never in all their lives cut up a man for eating unless they had killed him quickly and painlessly first. The other Maoris who squatted contentedly puffing at their pipes were dark-skinned, the tattooing on their faces and bodies less exquisitely designed than that of the four high-caste gentlemen. But they had the same charming manners and cheerful inconsequence, the same love for the interminable telling of tales.

"Yes, Kapua-Manga," said Marianne, seeing his bright eyes beseechingly upon her. "Tell us how you came to Aotearoa."

And Kapua-Manga, who was bilingual, lifted up his voice and told his tale in an admixture of pidgin English and his own language that was queerly intriguing and effective. For each race among his listeners some single beautiful phrase would leap up suddenly in the surrounding mystery. They clung to it, treasured it, waiting for the next, linking them together, not altogether understanding the recitation yet aware of its beauty and mysticism, its deep and reverent sense of the glory of the gods and the grandeur of man's soul.

Keeping the setting sun upon their left hand, said Kapua-Manga, steering by the stars, the great war canoes of the Maori people came to Aotearoa in the dawn of the world. They had migrated from the Pacific, "from the great distance," said Black Cloud, "from the faraway places, the gathering place of souls, from Hawaiki," drawn to the Long White Cloud by the tales that the sea rovers told of its beauty, its fine climate and fertile soil. Great and glorious were those war canoes, and Kapua-Manga sang their praises as he rocked to the rhythm of his tale on William's verandah. He must have got a little rum from somewhere before he came, William thought, for his narration was wonderfully mellifluous. Each canoe was hollowed from a great tree, Kapua-Manga told them, so great a tree that a hundred rowers could seat themselves within it, and was exquisitely carved, painted and inlaid, with the head of a majestic Taniwha, a magic sea-monster, carved at the prow to see which way they were going. These mighty men of valour had with them their shields and spears, war-trumpets, tomahawks and clubs, food, calabashes of water, and seeds to plant in the new land. Also they had their parrots (yes, even such fine parrots as the fine parrot Maui-Potiki had within his house) and their carved flutes made from the thigh bones of their enemies, to which they sang sweet songs when they rested, and told old tales. And so after many weeks of journeying, guided by the setting sun upon their left hand and the great stars overhead, they came to Aotearoa the Long White Cloud and saw the great forests, and the snow upon the mountains, and the white flowers and the red flowers, the raupo and the pohoutakawa, and heard the small birds singing like chiming bells, and saw the great bird, the moa, hopping this way and that, but not able to fly because he was too large, and the wild ducks and the wild pigeons, and the merry little lizards with jewels in their heads. And when they saw this beautiful country they shouted with a great shout of joy, and they pulled up their great canoes upon the white beaches, and they slung their tomahawks from their wrists, and took their spears and clubs and war-trumpets in their hands, and girded with the belt of scarlet feathers of the war-god Tu they went forth to do battle for this land, to conquer or to die. And they conquered, for each Maori was a Tino Tangata, a great warrior, and the few folk who lived in the land were a poor folk, and afraid, and were soon no more, their bodies eaten and their souls dispatched to Reinga to dwell with their ancestors. Then the Maori people made themselves fine villages in the forests and along the sea-shore, with strong Pas built upon the hilltops to protect them, and sowed their seed and reaped their crops, and for centuries they grew and multiplied, and formed themselves into tribes and fought each tribe with the other tribe just for the joy of the fighting. And they had their priests, their Tohungas, who could speak for them with their dead and beseech the gods for them, and each village had its house set apart where the wise men taught the young boys to repeat by heart the names of their ancestors, the dying messages left by the heroes of old, and all the songs, proverbs, funeral chants and incantations that were as precious to the Maori people as their very souls.

But now, said Kapua-Manga sadly, the fame of Aotearoa had reached the white man also, and he had come journeying out of the great distance in his canoes with the great white sails, and he too had landed on the white beaches and had taken his musket in his hand and gone forth to conquer, and when the Maori people had withstood him he had called to himself great warriors from across the sea who were not only girded with scarlet but coated with it also, and the Red Garment had prevailed, and the white man had cried to the Maori, "Fly away on the wings of the wood pigeon, and feed on the berries of the wood, for I have taken your land."

"That is not true, Kapua-Manga," insisted William. "It is only a part of your land that we have taken. Much land is still left you. The fight is over and now the white man and the Maori live here side by side in friendship and affection."

Kapua-Manga, refusing to argue, changed the subject with much courtesy and tact, took up his thigh-bone lute and sang the song of Reinga, the spirit land. Far to the north, upon the sea-shore where Tangaroa the great ocean and Tawhiri-Matea the wind strive always together, there is a cavern within a rocky hillside and through this cavern the spirits enter Reinga. Very sacred is this cavern, so sacred that the waterfalls cease to roar as they pass by, and Tangaroa is still when he stands upon the threshold, and Tawhiri-Matea falls silent with a great gentleness. The Tohungas can see the spirits of the dead flying northward, flying like the wild geese, sighing and lamenting because they must leave the sunshine of the sweet earth and pass from day to night.

> "*Passing now are the ghosts of the dead.*
> *The winds are hushed, the rude waves hide their head;*
> *And the fount flows silently,*
> *And the breeze forgets to sigh,*
> *And the torrent to moan*
> *O'er the rock and stone,*
> *For the dead pass by.*"

Kapua-Manga dropped his lute and sang no more, and one by one the Maoris arose, bowed, and passed away into the night. The white folk sat silent, listening to the voice of Tawhiri-Matea crying in the forest, and to the sound of the creek murmuring over the stones on its journey to the great god Tangaroa.

Then Tai Haruru spoke. "A queer myth, this of the immortality of the human soul. Strange how it persists."

"My friend, truth must always persist," said Samuel, swinging round, and defrauded of the souls of those dusky children who had slipped away into the night before he could recover from the mesmerism of Kapua-Manga's chanting, rise to his feet and speak to them of Christ, he fixed his burning eyes upon the heathen at his side. Tai Haruru immediately arose, and turning from Samuel with a gesture of courtesy almost identical with the gesture of Black Cloud when he turned with tact from the subject of the iniquities of the Red Garment, he bowed to Marianne and Susanna and went away also into the night.

William chuckled. "Slippery eels, these heathen," he said. "But isn't their faith as good as yours, Kelly? The Maoris worship their gods of wind and water and forest, and they die with magnificent courage believing that their souls will live on in Reinga. And Tai Haruru—he calls himself a heathen—but his reverence for life could not be deeper if he gave to life the name of God."

"The Maoris are without salvation," declaimed Samuel heavily. "They go to their spirit land sighing and mourning, they speak of the change of death as the change from day to night. They have not learned that to die is to live. They are without hope. As for your friend Haslam, he too, without salvation, is a man bereft of hope, a dead tree, a giant of the forest smitten by lightning whose leaves will never bud again."

They found that they were alone, for Marianne and Susanna had rustled away to the kitchen to wash up the dishes. William fetched himself a drink, for his misery and despair were heavy upon him, and then came back to Samuel again.

"Salvation's a fine-sounding word," he grumbled. "One of those big words you parsons are always using and don't yourselves know the meaning of."

"I know the meaning of salvation," said Samuel," and so do you. I offered it to you once before and you refused it."

He gripped his hands together again between his knees, praying for wisdom in his dealings with this man. His previous sermon, he remembered, had gone off William like water off a duck's back. But then he had offered William salvation through a way of life that was alien to him. "It is out of one's own sort of life," had said Susanna at the time, "that the gate of salvation opens." Well, William was living his own sort of life, and what with the drink and one thing and another a nice sort of mess he was making of it, as Samuel had foretold. Yet it remained his sort of life, that he had chosen, and from somewhere within it there must be the way out to the further country.

"You are making your good wife excessively unhappy," he said. He had not meant to say that. The words were drawn from him by the nauseating smell of William's whisky and by a sudden stifled sound from indoors, as though a woman wept.

William set down his glass. "It's a misfit," he growled. He had not meant to say that either. The worst of Samuel was that his sincerity always dragged forth the truth, as though upon a fish-hook. An uncomfortable little man to have to do with, though one couldn't help liking him.

"And the hell of it is," he continued, "that Marianne loves me and I've never loved her." He dropped his voice. "Since we've been man and wife I've come to hate her," he said heavily.

"Why did you marry her?" asked Samuel.

William sighed and was silent. He had vowed that he would never tell a soul of the mistake that he had made, for there was the danger that the knowledge might come round to Marianne.

Samuel looked at him keenly. It had struck him as odd that before the bride's arrival he should have been asked to call the banns of marriage between William Edmond and Marguerite Félicité, and that after she had arrived it should turn out that her bridegroom had been mistaken in her names and that she was Marianne Véronique. He had let the mistake pass at the time—there had been nothing else to do—and he asked no questions now. It was the future, not the past of this man, with which he was concerned. He counted William as one of his flock, and himself as responsible for his happiness as a father for that of his child.

"The thing is done now," he said sternly.

"Of course," said William with a touch of arrogance. "And I'm no quitter. Hate it or not, I've never yet made a bargain and not stuck to it."

"Yet to stick to a hated bargain with hatred is to damn your soul in hell," Samuel reminded him.

Poor William groaned in acquiescence.

"It is not impossible to cleave to it with love," continued Samuel. William emitted a contemptuous snort.

"No," insisted Samuel. "Most of the basic truths of life sound absurd at first hearing. If I say to you that hatred is only the reverse side of love you'll tell me that I'm a liar. Yet it's true. Could you understand the meaning of light if there were no darkness to point the contrast? Day and night, life and death, love and hatred, since none of these things can have any being at all apart from the existence of the other, you can no more separate them than you can separate the two sides of a coin. To possess one is to possess the other; only the indolence of human nature finds it so hard to pierce through to the other side."

"I don't want metaphysics," growled William. "I want practical instructions."

"We're not entirely human," said Samuel. "There's divinity in all of us. And as in the divine regard there is no shadow of hatred, there must have been some moment in your life together when you loved your wife?"

William rubbed his nose, considering. "There was that moment when I met her at Wellington," he said. "I didn't hate her when I saw her standing there on the deck of the Green Dolphin, with Old Nick in his cage beside her. She looked such a little bit of a thing—and she'd brought that damned parrot across hundreds of miles of ocean just to please me. I took her in my arms and kissed her. I've never felt more tender to a woman than I did to Marianne then."

"There was your moment of vision," said Samuel, "and from now on you will live your life by the light of it. In faith that what was then, is, that love is co-existent with hatred, you will take your married life with this woman and wrest it into conformity with that one moment."

"Eh?" said William.

"With all the strength that you have," said Samuel, "you will endeavour to give to your wife, through every moment of your life together, for however many years it may last, the same joy that I have no doubt you gave her when you took her in your arms on the deck of the Green Dolphin."

"Not possible," said William. "Just wild idealistic moonshine."

"I agree that the task is superhuman," said Samuel. "I did not say that you would accomplish it, I said that you should endeavour to do so with all the strength that you have. Fortunately for us men, when human endeavour is strained to the utmost it taps divine energy, and the two together are invariably sufficient for salvation. If you lend your life to this task in this way you will undoubtedly save your wife from disaster."

"Salvation again!" groaned William. "Always salvation. And who am I that I should set myself up to save Marianne? She's trying to save me, she'll tell you—from the drink and one thing and another."

"Give her the happiness of thinking that she's done it," said Samuel. "To think she's saved you will save her from the misery of her present sense of frustration. She's a proud woman and her sense of failure is poisoning her whole life. As for you, you're capable both of a self-abnegation and a humility beyond her power at any time; and there's no abnegation to touch that of letting another have the praise of what is in truth your own accomplishment, no humility so pleasing to God. Well, there is the choice. You can acquiesce in things as they are, or you can wrest them by the power of faith the other way round. It's the old choice between chaos and creation, darkness and light. Always the same old choice—which side of the coin do you want?"

He finished abruptly, knocked out his pipe and got up. Leaving William slumped in his chair, his mind swinging heavily this way and that between those two alternatives of chaos and creation, the one so vile and the other so impossible, he made his way through the heavy, sweet scents of the garden to that gate in the palisade that opened upon the primeval wilderness. He stood there holding to it, his knuckles showing white through the skin, the sweat standing out on his forehead as he prayed with desperation for the souls of men. Behind him in the house William was blundering to a choice that might be for him the choice between salvation and damnation, and before him it seemed to his fevered imagination that tall figures moved weeping through the fern, dusky children whose hearts were torn between the lust of killing and the grief with which they watched the heroes go down to the darkness of the grave. Sheep having no shepherd. He found that the gate was unlocked. He opened it and made his way between the walls of fern into the darkness of the forest. But he saw no one, he heard nothing except the sighing of the wind in the treetops, the crying of a night bird, the strange rustlings of small beasts in the undergrowth. Not yet. The darkness rose up before him like a wall, like the invisible frontier of which he had been told, that frontier that the white man crossed at his peril. Yet as he stood there, straining his eyes into the darkness as a man upon a mountain top strains forward to see a far-off glimpse of the promised land, the certainty came to him that one day he would cross it, carrying with him the saving knowledge of the love of God. He might cross it to his martyrdom, but martyrdom held no terrors for him. The only thing he had not relinquished, when he gave himself to Christ, was the right to follow his Master to the cross.

5

With sleeves tucked up and large aprons over their spreading skirts the two ladies washed up the dishes. There was scarcely room for two crinolines in the small kitchen, but they were accustomed now to achieving some sort of workable compromise between current fashion and pioneer life, and if it occurred to them sometimes that it would be easier to wear tattooing and feathers, as the Maoris did, the immodesty of the thought did not find expression on their lips.

"I hate the man!" said Marianne fiercely, scrubbing violently at a saucepan; and she burst into sudden tears.

"Which man, dear?" asked Susanna, wisely ignoring the tears, and gently and unobtrusively wiping away the soapsuds with which Marianne's enraged splashings had sprinkled her.

Marianne stopped, choked, and stood with one hand across her eyes, fighting her tears. Ridiculous to cry like this! Ridiculous and humiliating before this woman who was socially her inferior. She blew her nose violently, conquered the weakness and resumed her scrubbing. "Mr. Haslam," she said. "His influence upon William has been disastrous."

"Don't make him a scapegoat," said Susanna.

"A what?" demanded Marianne.

"A scapegoat. It's such an easy thing to do. It's such a comfort, always, to blame one's failure upon someone else."

Marianne ceased her labours for a moment and drew herself up to the full imperious height of her tiny figure, wiping the soapsuds off her fingers with incomparable dignity. Was Susanna presuming to preach to her? She took too much upon herself. She was not a parson, merely a parson's wife.

"My dear, in looks you remind me so much of Queen Victoria," said Susanna. "Here, let me do the washing, it's less tiring, and you're quite exhausted."

She pushed Marianne gently out of the way and had the saucepan clean in the twinkling of an eye. "I've been washing up all my life," she explained. "My father was a country doctor, you know, and he was so poor that we lived like a labourer's family. There were many children and my mother died giving birth to the last. I was the eldest. When my father died, and the children were all out in the world, there was no money for me, so I became housekeeper to an old clergyman in Manchester. I was not fit to teach, or do anything like that because, you see, I had never had any proper schooling. It was hard work in Manchester, but I did not mind, because I met Samuel there. So you see I have always been used to hard work—not like you, who have lived as a lady. You get too tired. You ought to let William help you."

There was humility in her tone but no subservience. It conveyed to Marianne that though in the old world one of them had lived like a lady and the other had not, yet in the new world they were equal. Marianne's figure relaxed a little, though she still continued to speak tartly.

"You have just told me I am a failure. It would be a humiliating confession of it, if I allowed my husband to do half my housework."

"It is not in the care of your house that you fail," said Susanna.

"You are being insufferable!" snapped Marianne.

"Yes," said Susanna. "I suppose I am. Forgive me."

"Now you've begun, Susanna, you'd better go on," said her hostess in a towering rage. "It's no good speaking half your mind and not the whole of it. Go on. Tell me. Why am I making a failure of my marriage?"

"You're too independent," said Susanna. "We love those whom we serve. You never let William serve you."

"He smashes everything."

"No Christian woman should love her china more than she loves her husband."

"Susanna, how dare you!"

"I really don't know how I dare," said Susanna, marvelling at herself. "I suppose it is because I am going away to-morrow and I am so sorry that you are not happy."

"I'd be happy if it wasn't for Mr. Haslam," fumed Marianne.

"You mean if it wasn't for hating Mr. Haslam. It's a pity you hate him when he's God's gift in your life."

"What on earth do you mean, Susanna? Are you suggesting that I should fall in love with Timothy Haslam?"

Susanna flushed crimson with painful embarrassment at the mere thought. "Oh no, no! I just meant that if you believe in God omnipresent then you must believe that everything that comes into your life, person or event, must have something of God in it to be experienced and loved; not hated."

"I definitely refuse to love Mr. Haslam," said Marianne. "And I refuse to insult Almighty God by thinking that any gift of His to me could take the form of that wicked old heathen. Susanna, that you should dare to talk to me like this in my own kitchen!"

"Forgive me," said Susanna. "You know, dear, it is very difficult for parsons and their wives. They must speak the truth as they see it, for that is the work to which God has called them, but when they are no better than those they preach to, and possibly worse, it is very irritating for their congregation and very embarrassing for themselves. I assure you, dear, that there are times when I wish with all my heart and soul that Samuel was a cattle-dealer. . . . Though to be sure he'd make a very bad cattle-dealer."

"And he makes a good parson," said Marianne with sudden generosity. "And you make a good parson's wife. You've said your say now, Susanna, and can rest easy."

Her anger had died out of her, its place taken by a sudden sense of weariness and hopelessness. Her mind turned this way and that, repudiating Susanna's reasons for her wretchedness, seeking others.

"If only we had a child!" she said suddenly. "I have a boxful of lovely little clothes all put away. Did you ever have a child, Susanna?"

"Yes," said Susanna. "It was in Manchester. We could not afford a good doctor, and the one we had was not very clever with me, and I lost the babe and could not have another."

"Poor Susanna!" said Marianne.

"I think that you should rest more, work less hard," said Susanna. "And you should not hate Mr. Haslam. You will not have a child while you hate."

Marianne laughed. "You know nothing of eugenics, Susanna!" she said.

"No," said Susanna. "I don't know what they are, even. But my Grandmother told me that a woman has more hope of a child if her heart and mind and body are soft and gentle like the earth in spring. My Grandmother was a country woman, a farmer's daughter."

Their work was finished and they went together to Susanna's bedroom door, and after a moment's hesitation they kissed each other, with affection and respect, and then Marianne went to her room.

It was filled with moonlight and the scent of flowers, and the long blue curtains of the four-poster stirred very gently. The air that blew in from the garden was cool and refreshing now, after the heat of the kitchen, and Marianne knelt down before the open window and with a sigh of relief lifted her heavy hair off her hot forehead. Frustration was still dogging her, even in this new land of opportunity. Was there anything in what Susanna had said? Would she have more hope in submission and helplessness? To cultivate weaknesses of her own seemed a strange way of winning her husband from his, but she had to own that in the eighteen months of their married life dominance and strength had utterly failed. And hatred? Her hatred and jealousy of Tai Haruru had not caused William to love her more, but less. William was faithful in friendship and incredibly obstinate. Yet how could she cease hating? She had always had strong and unswerving likes and dislikes and she did not see how she was to deny herself her hatred of Tai Haruru without denying her own nature. She must just act, she supposed, act all the time as she had been acting for a short while at supper to-night, be so consistently polite that William would cease to notice her dislike of his friend. . . . Keep up appearances. . . . Possibly that was more important than she had hitherto realized. She had wondered to-night if the deceptions of civilization were an achievement or an absurdity. Possibly they were an achievement; something creative. And would she care how much, or how exhaustingly, she must act if by her acting she won William? . . . If she won William. . . . Suddenly she remembered that night aboard the Orion when she had wondered if she would ever experience either the fairyland of mutual love, or the homely place beyond it where men and women who have so loved put a light in the window of the house of life and kindle a flame on the hearth. She and William had had no fairyland; for some reason or other the woman that she was had not been the same woman whom he had loved and dreamed of and idealized for so many years; and though they lived together there was neither brightness nor warmth in their life. She remembered that on that night she had suddenly for the first time in her life turned aside from the forcing of events into a mould of her own contriving, bent her head and taken her hand off the tiller, and waited for something outside herself to take her in charge. She had felt like a little child lost in the dark, she remembered, just sitting there weeping and waiting. But she had felt at peace, as peaceful as Susanna must feel when she took all that came as the gift of God. She dropped her head on her arms, stretched along the window-sill, and though she did not pray she abandoned herself, and wept and waited.

It was in this attitude of humility, sobbing with her head on her arms, that William found her.

"Marianne! Marianne!" he cried in consternation, and knelt

down beside her and took her in his arms. She said nothing, but clung to him like a child and sobbed on as he clumsily stroked her hair and sought desperately in his fuddled mind for the right words to comfort her, and to express aright the resolution that he had just made out there on the verandah, after Samuel had left him.

"See here, Marianne," he said at last, "I've been a clumsy fool since our marriage, a drunken selfish brute of a fellow, and I've made you wretched. But I see my fault and I ask pardon. If you'll forgive me I'll start afresh and do better. Please God I'll be a good husband to you yet. Say you forgive me, Marianne."

"Yes! Yes! Yes!" sobbed Marianne passionately. "If only you'll love me, William. If only you'll love me."

"I do love you, my girl," said William steadily. "When I do or say things that anger you and you doubt my love think of our wedding morning, when we met on the Green Dolphin and kissed each other with that blessed old parrot looking on. You did not doubt then that I loved you. When things go wrong between us think of that moment and say to yourself, 'That's William. That's what he really feels for me.' That was a good moment, my girl. That was our real marriage. We took each other then for better for worse. That was a good moment. That was the moment that must set the standard for our life together."

Marianne had ceased sobbing and was quiet in his arms, trembling a little, very small and subdued. "That and this," she said. "I'm sorry, William, that I've hated Mr. Haslam, and Scant and Isaac. I will try not to hate your friends."

William was altogether dumbfounded by the humility of her bent head and gentle childish words. If she could always be like this then perhaps it would not be so hard. But, of course, she wouldn't be. The childishness of Marianne at this moment was not a facet of her nature that could be expected to appear other than rarely.

"You fight the hatred and I'll fight the drink, my girl," he said. "And then maybe we'll not do so badly."

He lifted her to her feet and took his arms from her, but she was so exhausted that she nearly fell. She lifted her arms and then dropped them again. "I believe, William" she said weakly, "that you'll have to unhook me down the back."

He was once again dumbfounded. Never before had she even tolerated his clumsy presence in her room while she was dressing or undressing, and now she wanted to be unhooked down the back. Breathing stertorously, his hands shaking with his anxiety, he bent to his task, cursing himself for that last pull at the whisky that he had taken before he had come to her. A man needed to be cold sober for a job like this. But his good angel must have been in attendance, for somehow he got all the hooks out of the eyes without dragging more than a mere half dozen away from their moorings in the silk, and he took down her heavy hair and brushed it, and then tactfully withdrawing so that she could do it up in its curl papers (for he had the sense to realise that not if they lived to be eighty must he let out even by so much as a hint that he knew about those curl papers beneath her nightcap) he took her little shoes to the kitchen and polished them, and set out the breakfast china, and smashed the slop basin and hid the pieces, and hoped to God she would not storm and scold when she found them in the morning.

When he went back to their room she was already asleep, her cheek on her hand, her nightcap with its goffered frills tied demurely beneath her chin. He was reminded suddenly of that morning when he had looked out of his window in Green Dolphin Street and seen her leaning from her window in Le Paradis, her face transfigured by her passionate delight in the beauty of the morning. He had shared her delight and felt at one with her then. And they had had a jolly adventure together that morning. She was a good adventuress and a good comrade. Perhaps after all it would not be so bad.

CHAPTER TWO

1

Marianne dressed herself as quickly as she could. All was bustle this morning for William with his lumbermen was taking the timber down the creek to the sea to be loaded there upon a timber ship sailing from Wellington to Sydney, the Thrush, skipper Captain Parker. During the two years since the Kellys' visit something very like prosperity had come to the settlement, and Marianne was aware that William and Tai Haruru, just men, did not hesitate, albeit reluctantly, to attribute it to her own unresting ambition and creativeness. They had thought themselves doing well when she came to them, but now they were definitely prosperous. Whether the prosperity was worth the unending driving exertion of mind as well as body that she expected from them Tai Haruru was doubtful, and William in no doubt at all—it wasn't—but it was the price that both of them paid for domestic peace. Marianne knew it, and smiled as she dressed herself. She had gained enormously in self-mastery during these last two years. She had learned now not to let her sharp tongue run away with her but to use it as a tool for a set purpose, and when she had got her way with it the atmosphere of peace and gentleness that ensued was also her deliberate creation—the greater the yielding of the males the greater the subsequent calm in which she permitted them to bask.

It had been her suggestion that the timber should go down the creek by barge to the sea instead of being hauled slowly and laboriously overland by wagon to Wellington. She had plunged boldly for the expenditure of building the barges and erecting a strongly built stone jetty running out into deep water at the little fishing hamlet at the coast, with shacks for the men, and sheds and yards for the timber. She had also driven William and Tai Haruru into employing many more lumbermen in the forest, and shaping the whole business on a far more ambitious scale. There was even an office on the quay at Wellington now, with a trustworthy Scotsman named MacTavish in charge, and Marianne herself took the long journey into Wellington regularly, and stayed with Susanna, and put the fear of God into MacTavish and his clerks. The enormous increase of the business upon insufficient capital had been a gamble, but they had won it. "Haslam & Ozanne" was now one of the chief timber exporting businesses in North Island.

Marianne enjoyed putting the fear of God into MacTavish and the clerks, and she enjoyed dealing with the finances of the business. In spirit she was very near the Island of her childhood on those days of hard work in the office. One day, she thought, when she was an old woman, she would like to go back to St. Pierre, sail into the harbour and let down her anchor for ever. William could not go back, of course, because of that regrettable incident in his youth, but probably William would die first. Men usually did. There always seemed to be more widows than widowers. . . . Men succumbed earlier than women to the exhaustion of married life, William had told her once in a fit of temper. . . . But in any case, before she could know rest, she had her ambition to satisfy. She must win for herself and William that great house and wealth, and servants and flocks and herds such as Job had in the days of his prosperity. Well-to-do though they might be by pioneer standards she still had to work harder than any peasant's wife on the far-away Island, and her clothes were shabby and worn and she was always very tired. But it would all be worth while if she could get what she wanted in the end.

As she dressed she reminded herself happily of all that she had gained already. First of all there was William himself. She believed that by dint of many and most persevering scoldings she had more or less won him from the drink. He was a new man, healthier, happier, less addicted to bad company, full of admiration for her efficiency, touchingly grateful when following Susanna's advice she did violence to her own nature and invited his so-called co-operation in her house-work. He was grateful, too, for the effort she made to be more polite to Tai Haruru. Of course there were still times when he made her life wretched, when he was morose, rough-spoken, got drunk with Scant and Isaac, went to Wellington to fetch the stores and gambled away all the money she had given him to pay for them, came back to answer her reproaches with sullen silence or a sudden blinding rage that left her oddly shaken and afraid. Yet she said to herself that he knew now that he had a wonderful wife, and when the quick rage had passed, and his naturally sunny temper had asserted itself again, he would take her in his arms and tell her so, and she would forget that just for a moment she had been afraid. She never tried to analyse this fear. If ever she woke up in the night and heard a small in-sistent nagging voice asking deep in her soul if their marriage was really as satisfactory as she thought it was, she immediately silenced it. Of course it was. She had made a new man of him and he knew it. She had revolutionised the timber business and he and Tai Haruru knew it. She was a marvellous wife and he was deeply aware of the fact. . . . And now she was to bear him a son.

At last! She had almost given up hope, for she was now thirty-eight years old, but at last the miracle had happened. In another month William would take her to stay with Susanna in Wellington, where there was a good doctor, and soon after that the boy would be born. It was amazingly good of Susanna to have promised to take her in and nurse her, but she was not at all well and she needed the help of another woman. And Susanna was immensely interested in Marianne's little son. It was her opinion that his flame of life had been lit by Marianne's striving after gentleness. Marianne herself thought that was all moonshine. It was not gentleness but deter-mination that had produced the child. She had willed the boy with all the strength that she had, and had issued her commands to Almighty God during a very long period, and she was not accus-tomed either to having her will defeated or her commands dis-regarded. She always got everything in the end.

But it wasn't a very pleasant process getting the baby. For the first time in her life she felt really ill, and for the first time in her life she longed for her mother. But it wasn't any good now longing for Sophie, for Sophie was dead. She had become ill soon after Mari-anne had left the Island and after two years of pain she had died, and now Marguerite, still unmarried, was alone at Le Paradis with a totally blind father. If she found life hard she gave no sign of it, for her letters were always cheerful, and Marianne in her busy life took the letters at their face value and did not worry about her sister. As for William, he never mentioned Marguerite at all. When the letters came he read them in silence, and then handed them back to Marianne. But he had been very upset over Sophie's death, and had wept for her in the most foolish way, considering that she was only his mother-in-law. Marianne herself had not grieved overmuch; but now, as she waited for the birth of the child, she found herself thinking of her mother constantly. Even so, in this same sickness and weariness, had her mother waited for her.

It was Autumn, and the wind rattled the casement. She finished her dressing, opened the window wide and leaned out. The sky looked curiously veiled, as though it were dusty, and in spite of the wind it was stiflingly hot. It had not rained much lately and the queer dusty look that was in the sky was over the whole earth too. The woods looked desiccated, the autumn flowers in the garden dropped and had a dirty look; even the exquisite mountains had lost something of their clarity of form and purity of colour. "Earthquake weather," thought Marianne suddenly. "I don't like it."

She could never accustom herself to earthquakes. They left her as oddly shaken and afraid as did William's occasional rages, and before they came she had that same feeling of unease, the sense that all was not well, somehow, beneath the foundations. Vigorously she thrust the sensation from her. Of course all was well; with the weather, the timber business and her life. Everything was always well when a resolute spirit such as her own stood at the helm. She took a clean handkerchief from her drawer and went downstairs to give William his breakfast.

But he had laid the table himself and was just finishing his meal as she came into the room, his head tipped back and a huge blue teacup turned upside down over his nose. He absorbed the last sugary drop vulgarly from the bottom of it, set it down, wiped his mouth on a large and gaudy bandanna, jumped up and came to her. "Sleep well?" he asked her solicitously. He was hugely delighted about the baby, immensely patient with her, tender and understanding over her whims and petulances. "Hate to leave you," he growled now, sighing noisily, and took her in his arms.

But looking up at him she saw that his tawny eyes were dancing, and she felt a pang of intolerable anger and jealousy. It was always so when he was going off on his own on some rather lengthy expedition. Upon these occasions, when he should have been heartsick at parting from her, he looked like a schoolboy going home for the holidays, and it made it no better when he pulled a long face and sighed lugubriously like this, for always his eyes were dancing.

"It'll be hateful, left here alone with Mr. Haslam," she said pettishly, shutting her eyes that she might not see the merriment in his but only feel the strength of his arms about her. "He should go this time, not you."

"Taking the wood to the sea is always my job," said William cheerfully. "It needs no special knowledge, only goodwill and muscle. Old Tai Haruru has his work cut out here, training that new batch of men. A kauri tree must be felled just right, and there's no man in the world knows more about it than he does."

She withdrew herself from his arms. "You're always glad of an excuse to leave me," she said harshly.

"Now, sweetheart, that's not fair," he protested, mopping his forehead with the bandanna. "If I seem a bit cheery this morning it's for thinking that maybe down by the shore I'll be catching a glimpse of the old Green Dolphin sailing along to Wellington."

"Is she due in again?" asked Marianne almost eagerly, and sitting down she poured out a cup of tea and allowed herself to have her thoughts diverted. The Green Dolphin was still speeding gloriously about the seaways of the world, with New Zealand as the focal point of her activities, and they occasionally saw Captain O'Hara and Nat, and were always the happier for seeing them. The jolly old Green Dolphin was a spiritual power in their lives. That morning of their far-away childhood when they had discovered her had been the only time when they had been perfectly happy together. Though they never spoke of it to each other they often thought of it, and both of them with the realisation that what once had been might conceivably be again. For William the adventure, like the meeting on the Green Dolphin on the morning of their marriage, was like a lodestar by which, whenever he thought of the Green Dolphin, he tried to steer. If only, he thought, Marianne had retained her love of adventure for the sake of adventure, and not as a means to an end. But her life seemed to have settled not into this hard absorbed humdrum routine of house and business and the eternal, and to him hateful, striving for wealth.

"One day," he said, "you must come with me to take the wood to the sea. You've never been. It's a rough trip but you'd enjoy it."

"My dear William!" ejaculated Marianne. "I've not the time for unnecessary travelling."

"You're a good traveller," said William. "I'd like to travel with you in the bush one day. Right over the Maori frontier. It's a new world there. Make you open your eyes wide."

She looked at him over the rim of her teacup and he saw a sudden flash of excitement light her face. So she was still an adventuress at heart. He was glad. But all she said was, "The Green Dolphin is coming from China this time, isn't she? I'm glad of that. We're using the last caddy-full of tea."

The problem of overseas supplies was a perpetual one for housewives. In Wellington, when the tea was running low, Susanna lived with one eye on the tea-caddy and the other on the flagstaff that would announce the arrival of an overdue tea clipper, and when she saw the flag run up she used the last spoonful. But Marianne could not even do that. When the tea was finished she just had to wait in patience. One learned patience in a country where one's newspapers were eight months old, and it took five months for a correspondent in Nelson in South Island to receive a reply to a letter sent to Auckland in North Island and answered by return of post.

They finished their breakfast and went out into the garden where the hot wind seemed to meet them like a blow in the face. "Earthquake weather," said William briefly, and then forgot the menace in the bustle of departure.

A number of men were going with the great timber barges down to the sea; William himself, Scant and Isaac, Kapua-Manga, Jacky Poto and several young Maoris. The whole colony had turned out to see them off and when William and Marianne came out of the house there was quite a crowd about the jetty that had been built out into the creek. The last planks were rattling into place on the barges and upon the foremost one food and water and blankets were being loaded, for the journey to the sea sometimes took more than a day. Tai Haruru was there, standing with folded arms upon the jetty and running a critical eye over the barges. They had been Marianne's idea but he had seen to the building of them. The native war canoes had been his inspiration and each prow carried the proud head of a Taniwha. Each of these monsters was quite different, but each was equally imaginative, majestic and terrifying, for Tai Haruru did not become less of an artist as the years went by. Marianne could never look at them without a smile, and a remembrance of the carved chair in Captain O'Hara's cabin.

Tai Haruru saw her smile and came to stand beside her on the jetty. "So we're to be left alone together, Ma'am," he said politely.

"Not for the first time," replied Marianne tartly.

"As a rule I see little of you upon these occasions," said Tai Haruru. "This time I hope I shall see more."

She looked up at him, surprised at the unusual gentleness of his tone. He was looking at her very kindly. He had been persistently kind ever since he had known that the baby was on the way. She did not know if the kindness was for herself as herself, or simply for the vehicle that was to bring new life into the world.

There was a shout, and all was ready. William kissed her tenderly and jumped from the jetty to the foremost barge, where Scant and Kapua-Manga stood beside the great rudder. They had no need of rowers upon the downstream journey, for they would drift to the sea. On the homeward journey Maoris from the fishing hamlet would help to row them back. "We'll only be a few days gone," shouted William. "Good-bye!"

"Good-bye!" called Marianne. "Good-bye!" And she fluttered her white handkerchief as the mooring ropes were cast off and the barges pushed out into mid-stream amid the cheers of the settlement.

2

At last! A great sigh of relief broke from William. He was alone. Leaving the steering to Scant and Kapua-Manga he settled himself in the prow, his arm flung affectionately round the neck of the carved monster beside him, and was alone. For perhaps five whole days he would not see Marianne. For five whole days the fight upon which Samuel had started him was suspended. Lonely expeditions like this were his holidays. Without them it would have been very hard to go on with this perpetual wearisome acting of a part.

Yet he did not regret the decision he had taken two years ago. The drifting had been a council of despair, a negative thing, while this acting was positive and creative, an attempt to transform failure into success and hatred into love. He had perhaps not accomplished much in the two years but at least now he believed their marriage appeared outwardly successful. He was a healthier man too. To make Marianne happy he had fought the drink with all the strength that he could muster, and he hadn't done too badly, in spite of the scoldings that always awoke in him a wild desire to walk straight off and do again that for which he was being reprimanded. Suddenly he chuckled. What would Marianne say if she were to be told that the purpose of her rapscallion husband's life was the salvation of her soul? He was well aware that she imagined it was she who was saving him. She thought it was her tirades, and not his own efforts, that were slowly conquering his weaknesses. Well, let her think it. He was living now only to make her happy. The boy would help. Daily he gave thanks for the little son who was on the way, meanwhile vigorously crushing down within him the strangely violent desire for a daughter.

He must get it out of his mind that they were having a girl who would be the living image of Marguerite. They were not. They were having a boy, a sallow sharp-tongued little boy like Marianne. That little girl lived only in his dreams and his memories, where she danced over the sand at La Baie des Saints in her blue frock and flung her arms about him on the rock of Le Petit Aiguillon. What did Marguerite look like now, the woman of over thirty who had just nursed a beloved mother through a long and painful illness and now lived all alone in the house at Le Paradis with a blind father? Thought he never spoke of her to Marianne there was scarcely a moment of the day or night when he did not think of her, the thought of her no longer a torment but an amazing refreshment, and sometimes she seemed so near that he could have put out his hand and touched her. It was after one of these times, only a few weeks ago, that he had done an odd thing—he had sent her the carved necklace that he had bought for her in China. He had found it flung forgotten at the bottom of an old chest in his hut in the forest, a chest where he kept a few little possessions that he did not want Marianne's prying eyes to see—relics of his old sea-faring life and odds and ends that his Maori friends had given him—things which if found in the house she would have designated "rubbish" and thrown away. Taking it out he had marvelled afresh at the lovely carvings, and especially at the beauty of little Lung-mu hanging at the bottom. He remembered that once he had thought of it as a tainted thing, unworthy to be sent to Marguerite, and laughing at himself he had hung it out on the branch of a kauri tree that the fresh wind might cleanse it. Then, sitting down in the hut, he had written to Marguerite. Since his marriage he had done no more than scrawl affectionate messages at the end of Marianne's letters, but that day in the hut he had written her a long letter that would not be seen by Marianne. It had been an absurd childish letter, telling her the story of Lung-mu who protects sailor men, and the stories of the other little figures on the necklace, and he had described with picturesqueness and a wealth of detail, and an ease that had come to him from he knew not where, the lovely country where he lived and his life as a lumberman. He had told her about every detail of the long day's work in the forest, even giving her the time of day when various things were done, and about the barges with the sea monsters on their prows, and how the wood was taken down the creek to the sea. He had told her about the flowers and the birds and the fishes, and about the Maoris, and about Samuel and Susanna, and Tai Haruru and Scant and Isaac. And he had described the house and garden and the settlement, and drawn her an absurd little map to show her the lie of the land. He had not mentioned Marianne until the very end of the letter, when he had said, "Marianne is waiting now for her child. It is to be a boy, but I think I would have liked a girl with fair hair and blue eyes. Marianne will be an excellent mother, as she is an excellent wife and housekeeper and business woman. I am much blest in my wife. I try to live only to make her happy. Her welfare and that of her child is the reason for existence. She would send her love did she know that I am writing to you. Though you are so far away the bond between us is very strong. There is a saying I have heard somewhere, 'A threefold cord shall not be broken'. You have my love and devotion always. I think of you day and night. William." He had wasted nearly a whole day writing this letter, and Tai Haruru, who had been going on a trip to Wellington, had taken it with him to be sent to England upon the next ship, so that Marianne had known nothing about it. It had given him a strange feeling or reassurance to think that now Marguerite would know all about his life, and would know also that he loved her. He felt somehow that what was held within the consciousness of Marguerite was safe, and that therefore the mere fact that she knew about his life would be a guarantee that he would make a worth-while thing of it; and he felt too, fumblingly and vaguely, that her knowledge of his love would add joy to her consciousness, and so increase its depth and saving power.

Darkness overtook them that night a mere mile from the sea. William, straining his ears in delight, could hear the sound of the rollers on the shore. They camped in the forest, and while the Maoris lit a great fire of dried fern in a clearing among the trees William and Scant and Isaac fished for eels in a lagoon bright with phosphorescent lights. They always did this, grilled eel for supper being part of the ritual of taking the wood to the sea, and William always enjoyed it.

When they got back to camp the Maoris were roasting lizards on the fern, an unpleasant habit that William deprecated. He himself ate only eel, with roasted sweet potatoes and the bread he had brought from home; the lizards were such jolly little beggars it seemed a shame to eat them. He lay propped upon an elbow as he ate, lazy and happy, watching the absorbed Maori faces about him lit by the leaping flames. In the firelight the faces and long lithe limbs might have been forged out of bronze. They ate quickly, hungrily, with pouncing darting movements, and their eyes shone like living coals. They were savages when they ate, the firelight touching here and there upon a knife, a coloured feather, the red belt of the war-god Tu. They were children of the primordial forest, children of Tane-Mahuta the forest god, father and protector of birds. They might have been birds themselves, William thought, with their eagle faces and their coloured plumes. When the meal was over and Kapua-Manga picked up his flute and sang in his own language one of the war-songs of the heroes of old, the others rocking and humming to the refrain, William took up his blanket and withdrew a little to sleep by himself in the fern. Scant and Isaac and Tai Haruru, after almost a lifetime in this land, were very near now to the children of Tane, but he, even after those months spent in the bush, was still a white man, a Pakeha. As the night darkened and deepened he had felt himself mysteriously excluded from the circle by the fire. This pagan land was not his. His roots were not here but far away in a cool grey island where the Christian saints had lived and suffered, and Marie Tape-Tout, not Tangaroa, kept watch upon the waves. A nostalgic longing came upon him for the days of boyhood that would never come again and he fell asleep dreaming of the Island, hearing the sound of the waves upon the rocks below Notre Dame du Castel and the crying of the gulls in the wind.

He awoke with the sounds of storm still in his ears and lay for a little confused, not quite certain in which world he was. Then he was suddenly wide awake, aware that it was in the new world, not the old, that the wind was roaring through the trees with this tremendous and menacing note of warning. Then he heard Scant's voice in the darkness, "Are those damn barges firmly moored?" and Isaac shouting to awaken the Maoris, and he jumped up to join the other dark figures making their way through the trees to the steep bank of the creek.

Here they could see better what they were doing, for a fitful moon was showing through the hurrying clouds. Every now and again there was a squall of hot rain in the wind, and the creek was now flowing stormily, fed by rain in the mountains, the barges straining at their mooring ropes. Half the lumbermen were aboard them in a moment, throwing new ropes to the men on shore, lashing and knotting at furious speed. The precious harvest of their toil must be kept safe at all costs. There was no thought in any of their minds but the wood. But they were too late. William was standing on the bank, straining his eyes in the half dark to see the rope which a Maori was flinging to him from the foremost barge, when he felt the familiar and horrible tremor of the earth which however accustomed one was to it never failed to send an echoing throb of fear through one's body. A cry of dismay went up from the Maoris, and those on the barges jumped ashore, for this was what they called "the seeking and commotion, when Old Earthquake reigneth," and it was best to meet it neither sitting beneath a roof nor standing upon a ship, but lying flat on the ground.

There was a second slight tremor, and then a pause, and then it came, the worst that William had experienced in this land. One had the sensation that the earth was splitting and the forest falling, that the mountains were crashing down upon one, that the wind had the world in its teeth and was shaking it as a dog shakes a rat, that the sea was rising up to make war upon the heavens, while from the heavens there rained down fire and thunderbolt upon the sea. The elements were "seeking" each other in rage and confusion, and in the fury of the conflict boastful man was utterly humiliated, sucked down, drowned. William felt himself falling, falling, cried out aloud and knew he was not heard, clutched at the earth and felt it shudder away from his grasp, felt for foothold and found none, hurtled right over the edge of the universe into the darkness and nothingness of the chaos from which the world was born, felt the awful cold of it strike through to his bones and was engulfed in the darkness, his consciousness snuffed out like the flame of a pinched candle.

But not for eternity. Man is a tough creature, even when Old Earthquake is abroad. After what seemed like the passing of a century he was aware again of cold and darkness and pain, and clutched them to him almost with delight, because they were something, something, not nothingness yet, not nothingness. Hold on, hold on, he said to himself, gritting his teeth against the pain, steadying his mind against the darkness and the cold, trying to reach beyond them to what else might be within the grasp of his awakening senses. Then the roaring of the wind came back, the sound of a man moaning not far away, the taste of the blood that was running down his face from a cut on his head. For a little while he knew no more than that. Then he knew that the earth was steady again, that the first light of dawn was showing through the darkness, and that he was lying in shallow water tangled up in a mooring rope. He had been flung down the steep bank into the shallows of the creek and had hit his head against a barge. He shut his eyes, opened them again, and found fat little Isaac's round red face bent over him in considerable concern. "The wood?" he demanded at once.

"All the bloody barges except this one carried off down the creek," said Isaac, and swore savagely.

"Who's that groaning?" asked William. "Not Scant?"

"No. Scant's safe. Kapua-Manga. Branch of a tree fell on him. Scant's getting him out."

With Isaac's help William disentangled himself from the rope and struggled out of the water and up the bank. He was bruised and shaken, and the cut on his head was painful, but otherwise he was unhurt. Isaac bandaged his head and then, in pouring rain but increasing light, they set about assessing the extent of the damage. The world looked as though a naughty child had taken the contents of its toy cupboard and tumbled them out upon the floor. Trees had been uprooted, rocks had been hurled into the creek, the one barge that was left had had its side stove in and was filling rapidly, the bodies of two dead Maoris, killed by falling rocks, lay untidily upon the ground like broken dolls, and beside them knelt three dusky figures wailing out a terrible monotonous dirge. Until their dirge was finished no help could be expected from the mourning Maoris, and the white men did not expect it. They rescued Kapua-Manga, found him not seriously injured, bandaged his broken collar bone, fetched food from the barge and made a fire beneath a sheltering canopy of broken branches. Upon the appearance of food and warmth the mourners finished up the dirge at an increased tempo and joined the group by the fire with sudden resuscitated spirits. By the end of the meal, the two dead men not being their relations, they were chattering like starlings, rejoicing in their own escape from death. But the white men were silent, wondering what had happened at the settlement.

William got suddenly to his feet. "My wife," he said. "I must get back."

"How?" asked Scant, looking at the swirling creek. "You may get a canoe from the village, but you'll never get up-stream against that weight of water."

"I'll walk," said William.

"Man, it'll take you days to make your way through the wreckage in the forest."

William swore. "Then what the hell do we do?" he asked wretchedly.

"Lay hold of all the rope we can find and get down to the village," said Isaac. "See if we can salvage any of the wood. See what's happened to old man Parker and the Thrush."

"Old man Parker will have been too canny to leave Wellington," growled Scant. "An' if we'd had a grain of sense we'd have shipped this wood a fortnight back. . . . . Damn fools."

Punished, thought William. The wilds have lost patience this time, and no mistake about it. I always knew they would. And he wondered again about the settlement, and the huts in the clearing in the forest. And above all he wondered about Marianne.

They covered the dead men with branches and left them where they were, for later Tapu Maoris, outcasts who alone might handle the dead, would fetch them to the village for their burial with all due honour and the funeral rites of their tribe. Then they made a litter for the bruised and plaintive Kapua-Manga, took ropes from the barge and set out upon the mile-long journey. The going was appalling, climbing over the trunks of uprooted trees, fighting their way through the wreckage of the ferns and undergrowth. The rain poured down on them and the gale screamed in their ears, and as they came nearer to it they could hear the sea pounding madly on the rocks. But William, thinking of Marianne, was almost oblivious of the storm. It was not only the danger to her and her child that he feared for her, but also the set-back to her hopes and ambitions. There was not only the probable loss of a valuable load of timber to be reckoned with, there was the damage to property. It might be that that fine new office of hers in Wellington was a pile of rubble by this time. It would be a case of starting all over again, just when she thought that prosperity was well within her grasp. Those who had been living a pioneer life for as long as he had were used to starting all over again; he and Tai Haruru had done it several times; but in Marianne's cool grey Island this sort of thing did not happen, and she was not used to it. Poor girl, he thought, poor Marianne. And then was suddenly surprised by the depth of his pity and concern. Had he, then, already ceased to hate the little woman? The question came upon him like a burst of sunlight. He was not quite sure of the answer but it was a wonderful thing that he could even ask it.

"My God!" ejaculated Isaac suddenly.

They had left the forest behind them and reached the shore, and it was as though they had reached Muri-ranga-whenua, the last bounds of earth, and stood upon the brink of all things. Buffeted by the gale, clinging to the stark rocks of the headland, they stared in dismay. This coastline was never at any time soft or sentimental, it was always firm, clear-cut, cold, but in this storm it was so stark and terrible that it struck awe to the soul. Its great beauty, the exquisite opal colouring of rock and sky and sea, the glow of the blond grass and golden sand, had been swept away by the storm. Sea and sky were merged in a grey mist of driving rain and spume, the sandy bay was a boiling cauldron of white waves hurling themselves upon the splintering iron-grey rocks that were accustomed to rear themselves twenty feet above the water, and now showed only their bared fangs above the smother of foam. With the wind behind it the sea had come in like a tidal wave, leaping upon the land like a wolf at a sheep's throat. Where it met the creek in full spate there was a wall of furious water that flung great trees tossing upward as though they were mere twigs, and lashed at the sky as though it would drag that too to destruction.

"Where are those new sheds of ours?" shouted William above the roar of the storm. "And the jetty?"

Scant laughed shortly and harshly but said nothing, and a low wailing cry broke from the Maoris because once there had been a Maori village on this shore and now there was simply no sign of it at all. And there was no sign, of course, of Tai Haruru's beautiful barges. They and the timber had been matchwood long ago.

So great was the disaster that even in this land of disasters it struck like a stunning blow. After that one cry the Maoris were as silent as the white men, clinging to whatever handhold they could find to brace themselves against the storm.

"What's that?" asked Isaac suddenly.

Away to the left a gun had boomed. Then came the faint thin clanging of a bell.

"Ship in distress," said William, and started running along the cliff-top to the left. The others followed him, stumbling over the wet tussocks of grass, breathless with the wind, cursing the luck that had sent a shipwreck to top up all the other misfortunes of the storm. Guided by the signals of distress they ran on until the clanging of the bell seemed to come eerily from close beside them. Then they stopped, peering seawards through the driving mist and rain. The storm had moderated a little but at first they could see nothing. Then a gleam of sunlight suddenly tore the mist apart before their eyes, so that they looked as through a rent curtain over the drenched grass and stones of the headland where they clung and down to a patch of bright sea beyond. A reef of jagged rocks stretched out into the brightness like a long sword, and impaled upon the point of it was the wreck of what had once been a lovely and incomparable ship. Then the rain poured down again, and each man would have thought that what he had seen had been a dream had it not been for the evidence of the others, and of the clanging bell.

"Old man Parker and the Thrush?" asked Scant in horror.

"No," said Isaac. "It was a clipper."

"Bring those ropes!" yelled William, and then, running and stooping low against the wind, he disappeared into the rain. He was clambering down over the cliff, clawed at by the wind, numbed hands and feet clinging to the wet slippery rock and hard put to it to support his great bulk, in peril but uncaring. In that one moment of vision he had known without the shadow of a doubt that the ship was the Green Dolphin. It only needed this to fill up the cup of disaster to the brim. And he did not care in the very least if he flung away his life in attempting to save Captain O'Hara and Nat. His life would be only a small thing to give in payment of the debt he owed them.

CHAPTER THREE

It began as a halcyon voyage, decked out with all the trappings of a fairytale. They were late in sailing, for Captain O'Hara had been laid up with an attack of the gout and obstinately refused to leave Canton while still supporting his great bulk upon two sticks. A Skipper on two sticks was incapable of exercising a proper authority, he had averred to the protesting Nat. It might be late in the season, as Nat kept repeating so monotonously, but he was damned if he'd go to sea on two sticks. He'd wait till he had the use of his legs before he set sail, if he had to wait till kingdom come. Yet when at last the Green Dolphin left Canton the weather had not broken. It was a blue day of balmy weather and she sailed proudly between the green shores of the Estuary, past the lemon-sailed fishing boats and the men-of-war and merchantmen of many nations, conscious as always of possessing a presence and dignity second to none, and a beauty mellowed but not diminished by the passing of the years. In her hold were chests of tea and spices, bales of silk and fine muslin, and cedarwood boxes full of trinkets and adornments of jade and ivory. Captain O'Hara liked these romantic cargoes. The consciousness of treasure in the hold gave him a sense of affluence agreeable to his natural arrogance, and the thought of disgorging it in a needy country was pleasing to his generosity. He was well satisfied as he snuffed the air upon his poop. Increasingly, as he grew older, he liked the blue air of balmy days. He had told Marianne once that he never loved the sea so deeply as when he fought a storm victoriously, and if she had been beside him now and had questioned him he would have said the same again; but yet increasingly he loved the balmy days.

Getting old? The question came upon him suddenly as he stood beside Nat at the wheel. Land was out of sight now and upon every side of them a deep blue sea, scintillating with silver light, swept unhindered to meet the blue curve of the sky. It was one of those days when the whole universe seemed a crystalline bubble that enclosed one treasure only: a lovely white-winged ship.

"Am I getting old, Nat?" questioned Captain O'Hara. "Eh? Am I getting old?"

Nat hissed an affirmative through the only two rotting stumps of teeth that were now left in his head. It was a slightly surprised affirmative, for it amazed him that this obvious fact should not hitherto have come home to the Skipper. Doubtless it was his magnificent set of white china teeth from Paris that had prolonged the illusion of youth in Captain O'Hara. He could still masticate salt beef and Harrier Lane with enjoyment while Nat had to soak his Liverpool pantiles in his tea: it is when a man has to soak his biscuits in his tea that he knows he's old.

A sudden rage seized Captain O'Hara. "Old, is it?" he bellowed. "Devil a bit. An' who the hell are ye to go tellin' me I'm old, and you without a tooth in your head worth mentionin' an' bald as a tortoise beneath that bloody nightcap? You've never deceived the world with that nightcap of yours, Nat, any more than with that glass eye. 'Tis not for stylishness ye wear it day an' night. There's not a hair on your head, Nat, not a hair, begorra!"

The fair weather continued until they were only a couple of days from Wellington, when in the late afternoon they ran into a grey sea beneath a hazy sky and a queer oppressive atmosphere, as though the air were dust-laden. At nightfall Captain O'Hara would have made the ship snug against possible unpleasantness had not this course been suggested to him by the Mate, an arrogant young man from Aberdeen who always thought he knew better than his elders.

"Dirty weather?" boomed Captain O'Hara at the arrogant young man. "No, Sir. Wasn't I sailin' these seas when you were squawlin' in a cradle in that damned draughty town of Aberdeen that I've only set eyes on the once, an' hope never to set eyes on again, begorra? Dirty weather be damned. That haze is for heat, Sir. I don't take a rag off her for your moonstruck fantasies. I'm behind time on this voyage, an' I'll not dawdle through the night like a cow going home for the milking. Do ye hear, Sir? I will not, begorra."

He stumped below to his cabin and reached for the whisky bottle. The glass was falling but he disregarded the fact. A slight fall, nothing to be disturbed about. It was his pride that he was considered one of the most punctual skippers in the Merchant Service. Owing to the attack of gout that had delayed him at Canton he was now more behind time on a voyage than he had ever been, and he was damned if he was going to take a rag of her to-night to please an impudent nincompoop of a Scotchman young enough to be his own grandson. Damned if he was. The young needed taking down a peg or two. All the young nowadays needed to be taught their place. Impudent young devils. No respect for their elders. Made one wonder what the world was coming to. William, now, he'd never been impudent. And Marianne, the little green enchantress, though she was a proud piece and had always spoken her mind in a way unbecoming to a female, had never at any time made him feel like an old moulting cock who had outstayed his welcome in his own barnyard. But these young men nowadays, when you gave them an order they obeyed it, if they did obey it, with a cold gleam to their eye and a quirk to the corners of their mouths that made a man feel his trousers were slipping, or his wig on hind part before; moulting, in fact. William and Marianne had never made him feel he was moulting.

Slowly absorbing his whisky he gave himself over to thoughts of William and Marianne. Those two children—he still thought of them as children—had given to his life what he and Nat and the Green Dolphin had given to theirs, the brightness of a fairytale thread running through the sober fabric of everyday life. And this thread had had its beginning in one of the most perfect experiences of his life. In all lives there are moments that seem to detach themselves from the enigma called time and to travel along with a man through his whole life. It can scarcely be said of them that they are just memories, for this persistence is too vital and too vivid. It is as though they derive their life not from a man's memory but from some truth within them that makes them gleam and sparkle like the glass that contains the flame of a lantern. Such, for Captain O'Hara, had been that moment when he had come up on deck in the early morning and seen Saint Pierre reflected in the bright waters of the Island harbour. Shutting his eyes, swilling his whisky, he could see it now as vividly as he had seen it then. He saw the tall houses rising above the wharfs and the long line of the harbour wall, up and up, one behind the other, lit with the colours of the morning. And built above and around the first city was a second formed of piled golden cloud, both so drenched in light that it was hard to tell where one began and the other ended, and both reflected in the water of the harbour so that reality and reflection together made up a perfect circle, a habitable globe in miniature, the earthly city completely encircled by the heavenly.

That first time that he had set eyes on the vision that had accompanied him so persistently through life he had stood there gazing at it like a village idiot, his dressing-gown flapping in the morning breeze, his wig awry, his jaw dropping. Heaven alone knew for how long he might not have stayed in this moonstruck condition had not a slight sound made him glance downwards, and there, gazing up at him from a small boat rocking sedately on the bright waters of the harbour, had been William and Marianne, a beautiful bright-haired rosy-cheeked boy in a torn blue coat and a black-browed slip of a girl dressed all in elfin green like a changeling. Fairytale figures, both of them, inhabitants of one or other or both of the bright strange cities of earth and sky. As fairytale figures they had come on board and taken possession of his heart and of his ship, and as fairytale figures they had remained in his life ever since. . . . But the fairytale from which they had come was a true one, as true as the truth that had detached that moment of experience in the harbour of Saint Pierre from the normal time sequence and made it his companion for ever.

What they both were he had not as yet bothered himself to discover. Until just lately he had been a happy man, strong, prosperous and self-satisfied, with an excellent digestion and a will of iron. He had had no need to rout about for spiritual props to keep himself upon an even keel. He had even despised those who needed such props; poor anaemic creatures who fed their weak digestions on their bibles and whose knock knees sought the ground in prayer through sheer inability to maintain a vertical position without assistance. He had never counted himself one of that feeble brotherhood . . . not even during that last attack of gout.

He refilled his glass and turned up the lamp, for it seemed to him that his cabin was growing uncommonly dark and cold. And then quite suddenly he wanted Nat, good old Nat, who was also an old man and had companioned him through most of his seafaring life. He levered himself half up out of his chair to bellow for him, remembering just in time that at this hour Nat was standing his trick at the wheel again. A nice thing for the Skipper to start bellowing for the man at the wheel to come and hold his hand against the fear of the dark! He levered himself back again into his big chair, that beautiful carved chair that Timothy Haslam had made for him, and laughed and had another drink. And old Nat would scarcely have understood his state of mind, for Nat was growing old unashamedly. The thought of the humiliations of old age, nightmare beasts waiting to pounce just round the corner, did not seem to worry him at all. Probably, thought Captain O'Hara, a humble man does not fear humiliation. How did it go? "He that is down need fear no fall, he that is low no pride. . . ." He couldn't remember the rest. He'd never been a man for poetry and his head was muzzy and he was confused by the way the things in his cabin seemed dancing round him; the ribald dragons on the curtains that hid his bunk, the stuffed baby crocodile, the octopus, the three tattooed cannibals' heads; they were all swaying and surging as though the sea were flowing through the cabin, carrying them this way and that on its ebb and flow, endowing them with the movement of its own life. The ribald dragons put out their scarlet tongues at him, the crocodile snapped its jaws, the octopus waved its tentacles and the cannibals grinned. Even the carved creatures he was sitting on, Timothy Haslam's whales and dolphins and mermaids and fish and crabs, seemed alive, for he could feel them stir under him as though his body had lost its living weight, had become bloated like a balloon, so that it rose upward. . . . Terror seized him; he stumbled suddenly to his feet, his flesh pricking and his hands clinging to the edge of the old teak table. . . . Strange fish were swimming lazily through his cabin, fish with golden eyes and delicately laced thin bones showing through phosphorescent bodies, Timothy's fish off the chair. And all the creatures swaying this way and that in his cabin were singing, their myriad tiny voices making a music that one could hear and not hear, like the sound of bells that the wind is always catching away. "We're homeward bound, I heard them say. Fare ye well."

Captain O'Hara took a firmer grip of the teak table. "You're drunk," he told himself. "Drunk at sea with dirty weather blowin' up. Ye old fool. Better turn in. You're old and drunk, Denis O'Hara. Better turn in."

His familiar world steadied about him again. Timothy's fish swam back to the chair and stayed there. The cannibals' heads, the crocodile and the octopus were once more dead things nailed to the bulkheads, the dragons on the curtains swayed only with the motion of the ship. But as he fumbled at his clothes his fingers still shook. He'd take another tot before he turned in. Snug between the blankets, well primed with whisky, a man could forget the horrors and slip back in dreams to the great days when he had played ball with the world and never missed a catch.

He slept too well that night. When the storm broke and woke him his skuttle was already grey with the dawn. "But for that damn gout we'd have been in Wellington before this," was the thought that flashed through his mind as he tumbled out of his bunk, dragged on his oilskins and stumped up on deck into the murkiest, filthiest morning he had ever set eyes on. The sea was running half up the sky, moaning and hissing, and the wind came from the lowering clouds like a flail, steel-tipped with savage ice, slashing and clawing at the booming sails and the creaking timbers and the wavering nebulous shadows that were running leaping men.

The Mate was bellowing through the speaking trumpet, "Up! Damn you!" And the shadows were in the rigging. "Lay out!" And they were lying out on the yards, shadows upon shadows, shadows wrestling with shadows, all of them, even the Green Dolphin herself, dwarfed to nothingness by the mighty seeking and commotion of sea and sky. A sail, blown away and torn to rags, went by on the wind like a wounded bird. The great ship that a short while ago had sailed so securely within the crystalline walls of a balmy day was now a lacerated hunted creature tottering on the edge of chaos. Nothing would save her now, so it seemed to Captain O'Hara, but the exertions of shadows fighting with shadows, and the commands of an old man who was only the ghost of what he had been, who was silent like a ghost, bewildered like a ghost, lost in an alien world upon an alien sea. . . .

Suddenly he wrenched the speaking trumpet from the hands of the arrogant young man from Aberdeen and his orders rang out crisp and clear. He was once again the man he had been in his dreams not ten minutes ago, the vigorous man of mature age who had seen the two cities reflected in the water and the two fairytale children rocking in their rowing boat upon the silver ripples. That was who he was— not this old dodderer who had overslept himself when his ship was in danger. Well, it was in danger no more. The sea had never beaten him yet. It was his god, but he had never yet failed to match himself strength for strength and cunning for cunning against his god, and win.

"Better heave to, Sir," said the young man from Aberdeen un- wisely. "Better heave to, with this wind behind and the reefs of the coast ahead."

Captain O'Hara's jaw set savagely. "I'm behind on time," he snapped. "I'll give her a double reefed foretops'l and on we go. Nothing of a blow. Soon have spent itself." And he stumped away to his poop, pausing to swear at Nat, busy stretching life-lines across the deck. He, Captain O'Hara, had not give the order for the life- lines. Sheer jitters on the part of the young man from Aberdeen and Nat should not have obeyed the order. Nat, sworn at, grinned cheer- fully, and then crawled suddenly sideways and ducked in a futile attempt to avoid the sea that swept over the bulwarks. The move- ment was somehow a reproach to Captain O'Hara. Poor old Nat. He'd not have crawled like that, ducked like that, ten years ago. He'd kept him at sea too long, just that he might have the pleasure of his familiar company. Damned if he wouldn't suggest to him, when they made the port of Wellington, that he spend the rest of his life at the settlement with William and Marianne, squinting at the lizards and smoking his pipe in the sun. The Green Dolphin would not seem the Green Dolphin without Nat aboard, but the old chap would enjoy a good long smoke in the sun. He had no dignity to maintain, no prestige to bother about. The ignominy of such an ending would not hurt him because he would be unaware of it.

All that day he kept the Green Dolphin upon her course, speeding along with the wind booming in her sails and her decks awash. Her captain could feel in her body a desperate desire to twist and lay to, but the two vigorous young men at the wheel checked it and kept her upon her way. But her desire was a reproach to her captain, just as that sideways crawl of Nat's had been. . . . If he'd not, back in Canton, been too arrogant to come on board his ship on two sticks, they'd both of them have been spared this buffeting.

"All right, my girl," he said to his ship. "It's a devil of a blow, surely, but I've never failed to get ye safe to harbour an' I'll not fail ye now."

The sky cleared a little at evening but the wind increased and the ship plunged madly. It would not have been possible to heave to now even had Captain O'Hara desired to do so. He reckoned that with luck the wind would moderate during the night and that next day they would make Wellington. . . . During the night the wind would moderate. . . . He clung with increasing obstinacy to this conviction because it was his only justification for the bold decision he had taken in the morning. The sun sank in an angry red mist and the night closed down upon them. His world narrowed to the patch of streaming deck beneath his feet, the shadowy figures of the men at the wheel, a dim tracery of wet rigging lit by a swaying lantern to the brightness of a bediamonded spider's web, the roar and tumult of the storm and the misshapen figure of old Nat beside him. "Get below," he growled, but Nat did not obey the order and he did not repeat it, for he liked the companionship of Nat in this hour that he knew to be a peak hour of experience. The men at the wheel seemed only dream figures. The only reality was himself and Nat and the Green Dolphin speeding alone through the night.

Would she stay the course? As the hours went on the distress of his ship was very apparent to him. She was an old ship now and she was being pressed beyond her strength. But there was no more that he could do. They were at the mercy of the sea to break or save as it willed. He was glad that Nat was beside him.

He had believed that the storm would moderate during the night, but it increased, and a grey dawn of pouring rain and howling wind found them, as far as they could calculate, not far from the coast of New Zealand and in deadly danger. Yet the normal life of the ship went on as far as possible. The bells were struck and the watch was changed. Orders rang out. Nat went along to the galley and came back with two mugs of hot sugared whisky and water. As the returning light showed him the shadowy figures of his men Captain O'Hara lost the illusion that he and Nat and the Green Dolphin were alone in the turmoil of the waters, and in its place came an agony of self loathing and remorse. But for that delay at Canton, but for that refusal to take the Mate's suggestion and heave to, the lives of this gallant company of seamen would not have been in danger. His misery was increased by the cheery grins his men gave him, by the

quiet deference of the Mate, the almost pitying gentleness of his old
friend Nat. Their Skipper had got them into the hell of a mess but
it was no good crying over spilt milk. Better stand together now and
meet what came as one man. And the Green Dolphin herself was in
agreement with them. Helpless as she was she yet sped through the
storm with her rigging singing triumphantly, tearing through the
crests and racing down into the hollows as though she were not the
pursued but the pursuer. What was she after, the old Green Dolphin? Death with honour? Did she dread that final humiliation of
old ships, that slow disintegration in the shipwreckers' yard? Any
ship would dread that, especially his arrogant Green Dolphin. It
was death with honour that she wanted and was pursuing with such
fierce questing, death with her timbers still curving to the proud
curve of the prow's line, her raking masts still pointing to the sky,
her flags flying.

He jerked his head up quickly and the Mate, who was beside him,
understood his glance. "Wind would rip 'em to pieces, Sir," he said.
"But if our luck don't hold I'll run up the flags straight away." He
grinned at the old man; the old chap had aged twenty years during
the night; almost impossible to recognise him now, so broken was he,
so lost and drowned in humiliation. "Finest ship I've ever sailed on,
Sir," he said. "Finest Skipper I've ever sailed under. I'd not have
missed this voyage for anything you could have offered me." Then
he blushed scarlet and went away.

So you thought seamanship was deteriorating, did you? said Captain O'Hara to himself. Damned old fool.

An hour later there came to him quite suddenly the realisation that
the peak of the storm had been reached and passed. Very soon now
the wind would drop. He remembered trying to describe to Marianne this instinctive knowledge of the seamen. "Granted there's no
perceptible difference in the ragin' of wind an' water," he had said
to her, "yet somethin' tells ye ye've won." And he had inflated his
chest and grinned at her.

But he had not won this time and he knew it. The blows of the
adversary were slackening, but too late. For the first time in his life
Captain O'Hara began to pray; not with words, but with the agonised prostration of his soul. Struck down at the feet of God, accept-
ing his humiliation as his due, he gave himself up. Cast me away, me
and my ship, but save these men. He was unaware even of forming
the words in his mind, but the prayer was explicit in that creative act
of abnegation. And his action was not for a moment only. Minute
by minute, quarter hour after quarter hour, using the immense
strength of his will, he held himself resolutely in the place of sacrifice

in the hope that his death might be the bridge upon which others would cross to life.

Their first sight of land, a tall headland shaped like the gigantic figure of a man towering between sea and sky and glimpsed for a moment only through a torn sheet of rain, was followed almost at once by a splintering shock, the agonised shuddering of the ship, a sudden awful moment of stillness and then the leaping upon them of the hungry waves. The Mate shouted an order and looking up Captain O'Hara saw the Red Ensign and the green House Flag fluttering triumphantly in the wind.

And he, too, was suddenly triumphant. His offering was accepted. He had known it was the splintering spear of rock entered the Green Dolphin's side, seeming to pierce through his own heart too. That gigantic figure of a man, seen for that one moment through the mist, had the spear of death in one hand but in the other he held the gift of life.

"You're saved, boys!" yelled Captain O'Hara. "We're close in to the shore, begorra. Did ye see that fellow over there? Fire the gun, boys. Ring the ship's bell. Make a row like Hades and you're saved."

Was the old man light headed? wondered the Mate. He didn't look it. He looked himself again; red-faced, jolly, confident. Yet the sudden glimpse of the shore that the Mate had seen had shown him no signs of human life or habitation, only a landscape like that of the earth new risen from chaos, indescribably desolate and savage; the Mate had no smallest hope of salvation from the shore that he had seen. Yet he obeyed, as was his duty. He sent the Bosun to fire the gun and Nat to clang the ship's bell. It was their only chance. The one boat that had not been swept away during the night had been stove in by the collision, and for a swimmer to live in that boiling sea was clearly next to impossible. And the Green Dolphin was settling fast. Her decks already had an ugly list. It would not be long.

It seemed to some of the crew an eternity, to others the millionth part of a second, during which they fired the gun and tolled the bell, holding themselves ready the while to leap for it in the last resort. Yet there was no anger, cursing or despair. The lewd jokes and boisterous spirits of the old man on the poop, the fluttering flags overhead, lifted them all to a super-normal level of existence that alike transcended time and the passions of the body. In this timeless atmosphere of faith and courage the backstays were knocked clean away from fear, and he went overboard with all his attendant devils. The young mate from Aberdeen carried these hours, or moments, he did not know which they were, with him through the rest of his life just as Captain O'Hara had carried his vision of the two cities, not as memories but as a permanent possession alight with living truth; the spear had entered the Green Dolphin's side and the flags had run up almost in the same moment; the transition from death to life is as swift as the flick over of a spun coin.

"Here he comes, boys!" yelled Captain O'Hara. "Here he comes!"

Even Nat wondered, this time, if the Skipper was crazy. His one eye, peering out from under his dripping nightcap, could see nothing through the driving rain. Then he peered again, and bared his rotting old teeth in a broad grin. He had caught a brief glimpse of a huge man swimming outwards from the shore. He clanged the bell once more, not in supplication but in triumph.

They had all seen it, but they did not all share the triumph of Nat and the Skipper.

"He'll not survive once he gets among the rocks," murmured the Mate.

"Not survive?" shouted Captain O'Hara. "That fellow'd survive in hell itself."

Naturally. Captain O'Hara had not yet seen the face of the man who swam towards them, but he identified the fellow with the gigantic figure standing with death in one hand and life in the other that had been his first sight of the shore. He was the Saviour, saving sometimes by life and sometimes by death, but never failing to redeem. Failure and that fellow were not, like life and death, synonymous.

A huge wave seemed to submerge the swimming figure, but no groan went up from the watching men. They just waited breathlessly.

Then they saw him standing on the summit of a rock. Probably a wave had swept him there by a lucky accident, yet to the watchers it seemed as though he had risen up from the sea by the power of his own enormous strength. His figure seemed to tower to the sky as he stood upright and cupped his hands round his mouth. "Rope, you fools!" he roared at them across the waste of water. "Throw a rope!"

Even at that distance the voice, like the roaring of a genial lion, was vaguely familiar to Captain O'Hara. He seized his glass and clapped it to his eye. It gave him a shock, a shock that he greeted with a bellow of laughter, to find that his supernatural saviour was merely young William.

Yet why not? He had not been a sailor all these years without discovering that supernatural power works by natural means. And it was fitting that young William, whose earthly existence had been like the gold thread of a fairytale in the mundane weave of his own, should be present at the last throw of the shuttle.

The Mate flung a rope. Again and again it fell short, and again and again he flung it, until at last William caught it and made it fast to the end of the one he held. The rain was lessening all the while now, the wind moderating and the light growing. They could see the land quite clearly, and a group of gesticulating Maoris on the cliff top, with two white men on the shore below who had dared the dangerous climb down to pay out the rope to William.

The crew went ashore under Captain O'Hara's orders, the youngest first. Only two men, who had been slightly injured during the night, were swept away from the support of the rope, but William swam to their rescue and got them ashore. And all the while the Green Dolphin was slowly settling, and the Mate was in an agony lest she should sink before the men were all got off her. Captain O'Hara had no such misgivings. He knew they would all be saved.

And presently only he and Nat and the Mate were left on board. Leeward the Green Dolphin's bulwarks were under water, the sea was washing over her and the slant of her deck was so steep that the three men had to cling to the wheel.

"Now you, boy," said Captain O'Hara to the arrogant young man from Aberdeen.

The Mate gave him an agonised glance, like that of a dog commanded to go home against his will.

"Get on with you, begorra. Go to hell," roared Captain O'Hara genially, and the Mate saluted and went overboard along the rope.

Nat watched anxiously, hissing in a bothered sort of way, moving his head from side to side like a distracted old hen shepherding the last of the chickens to safety, but Captain O'Hara remained as imperturbable as ever.

"Rope's broken," said Nat suddenly. It was what he had feared would happen, for the rope had been fretted backwards and forwards over the sharp summits of rocks for a good half-hour or more. Then, just for a moment, Captain O'Hara was also slightly perturbed, for the breaking of the rope was not according to plan. But the Mate was beyond the dangerous strip of water between the ship and the rock from which William had shouted to them, and a few moments' anxious scrutiny showed him that the fellow was a strong swimmer, and safe.

But there was still Nat, and the old blackguard had never learned to swim. Captain O'Hara looked at him in consternation, for he had set his heart on the old fellow ending his days in peace with Marianne. Nat's answering grin was that of an impish child who has just circumvented the plans of its elders and got its own way in spite of them. . . . He and Captain O'Hara and the Green Dolphin were going down together.

But they had reckoned without William, who was battling his way towards them through that dangerous tract of seething water. "Go back, you fool!" Captain O'Hara roared at him.

But it was unlikely that William heard him above the noise of the waves. Anyway he came on. He was flung this way and that like a straw, and at any moment he was in danger of having his brains dashed out against a rock, but still he came on, every bit of progress an achievement of skill and daring, helped on by that touch of miraculous luck that is always generated like a bright spark of flame struck from flint and tinder when skill and daring meet. And presently the two old men could see his round red face triumphantly surmounting the crest of a wave quite near them, and hear his voice. "Come on, Nat," he yelled.

"Get on, Nat," roared Captain O'Hara.

Nat's face puckered like that of a distressful monkey, and he shook his head slowly.

"Get on with you for the love of mike," cried Captain O'Hara. "I'm followin' close behind ye. I'll be with ye in a moment." His great hand shot out, detached Nat from the wheel and sent him slithering overboard.

Once, in William's boyhood, when he had been struggling to climb aboard the Green Dolphin, Nat's hairy hand had gripped him in the small of the back and dragged him to safety, and in that moment they had liked each other. Now it was the other way round. It was William's hand that gripped Nat as he struggled and choked in the water, William's power and strength that were dragging him to safety. "Come on, Nat," he encouraged. "You first and the Captain next." There was triumph in his tone. . . . Very occasionally in this life one does manage to pay one's debts.

Captain O'Hara and the Green Dolphin were alone together. It seemed that both of them held their breath while they watched that epic struggle of the two men towards the land. William had had only himself to bring out to the Green Dolphin but on the return journey he had the dead weight of Nat, and there were times when it looked as though he would not succeed in his task of salvation. The minutes that it took seemed hours. Then he was in calmer water. Then a sudden gleam of sunlight showed him struggling through the shallows, bowed down by the weight of Nat upon his shoulders, like some old picture of Saint Christopher bent beneath the weight of the child who carried the sorrow of the world.

The Green Dolphin gave a great sigh and settled so low in the water that the sea was washing round her captain's waist. It never even occurred to Captain O'Hara to plunge overboard and take his chance. He and the Green Dolphin together made up the one sacrifice.

He thought for a moment with satisfaction of the treasure in the hold. Chests of tea and spices, bales of silk and fine muslin, and cedarwood boxes full of trinkets and adornments of jade and ivory. That was a fine cargo with which to sail into Davey Jones' locker. He'd always liked sailing with a fine cargo.

Suddenly the sun came right out and the colours of dawn bathed the whole world in the same pristine loveliness in which he had first seen the town of Saint Pierre. The towering rocky cliffs were no longer grey and forbidding, they were walls of pearl, turrets of amethyst and jade, star-hung towers of a fairytale city. And above them great storm clouds, riven by shed rain, piled one upon the other by the wind, lit by the fires of dawn, climbed up and up into the sky in the semblance of a second city. Below the cliffs a stretch of smooth sand, its wet surface shining as glass, reflected the two cities one within the other, making of the two of them a circle of light as perfect, complete and unbroken as the aura of God's love. Captain O'Hara knew then, as the vision that had accompanied him through so many years of his life flamed up before him as eternal reality, what were the fairytale and the truth that had hitherto eluded him. This was the fairytale; that man is a citizen of two worlds. This was the truth; that neither in the height of Heaven nor the depth of Sheol, neither in the furthest places of the earth nor in the uttermost parts of the sea, can a man be separated from the love of God, because like a fish in the sea or a bird in the air it is in that element alone that he lives and moves and has his being. Withdrawn from it arrogant man has no more existence than an unborn thought. High and wonderful knowledge, so high that only those beaten to their knees in childlike humility can attain to its height.

As the great ship heeled over the brightness was blotted out for Captain O'Hara by a whirling rushing darkness; but he was not afraid as it took what he had freely offered.

> *If I say, Surely the darkness shall overwhelm me,*
> *And the light about me shall be night;*
> *Even the darkness hideth not from Thee,*
> *But the night shineth as the day.*

CHAPTER FOUR

1

It was a hateful wind. Marianne, lighting the lamp in her parlour and drawing the curtains to shut out the sight of the sickly grey evening, found no companionship in the sound of its voice in the forest, or in the voice of the creek racing along at the bottom of the garden. Surely it was flowing faster than usual to-night? It must be raining hard up in the mountains. She sighed, for if the current was too fast William would have trouble with the barges. She wished he was safely home again. She was anxious about him and she was lonely. A Maori woman, Kapua-Manga's beautiful wife Hine-Moa, was sleeping with her in the house, and Tai Haruru was only a stone's throw away, but they were not William, and she was deadly lonely, almost as lonely as she had been on her first night in this house when she had lain alone in her big bed and been grateful to the wind because its voice had drowned the sound of her weeping. Well, she never wept like that now. Things were better between her and William. But still they were not quite right. He did not really seem to appreciate being saved. He did not seem to enjoy being turned into a sober, solvent, prosperous business man against his will. Well, it would be all right when the boy came. For the boy's sake, then, he would want wealth and a decent reputation.

The thought that it would be for the boy's sake, even more than for hers, gave her a sharp pang. To forget it she pulled her work-box towards her and took out her sewing. It was a quilt for the boy's cot, a gay affair of birds and butterflies surrounding a nursery rhyme, worked on a pale blue ground. It reminded her of the sampler she had worked long ago, only then the embroidered border had surrounded three verses from the 42nd psalm. "Like as the hart desireth the water-brooks so longeth my soul after thee, O God. . . . One deep calleth another, because of the noise of the water-pipes. All thy waves and storms are gone over me. . . . My soul is athirst for God, yea, even for the living God. When shall I come to appear before the presence of God?" Why put in the bit about the water-pipes, Sophie had asked when she was working the sampler, why not have just the first and third verses? But the bit about the water-pipes had appealed to the stormy soul of the young Marianne. She had liked it. She had realised perhaps that for her the way to the quenching of thirst lay only through the storm.

She dropped her work and covered her face with her hands. One of her rare and hated moments of humble sincerity had got hold of

her, when she found herself acknowledging a measure of failure . . .
just for a second or two, because somehow or other she had let her
habitual armour of self-esteem slip out of place. . . . She had passed
through so many storms already and still she was parched and unsatisfied. Everything she wanted seemed to elude her somehow.
Though since their reconciliation on the night of the supper party
she had not doubted that William loved her, yet he still did not love
her in the way that she wanted to be loved. They were not really rich
yet. She had not even attained to the negative sort of peace that Tai
Haruru had. And yet she was a splendid wife, a good manager, an
upright and God-fearing Christian woman. Surely God was not
treating her quite right. It was very odd. . . . But she was going to
have a son. That longing at any rate was going to be fully satisfied.
And it was wonderful of her to be having a son at her age. . . . She
picked up her sewing again, once more armoured against the hated
humility, worked for a little longer, then put out her lamp and went
to bed.

She kept the candles burning in her bedroom and slept only fitfully,
for she felt sick and feverish and the wind and rain disturbed her.
And she was more anxious than ever about William and the wood,
for she could hear that the creek was in spate now, fed by swollen
streams up in the mountains. The sense of coming disaster pressed
heavily upon her. Truly this was at times a nightmare country. She
loved its space and beauty but dreadful things could happen in it,
things that would never happen on the Island at home. She was
thinking of the Island with nostalgia, of the beautiful house in Le
Paradis, of soft-footed Charlotte waiting upon her with such dex-
terity, of the carriage and Pierre and all the comfort and luxury that
she had never appreciated while she had it, when the first earthquake tremor shook the room. I'll stay here in bed, for it's only a
little shake, she said to herself, and was ashamed of the fear that, as
always, gripped her. But the second tremor was more violent, and
all the crockery jangled in the kitchen as though a giant had taken
the house in his two hands and was rocking it to and fro. She got
out of bed that time, flung her wrapper round her and ran to stand in
the doorway, calling to Hine-Moa. The Maori woman just had time
to jump up from her mattress on the parlour floor and run to her
and then the third tremor was upon them, the worst that Marianne
had known, shaking the whole world. The house seemed tumbling
about her like a pack of cards, and she heard a woman screaming
and did not know it was herself.

"All is well, Ma'am, all is well," said Hine-Moa's gentle voice, and
she found she was sitting on the floor with the Maori woman's arms

about her. The candles had gone out in her room and they were in darkness, but though she could see nothing she had the sense of dreadful desolation all about her. From somewhere or other a chill rain was beating in, and she was crying.

"What has happened, Hine-Moa?" she asked through her sobs. "Whatever has happened?"

"I think the house is hurt, Ma'am, but here in the doorway we were safe."

"Hine-Moa, how dreadful! Was it you who screamed like that?"

"I think, Ma'am, that it was yourself," said Hine-Moa politely.

"Disgraceful," whispered Marianne. "I never screamed on the Green Dolphin." And she rubbed her knuckles in her eyes like a child and tried to stop crying. It was not only disgraceful, it was humiliating to behave like this in front of a native woman. And Hine-Moa was so calm. She was, of course, used to this sort of thing in her appalling country.

"Poor lady! Poor lady!" said Hine-Moa, stroking Marianne's wet cheek. "Do not cry, Ma'am. Soon Tai Haruru, the Sounding Sea, will be here to liberate us with his great axe."

"If he's not dead himself," said Marianne.

"No, he will not be dead," comforted Hine-Moa. "Tai Haruru will not be dead while there are those who have need of him."

Never had Marianne longed for anyone as she longed now for the hated Tai Haruru. But her courage and control had come back to her and she longed for him silently, with no more sobs and lamentations, and she said no word to Hine-Moa of the awful feeling of illness that was growing upon her. She sat propped against the door jamb, her eyes closed, her teeth clenched against the waves of sickness that swept over her. It was bitter cold and the roar of wind and water seemed to her deafening.

So deafening that though she longed for Tai Haruru it seemed that she did not hear him coming. When next she opened her eyes it was to find herself lying in a pool of lantern light with Tai Haruru kneeling beside her. She had never seen such kindness in any man's eyes, not even William's, as there was in Tai Haruru's as he looked at her, and when his hands touched the heavy lump of feverish pain and misery that was her body she was suddenly so strengthened that she looked up and smiled at him.

"You're a brave woman," he said as he lifted her. "Take the lantern, Hine-Moa. We will carry Mrs. Ozanne to my house."

As her sickness increased her surroundings seemed strangely to withdraw themselves, so that her consciousness seemed only to operate within the small world of her agonised body. She vaguely noticed as Tai Haruru carried her out of it, that her home was in ruins, but the sight seemed to have nothing to do with her, and the scene of desolation out of doors, only half revealed in the pouring rain and the sickly struggling dawn, seemed as far away from her as though it were upon another planet. "My son," she heard a voice saying. "I shall lose my son. I thought at least I should have had my son."

"You will have your son," Tai Haruru assured her.

"But it is too early," she said.

"Seven months," said Tai Haruru. "Not too early to bear a living child."

Tai Haruru's small house had not been so badly shaken as others in the settlement and his austere little bedroom was still habitable. In no time at all he and Hine-Moa had established Marianne on his hard camp bed and had lit a fire and done all they could to ease her. But she was oblivious of her surroundings, drowned in pain more dreadful than anything she had ever conceived of. "The doctor," she commanded, "get the doctor quickly," and did not remember that this was not a country in which the doctor lived in the next street but one in which he lived some days' journey away.

"I am your doctor," said Tai Haruru gently. "And Hine-Moa is your nurse."

For a moment then she realised her situation, and cried out almost hysterically in shame and fear.

Tai Haruru stood beside her and held her hand. "Listen, Marianne," he said, when there came to her an interval of peace from pain. "I have skill as a doctor. When I lived in the bush Maori women would often accept my help in their extremity. I have brought many babies into the world, and so has Hine-Moa. Put yourself in our hands trustfully, be brave and obedient, and you will bear your son alive."

Beautiful Hine-Moa was upon her other side, smiling at her, plunging a bunch of some strange aromatic herb into a bowl of hot water. "What will they do to me?" wondered poor Marianne. "They're just savages, both of them. What awful pagan sort of thing will they do to me? I wish Mamma was here. . . . But Mamma is dead. . . . What have I done that this awful thing should happen to me when Mamma is dead?"

Tai Haruru was still holding her hand in a firm reassuring grip. "Forget that you dislike me, Marianne," he said. "Remember that I like you and love William, and that I have skill as a doctor. This is the sort of thing that happens to women in a pioneer life, my dear. You chose it."

That steadied her somehow. Yes, she had chosen it. Sophie, weep-ing in the parlour at Le Paradis, had warned her. But still she had chosen.

"I trust you," she said to Tai Haruru. "And I will give as little trouble as I can." And then the rhythmic pain swept over her again and scarcely aware of what she was doing she clung to his hand as though it were all she had in the world.

Mamma. Mamma. As the dreadful leaden hours went by she thought of her mother constantly. Had her mother endured this same torture for her and had she rewarded her with so little love? But it was too late to love Sophie now. She was dead. Did all women go through this agony whenever a child was born? Then women were greater than she had thought. Hine-Moa had had six children and was still beautiful and serene. And Charlotte had had many children. She must not scream. She was sure that neither Charlotte nor Hine-Moa had ever screamed. No, she must not scream, for this was what she had wanted. This was what she had desired when she had first seen Charlotte in Dr. Ozanne's waiting-room. She had wanted the pride and dignity of motherhood. She had known then that there were things one was more afraid of being without with ease than possessing with pain. But such pain! If it went on much longer she was sure she would die.

Tai Haruru allowed no such fears to weaken his determination that she and her child should live. She was having a very bad time, she was not young, but she was tough. And he had faith in his own gift of healing. What exactly this power was that was in him he did not know, but he reverenced it almost as though it were something outside himself that took possession of him by no virtue of his own, and he had hardly ever known it to fail. Suffering men and women, children, animals, birds, if he could only hold their bodies between his hands, that were the most vital part of his vital body, and empty from his spirit to theirs his passionate love of life, then he could generally save them, In the last agony, confused though she was by some herbal drink that he had given her to dull the pain, Marianne was aware of the strength of his hands, of the reiteration of his soul upon life, life, life, of Hine-Moa's voice crying aloud some mystic words of Maori exhortation. Then her groaning body obeyed the command of his hands, her soul clung to his, anchored to his against the pull of death, and the child was born.

The room was full of sunset when she returned to possession of herself. Her body was weak and bruised and feverish, but the child had left it, Tai Haruru's hands no longer commanded it, she alone possessed it again; it was bathed and slim and clean and no longer a thing that repulsed and horrified her. Her soul too was her own again. She was no longer anchored to another. She was escaping from the depths of her humiliation. It was not the pain that had been the worst of it for her, it was the shame.

Tai Haruru was standing beside the bed, smiling down upon her, this man whom she had so hated, and who had performed this tremendous office for her and seen the fearful humiliation of her body. "I am ashamed," she whispered.

"You should be proud," he said. "We've done a good day's work, you and I. There's a new life in the world."

Suddenly she remembered her son, her precious son who had been fighting for his life even as she had been fighting for hers. "Let me see him," she said. "Is all well with him?"

Tai Haruru's smile broadened and became just very faintly tinged with mockery. "All is well with him," he said. "Except that he's a girl."

2

Marianne's physical toughness showed itself in the rapidity of her recovery. For a few days she fretted desperately over William, but a little note from him, brought back by the Maori boy, Hine-Moa and Kapua-Manga's eldest son, who at the risk of his life had gone down the swollen creek in a canoe with the news of their safety and of the birth of the child, set her mind at rest. William's scribbled note said that he was overjoyed to hear of her safety and that of the child, that he was safe himself and would soon be home, but the Maori village at the coast had been devastated, and there had been a wreck, and there was much to do before he could start back.

"I hope no damage has been done to the barges, or to the jetty and the sheds at the coast," Marianne said to Tai Haruru.

"They were all of stout workmanship," he told her with a smile. She had not realised yet the extent of the damage wrought by the earthquake, and until she was stronger he did not want her to realise it. He guessed that their prosperity, for which she had worked so ambitiously, had received a serious set-back. That would not disturb himself and William but it would seriously disturb her; and she had already received one very severe disappointment in the sex of her child.

With a mind at rest and a body at last at ease Marianne was able to concentrate upon her appearance. Little had been done about it during the first few days, for the wreckage of her house had lain on top of her wardrobe, and though she had issued urgent instructions that the rescue of the box containing her nightgowns and wrappers and lace caps and the baby's layette should be the first bit of salvage work undertaken by the settlement, the settlement had disobeyed her commands and had thought there were other things more important to do first. But at last the box was found and brought to her, and upon an afternoon of sunshine and warm peace she set about making herself presentable. Tai Haruru's bare little bedroom, where she still had her bed because it was the only habitable room left in the settlement, had been made tidy and filled with autumn flowers, and a large cracked looking-glass had been propped at the foot of the bed. "Now go," she said a little sharply to Hine-Moa, "and take Baby with you. I know it is good for her to exercise her lungs as much as possible but the noise she makes is not good for the tympanums of my ears, which are exceptionally delicate."

Hine-Moa departed in some dudgeon, the baby cradled in her arms with passionate affection. Certainly the little thing made a noise out of all proportion to her size, but she was a lovely child, white-skinned and blue-eyed, and Hine-Moa deeply resented Marianne's indifference to her. Though naturally the bearing of a male warrior to the tribe, a true Tua, is the goal of every woman's ambition, yet girl babies also must be born to be the mothers of the Tuas of the future, and they should be borne with as good a grace as possible and not sent out of the room when they roar. . . . Hine-Moa closed the door with the slightest suspicion of a bang and the baby's yells died away in the distance.

Marianne gazed into the glass with concern. She looked absolutely frightful, and Tai Haruru had been seeing her looking absolutely frightful. Never, she thought, until she died, would she get over the humiliation of having had Tai Haruru, of all people, as her doctor during her confinement. . . . Yet if he had not been here probably she would have died. . . . What was it that Susanna had said about the tiresome man being God's gift in her life, part of the plan of it? Well, if he had saved her and the child she supposed that that was exactly what he was, and to continue to dislike him would be simply silly. I suppose it's always a mistake to hate, she said to herself, because when the people you hate suddenly turn round and do great things for you it puts you at such a ridiculous disadvantage.

She did her hair in elaborate curls and put on an elegant lace-trimmed wrapper and a cap with lavender ribbons. Then she looked at herself critically in the glass, pinching her lips and cheeks to bring colour into them. It occurred to her that it was a great comfort not to have that wretched parrot squawking at her derisively while she did it. Old Nick was presumably dead beneath the ruins of the house, and it was not a bit of good saying his demise was not a relief to her, because it was. When there was no more that she could do for her appearance she clapped her hands for Hine-Moa and sent her to fetch Tai Haruru. He must see her looking elegant. She must do her best, now, to make him forget what she *had* looked like. She must try to get their relationship back on the right footing again. Her need of his skill had made of her a little child clinging to the strength of a superior being. But the phase was past. They must be once more lady and lumberman.

"A most exquisite toilette, Ma'am," said Tai Haruru, when he had knocked and entered. "I congratulate you." And he bowed very courteously and remained standing.

"Do sit down, Mr. Haslam," she said with dignity.

"How very kind of you, Ma'am," he said, and sat. "What a very comfortable chair this is."

"You should know," said Marianne sharply. "It's your chair."

"Why, so it is, Ma'am," he said in surprise.

She looked at him suspiciously. Was he laughing at her? No. The solemnity of his countenance was quite untouched by mirth.

"I must thank you, Mr. Haslam, for all that you have done for me," she said graciously. "I should like you to understand that I am most deeply grateful."

"I am deeply grateful for your gratitude, Ma'am," he said. "And now the incident is closed, eh? We go back to where we were."

And now there was no doubt about his amusement, for the corners of his lips were twitching with it. Marianne opened her mouth to speak, suddenly floundered and dropped her eyes. How she disliked this man! And just a moment ago she had been making up her mind that it would be silly to dislike him any more. The fact was that he was literally the only human creature she had ever encountered who knew how to put her at a disadvantage. Why must he use his knowledge? Why wouldn't he keep it to himself and stay where she put him? If only he would do that she thought she might manage to like him.

"It's no good, Marianne," he said. "Face it."

"Face what, Mr. Haslam?" she asked him coldly.

"We can't go back to where we were. In spite of your pride you had to turn to me in your extremity, and now there is a bond between us that does not allow you to put yourself upon a pedestal. It holds us side by side as equals, you and I. Why not be friends?"

"I was not aware, Mr. Haslam, that we were not friends," she said stiffly.

"Don't lie, Marianne. We've been excellent antagonists, but

hardly friends. You are jealous of my friendship with William and you think I've had a bad effect on him all these years. In some ways, perhaps, I have. But I've taught him not to quit. If he's taken on a tough job he sticks to it. It may be that that perseverance of his has stood you in better stead than you've any idea of."

His eyes were twinkling. Then he left the room to fetch something and now he was back again, setting it beside her bed. It was a baby's cradle, made of kauri wood. "I only finished it this afternoon," he said. "Your little lass was beforehand with me."

Marianne gave a cry of astonished delight. It was an exquisite thing. It was carved with all the enchanted things, stars and cherubs, moons and suns and unicorns, lambkins and butterflies, robins and daisies and little sea-horses with frisking tails. It must have taken him months of patient labour to make, his fingers feeling through the wood for all the beauty that he could conjure from it to garland the sleep of a little child. And Hine-Moa had put the baby in it, dressed in one of the lovely embroidered robes that had now come to hand, wrapped in her fleecy shawl and laid upon her little lace-trimmed pillow. And she was not howling any more but was lying deeply asleep, her crumpled face no longer flushed with her wrath but delicately tinted as a flower, and old and very wise, the microscopic nails on her tiny groping fingers reminding her mother quite suddenly of the shells that Marguerite had long ago brought back from La Baie des Petits Fleurs.

"But she's a little darling after all!" cried Marianne. "She's sweet. . . . And, next time, I'll have a boy."

Tai Haruru went out laughing, before she had time to thank him for the cradle with more than that one cry of delight. She was going to love her daughter now but she'd not rest until she got the boy. Any other woman, who had been through what she had, would have said, "Never again!" But not so Marianne, baulked of her will. She was incorrigible. But she was going to love her child now, and cease to hate himself, and he was not dissatisfied with his afternoon's work. Poor old William would have a better time of it now. Years ago the young man who had been Timothy Haslam had vowed that no human being should ever again get a stranglehold upon his affections, but the man who was Tai Haruru had broken that vow when he had looked up that night at Hobson's saloon and seen the boy William sitting at the other side of the table staring at him. He wanted William's happiness as he had never expected to want anything again in this world. A funny business, this of William's marriage. He had not listened with much attention to William's rhapsodisings upon the subject of his bride before her appearance, but even so he had found it difficult to reconcile Marianne as she was with Marianne as he had expected her to be. . . . Though he preferred Marianne as she was. . . . He liked her particular brand of obstinate courage, and her character was sufficiently complex to make life with her interesting. And above all he liked the changeling in her. . . . He loved that elf, half merry and half afraid, confident and yet lost, who peeped out sometimes from the brightness of her eyes.

Marianne for the next two days slept and woke and slept again, and enjoyed the peace and the cessation of perpetual striving. She was prepared to begin it again, with gusto, very soon, but meanwhile it was pleasant to rest. That afternoon with Tai Haruru had so completely shattered the remnants of her stupid hatred and jealousy that now she did not feel humiliated any more by what he had done for her, only humbled. To feel so humble made her feel extremely chastened and odd, as though she were a little girl again, punished and forgiven and tucked up in bed with a sweet to suck. I believe there is a lot of the little girl still in me, she thought, and I believe I am nicest when it shows.

It was sunset, and the baby slept beside her in the cradle, when she heard the sounds of arrival. Tai Haruru's house was very close to the creek and she could hear the splash of paddles in the water, the excited cries of the Maoris, and William's voice issuing orders. She looked at herself in the glass, the colour rushing into her cheeks and the light into her eyes. She was trembling all over. William! Yes, she was looking almost pretty, almost like the excited small girl that she felt. Surely he must love her now in the way that she wanted. She had borne him a child and she was looking pretty.

His fumbling knock came at the door.

"William! William!" she cried eagerly. Why must he knock? Why could he not come straight in, stride across the room and take her in his arms? He was inside the door now, but standing sheepishly upon the mat, embarrassingly conscious of his disreputable appearance, half afraid of her because she had suffered so much for him. "William!" she cried again, and now there was a note of sharpness in her voice.

He came to her then, stumbling and rucking up the mat, and knelt beside her and kissed her gingerly as though she was a piece of Dresden china. "Poor Marianne!" he whispered shamefacedly. "Poor girl! Shocking time you've had. Shocking. And look at me in this filthy state. Should have changed and washed before I came to you."

"In too much of a hurry to see your child, William?" she asked lightly, and a little coldly, for he was, she noticed, keeping his eyes fixed firmly upon her and not upon the cradle with considerable effort. "She's there, William. Look and see."

"*She?*" almost bellowed William. "*She?* Is it a girl?"

"Yes, William, I'm afraid it is."

"Good God, why did nobody tell me? A girl! Why wasn't I told it was a girl?"

"I didn't know you wanted a girl, William," said Marianne. "Why did you want a girl?"

But he was not listening to her. He had suddenly forgotten his embarrassment, his dirt, his fatigue. He was kneeling by the cradle, his coarse red face beaming like the sun, chuckling and chortling to his daughter, one of her tiny hands clutching his finger. Never, since the day of their marriage, had his wife seen him look so happy, and once more jealousy stabbed her. Must she always be jealous where William was concerned? Had she lost her jealousy of Marguerite and Tai Haruru only to feel jealous of her own baby? Oh, it was too bad!

"Blue eyes and fair hair!" boomed William triumphantly.

"They always have blue eyes when they're born, and the first lot of hair always comes off," Marianne told him flatly.

"But you can tell she's going to be fair," exulted William. "Look at her skin. Like white satin. What shall we call her?"

His eyes had at last left the baby and were fixed eagerly upon his wife. Marianne, who had never at any time permitted herself to contemplate the disaster of a daughter, had given no consideration at all to female names. "I don't know," she said a little feebly. And then, from somewhere far away, a voice that did not seem to be her own said, "Mr. Haslam has carved daisies all over her cradle. I've worked daisies on her cap. Shall we call her Marguerite?"

He kissed her then almost as she wanted to be kissed, almost with eagerness. "But she must be named after her mother too," he said. "We'll call her Marguerite Véronique. After you and Marguerite."

She felt most horribly tired suddenly, and had a frantic desire to get rid of the baby for a bit and be alone with him, the only one he looked at. "Put the cradle outside," she said. "It's time Hine-Moa bathed her. And then come back and tell me all you have been doing."

He did as she told him, though very reluctantly, and then came back and sat down beside her and took her hand. He looked very grave suddenly, and she noticed the deep lines of fatigue running from nose to mouth. He looked all at once like a thoroughly wretched Newfoundland dog.

"What's happened, William?" she asked sharply.

"Maybe I should not tell you for a day or two, not till you're stronger," said William uncertainly. "Let's go on talking about the baby."

"Don't talk nonsense, William. Bother the baby. It's far worse for me to have you sitting there hinting at things than to have you tell me the whole thing straight out. Go on, William. What *has* happened?"

William cleared his throat, scratched his head, sighed, and came out with it at last. "Captain O'Hara is dead, Marianne."

The room swayed about her. No, she had not been quite strong enough for this. Nothing seemed certain except William's strong clasp on her hand. Dr. Ozanne, her mother, and now Captain O'Hara. Well, she was middle-aged now. She had reached the time of life when she must expect to see the older generation pass from her one by one. But Captain O'Hara! He and the Green Dolphin had seemed such an integral part of her life and William's. "The Green Dolphin?" she whispered anxiously.

"Gone too," said William, and he held her hand and stroked it while she fought to overcome the shock and weakness.

"Tell me," she said at last. She felt steady again now, and she was loving the grip of William's hand. In their love for the Green Dolphin they were at least always at one. In that nothing ever came between them.

"There's not much to tell," said William heavily. "She was wrecked on that hideous reef of rocks that runs out into the sea from the coast down by the fishing village. I've told you about it. It's a death trap in a storm. We found her there. She was almost broken up by the time we found her. But we had rope and I got out fairly near to her with a coil of it."

"You got out near to her?"

"Yes," said William sheepishly.

Marianne had a sudden vision of the awful sea and William fighting his way through it from the shore. One end of a rope held by his men would have been round him but even then the danger must have been deadly. "How dared you, William?" she demanded passionately. "You might have been killed. You should have thought of your wife and child."

"There wasn't time," said William simply. "It had to be done quickly, you know, if it was done at all, because the poor old Green Dolphin was breaking up so fast. But I couldn't have done it if I hadn't been the strongest, stoutest chap God ever made. I got out as far as I could and they flung me a rope. They flung it again and again and at last I got it and made it fast to mine. They were uncommon glad to see me, those poor chaps. They were pretty well knocked about, and pretty blue, all except Captain O'Hara. I could see him there bellowing away on the quarterdeck . . . laughing . . . he was just the same. . . ."

"Even though he'd wrecked the Green Dolphin? I expect it was his own fault. I expect he took a risk once too often."

"If he had it wasn't bothering him. He was as jolly and confident as though the whole thing were just a picnic. Maybe he knew there'd be no life lost except his own. All the men got ashore holding to the rope—not one of them was swept away. Nat got ashore the last of all. He didn't want to leave Captain O'Hara but the old man ordered him overboard. I go Nat ashore myself, and then just as I turned round again the Green Dolphin suddenly heeled over, and before one could say Jack Robinson she was gone, and Captain O'Hara too. Just gone. Vanished as though a wild beast had opened its mouth and swallowed them down whole. Marianne, the sea's a devil. You'd have known it was a devil if you'd seen it then."

He broke down and sobbed a little in the silly childish way that had so exasperated Marianne when he had wept for Sophie. But she was not exasperated now. She stroked his untidy bent head with a gentleness he had never yet experienced from her.

"For Captain O'Hara, that was the best way to die," she comforted him. "He was getting old and he wouldn't have known what to do about being really old. Yet if he had time to think I expect he was surprised when it happened like that. He was arrogant, you know. He'd never have expected the sea to beat him." She stopped, wondering exactly what he *had* thought in the very last moment. Then she remembered Nat and his humility, that she had so deeply loved. "I'm glad you saved Nat, William. I'm so glad you saved Nat."

"Nat's nightcap's gone," he told her lugubriously.

She laughed, and amazingly comforted by the touch of her hand he ceased sobbing. They were nearer to each other than they had ever been.

"It's not only the Green Dolphin that's gone, Marianne," he told her hesitatingly. "The barges are swept away, the sheds, the jetty, everything, all that you've worked for. And the settlement here is in a great mess, too. Years of work have gone in a night. That's the way of it in this damn country."

She took the bad news calmly. "Never mind, William," she said. "We'll begin again. In every sort of way we'll begin again and do better. We'll never forget the Green Dolphin and we'll do better."

He kissed her and left her and she wept for a little; for Captain

O'Hara and the Green Dolphin and for a happy chapter closed for ever in her life. That lovely ship! It was as though her own childhood had gone down on it. And she wept too for the loss of so much that she had planned and striven for. But it was no good crying. They must just pick themselves up and start again. That was the meaning of pioneer life, starting again. As they used to say on the Island at any fresh beginning, "Au nom de Dieu soit".

She dozed for a little, tired by her weeping. She was awakened by a rustling sound, and by a touch upon her body. She looked up and there was Nat standing by her bed, one hand laid caressingly upon her left ankle. "Nat!" she cried. "Nat!"

He looked at her, trying to speak, the very depth of what he felt making his noises even more unintelligible than usual, yet fully expressive of his love and sorrow. He was the same Nat, if perhaps a shade sadder, a shade more wizened because he had lost Captain O'Hara, much more like a monkey than ever without his ridiculous nightcap. But he was the same Nat, and he did not fail, as ever, to touch the spring of tenderness in her that only he could touch.

"You're not to go to sea again, Nat," she said decidedly. "You've had enough of the sea. You're to stay here always with Mr. Ozanne and me and my baby. We'll all be so happy together. No more storms and scoldings. Just happiness and peace together."

"You don't say!" a voice ejaculated, a detestably mocking and incredulous voice. "Oh my! You don't say!"

Vaguely Marianne had been aware of that rustling sound by the window. Now she looked towards it and there on the window ledge was Old Nick, preening himself.

PART IV

THE NUN

*The high goal of our great endeavour is spiritual attainment,
individual worth, at all cost to be sought and at all cost pursued, to be won at all cost and at all cost assured.*—ROBERT
BRIDGES.

CHAPTER ONE

1

The Autumn wind and rain were battering at the window of the old
schoolroom, that was now Marguerite's bedroom, and she was restlessly aware of the tumult as she sat before her dressing-table, turning out its drawers so as to give her restless body and chaotic mind
something to do. It was so unlike her to be either restless or chaotic
that the very unfamiliarity of her state in itself frightened her. Or
rather it alarmed that detached observer who seems to accompany
us through life and to be one half of ourselves, while the other half,
the suffering, striving, growing self, is the thing observed. The observer half of Marguerite did not recognise the observed half any
more, was full of consternation, drew back and strained away, so
that there was disunion in the woman Marguerite Le Patourel, and
threatened disintegration.

"Who am I?" she asked, and looking up she unexpectedly saw
herself in the glass and did not know who this woman was who
looked back at her. Who was it? She was not beautiful with her
thin face, her slack exhausted mouth, her frightened eyes and greying
hair. The beautiful young Marguerite did not know who she was
until as she leaned forward to look more closely she saw a familiar
black dress, and the gold locket that she was herself wearing hanging
about the neck of this other woman. Then terror gripped her.
How many more people was she becoming? Who was she of all
these different fragments into which her personality seemed fraying
away? Would she soon have frayed away into nothingness, and not
exist any more? Nothingness. It was the old nightmare back again,
that had never quite left her since that night five years ago when she
had lost all the treasure of her life; her sense of the immanent
presence of God, her blessed quietude, her sense of one-ness with

William, her delight and pride in her own power to comfort, her faith that her life was a complete and timeless thing rooted in eternity; every single thing, in fact, that had once made life worth living. Except one thing. It had only been at the blackest hour of that dark night that she had ceased to believe that God is. When He had given back to her night and morning, birdsong and the scent of earth, she had believed in Him again; with no joy, no adoration, just a blind reliance upon the fact of Him, that same blind reliance that was hers when she got out of bed in the morning and knew that some solid surface would support her feet. That was all. For the rest, her own life and the universe seemed just a tumbling chaos.

It had been worse these last two weeks, for a fortnight ago Octavius had died. She had been thankful to see his misery ended, thankful that he had not had to linger too long without Sophie, but their need of her had given some sort of cohesion to her life, and now that they had both gone its disintegration seemed complete; and all the greater because their need had been so great.

And the extraordinary thing had been that she had fulfilled it. This astonished her, for though the outward forms of her service to them had been just the same, and her love for them had been the same, and she had fought almost madly to appear just as usual, it had seemed to her that her inward humiliation and misery must surely destroy the strength and comfort that once they had drawn from her presence. She had felt strong, in those days that now seemed a thousand years ago, because somehow or other she had dared to believe her small sinful self worthy of an indwelling of the presence of God, and the unspeakably selfish delight that she had taken in that strange fantasy of hers, that extraordinary notion that her muddied soul was capable of radiating God's power and laughter, had no doubt made her cheerful, and therefore comforting, company. But not for one moment had she expected that her parents would continue to find her good company once she had seen herself for what she was, a woman so self-deceived, so egotistical, that there could be no humiliation too great for her overweening and most horrifying pride. Yet they had continued to rely upon her exactly as before. She had only one explanation; that God had no intention of leaving them comfortless in their extremity because the only instrument He had to hand was the worthless thing that was herself. In default of a gold chalice He could yet pick up an old cracked earthenware jar and patch it up sufficiently to hold the waters of comfort. But how shamed she had been, how utterly and horribly shamed, that after thirty-three years of life in this world, that was all she was. "How can You touch me?" she had cried out in dismay. "Go away from me. Fling me down. Leave me alone."

No wonder that now, when it was all over, she seemed to herself to be falling to pieces. She was too paltry a thing not to crack under sorrow. . . . And such sorrow. . . . Sophie's pain would have seemed impossible to bear, either by herself or Marguerite, had it not been that it had to be borne. Marguerite, now, would have liked to have stopped thinking about it, to have thought only of Sophie's amazing patience under the humiliations of dying, had it not been that her will, once so strong, was now as weak as water. She could no longer direct her thoughts. They hovered all the time between Sophie's pain and Octavius' long misery of doubt, that had been almost as bad, and she could rid herself of the memory of neither.

For not until the last week of his life had Octavius been able to make up his mind which of the two deities in whom, until misfortune came upon him, he had believed simultaneously, must now go by the board, God or the Octavius Le Patourel whom his benevolent mind's eye, inwardly inclined, had beheld in such a rosy light. The utmost that Marguerite had been able to do for him had been to continue to keep him in a state of balance, to give him time. She was not absolutely certain even now that he had come to any definite conclusion, she only knew that on the day when he took to his bed with a bad chill that rapidly became pneumonia he had asked her, "Who was it of whom it was said that he walked humbly with his God?" And before she could answer he went on, "Not much time now." And then he had fallen asleep and had not spoken to her coherently again. Yet through the days during which he had been still with her upon this earth she had had the feeling that she was not alone in the valley of humiliation. She had had a strong sense of companionship that had made her almost happy; though when he had died and she was by herself again she almost wished that she had not had it, for by contrast the returning loneliness seemed doubly impossible to bear.

There was a knock at the door and mechanically she straightened herself, turning to the door with smiling lips as Charlotte entered.

"The packet is in harbour, M'selle, and there is a package and a letter from New Zealand," said Charlotte, smiling broadly. "It is, of course, too early for us to have news of the birth of the little one—but there is the letter as well as the package."

"Wait while I open them, Charlotte," said Marguerite.

Charlotte waited eagerly, for though it was Marguerite whom she loved the best of the two sisters she was nevertheless deeply attached to Marianne and eternally grateful to her.

Marguerite opened the package, where a bulky letter was folded about something knobbly wrapped in moss, and then opened the second letter. The dates of the two were separated by several weeks, but that was nothing unusual, for a letter waiting at Wellington for a homeward-bound ship was often joined by a second package before the ship arrived, but what was unusual was that both letters were written by William, who usually contented himself with a few scrawled lines at the end of Marianne's epistles. The first one was so long that after one glance she set it aside, looked at the second and then read it aloud to Charlotte.

"My dear Sister,

I hasten to tell you of the arrival of our infant daughter, and to assure you of the safety and well-being of my beloved wife. I am sitting beside Marianne as I write and she wishes me to tell you that both she and the child are doing excellently, that our daughter is a fair-haired blue-eyed infant of exceptional beauty and intelligence, and that she is to be named Marguerite Véronique after both her mother and her aunt. As you will immediately realise, upon seeing the date at the head of this letter, the birth of the child was premature, caused by the shock experienced by Marianne as the result of a severe earthquake that has done great damage to the settlement, to our office at Wellington, and to the sheds and jetty at the coast of which we have told you. But these material losses are nothing in comparison to the happy fact that Marianne and her child are safe and well. For this fact we give most humble and heart-felt thanks to Almighty God. No more at present, my dear Sister, and I ask you to forgive the hurriedness of this note. We have just heard that a neighbour is leaving for Wellington this very hour, and we wish the happy news to reach you at the first possible moment. Your next letter will be from Marianne herself, and will contain all those domestic details for which you must long, but to which the pen of a mere male is incapable of doing justice. Marianne sends her love to you, and I remain always, my dear Marguerite, your affectionate brother William Ozanne."

The Autumn seemed to turn to Spring, and the wind and rain to sunshine, as the two women exclaimed and ejaculated and read and re-read the letter. That jubilance that seizes every human being at the news of a birth had hold of them. There must be some great worth-whileness in human existence, thought Marguerite, or why this instinctive joy? "Marguerite Véronique." The letter had been five months coming from New Zealand, and though it was Autumn on this Island, on that Island it was Spring, and Marguerite Véronique was five months old. She had learned to laugh by this time, to open her blue eyes wide when she saw bright colours, to know her father's voice and her mother's arms. "Marguerite Véronique." Two dead childhoods lived again, and as the rain spattered on the window Marguerite remembered another Autumn storm, and two small girls lying on their backboards in this very room and wondering what the packet had brought. So vivid was the recollection that it was not a recollection at all but a present experience. She was no longer the exhausted, frightened and unlovely woman whom she had been ten minutes ago, but the golden-haired, blue-eyed, happy little girl who had sat bolt upright on her backboard to watch the packet come in. It was the same little girl who cried out now to Charlotte, "We'll all have tea together in the dining parlour, Charlotte, you and I and the children. We'll put on our best frocks and it shall be a birthday party for Marguerite Véronique. Light all the candles, Charlotte, and see that there is lots to eat."

Charlotte looked at the French clock on the mantel-piece, noted the time and laughed. "I have two hours," she said. "I and the children, we have two hours to prepare. Do not come down, M'selle. We will prepare a surprise for you. Do not come down until I ring the bell."

The ghost of a dimple showed in Marguerite's thin cheek. "Will there be gâche à corinthes, Charlotte?" she asked. "And anglicé currant cake?"

"There will be all the good things that you like, M'selle," Charlotte assured her. "I have two hours." And she left the room still laughing. Was it possible that her beloved M'selle was going to recapture her love of life and her delight in little things? Was she once again to see good days? Always the good days come back, just when we think they have gone forever, said Charlotte to herself as she hurried downstairs. If it were not so we should not be able to rejoice when a child is born.

Marguerite spent a curious two hours. For a moment or two she sat at her dressing-table, laughing and crying together, aware that she was crying because Sophie and Octavius had not lived to know of the birth of their grand-child, but unaware, even though a transfigured face looked back at her from the mirror, that she was laughing because the little girl whom once she had been had come alive again; and with her that belief she thought she had lost, that certainty that one's life is a complete, rounded, timeless thing rooted in eternity, that what we once had is ours forever, that what we will have is already present with us, that at no time in our lives are we ever anything but immeasurably and inconceivably rich and blessed.

Then she dried her eyes and opened the package that had been wrapped in the long letter from William that she had not read yet. "A rosary!" she cried at first sight of it. And then she held it up and saw the wonderful carvings of flowers and birds and butterflies, monkeys and gods and men, and smiling little Lung-mu hanging at the bottom. It was a perfect thing, and the little girl whom she had once been, and who had come back to her once more, laughed aloud at its beauty, and then the woman whom she was stopped laughing and looked at it very gravely. Though it was not a rosary it was shaped like one. As she looked at it, and fingered its exquisite diversity, all the created loveliness of the whole world seemed flowing in to her, without barrier of time or space, and as the tide of it lifted her she felt again that glorious upward movement of speechless adoration that she had been accustomed to think of in old days as the reward of persistent and persevering prayer. It had not come now as a reward, for she had not prayed for years, it had come simply as an unasked, unexpected gift to a woman so astonished that this should come again to her unworthiness that she could only recoil from the joy with a sort of dismay, just as she had recoiled when the clay of her spirit had been picked up and used as though it were gold.

Trembling all over, still holding the necklace, she picked up the letter. Slowly and deliberately she read it right through, then turned back to the beginning and read it again. Why had he written of his life in such detail? It seemed to her as she read that she could hear the rasping of saws in the forest, the shouted orders, the ripple of water against the sides of the barges, the rustle of Marianne's dress as she went about her work. And she could smell the kauri trees, see the mountains, hear the chiming of birdsong. Why did he want her to know all this? Why had he sent her across half the world, garlanding the goddess of protection, these exquisite little carvings that had suddenly given back to her for a moment the power of prayer? Out of her childhood came a picture that she had not thought of for years, the white gull flying backwards and forwards over La Baie des Petits Fleurs, weaving a pattern of protection in the air. Did he want help? Had this necklace come to her with a command? It had banished space for her; had she to answer with a similar reaching out of power across the world? I'm crazy, she thought. William would never think about things in this way; or if he did it would only be vaguely and fumblingly, not knowing quite what it was that he wanted. Then she read the concluding words of his letter over again.

"Marianne is waiting now for her child. It is to be a boy, but I think I would have liked a little girl with fair hair and blue eyes.

Marianne will be an excellent mother, as she is an excellent wife and housekeeper and business woman. I try to live only to make her happy. Her welfare and that of her child is the reason for existence. She would send her love did she know that I was writing to you. Though you are so far away the bond between us is very strong. There is a saying I have heard somewhere, 'A three-fold cord shall not be broken'. You have my love and devotion always. I think of you day and night. William."

It struck her suddenly that this was not the letter of a man who was happy in his marriage. Her sister's character seemed to leap up at her from the careful phrases. "It is to be a boy." But for once Marianne's strong will had failed to get her her wish, and Marguerite only hoped she had not taken a dislike to the poor babe in consequence. "An excellent housekeeper and business woman." Surely there was something rueful about the easy-going William's description of his efficient wife? "I try to live only to make her happy." Yes, it had always been hard to make Marianne happy. No doubt William was finding it a stiff job, as she had too in the old days. But why had he written her this long letter without his wife's knowledge? "I would have liked a little girl with fair hair and blue eyes. . . . Though you are so far away the bond between us is very strong. You have my love and devotion always. I think of you day and night." No, the jealous Marianne would not have liked him to write in that way to her sister.

She sat there staring at the letter. Had she after all not deceived herself when she had imagined that there was a special union between herself and William? Evidently not. He said that she had his love and devotion always. He had chosen Marianne for his wife, and perhaps he had shown good sense there, for Marguerite acknowledged frankly that Marianne's adventurous spirit was more suited to pioneer existence than her own, but it seemed that he had a special love for her too, and that he needed her still. He was asking that she should hold him and Marianne day by day in her consciousness and help him to make a fine thing of his marriage.

But it's no good, William, she thought, as she locked away the letter and the necklace; in the old arrogant days I would have felt sure that I could help you, but now I know that I am useless . . . nothing . . . nothing at all.

She stood up to take off her heavy black dress, that was most unsuitable for a birthday party, and then suddenly the arms she had lifted to unhook her dress fell again to her side, and she stood still, thinking hard. On that dark night five years ago, when everything in which she had believed had seemed to fall away from her, she had thought herself arrogantly self-deceived alike in her faith in an earthly and a heavenly union. In this last hour, in the matter of the earthly union, as well as in the matter of the wholeness and completeness of her life, she had been proved self-deceived the other way round. Had she, when she imagined herself cast out from the presence of God, also deceived herself? Was it possible that in these last five years of darkness she had after all lost nothing whatever except her pride?

The mere possibility of such joy was too much for her to face just at present. She had to push it away from her, hold it off like some dazzling dream that she must not think of yet. Now there was the birthday party to consider. Now, the happiness of Charlotte and her children was what she must think of. Yet as she unhooked her dress and took it off the blood was tingling through her body, her cold hands and feet were suddenly warm and glowing. The dark night was over and the sun was rising in the east.

She did her hair in festive ringlets and put on a frock of sky blue. To-morrow the proprieties would demand that she wear black again, but she could not wear black for Marguerite Véronique's birthday party. Marguerite Véronique was herself, she felt. As she hunted through her drawers for a blue ribbon to tie round her hair she was seeing a picture of a little girl in a blue frock kneeling on the sand at La Baie des Petits Fleurs, laughing in delight as she picked up handfuls of the exquisite shells and let them fall again in drops of brightness through her fingers. A second visit to La Baie des Petits Fleurs had been forbidden by her parents after her childhood's escapade, and she had not been there again. Until to-day she had almost forgotten about it. But on the first fine day she would go there at low tide and gather shells for Marguerite Véronique.

She found the ribbon at last, and under it, pushed away forgotten at the back of the drawer, that little book by the French barefoot Carmelite that had first started her on the path of spiritual discipline, and that had been the cause of so much torment and so much joy. She opened it and turned the pages at random. "I always thought that He would reduce you to extremity. He will come in His own time, and when you least expect it. . . . But those who have the gale of the Holy Spirit go forward even in sleep. If the vessel of our soul is still tossed with winds and storms let us awake the Lord who reposes in it, and he will quickly calm the sea."

She put the book back, and smiled. Even in sleep, even through the night, the vessel had been carried forward by no virtue of her own; and God had been within it all the time.

She ran downstairs lightfooted and flung open the door of the dining parlour. All round the room the candles were blazing and the table was loaded with the full astounding indigestible munificence of an Island high tea, with nothing forgotten, neither the crab nor the gâche à corinthes, nor the curds nor the strawberry jam. The children stood in their places with laughing faces shining with soap and water, dressed in their best, and Charlotte wore her scarlet festival petticoat and a flowered chintz gown that had belonged to her great-great-grandmother. She had sprinkled white sugar over the cake and on top of it burned one scarlet candle.

2

I was the greatest idiot ever made, thought Marguerite, not to have come here before. She was sitting in La Baie des Petits Fleurs, her lap full of shells, looking out across the exquisite little bay towards the distant shining line of sea. She was keeping a wary eye upon it, for it was just such another perfect Autumn day as it had been on that first visit of her childhood, it was as though the occasion were repeating itself, and she did not mean to be caught by the tide again. She had forgotten how lovely it was here. She ought to have come before. My mind was always so full of other things, she thought, and until now I have had no little niece for whom to gather shells.

What to do with herself was still her problem. Sophie and Octavius had absorbed every minute of all her days for the last five years, and in consequence she had lost her girlhood's friends and gradually dropped out of the social life of the Island. She could have got back into it again, she supposed, but she found that she did not want to, for she had lost her taste for society and the urge was in her to move not backwards but forwards; though as yet she did not know to what. I must just wait and see, she said to herself. One has to have these waiting times in life, when one just sits back and gathers one's strength. It is silly to be impatient when one has the whole of eternity.

And in this fairytale bay there was less temptation to be impatient than there was at home. At Le Paradis, with carriages rattling by over the cobbles, Charlotte's children growing up even as she looked at them and her own ageing face confronting her every time she passed a mirror, she was continually aware of the thing called time. Here it did not exist. In twenty-two years nothing whatever had changed in this bay. There was Marie Tape-Tout looking out to sea, and the rock of Le Petit Aiguillon, and the pools full of anemones, and the silver sand and opal-tinted stones and purple-brown seaweed all just the same. It was true that she was not now conscious of the myriad tiny voices of the shells making a music that one could hear and not hear, like the sound of bells that the wind is always catching away, and the pebbles no longer seemed to her to have fat smiling faces, or the anemones mad bright eyes above their frills, but that, she knew, was due to a change in herself, not to a change in La Baie des Petits Fleurs. She did not doubt that fairy creatures still inhabited this place, but the gates of her childhood's fairyland had clanged shut behind her now and she could no longer see them. Yet what did that matter? If the gates of fairyland were shut against her the gates of Paradise were open wide. The one was a parable of the other, and both of them synonyms for something that had no name.

It was as warm as summer in this sheltered bay. She took off her bonnet, leaned back against the sun-warmed rock behind her and closed her eyes. It was so strange, so amazingly restful, to feel so happy. Ever since the day of Marguerite Véronique's birthday party she had been slowly passing out of the darkness into a state of liberation that for want of that unknown name she called Paradise. Her first tentative efforts to pray again had been made for William's sake and had been her answer to the command that was certainly present in his letter and his gift, whether he was aware of it or not. It had been hard at first, so inhibiting had been her sense of her own nothingness, so rusty her mental machinery. But she had persevered, giving her worthlessness bravely into the hands of God, and gradually all the old power had come back. Only it had come back with a difference. In old days she had felt as though the laughter and strength that she brought away from her hours of prayer had flowed out from herself, and the knowledge of her own power had delighted her; now she knew that they flowed only through her, and what delighted her was the miraculous power of God that could pick up even an empty straw and make it the channel of His grace. Such a glorious and loving condescension had called out the love of her whole being, prostrated in humility, and to it she had surrendered herself utterly and forever. "Intreat me not to leave thee, or to return from following after thee." That was the true cry of love, born of humility, and it had liberated her from the burden of her own selfhood and unlocked for her the gate of Paradise.

Yet in spite of her happiness she was scared. She was afraid sometimes lest the old sinful pride might come back, to be followed again by the darkness. Now and again came the shadow of an even worse fear; that perhaps the whole experience was a figment of her imagination; that perhaps she was not quite normal. It would have comforted her if she could have known that other people had had this same experience. She was so ignorant. She had read little and been taught little. An empty straw was not usable unless one could learn how to keep the channel of its emptiness unblocked by sin, and in this business of following after one needed signposts. She felt a desperate need of help and guidance.

She opened her eyes and saw that the bright line of the sea had drawn a little nearer, and that she must go. She put the cover on her box of shells, slipped it in her pocket, got up and walked slowly and reluctantly away over the silver sand. Standing in the narrow rocky entrance that was the gate of this enchanted place she stopped and looked back, seeing it again in imagination as she had seen it in her childhood, with the pebbles laughing and the anemones staring with their mad bright eyes, and the white gull flying backwards and forwards overhead. Good-bye, fairyland of childhood. I'll not see you again till life comes round full circle and the gate that a growing child came out of will be the gate where an old woman enters in.

She made her way back to La Baie des Saints and the village, and slowly climbed the long steep road to the cliff top. She had walked all the way from Le Paradis, she was ridiculously tired, and when she reached the summit she had to stop and get her breath back. The pinnacles and bastions of grey granite fell away below her, grand as ever, and there, across the bay, was Notre Dame du Castel towering up against the sky, as it had towered for centuries, a great fortress of the spirit that time had never touched.

Looking at it Marguerite found herself thinking about Reverend Mother who had been so kind to her. She was still there, she had heard. It seemed only yesterday that she had sat warming herself in that small fire-lit cell that she had thought was like the inside of a seashell. The shabby little book that Reverend Mother had given her was even now in her pocket with the box of shells. "I should be sorry not to see you again," Reverend Mother had said, "for I am your friend."

She had quite forgotten those courteous words, but now they came back to her. And she remembered too what Reverend Mother had said about liberation. She had not known what the word meant then, but now she did know, because she had experienced it. Had Reverend Mother passed through the same torments and joy which she was now experiencing with such bewilderment and happiness and fear? Probably she had, thought Marguerite. We are never so unique as we think we are. All our experiences are common to the human race; and common too is the longing to turn round on our path and hold out a helping hand to those who are floundering along the self-same way that we have trod ourselves.

Marguerite did not hesitate. She smoothed her bonnet strings, gathered her black cloak more firmly round her shoulders, and made her way along the cliff top to the narrow road that approached Notre Dame due Castel from the landward side.

3

It was once more the hour for correspondence, and Reverend Mother sat at her desk dealing with it. She had changed very little and she bore her years lightly. The pencilling of lines about her brilliant keen grey eyes was more noticeable, her smooth olive cheek was more hollowed and her delicate eyebrows were now grey, but that was the only difference. The years from forty-three to sixty-five had set little mark upon a body so consistently disregarded by its owner that it had been able to carry on its orderly functions without let or hindrance from vanity or fear. The vagaries of her mortal body did not interest Reverend Mother.

But nevertheless she was aware of a slight fatigue this afternoon. There was this problem of the Notre Dame du Castel Orphanage. Years ago a rich and devout old lady had left the convent a substantial legacy, with the instructions that it was to be used for the founding of some charitable institution on the Island, the nature of which she left to be decided by the discretion of the Order. The Order had shifted the responsibility of decision on to the shoulders of Reverend Mother, who, in doubt as to whether a hospital, a home for the aged of a children's orphanage was most needed by the islanders, had upon an autumn day some twenty-two years ago gone down to the chapel to lay the problem before Almighty God. She had not at that moment had the opportunity of doing so, however, for a commotion in the chapel had distracted her attention, and the discovery of a wet and dirty child as the cause of it, a child who had been cut off by the tide in La Baie de Petits Fleurs and had had the temerity to climb up the cliff at the risk of her life and batter for entrance at the west door of the chapel, had for the moment put the whole problem out of her mind. Later, however, when the child had been fed and dried and restored to the arms of an agitated Papa, and she had once more gone down to the chapel with her problem, she had seen the advent of the child as a definite piece of guidance. On her knees before the altar she had recoiled at the thought of the dangers to which children are constantly exposed, especially those children who have no agitated Papas to whose arms they can return at the completion of adventure. She had shivered at the thought of orphans exposed to the corruption of a wicked world, of orphans exposed to the elements, of orphans permanently wet and dirty and hungry, and (under the guidance of Almighty God, so she had said)

she had decided for the orphanage. A suitable house had been procured upon a twenty-two years lease, with the option of renewing
the lease at the end of the period, and the orphanage, if a constant
responsibility and source of anxiety, had become nevertheless a most
flourishing concern. But now, in a few months' time, the lease
would be terminated, the owners were unwilling to renew it, and
nowhere upon the Island could Reverend Mother find another vacant
house large enough to house twenty female orphans; devout happy
little orphans who went to Mass on Sundays walking two by two,
clothed in dresses of Madonna blue with white tuckers at the necks,
blue cloaks and black bonnets tied beneath their orphaned chins
with neat blue bows. As Reverend Mother sat at her desk, with a
letter from a despairing house agent held in one hand, her mind's eye
was seeing those blue-clad orphans returning from Mass two by two,
hungry as hunters . . . with no home to which to return.

It was at this moment that Soeur Angélique knocked and entered.

"What is it, Sister?" asked Reverend Mother.

"A lady to see you, Mother," said Soeur Angélique, her little
black eyes popping with enthusiasm. "And she is beautiful as the
Mother of God."

"No doubt," said Reverend Mother drily. "But it is neither the
day nor hour for visitors. You should have told the lady to make an
appointment and come again at the correct time."

"But I did, Mother," protested Soeur Angélique. "I told her that
you received no visitors except at the correct hour for visiting, and
by appointment. She is obstinate, that one, though beautiful as the
Mother of God. She said that her name was M'selle Le Patourel and
that you would see her."

"Go down again," said Reverend Mother, "and tell Mademoiselle
Le Patourel that I shall be delighted to see her on visitors' day, and
ask her to make an appointment.

Marguerite, however, had no intention of being removed from the
doorstep, for she was every whit as obstinate as Reverend Mother
herself. What she was doing required courage, and if she was not
allowed to do it to-day she was afraid she might falter in the doing of
it to-morrow. She smiled sweetly at Soeur Angélique and sent her
back once more to Reverend Mother, this time carrying a book in
her hand. It was perhaps too much to hope that Reverend Mother
would remember the little girl who had once knocked so persever-
ingly upon the seaward door of the convent, as the grown woman
was now knocking on the landward door, but there was just a
chance.

Reverend Mother took the little volume. It opened at familiar

words. "To arrive at this state, the beginning is very difficult. . . .
Knock, persevere in knocking, and I answer for it that He will open
to you in His due time." She turned to the flyleaf and saw her own
name, Marie Ursule Lamonté, written there in the spidery handwriting of the old village curé who had given it to her, and below it
was written in the round handwriting of a child, Marguerite Félicité
Le Patourel. Twenty-two years flashed away suddenly and the child
sat there in her blue dress, warming her toes at the fire.

"Ask Mademoiselle Le Patourel to come up instantly, Sister," she
commanded. "Quickly, Sister!"

Mon Dieu, there is no accounting for the holy ones, thought
Soeur Angélique, as she once more waddled away. One thing one
minute and another another, until those who are not so holy are out
of breath bustling this way and that fulfilling their incomprehensible
commands.

It was natural that Soeur Angélique should not have recognised
her, thought Reverend Mother, as she stood up to greet Marguerite.
She would not have recognised her herself had it not been for the
fearless glance of the blue eyes, the carriage of the head, the childish
way in which, after she had greeted her hostess, she put her hands
behind her back and stood straight as a poplar tree. But it was to
Soeur Angélique's credit that she had described this woman as
beautiful, for her greying hair and worn face might not have appeared
beautiful to many.

"Sit down, my daughter," said Reverend Mother gently. "Take
off your cloak and bonnet."

Marguerite took them off and then sat down easily and gracefully
on the stool, her hands linked round her knees. She was more easily
recognisable without her bonnet. Her curly hair and her white neck
were still lovely, and her gravely appraising glance was just the same
as she looked about her, verifying the whitewashed walls lit to rose-
colour by the firelight, the crucifix and prie-dieu, the statue of the
Virgin in the niche on the wall, and the blue of the Atlantic seen
through the narrow windows in the thickness of the wall.

"It is all just the same," she said.

"Convents don't alter very much," said Reverend Mother, smiling.
"Nuns do not follow the latest Paris fashions in clothes or furniture.
The wimple and gown of the 14th century, and tables and chairs that
have been here longer than we have, satisfy us and do not tempt us
with vanity or comfort."

"You are fortunate," said Marguerite. "In the world we are afraid
of vanity."

"You do not look vain," said Reverend Mother. "Sitting on that low stool in your mourning garments, you look both humble and sorrowful. Are you in trouble?"

"I loved my parents, and I have lost them," said Marguerite. "But that is a common trouble, isn't it? In that I am not unlike other women. I wish I knew if I have been like others in my vanity and humiliation, and joy and fear. If others have passed the same way then I am not going crazy, and I am not alone, and there must be a way to live that will suit the kind of person that I am."

"Your experience does not sound phenomenal, my daughter," said Reverend Mother. "But I could judge better with a few more details."

Her voice, that chilled so many by its coldness, did not chill Marguerite. She felt exactly the same liking for Reverend Mother that she had felt when she was a child, for she was subconsciously aware that the nun's apparent coldness was not the result of want of feeling but of iron control clamped down upon too much. And she did not want emotional sympathy. She was worn out by emotion. She wanted a cut and dried explanation of her condition that should serve as some sort of map for the future. So badly did she want it that she did not find it so difficult as she had expected to break her reserve and give this woman, who was almost a stranger to her, a completely honest account of her life for the last fifteen years. Now and then Reverend Mother slipped in an extremely searching question, but she gave straightforward answers to straightforward questions as she had twenty-two years ago, and her eyes never faltered, however deep her shame.

"And so you did not really read that book I gave you, you did not turn to the comforts of religion, until after your lover had sailed away without declaring his love?" asked Reverend Mother.

"No," said Marguerite.

"You want to know that your experiences are not uncommon. I am happy to inform you that it is quite common for women to turn to the Heavenly Lover as a second best," commented Reverend Mother with excessive dryness.

Marguerite's face was crimson.

"And when it appeared to you that the earthly lover had failed you spiritually as well as physically you imagined that God had also withdrawn His presence? Wasn't that tantamount to judging God by man?"

"Yes," said Marguerite.

"The way in which our sex perpetually insults Almighty God in this way is quite deplorable," said Reverend Mother.

"Yes," said Marguerite, and now her neck as well as her face was crimson.

"Yet it appears that all is now well," said Reverend Mother, in a voice now so dry that it sounded almost brittle. "This man, William, apparently has some feeling for you after all, and so God, too, has returned."

"Yes," said Marguerite, and she could hardly articulate.

Reverend Mother stretched out a hand and touched her lightly on the shoulder. "I think, now, that you should cease to brood upon your shame," she said. "You have experienced your own nothingness. You know of it for all time. You will not forget. No, your experience is not uncommon. Should I be a nun to-day if I had not discovered the man I loved to be so great a sinner that my pride revolted from marriage with him? Possibly not. And so great is the magnanimity of God that if we come at last to His feet I think He cares little how we came. . . . Divine humility is a strange thing for proud humanity to contemplate. . . . As for your spiritual experiences, they have been normal for a woman of your temperament, setting out upon the age-long quest for reality. We glimpse reality in childhood, in those sudden flashing moments when the veil of appearance suddenly slips and we are aware of something behind, something indescribable and incomprehensible, but incomparably lovely. If you remember your childhood at all you will remember those moments. All our life afterwards is a search for the reality we saw then —saw without understanding and then lost. We think of it as a place, a person, a state, according to our temperaments."

"My sister used to have what we called her 'moments'," said Marguerite, gazing into the fire, thinking herself back into her childhood. "But I don't remember that I did. The whole of life was so shining and beautiful to me then. I don't think one moment seemed more glorious than another."

"You loved life and saw good days, did you?" asked Reverend Mother, her voice softening into a slight suspicion of tenderness. "Not isolated moments but a perpetual experience of felicity. I expect your sister, whose moments came only now and then, was more aware of the unearthliness of that childhood's felicity than you were. Was she a restless woman, your sister, that she has been so eager to travel to the other side of the world?"

"She was always restless," said Marguerite.

"It is that conception of reality as a place that makes some souls pilgrims and wanderers," said Reverend Mother. "They must always go out from the environment in which they were born in search of a better country. They are the creators, the pioneers, the builders of new worlds. Yet I think they are often unsatisfied. They can never build the perfect thing. The country they want is both within them, and beyond the confines of this world, and in neither place does it occur to most of them to look for it. The lovers of this world, those who conceive of reality as a person, are generally more fortunate, I think. If the craving of the soul for its perfect mate remains unsatisfied they find salvation in the service of others, in saving others."

"They are the best of all, surely," said Marguerite softly.

"Not necessarily the best. You find the saints in each person of this trinity of search. Yet perhaps life is less hard for them than for the rest of us. They are friendly people, at their best in personal relationships, liked wherever they go. The atmosphere they breathe is warm and glowing. Ours, my daughter, is colder and more rarefied."

"Ours?" asked Marguerite.

"Ascetics like ourselves conceive of reality as a state. We long for inward perfection. Do not think that I do not understand what you have been through. I and countless others have passed the same way. First the completely selfish delight in the discovery of religion, then the apparent falling away, the loss and humiliation and chaos. 'I was swept up to Thee by Thy beauty and torn away from Thee by my own weight,' said Saint Augustine. You were born again, my daughter, you escaped from the weight of the old self when you passed through that terrible humiliation. Though you did not realise it the new self was growing as a child in the womb during the time of chaos; destruction and construction go always hand in hand, the one the price that is paid for the other; they will go on through your whole life, for until you die sin and judgment and rebirth will be an integral part of your growth. But you need not fear that that particular depth of suffering will come again. Something was destroyed in you then that will not need to be destroyed again. Now you are made anew. Now you will breathe in the air of another country not for your own delight but to breathe it out again in prayer for others."

"I remember saying when I was a child," said Marguerite, "that if I were a nun I'd pray all the time for people to be happy. I said I'd pray all day and all night for everyone, birds and animals and people and the whole world, just to be happy."

"It seems that even then you were aware of your vocation," said Reverend Mother. "And I remember that I also, when I first saw you, was aware of it. 'Une vraie religieuse,' I said of you."

Marguerite looked up, startled, her eyes widening. Then she got up, reaching for her cloak. This was travelling far too quickly. It was enough, for now, to know herself a normal creature following a normal path.

"Is it wrong to feel as happy as I do now?" she asked.

"Why should it be wrong? Happiness is your birthright, and those who pray with joy pray with power. Happiness is only sin when it springs from delight in self rather than in God."

Reverend Mother had got up also, for she was too wise a woman to say more now upon the subject that had suddenly become the subject next her heart.

"You will be amused to hear that twenty-two years ago you caused me to found an orphanage that has been a perpetual nuisance to me ever since," she said lightly.

"*I* caused you to found an orphanage?" asked the astonished Marguerite.

The two tall women stood facing each other in the sunlight that shone through the west windows. It had gathered the brightness of the sea up into its own light and their two pale worn faces shone each to the other as though radiantly alight. They loved each other in that moment. They understood each other as only those understand who have suffered the same pain.

"Tell me about it, please," said Marguerite, and Reverend Mother told her. "You might hear of a suitable house," she finished.

"Yes," said Marguerite, "I might. Indeed, I will. I'll not rest till I've found it for you."

"Thank you," said Reverend Mother. "Come and see me again when you have found it. Now I'll take you down to the chapel, for I don't doubt you'll like to look again at the scene of your youthful escapade. The west door is always kept open now. I often spend my meditation hour on the ledge of rock under the statue of the Madonna."

"Mère Madeleine who let me in that day is still alive?" asked Marguerite, as they went down the worn stone steps to the chapel door.

"She's still alive, poor soul, but very old and rather wandering in her wits, and something of a trial to us all. She says the good God must have forgotten to call her home, and we are all inclined to agree with her. You shall see her next time you come. Now I will leave you here in the chapel. Stay as long as you like and then let yourself out. Good-bye, my daughter. Allez en paix, vivez en paix, et que le Dieu de Paix vous bénisse."

Her slim cool hand touched Marguerite's cheek for a moment, and then she was gone. What beautiful hands she has, thought Marguerite, beautiful indolent hands. Who was she before she became a nun? A very great lady, surely, born to luxury. It cannot have been easy for her to take the holy habit of religion.

Then she lifted the latch of the chapel door and went in, greeted by the remembered musty smell of antiquity, incense and lilies. It all looked just the same, dim and most powerfully old, with the faint light from the deep-set windows touching the dull gold and dim blues and crimsons of statues and embroideries. The sanctuary lamp burned before the altar and a motionless nun knelt praying before the statue of the Holy Child. Marguerite stood and looked about her for a moment, attentively, comparing reality with memory and finding them less divergent than usual, for with the passing of the years the place had lost for her neither its awe nor its welcoming homeliness. Then she went out through the door of the tower and stood on the ledge of rock beneath the great worn statue of the Madonna and Child, looking westward out to sea. There was no mist to-day and the horizon line was drawn straight and clear against the sky. Beyond it, at the other side of the mighty ocean, were William and Marianne. Yet though their bodies were hundreds of miles away their souls seemed very near to hers. They sought the same thing and their trinity of search made up a unity. "A threefold cord shall not be broken," William had said. No, it should not. She went back into the chapel and knelt down to pray for them.

CHAPTER TWO

1

Marguerite sat upon the floor of the dismantled parlour and wondered what to do with the three last worldly possessions that she had not yet disposed of. She held them in her lap, a sampler, a wooden mouse and a string of carved beads, and couldn't imagine what to do with them. Ten months had gone by and beyond the windows the garden burned in the afterglow of a summer sunset. It was the last evening of her life in the world. To-morrow she would receive the holy habit of religion in the Chapel of Notre Dame du Castel, and a few days later, accompanied by three other novices, she would set sail for France to spend the time of her novitiate in Paris. Perhaps she would one day be sent back to her beloved Island, perhaps she would never see it again. Perhaps she would never see Reverend Mother again, whom she now loved more than anyone else in the world except William. The saying good-bye to old friends, and to the houses and the streets and the bays of the little Island that had been her world since babyhood, had been very bitter, and for the last week she had scarcely slept for weeping, but this evening she was at peace and worrying about nothing at all except this trivial ridiculous problem of what to do with a sampler, a mouse and a necklace. Her letter from William she was taking with her, folded inside the little book Reverend Mother had given her. That, she thought, did not rank among the worldly possessions she had renounced, but the sampler, the mouse and the necklace most certainly did, and she could not turn up at the door of the convent with them clasped to her bosom.

What to do with them was her only worry, for if the partings had been bitter there had been no doubt at all in her mind about their necessity. Throughout these last ten months she had come step by step to a conclusion that seemed to her inevitable. The renunciation of outward circumstances that she was making was only the symbol of the renunciation of an outworn self that she had made months ago, but for her it was a necessary symbol because she could not see how to keep the new wine safe in the old bottle. She was still fearful and hungered for discipline and guidance.

The first step had been an unsuccessful search for a house for the orphanage, and then the decision to offer Reverend Mother No. 3 Le Paradis. She could scarcely afford to live there by herself, for Octavius, with his love of comfort and display, had always spent nearly everything that he earned and had left very little money to his daughters. And the arrangement had provided for Charlotte, who as a Catholic had been delighted with the suggestion that she should stay on as cook to the orphanage. Her boys were old enough now to go out to work and her two little girls could don the blue dresses and bonnets and cloaks and attach themselves to the tail of the crocodile that walked two by two to Mass on Sundays. Marguerite would have liked to sell No. 3 outright to the Order but the house and the furniture had been left jointly to her and Marianne, and when she asked Marianne's permission to do this it was refused in an extremely dictatorial and Marianne-ish letter. "Certainly not," Marianne had written. "Let the house by all means, if you can get a good price for it, but do not sell, for I shall probably be requiring it in my own old age." How could she possibly ever require it? Marguerite had wondered. William had said it would never be possible for him to return to the Island. Well, no doubt Marianne would manage things to her liking somehow. She always did. "And be certain you *do* get a good price for it," had gone on Marianne's letter. "You must not let it for less than its value. I enclose a list of the furniture and china I should like you to keep and the rest you may sell. And I insist, my dear sister, that you *do* sell, and for a fair price. I do not wish you to part with articles of value as gifts to friends. Your tendency to lavish and wholly unnecessary giving, which merely tends to embarrass the recipient, was one which caused pain to dear Mamma and Papa and should not be indulged. I refer, of course, only to those articles which have been left to us both conjointly. In the case of your own personal possessions I have of course no right to command you, though I could by no means approve the sale of the lacquer desk that Aunt Louise gave you, or your Chinese workbox, or of course any of your jewellery. You have, I know, never cared for jewellery, but you must remember that you now have a niece."

So slow were the posts that Marguerite had not received this letter until a month ago. But she needed no reminder about her niece. She thought lovingly of little Marguerite Véronique every moment of the day and night, and all her personal treasures were now lodged in the bank, waiting until that young lady should be of age to claim them. And the furniture and china Marianne wanted kept was in store, and the rest sold, and the house let to Reverend Mother's Order at a rent so low that Marguerite thought with compunction of poor William, who would doubtless have a bad time of it when Marianne got the news. And perhaps William would also have a bad time when Marianne heard that her sister had become not only a Catholic but a nun as well. But Marguerite had no idea how her sister would react to that piece of news. . . . It was just possible that she might be glad. . . And what would William think of the step she was taking? She did not know that either. She had written the news in a letter beginning, "My beloved Brother and Sister," and ending with the words, "I picture you in every detail of your daily living and think of you surrounded by strange birds and beasts and butterflies that make a necklace of beauty about your day. I shall pray fervently for your happiness. Though you are so far away the bond between us is very strong and a threefold cord shall not be broken. You have my love and devotion always. I think of you day and night. Marguerite." The repetition of his own words would tell William that she had received his letter.

Looking back she marvelled at the skill and gentleness and patience with which Reverend Mother had helped her. She had gone often to the convent (at the correct time and hour) with details of unsatisfactory houses that would not do at all, and always they had talked deeply and intimately. Independent as she was herself Reverend Mother had respected the independence of the younger woman. She had never tried to force her guidance upon her, she had merely answered questions and for the first time in her life thrown her precious reserve to the winds and talked to Marguerite of her own past life. She had told her of the old Chateau in the pinewoods of Normandy where she had been born, of her mother's salon in Paris where she had met the most brilliant men of her day and had not been eclipsed by the most beautiful women, of her betrothal and its disastrous ending, of subsequent illness and breakdown and her return, shattered in mind and body, to the Chateau in the woods.

"I lived in the Chateau for three months, with my dear old peasant nurse to look after me," she had told Marguerite. "I was sick, I think, chiefly of humiliation. I was twenty-five years old then and an exceptionally proud woman. The fact that I had been so brilliantly and successfully hoodwinked by the man to whom I had given what I considered the inestimable treasure of my passionate love, the knowledge of how ribald must have been his skilfully hidden amusement, and that of the world that knew him better than I did, when I accepted his devotion as a natural tribute to my beauty and personality, rather than to my wealth and the great name I bore, was I think an even greater shock to me than the discovery of his vileness; though that too, by convicting me of a fastidiousness that was without true discernment, struck as shrewd a blow at my pride as at what, without a shadow of a smile, I then called my purity. For I considered myself to be an exceptionally good woman, my dear. When people told me I was a saint my disagreement with them was verbal only. I was better read in Theology than any woman in Parisian society and would discourse fluently with learned Abbés in my mother's salon for sheer joy of hearing my own melodious voice. I gave my cast-off clothes to the poor and even visited them in their homes if it could be first ascertained that there was no contagious disease in that quarter of the town. I attended Mass and read the Scriptures regularly and assiduously, thanking God that I was not as other women, and utterly failing to notice that profligacy and thieving washed the feet of Christ with their tears and companioned Him through the agony of the Cross, while pride and hypocrisy made but little contact with Him. When I lay in my big carved bed in the Chateau, half-crazed with humiliation and despair, and the old curé from the village who had known me since my childhood came to visit me, I told him imperiously to go away because, I said, I had lost my faith. . . . Also he was only an old peasant and I was revolted by the snuff stains on his soutane and the wart on his nose. . . . He went at once, of course, sadly and humbly, for in all his dealings with the Chateau he was always most painfully conscious of his own humble origins, but he paused at the door and coughed a little, and went very red, and then said gently that when people said they had lost their faith it sometimes meant that they'd never had it; and that in another fortnight the bilberry leaves would be scarlet under the pine trees.

"That was what I remembered of what he had said to me—that the bilberry leaves would soon be scarlet under the pine trees. In my childhood I had loved to pick bilberries, but I had not been in the woods for years because I had scarcely been at the Chateau at all since my twelfth birthday. Indeed I had hardly been in the country at all. I had become a completely sophisticated town dweller. But now, as soon as I could leave my bed, I had the servants carry a rug and cushions out into the woods and I spent most of my day there lying under the trees. As the old curé had said, the bilberry leaves were scarlet and the pine trees pungent in the Autumn heat. The sun, striking down through their branches, made a chequered pattern on the floor of the forest and there was always a low humming of insects in the air. After a while the old curé used to come and pay me little visits, and I did not drive him away now because he had the sense not to talk of anything except the birds and flowers and insects. He had an immense knowledge of natural things and away from the Chateau he was not so shy and embarrassed and not afraid to talk of what he knew. He would sit beside me and tell me of the habits of dragon flies, or whatever it might be, and sometimes I would listen and sometimes I would not, And then he would get up quietly and go away, but always he would leave some absurd little gift for me, an apple or a sugar biscuit, or a little bunch of sun-warmed grapes from his garden. In the Chateau I should have been annoyed at his treating me like a child in such a ridiculous way, but out there in the woods it only amused me. I could see that in his mind I had joined the company of the peasant children whom Sunday by Sunday he taught to say their prayers in the village church. I had become one of his flock to him. It was such a comic idea that it made me laugh, and though my illness had entirely destroyed my appetite for the exquisite dishes they cooked for me in the Chateau, yet I ate the funny odds and ends he brought me and under the pine trees they tasted good.

"Marguerite, out there in the woods I recaptured my childhood. Perhaps it was the way the old curé treated me, perhaps it was just the fact that I had not been in the woods since I was twelve, but whatever the reason I became a child again. I recovered the lost piercing senses of childhood, those senses that can pierce through appearance to reality. And like a child I did not bother myself as to what it was to which my vivid apprehension of sound and scent and colour was admitting me; but like a child I breathed it unconsciously into my being as a pine tree absorbs the sun and rain and air. And I learned to experience a sharp delight in little things, such things as bilberry leaves and butterflies' wings and the taste of a ripe apple, that I had never known before. I never would have known it, Marguerite, had I not been stripped of what I had hitherto believed to be my wealth, because that increasing delight in the riches that are for us all only

comes when we have renounced the wealth that is for the few. . . .
Well, that was all. . . . What happened to me in the woods was nothing at all except a change of taste—no vision or miracle—just a
gradual change of taste. When I went back to my old life in Paris
again I found I had lost my taste for it, and as one by one I slowly
let go of the activities and habits and possessions that I no longer
cared for, so I slowly drew nearer step by step to the inevitable conclusion of it all. On the eve of my novitiate the old curé sent me the
only present he had ever given me that was not something to eat—it
was the little book that I have now given to you. 'In this book,' he
said in the blotted ill-spelt letter that accompanied it, 'you will not
find a single word that a child would not understand. That is natural,
since the man who wrote it was in his youth an unlearned peasant,
such as I am myself, and was converted to the Love of God and our
holy religion by such a little thing as beholding a dry and lifeless
winter tree and thinking how changed it would be when it was born
again in the Spring.' My mother laughed when she read the letter.
She thought the little gift a most unsuitable one for a woman whose
reputation for intellectual brilliance was known to all Paris. I did
not laugh. The old curé was the only one who understood that I had
recaptured my childhood in the woods."

That had been Reverend Mother's story, and it had helped Marguerite also to let go and to move forward, until here she was now
with nothing to dispose of but this comic collection of odds and ends.

Then she put the sampler and William's two gifts into a cedarwood box of her mother's that she had meant to give to Charlotte,
and stowed it away at the back of a dark cupboard beside the fireplace. This solution of her problem was a poor one, she realised, in
fact it was no solution at all, but she did not want to destroy her
treasures and she could not think what else to do.

2

Even the most well-trained minds are guilty occasionally of the
most ridiculous and lamentable wanderings at the most unsuitable
moments. Next day, as she knelt with the other novices in the Chapel
of Notre Dame du Castel, clothed in the black serge gown and the
white linen wimple, the holy habit of religion that would be hers now
until she died, with the sweet high voices of the nuns rising about her
in the Kyrie eleison, she opened her eyes suddenly and saw a mouse
run across the chapel floor. It was an exceptionally comic mouse,
with a very long tail, and Marguerite, at this most solemn moment of
her whole life, had to cover her face with her hands to extinguish an

irrepressible giggle. And then, thick and fast, her girlhood's memories came tumbling about her. It was a stormy day, and the rushing mighty wind that was sweeping in from the sea beyond the convent walls, the tumult of it almost drowning the chanting of the nuns, took her back easily to another stormy day, and the wind was banging the door of the Le Paradis garden shut behind her and Marianne, and she was running over the cobbles of Green Dolphin Street and chasing her brown beaver bonnet with the pink ribbons up the narrow passage of the Ozannes' house. And then she was running into the doctor's arms, and he was picking her up and carrying her into the parlour, and there was William in his gay mad green clothes standing laughing in front of the fire. And then she was sewing her sampler in the parlour, with William's mouse hidden in the folds of her dress, and then she was weeping stormily because Marianne and William had had some wonderful adventure together and had not taken her. And then she was racing over the sands with William, climbing with him up the slippery sides of Le Petit Aiguillon, holding out her arms to him at the top. Then she was La Môme, crowned with the chaplet of flowers, and William was lifting her to her feet and kissing her beneath the canopy of pink and white lilies. And then, the last memory of all, she stood beside William on the Orion, her hand trembling in his, and heard the quiet water murmuring against the ship's hull and the harp-thrumming of the breeze in the rigging over her head, and knew that from ages past she had loved this man and would for ever continue to love him. They were one flesh, one mind, one soul, a unity that nothing could divide, but just as William leaned towards her to tell her something there was an interruption and the words were never said. . . . And now she was here, doing the banal, the melodramatic, the obvious thing that women had been doing for centuries, and renouncing the world because a man had renounced her. . . . Only that was not the whole of it. By whatever devious and humiliating steps she had come to this place she had nevertheless come to the right place. Clothed in these austere garments, with the cold wind rushing by outside this old fastness of the spirit built high up among the clouds, facing a life of poverty, chastity and obedience, she was at home. A surge of joy went through her. If the wind was tearing the golden fruit off the trim little trees in their tidy pots it was with the perpetual sweep of its wings burnishing the stars. "Au nom de Dieu soit."

BOOK THREE

THE WORLD'S END

VÉRONIQUE

See with what simplicity
This nymph begins her golden days!
ANDREW MARVELL.

CHAPTER ONE

1

Véronique sat upon a small three-legged stool under the pohouta-kawa tree in the garden and stitched placidly at a cross-stitch kettle-holder for Mamma's birthday. She had designed it herself, her inspiration being the tattooing on Nat's chest. Her life was full of wonderful things, and one of them was undoubtedly Nat's tattooing. The kettle-holder had an anchor in one corner, a heart pierced by an arrow in another, a mermaid in the third, a dolphin in the fourth and a ship in full sail in the middle. Nat, his chest bared, had sat upon an upturned bucket as model while Papa had sketched the design for her upon the canvas, but the stitching was being executed entirely by herself in scarlet wool upon a blue background. Mamma knew nothing about it at all. It was to be a complete surprise. She would like it, Véronique knew, because of its being copied from Nat's chest. For Mamma loved Nat as much as Véronique did herself, and she did not seem to mind how much Véronique loved Nat, or Nat Véronique. This was pleasant. If she was sitting on Nat's knee he did not have to put her down suddenly when he heard Mamma coming, as Papa and Uncle Haruru did, because Mamma did not lift her eyebrows or make her mouth go tight when she saw Véronique on Nat's knee, she only laughed and was pleased. The whole of life was different when Mamma was pleased. Though she was only seven years old, rising eight, Véronique had already learned how to direct her life to that end, just as Papa and Uncle Haruru did. Nat didn't have to try so hard to please Mamma because all that he did and said was generally right in her eyes, just as what Véronique and Papa and Uncle Haruru did and said was generally wrong. And as for Old Nick, he never tried to please Mamma because he didn't care about anything at all except eating and saying what he thought in a loud voice. Hine-Moa, who lived in the village of raupo houses in the forest beyond the palisade, and came sometimes to help Mamma with the housework, was rather like Old Nick in that she too did not mind Mamma. In her dealings with Mamma she was fortunate in that she was a Maori. This meant that when Mamma told her to do something she did not want to do she could pretend she did not understand a word of English, and when she wanted to insult Mamma she could do it very fast in a native dialect of which Mamma understood nothing at all except the tone of voice. No, neither Nat nor Old Nick nor Hine-Moa minded Mamma, and neither did Uncle Haruru, really, though for all their sakes he was always very careful not to make her annoyed. . . . It was only Papa and Véronique who minded. . . . But they loved Mamma, so Papa was always telling Véronique. She was a wonderful woman and they loved her very dearly.

It was natural to Véronique to love people very dearly. She was made that way. She looked up now to see which of these six people, who made up her whole world, were safely within call. Nat was quite close, weeding Mamma's flower border.

"Nat," she called, "I'm doing the mermaid's tail."

Nat's head, its baldness covered by a red nightcap that Mamma had knitted as an exact replica of one Nat had lost in a wreck, lifted itself above the bushes. He straightened himself and grinned at her, then bent again to his work, hissing softly through his teeth, as he always did when he was feeling affectionate and happy. Véronique hissed in reply. They had developed a sort of hissing language, he and she. No one else could understand a word of it but they were quite comprehensible to each other.

"Old Nick," said Véronique, "I'm doing the mermaid's tail."

He had been let out of his cage and was sitting just above her in the pohoutakawa tree, eating a sweet potato. "Oh my," he said, winked an eye at her and went on eating the potato.

"Hine-Moa," called Véronique, for she could see Hine-Moa moving about in the parlour, laying the table for the evening meal. "Hine-Moa, I'm doing the mermaid's tail."

"Are you, my duckling?" asked Hine-Moa. "Don't you speak too loud for your Mamma is in the kitchen and it's past your bed-time."

Véronique nodded her head, folded her sweet lips and said no more. Hine-Moa knew that she wanted to stay up late to-night. Not only was Papa not yet back from the forest, but Uncle Haruru had been for a journey to a settlement up north along the coast, prospecting for timber, and to-night he would be home again and coming to supper and she wanted to see him before she went to bed. He would have some little gift for her, she knew. He never went on a journey, however short, without bringing her something, a carving of six little birds sitting on a bough, or a tuft of bright feathers to stick in her bonnet. Mamma said it was spoiling and didn't hold with it.

Indoors a door opened and shut, there was a tapping of determined footsteps and a voice enquired sharply, "Hine-Moa, have you put the child to bed?"

"Yes, Ma'am," said Hine-Moa in honeyed tones. Old Nick said never a word and Nat stopped hissing. Véronique folded up the kettleholder, put it away in her hanging pocket, arose and shinned up the pohoutakawa tree. Quite hidden by the green leaves she settled herself comfortably in the angle of a branch, folded her hands in her lap and looked about her. She liked sitting still and being what Mamma called "disgracefully lazy". But she wasn't really being lazy because she was looking about her. The rays of the sun were long and golden and lay across the garden as though they loved it, and all the flowers lifted themselves up with cupped petals and drank the golden light, while the green leaves about Véronique took to themselves an edging of pure gold, and Old Nick sitting just below her in the tree fluffed out his feathers and let the light shine through them so that he had an aureole all about him as though he were a saint, which he was not. Peeping through the leaves Véronique could see the crests of the hills blazing with colour and the forest below them motionless as a still lake. There was no sound except the ripple of the creek and the beating wings of the wild geese flying homeward. It was one of those hours so hushed and shining that it gave one a sense of safety. It did not seem possible that anger or clamour could ever again break in upon such peace.

Véronique, one way and another, had known a good deal of both in her short life. She had awoken to consciousness in an atmosphere of stress, for it had taken her parents years of struggle to make good the losses caused by the earthquake and to fight their way back to some measure of prosperity again, and always she had been subconsciously aware of her mother's ambition restlessly striving with her father's lack of it, and of Uncle Haruru's desire to let his genius lie fallow while he sat and meditated in the sun, for no one's good but his own, at odds with her mother's determination that it be kept in perpetual action for the good of all. She had been aware too of quarrels between her mother and Hine-Moa, between her mother and Scant and Isaac, even between her mother and the parrot. And then three years ago, when she had been only four years old, there had been a series of most alarming nightmares. She had been awakened in the night by unfamiliar noise and light and running to the window had looked out upon an angry darkness streaked by fire.

The thatch of several houses in the settlement had been blazing and by the light of the flames she had seen the Maoris from the village running by, not friendly and smiling as she had been accustomed to see them but brandishing guns and clubs and spears, wearing the red belt of the war god Tu, looking horrible and angry and yelling out their war-cry, "Ma! Ma! Mate rawa!" which meant that they had already drawn blood from the enemy, She had wondered what tribe they were fighting, for Hine-Moa had told her about the different tribes and their feuds, and then she had seen a man lying on the ground, and he hadn't been a Maori, but a white man. And then her mother had come running and had pulled her away from the window and wrapped her in a blanket and taken her downstairs, and sat for a long time in the big armchair holding her in arms that felt tight and hard as iron about her. There had been a horrible noise going on all the time but she had not felt too frightened because Nat had been standing by them with a gun in his hand, and her mother's arms had not trembled, and she was never afraid of anything when her mother or Nat were there. And then it had become quiet again and her father and Uncle Haruru had come in, very untidy and dirty but not hurt at all, and had said it was over for the moment. And her father had said he had known all along that the fire in the fern was only smouldering. Then she had been given a drink of hot milk and put to bed again.

But the next morning the big wagon had been brought round and she and her mother, and two other white women who lived in the settlement now, had been lifted into it by her father and Uncle Haruru, together with Old Nick and his cage, and a kitten belonging to one of the other women, and boxes containing their best clothes, and a few bits of furniture that they were particularly fond of. And then Nat had climbed up to the front of the wagon and taken the reins and they had rumbled off across the wooden bridge that spanned the creek and up the hill towards Wellington, with Papa and Tai Haruru riding beside them carrying their guns.

At Wellington Véronique and Mamma, and Nat and Old Nick, and the other two women and the kitten, and the boxes of clothes and the furniture, had all been emptied out upon the doorstep of Uncle Samuel and Aunt Susanna, who had been surprised at first but had kept very calm considering, and then Papa and Uncle Haruru had kissed Véronique and Mamma good-bye and ridden off home again to do what they could to defend the settlement.

Véronique and her mother had stayed at Wellington for some time, and Véronique would have enjoyed the unfamiliar excitement of seeing so many houses and people all together in one place, and the great harbour full of shipping, and soldiers being landed at the quay and marching through the streets in their red coats, and having dough babies with currant eyes made for her by Aunt Susanna, and being taught to say the 91st psalm by Uncle Samuel, had it not been for the peculiar state of turmoil in which all the grown-ups had seemed to be living. There was a war on, she had understood, not a new one but an old one broken out again. It was about the land. Somewhere up north of the settlement some Maoris coming back from a long journey had found white men living on what they said was their land, though the white men had said it wasn't, and there had been a great deal of unpleasantness, and now up north everybody was fighting everybody else. The Maoris who wanted to sell land to the white settlers were fighting with them against the Maoris who did not, and the soldiers in the red coats were trying to stop them and only getting killed for their pains, and no one knew how far the fighting might spread.

There had been a certain amount of fighting even in the Parsonage, for Mamma and Uncle Samuel had not been able to agree about the war. Mamma, as well as a lot of other English people, had been very angry with Bishop Selwyn, the Bishop of New Zealand, because he had taken the part of the Maoris who had come back from the long journey and not been pleased to find English people living on their land. Mamma had said that she loved the Maoris as much as the Bishop did, but after all they were not white, and must be kept in their places, and the Bishop's championship merely encouraged them to get above themselves. But Uncle Samuel had said that the Bishop was quite right, and that the people who must not get above themselves were the English. And then Mamma had said that the way the Bishop behaved, tramping about the country on foot to visit the lonely settlements and the Maori villages, wading through swamps and swimming across rivers, and getting home again in such a disreputable condition that he had to wait until dark before he could enter the town, was most undignified and a disgrace to his cloth. And Uncle Samuel had said that it might be undignified but it was very Christ-like, and he hoped to do the same himself one day, and then he and Mamma had made such a noise arguing that Véronique and Aunt Susanna had fled to the kitchen to make dough babies, and the next morning Mamma had said she was going home.

Papa and Uncle Haruru had been none too pleased to see them arrive, for half the settlement had been burnt down, and the Maoris had smashed up the inside of their house and rooted up everything in the garden, and even though the worst of the disturbances seemed over Papa and Uncle Haruru were just living in the middle of the desolation and smoking their pipes and drinking their rum and water and not bothering. But Mamma had soon made them bother. Véronique, sitting up in the pohoutakawa tree, looking about her and recalling what she could remember of those past days, preferred not to remember too vividly the dreadful state of turmoil in which they had lived until Mamma had got things to her liking again. After all, it was over now, and the grown-ups said the fighting in the north was dying down, and here she was sitting up in the pohoutakawa tree lapped about in this lovely golden peace, waiting for her father to come home from the forest and Uncle Haruru to come in to supper after his expedition up the coast.

Véronique was a very lovely little girl. In looks she had taken after Sophie and Marguerite, except that she was thinner and frailer and her colouring was more delicate. Her hair, that her mother brushed into ringlets round her finger every morning, rejoicing in its natural curl that would never need curl-papers, was a very pale gold, almost silver in the sunlight, and her cheeks had the dainty colour of a tea rose, not the blatant pink of rude health that had been Marguerite's. When she was tired there were dark smudges under her deep blue eyes and a poignant droop to her mouth that sent her father into paroxysms of quite unnecessary terror; because though she tired easily she never ailed at all.

Her mother dressed her beautifully in frocks that she made herself, full muslins and ginghams in the pale pinks and blues and lavenders that suited her silvery curls. She was in pale blue to-day, exquisitely tidy and fresh though it was past bed-time. She had learned to keep herself clean and neat, however many times she shinned up the pohoutakawa tree, because Mamma scolded if she hurt her clothes, and she loathed being scolded.

Though she was a naturally happy child she was not so radiantly happy as Marguerite had been. The love of peace and quiet that she had inherited from her father had not been gratified by the uncertainties of her days, and she was always slightly apprehensive as to what was going to happen next. That was what made her cling so tenaciously to the six who made up her world. It was only when held in the arms of one or another of them that she felt that things were really safe and satisfactory. Old Nick, of course, couldn't take her in his arms, but when he sat with her in the pohoutakawa tree and said, "Oh my!" in that kindly tone, it was really almost as good.

Nat raised himself, hissed softly and nodded in the direction of the gate in the palisade that led into the forest. It was Papa, and Uncle Haruru was with him. He must have come home earlier than they had expected and walked out into the forest to meet Papa. Véronique giggled softly and then sat still as a mouse, while Nat bent to his work again and made no sign.

It is strange watching people when they don't know you are watching them. Papa and Uncle Haruru were aware neither of Nat nor herself as they came through the garden, and they looked so different that she hardly recognised them. Papa's heavy red face was troubled, he was frowning and his shoulders sagged, and he came trampling across one of Mamma's new flower-beds and smashed off a peony head without apparently noticing what he was doing, though surely he must be aware of the scolding he would get later when Mamma saw what he had done. And Uncle Haruru was looking more like a twisted old kauri tree than ever, and there was a look on his face that she had only seen there once before, when they had been in the forest together and had found a young animal caught in a trap. ". . . every man-jack of them in the settlement murdered," Véronique heard him say as they drew nearer. "A hideous sight. God, how I hate the smell of blood! Worse than ever, just when one thought the Governor had got the thing in hand. He went quite alone into the Ngati-Maniapoto country, no one with him but an interpreter. That was courage, if you like, and courage usually wins 'em. Why didn't he win 'em?"

"He bungled it when he sent those troops to turn 'em out of Tataraimaka," said Papa sombrely. "Rewi knew he'd no right to Tataraimaka, but Grey didn't tell him first that we were resolved to give up Waitara. He bungled it. His mana has always been high but he's lost it now."

They had seen Nat now and they straightened and grinned and suddenly looked like themselves again. And Nat grinned back and gave his head a tiny jerk towards the tree. They were both preternaturally solemn as they strolled beneath its branches.

"Did you think you saw a blue bird up there?" asked Papa.

"It's only Old Nick," said Uncle Haruru. "Ugly old fellow."

"Not an ugly old green parrot but a beautiful blue bird with a silver-gold topknot," said Papa, staring upwards in a vague sort of way. "Pretty! Pretty! Sweet! Sweet! Where are you?"

"This'll fetch it," said Uncle Haruru, and he took from his pocket a necklace of scarlet berries, such as the Maori children wore.

Véronique could hold out no longer. She went off into a peal of laughter, reached for the necklace, over-balanced and fell out of the tree into Papa's arms. It was wonderful to be in Papa's arms again, though it wasn't really very many hours since she had last been there. Perhaps of all the people whom she loved he was the one she loved best of all. And when Mamma was not there she could hug him just

as much as she wanted to, for Uncle Haruru and Nat never seemed
to mind how much she hugged him. They only laughed and then
strolled off and left the lovers together.

"Mamma thinks I'm in bed," whispered Véronique.

"Mum's the word," whispered Papa, and then hand in hand they
stole softly round the house to Véronique's bedroom window.
Though Papa was a naturally clumsy man he had learnt to be very
cat-footed when they were eluding Mamma. . . . Nat, Véronique
noticed, had already removed the peony head, and cut away the
broken stalk. Nat was wonderful in smoothing away these little
difficulties.

They climbed in through the window, and Papa unhooked her
down the back and brushed her hair, and when she had got into bed
he folded up her clothes neatly and laid them on the beautiful little
chest that had been made out of a cradle Uncle Haruru had carved
for her in her babyhood, and then he sat down beside her and held
her hand, and she lolled her curly head against his arm and said,
"Tell about the Island."

She and Papa had two wonderful worlds in which they lived together, worlds which were as real to them, and decidedly more enjoyable, than the world in which they ate and dressed, went to bed and
got up again, did the wrong thing and were scolded for it by Mamma,
and never felt safe because of the Maoris. Papa told Véronique tales
of these worlds when she went to bed, but that was not the only time
when they lived in them. They were really in one or other of them
always; in their dreams at night and during the reveries that Papa
had while he was working in the forest and Véronique while she was
sewing her sampler under Mamma's eye. In this way, though their
bodies were separated most of the time, their spirits were always together. Even during those months when Véronique had been in
Wellington she had not felt separated from Papa because she had
only to run into one or other of the worlds and there he was.

The first world was called Green Dolphin Country and was a
laughing merry world where Papa felt particularly at home, where
they sailed upon a great ship whose crew consisted of Véronique and
Papa, Nat, Old Nick, and a jolly old gentleman called Captain
O'Hara, who was the chief person in this world and whom Papa had
described to Véronique so many times that she knew him as well as it
is possible for one person to know another; far better, in fact, than
she knew many people in her everyday world. Upon this ship they
had the most incredible adventures, all rendered highly enjoyable
by the knowledge that whatever happened everything would come
out all right in the end.

No one was ever unhappy in Green Dolphin Country. There were no quarrels there, no scoldings and no misunderstandings. It was in fact, so Papa had said one day, Paradise.

"Mamma says Paradise is where the angels live," Véronique had replied to this remark of Papa's.

Papa had scratched his head and looked puzzled.

"Maybe lots of different countries make up Paradise, like lots of different countries make up the world," Véronique had suggested. "Maybe it's just the place where your spirit can go without your body."

And Papa had looked relieved and said maybe it was.

Green Dolphin Country was Papa's favourite, but Véronique, though she loved it dearly, loved the second world, the Island, even more. It was the Island where Papa had lived when he was a little boy, and where Mamma and Aunt Marguerite had been born, and it was made very real to Véronique by the fact that her most precious treasure, the box of shells that Aunt Marguerite had sent her, had come from there. She adored these shells, and every night after Papa had left her she would jump out of bed and get them out of the carved cradle-chest and spread them out on her pillow and play with them. The biggest shells represented to her the different stories Papa told her about the Island. The grey-blue shell shaped like a curling wave was the story of the Sargousets who rode on the sea and dined in the cave in La Baie des Petits Fleurs, and the one shaped like an elf's cap was the one about the peasant who was very poor and when he went to bed asked the fairies to help him, and when he woke up in the morning every flower on the gorse bush under his window had turned to a gold coin, and the one like a rose-petal was the one about the little girl who looked in a wishing well and wished for a baby brother, and there he was rolling about in the buttercups. And there was a shell like a grey cowl that was the story of the monks who came from Mont St. Michel in their little boats, and landed at La Baie des Saints and built Notre Dame du Castel. And there was a shell like a drop of starry light that was the animals all kneeling down in their stables at midnight on Christmas Eve to worship the manger, and a lavender-coloured one shaped like a distaff that was the old Island woman who spun a magic carpet that carried her away to fairy-land.

Véronique knew the landscape of the Island as well as she knew the landscape of her own home. She knew the old houses of Saint Pierre climbing the steep rock above the harbour, the deep gardens with their magnolia trees and hydrangeas and bushes of jessamine, the rocky bays and cliffs covered with purple heather, the windmills on their green knolls and the sandy roads arched over by storm-twisted stunted oaks. Three children played with Véronique on the Island, Papa, Mamma and Aunt Marguerite when they were little. Papa had described them so vividly that Véronique was well acquainted with the rosy-cheeked boy with the torn, untidy clothes, the small brown girl whose nurse had said she was a fairy changeling, and the other little girl who was very like Véronique herself, except that she was fatter and laughed louder. It was this little girl, Marguerite, who was the most important person in the Island world, as Captain O'Hara was in the Green Dolphin world. She was so important that the whole of the Island world seemed to group itself about her, and she was in the centre of it all like a picture in a frame.

But the odd thing about her was that she did not stay in her frame. She was not only with Véronique in the Island world but in the every-day world too. If Véronique was playing by herself in the garden and suddenly felt lonely she would find that Marguerite in her blue frock was running up the garden path beside her, tossing the curls out of her eyes. And if she woke up in the night and was frightened she would see Marguerite sitting on the bed, laughing and swinging her legs in their long white pantalettes. She was always laughing and when she was there one did not feel afraid. Véronique's instinct had been to tell no one, not even Papa, about Marguerite coming out of her frame, but one day when she had been talking to Marguerite Mamma had come in and said, "Who in the world are you talking to, child?" And Véronique, a truthful little girl, had replied instantly, "Aunt Marguerite." And Mamma had looked startled and then had said sharply, "Nonsense! Aunt Marguerite lives on the other side of the world. She lives in France in a convent. She's a nun. You must not talk to people who aren't there, Véronique. It's very silly."

But Véronique had not been discouraged by Mamma's sharp re-marks. She understood perfectly well that there were two Aunt Marguerites. One was old, nearly as old as Papa, and was called Sister Clare and lived in France, and wrote her rather boring letters in a beautiful pointed handwriting about being a good girl and say-ing her prayers, but the other was the little girl Marguerite, who was never boring but the most exciting person in the whole world. But she was very careful never again to mention Marguerite to Mamma. And neither she nor Papa ever spoke of their two countries to Mamma. They had decided together that it would be better not. They did not suggest to each other any reason why it would be better not, they just said—better not.

2

Marianne sat at the round table in the parlour and dispensed a perfectly cooked supper to two men who were for once too pre-occupied to appreciate it. Nor were they in a frame of mind to appreciate the fact that she had made herself one of the new crino-lines, shaped like an isosceles triangle, and was wearing it under her voluminous rose-pink skirt, or that she had dressed her hair in a new style, gathered up into a net in the nape of her neck. Though she lived in the wilds she always managed somehow to keep more or less abreast of fashion, for Sophie's London friend sent her a packet of fashion-plates monthly, so that she had never had to sink into the dowdiness of most pioneer women, and it was most annoying when her efforts were not appreciated, were not even noticed, by her men folk. Tai Haruru generally noticed, even if William did not, but he had come back from his trip up the coast in so heavy a mood that it brooded over the whole room like a thundercloud. Marianne bit her lip and straightened her shoulders. It was her cross to be for ever unappreciated, and she must bear her cross. Even her own child did not appreciate her. She had a dreadful suspicion that Véronique and William were more to each other than she was to either of them, even though she had borne Véronique with so much pain and com-pletely saved and reinstated William. He was seldom drunk now, had apparently given up gambling and other vices of which in the past she had shrewdly suspected him, and had become a husband against whom she could lodge no reasonable complaint except the over-whelming one that he seemed entirely unaware to whom it was that he owed his salvation. If only she could have had a son! But she had never had hope of another child, even though she had willed him with all the strength of which she was capable. Oh, to have had that son! A son would have appreciated her, would have seen where credit was due, would have given her at last the love that she deserved. He, if she had left him as she had been obliged to leave William when she went to Wellington, would not have been obvi-ously sorry to see her back again. She was not going to leave William again. Never again was she going to give him the opportunity of hurting her as he had hurt her then. Never would she forget the blissful relaxation of his attitude, lying there in a long chair on the shattered verandah, his coat unbuttoned and his chin unshaven, his pipe in his mouth and a drink beside him, nor the look of dismay that had spread over his face when the wagon drew up at the gate.

". . . so you and Véronique must go back to the Kellys again, Marianne."

William was speaking and she came back abruptly to the present.

"Why?" she demanded.

"I'm afraid the Governor has blundered over the peace terms. It's blazing up again and you're not safe here."

"I'm not going back to live with the Kellys," said Marianne decidedly. "I like and admire the Kellys but I can't live with them. They're so narrow-minded and Susanna's cooking is most indigestible. No, William, Véronique and I stay here. There are plenty of men in the settlement and plenty of weapons. If you build ditches and stockades round the house and garden and defend the place properly we shall not be attacked. Most of the Maoris round here are well disposed and will not cause much trouble unless they are tempted, as last time, by indolence and lack of resolution upon our side. Last time you did not take sufficient trouble and when you were attacked you were not prepared. If I leave you it will be the same story all over again—you will not take sufficient trouble."

"We should be making the worst mistake possible if we turned the place into a fort, Marianne," said William. "I doubt if any fortifications we should have the time to make would be proof against an overwhelming attack, and it would immediately alienate the friendly Maoris by showing a lack of trust in them."

"You are merely making excuses for your laziness," said his wife. William shrugged his shoulders and Tai Haruru leaned forward.

"I've not liked the look of things up north, Marianne. I went a good deal among the Maoris and I came across some men of the tribe who knew me in the old days, and who look upon me as one of themselves, and they told me ugly things."

"Idle tales," said Marianne. "They are out to frighten us. If they can get what they want by threats only that is to their advantage. They fear the Red Garment."

"They fear nothing," said Tai Haruru tersely, for the Maori honour was intensely dear to him. "And I did not only hear ugly things. I saw them. I passed through a settlement in which there was not a white man left alive."

Marianne's eyes widened for a moment but she was not shaken from her resolution. "That was far out in the bush. They would not dare to do that sort of thing here, only a few days' journey from Wellington barracks."

Supper was finished and Tai Haruru rose abruptly. "I leave you to argue with your wife, William," he said. "She will not, it appears, listen to me." And with a curt bow to Marianne he went out. She was bitterly hurt by his rudeness, for they were friends now, and he might at least have expressed thanks for his beautifully cooked meal, and have paid her the compliment of just one glance at her new gown. No, of course she was not going to listen to him. She was near to hating him again.

William came blundering round the table and laid his hand caressingly on her shoulder. "You must go, Marianne. Véronique must be kept safe."

She jumped up and backed away from his hand, Véronique, always Véronique, whom he loved better than his wife. "You know perfectly well that if we take proper precautions there will be no danger here," she flashed. "You want to get rid of me. You want to turn the whole place into a beer garden, like you did before, and drink and smoke and gamble behind my back, and have native women in, and . . ."

"Hold your tongue, Marianne!" he shouted at her, stung to fury. Not a single Maori woman had crossed his threshold while Marianne had been away. He had indulged in no weaknesses that he needed to hide from her, except that one bout of drinking in which she had caught him on her return from Wellington, since . . . since . . . that letter to Marguerite. And she knew it. She was merely, for some reason that he could not fathom, trying to drive him mad.

"If you shout so loudly you will wake your precious child," she said coldly.

So that was it. She was jealous of Véronique. She had found out at last about that story-telling hour and she was jealous. Poor Marianne! His anger vanished and his immense kindness took its place. He turned and flung his arms round her.

"You know I always want you with me," he lied gloriously. "You know I'm wretched away from you."

"You were sorry to see me come back from Wellington."

"I was sorry to see you come back into danger."

Their quarrels, though frequent, were always short-lived nowadays, and she yielded to the pressure of his arms. "We'll see it through together, William," she whispered. "We won't be parted again."

"Let's leave it for to-night and decide to-morrow," hedged William. This was his invariable remark when he and Marianne could not agree. He always hoped that meditation during the night would make her see the wisdom of his point of view, and the fact that she usually slept the whole night through, indulging in no meditation whatever, and woke up the next morning in exactly the same frame of mind in which she had gone to sleep, did not seem to prevent his tentative hope from once again thrusting up its head at every fresh disagreement.

"You see, dearest, don't you, that it would be best for you and Véronique to go back to Wellington?" he said hopefully at breakfast the next morning.

"I see nothing of the sort, William," said Marianne tartly. "Véronique and I stay here and you and Mr. Haslam start this very morning erecting your defences. The work in the forest can wait. Get every man you have upon the job."

"Marianne!" pleaded William. "I do not think it would be wise to defend the place."

"You know perfectly well, William," she said, "that whenever you neglect my advice you regret it. I have more common-sense than you, dearest. You know that. I am as concerned for the safety of Véronique as you are and I am aware that I am doing the sensible thing. Véronique and I are far more likely to be set upon and murdered during the journey to Wellington than we are if we stay well-protected here."

Marianne had thought of this additional reason for doing what she wanted while doing her hair that morning, and she entirely believed in it.

"You understand, don't you, that I cannot face the danger of the journey for Véronique?" she said later to Tai Haruru, at the end of a long and rather exhausting argument which left her with the uncomfortable suspicion that it was his hatred of scenes rather than her stronger will that had left the victory with her.

"I understand you perfectly, Marianne," he said suavely. "The creditable reasons with which you support your actions always do equal justice both to the nobility of your nature and the adroitness of your mind. May I do anything for you in Wellington?"

"Do anything for me in Wellington?" she gasped.

It was Tai Haruru's habit, if he had just paid her a compliment which might be suspected of a sting in the tail, to follow it by a change of subject so abrupt that it deflected her from examination of his previous remark.

"Yes. I am riding to Wellington at once."

"Whatever for? You said nothing of it last night."

"The necessity for the expedition has only become apparent to me during the course of the morning. Won't you change your mind, and bring Véronique, and come with me?"

"No, Mr. Haslam, I will not. And I see no need whatever for your dashing off to Wellington in this way. You are needed here to see to the erecting of the stockade."

"I agree with William as to the foolishness of that stockade, but if you insist upon it he is perfectly able to attend to the matter without my assistance. Good-bye."

He was gone, and a moment later she heard the pounding of his horse's feet as he cantered over the wooden bridge which spanned the creek. She felt a little sinking of the heart when the sound ceased. . . . She would not feel so secure without him, for he was so beloved by the Maoris, so good at reasoning with them if there was any trouble. . . . And she feared for his safety upon the journey. . . . She decided to choose the second of these reasons to account for that momentary sinking of the heart, for it buttressed her conviction that Véronique must not be taken to Wellington. Having done so she banished misgivings and set about her housework with vigour and determination. She had only just got her home into apple-pie order again; for the second time; first the earthquake, then the civil war. But her spirit was not even bruised, let alone broken. She hummed a little tune as she worked, and glancing out of the window noticed with satisfaction that William and his men were already working at the stockade.

CHAPTER TWO

1

This time, with Marianne and Véronique to protect, no one could have accused William of indolence. He and his men worked like slaves, and a couple of days later, when he and Marianne went to bed, they had the satisfaction of knowing that to-morrow the stock-ade would be finished. Just one more day's work and their house and garden would be entirely protected by a strong wooden wall made native fashion of stout stakes lashed with a tough rope-like plant called toro-toro. The lumbermen were all camping out to-night in the garden within the almost completed stockade, and they had a good stock of food and arms. William's doubts about the wisdom of the stockade had been quieted by Marianne's arguments, but not quite killed. He had been disturbed by the abrupt dis-appearance of Hine-Moa, Jacky Poto and Kapua-Manga, who had apparently vanished into thin air with the erection of the first stake. Marianne was not worried about this at all. She had heard reports of an epidemic of illness in the Maori village in the forest. "Hine-Moa would not wish infection to be brought to Véronique," she said.

"The men have worked damn well," said William from his side of the four-poster. "But this time to-morrow the place will look a good stout Pa from the outside. There should be two more rings of inner fencing, and ditches such as the Maoris have. We'll get those done next, as quickly as possible."

Marianne moved her night-capped head a little restlessly on the pillow to get her curl-papers as comfortable as might be. "Just the outward appearance of strength will be sufficient to ward off unpleasantness," she said. "But certainly we'll have the inner fences and ditches too. Mr. Haslam should have stayed to help. He's afraid, I think. I see no reason except cowardice for dashing off on this mysterious expedition to Wellington."

"Tai Haruru a coward?" ejaculated William, raising his head abruptly from the pillow, his face crimsoned with rage below a nightcap comically askew. "A coward? Tai Haruru?" He gobbled for a moment like a turkey cock, then laid his head quietly on the pillow again and fought down his anger. Ten minutes later, just when Marianne was dozing off, he said in level tones, "He rode off alone to Wellington. You, if you remember, decided that the journey was too dangerous for you to attempt even with protection."

"Don't answer me back, William," snapped Marianne.

Her husband turned over on his side and hunched his shoulder at her. He was soon snoring but Marianne lay awake staring into the darkness. She knew perfectly well, really, that Tai Haruru was no coward, but that she might be justified of her remark in her own eyes she must now lie awake for perhaps hours, thinking up all the occasions in the past when actions or words of Tai Haruru's might be construed as indications of fear.

But as it happened her wakefulness was to some purpose, for it was she who in the first grey of dawn was suddenly aware of danger. She had been lying on her back, busy turning Tai Haruru's hatred of all forms of violence into cowardice, when all of a sudden she found herself sitting bolt upright, listening intently. She did not know what is was that she had heard but Captain O'Hara's advice, given long ago on the Green Dolphin, came back to her. "Never lay an' listen when a twig snaps in the forest—ye should be up an' doin' with your musket ready," and in a moment she was out of bed and had awakened William.

"Eh?" grunted William.

"Quick, quick, William! There's something not quite right outside. I heard something."

In a moment William too was out of bed and dragging on his clothes. Then he seized his gun and went to awaken Nat, while Marianne hastily dressed, quickly but carefully, with full attention to detail. She had just fastened her ear-rings in her ears when a horrible raucous moaning sound seemed to tear the grey veil of the dawn into shreds. Her heart missed a beat, for it was the tetere, the Maori war-trumpet, and hard upon its clamour came a hateful din; men shouting, dogs barking, and the rattle of musket fire. She ran into the next room and found Véronique sitting bolt upright in bed, wide-eyed. "It's nothing, darling," she said. "Only the Maoris making a silly noise to frighten us. We won't *be* frightened. Get up and put your clothes on, and keep away from the window."

"We won't *be* frightened," repeated Véronique steadily, thrusting her pink feet out of bed and feeling beneath her pillow for her box of shells. "Captain O'Hara wasn't frightened when we were wrecked on that whale."

"No, of course not," said Marianne, unaware of what on earth the child was talking about. "It's just a noise."

And then she ran out to the verandah. Here, by dint of climbing on a chair at the top of the steps, she could just see over the fencing in front of the house, and in the struggling light of the dawn she could see more Maoris than she had ever seen before in one place. The whole male population of the village in the forest must be here, with many more besides. They were milling about uncertainly outside the stockade, making all the noise they could and occasionally firing their muskets into the air.

"Get down, Marianne!" William shouted at her angrily. "Get down, I tell you!"

He and Nat and his lumbermen, their guns in their hands, were standing ready for any eventuality. When the full light came it might be apparent from outside that there was only one ring of fencing, and that with a weak spot in it, and no ditches yet.

But Marianne stayed where she was, her heart beating now not with fear but with excitement. Her whole being was almost exploding with excitement, just as it used to do sometimes when she was a child and some thought of adventure lit up suddenly like a flame in her mind. She felt as light as air and as mad as a hatter. This wasn't only the thought of adventure, it *was* adventure, and adventure decked with a strange wild beauty. It was dawn now, with the flames of the hidden sun licking up behind the mountains and the sky a glorious gradation of pulsing light. The forests were still drowned in night and the mist was milk-white in the valleys, but the great hills, rising above, had a reflected light upon them that turned their flanks to lacquered gold. The Maoris had feathers in their heads and wore their red war-belts, and the morning gleamed on their tomahawks and muskets and fine bronze polished limbs. During the brief moment that she watched the sun lifted above the mountains and the whole scene suddenly blazed up into a fierce unearthly brilliance that seemed to turn the blood in her veins to fire and set her pulses throbbing like drums in her body. She was laughing aloud, she found, and she only laughed the louder when a bullet pinged into the woodwork beside her.

But William leaped up the verandah steps snarling like a wild beast, lifted her down, pushed her into the parlour and slammed the door on her. Then from the top of the steps he cried out to the Maoris in their own language. Was he not Maui-Potiki, their friend, he asked? In his youth he had lived among them in the forest, and he had never lifted his hand against them. Why, then, must the peace of himself and his wife and child be thus disturbed? They desired only to dwell in peace among their Maori friends. They wished them nothing but good.

But William had been infuriated by the pinging bullet so near to Marianne, and his peaceable words did not issue in a very peaceable tone. Perhaps the Maoris did not hear what he said and were aware only of his angry shouting and the scarlet fury of his face, or perhaps that sudden blazing up of light and colour had whipped their blood to madness, as it had Marianne's. In any case their mood abruptly changed from uncertainty to the red-hot lust for destruction. A shower of bullets came over the stockade and the battering of their clubs against the wood was like the roaring of thunder.

Although until the end of her days Marianne shuddered dramatically when recounting the history of the next half-hour she nevertheless enjoyed it enormously. Picking herself up from the floor, where William's vigorous push had landed her, she ran to Véronique's room to tell her to stay where she was and not to be afraid, and then ran back again to William and Nat and the men in the garden. "Keep indoors!" William shouted at her. "No!" she answered, and seized a gun and cartridge box and stood beside him and Nat. She knew how to handle a gun. At her request William had taught her when she first came to New Zealand.

"Six men here, where the stakes are not lashed," commanded William. "The rest of you spread out round the garden and watch the stockade. Shoot on sight if any Maori attempts to scale it."

There were not enough of them, of course. Their numbers would have been adequate against the small raiding parties that had come against them last time, but with their defences incomplete they were not adequate for the bronzed army that now entirely surrounded them. With six men concentrated at the weak spot it was quite impossible to watch every part of the single stockade. Marianne knew this, but she was not yet dismayed.

"Not here, Marianne," said William, who with Nat had constituted himself one of the six who guarded the weak stretch of fencing. "If they break through badly it will be here. If you must play the fool with that gun, my dear, get away from here."

"Go, Ma'am," said Nat gently, his one eye fixed pleadingly upon her. "There is the child."

She withdrew a little and crouched down with her gun among the bushes beneath Véronique's bedroom .window, with William's broad back well within her sight. His rough tones had thrilled, not angered her. There had been a comradely admiration in them. They were surely closer together now that they had been since that morning of adventure when they had found the Green Dolphin.

"Who is it?" queried Véronique from inside the room, and there was an edge of terror to her voice.

"It's Mamma," said Marianne. "Stay where you are, darling. Don't come to the window. You're quite safe with Mamma."

Véronique gave a little sigh of relief and satisfaction and that, too, thrilled Marianne. She might not be loved as other mothers were loved, but at least her child felt safe if she was there.

The babel of noise continued but from where she crouched she could see nothing above the high stockade. Now and then there would be a gleam of bright feathers as a Maori leaped into the air to get a view of the garden, but the gleam was immediately followed by the flight of a white man's bullet, and after a few moments they leaped no more. They were discouraged, Marianne guessed triumphantly. Those who had leaped had not been left alive to disclose how few white men were within the enclosure, and that there was only one fence and no ditches. They were quieter now. They were discouraged and soon they would go away. She knew very little, really, of the Maoris, and she saw nothing ominous in the silence.

The horror burst like a thunderstorm or an earthquake, like any of the upheavals that were forever devastating this appalling country. One moment there was quiet and the next there was a roar as of a breaking dam. She saw the weak strip of the stockade give way before the determined onslaught of shouting men, while all round the enclosure other Maoris, steadied on the shoulders of their fellows, came leaping over the one fence and down into the garden. Marianne did not look at that handful of white men stemming the onslaught in the breach, she steadied her musket and fired at the men leaping the fence. She took aim carefully and fired again and again. She scarcely even thought of William now. Every thought, every nerve in her body, was concentrated upon the child in the room behind her. When a leaping bronzed figure toppled and fell she felt no

sense of horror at what she had done, only exhilaration because of
Véronique. Nothing lived in her now except her motherhood. She
should have taken Véronique to Wellington and she had not done
it. Because of her jealousy and pride she had endangered the life of
her child. . . . The little thing had crept to the window and was
crouching down close behind her mother. Marianne could hear her
panting. . . . For one blinding instant she saw herself for what she
was and loathed what she saw.

Her round of ammunition was finished now and the Maoris were
on top of her, coming down upon her like a tidal wave that had
already swept away the white men strung out round the stockade.
The stench of their bodies choked her and she was deafened by their
shouting. She stood up straight before the window, her arms
stretched wide to shield Véronique, and waited for their spears in her
breast. It was a futile gesture, for her child would remain hidden
only while the life was in her, but she had become now merely a
creature of instinct and her instinct was to hide Véronique with her
body while she could. Yet she closed her eyes while she waited for
the thrust of the spears, because it would be easier if one did not see.

But there was no sharp pain, only a hand that grasped the bodice
of her dress and dragged her roughly away from the window. And at
the same moment that the hand touched her she felt Véronique
scramble up on the window-sill and wind her arms round her neck
from behind. She staggered a few paces and opened her eyes. She
was standing in the middle of a crowd of Maoris with her child on
her back. Of course, she thought, all the ghastly stories of Maori
atrocities that she had ever heard flooding through her mind. Of
course. They would not kill at once. They would not kill until they
wanted meat. She had a little time yet, and the more time there is the
more room for hope.

And meanwhile they were more curious than unfriendly. They
were wild Maoris from deep within the forest whom she had not seen
before, and from their astonished exclamations she guessed that
they had never yet seen a white woman or child. They dragged the
cameo brooch out of her dress and snatched at the chateleine that
hung from her waistband. They were not interested in her green-
stone earrings, for they were such as their own women wore. They
touched Véronique's flaxen curls with astonished fingers, those in
the background thrusting forward for a better view and those near to
the white lady and her child refusing to give ground until they had
thoroughly examined the phenomenon in their midst. Marianne's
black eyes, gazing into theirs, never wavered, and though Véronique
was trembling all over she did not cry. She was holding her box of

shells hidden in a fold of her dress and they did not take it away from her. Neither of them could see anything beyond the wall of tall figures that surrounded them, and they had lost all sense of time. It might have been hours that they stayed like this, with the alien fingers plucking at them, or it might have been minutes, and then the bronzed bodies about them were caught up into sudden movement, as forest trees when the wind blows, and they were being carried away over the ruins of the garden they knew not in what direction. Véronique had scrambled down from Marianne's back now and was stumbling along beside her, holding her hand. Presently they halted again, and Marianne knew why they had moved. For acrid smoke was blowing over them and it was very hot. Her home was on fire. She could hear the crackle of the flames above a roar of triumphant shouting. Doubtless they had pillaged the house before they set it alight and now they were dividing the spoils.

"Mamma, where is Papa?" asked Véronique. She was not too desperately frightened because she always felt safe when her mother was with her, but she was terribly anxious about the other people whom she loved, and longed, as always, to have them all with her. "And Nat?" she went on. "And Old Nick and Uncle Haruru?"

"Uncle Haruru is safely in Wellington," said Marianne with bitterness, "and Papa and Nat will be here very soon."

And then, every vestige of her brief mad enjoyment gone, anguish swept over her. For where was William? And where was Nat? When she had seen them last they had been two of that little party of six withstanding the onslaught of an army in the breach, and it did not seem possible that they could be still alive. She seemed to herself to stand there drowned in anguish for hours and hours.

Then they were moving again and presently the fronds of great ferns showed above the shoulders of the Maoris and over their heads was the grateful green of mighty trees. The scent and sound of the burning were dying away and they were in the forest.

A hand gripped her arm and Marianne looked up and found Kapua-Manga striding beside her, his eyes upon the ground.

"Kapua-Manga," she cried to him reproachfully, "you have been false to Maui-Potiki."

"Maui-Potiki was false to his friend Kapua-Manga," said the Maori defensively. "Why did he erect that fence against his friend Kapua-Manga, and his friends Jacky Poto and Hine-Moa?"

So they had resented the stockade. William had not wanted it but she had insisted. Her grief and self-loathing were so intense that they affected her body like a physical illness. Her head began to swim and she stumbled so much that she would not have been able to go on walking had it not been for Kapua-Manga's hold upon her arm. "Does Maui-Potiki still live?" she asked him over and over again. But he gave her no answer. He was bitterly angry and resentful and he was not going to speak to her again.

Yet he continued to help her along and presently, when her nausea and dizziness passed and she was able to walk without stumbling, he picked up Véronique and carried her. He was very gentle with the little girl whom his wife had nursed, and hope for Véronique, if not for William and Nat and herself, gave Marianne fresh energy. Yet even so the journey was a nightmare of mental agony that she would never forget. It was all her own fault. Why had William and Tai Haruru and dear old Nat suffered her all these years? Why had they given in to her? They should have taken her pride and smashed it before it smashed them. "All thy waves and storms are gone over me." No, not all of them yet. Terrible as the pain was now there must be much more yet to come. And she would welcome it and not flinch. She deserved it to the last drop.

They passed the little village in the forest where Kapua-Manga and Hine-Moa lived and Marianne saw that it was deserted. Evidently the villagers feared the Red Garment and had taken refuge deeper in the forest. They passed through the lumbermen's clearing and she saw that William's sheds had all been pulled down and she guessed that the Maoris had wrecked them on their way to the settlement. As with the earthquake, just one dawn had destroyed the work of years. And if William was dead, if she was to die, there could be no fresh rebuilding. Never now would she have the fine house, with servants and flocks and herds like Job in the days of his prosperity. Well, she did not deserve it.

They rested through the worst heat of the day and then went on again, and soon for Marianne the mental pain was blessedly dulled by the physical. She became aware of nothing at all except the aching body that by sheer will-power must be dragged over the ground. Then came another rest and another start and presently the physical distress was less severe and she seemed to herself to become a sort of walking machine. Her body became adjusted to the rhythm of pain and effort and she moved like a sleep walker. They camped that night beside a stream and when she had wrapped the blanket that Kapua-Manga brought her round herself and Véronique she was asleep almost before she knew it.

The next day's travel was easier because now and again Kapua-Manga and another Maori made a chair of their arms and carried her. Though he still would not speak to her Kapua-Manga was roughly kind.

Late in the third day she found that she had got her second wind and was noticing the way they were going. She had never been as far in the forest as this before and the intensity of its depth and power touched her to awe. The trees here rose to such a height above her that there was no sky to be seen and the light fell dimly, suffused, tinctured by the filigree of leaves that had admitted it, with just a faint coolness, a faint sparkling of amber dust in the green, to tell of the sunset that far away above their heads must be burning along the bare mountain tops. Though she could not see them Marianne's second sense was aware of those mountains, godlike in constancy, that were the perpetual theme of the landscape in this country, and the thought of them steadied her in the awful depths of this tropic green. The ferns, now, were like a green sea flowing in from a distance so far away that its existence could not be grasped by the mind, flowing with a movement slight but inexorable, that spared for the moment only the bright cavalcade winding in and out between its billows that were piled up poised and trembling, as the waters of the Red Sea were poised above the ranks of the Egyptians before they fell and swept them to annihilation.

Against that background the feathered heads of the Maoris, their weapons and clean-cut limbs, were so clearly etched that it seemed to Marianne that she saw each separate thread of each separate feather, each drop of light upon each spear-point, every ripple of every muscle beneath the polished skin. Death is abroad, she thought. It is death that makes life live. Soon, in a moment now, the waves will fall.

But if death hovered over this place the descent was not yet. The fern swept not down but away, showing an islet rising up out of its green like a child's sand castle on the shore. A small hill in the forest had been cleared of its trees and a Pa had been erected on its summit, with the thatched roofs of a village clustering below. The ground immediately round the village had been cleared and planted with potatoes. Pigs rooted peacefully under the trees, dogs lay sleeping before the doors of the houses and smoke curled lazily up from the chimney openings in the thatched roofs. The clear space overhead was itself like a chimney in the great green roof of the forest. Through it the golden light poured down and one could see, at last, the blessed sky, and the heavenly rose-flushed peak of a mountain. The women and children were all indoors preparing the evening meal, and stillness brooded over the village.

Then one of the Maoris raised his tetere and blew a blast upon it, and instantly the whole village wakened to life. Women and children came running from the houses, dogs barked, pigs squealed. Most of the Maori warriors ran towards their houses, shouting lustily, but Kapua-Manga and five others, surrounding Marianne and Véronique and keeping off the importunate curiosity of the Maori women at spear's length, led them away from the village and up the steep path to the Pa. Looking back Marianne saw that the Maoris who had scattered to their homes were laden with treasures stolen from her house.

"Where are we going, Mamma?" whispered Véronique, pulling at Marianne's skirts. "Where are Papa and Nat?"

"It's all right, darling," said Marianne gaily. "Soon we shall all be together again."

Yet she felt anything but gay as they passed in through the narrow opening in the outer wall of the Pa, the pekerangi, already guarded by four warriors in full war paint, and crossed the plank across the first ditch. If the forest had seemed asphyxiating what would it be like to be shut up within these wooden walls? There were three of them, of great strength, lashed with toro-toro, and three ditches so deep that warriors could stand in them with faces level with the ground and fire through the loop-holes in the fences. Inside was an open space on the summit of the little hill, where the whole community would gather if attacked, and in the centre of it were the ruins of an earlier village, overgrown with bushes, with two raupo-walled, reed-thatched houses still standing intact at some little distance from each other. Marianne remembered that William had told her that in earlier days the villages were always built within the walls of the Pa, but now, when there was less fighting between the tribes, they built them beside their potato fields. She and Véronique were pushed inside one of the houses and then their escort abruptly disappeared. Holding hands in the dimness they looked about them. There were no windows but there was a fireplace made of four flat stones sunk edgeways in the ground and fresh fern was piled on the floor. Two bright clean native blankets were laid on the fern and beside them was a gourd of water and a dish of sweet potatoes, with dried fish laid daintily on top. The sight of the fresh fern, the clean blankets and the carefully prepared food gave a sense of welcome that eased Marianne's misery and made Véronique suddenly laugh and clap her hands.

"A picnic!" cried Marianne, quick to echo and encourage the little girl's mood. "What fun. We'll carry it outside, shall we? It's too hot to eat in here."

They carried the food and blankets outside and sat down together on the threshold of the little house. They ate and drank and then, sitting on one blanket with the other pulled over them because the evening was growing cool, they wound their arms about each other and waited for what should come next. The excitement of the village came to them only as a distant murmur. They could see nothing at all above the high wooden fences except the tops of the forest trees, the beautiful clear evening sky and that one mountain peak flushed with the sunset. As they waited Marianne gazed at the mountain peak and suddenly felt more hopeful, for it was like a presence watching over them. . . . And the preparations made for their comfort in the little house did not look like the work of an enemy. . . . She looked down at Véronique and found that the little girl was fast asleep.

Exhausted as she was she must have slept too, for with a sudden start she was aware of a cricked neck and aching limbs and looking about her found the ruins of the little village lying in shadow. Over her head the sky was a deep translucent green. The sunset fires had left the mountain peak and its snow glittered coldly beneath the diamond spikes of the first star. The village was utterly still but some sound, she thought, had awakened her. She listened and it came again, the faint crackling of burning wood beyond the thick bushes that separated her little house from that other on the far side of the ruined village. So she and Véronique were not here alone after all. Who was it here with them? Kapua-Manga? She must know.

She laid the deeply sleeping Véronique down upon the blanket and crept forward through the bushes, guided by the faint glow of the fire, until she could peep from behind a ruined raupo wall and see the other house. A fire of twigs had been lit just outside its door and between her and the fire a man sat brooding, his silhouette dark against the flames. He sat bowed down as though with sorrow, head bent, but there was a suggestion of power in the heavy slumped figure that took her back instantly to the moonlit night on the verandah when she had seen William sitting just so and had marvelled that so weak a man could give her such a sense of strength. It was the same now. Almost before she had realised that the man sitting there was William himself she knew fleetingly that she was saved.

"William! William!" she cried, and did not know how she got over the uneven ground that separated her from him.

He got to his feet, peered a moment, then held out his arms with a great bellow of joy strangled midway lest the Maori guard at the pekerangi should hear it. Even in the twilight dimness she could see how his face was on fire with a delight and thankfulness near to ecstasy. Never, in all their life together, had he given her a welcome of such spontaneous joy. "Véronique is safe," she said as she ran into his arms. It was perhaps the only unselfish utterance of her life.

"Nat too," said William. "He's here, asleep in the hut. Holy Moses! My darling girl, my precious darling girl, how in the world did you get here?"

Then he stifled any possibility of reply with passionate kisses and nearly smashed her ribs in with the warmth of his hug. She would not have cared if he had. This was the embrace she had expected on board the Green Dolphin. This was what she had always longed for. This at last was the satisfaction of her life-long hunger. For one perfect moment she was utterly happy. She pressed herself against him as though she would have forced her being into his, lost her own identity in his. What did it matter if they were soon to die a hideous death? She would not care, for life, after all, had not defrauded her. She had had her moment of supreme and perfect joy.

"Véronique safe, you said? Not hurt at all?"

It was his first coherent utterance since he had taken her into his arms. A little while ago it would have plunged her into jealousy, now it plunged her into a fresh paroxysm of self-loathing. . . . For just for the moment she had forgotten Véronique, thrust into such deadly danger by her fault. . . . She broke into a storm of tears, her hands covering her face as she leaned against his breast.

"Forgive me, William. It's all my fault. I would not go to Wellington. I made you put up that stupid stockade."

"No more of that, girl," said William gently. "If you were headstrong I was weak. Nothing to choose between us. Where's Véronique? Not for one moment must she be left unguarded."

They made their way back to the other hut, where Véronique slept in her blanket, watched by the spiked star above the snow mountain. She woke when her father lifted her, gave a sleepy cry of joy and wound her arms tightly round his neck.

"A grand joke, this, eh sweetheart?" he whispered to her. "A regular Green Dolphin Country adventure, eh?"

She laughed and yawned. "Where's Nat?" she asked. "Nat and Captain O'Hara?"

"I'm taking you to Nat," said William. "Captain O'Hara's gone down to the village for a drink."

Marianne stumbled along a few paces behind her husband and child as they made their way back to the other hut and the gay crackling bonfire, vaguely aware that they had entered some private country of their own where she did not belong. Yet she felt no sense of resentment for she was still drowned in humility.

"Nat! Wake up, Nat!" cried William. "Come out, old fellow. See what I've got here."

And Nat appeared in the low entrance to the hut, on all fours like a wizened old monkey, a bandage made from the tail of William's shirt bound about one leg. He scrambled to his feet, rubbed his eye, gazed and gazed again, grinned, and relapsed into soft and thankful profanity that progressed by easy stages, as he took Véronique from her father's arms, into those gentle hissing noises that denoted with him the utmost and most supreme content.

But he would not permit that Marianne should be outlawed and his one eye sought hers above Véronique's golden head, drawing her out of the shadows into the charmed light of the crackling fire. "Good evening to ye, Ma'am," he said with an ordinariness so delightful that quite suddenly the little house, the fire, the high wooden walls that shut them in, the treetops above and the mountain peak with the bright star impaled upon its summit, were to the four of them home.

2

With William and Marianne this sense of security did not survive the night. They awoke sore and cramped, and cold in spite of the sun-warmed golden air that showered down upon them out of a clear sky. It was also disturbing to have their morning meal brought to them by a silent Hine-Moa who would not meet their eyes. The meal was piping hot and as carefully prepared as that of the night before, and she brought also two large calabashes of water, but she would not speak to them and her eyes were inflamed with weeping. "Hine-Moa!" they cried to her, but she shook her head and turned away, stumbling over the rough ground. When they had washed and eaten they left Nat to amuse Véronique and strolled away out of earshot. Then Marianne sat on a fallen tree trunk while William prospected.

"As I thought," he said when he returned. "There is still a guard posted at the pekerangi. And since you came it has been increased from four to six." He smiled at her as he sat down beside her and took her hand. "They seem to think you the equal of two men, my dear. And so you are. A darned stout-hearted courageous woman. I said I'd like to adventure with you in the bush one day. Remember?"

"But not like this," said Marianne, gripping his hand hard. "Not like this." Her voice died out and she hung her head, looking at their intertwined fingers. For however courageous she might be in this mess it would remain her own self will that had got them into it.

"I'll tell you how I got here," said William suddenly, for the spectacle of Marianne in this condition of humility was so startling as to be almost disturbing. "Nat and I were here a good twenty-four hours before you and Véronique. It was a bad business, Marianne, when they saw that weak place in the stockade and rushed it. They were too many for us. Scant was killed, and the other fellows too I shouldn't wonder. I wish I knew what had happened to Isaac. Good fellows, all of them. They stabbed Nat in the leg, but not badly, and Jacky Poto knocked me silly with a blow on the head with the butt-end of his gun. Seemed as though they must have wanted to save Nat and me alive. Next thing I knew we were in the forest, travelling pretty fast, Nat and I carried in litters, with our hands tied. Jacky Poto was in charge but he'd not speak or even look at me; and he'd taken my Maori knife from me; I saw it in his belt. As soon as I was myself again I rolled out of the litter, kicked out and refused to budge, but there were so many of them they just picked me up like the carcase of a dead ox and carried me along, and in the end I just legged it with the rest. They tied us up at night but otherwise they treated us well. They fed us and let me attend to Nat's leg. But we were just about crazy, thinking of you and Véronique, and all those good fellows dead, and getting no answer to any of our questions. I never ought to have brought you out here, my girl. The country's too raw, too savage. Forgive me. I'd have done better to leave you on the Island."

"No," said Marianne. "I was never so happy as when you took me in your arms last night. It was the best moment of my whole life. If I am to die now, I thought, at least I have had one perfect moment. I am still happy. Happier than I have ever been."

He looked at her strangely. To make her happy had been his life's work for years past. Odd if he should apparently be succeeding at the very moment of her greatest danger and discomfort.

"What'll they do to us, William?" she asked him, but with more curiosity than dread, so armoured against misfortune was she by her joy. "Why have Hine-Moa and Kapua-Manga and Jacky Poto turned against us in this way? It is all so puzzling."

"This is how I see it, girl," said William steadily. "The feeling against the white man is very bitter now, so bitter that even Kapua-Manga and Hine-Moa and Jacky Poto have had their loyalty to us submerged by it. You can't wonder at that. Race feeling is bound to be a stronger thing than affection for strangers of just a few years' growth. And this tribe here is their tribe, with the right to command them, and this tribe is so hot against the white man that it has taken the trouble to go a three days' journey through the forest to attack the nearest white settlement. And mind you, Marianne, they've shown great courage, for they're likely to bring down upon themselves a pretty severe vengeance. We're not far over the Maori frontier here, if we're over it at all, and the Red Garment, marching from Wellington, could find this Pa and wipe it out without putting itself to too much trouble."

"But why have they saved us four alive?" asked Marianne.

"I couldn't say, girl," said William slowly. "Maybe Jacky Poto and Kapua-Manga insisted on that. You can tell they're doing all they can for us."

"If they have saved our lives merely from kindness why bring us here?" asked Marianne. "It would have saved trouble to leave us alive in the ruins of the settlement. Hine-Moa had been weeping, William. Don't you think it's possible we've been brought here to give the village the pleasure of seeing us tortured?"

"It's possible," admitted William heavily. "There's a new form of religion growing up among the Maoris, Tai Haruru was telling me. They've picked out the worst elements in the beliefs of the various white men they've come across and added them to the worst elements in their own. He described their goings-on at present as an unpleasant mixture of Judaism, Mormonism, mesmerism, spiritualism and cannibalism. Things are being done that are not at all in keeping with the Maori character. Seems as though once men start killing each other the devil breaks loose. I don't blame old Tai Haruru that he never kills if he can help it."

Marianne raised her eyes from the linked hands of herself and her husband and looked up at all she could see of the outer world above this round chimney of wooden walls; the feathery tufts of motionless trees, the deep blue sky, the peerless snow of the mountain peak with a wisp of white cloud trailing from its summit like a feather. The only sounds to be heard were peaceful village sounds, the voices of children, the distant bark of a dog, the rasp of a saw on wood. The violence of three days ago seemed like a bad dream, and it was difficult to think of it coming alive again in this peace and beauty. It was still harder to imagine oneself being tortured. Torture was the sort of thing that happened to other people, to early Christian martyrs and people of that sort, but not to oneself and one's relations. Yet why shouldn't it happen to oneself and one's own? Out of what congenital arrogance had sprung this sense of immunity? This to them, not to me and mine, way of thinking, that she had hitherto taken as quite natural, was a shocking and dreadful revelation of human callousness. Pride and selfishness, they were the same really. If torture could root them out of her then let her be tortured.

But not William, not Véronique. She turned to William, suddenly breathless as though there was no air to breathe. The worst thing about sin was that its punishment could not be borne by the sinner alone. Why did one not realise that before it was too late?

"There, there, my girl," said William soothingly. "I spoke too openly. Clumsy ass. You were happy a moment ago and now I have you all of a twitter."

"I'm still happy," said Marianne. "One can be happy and miserable both at once, you know."

"No, I didn't know," said William. "Sounds silly to me. We've been looking on the black side, girl. Doesn't do to dwell on that. There's always a silver lining. In our case, two. Kapua-Manga and Jacky Poto, now, I can't think they'll fail us altogether. I remember Tai Haruru saying to me as a young lad, 'They'll be your friends if you always speak courteously, always keep your word and never show fear before them.' Well, we've lived up to that, you and I, and we won't fail now. And then there's old Tai Haruru himself. What's he up to at this moment?"

"Yes, what?" asked Marianne tartly. "Is it a silver lining that he left us in danger and went off to Wellington on his own selfish concerns?"

"He didn't do that, my dear. He went to Wellington to fetch a detachment of red-coats to conduct you and Véronique there in safety. You wouldn't go, you remember, because of the danger of the journey for Véronique."

"Oh, why was he so weak?" demanded Marianne. "He knew I was just making excuses. He should have taken Véronique and me with him by main force."

"Well, he doesn't like scenes, and you'd have made a scene, Marianne, you know you would. And he thought we had plenty of time. He didn't expect the tribes hereabouts to turn unfriendly. What he expected was a migration of unfriendly Maoris from further north."

"Oh, what a headstrong fool I was!" lamented Marianne.

"Don't think of that, girl. Just think that Tai Haruru will be turning up at the settlement with his red-coats, and when he finds us gone he won't be the man I think him if he doesn't come on in pursuit."

Marianne smiled. It was her private opinion that for the Red Garment to attack the Pa would be immediately to seal the fate of the prisoners inside it. Nor could she imagine Tai Haruru leading English soldiers to slaughter his beloved Maoris. And in any case how long would it take him to find the Pa? She did not see what he could do to help them. But she did not speak of her doubts to William, who was resting upon the thought of Tai Haruru like a young child upon the thought of its father's strength. She too rested, leaning against William's shoulder. The sun was hot now and its eager blaze had dispersed the feathery cloud that had clung to the mountain top, leaving its beautiful outline clear-cut against the blue. That ever-changing yet ever-constant mountain was an unspeakable solace. Life is so brittle, so soon broken, she thought, that our thoughts must find some sort of permanence to cling to. A child's thoughts to its father, William's to his friend, mine to the mountain. It's queer, I've never needed to cling before. I don't think that I've ever before felt that I needed God.

CHAPTER THREE

1

Véronique was happy. She and Nat were sitting together in the sun and Nat was carving a bit of wood into a toy for her with his jack-knife. She still had her precious box of shells but it was nice to have other things to play with too, and Nat's toys comforted her for the fact that the kettle holder she had been making for Mamma had been left behind at home, mermaid, bleeding heart and all. Nat could not carve so well as Uncle Haruru. One could not tell what kind of birds his carved birds were meant to be, but one could tell that they were birds, and not monkeys or elephants, and that was something; more than enough, in fact, to please Véronique. She liked having Nat entirely at her disposal like this. His leg was better, but not quite well yet, and he could not pace up and down and talk as Mamma and Papa did, he had to sit still with her and make her toys and tell her stories. His stories were not the equal of Papa's, of course, but she found them very enthralling all the same. He told her about when he had been a little boy. It was almost impossible to imagine Nat as a little boy, and she had not known before that he had ever been one, but he assured her that he had. His stories were somewhat involved, and anyone who was not accustomed to his queer speech would have found them difficult to follow, but Véronique could always understand Nat and by the time he had told her every incident ten times over she had a very clear idea of Nat's boyhood. . . . And so had Marianne, who sometimes left the pacing William and sitting at a little distance from Nat and Véronique, often unnoticed by them, listened intently to Nat's tales. She was always greedy for knowledge of those she loved and hitherto she had known nothing of Nat's beginnings.

The little boy called Nat had never as far as he knew had any other name, Nat told Véronique. He lived in the city of London and swept chimneys. He supposed he'd had a father and mother but he couldn't remember them. Both past memories and present experience consisted only of soot, and having sore eyes and being beaten by his master, and playing in a back yard with two other boys who got beaten too, and washing the nasty mess on their backs for them with water from a pump, and giving them most of his food because they were always hungrier than he was. He was a thin and bony boy and very ugly, and it is well known that the ugly don't have such hearty appetites as the beautiful. Chimneys in London in those days were great towers of stone with steps inside and little boys climbed up them to sweep the soot away.

The little Nat did not know that there was anything in London, or the world either for that matter, except chimneys; he thought they just went on and on for ever. And then, one fine spring morning, he suddenly wondered if they did. He wondered if there were other things to see in the world besides chimneys, other things to do besides clean them. He wondered so much that quite suddenly one morning, without in the least realising that he was going to do it, he ran away. It was not to escape from the beatings and the sore eyes that he ran away, because it was not in his nature to run from things, but simply to see what there was in the world besides chimneys. And he would not have gone, of course, had the other two boys whose backs he had washed, and to whom he had given most of his food, not caught the fever and died, because it was not his habit to leave anyone who wanted him. So there being nothing to keep him off he went and found to his astonishment that there was a great deal in the world besides chimneys. To begin with there were the streets of London below the chimneys. He had known they were there before, of course, but he had only trod them in the half dark going to work, or coming back from work when he had been too tired to notice anything. Now, exploring them in the full brilliance of a spring day, he found them full of wonder. There were barrel organs in them and the scent of lilac, and grand ladies and gentlemen bowling along in fine carriages, and people of all sorts and shapes and sizes walking along on foot, and shop windows and crossing sweepers and boot-blacks. All that spring and summer he lived in these glorious streets, picking up a living holding the heads of horses.

And then one fine autumn morning it suddenly occurred to him to wonder if walking along a street or bowling along it in a carriage was the only way of getting about the world. Did a street just go on for ever or did it sometimes turn into something else? And if it did turn into something else what was this something else and where did it take you? Obviously the only way of answering these questions was to start walking along a street and to go on and on in the same direction and see what happened.

So very early one morning he put a crust of bread and an apple core into his pocket and started walking eastward into the dawn. He said to himself that if he kept the rising sun in front of him always then he would keep straight and not go round and round in circles. He chose a narrow cobbled street, with high walls on either side. There had been rain in the night, but the sky was clear now, and the rising sun made the cobbles gleam and shine like the jewels that he had seen in the shop windows, and turned the high wet walls to sheets of gold. This was suddenly not London any more. It was not even in the old world that he had hitherto known. It was a new world altogether. He had often wondered how far London stretched but he had not known it was as easy as all this to step out of. He walked on and on into the sun for what seemed like hours but he was so excited that he did not get weary at all.

And then the miracle happened and the street turned abruptly into something else, turned with such startling suddenness that he nearly fell headlong down a flight of steps into the new sort of street that it had turned into. For it was still a street, going along at right angles to the street he had come down, he knew it was a street because he could see the houses on the other side, but it was a street that moved, a street composed of brilliant flashing liquid diamonds, flowing and rippling under the sun. He had never been so astonished in all his life. He just stood there and gaped. And then he stopped gaping and laughed, because he knew in his soul that the discovery of this new sort of street was the most wonderful discovery that he would ever make in all his life.

He went down the steps and cautiously felt the rippling diamonds with his dirty bare foot, and they were cold and wet like rain, and soft, and it was not possible to stand upon them. And then he knew that this new sort of street was composed entirely of water, that it was a gigantic edition of one of the streams that ran down the London gutters after a thunderstorm. But if one could not stand on it how did one get anywhere upon it? He straightened himself and looked about him and found to his stupefaction that houses were floating on it as he had seen bits of paper floating upon the streams in the gutters. They were odd-shaped houses, with small round windows in their wooden walls, and immensely tall thin chimneys going up at a slant, with washing hanging out between them. But no, they weren't chimneys, they were wooden poles, and the washing did not look so much like washing as immense birds' wings. Did these wooden houses fly? There was one not far away from him, quite near to the stone wall that bounded the water-street upon the one side, and a plank was leaning at a steep slant from the wall to its roof. It was the work but of a moment for Nat to run down the wall and nip up that plank.

The roof of this wooden house astounded him, cluttered up as it was with coils of rope, and a huge wheel with spokes, and buckets and all manner of things that he had not been accustomed to see upon the roofs of houses. And though all the houses he had hitherto known had had their front doors at street level, with stairs going up, this one had its front door on the roof with the stairs going down. He longed to explore the inside of the house as well as the outside, but deep down in the darkness of the house he heard voices, and he was afraid to go in. He would hide on the roof, he thought, until the people of the house went out to do their morning's shopping, and then he would nip in at the front door and have a good look round.

There was a cat upon the roof of this house, as there is upon the roofs of most houses, a ginger cat with silver whiskers and a tail that stuck up straight as a ruler, and it took a great fancy to Nat, as cats always did, rubbing itself against his legs and purring. It had a sore patch on its leg and he tore a bit off his ragged shirt and bound up its leg for it, because he remembered from the days when he had had sore eyes and been beaten how uncomfortable it is to be sore. When he had finished bandaging the cat it suddenly stalked off, as cats will when they think there is no more to be got out of you for the moment, and disappeared among some barrels that were lashed together upon one part of the roof. Nat followed it because he thought that among the barrels would be a good place to hide, and squeezing himself through a space so narrow that one would have thought not even the thinnest and most starved of human boys could get through, he found that within the ring of barrels was a pile of crates full of live chickens, all squawking distressfully because the cat was sitting looking at them, twitching its tail from side to side and licking its lips.

Now here was another wonder. Nat had seen dead chickens often enough, hanging upside down in poulterers' shops, but he had never seen them right way up and alive, and he had never yet seen that majestic bird, the cock. There was one in a crate all by himself, with a magnificent scarlet comb and feathers scintillating with every colour of the rainbow. Trembling with awe Nat sank down on hands and knees before this glorious creature and offered him the apple core that he had been keeping for his own consumption. He talked to the cock for a long time, because he could see it was not altogether happy, and then noticing again the fright of the chickens he put the cat inside his coat, to keep it from lashing its tail and licking its chops in that unpleasant way, and talked to them too, and crumbled up his bit of bread among them, and very soon had them happy and quieted. He had been afraid when he left the old sort of streets that morning that perhaps the horses would miss him, and it was comforting to find that in this new street the poultry's need of companionship was just as great. He was so busy talking to them that he quite forgot about listening for the people of the house to go off and do their shopping, and he took so long about it that the sun rose high in the sky and it got very hot, and presently he curled himself up with the cat still in his arms and went to sleep.

He woke up to hear a great noise going on all about him, a clanking and grinding and booming that was very startling, and the shouts of men and the tramping of their feet. The wooden house was moving and looking up over his head he saw that on the slanting wooden poles that he had thought at first were chimneys there were many more white wings than there had been before. There were men up there among them, lashing them fast to the poles, men who if they were to look downward might see him crouching among the crates. Quick as thought he wriggled under a tarpaulin that was lying there, cat and all, for he did not want to be found and perhaps flung back to the old life again. The wooden house *was* flying and more than anything else in the world he wanted to see where it was flying to.

He stayed for a long time under the tarpaulin, terribly hungry and thirsty but scarcely noticing that in his excitement, until he no longer heard shouts overhead, and peeping out saw the great white wings carrying the house along with them without apparent assistance from humankind. Then he emerged and sat cross-legged among the chickens, staring up at the blue sky above. He felt thoroughly at home, because with the wall of crates and barrels about him, and not being able to see anything but the sky and the white wings overhead, it was just like being inside a chimney at that lovely moment when you knew the climb was nearly over and that in another moment you would come out into the fresh air. . . . Only the air above the chimneys he had been accustomed to had not been as gloriously fresh as the air that was blowing about him now, nor the blue sky so clear.

The hours sped on and Nat longed to know what was beyond the walls of the chimney. Yet he did not move, for instinct told him that the longer he could stay undiscovered the more likelihood there would be of his being permitted to continue his voyage of discovery. But it was hard to stay where he was when he was devoured not only by curiosity but by hunger and thirst too. Some rain water had collected in the folds of the tarpaulin and he lapped this up like a dog, and the chickens had disdained a bit of his crust, and he ate that, but even so the hole in his inside seemed to grow larger and larger and to ache more and more the larger it grew. The wind increased, whistling and singing and bellying out the great wings overhead, and they flew faster and faster. The sun wheeled across the sky, burning hot, and then it grew cooler, and then the sky was all pink like a rose, and the wooden house began lifting and dipping as though it were curtseying. Nat had once seen royalty passing in the streets, and all the ladies curtseying. Were they approaching royalty now?

But he hadn't time to wonder much about that because there was a grating sound and looking up he saw a tall ferocious-looking man with a matted black beard, horribly like the sweep who had beaten him, moving aside the barrels and coming towards him with a bowl of grain in his hand. He was going to feed the chickens. Nat did not attempt to hide. What would have been the good of that? He did what he always did when disaster threatened, stayed mousy quiet in the hope that it would pass him by, meanwhile facing with serenity the extreme unlikelihood of its doing anything of the sort. Nat was always serene in disaster because he was completely unresentful. It had never even occurred to him that he merited immunity from misfortune, because his merits had never at any time received his attention, invariably riveted elsewhere.

"Eh? You young devil, you! Stowaway, is it? I'll stow you away, you young varmint! I'll give you something you won't forget in a month of Sundays! It's swung by the neck from the yardarm you'll be, swing by the neck until you're dead, you young——"

The blows were already falling but this time Nat did not submit as calmly as usual to the inevitable because behind the man's great figure, through the gap in the barrels, he could see something the like of which he had never seen before. Like a little eel he slithered along the wooden boards, wriggled between the man's legs and crawled out through the gap in the barrels towards the thing that he had seen. Then he leaped to his feet and ran into the bows of the ship that he might have a good long satisfying stare before he was collared.

Upon either side the banks of the estuary were melting away into the rosy sunset mist and were seen by Nat merely as vague shadows, and in front of him, where river and sea became one, was a vast expanse of wind-rippled water stretching away as far as the eye could see, glittering with gold, streaked with the colours of the sunset sky, not a street any more but something vast and mystic for which Nat could provide no analogy because his previous experience had provided him with nothing with which he could compare it. "Royalty" was the only word that came into his head, and it seemed to him quite fitting that with a well-aimed kick from behind he should fall prostrate before it.

Quite a crowd of men had gathered now, laughing and jeering. They picked him up and pinched him and then boxed his ears and knocked him down again, and did a good many other things to him that Nat did not mention when he told the story to Véronique. Used as he was to this sort of treatment he had never before taken quite such severe punishment, and a vast fear was rising in his soul, a fear that threatened to submerge him altogether, when suddenly there was a bellow of rage and a lusty young voice cried out, "Here, you swine, what are you doing? Begorra! It's murdered the boy is already. Get to hell out of here, or I'll have the life of every mother's son of you."

Nat dragged himself to his knees, one black eye closed up, blood streaming from his nose. A boy a few years older than himself, wearing a dark blue jacket with brass buttons, with a head of startlingly red hair and bright blue eyes, was laying about him with whirling fists. As Nat stared at him he lowered his red head, charged like a goat, butted the chief of Nat's tormentors, the man with the matted black beard, with tremendous force in the stomach and sent him over with a crash upon his back. Then he laid about him with his fists again, letting fly a volley of Irish oaths that seemed to turn the sunset air blue with the violence of their profanity. It was Nat's first experience of the immense force of righteous anger, especially Irish righteous anger, backed by great strength and fearlessness. The crowd of bullies melted away before the rage of a boy only half the age and size of the youngest of them, and Nat was jerked to his feet by a powerful grip upon his arm, and encouraged to exert himself by a bellow of great kindliness, if of a volume calculated to split the tympanum of a delicate ear.

"Here, you ugly little toad, come along with you. Stowaway, is it? It's the broth of a boy you are entirely, but the dirtiest young devil I ever clapped eyes on. Come on with you now. Come on."

The red-headed boy was striding along the deck with Nat more or less suspended from the grip of his freckled hand. He clattered down below and kicked open the door of the apprentice half-deck, entering with a noise and suddenness, a majesty of demeanour and an utter disregard of who or what he was trampling upon that bespoke him the lord of that domain. Five other young boys, employing this evening hour of brief leisure in getting themselves, their sea chests and their apartment neat and ship-shape, gazed up at him and hastened to remove themselves and their belongings from his path.

They also gazed at Nat and one of them, the eldest, ventured a protesting, "What next, O'Hara? What on earth have you got there?"

"Stowaway," said Denis O'Hara. "Gimme a bucket of water."

It was produced and Nat's head was inserted in it. His filthy rags
were also stripped off him and he was clothed with garments wrested
from the protesting but subservient youngest apprentice, while the
youngest but one was sent to fetch a mug of hot sweet tea and a ship's
biscuit from the galley. With the utmost kindness and condescension
Denis O'Hara tipped the hot tea down the throat of his protégé,
shoved the biscuit between his teeth and smote him upon the back
when he choked, what time Nat gazed up at him with a worship and
adoration that were never to falter throughout his life.

"What are you going to do with it?" asked the youngest apprentice, a white-faced little creature with a button nose.

"Put it in care of the livestock," said Denis O'Hara. "Make it an
extra cabin boy. Feed the poultry. Brush the cat. Scratch the pig.
Clean out this stinking hole. Polish my shoes."

"What'll the Skipper say?" asked someone else.

Denis O'Hara shrugged his shoulders. The Skipper of this merchantman was his own uncle, and as well trained as were all his relatives in habits of obedience and docility. His shrug indicated that
such a little matter as persuading the Old Man to engage an extra
cabin boy could easily be left to his discretion.

And he had little difficulty in the matter. After only a short burst
of lively argument Nat became a member of the Merchant Service.
The small boy who had wondered what, if anything, lay beyond the
chimneys of London sailed to the other side of the globe. The gateway of one new world after another swung open before his astonished gaze, and in the person of Denis O'Hara he discovered an
object of worship and service worth more than all the cats and all
the horses in the world. His devotion to his benefactor never wavered. It was a white-hot flame of dedication that years of hardship,
toil and injury did not cause even to falter. Not even Denis O'Hara's
death put it out. It was merely transferred to burn before the altar
of Marianne, who had been Captain O'Hara's special protégée, her
husband and her child.

2

"You've had a lovely life, Nat," said Véronique on this particular
morning when she was feeling so happy, Nat having just recounted
for the eleventh time the story of his first meeting with the amazing
and wonderful Captain O'Hara.

"Ay," agreed Nat whole-heartedly, whittling away at the wooden bird he was making for her.

"I like it in this funny place, don't you?" she continued, looking up at the great clouds overhead that were like sailing ships drifting on a calm ocean.

"Ay," said Nat. "Puts me in mind of a chimney. Always feel at home in a chimney."

Then he began hissing softly through his teeth and Véronique hissed too. Marianne, sitting near them, listening and watching, supposed that they were saying something to each other that was perfectly comprehensible to them though not to her. . . . Probably that though you are imprisoned in a place like a chimney, and do not know what is going to happen to you before the day is out, still life can be remarkably pleasant when you are in congenial company. . . .

But suddenly, most unexpectedly, Véronique began to weep. Nat gazed at her horror-struck, then, looking down at the bit of wood in his hands, realised what he had done. His ignorance of ornithology was abysmal, and he had not made any attempt at portraiture in the bird he was carving for her, yet quite without intention on his part it had come out with a parroty head, and parrots were a subject that had to be avoided just now with Véronique. No one knew what had happened to Old Nick when the settlement had been attacked and the little girl wept upon every remembrance of him, by no means comforted by the assurances of the grown-ups that he'd be bound to turn up soon. Their assurances lacked conviction and she knew it.

"Old Nick!" she sobbed now. "Poor Old Nick! You're here, and Papa and Mamma are here, and Uncle Haruru is safe in Wellington, but where's Old Nick?"

Nat began to make rumbling noises of exquisite tenderness but doubtful meaning deep in his throat. Then he touched the little girl gently with his forefinger and bared his tattooed chest for her inspection. Nat's tattooing was a source of comfort that had never been known to fail and Véronique's sobs stopped instantly.

Marianne got up and stole away. She felt suddenly that it was not seemly that she should be present while Véronique sought comfort for a bereavement over which her mother was less grief-stricken than she was. It was no use Marianne pretending to herself that she was missing Old Nick because she was not.

She settled herself in a quiet nook screened by bushes. They had been held prisoner for a week now, without any indication of what was going to be done with them, and she often came here to be alone, leaving Nat and Véronique to their story-telling and William to the repairing of their hut, which had several weak places in it and was likely to leak like a sieve in a thunderstorm. The back of it gave on a thicket of bushes and was protected, but the sides were exposed to the weather.

Not for years had she had so much leisure as she had now and she wanted very much to use it sensibly in putting herself together again. She had been so horrified at the results of her folly, so humiliated, that she had begun to feel as though she had disintegrated completely and fallen to pieces. She might, of course, be going to die very shortly, or she might not, but in any case the shattered woman that she now was must be integrated once more to face whatever might come. But she did not know which bit of herself to pick up and put into position as the corner-stone; pride, selfishness, ambition, jealousy, anger, self-deception; they were all of them equally useless. There was, of course, her love for William, and the joy that she felt in the new freshness and spontaneity of his response, but she felt both the love and the joy to be so deeply tinged by the selfishness of her life-long wish to find satisfaction for all her desires before she died that she had no faith in them. Her courage she did not consider because it was instinctive with her, a virtue of which she was largely unaware, and in her present mood she looked upon her initiative as a sin, scarcely to be distinguished from ambition. After a few moments' search for a corner-stone a rather scared hopelessness would take possession of her mind and she would turn away from contemplation of herself to contemplation of Nat.

From his constantly repeated stories, added to her previous experience of him, she had pieced together a picture of his life and personality that staggered her. She supposed that he was the most perfect character that she had ever known and that that was why the love he had won from her had been the least tainted of any of her loves. . . . She had never been jealous of Nat. . . . She remembered how upon the Orion she had realised that there was a way to live that she had never discovered, a love whose meaning she did not understand, and she had wondered if the poor would be able to teach it to her. She had always loved the poor, though the arrogance of her philanthropy upon the Island seemed to her now a detestable thing. And what had she said once to Captain O'Hara about the poor being malleable metal upon which one could stamp one's own image? She forced herself to remember exactly what she had said, and squirmed. I'll learn of Nat, she said to herself abruptly. That's what my corner-stone must be—to learn of Nat. I'll be a child again and learn of Nat. I've been humble a few times in my life, on the Orion, that night at the settlement when William found me crying, and now. For the rest of my days I'll be humble all the time. I'll be a child again and learn of Nat. . . . That is the secret. To live and love as a child. . . . Of such is the kingdom of heaven.

Whatever was that? Something had hit the ground with a soft thud just a couple of feet in front of her. It was a Maori arrow. She jumped to her feet, her humble mood boiling up into sudden anger. Some wretched Maori was evidently going to amuse himself by shooting arrows into the Pa. This one might have hit Véronique. She picked it up in a rage, then paused, her rage turned to wonder. "William!" she cried. "William, come here!"

He came to her and took the arrow, turning it slowly over and over in his hands. Its tip had been carefully blunted, there was faint delicate ornamentation on the shaft and its feathers were unusually gay, bright green, buff and rose colour.

"Nat!" called the mystified William.

Nat came, Véronique holding to his hand.

"Did you ever see an arrow like that?" William demanded of him.

"Prettiest arrow I ever seen," Nat averred.

But it was Véronique who knew at once what it was about this arrow that was different from other arrows. "Its feathers are like Old Nick's," she cried. "Oh, Papa, Papa, Old Nick's dead! That arrow has been made out of Old Nick!" And she once more dissolved into tears of inconsolable grief.

William picked her up to comfort her, and Nat shook his head sadly, but Marianne snatched the arrow and looked at it again. It was most exquisitely fashioned. Excellent craftsmen though the Maoris were she was sure they had never made an arrow as beautiful as this. And the artist had signed his work. The carved pattern along the shaft began and ended with the two letters, T.H.

Marianne felt as though a tight band that for days and nights had constricted her chest had been loosened, and as though a leaden weight had been lifted off the top of her head. She let out a great sigh. "My dears," she said, "I believe that we are delivered."

CHAPTER FOUR

1

Véronique sobbed herself to sleep that night but the grown-ups, though they had to dissemble their joy before her, were happy, and when they had lain down slept instantly and deeply. True, Tai Haruru was merely a human man, with no miraculous powers to save and defend, yet the fact that he was apparently near to them gave them a sense of wonderful security. His mana was indeed high with them; perhaps until this night they had not realised just how high. "One can rely on him," Marianne said to her husband before she slept. And in her dreams she saw that constant mountain top above the Pa, and a tall figure standing upon its summit fitting a feathered arrow of deliverance into a bow. The figure was that of Tai Haruru, yet when she looked more closely the face became suddenly the face of Marguerite. And then, with another of those queer changes that come in dreams, the mountain was the rock of Marie Tape-Tout. She could hear the breaking of the waves on the rocks and the raging of the wind around it; and awoke suddenly in a darkness lit by flame to find the raging tumult actually with her in this hut on the other side of the world. "That sea of green fern has crashed down on us," was the thought in her sleep-confused mind. "I knew it would. Véronique? Véronique?"

Her child's hand touched hers and immediately she was sitting up and fully conscious. Nat had come creeping into the hut and was shaking William awake.

"What's the matter?" mumbled William indignantly.

Nat croaked out some unintelligible remarks but it was Marianne who gave her husband precise information. "The whole village seems to be coming inside the Pa, William," she said calmly. "They must think themselves in danger. Hand me my corsets."

As they had no night-wear they had to sleep in their torn and crumpled clothes, but Marianne always removed her gown and corsets before she slept, for to sleep in Victorian corsets was simply not possible. William looked at his watch in the torchlight that shone through the low door of the hut. . . . Midnight. . . . He put on his coat and went outside with Nat while Marianne laced up her corsets with precision, hooked up her own gown and Véronique's with care and stowed her hair tidily away inside its net. This gathering of one's back hair inside a large net, the new style of hairdressing that William and Tai Haruru had failed to notice on the last peaceful evening at the settlement, was excellently adapted for civil war in the primeval forest, she thought, though possibly the Parisian hairdresser who had devised the fashion had been unaware of the fact. She blessed him, all the same. It would be nice to die tidy. For it looked, now, as though they would have to die. If the Red Garment was attacking the first thing the Maoris would do would be to slaughter their white prisoners who had brought the attack upon them. If Tai Haruru had instigated the attack he was not being very subtle, and her last night's faith in him had been mistaken. But had he? Was it like him to bring death upon his Maoris? Her eye fell upon the green feathered arrow, lying on the floor of the hut, and she found that though appearances were against him yet his mana was still high with her. If ingenuity could save them they would be saved. Telling Véronique to stay where she was she joined William and Nat at the entrance to the hut.

In the mingled light of moon and flaming torches the whole village was surging into the Pa, warriors in full war panoply, old men and women, children and dogs. The din was indescribable, war drums tapping, teteres braying, men shouting, children yelling and dogs barking. But in spite of the noise and confusion there was no sign of fear, for the gathering of the tribe within the Pa in time of danger was an age-long ritual and the Maoris were always brave in battle, whatever the odds against them. And gradually the confusion sorted itself out into ordered activity, the able-bodied women running backwards and forwards bringing in fuel, provisions and household possessions from the village below, the children and old people building fires of brushwood to increase the light, the warriors working like furies cleaning muskets, strengthening the fences, clearing out the ditches and hacking down the ruins of the old village that impeded movement within the Pa.

Presently the ebb and flow of movement steadied a little as the women and children settled down in family groups with their cooking pots and household goods. But the men worked on, the savage light of the flames gleaming on their fine naked bodies, tattooed from knee to waist, their red war belts and the feathers in their heads. Cartridge boxes were fastened to their belts and short-handled tomahawks were thrust into them in the small of the back, for close fighting and to finish the wounded. Each man had his musket and now and then there was an explosion of angry sound as they experimented with them to see if they would go off. Once Marianne thought she caught a glimpse of Kapua-Manga and Jacky Poto but in the strange fitful light it was difficult to be certain.

Suddenly William caught his breath. "Look at that Tua sitting on the stone to the left," he whispered to Marianne. "Take a good look at him and then look away." And then he himself looked to the right that they might not both be seen gazing at the same man.

At first sight Marianne could see nothing outstanding about the warrior seated on the stone cleaning his musket. He was not a young man. His brown body was long and lean, his hawk-like features fine-drawn and clear-cut against the glow of the fire behind him. He gave the impression of having been shaped from some tough old kauri tree, an effect increased by a tattooing of limbs and face as elaborate and precise as fine carving upon wood. Utterly detached from the noise all about him he was so absorbed in his task that his serenity spread even to Marianne, stilling her madness and quieting her hammering pulses. Then the fire behind him sent up a bright tongue of flame and she saw that he had green feathers stuck in his grizzled hair, and again her heart was beating and her pulses throbbing, and like William she looked away.

They drew back into the shadows of the hut and held tightly to each other.

"Is it—is it——" she whispered.

"Yes," said William.

"But the tattooing," she said.

"He was always tattooed like that from waist to knee. Had it done years ago to please the Maoris. But the tattooing on the face is new. It would be a perfect disguise if we did not know him so well."

They allowed themselves another brief glance. He was strolling towards them and what he had been sitting upon was not a stone but a bundle that he now carried fastened to his belt behind in place of a cartridge box. By a very circuitous route he reached them and passed them without a glance, a knife falling from his belt. Marianne covered it with a fold of her gown and presently William took it and put it in his own belt. It was his own knife, that Captain O'Hara had given him long ago, and that Kapua-Manga had taken from him.

Then for a good hour they saw nothing of Tai Haruru except a distant brown back, the muscles rippling and knotting as he worked like a maniac lashing the inner fence. Then he seemed to disappear altogether and the minutes went by leaden-footed. The desperate activity seemed slackening now and many warriors joined their families round the fires to rest and eat. Then Kapua-Manga appeared, carrying a couple of heavy cooking pots to a family group round a fire near the hut. As he passed William and Marianne he tripped over the root of a tree and fell. When he had picked himself up and gone on they saw that he had forgotten to pick up one of the pots. After a few minutes William lifted the pot cautiously inside. It was filled with some thick sticky red soup that smelled disgustingly of rotten fish. "I couldn't touch it, William," whispered Marianne in horror when he showed it to her. William made no answer but she saw the shadow of a smile on his face. Perhaps he thought Kapua-Manga had left the soup there on purpose. She doubted it, for the Maori had had a very ugly look on his face when he had picked himself up after his fall. Now that the activity was slackening there had been many ugly looks, and she found herself watching the faintly glimmering mountain peak anxiously. The conviction had come to her that when the dawn touched its snows to rose-colour the preparations within the Pa would be complete and the Maoris would have time to turn their attention to their prisoners. Dawn was the time for death. It seemed an instinct with the human race to dispose of its captives at dawn. It was very dark now. It was surely the hour before the dawn. If Tai Haruru was going to act he had better act quickly.

Véronique was sleeping peacefully now within the curve of Nat's arm. The slow minutes went by again, with a renewed outburst of activity as the warriors finished their meal and went back to work, and with a beating heart Marianne saw the mountain peak suddenly silhouetted against a lightening sky. And in another moment she saw Tai Haruru again, staggering as though drunk with weariness. He came past the hut, his face turned from them, wiping the sweat off his forehead with his forearm, and the bundle fell from his belt.

William acted with astonishing speed, almost as though his slow body and brain had sucked energy from the man passing by. Pulling Marianne back into the hut he seized the bundle, tore it open, looked at the contents, then hung a blanket over the entrance to the hut and began hacking at the roof with his knife, undoing all the good work of the last few days. Then he pulled the thatch away in handfuls and let in the first grey glimmer of dawn.

Marianne bent over the contents of the bundle. "Rags!" she exclaimed in disgust. "Filthy rags!"

"Strip!" William commanded. "Daub yourself with that red paint all over. It's not soup. It's paint."

"William!" gasped his outraged wife. "*Take my clothes off?* Are you mad?"

"Do as I tell you," he said. "Quickly!"

He had already woken up Véronique and was fumbling clumsily with her clothes. "We are going to dress up, sweetheart," he was whispering to her. "We're going to dress up as Tapu Maoris and run about in the forest with red paint all over us. It'll be grand fun. It'll be the grandest Green Dolphin Country adventure we've ever had."

But William was clumsy with the hooks and eyes and Nat pushed him gently aside and in a moment had Véronique's clothes off. He dipped a bit of rag in the pot and with a shudder of revulsion Marianne saw the filthy red stuff trickling over her child's little white back. Véronique was not too enthusiastic either. "It's cold," she complained. "Is Mamma going to undress and be painted too?"

"Yes, Mamma too," said William.

"Never," declared Marianne.

She had her back against the wall of the hut. Undress before these men and be smeared with the filthy paint of a Tapu Maori? Her Victorian prudishness revolted utterly. Never. She'd sooner die.

She saw Tai Haruru's idea now and she thought it the most revolting idea of which in the circumstances it was possible to conceive. Tapu. Unclean. They were to disguise themselves as Tapu Maoris, outcasts, untouchables, and so get away.

She knew all about these wretched outcasts. They handled the dead and were unclean. They were supposed to be possessed by devils and anyone coming in contact with them was also bedevilled. They were not allowed to touch food and had to eat what was thrown to them from the ground like dogs. They must enter no house and speak to neither man nor woman of the clean. They were dressed in rags and daubed from head to foot with a red paint made from stinking shark oil and red ochre mixed, red being the funereal colour. If they were not insane to start with they soon became so.

"No, William," she said hoarsely to her husband, who was advancing with intent to unhook her down the back. "I refuse utterly to be put to this humiliation."

He took her roughly by the shoulders. "It is this or the most horrible death of which you can conceive," he told her. "You may prefer death but I do not—neither for myself nor Nat, and least of all for my wife and child. Never in all our married life have I commanded you. I command you now. Do as I tell you."

This was the first time she had encountered William in this mood. That hidden depth of strength in his weakness, revealed to her hitherto only by a chance attitude, had now taken possession of his whole personality. She had not seen him when he had fought for the life of Captain O'Hara and Nat. She had not the slightest suspicion that it was his heroic striving for her happiness, and not her own efforts, that had brought about his moral redemption. She did not understand at all that in the saving of life this man fulfilled the purpose of his birth; she only knew that in William at this moment she had more than met her match, and she gave in. With flaming cheeks and bent head she suffered him to unhook her down the back. It was not by torture that her pride was to be rooted out of her but by this shameful insult to her woman's modesty.

Never was so complete a transformation wrought in so short a time. William and Nat worked fast, and Marianne, once she had yielded her will, worked faster than either of them. They covered their bodies with the filthy-smelling red paint and draped their nakedness with the rags. They sheared off Véronique's curls with the knife and bound rags round William's head and hers to hide their bright hair. Then Nat flung Véronique's curls and their clothes in disorderly fashion upon the ground and cut his arm and let the blood run out upon them, so that to any entering Maoris it would seem that without doubt other murderers had got there first. And all the while, as they worked, they were conscious of a steady gentle rasping sound at the back of the hut, as though someone were sawing at the wall from the outside, and once Marianne and William looked at each other and smiled. It did not surprise them when the frail raupo wall gave way and Tai Haruru's tattooed face looked serenely in upon them. He looked at the blood-stained clothes upon the floor and nodded in appreciation of Nat's inspiration. "Bring the paint pot," he said briefly.

They climbed through the hole in the wall and found themselves in the thicket behind, where Tai Haruru hacked a hole in the ground and buried the pot. "Now I leave you," he said. "Push your way straight through the thicket to the other side and crouch down there. When you're seen you'll be hounded from the Pa. The rest is with the gods. Good-bye."

He left them, struggling through the bushes to the right, while they obediently pushed their way forward. The bushes were so thick that the thorns tore their skin and Marianne's black hair was pulled over her eyes in wild disorder. Véronique, though her father carried her in his arms, was never the less considerably scratched and had hard work not to cry. But she didn't because William was whispering to her that she was not to be frightened whatever happened. Didn't all their Green Dolphin Country adventures come out all right in the end? The end of this adventure was going to be that wonderful ship with white wings in which they had so often sailed before, and in it they would travel to a fairy country more beautiful than anything Véronique had ever seen.

William had no time to describe this country because they had come to the further side of the thicket and crouched down in its shadows. The Maoris were all about them now. To right and left of them family parties were squatting round cooking pots hanging over fires, and just in front of them several warriors, of whom one was Tai Haruru, were at work cleaning out the inner ditch. The dawn had come now and the flames of the fires, and of the torches that had not yet been extinguished, were only the ghosts of themselves against its light.

Tai Haruru straightened himself in the ditch, rubbed an aching back and turned towards them. For a moment his gaze was fixed in speechless horror, then he let out a yell and pointed a shaking finger at them. "Tapu! Tapu!" he screeched. "Unclean! Unclean! Devils in the Pa! Devils in the midst of the Pa bringing bad luck. Hound them out! Hound them out! Tapu! Tapu!"

Pandemonium suddenly broke loose. Men and women and children came running, looked and screamed. Tai Haruru, Kapua-

Manga and Jacky Poto, shrieking out imprecations and curses, leaping up and down and brandishing their tomahawks, gave no Maori any chance to exercise any wits he might possess. Distracted with superstitious fear not a single man or woman connected these terrible devils in their midst, who must have crept into the Pa for protection under cover of darkness, with the prisoners in the hut. Their one idea was to get them out before they brought terrible evil upon them. They might not touch them with their hands, and to kill them would be to have their dead bodies in the Pa, but they could be driven out with spears and stones.

"Run!" commanded William, leaping to his feet and leading the way with Véronique in his arms.

They were not far from the opening in the first fence and it was a short run, but even so Marianne was to repeat it in her nightmares for the rest of her life. The shrieks and curses seemed like a suffocating evil smoke through which one had to fight one's way out of this terrible chimney. Stones whizzed in the air and once a spear point pricked her body. Bent low to the ground to avoid the stones she fixed her eyes upon William's back and ran. She could hear Nat stumbling and panting behind her. She saw William leap the first ditch with Véronique. There were three ditches. Could she possibly jump them? Could Nat, old as he was, with his wounded leg not yet healed? Yet before she realised it her desperation had carried her across the first ditch with ease, and then the second. At the third leap she missed her footing and would have fallen, but William swung round and grabbed her wrist and pulled her to safety. Then they were through the opening in the last fence, the pekerangi, and running down the hill towards the deserted village. Nat had managed the ditches. He was running beside her, grinning at her, looking like a great red hairy ape, the most hideous spectacle she had ever seen. Stones were still whizzing through the air about them and one grazed her shoulder and cut it, but the dreadful sound of the curses was dying away. . . . Only one Maori was still following them. She could hear his padding bare feet and his insults shouted in the Maori language, that changed quite suddenly to injunctions in English. "Straight on. Through the village and into the forest. Don't stop till I tell you."

The village was left behind and they were stumbling along a rough track through the ferns and great trees. Their unaccustomed bare feet were soon bruised and painful but Tai Haruru, driving them on from behind, gave them no respite. "Go on," he said. "Right away out of this as far as you can. Go on. Go on."

Presently, when they were out of sight of the Pa and he had satisfied himself that there were no pursuers, he sped on ahead of them and led the way. The going was fast and hard but the mad impetus of their escape kept them at it, and presently the track began to wind uphill and Tai Haruru's loping run slackened to a swinging walk.

A harsh rattling sound broke the stillness of the woods and Tai Haruru stopped and swung round. His face was suddenly contorted, then became immobile as a mask. "No need to hurry now," he said in an expressionless voice. "They'll have their hands full at the Pa. The Red Garment has attacked."

He turned round and went on again, but very slowly this time, and while he had moved before with the grace of a wild creature he moved now like an old man. None of the others dared speak to him. It seemed that in saving them he had not been able to stave off death from the Maoris after all.

They climbed on and on and up and up, and the sun rose high and it was abominably hot, yet with Tai Haruru in his present mood they dared not ask him to let them stop and rest. Nat was now so lame that he could scarcely drag himself along, yet whenever Marianne looked back at him anxiously over her shoulder he grinned cheerfully. His appearance was indescribable and so was William's. As for her own, Marianne dared not let her mind's eye contemplate it for a moment, or she would have dropped down dead in her tracks with shame. A huge cliff loomed up above them and the fern fell away like waves foiled by an obstinate island thrusting its grey head up through the sea. They entered a cleft in the rock and had to climb now clinging with hands as well as feet. William, who had had Véronique riding upon his back, had to put her down and let her climb by herself.

The gully brought them out abruptly upon a narrow ledge of rock before the entrance to a large cave, and Tai Haruru spoke at last. "Turn your heads away and pass it quickly," he commanded them. "It is a Torere."

Marianne shuddered as he led them quickly past the cavern's mouth. A Torere was a cave where the bones of the dead were flung by the Tapu Maoris and it was a haunted spot, seldom visited by the living, and for that reason a good hiding-place. To the right of the cave they climbed again, and here there was no gully and they had to scramble up the sheer rock face. It was lucky, Marianne thought, that as a child she had learned to climb cliffs, and that Véronique had the Island heritage in her blood; she was climbing like a little monkey, as bravely and cleverly as Marguerite had long ago climbed the cliff above La Baie des Petits Fleurs.

Panting and exhausted they came out at last upon the summit of the Torere and found a small and beautiful amphitheatre in the rocky hillside, carpeted with grass and flowers, a place so lovely that it might have been the anteroom of Paradise. Wind-tossed mountain larches, bending over from the serried ranks of them that covered the hill above, gave shade, and far up above the larches, nearer to them than it had been in the Pa, was that glorious snow-covered mountain peak lit with the sun. The little amphitheatre was backed by a wide shallow cave. Blankets were spread upon its floor and in front of the entrance a pot hung over a fire. Hine-Moa was cooking something in the pot, while swinging on a branch over her head was a truncated green object which upon closer inspection proved to be Old Nick without his tail. He gazed in dumbfounded astonishment, not untinged with mockery, at the spectacle presented by his family, opened his beak wide but for once found himself deprived by shock of the appropriate comment. Yet he showed undoubted pleasure in the reunion and flew at once to the little red-limbed creature with the filthy rags bound round her head who cried out with such joy at the sight of him. Véronique's delight was sweet to see. Now she was happy. Rags and dirt and fatigue and hunger meant nothing to her now that all the people she loved were once more gathered together in one place.

2

Sweeter even than the safety, more full of comfort than food and drink, was the knowledge that Hine-Moa's friendship had never wavered. She was too full of lamentations over their pitiable condition to have any coherent explanations to offer, but when they had eaten and rested and she had bathed their sore feet Tai Haruru sat cross-legged with his pipe in his mouth and filled up the gaps in their knowledge of what had happened.

At Wellington he had asked for a small detachment of redcoats to ride with him to the settlement and bring back a white woman and her child to safety. But the officer in command of the garrison had thought the plea unnecessary, much valuable time had been spent in argument and a whole day wasted before Tai Haruru got his own way and rode off again with a young officer named Ellis and four men, and when they got to the settlement it was only a heap of smoking ruins.

"Nothing left?" asked William.

"Nothing at all," said Tai Haruru sombrely. "Every man dead. Every building reduced to ashes. Every barge destroyed. Our situation is far worse than after the earthquake."

William and Marianne said nothing. There was nothing to say. Houses can be built again but nothing brings back murdered men.

The young officer, who had ridden with Tai Haruru in tolerant amusement, unconvinced by the older man's misgivings, had blazed out into furious anger at the sight of the devastation, and when he had helped Tai Haruru to bury the dead, and to satisfy himself that William and Marianne, Véronique and Nat, were not among them, had immediately ridden off to Wellington again to arrange for a punitive expedition.

"I asked him not to do that," said Tai Haruru heavily. "I knew of this Pa in the forest and I said that if, as I imagined, you had been captured and taken to it that to attack it would probably be to seal your death warrant. I asked him, in order to save unnecessary bloodshed, to let the matter rest and to let me go alone to the Pa and see what I could do. He would not agree to that. He said, with reason, that if it was possible for me to get you out single-handed I would have time to do it before he and his men arrived, and that the destruction of the settlement must not go unpunished, though he would be as merciful as it was possible to be. Then he rode back to Wellington, taking with him a letter to Samuel Kelly, telling him and Susanna that you were not among the dead at the settlement and to expect us soon. We are making now for a settlement I know of north-east of Wellington, at the edge of the forest. There we'll borrow clothes and food and a wagon for the rest of the journey."

Tai Haruru went on with his story. With his plan of rescue already shaped in his mind he had made his way into the forest to the nearby village, hoping to find Kapua-Manga and Jacky Poto. He had found it deserted except for Old Nick, who had been perched upon the thatched roof of the chief's house swearing horribly. With Old Nick upon his shoulder he had journeyed on. He had known the direction he must take to reach the Pa but in any case it had been easy for a woodsman to follow the trail of the Maoris and their prisoners, and as he went he had broken branches along the way to guide the Red Garment. He had almost unbelievable luck, for only a few hours' journey from the Pa he had found Kapua-Manga wandering disconsolately after game and learned from him that Maui-Potiki and his family were prisoners within the Pa and still alive. With much bitter lamenting Kapua-Manga had told Tai Haruru that he and Jacky Poto and Hine-Moa had been powerless to help their white folk. Before the attack on the settlement they had been summoned suddenly to a meeting of their tribe at the village and in duty bound had obeyed. Hine-Moa had been sent to the Pa and Kapua-Manga and Jacky Poto had been held bound in the forest until the fight at the settlement was over.

"You should have told Maui-Potiki that you had been summoned to that meeting," Tai Haruru had said severely. "To leave him without a word was discourteous."

And Kapua-Manga had looked sheepish and had replied that Maui-Potiki had erected a stockade against his Maori friends. Did a man who did not trust his friends deserve consideration from them? But he and Jacky Poto and Hine-Moa were still the friends of Maui-Potiki and his wife and child, and also of the hairy one with the long arms. They had persuaded their chief not to put them to death just yet but to feed them and fatten them well in preparation for the next feast day, and they were meanwhile seeking for some means of delivering them.

Tai Haruru had expounded his plan to Kapua-Manga and the Maori had thought well of it. He had left Tai Haruru to sleep that night in hiding in the forest and early next morning he had come back to him again, and had tattooed his face for him, and had helped him to change himself once more into a Maori of the northern tribe to which he had once belonged, and together they had deprived the infuriated Old Nick of his tail feathers and Tai Haruru had made the fine arrow that in good time was to be a message of hope to the prisoners in the Pa. Tai Haruru had remained in hiding in the forest until his tattooed face had looked as it should do, and then he had come running to the village, a Maori escaped from the fighting in the north, with the warning that the Red Garment was everywhere sniffing the air for battle and that it would be wise to put the Pa into a state of defence.

"That at least I could do for them," he said. "I could not save them from young Ellis' attack but I could warn them that attack was not unlikely. They sent out their scouts immediately and prepared themselves to move into the Pa. They were not afraid and they trusted me, so completely is it my second nature now to speak and act and even to think as a Maori."

He had had one day in the village, the day when he had shot the arrow into the Pa and given his instructions to Hine-Moa. On the evening of that day the scouts had returned with the news that the Red Garment was advancing through the forest, and the whole village had moved into the Pa.

3

They slept that night in the cave above the Torere, and for Marianne it was a fitful, poor sort of rest. It was not until the night was

nearly past that she fell asleep, and then it was to pass not into restful unconsciousness but into one of those nightmares that are all the
more terrifying because they offer no adequate explanation of the
terror that one feels. She was not even aware that she was asleep,
because in her dream she was lying in the same lovely amphitheatre
hollowed out of the hillside where she had fallen asleep. The moon
was up, turning each flower petal to a sea-shell of mother-o'-pearl,
each blade of grass to a tiny silver sword. Infinitely high above her
the great stars hung motionless in the sky, far down below she could
see the tops of the forest trees lying like a shroud of silvery cloud
upon the floor of the world. There was neither sound nor movement and the unearthly silver stillness was so benumbing that she
felt as though her whole body were encased in ice. And then she
found that she was quite alone. The others had all gone away and
left her. She would have liked to have cried aloud to them but the
cold seemed to have paralysed her voice as well as her limbs, and she
could not. Then it seemed to her that the visible world, the great
stars, the moonlight, the cold still sworded grass, the motionless
flowers and trees, were leaving her too. They did not move but yet
they were passing away, thinning into nothingness, and beyond
them there was a great and appalling darkness, the kind of darkness
that little children are so afraid of, that kind that dwells behind a
drawn curtain in a lighted room and holds they know not what. She
knew she would be in it in a moment, every familiar thing left behind
on the wrong side of the curtain. Her nightmare terror rose to the
peak where it could not be borne and broke like a wave in a storm of
childish tears.

It was over and she was awake and Tai Haruru was bending over
her, holding her cold hands tightly in his. That terrible moonlight
had gone, leaving the first sweet grey dimness of the dawn. The
silence had gone and there were bird rustlings in the trees and a few
clear notes of song. And, best of all, the others were lying peacefully asleep as she had last seen them. They had not left her after all.
And Tai Haruru was bending over her, soothing her as though she
were a frightened little girl. . . . And like a frightened little girl she
clung to him and was not ashamed.

"A nightmare?" he asked. "Tell me."

"There's nothing to tell," she said, half laughing, half crying. "I
just dreamed that I was alone here at night and everything went
away. It was dreadful; like dying." She paused, fighting the last of
her terror, still holding his hands. "I felt like it once before, on the
Island, after William's father died. I wondered if he'd felt that way.
Is it very terrible to die?"

"I think there is just one moment when it is terrible," said Tai Haruru judicially, as to a child of eight. "But it is a moment that is soon gone."

"Why did I dream of death in this place?" she asked.

"How can I tell you?" he said, smiling. "Perhaps because there is a Torere just below."

But she shook her head, unsatisfied by his explanation. The dead Maoris in the Torere had none of them died here, and she believed that she had once again shared in the experience, past or to come, of a dying man.

"Go to sleep again," said Tai Haruru. "It's the best sleep, the dawn sleep. You're not alone."

She lay down again and he tucked her blanket round her. Then he fetched his own blanket and lay down near her. She did not mind, she was glad to have him so close; closer even than William was. As she drifted again towards sleep she found herself saying his names over and over again. . . . Timothy Haslam. Timothy. Tai Haruru. The Sounding Sea. . . . They none of them seemed quite right somehow. He had had another name once but she had forgotten it. She had known it long ago, but now she had forgotten it. Once again came the feeling that things were slipping away, but there was no terror in it now, only joy, because they were leaving her not alone by herself but alone with—with—the man whose name she had forgotten. . . . And that was what she wanted.

She woke up in broad daylight, and she had almost forgotten both the terror of her dream and the utter content that Tai Haruru's comfort had brought her. Yet enough memory remained to make her sit up quickly and count the sleeping forms about her. And there was one missing; Hine-Moa was no longer with them. She must have slipped away in that hour of the dawn when Marianne had slept so deeply. Her cry of consternation awoke the others, and brought them crowding round to look at the tokens of love that the Maori woman had left behind her. Upon the blanket that covered Véronique she had laid a little amulet that she had always worn round her neck, and upon Marianne's blanket lay a beautiful carved bracelet that her mistress knew had been her most precious possession. She had gone back to her own people and what now remained of the Pa and the village, careless of what might happen to her if the Red Garment had conquered. Tears were pricking fiercely in Marianne's eyes as she slipped the bracelet on to her arm, for instinct told her that she would not see Hine-Moa again.

After they had eaten, and had turned Tai Haruru also into a Tapu Maori with the contents of a second pot of paint that Hine-Moa had left with them, they set out again upon the journey back to civilisation. They travelled slowly and painfully, hampered by Nat's lame leg and Marianne's exhaustion. She had a pair of skin shoes to wear now, that Hine-Moa had brought for her, but they did not seem to ease the pain of her swollen feet very much, and the vertigo and nausea that were continually overwhelming her made her afraid lest she should collapse altogether and have to be carried. . . . And William was already burdened with Véronique and Tai Haruru with the blankets and Nat with the cooking-pot and Old Nick. . . . Yet her bewildered mind, reeling with fatigue, remembered that she was rebuilding her shattered existence upon the fact of Nat. Out of the abyss of utter loss into which she had fallen, an abyss where even her modesty had been stripped from her, she watched Nat as a small child watches a teacher from whom it must at all costs learn. He took to himself each day as it came with child-like trustfulness, and so did she. He never complained and neither did she. He took every misfortune with a grin and so did she. He took upon himself all the hardest and most unpleasant duties as a matter of mere routine, and she tried to do the same, only William would not let her. She noticed that her husband seemed a trifle bewildered by this sudden transformation of his self-willed wife into a very fair imitation of a saint; one of those dirty medieval saints who lived in caves in the desert or sat upon the tops of pillars and never washed in a lifetime. Yet never, in spite of her appalling appearance, had he behaved more lovingly towards her. His protecting enveloping tenderness had a quality of intensity that it had never had before. . . . He even seemed to be more concerned for her than for Véronique. . . . So I have not lost everything after all, she said to herself. Out of all the world he chose me to be his wife, and now I am not only his choice but his best beloved. Better beloved even than Véronique.

Tai Haruru seemed less astonished by her virtue than was William. "It is wonderful to what heights one can momentarily reach when put to it," he said drily one day. But he did not withhold his admiration. "Marianne," he said to her upon the last evening of their journey, "I don't believe there is another woman of your upbringing and your generation who could have borne herself with the fortitude that you have done. You will not lose your reward, my dear. I know where we are now. By this time to-morrow you will once more be able to lay your hands upon a pair of corsets."

Marianne, lying by their camp fire, feverish and almost light-headed, smiled faintly. The distance they had covered had actually been shorter than the distance from the settlement to the Pa but because they had travelled so slowly it had taken three days longer, days that had seemed like years, so full of hardship and danger had they been. The food Hine-Moa had brought for them had soon given out and Tai Haruru had had to shoot game for them, and they had cooked it as best they could over their camp fire. There had been no definite trail to follow and their only compass had been the position of the sun. Often they had been confronted by a bog, or by a cliff too steep to climb, and had had to retrace their steps and try again. For a whole day they had found no water and had been nearly frantic with thirst. Twice they had met bands of Maoris, fully armed and in ugly mood, and had thanked heaven for the hateful disguise that kept these warriors at a distance. Véronique had been very good all the way, riding upon her father's back, listening to his enthralling tales, prattling ceaselessly about the ship with the white sails that was going to carry them to fairyland, and she had not grumbled at the tummy aches caused by the queer diet of smoked meat and berries, and she had seemed quite fearless when they met the Maoris. Yet during the nights that had followed those meetings she had cried out in nightmare and woken up sobbing and trembling. It was obvious that the day at the settlement, and their terrifying escape from the Pa, had left their mark upon her. Lying beside the camp fire that last night Marianne came to a sudden decision. They would not go back to the ruined settlement. They would leave North Island and go south, where there were hardly any Maoris and no fighting to frighten little girls half out of their wits, and where there was no excessive heat to burn the roses out of their cheeks. . . . Only last night, Marianne vividly remembered, she had had a queer dream in which she had been standing in the centre of a flock of sheep in a green pasture, and beside her, staff in hand, had stood her husband Job.

The decision taken Marianne stretched herself more comfortably beside Véronique in their nest of blankets, looking up at the great stars that she could see glimmering faintly through the treetops over her head. "The stars at night so big and silver bright they might every one of 'em have been a moon," had said Captain O'Hara. She had felt very near to him all through this journey, that had been so like the one he had described on board the Green Dolphin, and once or twice she had fancied she had seen his great figure striding on ahead of them leading the way, his head tilted back to catch the gleam of mountains above the swaying treetops, listening to the chime of birdsong and the wind in the trees. . . . Doubtless she had been as feverish then as she was now. The faces of William and Tai Haruru and Nat, sitting smoking by the fire, discussing their plans for the resuscitation of the timber business and blissfully unaware that she had already decided it should not be resuscitated, kept appearing and disappearing in a very odd way, seeming now very near to her and now very far away. To shut out the unpleasant phenomenon she closed her eyes and tried to send herself to sleep by counting sheep—Job's sheep—jumping over a gate.

4

It was the evening of the next day, and long spears of golden light had been flung down by the sun across the path they followed. Marianne found herself stepping over them, so that they should not hurt her feet. Throughout this day she had found herself doing the oddest things: stumbling over the dead body of the Maori whom she had shot in the settlement garden, only it wasn't him at all but a log of wood; gathering her strength for just one more leap over the last of the ditches in the Pa, only it was just a stream that crossed the path; running down the hill with screams and curses still sounding in her ears, only she wasn't running but crawling at a foot's pace with William's arm round her. He had no idea, of course, of the odd things that she kept doing, though he realised that she was very tired.

He and she were at the tail end of the procession wandering in single file along the path, and Nat was just ahead with Old Nick perched upon his shoulder. She would not have been able to get along at all had it not been for Nat. She fixed her eyes upon him and when he put a foot forward she put a foot forward, when he stopped to rest she stopped to rest, when he grinned back at her over his shoulder she grinned too, and when he cracked a joke with Tai Haruru, on ahead of him, she made a raucous noise in her throat which frightened poor William nearly out of his wits.

And ahead of them all, recently set down after a long refreshing ride on her father's back, pranced Véronique on her way to fairyland. She was the only one of the party whom a costume of rags, fish oil and red ochre had not rendered an object of terror and repulsion. She looked like a red-brown forest elf dancing effortlessly over the golden spears that so impeded her mother, her body now mysteriously shadowed, now shining like a flower. They were all following her now, even the men so weary that they were scarcely conscious of where they were going. She knew, it seemed. She danced on and on, and suddenly there was a blaze of golden light and she had danced right away into it and vanished.

For a moment the grown-ups halted, appalled at her disappearance. Then Tai Haruru laughed. "We've come to the edge of the forest and the sun's in our eyes," he explained.

Huddled under the last of the trees, the forest with its darkness and dangers behind them, they stood and looked out at the fair prospect as Christian and Hopeful, worn by their travels, must have looked out over that valley where ran the river of the water of life. From their feet a green meadow sprinkled with flowers sloped down to a stream crossed by a wooden bridge, and on the further side of the stream the thatched roofs and wooden walls of a prosperous-looking settlement showed among the fruit trees of pretty gardens. Beyond the settlement was a patchwork of harvest fields backed by low green hills that curved protectingly about this enchanted valley, shielding it from the mountain winds and the storms from the sea. The whole lovely scene was bathed in a golden sunset haze that softened every outline to grace and muted sounds as well as colours to a gentleness that was of the essence of peace. There was music even in the distant sound of a cock crowing and the scraping of a saw, as well as in the chime of birdsong and the ripple of water and the gentle sound that two old horses made as they cropped the grass of the green meadow beside the stream. Beside them a wagon rested with shafts tilted skyward, with a woman in a grey gown sitting in the shade of it reading a book, unconscious as yet of Véronique running towards her through the grass and flowers and sunshine. Into Marianne's bewildered mind drifted words from the Pilgrim's Progress learnt long ago in the schoolroom at Le Paradis. "The water of the river was pleasant and enlivening to their weary spirits. Besides, on the banks of this river, on either side, were green trees with all manner of fruit, and the leaves they eat to prevent surfeits and other diseases that are incident to those that heat their blood by travels. On either side of the river was also a meadow, curiously beautified with lilies, and it was green all the year long. In this meadow they lay down and slept, for there they might lie down safely."

Véronique's clear voice added its note of beauty to the cadence that rose from the valley as though the earth itself were singing. "We've come," she called, as though they were the rightful owners of this enchanted place. "It's us."

The woman in the grey dress dropped her book, looked up, stared for a moment in astonishment, then jumped up and held out her arms; for she was Susanna.

CHAPTER FIVE

1

In the bare little guest room of the Parsonage at Wellington Marianne was making a leisurely toilet, and sniffing appreciatively yet critically the scents of roast mutton and mint sauce that floated up from below. But the appreciation outweighed the criticism; which had not been the case upon her previous visits to Susanna. She had been ill, and now she was convalescent and excessively hungry, and not disposed to cavil at good food, even though it had not been prepared according to her own methods. Moreover she was not the Marianne she had been. Although with returning health and strength sufficient of her old self-will had reappeared to assuage any anxiety her husband and friends might have been feeling upon her behalf, yet it was self-will with a difference. Before taking her own way she now subjected it to a very strong scrutiny. The shocking discovery that her way was not necessarily good because it was hers had been epoch-making in her life, and now she did her best to put all her wishes to the touchstone of objective excellence before imposing them on her family.

She doubted if her decision to leave North Island and the timber trade and start their life afresh in South Island as sheep farmers would be popular with that family; William had never been to South Island, he knew little or nothing about sheep, and he was intensely conservative, Tai Haruru would hate leaving his Maoris, and Nat now hated journeys of any sort or kind; but she was quite convinced that to put her child's welfare before everything else was what every mother ought to do. Her decision was therefore the right one, and she would break it to them all at dinner time.

She looked at the cheap clock on the mantelpiece. Another ten minutes. Shocking to think that she had only left her bed in time to dress for dinner. To-morrow she would get up for breakfast, for she was well now, and there must be an end of this laziness. She had been doing nothing for a week, first at the settlement at the edge of the forest where Susanna, guessing that this was the spot Tai Haruru would make for, had come to meet them, and where kind folk had taken them all in for three days because she was too ill to travel, and then for three more days at the Parsonage, and that was far too long a period of idleness in a life that materially as well as spiritually had to be rebuilt from the foundations.

For they had just nothing now, she and William, except a small sum in the bank that might, or might not, suffice to start them in the new life. Even their clothes had gone this time. The hideous dun-coloured gown she was wearing was Susanna's. Nothing that she had on was hers except the green-stone earrings which had hung fantastically in her ears all through their adventures, even when she had been disguised as a Tapu Maori. She looked at herself in the glass with a shudder of distaste when her toilet was finished. Her hair was grey now and her sallow face lined. She looked an old woman. Impossible to imagine that she was the same Marianne as the girl who had dressed herself in green and cherry red and painted her cheeks with geranium petals on the day of the review. And Marguerite, who had gone whirling round the room on that far-off day in white frills and blue ribbons, how did she look now dressed in black serge? She did not think of her sister very often nowadays, and with the passing of the years found the duty letters that she wrote to her more and more difficult to compose, so great was the separation between them now that Marguerite was both a Catholic and a nun. Yet though the news that Marguerite had taken the habit of religion had caused her to express herself to William in terms of outrage and horror she had not in her heart been sorry about it. She had not stopped to search for the reason for this content, she had just felt vaguely that now William was more completely hers than he had been. William himself had taken the news in silent stupefaction, though he had read Marguerite's letter twice over, the final paragraph several times, and then without a with-you-leave or a by-your-leave had decamped with it into the garden. In some dudgeon she had asked for the letter back again next time she saw him, but meanwhile the tiresome man had been into the forest and had lost it there. He showed little interest in Marguerite nowadays.

The dinner bell sounded and she rustled her way down the steep stairs to the living room. Somehow or other, by some personal magnetism, she could get a rustle out of the calico petticoats from which Susanna herself could only coax a faint whisper, and, positively, as she came into the parlour, she looked almost chic. Susanna gazed at her in admiration. By turning up the hem and taking tucks round the bodice she had given to the dun-coloured gown a fit it had never had when it draped Susanna's lanky form. She had dressed her grey hair quite perfectly and tied a green ribbon round her waist to match her green earrings. They all, with the exception of Samuel, who was not there, and Old Nick, who was eating a lump of sugar in his new cage and taking no notice of anybody, rose respectfully to their feet as she made her superb entrance.

"Well done, Ma'am," said Tai Haruru. "That is a more becoming costume than rags and paint."

She put him in his place with a cold glance, for why must he remind her of past humiliation? Then she laughed, for she did not resent her humiliation. For some unknown reason she was a happier woman because of it.

"Are we waiting for Mr. Kelly?" she asked, meanwhile motioning to William to take his place at the head of the table.

"I expect he has been called to some sick person," said Susanna in her gentle voice. "So we won't wait. Please to be seated, Marianne."

She need not have spoken, for William, automatically obeying his wife, was already sharpening the carving knife, and Marianne was already seated. She slipped deprecatingly into the chair at the end of the table, opposite William, feeling that the place should have been Marianne's, wishing that Mr. Haslam would not push her chair in for her with quite such an air, or Nat bother to bring her a footstool. The joint was as Marianne liked it, she thought, but she was terribly afraid that she had overcooked the apple pie.

And so she had. But Marianne, when it came, did not comment upon the fact; merely set aside upon the edge of her plate those portions of pastry that were a little burnt. Unquestionably she had changed. Though she was still Marianne she was a much nicer Marianne, thought Susanna.

"I've been thinking about our future," Marianne said presently. "It would be best, I think, to leave North Island and go south. Véronique, darling, have you finished? You may run out into the garden and play with the cat. Aunt Susanna will excuse you. . . . It is for the child's sake," she said to the four grown-ups when Véronique had gone. "She has such dreadful nightmares. I would like to take her right away south where there will be no Maoris and no fighting. It is for the child's sake."

Old Nick dropped his sugar and gave a derisive squawk with a twist to it, that somehow sounded like a question mark.

"For the child's sake," Marianne repeated a little louder. Then she glanced at Nat, who sighed, and then nodded and smiled at her. Yes, he approved. It would mean another of the long arduous journeys that he hated but what of that when it was for the child? William's mouth had fallen open in stupefaction. Tai Haruru, smiling faintly, was applying himself to a second helping of apple pie and from all the evidence that his inscrutable face gave to the contrary she might not have spoken.

"South Island?" ejaculated William. He turned to Tai Haruru. "What are the timber prospects in South Island?"

"Not too bad," said Tai Haruru laconically. "Mrs. Kelly, this is the best apple pie I have ever eaten."

"There's a great future for sheep farming in South Island, so I'm told," said Marianne. "I think we should find wool more profitable."

"You're talking nonsense, Marianne," said William, suddenly recovering himself. "What lumbermen know about sheep could be put into a thimble, and then there'd be room for a pint of beer."

"You can learn," said Marianne. "Neither you nor Mr. Haslam are devoid of intelligence."

"What exactly are your plans, Ma'am?" asked Tai Haruru in a voice of silk.

"Sell our land at the settlement," said Marianne. "Then take ship to South Island. When we're there buy a wagon, horses, cooking utensils, all that's needed for a long journey. Then trek south."

"Sounds like the migration of the Children of Israel to the Promised Land," said Tai Haruru drily. "I did read the Bible once. It bored me but portions of it are still in my memory. What'll you eat in the wilderness, Ma'am?"

"Better take all the food we can with us in the wagon," said William gloomily. "And where did you think of settling, Marianne?"

"Oh, we'll light upon some pleasant pastureland," said his wife airily. "And spend our bit of capital on it, and upon the hire of expert labour, and there'll soon be nothing about sheep that we don't know."

There was a short silence.

"But why sheep?" asked William dismally. "If it's for Véronique's good that we should go south, why then, go south we must. But why wool? I know timber. I love it. Why can't we stick to timber?"

"Because there's a bigger future for wool," said Marianne.

"How do you know that?" demanded her husband.

"Whenever I come to Wellington I listen to men talking," said Marianne. "I don't go about in a dream, as you do. I make it my business to listen and learn. And you know, William, I've an instinct for these things. I just know we could make money in wool."

"You're sure what you call your instinct is not just association of ideas?" asked Tai Haruru. "As I told you, I once read the Bible, and now I can never think of sheep without immediately connecting them with the prosperity of Job."

"At one period he lost the lot and had boils," said William.

"Just a bad year," said Tai Haruru. "Taken as a whole he found the sheep farming business highly satisfactory. Eh, Marianne? And if I remember rightly a short period of humiliation and poverty did not, as with so many, have any permanent effect upon his natural aptitude for possessions. Am I right, Marianne?"

She observed him intently. It was uncanny, the way he always brought the hammer down on the nail. There was another silence, broken by Susanna speaking for the first time.

"Samuel and I have friends living at Nelson," she said in her gentle voice. "We had meant to go to them in a few weeks' time for a little holiday. You could go instead. They would take you in, Marianne, and give you all the help possible."

"That would be very kind," said Tai Haruru. "Well, Ma'am, I hope matters are now settled to your satisfaction." He poured himself out a glass of water (there was never anything stronger than water on Susanna's table) and held it up. "Here's to the flocks and herds of Job," he said, and drained it to the dregs with a wry face.

2

It was evening before Samuel returned. Véronique was in bed and Marianne and Susanna were sitting in the back porch stitching at new little dresses for her. Susanna, a laborious needlewoman, was utterly absorbed in what she was doing, but Marianne, though her clever needle never ceased to dart to and fro like lightning, looked up now and then at William and Tai Haruru, deep in conversation at the bottom of the garden. She was astonished, and a little puzzled, at the way the two men had taken her decision. She had expected vehement opposition from Tai Haruru, so passionately attached to his kauri trees and his Maoris, and easy compliance from William, who was always compliant. But it had been the other way round. Tai Haruru had received her proposal with the sleek acceptance of a cat invited to a bowl of cream, while William had argued the point. And now Tai Haruru was smoking his long curved pipe with an air of peace and serenity while William's shoulders were bowed and his face furrowed with distress. She felt a little annoyed with him, as well as puzzled, for he had nothing, as far as she could see, to be grief-stricken about. She felt troubled when she looked at him, and the sudden eruption of Samuel into the porch was a welcome distraction.

"Has anything happened, dear?" asked Susanna anxiously, for Samuel's eyes were blazing in a face whose pallor was almost luminous with intensity of feeling. His wife knew the signs only too well. Samuel was on salvation bent. In another minute she would be asked to receive some poor derelict soul into the house, feed him and shelter him, regardless of the fact that William, Tai Haruru and Nat had finished the whole of the joint at dinner, and that Samuel was already sleeping in the passage that Véronique might share Susanna's bed. . . . Or else she was to be seized by the arm and haled off to the dirtiest quarter of the town to attend the accouchement of some poor drab of the streets. . . . Or else (worst thought of all) he had suddenly received a Call.

He had received a Call to set sail for New Zealand, and only Susanna and her God knew what it had cost her to drag her roots up out of English soil and follow him. . . . Or how intensely she had disliked pioneering life in this wind-swept God-forsaken country all these years. . . . She realised, of course, that it is the cross of a parson's wife that her husband's Calls may not always seem to her to be her own, and she had borne her cross in such a manner that only she and God knew that she had it. But that did not prevent her dreading changes and, even more than changes, partings. She looked up at her husband's face now with her hand to her throat to hide the little pulse that always beat there very fast when she was afraid. . . . And she was very afraid. . . . For a long time now she had felt that a Call was on the way. They had been in this little parsonage for some years and by pioneer standards the life they had lived in it had been comfortable and undisturbed. Too comfortable. Samuel had been bound to feel sooner or later, even though he slept in the passage more often than not, that he was far too comfortable.

"Yes, Samuel?" she asked tremulously.

It appeared that Samuel had been spending the afternoon at the hospital. The English wounded had been brought back from the forest, and at last they knew what had happened at the Pa. The word "Pa" reached at once to Tai Haruru at the bottom of the garden and he and William joined the group on the porch. "Tell us what you know as coherently as you can, Kelly," he commanded the excitable little man. And Samuel, subduing with iron control the fires that had been lit in him by what had happened, sat down on the porch steps and confined himself to surface events with commendable lucidity.

It had taken the Red Garment three days to subdue the Pa, and the fighting had been bloody and magnificent. Young Ellis, who was himself among the wounded, had been astonished at the vigour of the Maori defence. It had been his first experience of the toughness of the Tuas and it was his earnest hope that it would be his last. "For it's a damn shame to have to shoot down such fine fellows," he had said to Samuel. "They may be cannibals and bloody heathen but, by God, they fight like Christians."

Underestimating the task before him, and urged by the instinct for fair play, Ellis had not at first made use of the rocket gun he had brought with him, he had left it guarded in the forest and had relied on musket fire only. For the whole of the first day he had blazed away at the Pa, and the Pa had blazed back with great spirit but

inferior ammunition, and at evening he had sent a man who knew the
Maori language and had come with them as interpreter with a flag of
truce to demand surrender; but the answer to that had merely been
shouts and yells of a most abusive character. That night his men had
crept up the hill under cover of darkness and at dawn they had
attacked. He had expected that first charge to decide the issue but it
had done nothing of the sort, for after savage hand to hand fighting
his men had been driven back. The discomfiture of the Red Garment had been bitter indeed, and on the morning of the third day
they had brought up their rocket gun. But Ellis had not used the gun
until he had sent his messenger again with the flag of truce, to explain that this was a very terrible gun, that it would destroy the Pa
utterly, and that if the Maori warriors would yield now their lives
would be spared. But the answer to that had been, "Ka whaiwhai
tonu ake! We fight on for ever!" He had sent the messenger once
more with the demand that the Maori women and children be sent
out into safety, and the answer had come back, "The women will
fight on with the men". After that there had been nothing for it but
to fire the rocket gun.

The first rocket had fallen to the left of the Pa, and cheers had risen
from within, and the second had passed right over it and howls of
derision had been added to the cheers, but the third had struck the
pekerangi, and the fourth had alighted in the very centre of the Pa,
and after that the flaming stars had fallen thick and fast and soon
the whole fortress had been blazing. The Maoris had fought the
flames as gallantly as they had fought the Red Garment on the previous day, but a hot wind had whipped the blazing fences to fury, and
on the evening of that day they had had to yield.

But only to the fire, not to the Red Garment. When twilight fell
warriors, women and children, carrying their wounded with them on
their backs, had come running through the flames and down the
slope of the hill, had hacked their way through the soldiers with
magnificent courage and fled into the woods.

And they had by no means finished with the Red Garment. For
days on end the warriors still left alive had harried the British as they
attempted to force their way back through the forest, so that what
should have been a victorious march had begun to look remarkably
like a fighting retreat. When their ammunition had given out the
Maoris had continued to harass the white men with arrows and
tomahawks, and they had kept up their attacks until the ruined settlement had been reached.

The rest of the journey back to Wellington had been a continuing
nightmare for Ellis and his men, short of food as they were and able

to travel only at a foot's pace because of their many wounded. Altogether it had been a costly expedition and though they had destroyed the Pa the last word had undoubtedly been with the Maoris.

"Undoubtedly," said Tai Haruru, and smiled.

"What I would give to know that Jacky Poto and Kapua-Manga and Hine-Moa are still alive!" cried Marianne.

William grunted in agreement. "I'd give ten years of my life."

"I may be able to send you word," said Samuel, "for it so happens that I am leaving for the Pa to-morrow. I've a holiday owing to me, you know. The first long holiday I've had since we came to Wellington. I'd meant to spend it at Nelson with Susanna. But I've changed my mind. I shall spend it at the Pa." He spoke quietly, but now that the restraint imposed by the telling of the tale was lifted his inner excitement had blazed out again and his face was once more alight. "There must be great suffering in that Maori village. Wounded men and bereaved women. Suffering both of mind and body caused by white men. I shall go on horseback with a case of medical supplies."

"Mr. Kelly, are you mad?" ejaculated Marianne. "You'll be murdered. Spare a thought for your poor wife, for goodness sake."

But Samuel, his fanatical eyes already looking across the garden in the direction of the forest, was not considering his poor wife. As Susanna had guessed, he had had a Call. Or rather, the way had suddenly been opened for him to answer the Call that had come to him on that night when he had looked through the palisade at the settlement and fancied he had seen weeping figures moving through the fern. Susanna's face had blanched, but she said nothing. She knew it would be no use.

"How well do you know the Maori language?" asked William. "You can speak it a little, I dare say, but without a thorough knowledge of it you'll get yourself nowhere except into your grave. You couldn't attempt a task such as you propose without a first-hand interpreter, and where will you find a man crazy enough to want to run his head into the hornets' nest of a bereaved cannibal village?"

"God willing, I shall find him," said Samuel confidently.

"You needn't look far," said Tai Haruru, "for he's here."

They looked at each other, and the comradeship of their meeting glance was familiar to Marianne, for they had looked at each other in that way on the verandah at the settlement.

"Mr. Haslam, I must tell you that I do not intend to take with me medical supplies only," Samuel said formally. "I shall take also the Gospel of Christ. I shall take salvation."

"No harm in that," said Tai Haruru tolerantly. "With only a smattering of the Maori language at your command you'll not make much headway with it. But I'll not interfere with you. If you'll let me have my way first with the sick bodies of men, about which I suspect I know a great deal more than you do, you can have your way later with their souls. That's only fair and right; though I shall have the advantage of you, the bodies being existences in actual fact and the souls mere figments of your imagination."

"We differ," said Samuel belligerently.

"We do indeed," agreed Tai Haruru pleasantly. "We shall not lack subjects for argument during the long hours of our journey. Shall we walk down to the hospital and see about those medical supplies? And we'll need to find two tough horses."

They got up, absorbed in each other and the coming adventure, though Samuel had by this time recalled the fact that he had a wife and in passing he laid his hand gently and lovingly upon her shoulder. "I'll not be long away from you," he whispered to her. She covered his hand with her own but still she said nothing, so inhibiting was the chill of foreboding that had made her ice-cold all over as though it were mid-winter.

But Marianne was not so inhibited. "Mr. Haslam!" she cried out indignantly. "I never heard such crazy nonsense in all my life. The summer is already passing and William and I cannot wait here indefinitely for you to come back from this mad expedition. If we are going to South Island at all we must start as soon as possible."

"Certainly, Ma'am," said Tai Haruru equably. "I agree that you and William should lose no time in starting. I'm not preventing you. My best wishes will go with you."

"But surely——" She faltered and stopped, gazing at him in mingled distress and perplexity. "But you are William's partner. Surely you will come with us too?"

"How little you know me, Marianne," he said gently. "I find no value in life apart from personal independence. That you and William should join me in my lumber business—that was one thing. That I should follow along at the tail-end of your Israelitish migration like your tame tabby cat—that is another, and can hardly be expected of me."

He smiled at her and was gone after Samuel.

3

So that was why William had looked so bowed down with sorrow. He had known Tai Haruru was not going with them. Supper was over and Marianne was out on the porch again. The wind had risen, sweeping clear the face of the moon and whipping the stars to flame, so although it was late it was not dark. She was alone. Susanna was in the house, Nat had gone to his lodging, William had gone to see the notary about selling their land. . . . At least so he had said, but his wife suspected him of a visit to Hobson's saloon to drown his sorrows in whisky. . . . Samuel and Tai Haruru had not yet returned.

She was most desperately unhappy, and amazed at her own unhappiness. Once she had hated Tai Haruru, and now here she was unable to face the fact that she and William were going to have to live without him. Looking into her soul she realised that of late years she had come to lean very heavily upon his strength. Her dependence upon him had begun as long ago as the birth of Véronique, and now that she was not as physically strong as she had been, and not so self-confident, it was increasing daily. Her bitterness against him, when he left them at the settlement and rode to Wellington, had been because she did not feel so safe without him. When he had shot the arrow into the Pa she had believed that they were saved. She had felt confident and happy in her decision to go to South Island because Tai Haruru would be with her, and when he was with her all was well. . . . And now he would not be with her. . . . William would, William without whose courage and resource on that last dreadful night in the Pa Tai Haruru could not have rescued them, but William without Tai Haruru was not enough. William could be very stupid sometimes. It took a great danger, a great crisis, to set free that strength that was deep as a hidden well in him, while Tai Haruru's creativeness, that led him to counter every perplexity of the passing moment with imaginative and vital action, was always rising freshly to the surface of life like a spring of clear water.

Should she change her mind, wait here until there was peace and then go back to the ruined settlement and start again as they had after the earthquake? Her new weakness, that clung to Tai Haruru, wanted to do that, but her pride rebelled. She had said it was best for Véronique that they should go, and if she were to change her mind now she would stand convicted of insincerity in advancing Véronique's welfare as her motive for the journey. And she did really believe that a change would be best for Véronique, even though Tai Haruru's sarcasm at dinner, putting a fresh polish upon her new clearness of sight, had made her see that her own character had been chiefly responsible for her decision. . . . She loved to journey on, to adventure just a little further, to create afresh. She could escape from herself best in those moments of vivid experience that fresh scenes gave her. She always felt that the hunger of her heart for perfection would be satisfied if she were in some other place, not this one. She could not endure to have her ambition thwarted, and she had decided long ago that she would enjoy prosperity before she died. She hungered for the flocks and herds of Job.

A tall figure came suddenly from the house and loomed up beside her. "And so you are hurt, Marianne, that I am not coming with you to South Island?"

"Yes," said Marianne. "I am hurt. I thought that you loved William and Véronique, and that you liked me."

"You thought quite rightly," said Tai Haruru. "You are mistaken only in one thing; I love you as well as William and Véronique."

Marianne looked up at him but she could see little of his face in the shadow. "Then why?" she murmured.

"The reason I gave you. I love my independence more than any of you."

"You talked nonsense when you said you would have to trail after us like a tabby cat," she flashed. "If you came with us you would be what you have always been, the central figure in the picture."

"I thought it was Marianne Ozanne who was always that, Ma'am," he said mockingly.

"No," said Marianne sombrely. "I know myself better than I used to do. I lack your aristocracy. You were right when you said once that I was a vulgar woman. I am. Nor am I as strong as I thought I was. I don't really know how I shall manage without you."

"Marianne!" he cried with mock horror. "You don't know what you are saying. To speak like that is to be in danger of salvation."

"Salvation? What's salvation?" she asked wearily.

"As far as I can make out from Kelly it is a curious process of divine burglary. The first thing to be wrested from one by a God who said 'Thou shalt not steal' is one's good opinion of oneself."

"We are talking of independence, not salvation," Marianne interrupted tartly. "You will not lose it by becoming my prop and stay in South Island."

"A man in love has no independence worth mentioning."

She could only stare up at him, stupefied.

"Years ago I swore never to love a human creature again," said Tai Haruru irritably. "Then I saw the boy William sitting on the other side of the table at Hobson's, and I loved him. Then I loved you. There's nothing for it now but to cut myself adrift from the two of you."

"I think you have gone quite crazy," said Marianne. "I was not without attraction when I came here as a bride, and you did not love me then, but now that I am getting old, with any vestige of good looks I ever had completely vanished, you tell me that you love me."

"I love the child in you," said Tai Haruru. "The adventurous, brave, stubborn little child. She is a changeling child, lost and lonely but passionate, vital, conscious like all the fairy folk of her superiority to the common herd. . . . Oh yes, you are, Marianne. This new humility of yours only goes skin deep, you know. You stand in no danger of conversion at present, thank God. . . . You see, I am as enslaved by the changeling's faults as by her virtues, for they're all part of her. I should hate to see Samuel convert her into one of those detestable little cherubs with head and wings but no body. Mercifully I think there's little danger at present."

"But I tell you I'm not proud now," protested Marianne. "Out there in the forest I was utterly humbled. It was not skin deep. It went right through to my soul."

"Really?" he asked mockingly. "Do humble women long for the flocks and herds of Job?"

She covered her face with her hands. "You know me through and through," she murmured.

He put his hands under her elbows and lifted her up to stand before him. "That's why you love me," he said. "At first you hated me because I saw too much. Then the subconscious knowledge that you could not deceive me made you find me restful company. Now when you are with me you are utterly at peace."

"I suppose that is why the humbled are the happy," she murmured. "Not to have to pretend any more—even to yourself—that you are nicer than you really are—it is certainly very restful." Then she took her hands from her face and laid them on his breast. "Yet I am William's," she said. "Though I love you yet I am William's. He and I have belonged to each other since we were boy and girl."

"That is your conviction," he said, "and you are stubborn in it. Do you know, Marianne, I believe that the breaking of that conviction is the only thing that would ever break your pride."

"But it is true," she cried. "I have always loved him. His love is the only thing I have ever wanted. Don't you believe me?"

He put his hands over hers and smiled down at her. "I believe you," he said. "And it is partly because I believe you that I am not going with you to South Island. You'll have more chance of getting what you want if he has no one to turn to but you."

"But he does love me!" cried Marianne. "He loves me now with all his heart and soul. He loves me now as he has never loved me."

"Good-bye," he said. "I'll think of you often and you'll not forget me though you live to be a hundred. If I believed in souls I'd say that yours and mine are well matched and of very long acquaintance."

He took her in his arms and kissed her and she did not struggle because his embrace was cool and passionless. She stood leaning peacefully against him and there came to her a strange home-like sense of familiarity, as though this were not the first time that he and she had stood like this in the summer night with the warm wind burnishing the lights in the sky to flame, as though he knew her so well because he had known her under other stars. When he withdrew his arms and went away there fell upon her an awful sense of desolation; and pain as though she'd been reft in two.

4

William did not stay long at Hobson's. The Red Garment was in preponderance there to-night, nearly swamping by its numbers those primeval men of the earth whose company was always so congenial to him, and the sight of the Red Garment was not bearable to him just at present. . . . Because he had been fool enough to let himself and his family be taken prisoner by the Maoris a rocket gun had been trained upon the Pa in the forest, and his mind was a nightmare kaleidoscope of smoking ruins and mangled brown bodies and women lamenting and cutting themselves with flints because the Tuas had fled to Reinga and there was no more joy left for them upon the earth.

He downed only a couple of drinks and then went outside again, where the radiance of the rising moon had turned the water of the harbour to silver and the mountains to crystal. "It is well with thee, O moon! You return from death, spreading your light on the little waves. Men say, 'Behold, the moon reappears', but the dead of this world return no more."

He climbed the hill and paced up and down in front of the Parsonage, as he had done on that night of deadly homesickness when he had first met Tai Haruru, and again on his wedding night when he had felt that married life with Marianne was a thing that could not be faced. He had been wretched then and he was wretched now. At Marianne's command he was leaving Tai Haruru, whom he loved as greatly as one man can love another, and North Island that had grown nearly as dear to him as the Island of his boyhood, and the kauri trees of his trade whose scent and shade and deep voices talking in the wind had somehow become a part of his very soul. Yet work and friendship and familiar soil, though three of the most precious possessions of man in this world, are not the final treasure; they are not that one love of a man's life which to him is the justification of the pain of living. In spite of his wretchedness William was sacrificing home and trade and friendship to Véronique's welfare as a mere matter of course; and deep below the surface wretchedness, with gladness.

His heavy sagging shoulders straightened and the sadness went out of his eyes at the thought of his child. . . . Marguerite Véronique. . . . He had not known, until his child had been born, that a love as complete and exquisite and perfect as that which he felt for her could exist upon this earth. She was his child, bone of his bone and flesh of his flesh, beautiful and loving, and that fact alone surely had enough in it of felicity to justify the fact of his life. But she was more even than that. She was Marguerite as well as Véronique. In some way that he did not attempt to understand she was not only his child but also the little blue-eyed girl who had played with him in his boyhood, and the tall fair woman whom he had loved as a man. She was child, playmate and lover, the perfect companion. She made everything in his life worth while; the daily toil for which she was the chief incentive, the once-hated marriage that was blessed now because it had brought her to birth, the dream life that she dominated, the hidden scarcely considered life of the soul which it seemed she must have companioned in some way from the beginning of time; so perfect was she that she sometimes seemed to him to sum up in herself the whole of reality. He need look no further now.

So thought William as he blundered up and down and listened to the wind with its multitude of voices, and watched as the sweep of its wings burnished the stars to flame. Increasingly with the years he had loved this wind, increasingly he had worshipped its godlike immanence of power. . . . It was Marguerite's wind. . . . Because the woman who was now a nun had become mysteriously one with the little girl asleep in the house behind him he had not for that reason forgotten her. The letter that she had written to him and Marianne, telling them of her decision to take the veil, was in the wallet at his belt at this moment. He had not spoken the truth to Marianne when he had said he had lost it in the forest, and he had taken very good care not to discard the belt when he threw off his clothes at the Pa. The closing words of that letter, that were also his own words, were never out of his mind. "Though you are so far away the bond between us is very strong. . . . You have my love and devotion always. I think of you day and night." No, he would never forget her. Through the child, through the wind, through the strength of her prayer, she was always with him, and his response to her power was continuous.

A step crunched on the road and Tai Haruru was beside him.

"Well, lad, so this is good-bye, eh?"

Tai Haruru, his pipe in his mouth, his hands deep in his pockets, spoke serenely, but his rough deep voice had in it once more that note of mourning and of angry resignation, echoed from the trumpet notes of nature, that had so caught William's attention at their first meeting, and his face, seamed now with the lines of tattooing, had more than ever that look of being graven from hard wood. William could feel, without being told, how his whole nature, constrained for so long by the bonds of human companionship, was now straining out and away, angry and sorrowful yet eager too. It was with self-knowledge that he had carved his pipe in the form of a bird in flight. His body might have taken to itself the likeness of a kauri tree but the spirit of the man was winged.

William groaned and swore. "On the whole you're glad," he said.

"Glad? Sorry?" said Tai Haruru. "I'm both. To be sorry and glad together is to be perceptive to the richness of life."

William grunted in agreement. Marianne had said something the same at the Pa and he saw now that it was true. Only at the very centre of pain or joy was one wholly wretched, wholly joyful. There was only one hour of the night in which sunset or dawn were not present to the mind in memory or hope, only one hour of the day when the sun seemed neither rising nor declining, and the intensity of those hours dulled and blinded.

"After the Pa what next?" he asked. "Back to what's left of the settlement?"

Tai Haruru shook his head. "Back in the old haunts I'd miss your company. After the Pa I've a fancy to travel towards the sunrise, travelling light, and take my chance of what comes. That's a part of the country I don't know yet and I'm not too old for fresh discovery."

William forbore to question his independence further, and he was without anxiety. Wherever Tai Haruru went, whatever he did, he'd be at home. Life, that he loved as most men love the fire upon their hearth, burned everywhere.

"I'd not have missed these years with you and Marianne," said Tai Haruru. "My only taste of family life since my boyhood."

They were pacing up and down now. "Not always happy," said William awkwardly. "In the early days—all those rows and arguments—I used to wonder how you stood it."

"I like you both," said Tai Haruru. "And the maladjustments as well as the adjustments interested me. Obviously you were never in love with Marianne and why you married her is still to me an unsolved problem. But having done it you made a damn good job of her."

William was startled. He knew it was the opinion of most people, including Marianne herself, that she had made a good job of him.

"I'm for the wilds to-morrow," said Tai Haruru, "and secrets are as safe in the wilds as in the grave. . . . Why Marianne?"

William told him; the only human creature he had ever told. Tai Hariru smiled broadly when the story was done but showed little surprise.

"Like you," he commented. "Only the damn fool that you are at times could have made such a blunder, and only the fine fellow that you also are at times could have given your life to saving the woman from disaster because of it. For that's the plain truth of it, William. If you'd not turned your life into a living lie Marianne would certainly have foundered."

He said no more, and they walked up and down smoking in silence, for awe, touched by mockery, made him feel oddly shaken; jerked right out of the rut of his usual peaceful disillusionment. For if the young fool William had not made that idiotic mistake in a girl's name he himself would never have known Marianne. He would not have stood in the summer night with her in his arms, he the sceptic who had believed life divorced from the experience of it by the senses to be just nothingness, and known with sudden absolute conviction that it was not for the first time. Just a fancy, this conviction? If so it was a fancy that threatened to turn his life upside down.

5

Véronique, holding tightly to her father's hand, stood wide-eyed in the stern of the ship that was carrying them from North Island to South Island. She was dressed in the warm pelisse and bonnet of periwinkle blue that Mamma had made to protect her from the sea breeze, and her face was pink with ecstasy. The white wings of a sailing ship had carried her upon many thrilling journeys in Green Dolphin Country, but never yet in the real world.

She glanced back over her shoulder. Mamma was there, just behind them, sitting on top of a pile of luggage, wearing a purple porkpie hat with a grey feather in it, Old Nick beside her in his cage, and Nat was rolling delightedly round the deck, gazing up at the white wings overhead with a broad grin on his face, just as she had seen him so many times in Green Dolphin Country, and beside the sailor at the wheel stood an immensely tall old gentleman with a round rosy face and a merry eye and lots of brass buttons down his bulging front, who was quite certainly Captain O'Hara.

"There's Captain O'Hara," she whispered to her father.

Papa swung round, glanced at the old gentleman, then looked down at her and smiled and nodded. "That's him," he said. "That's the Skipper. One's always safe, Véronique, with the Skipper at the wheel."

Safe. Véronique heaved a great sigh of happiness. Safe was a word that Papa and Mamma were perpetually using to her nowadays. . . . There were hardly any Maoris where they were going and they would be safe. There were no earthquakes where they were going and they would be safe. There was no fighting where they were going and they would be safe. . . . Yes, without doubt this was not the real world. She jigged up and down with delight and looked about her. The sea was turquoise blue, spread all over with diamond-crested ripples, and the sky overhead was blue too with small clouds like pink seashells sailing along on it because it was so early in the morning. Wellington in the distance looked like a toy town, very tiny and pretty against a mountain background so clear and cold and beautiful that it gave her quite a pain in her middle. Funny to think that folded up within that beauty were brown men who yelled at you, and fired noisy guns and set your home on fire, and hurt Nat's leg, and made you so dreadfully frightened that you had to take your clothes off and run away into the forest with next to nothing on. And funny to think that Aunt Susanna was still there. Véronique could no longer see her standing on the quay and waving to them, so perhaps she had gone home. What would she do to-day? Would she wash and iron the sheets that Véronique and Mamma had used, and would she cry as she did it, so that the tears falling on the hot iron made a funny sizzling sound, as they had done when she ironed the sheets that Uncle Samuel had used before he went away with Uncle Haruru?

A shadow fell upon Véronique's joy, for that memory of Aunt Susanna crying sizzling tears on her iron was not a good one. The memory of Uncle Samuel and Uncle Haruru riding away was not a good one either. She had stood outside the front door of the Parsonage, with Mamma and Papa and Aunt Susanna, and she had watched them ride away and she had not liked it. Mamma and Papa and Aunt Susanna had been laughing and talking but she had known all the same that they were not happy.

Uncle Samuel and Uncle Haruru had not been unhappy but they had been unlike themselves, odd, with eyes that looked very dark and deep in the lightness of faces that shone as though the sun was on them; which it wasn't. And when they had sat upon their horses and looked down on the group by the door they had seemed to look down from a great distance away, almost from a mountain top. And then they had smiled, and raised their whips in a last greeting, and clattered away round the corner and disappeared into nowhere.

Véronique pulled at her father's hand, for suddenly she did not want to look any more at that beautiful cruel real world that held people crying and people killing each other, and people riding away to nowhere, hidden in its folds. She wanted to look at the new land, where she had been assured that no unpleasant things would ever happen. She wanted to look at the coastline of Fairyland.

In the bows of the ship the wind was so strong that it pushed Véronique's blue bonnet off, and lifted the short fair curls that had taken the place of her lost ringlets right up from her head as though it had endowed each one with a joyful life of its own. She had never felt a wind like this and she laughed in her joy. It blew so hard that she could feel it even on the skin of her body through her clothes. The strength and cleanliness of it thrilled her through and through. "I like wind," she said to her father.

He gripped her small hand tightly, smiling down at her. Of course she liked wind. She was his daughter through and through, and the niece of Marguerite who had felt at home in her special country when the light was clear and the wind cold and there were no lies or subterfuges. He picked his little daughter up in his arms and pointed to the faint lovely coastline ahead of them. "Look, Véronique," he said. "There's *your* country, your own special country where you will grow up to be a happy woman. It is called the Country of the Green Pastures."

"Not Green Dolphin Country?" she asked.

"Green Dolphin Country is my country," he said. "Though of course it's yours too, just as Aunt Marguerite's Island Country is yours too, because we love you and all that is ours is yours. But this country is your very own. You'll like to have a country all your own, won't you? Green Dolphin Country is a bit rough and adventurous for a little girl sometimes, but in the Country of the Green Pastures, where the sheep feed beside the waters of comfort, there is never any fear. It is the perfect country for little children."

The new land ahead rose up sunlit out of the sea.

"Tell about what we'll do when we get there," cried Véronique excitedly. "Tell about where we'll live. Tell about the sheep."

"First we shall go and stay with a friend of Aunt Susanna's," said William. "And it won't seem very exciting at first because we shall be staying in a town rather like Wellington, and the people there won't know that you are the Queen of the Country of the Green Pastures and so though they will love you I doubt if they'll curtsey or kiss your hand. You will, of course, realise that it is just their ignorance and make allowances. And then when we have been there for a little while we will buy a wagon and horses and set out on a long wonderful journey. I expect we shall get very tired on the journey but the home we are going to is so lovely that it will be worth it. At first we shall travel through great plains where because it is your own country the rivers will be blue like your eyes and the blond grass the colour of your hair, and the flax will bow to you because you are the queen, and the wind will kiss your hand. On one side of us, as we travel through the plains there will be wonderful lagoons, and on the other side there will be a rampart of mountains that touch the sky. Then we shall leave the plains and travel up a rough track into the foothills of the mountains, and the grass will be green and there will be flowers, and you will hear the birds singing. Then the track will run into a narrow gorge with rocks on either side, and we shan't see anything except the rocks until we get to the top, and then——"

William paused, slightly worried. A frightful thing it would be if the portrait of their future home which he was about to paint were not later to be substantiated.

"Yes?" prompted Véronique excitedly.

William took a deep breath and went on.

"And then, Véronique, we shall go in through a gateway of rock and find ourselves in what is about the loveliest thing God ever made, an upland valley ringed about by mountains. It will be rather like that valley that we came to when we left the forest, because as one journeys along through life the valleys of comfort perpetually recur, but it will be much more beautiful even than that. Stretching up the sides of the mountain you will see the Green Pastures with the sheep feeding on them, and the water in the streams that come down from the mountain tops will be so clear that you will see every pebble at the bottom, and the reflection of the mountains, and your own happy face. In summer the air will be warm, but it won't be too hot like it used to be sometimes at our old home, for the Green Pastures are nearer to the mountain tops than the settlement was and the lovely tang of the snow will always be with us. Véronique, in that lovely safe valley in the hills there will be a house for us, for you and me and Mamma and Nat and Old Nick. In summer the door will stand always wide open and through it you will see the sheep feeding on the mountain sides, but in winter when it is snowing in the mountains, and the sheep have been brought down to the valley, it will be closed and we shall light a large fire of blazing logs on the hearth, the sort of fire that you have never seen, and we shall sit before it and tell each other stories, and be the happiest four people and the happiest parrot in the whole wide world."

KNIGHTS OF GOD

I heard them in their sadness say,
"The earth rebukes the thought of God;
We are but embers wrapped in clay
A little nobler than the sod."

But I have touched the lips of clay,
Mother, thy rudest sod to me
Is thrilled with fire of hidden day,
And haunted by all mystery.
GEORGE WILLIAM RUSSELL.

CHAPTER ONE

On some days it seemed to Marguerite, enclosed in the stone cell of her French convent on a hill top, that those who live the life of prayer live it in a great void, a desert of emptiness where is nothing but one-self and the winds of God; but on other days it seemed to her that they live it in a suffocating crowd of devils, so pressed upon and jostled that it is hard for the labouring lungs to catch enough of the foul air even to breathe.

It depended, of course, simply upon the mood of the moment. There were days when the impossibility of seeing the result of one's prayer was disheartening almost to the point of faithlessness. One prayed for those in peril, but though one might seem to hear the beating of wings in the wind the eyes of the body could not see the angel who took the prayer from one's outstretched hands, and held it as a shield between some human creature and the death that it was not yet the will of God should come upon them. One prayed for courage for those who had turned back upon the path, that they might turn again, but one's own body did not experience the shock of realisation, the reversal, the regathering of strength. One prayed for the faithless but it was not granted to one's ears to hear the crumbling of the walls and the shouting of the trumpet and the "I believe . . .". These were the great void days, when prayer was torn out of one by the wind and vanished into thin air. They were days of intense cold, and the numbness seemed to grip body as well as soul, so that one's lips could scarcely form the words that seemed so useless or one's weary body maintain the rigid attitude of prayer. They were days of self-loathing and of that recurrent humiliation that Reverend Mother of Notre Dame du Castel had taught her to expect. They were dreadful days. One could expect no relief upon them except, sometimes, the relief of finding one's straining body and aching arms curiously supported, as though upon a stark two branching tree.

Dreadful days, yet not so hard to endure, perhaps, as the suffocating days. "If I were a nun I'd pray all the time for people to be happy," she had said in her childhood. "I'd pray all day and all night for everyone, birds and animals and people and the whole world, just to be happy." She'd not known in her childhood what that would mean. She'd not known that to fight with the weapon of prayer that which destroys happiness is to have it round upon yourself. "For we wrestle not against flesh and blood, but against principalities, against powers, against the rulers of the darkness of this world, against spiritual wickedness in high places." To pray for the diseased, the wicked, the insane, was to be bound with their chains and tortured with their fears, it was to stagger beneath a load as heavy as that of Atlas, and yet somehow find the strength not to be bowed down to the earth by it but to lift it up and up, to straighten oneself with it, until again there came that sense of support. But it never seemed to come until it seemed that the last moment of endurance had been reached. One had to reach and pass that moment before one could feel the strength of the wood.

Battered between these two mighty experiences of prayer one could not have lived, surely, without those other experiences at the other end of the scale, that were homely and sweet and sometimes extremely funny, experiences bound up with specific prayer for those who companioned one's everyday life, for the other nuns, for the peasants in the village at the bottom of the hill. It was sweet when a sick child recovered, a lost cow was found, after one had prayed, intense happiness to feel again that old sensation of being picked up as a tool and used. And if pride reared its head it would immediately be laid low by some little happening of sheer comedy that reminded one how God laughed at the self-importance, the self-conscious business of His tools, mere dead things bereft of warmth or sentience without the hand that lifted and gave life.

She had prayed once for comfort for a little lay sister, inconsolably homesick, and could only dissolve into hopeless laughter when next day a stray kitten scaled the convent walls and jumped through the refectory window straight into the outstretched arms of the little sister. . . . But surely they must keep the kitten, she had said later through gales of mirth to their Reverend Mother, who did not like cats and was all for putting it out, for as it had come in answer to prayer surely it was here as divinely appointed mouser, and to cast it out would be to run directly counter to the will of God? . . . Reverend Mother had yielded, meanwhile eyeing Sister Clare with that slight uneasiness which her laughter always caused her superiors. For was it right that so spiritually gifted a nun should be at times so extremely flippant? Was it right that she should enjoy the little things of life, the taste of a ripe apple, a beam of sunlight, a kitten, a bird's song, with such abandonment? Quite right, Sister Clare had once said in answer to this question. It was her opinion that the compensatory intensification of delight in little things that comes when larger things have been renounced is God-given. Why should He have scattered such playthings as sunbeams and kittens along the thorny way if they were not to be exclaimed over and enjoyed?

And between the terrible and the comic there came that prayer for those one loved but from whom one was parted; for William and Marianne and little Véronique. There again the prayer life had to be lived by faith for no word ever came back to her that God in His mercy had let her share in their lives. William never wrote to her at all and Marianne's duty letters were so stereotyped as to be almost completely non-informative, and Véronique's exquisitely written little epistles, occasionally blotted with tears and always obviously dictated by her mother, told her nothing whatever about the child except that she must be obedient and good, or she'd not have consented to be kept from play to trace so carefully, and with tears, those ridiculous, laborious, stilted phrases to an unknown aunt. Poor little Véronique! If that was the kind of letter that Marianne dictated to her then she doubted if Véronique had quite the right kind of mother. And William, who was no doubt a most indulgent father, must be away from Véronique through the greater part of every day. Surely the little thing was frightened sometimes, playing alone in a garden that Marguerite pictured as entirely surrounded by dark forests full of prowling beasts and marauding savages? Through many hours did she pray for the child that she might not be afraid, trying to send that little girl Marguerite Le Patourel to play with her in the lonely garden. She felt sometimes emptied of all joy, old and weary beyond words, as though the little girl in her who so scandalised her superiors had gone away. But she could not see her running up and down the garden paths with Véronique, or sitting on her bed when she was frightened in the night. She could only have faith that her emptiness and weariness were endured to some purpose for this child with whom she felt so curiously at one.

She knew, though she had never been told, how greatly William loved Véronique, and she imagined sometimes that she felt the intensity of his love reaching out through the child to herself. Though he never wrote to her at all she had never lost her sense of union with him, only now she felt it not directly but through the child. That was as it should be, she thought, for she had never ceased to pray, as she imagined he had commanded her, that his marriage to Marianne should be blest; and the right recipe for a happy marriage was surely the fruit of a loving and beloved child. She found no cause for jealousy in the thought that she reached him now through the child. As day by day and night by night she held him in her consciousness, following his doings, saying, "Now it is morning on the other side of the world and he will be going out to the forest. Now it is mid-day and he will be felling his trees. Now it is evening and he will be turning homeward," it was hand in hand with Véronique that she was with him, and it is not possible to be jealous of a child whose hand has been put trustingly into one's own. . . . But sometimes she felt she would have given years of her life to have known that life was the easier for him because she lived and prayed, that sometimes in his thoughts of Véronique she had a part, that just now and then, when the stars were bright as they had been that night on the Orion, that he remembered that night. . . . But this latter wish was not seemly in a nun who had vowed to live her life by faith, and when it thrust itself into Marguerite's mind Sister Clare resolutely put it from her.

And turned with considerable effort to think lovingly of Marianne. The thinking of Marianne did not require effort, but the thinking lovingly. It was disgraceful that effort should be required after all these years, and when she did most truly love her sister, but thoughts of the Orion always touched up that sore place that Marianne's behaviour that night had left in her heart. . . . If Marianne had just not turned up at that particular juncture that moment of perfect union that she had had with William would not have been torn off in the middle, leaving this sore that had never quite healed. . . . Poor Marianne, how could she possibly have known that she was interrupting something that ought not to have been interrupted? Marguerite was sure that her intentions upon that occasion had been only all that was kind, and whenever she was having difficulty in tinging her thoughts of her sister with the right depth of the rich red colour of love she hated herself and redoubled the intensity of her prayers for her.

She was praying for her in her cell one winter's day, conscious that though it was daytime and winter in France it was a summer night in

New Zealand, when there slid before the dark curtain of her closed eyelids one of those strange little pictures that often came to her when she was praying, or when she was lying on her bed in the darkness between sleeping and waking. They were puzzling pictures of some unknown scene, some unknown face, and seemed to have no sense in them and no connection with anything or anybody she knew.

To-day the picture that sprang up as she prayed was that of a snow-covered mountain peak crowned by moon and stars. She stood upon this peak and the air was cold and rarefied, the air that she loved, and the austerity of the snows was the austerity of her own especial country. From this height she looked down upon the darkness of a great forest, a darkness that she felt to be full of danger. Far down at the foot of her mountain there was a sort of chimney in the forest roof, and inside it, lit by the moonlight, she could see a conical hill crowned by some queer fortification of fences and ditches, and at the foot of the hill was a village of thatched huts. As she watched dark figures came out of the huts, running towards the hill. . . . Marianne. Marianne. . . . The little picture faded as quickly as it had come but it left the thought of danger coupled in her mind with the thought of her sister for whom she was praying. With all the strength that she had, her whole being reaching out towards Marianne in love, she prayed that she might be preserved from harm.

A bell tolled. It was the recreation hour when she might if she wished take the air in the terraced garden below the convent. She got up from her knees, feeling uncomfortably weak, for virtue had gone out. She stopped and rubbed her knees, often painful now-adays with rheumatism, that special enemy of those who kneel for long hours together in cold and draughty cells. How old was she now? She paused to think. Forty. That was a good age, of course, but not quite old enough to justify rheumatism. It would be terrible to become as crippled as poor old Mère Madeleine of Notre Dame du Castel. The Reverend Mother of Notre Dame, who wrote to her regularly, had reported recently that poor old Mère Madeleine had died at last aged ninety-nine and so crippled that she could scarcely move; and lamenting with her last breath, poor old soul, that she would never see France again. Except for these twinges Marguerite was still extraordinarily strong and healthy and shrank from the thought of illness with horror. . . . Pain made it so hard to pray. . . . She took her cloak from its hook on the wall and went quickly down the stone passage into the garden. She must take all the exercise she could, for walking, they said, was the best way of keeping the enemy at bay.

The winter afternoon was mild and clear, and the long level beams of a golden sun streamed with benignity over a fair landscape. Terraces of vines fell away below the old grey convent upon its hill, and down below them the small village of white-walled cottages nestled among orchards, with woods beyond that were a paradise of flowers in the spring. The peaceful valley was protected to the north by low blue hills, but over this barrier there always fled at nightfall the homing thoughts of Marguerite.

For northward was the Island. She had never gone back and her only links with it now were the letters of her great friend the Reverend Mother of Notre Dame du Castel. She had never seen Reverend Mother again either, but through their letters their friendship had deepened and strengthened and become one of the best things in both their lives. Each understood the hunger of the other for her own land. Marguerite sent Reverend Mother, exiled upon her grey rock, detailed descriptions of the fair land of France where she herself was exiled, of the budding and blossoming of the vines, of the ripening of the apple harvest, of the murmuring heat of summer days and of the golden calm of the mild winters when one could hear the angelus ringing in a village miles away, and the distant hills would draw so close at evening that one could have stretched out a hand and touched them. And Reverend Mother in return told of the spindrift that clouded the windows of her cell, of the gulls crying and circling about the convent walls, of the light that was still always kept burning in the west window of the tower to guide the fishermen at sea, of the battering of mighty winds and the gathering of vraic upon the shore of La Baie des Petits Fleurs.

"To put away all hope of seeing one's native land again is not easy, my daughter," Reverend Mother had written at the end of her last letter. "Of all the hopes which we nuns may be called upon to lay aside it is perhaps the hardest from which to part. I am an old woman now and I shall not see France again, but you are still only in middle life and I pray unceasingly for you that one day God in His goodness will grant you to see again this Island of your birth. That is a prayer that you could not pray for yourself, but I can pray it for you. Adieu, my daughter. Have you still that little book I gave you? When I think of you these words come always into my mind, 'Those who have the gale of the Holy Spirit. . . .' You are one of those. The thought of you always brings a clean fresh wind to my mind. I have not enjoyed good health of late and have often and often turned with gratitude to remembrance of your health and strength, which I pray God always to preserve unto you. Adieu again, Marguerite. Let us pray for one another. I am, in Our Lord, your friend Marie Ursule."

Marguerite was thinking of this letter as she walked up and down. "Marguerite. Marie Ursule." It was the first time in their correspondence that Reverend Mother had used the names that had been theirs when they lived in the world. It was of a piece with the expression of her nostalgic longing to see France again; as though she were reaching back into her youth, gathering up what she had been into what she was, putting together all that she had like one who makes preparation for a journey.

Marguerite was seeing her friend very vividly as she paced up and down; the tall supple figure, the beautiful humourless face, alight with holiness yet chill and a little frightening. Shining and cold, supple and strong, she had been like a sword.

Marguerite looked up sharply, a little confused by the suddenness with which the sound of hurrying footsteps had jerked her back from the Island to this vine-terraced hillside in France. It was a stout little lay sister, panting in her hurry, slipping and stumbling over the stones in the steep path. "Reverend Mother wants you, Sister," she gasped. "In her study. Vitement!"

Marguerite walked without haste back up the steep path, smiling at the other nuns again as she passed them. In Reverend Mother's white-washed study she stood very upright, hands linked behind her back, and waited for what should come. This Reverend Mother was very different from the Reverend Mother of Notre Dame du Castel. She was circular in figure, with a little round red nose like a cherry beneath her anxious short-sighted round eyes. She was of peasant stock and always felt a little uncomfortable with Marguerite, whose tall slim figure, looming over her like a poplar tree, made her feel like a cabbage at its foot. Yet she loved her. Marguerite's power of enjoyment, though disconcerting at times, seemed to set such a bright polish upon life when one was with her.

"Sit down, Sister," she said.

With the tall nun sitting on a lowly stool Reverend Mother felt less like one of the humbler vegetables and was able to say what must be said.

"Sister, I have news for you that will cause you both grief and joy. I am sorry to inform you that the Order has suffered a great loss in the death of your old friend Reverend Mother of Notre Dame du Castel. I am happy and glad to be the one to tell you that upon her earnest recommendation the Order has appointed you Mother Superior in her place. Tonight, Sister, we will sing Te Deum in the Chapel. It is an honour for us all that you have been chosen."

At the news of the passing of her friend Marguerite had crossed herself and bowed her head in prayer for her soul. She had known, she thought, that that last letter was the letter of a dying woman, and so she had been prepared, yet all the same a stab of pain went through her that she would not, in this world, see her friend again. Yet when she lifted her head and smiled at the round little woman on the other side of the table her face was luminous with joy.

"With God's help, dear Mother, I will be worthy of this honour," she said, adding under her breath, "Au Nom de Dieu soit."

CHAPTER TWO

1

Mounted upon their horses Samuel and Tai Haruru had seemed to Véronique to look down upon those they were leaving as though from a great distance, like two men upon a mountain top looking down upon the dwarfed littleness of their homestead in the valley below, and hard put to it to convince themselves of its reality.

"Always so much harder for those who stay behind," said Tai Haruru as they jogged upon their way, remembering the blank dismay that had been upon Marianne's face as he and she had looked at each other for the last time, the appalled dismay of a woman who sees a treasure for which she has been searching given at last into her hands, only to have it withdrawn again before she has had time to do more than recognise it with that recognition of eternal values that comes only once or twice in a lifetime. "For those who journey on the past fades away into the distance, while for those who remain behind it is an ever-present torment. Poor Marianne. Poor girl."

"I was under the impression that Mrs. Ozanne, by her own choice, was also about to journey on," said Samuel with a sarcasm unusual with him. . . . For in front of him, obscuring the sun, floated the picture of a woman who was journeying nowhere, a lonely woman weeping in a house whose only unfamiliarity was its intolerable emptiness.

"Like a snail carrying his shell she bears her normal responsibilities with her," said Tai Haruru, still musing upon the woman he loved. "The marriage bed, the nursery, a household cares, however far she may wander they are present with her in the persons of husband, child and servant. That's not true journeying, Kelly, that's just moving house. The authentic journey, the adventurous cleaving of the air with wings, is made alone."

"We are together," said Samuel.

They looked at each other.

"Only for a short time," said Tai Haruru.

They looked at each other again, a strange look, for they knew instinctively that for each of them this was to be an authentic journey. The end of it would be a new state of being, and from it there would be no return.

They rode for some fifteen minutes in complete silence.

"It must be alone," repeated Tai Haruru then, still following the same train of thought. "And until now I have never even wished that any journey of mine should be other than lonely. This queer sensation of being only one half of a whole, of finding completeness only with another's help, is mere illusion."

There was the hint of a question in his statement and Samuel answered it. "Migratory birds fly alone across the sea," he said, "but on the further shore there are meetings and matings and nest-building once again."

"As though the two halves of a circle sprang apart, travelled the orbit alone, came together, parted once more and so on for ever," mused Tai Haruru. "The circle of immortality. It is such a tiring idea that I don't accept it."

"Luckily the basic truths are not dependent for their validity upon your acceptance," said Samuel drily. "As for fatigue, it is a thing that passes, the corollary of approaching finality and good news of a fresh beginning."

"The trouble with you, Kelly," said Tai Haruru, "is that you will not permit finality to be final. That's your arrogance. Only the arrogant think that they will live for ever."

"On the contrary," retorted Samuel, "it is you who are arrogant with your insistence upon your right to say the last word. I have now been in company with you upon many occasions, and never can I remember that you permitted a conversation to be brought to a conclusion by any except yourself. Let me now tell you, my good Sir, that you will one day discover to your chagrin that in this matter of the length of life of the human spirit the right to say the last word is not yours but God's."

Tai Haruru laughed, and then a few moments later laughed again at the realisation that in this particular conversation the last word had been not his but Samuel's. And he let it rest so, for the experience had the freshness of novelty, that very same freshness of which Samuel had been speaking.

Indeed the whole journey had a dewy freshness about it that made the two men boys again. The faces of Marianne and Susanna soon ceased to haunt them, for these women whom they loved had companioned their manhood and they were journeying now backwards into a lost youth.

"Or forwards," said Tai Haruru, his mind still busy with that analogy of a circle that had haunted him ever since he had held Marianne in his arms and there had come to him the conviction, cutting straight across all previous belief, that their souls were long acquainted.

Samuel, riding along a forest path dappled with sunlight, answered mechanically, "Yes." Stray unrelated sentences were always drifting towards him from Tai Haruru like floating leaves that show which way the wind is blowing, and though he made little comment he understood, having travelled this way himself. There'd be a great wind presently, the wind of an authentic journey that lifts a man into the air like a bird, but the time was not yet. And meanwhile he was enjoying himself as never before, with a trembling astonished enjoyment that had come to him hitherto only in the deeps of prayer. Tai Haruru's boyhood in Cumberland had been the right kind of boyhood. He had run wild in the woods as soon as he had had the use of his legs. The white peace of the snow-covered fells, the scent of wet moss, the pattering of rain upon leaves and the voice of the wind in the branches had from the beginning been as much a part of him as his own hands and feet. But Samuel had been defrauded of that heritage. He had only seen snow trampled to filth in city streets, wind and rain had hardly been more to him than the harbingers of cold and discomfort. The beauty of England had from afar stabbed him now and then with a flash of sunlight, a phrase of birdsong, but he had left her before he could become acquainted with her loveliness, and he had been too preoccupied with the saving of souls for the beauty of New Zealand to touch him very nearly. But now, as the great trees of the primeval forest closed about him, shutting away past and future, leaving him with nothing but a couple of saddle-bags, a horse and his bare existence, the earth his mother for the first time held out her arms and pulled him close. As with his spirit in the deeps of prayer so now with his body in her arms, separateness vanished. The same ecstatic life that pulsed in his body throbbed also in the body of his horse, blazed in the sunlight, chimed in the birdsong all about him, sang in the wind in the treetops, aspired in the delicate veining of leaves and grasses and the silent miraculous unfolding of the flowers. He was in them and they in him, and yet he was still himself and still in some sense hungry; that did not surprise him, for he had learned in prayer that union is not sameness and that in this world the core of longing is never satisfied; what did surprise was the sense of awe and reverence that possessed him, reverence that he had felt hitherto only for God. Reverence for a flower petal that would be dust to-morrow? For a repetitive bird phrase, the opening bars of a statement that was always left unfinished? For such trivialities? And, as in prayer, reverence brought peace and peace dedication. "Then shall the dust return to the earth as it was and the spirit shall return unto God Who gave it." Almost he could imagine that in the supreme self-giving of death there could be as great an exultation in the surrender of the body to the earth as in the surrender of the soul into the hands of God the Father. For the first time in his life he considered earth the mother. Most grievously had he hitherto neglected her. Never had he commented upon the different facets of her beauty as a good son should. Had he said they were trivial a moment ago? The scales as yet had scarcely fallen from his eyes. Stray phrases began to float from him to Tai Haruru, once more like drifting leaves, and Tai Haruru, though paying little attention, yet answered with a comprehension born of his own experience.

"One seems never to catch a flower at the moment of unfolding."

"Flowers are alive, man," murmured Tai Haruru. "You can't watch life, it's divine. The movement of divinity has so miraculous and perfect a rhythm that it is beyond human perception."

"The birds do not finish it," complained Samuel at another time. "They perpetually repeat the question but they give no answer."

"Like all religious men you read more into a thing than its content," said Tai Haruru. "That bird phrase is not the opening bar of a symphony but a lyric, a thing complete in itself. And earth neither asks nor answers questions. Why should she? She herself is finality."

"There is no finality," reiterated Samuel quietly. And indeed he recognised none in this new-found beauty of earth the mother. Every sensual experience of her loveliness was coming to him not as an end in itself but as the shadow of a hint about something beyond comprehension or definition, greeting him as the perfume of a rose growing round the bend of the road would greet a traveller who had never seen a rose. "We have both been unworthy sons of earth," he said to Tai Haruru. "I unobservant of her beauty, you of the purpose of it."

"Laziness?" suggested Tai Haruru lightly. "Too much trouble to take a country walk? Too much bother to pursue the will-o'-the-wisp of beauty to some probably quite imaginary bourne?"

"And pride," said Samuel. "The overweening pride of thinking ourselves capable of a discovery that is sufficient. Enough, you said, when the life in you made contact with running water and the shimmer of grass. Enough, I said, when I found my God in prayer."

"Cowardice too then," mocked Tai Haruru. And then he fell into a muse. He knew himself to be a proud man and he knew, too, that there was a streak of indolence in him. But a spiritual coward? He had not suspected that. Was disillusionment another name for cowardice? Perhaps. Yes, most certainly, for it was the line of least resistance. . . .

It was perhaps the sense of danger ahead that gave such a passionate intensity to their experience of earth's loveliness upon this journey. At the back of both their minds was the knowledge that contact with loveliness through the medium of the physical senses was one that might soon have to be laid aside for ever; for another; or nothing.

2

It was evening when they reached the village and the Pa, riding their weary horses through the sea of fern that had so frightened Marianne. The Pa was a blackened ruin upon its hill top and many of the houses in the village had been destroyed. At first sight it looked deserted, but a second glance showed a few coils of smoke rising up through chimney holes in roofs that were still intact, and a few dogs lying dejectedly in the last pools of sunlight.

Tai Haruru might be a spiritual coward but he was no physical one. After they had dismounted and tied their horses to a tree he made his way straight to the heart of the village and cried aloud, and there was a note in his voice that reminded Samuel of some wild old lioness roaring to her young. There was a brooding savage pity in Tai Haruru's face, as he called aloud to his dusky children, that was as elemental as the deep undertones of his voice. Samuel had scarcely noticed the peculiar quality of Tai Haruru's voice before, but he understood now why they called him Sounding Sea. Straightening himself in an instinctive bodily reaction to a tremor of fear that went through him in this last moment of peace before the storm, Samuel looked upwards and saw towering above the trees a snow-capped mountain peak flushed with the fires of sunset. It was like a beneficent Presence in the sky. At the same moment Tai Haruru took hold of his arm and a tide of strength mounted steadily both in his body and his soul, so that when a moment later he found himself the centre of a storm of almost devilish hatred he knew no fear.

They had come pouring out of their houses at the first sound of Tai Haruru's voice, old men, children, women with their bodies lacerated by the savage rites with which they had mourned their dead, wounded men with dirty bandages bound round their limbs, unkempt, half naked, maddened with pain, yelling aloud in a frenzy of mingled hatred and delight. They had been hurt almost beyond enduring but

here at last was vengeance within their power. Two white men, unarmed and at their mercy, one of them easily recognisable as the very
same pakeha with a tattooed face who had passed himself off as a
Maori and whom they suspected of spiriting away their white
prisoners and betraying them to the Red Garment. Samuel had once
seen hounds closing in upon a hare and had sickened at the sight.
Now he and his friend were as defenceless. More defenceless, because the hunters were human and to the blood lust of an animal
body was added the demoniac madness of the spirit's hatred.

No, he was wrong. Not more defenceless, but less, because the
hunted also were human, and the man beside him had a reserve of
spiritual force immeasurably stronger than the squandered frenzy all
about him. Samuel found himself trembling, not with fear but with
astonishment at what had happened. For with the inhuman distorted faces as close to his own as faces in a nightmare, with the
stench of unwashed bodies and foul wounds nearly choking him and
the gleam of weapons a brightness of death in the air, there was a
sudden pause. A way had been made into the core of quiet at the
heart of the cyclone by the sheer power of a man's goodwill. Tai
Haruru was speaking now, slowly and persuasively, swinging his
pack off his back and showing the Maoris the bandages and salves
he had within it. Though he could not always follow the words
Samuel could sense the passion of pity that ached in them, could see
how it ate its way into the surrounding filth of hatred, cathartic, inexorable, destroying to create. But this was not pity only, that
smacks of contempt, nor kindness only that looks no further than
the passing moment, it was goodwill, love stripped of mawkishness
and sentiment and lust down to the bare naked steel of action that
sticks at nothing and pays any price. He doubted if he had ever seen
this weapon put to quite such powerful use before. If he could wield
it so perfectly, himself, just once before he died, he thought that he
would die happy.

The crowd was suddenly in movement and they were being carried
along towards the far end of the village, led by a tall Maori with
many feathers stuck in the hair above the bandage tied round his
head, and fine weapons strung about him. He was the war chief,
Samuel guessed, and it came to him that they were to be put to the
test. If they won the first round they would be permitted to live.

They came to a house a little larger than the others and went in, as
many of the Maoris as possible pressing in after them. On a bed of
rushes lay a young boy of fifteen or sixteen, the chief's son. A wound
in his arm had become infected. The arm was swollen to three times
its normal size and was of a terrible greenish hue. The boy was

unconscious, lying with eyes half closed and lips drawn back from his teeth. After one glance at him Samuel's heart sank.

It was evident that the Maori people had themselves given up hope, for the scene was set for a spectacular dying. The boy was covered with a fine blanket and at his right side lay his spear, musket and tomahawk. At his left side lay his red war belt and over his head hung his greenstone mere. Young though he was he would pass to Reinga as a true Tua, killed in battle, bearing his weapons with him. Around the bed, upon the rush-strewn floor, sat sobbing women, and at the foot of it stood an emaciated savage with fanatical deep-set eyes that blazed with hatred at sight of Tai Haruru. He was the Tohunga, the village priest whose prayers and incantations had not availed to heal the boy's wound.

Tai Haruru issued his orders. Part of the roof must be removed to give more light and air. A fire must be lit and a cauldron of water set to boil over it. The wailing women must cease their noise instantly, go away to another house and prepare nourishing soup to be given to young Tiki upon his awaking. All must go away, yes, even the Tohunga; he and his friend must be alone while they called back the spirit of Tiki, already nearly departed, to inhabit his body again. The words were repeated by the boy's father and obeyed by all but the Tohunga, who lingered till the last moment, muttering under his breath. Urged towards the door by Tai Haruru he swung round, threw up his arms and screamed aloud, "Kai kotahi ki te ao! Kai kotahi ki te ao! Kai kotahi ki te po!" while all the people outside broke into a hopeless wailing; for these were the words always cried aloud by the priest at the approach of death.

"Be silent!" said Tai Haruru, and seizing the Tohunga by the shoulders he summarily put him forth. Then taking the blanket that covered young Tiki he hung it over the door. "Now," he said angrily to Samuel, "do exactly as I tell you and you also be silent. It is you chattering priests who kill all the patients and drive the doctors mad."

Samuel, whom ignorance of the language had kept entirely silent throughout the proceedings, swallowed this insult to the priesthood in a further silence, rolled up his sleeves and stiffened his nerves for the coming ordeal.

He was sensitive and fastidious, possessed of an instinctive repulsion from the ills of the body, and he found it a greater ordeal even than he had expected. His knees seemed to turn to water as Tai Haruru's knife incised the boy's poisoned flesh, and the oozing out of the evil-smelling viscous fluid sickened him nearly to nausea. Yet he held the limb steady for Tai Haruru and handed him what he needed without faltering. When the operation was over and the limb bandaged the two men smiled at each other. "Well done, little parson," said Tai Haruru. "Now, if you like, you may pray."

He seemed confident but to Samuel the figure lying on the bed in the pool of brilliant light seemed now scarcely more than a wraith. It was as though the sun were slowly absorbing the boy's being into itself, and leaving only the mortal shadow of its immortality lying on the bed. Samuel fell on his knees and prayed. It meant so much that young Tiki should recover. It meant not only the life of himself and Tai Haruru, which was a small matter, but the salvation of the whole village. . . . Or so Samuel believed. . . . He prayed with a great intensity, only vaguely aware of Tai Haruru moving deftly about his doctor's business, coaxing soup between the boy's lips, wrapping him warmly in blankets, placing stones heated at the fire and wrapped in rag against his feet. He was hardly aware either of the fading of the sunshine and the coming of the night, and only came to himself when Tai Haruru shook him roughly by the shoulder and put a bowl of hot soup into his hands.

"Wet your whistle with that," said the older man kindly. "You must be ravenous after so much entreating of Almighty God. And the battle has only just begun."

He turned away and lit the lantern, then sat down by the bed and took the boy's hands between his own, speaking to him softly in his own language. Tiki was stirring and muttering occasionally now, and Samuel had the feeling that he was trying to go free, pulling against the hands that kept him. Sometimes Tai Haruru took the boy's body between his hands, sometimes he gently laid them on the head and breast. He had spoken with contempt of the Tohunga, but it occurred to Samuel that though his skill with the knife had been equal to that of any trained surgeon his present manner of healing was more analogous to Tohunga methods than to those of modern science. What was this power that he had in his hands? It struck Samuel as being all of a piece with that primeval earthy quality of the man, and yet at the same time to be a power that was of God. Had all men at one time had this power of compelling the body through the spirit? Perhaps they had, far back in that lost age when conflict had not been born, when man had neither rebelled against God nor lifted his hand against his brother, nor slain the animals to be his food, when the worshippers of God the Father and earth the mother had not been two men, like himself and Tai Haruru, but one man, Adam. So he thought, drawn towards his friend as he had always been since the first day he had seen him, fumbling towards the lost principle of co-ordination that if found again would bring back Paradise to earth. He prayed once more, striving through union with God for a one-ness with his friend that should make them again one man with the power of two.

3

"Sunrise and all's well," said Tai Haruru, once more administering a shaking, and Samuel came to himself from the stupor of exhaustion into which he had fallen to find the sunlight shining through the roof again and Tiki sleeping as peacefully and healthfully as a child.

"Have I slept?" he asked. He had only the vaguest remembrance as to how he had lost consciousness last night, but he found himself now stretched out comfortably upon one rug and covered with another, and he scrambled to his feet with horror at his own laxity.

"Why not?" asked Tai Haruru, laughing. "You permitted yourself to be put to sleep as obediently as Tiki himself."

"And you yourself have not closed your eyes the whole night," cried Samuel in self-reproach.

"I'm no townsman," said Tai Haruru contemptuously, "accustomed to sleep and eat and pray and work at certain hours, and all at sixes and sevens when my routine's broken. I eat and sleep when it is convenient, as the animals do."

"All's well with the child?" asked Samuel.

"All's well with careful nursing," said Tai Haruru.

A shadow darkened the sunlight in the doorway. It was the chief, Hongi, with Tohunga beside him and the villagers behind at a respectful distance.

"Enter Hongi only," said Tai Haruru.

Hongi entered and stood at the foot of the bed looking at the bandaged arm from which undoubtedly a devil had departed, for it was of a normal shape again, and at the boy's face from which the shadow of death had lifted. Then he strode out of the hut and cried to the assembled villagers that these pakehas were good pakehas, each was a tino tangata, a right good man, and should be treated accordingly. If Tai Haruru had sinned in the matter of the Red Garment his sin should be forgiven him, for he had repented of it, and he had healing in his hands.

Only the Tohunga, though he bowed to the pakehas and congratulated them volubly upon the success of their night's work, was without friendliness. Their mana was now high and his correspondingly weakened, and what does it profit a Tohunga if he gain the whole world if that mysterious and precious thing, his mana, is departed from him? Without it he is no Tohunga, for he is without reverence, honour or authority. His eyes were blazing with hatred as he turned away after his courteous speech, and Samuel shivered.

When he had told the good news Hongi returned to the hut again and sat down cross-legged to feast his eyes upon the healthful sleep of his son. What could he do, he asked, to reward the pakehas? He was a poor man now, his other sons and his wife had been slain in the battle, his pigs had fled into the forest, his young daughters likewise—though their loss was less severe than that of the pigs—so that he could neither entertain the pakehas, nor feast them, nor give them his daughters to wife. Yet reward the pakehas must have, for they had saved the life of his only remaining child.

"Where are Kapua-Manga, Jacky Poto and Hine-Moa?" demanded Tai Haruru.

Hongi looked vague, and Tai Haruru repeated the question.

Hongi said he had never heard of them.

"If you think that they gave any assistance to the Red Garment you misjudge them," said Tai Haruru. "Their loyalty to their tribe was unblemished. I, Tai Haruru, am a magician who knows the hearts of men, and I know that this is true."

Hongi asked to be told who these loyal ones were, that honour might be done them?

"Your son Tiki is by no means recovered from his sickness," said Tai Haruru. "If he does not receive very careful nursing he may yet die. The woman Hine-Moa has much skill in nursing. If she is not here within the next ten minutes to assist me in my labours I and my friend the white Tohunga will leave the village and Tiki will die."

Hongi arose with slow graceful dignity and said he would enquire among his people if there were any woman of this name.

Five minutes later Hine-Moa stood in the doorway, a dish of steaming sweet potatoes in her hands. She was smiling, but tremulously, and her wrists had been chafed raw by the rope that had bound them until a moment ago. But a quick glance showed Tai Haruru that her breast had not been cut by the flints. She was not a widow.

"Kapua-Manga lives," he said with satisfaction. "Is he also now unbound?"

Hine-Moa nodded. "He is wounded but alive," she said. "Jacky Poto was killed by the big gun. But what is that to me? He was not my husband. Now that we are freed when Kapua-Manga is well again we will go back to our own village. We do not like it here. The potatoes are good. Eat them. The sun is warm and light a blessing to the eyes but there are many who will go down into darkness unless you aid them. Eat and come quickly."

CHAPTER THREE

1

Samuel was a man unaccustomed either to sparing himself or being spared, yet never had he lived at such full stretch as during the next few weeks.

He and Tai Haruru threw two huts into one and turned them into a hospital for the wounded. They sent the few able-bodied men left into the forest to round up the scattered pigs, for the village was near to starvation but had hardly had the heart even to dig potatoes, and they set the women to cooking savoury stews and washing bandages and making splints. A third hut became a crude operating theatre where Tai Haruru reigned supreme, and a fourth a dispensary where Samuel dealt with minor ailments such as cuts and bruises and sore eyes. Kapua-Manga was soon healed of his wound and he and Hine-Moa and their children went away to their own village. Tai Haruru was sorry to see them go, for not only was Hine-Moa a good nurse but they would have been staunch friends in adversity. Some of the wounded were in too desperate a case for even Tai Haruru's skill to save them, but Tiki recovered, and the percentage of recoveries was so high that the mana of the white men remained high also. For a short space the grateful village was theirs to do what they liked with. They moved as gods, but delicately, for they were well aware, both of them, that the worship of mortal men by other men lasts only until the first bad failure.

Tai Haruru, knowing this, worked untiringly, giving himself to the last ounce, but steadily and without distress, for his aim was merely the easing of pain as some reparation for the rocket gun that had been the cause of so much misery, and he had already done so much that at whatever moment the crash came he would feel that he had accomplished his object. But Samuel's purpose was so immense that he felt the constriction of the time like an iron band about him, goading him nearly to frenzy. He had to fight not pain and dirt and disease but that almost ineradicable human tendency to think in terms of finality. The spirit of worship was abroad in the village and he wanted somehow to teach these dusky children that what they were adoring, what all men loved when they worshipped a man dead or alive, was not the man himself, nor even his virtues, but the one God beyond of whom they told good news. When he and Tai Haruru crashed that must not be the end. He had to see to it that the good news would not be discredited together with the tellers of it. . . . And he was still speaking almost solely with the labour of his body and the dedication of his spirit, not with the words of his mouth, for he had discovered that he knew even less of the Maori language than he had imagined. How in the world was he to learn enough of it to preach salvation to these people? He had thought it would be easy to become proficient in a primitive tongue. It was not. The Maori language was an abominable language. Trying to get the gospel of Christ within it was like trying to force a man's foot into a child's boot. He went nearly distracted trying to master the outlandish and inadequate words, while meanwhile his unused Bible seemed to him to be burning a hole in his pocket, so red-hot was it with the passion to be put to use.

But something he could do, in the intervals of slaving in hospital and dispensary, he could build a Christian church. Near the Tohunga's house, flanked by its totems upon posts, with the head of the god Tumatauenga carved over the triangular lintel, was a deserted and half-ruined hut. This he repaired as well as he could, setting a cross over the lintel. Inside he placed a wooden table with his bible upon it, and he strewed the floor with fresh rushes. Twice a day, at sunrise and sunset, he knelt within his church in full view of the village, and prayed.

The village, still under the spell of the white men's skill and devotion, still needing their help, crowded round the door while he prayed and regarded his devotions with tolerant amusement. And when he rose from his knees and struggled to speak to them of his God they listened with the utmost courtesy, scarcely understanding a word of the gibberish he was making of their language but understanding their duty as hosts very well indeed. It was not they, Samuel knew, who under cover of darkness removed the cross. It was the Tohunga. But he said nothing to the Tohunga. He just made a second cross.

Tai Haruru argued fiercely with Samuel. "Let it alone," he commanded. "Tumatauenga is the Father of Men. Is he not as good a god as your god?"

"Tumatauenga is also the god of war," retorted Samuel. "While my God is the Prince of Peace."

"Worshipped by the Red Garment and its rocket gun," said Tai Haruru acidly. "Of the two I think I prefer Tumatauenga. He at least seems to have less trouble in bringing round his worshippers to his own way of thinking, and I like efficiency in gods. Don't fight the Tohunga, Kelly. He's dangerous."

"Error must be fought wherever it is perceived," said Samuel sententiously. "These children are in error when they worship their nature gods of wind and wood and water. These gods are merely the personification of their own longing to be one with the beauty of earth. They in their earthly bodies cannot pass into the grace of a kauri tree, or the majesty of wind or the splendour of the sea, but Tane-Mahuta can, Tawhiri-Matea can, and Tangaroa. When we rode through the forest together I understood for the first time why men make these nature spirits, these sprites and elves. Yet I have to teach these children that their gods are only man-made. I have to teach them the real meaning of their hunger and thirst."

"Any success?" asked Tai Haruru drily.

"Lack of even the likelihood of success in the performance of a divinely commanded task does not absolve a man from the duty of making the attempt," said the little parson with dignity. "The attempt is what God demands of man, the success follows as and when He pleases, and seems to bear little relation to human notions of it. And why this argument? We had a bargain. I was to let you alone and you were to let me alone. I have not only let you alone, I have helped you, while you are interfering with me in the most unpardonable manner."

Tai Haruru laughed, for Samuel's impressive pulpit manner always consorted most comically with his small physique. Then he was suddenly grave again. "I'm damned fond of you, Kelly," he said soberly. "And damned nervous of the Tohunga. Some of these Tohungas are fine men, genuine seers and prophets, but others are devils. There's a devilish side to the Maori religion, you know, Kelly. There always has been and lately, under our influence, it's got worse. Don't forget that when the first—so-called—Maori Christians were given bibles they lapped up the blood and thunder of the Old Testament like a cat lapping cream, but they made the New Testament into cartridges to shoot the white men with. They're like that —especially just lately."

"I know perfectly well," said Samuel, "that the Maori religion has to a certain extent been polluted, not cleansed, by the white man. That's partly why I'm here."

Tai Haruru shrugged his shoulders and turned away. It was little use to argue with Samuel, for the strength of the little parson's will was out of all proportion to the size of his body.

Samuel was not deceived when the Tohunga suddenly turned friendly, asking that they might speak together, assisting him in his care of the sick, bringing him dishes of carefully prepared food, joining Samuel's amused little congregation and listening to his halting sermons with the kindly condescension of a grown-up consenting for the moment only in the make-believe of a child. He could still sense the man's hatred, his wickedness. He knew that this friendliness was merely an attempt on the part of the Tohunga to win favour again with his own people, for the favour of his people was necessary if he was to destroy the white Tohunga without bringing harm upon himself. He was genuinely and fanatically jealous for his gods, as jealous as was Samuel for his God, but at the same time he was determined to come to no harm himself. And he was expert in avoiding unpleasantness, as only those can be who live their whole lives among bloodthirsty and courageous people. In only one thing had Samuel the advantage of the other; in this fight that had been forced upon him he cared very little what might happen to himself; he did not care nothing, for there was Susanna, and there was the natural shrinking of his human flesh from danger and pain, but he cared very little.

Yet he chose his weapons with care, mindful that upon the weapons used by his servants the king is judged. He set aside guile and caution and chose instead friendliness, courage, and a gentle patience foreign to his fiery nature, and that immense goodwill that he had seen in action when Tai Haruru had surmounted that first wave of hatred that had met them on arrival. . . . Only this hatred of the Tohunga's was much more subtle, much more difficult to counter, because it was running underground. His task was far more difficult than Tai Haruru's had been.

And so he invited the Tohunga to halting conversations beneath the trees, teaching him English at his request—which he picked up far more quickly than Samuel picked up the Maori tongue—expounding to him the Christian religion, welcoming him in his little dispensary and teaching him all that he knew about the white man's methods of healing. Most especially, remembering the Tohunga's failure with Tiki, did he teach him about the cleansing of wounds and the avoiding of tetanus. And he ate of the Tohunga's oily dishes, hiding his fear of poison, and instead of spending his nights with Tai Haruru in his little hospital he insisted on sleeping alone and unarmed in a lean-to hut at the side of his miniature church. . . . During sleepless nights he thought of Samuel Marsden, who on Christmas day had wrapped himself in his great coat and lain down to sleep among Maoris who had just massacred and devoured a whole ship's crew of white men. And of Bishop Selwyn, perhaps at this very moment travelling unarmed through the bush. And of Saint Paul enduring the stocks and the stoning and the beating. . . . Missionaries, he told himself, are always in good company.

2

He awoke suddenly one morning to find the Tohunga bending over him. Was this the end, he wondered? He lay still, steeling himself against the descent of the knife. But no, the Tohunga was merely awaking him with the news that some inexperienced young Tuas had been out after wild boar and two of them had been gored, and Tai Haruru required assistance at the hospital.

"We will go together," said Samuel.

He had slept late and he stepped out of his little hut into the fresh loveliness of a most brilliant morning. The snow-covered mountain peak, that from the first moment that he had set eyes upon it had symbolised for him some watchful and prayerful presence, was so dazzlingly lovely against the depth of blue beyond that for a moment he shielded his eyes. It had rained in the night and the leaves of the forest caught the early sunlight on their polished surfaces with such brilliance that each leaf seemed a tongue of flame. The chiming of bird song was all about him and the scent of flowers. This new-born delight in the beauty of the earth became suddenly so piercing an ecstasy that all his senses strained like hounds on the leash, reached an intensity of awareness that he had not thought possible, then checked and fell, leaving him stumbling forward over the grass shaken by an almost intolerable longing. Yet he thanked God that he had tasted of the love of earth. But for this journey with Tai Haruru he might never have seen the promise in her face.

They reached the hospital. One boy, Taketu, had only a slight flesh wound in the leg, but the other, Te Turi, was so seriously in-jured that Tai Haruru had taken to himself the deliberation of movement, the half smile, that were always his in moments of extreme danger. Both boys were relatives of the chief, well-born and of im-portance to the tribe. "I'll need you, Kelly," he said briefly.

Samuel told the Tohunga to take Taketu to the dispensary and care for his wound himself. "Your skill is as great as mine now," he said to his enemy with a courteous bow. And the Tohunga returned the bow with equal courtesy and went away with the boy.

It was a good hour before Tai Haruru had finished with Samuel and he was free to go to the dispensary. The Tohunga and the boy were still there and nothing had been done.

"He refused to let me touch him," said the Tohunga suavely. "Only in the white healers has he any trust."

"You should have trusted your Tohunga," said Samuel to Taketu.

The boy grinned and shook his head. "He bound up the arm of Tiki," he said, "and from his heart there flew a devil into the arm of Tiki, and swelled it up like a gourd. Had the white healers not come and slit the arm and let out the devil Tiki would have died."

"There was no devil in the arm of Tiki," said Samuel patiently, for the hundredth time. "It was merely that dirt got into the wound.

Wash your wounds, cleanse them well, and there will be no swelling."

"I have here the warm water and the antiseptics," said the Tohunga in a voice like silk. "All is ready for the white Tohunga."

He had prepared everything most carefully. Nothing was forgotten, not even the small dose of cordial in a medicine glass that Samuel sometimes administered at the end of a painful dressing. He had nothing to do but cleanse and bind up the wound. "In three days you will be well," he said to Taketu.

But three days later both boys were dead, Te Turi of his mortal wound and Taketu in an agony of pain that could not be accounted for. Both deaths had been shocking and distressing and the tribe had lost the two young men who, after Tiki, were their most promising Tuas. The funeral rites were inaugurated amid a wailing and grief that were deafening, and the two white men were forbidden to attend. The Tohunga was profuse in his apologies for this exclusion. "The people will have it so," he explained. "It seems that for the moment, for the moment only, they have lost their faith in the skill of the pakehas."

That night, when Samuel was alone in his little hut, courting a sleep that would not come, Tai Haruru came and sat in the doorway, leaning against the jamb, smoking his long pipe. Samuel lay and sniffed the strong pungent tobacco and looked at the eagle features, dark and clear cut against the moonlight outside, and was as comforted as a child who wakes from nightmare and finds his mother beside his bed.

"You've been a fool, Kelly " said Tai Haruru.

"You think that in caring for Taketu's wound I should not have used things prepared by the Tohunga?" asked Samuel humbly.

"You played straight into his hands," said Tai Haruru. "There was poison in the water, or the cordial, or both. What these Tohungas do not know about poison is not worth knowing."

"I am a great sinner," stated Samuel with grief.

"Sinner? Merely a fool."

"It is a sin to serve the most high God with foolishness."

"Then are all the saints steeped in sin," said Tai Haruru. "For I've never met a real downright good man yet who was not also a real downright god-damned fool." He sighed, but without bitterness. There was resignation, and even a hint of affectionate amusement, in his deep voice. He had evidently accepted the idiocy of good men as one of the facts of nature, like earthquake and flood. No use cursing it. Better to keep one's energies for dealing with the lamentable results of the phenomenon.

"You must get out of this, Kelly," he said. "To-night. The funeral rites will go on for another day, and to-morrow night the Tohunga will hold a spiritist séance and raise the ghosts of the dead boys to speak with the relatives. This Tohunga is especially gifted in the calling up of spirits and if he stages a really effective séance his mana will be sufficiently restored for him to consider administering one of his little potions to you without stirring up any resentment from the tribe. . . . But you'll be a couple of days journey away by that time. Have you your things packed? I've got your horse handy."

He turned to knock out his pipe, but Samuel checked him. "And you?" he asked him.

"I'll stay a while longer," said Tai Haruru. "I've not brought down upon myself the hatred of the Tohunga to the extent that you have, for I've not cast aspersions on his precious gods. And I know the Maoris. I can handle 'em, To quit now would be to do the mana of the white man no good at all. When I've restored it I'll go—eastward. No point in staying here indefinitely. My work's done."

"Which is more than can be said of mine," said Samuel.

Tai Haruru eyed him with benevolent exasperation, and then looked away to where the moonlight lit the distant snows. "After what has happened you've about as much chance of converting this village to Christianity as of removing that mountain and casting it into the sea," he said.

"We have had a conversation much like this before," Samuel reminded him. "Granted that what I am trying to do seems humanly impossible, nevertheless my work goes on until it is no longer possible for me even to make the attempt."

"Do you ever consider Susanna?" asked Tai Haruru suddenly.

Samuel flinched and was silent. "She is my wife," he said at last. "She is the complement of myself. If I fail in my duty she shares my shame."

"The complement of a murdered man is generally a heart-broken widow," said Tai Haruru angrily. "And I wish to God I'd never set eyes on you. I wish to God I'd never brought you here with me."

"I was under the impression that it was I who had brought you," Samuel reminded him drily.

Tai Haruru laughed. "So it was, little parson," he conceded. "Yet you'd scarcely have found your way here without me. You owe me a debt of gratitude and you're not the man to deny it. Will you repay me by the death of my friend?"

This was an aspect of the matter that Samuel had not yet considered, and he considered it, together with the picture of Susanna that Tai Haruru's remarks had conjured up.

"I will wait for another couple of days," he said, "and then I will give you my decision."

"You may wait a couple of days too long," Tai Haruru cautioned him.

"I will wait another couple of days," said Samuel with so gentle yet tough a stubbornness that Tai Haruru knew he had gained the utmost that would be conceded at present. He knocked out his pipe, took the Maori blanket that hung over his shoulder and spread it out on the ground beside Samuel. "At least I do not leave you while you consider of the matter," he said, and lay down on it.

Samuel opened his mouth to protest, then realised that he also was halted. The figure of Tai Haruru, stretched beside him, had taken to itself such a look of reposeful stolidity that it might have been made of iron. Nothing short of an earthquake would remove that figure from that doorway that night. . . . And in a moment the man was asleep.

Samuel remained awake, pondering that everlasting problem of the knights of God—how to forsake all and follow Christ without bringing too much desolation upon friends and relatives. "He that loveth father or mother more than me is not worthy of me." Yes. But on the other hand, "Son, behold thy mother." The chief puzzle of life always had been, was, and always would be, the right striking of a balance.

In the end, though he prayed and pondered for an hour, he saw his way no further than that spiritist séance of to-morrow night. He must be there, of course. Recalling the witch of Endor he was convinced that the attempt to call up the dead was contrary to the will of God. He must therefore attend the séance and make his protest. He had no doubt whatever about that. Wherever the Christian warrior saw the command of God abrogated there must he take his stand and cry aloud. And unknown to Tai Haruru he had specifically been invited by the Tohunga to attend. "Come if you have the courage," had said the Tohunga, "and if the friendship which you have shown towards me was true friendship and not assumed. Upon your appearance or non-appearance will I judge your friendship." In other words, by his choice of weapons he had told good news of the nature of his God, and now he was invited to set the seal upon his statement—if he had the pluck. It was a challenge which could not be ignored. The séance was undoubtedly the next step; in all probability it would solve the problem of the one beyond; the next step had that habit. But how to evade the vigilance of Tai Haruru? He was aware that the sleep of the man by his side was not as deep as it looked. Trained to the wilds as he was he would be wide awake at the least hint of any unusual sound or movement. There was no hope whatever that he would remain asleep if Samuel attempted to step over his body to-morrow night. Astuteness would be necessary, and Samuel was not astute. He sighed deeply, then turned to see the first light of the dawn filtering reassuringly through the dark leaves of the forest. There is no more comforting sight in the whole universe than the renewal of the dawn. At sight of it he almost instantly fell asleep.

And the next day things happened with an inevitability that surprised him. It had so often been like that with him in his life—just when he had expected the carrying out of a resolve to be beset with difficulties the way became suddenly clear.

The day passed much as usual. No patients had attended the dispensary since the deaths of the two young Tuas, but there were still a few patients in the hospital who had not lost their faith in Tai Haruru's power to heal. He was busy with them most of the morning, while Samuel cleaned out his dispensary, as though he expected a flood of patients next day, prayed at the usual afternoon hour in his little church and preached to a congregation composed of two old women, five pigs, a nanny-goat and, for the first time, Tai Haruru. He had finished with his patients and was afraid to let Samuel out of his sight, for he had been told by an obstinately loyal Tiki that the Tohunga, who had some reputation as a soothsayer, had predicted that before the next day's dawning the Maori gods would have shown what they thought of the white Tohunga. "He will perish, and yet not perish," had said the Tohunga, making his prediction, like most Tohungas, in words of doubtful meaning, so that whatever happened he could scarcely be proved wrong.

The nanny-goat, the property of one of the old women, did Samuel great service. It lamented with many lamentations, and so did the old woman, making so much noise that Samuel was obliged to break off his discourse to ask what ailed them. With the help of Tai Haruru he made out that the goat had a kid, a piece of valuable property to the old woman, and that it had pulled its stake up out of the ground and wandered off into the forest. The old woman herself was too infirm to retrieve it, and the rest of the village too much engrossed in the still continuing funeral rites to do it for her.

"I will find your kid for you, Mother," Samuel assured her, and continued his discourse to a somewhat quieted congregation.

In the afternoon he set out to look for the kid, Tai Haruru dogging him like an obstinate shadow. "Looking for a kid in the primeval forest is like looking for a needle in a haystack," he said, laughing.

"The walk is a delight," said Samuel quietly, and then said no more, awed to silence by the majestic curtains of green shade that fell sheer about him, suspended from the blue ceiling of the world, motionless until the statuesque lines of the trees softened imperceptibly into the faint sway and rustle of the fern. And he was penitently conscious that he had only a little time left in which to worship beauty. He had left it very late. It was consoling to think that the loveliness of earth was in very truth a curtain. At death one stepped through it and worshipped afresh from the other side.

"We're travelling eastward," said Tai Haruru suddenly, after a long period during which they had spoken little but had enjoyed a comradeship as intimate as any either of them had ever known. "Odd. I chose no particular direction."

"You followed to-morrow's sun," said Samuel. "And so, apparently, did the kid."

They stood at the edge of a small dell carpeted with flowers, with a stream running through it. There was a break in the forest roof above, for the curtains of green shadow stayed themselves upon the edge of the dell, giving free passage to the sunlight that poured down from above, lighting to a pearly whiteness the body of the little kid lying among the flowers beside the stream. It had caught one hoof in a twisted root and was bleating pitifully.

It was the first time in his life that Tai Haruru had not gone quickly to the aid of a creature in distress. He stayed where he was, in the shadows that surrounded the dell, and watched the other man perform the office that was usually his. For the life of him he could not have moved. He was oddly shaken as he watched Samuel go down through the sunlight to the stream, kneel among the flowers and gently free the small hoof, lift the kid to his shoulder and turn back again, his figure bent over by the weight as he toiled up the steep side of the dell. The exquisite circle of flowery brightness, the bent figure, awoke in Tai Haruru confused memories of a lost childhood. . . . Waters of comfort. . . . The lost sheep. . . . The good shepherd. . . . Lovers, living together through long years, sometimes grow to resemble each other. . . . Samuel Kelly seemed to Tai Haruru something more than a man as he toiled up the side of the dell.

Yet when he had left the halo of light and was once more beside his friend under the trees he was merely a comic figure of a little man, panting and perspiring beneath a load too heavy for him.

"Give the little fellow to me," said Tai Haruru, and transferred the kid to his own shoulders. It had bleated and struggled a little in Samuel's inexpert grasp but with Tai Haruru it lay still, and as they walked back through the forest he caressed it now and then.

"You've a way with wild creatures," said Samuel, watching him.

"I take no credit for it," said Tai Haruru. "My hands seem not my own at times."

Samuel smiled but said nothing. He was too weary for speech. He was unaccustomed to walking in the sub-tropical forest and impeded as he was by his lame leg it was all he could do to drag himself along. They had come much further than they had realised and when they drew near to the village again it was quite dark.

"The recovery of the kid may restore your lost mana," said Tai Haruru. "We found it with the help of your powers of divination, of course, not through a sheer fluke. You'll remember that, won't you?"

But Samuel was not attending to him. "Is the village on fire?" he asked. There was a smell of smoke in the gloom, and a fitful light showing between the trunks of the trees.

Tai Haruru stopped, then strode quickly forward, Samuel following him. But it was not the village, it was only Samuel's little church and dispensary. When he saw the fire a chill of sadness took hold of him, for it was as though his own hopes were going up in smoke and flame. Then he passed from sadness to passive acceptance. It was just the next thing, and he must make use of it.

But there was no passivity about Tai Haruru. He was taken hold of by a fury such as had not visited him for years, and he was nearer hating his beloved Maoris than he had ever been. Couldn't they have left the harmless little man's harmless little church alone? What had he ever done to them but good? Surely it needed only a rudimentary intelligence to lay the blame of Taketu's death where it belonged—at the Tohunga's door? They were fools and worse and he'd teach them a lesson they'd not forget in a hurry.

"Here, take the kid," he said to Samuel, heaving it back to the little man's shoulder. "Take it to the old dame and then stay in her hut with her, out of harm's way."

Then he ran towards the blazing church, and the Maoris who were dancing and yelling and gesticulating round it. The flames were licking up the walls but they had not yet reached the wooden cross over the lintel. The cross meant nothing to him but it meant a great deal to Samuel. Careless of the fire he leaped and pulled it down, then jumped back, scorched and singed by the flames, to tell his Maoris what he thought of them, and his bellowings of rage were like the bellowings of waves crashing on the rocks. "Sounding Sea!" they cried out in fear when they saw him. They were many and he was one but yet they were afraid of him. A pole supporting a totem was not far from the burning hut, and Tai Haruru wrenched it out of the ground as though he had the strength of ten men and laid about him with all his strength. He did not care how many crowns he broke.

Then a deeper cry of alarm arose. Some flying sparks had lit the thatch of the chief's house. Now the village was alight in good earnest.

CHAPTER FOUR

1

Samuel thrust the kid through the doorway of the old dame's hut and without waiting for her thanks walked away from the village, down the path that Marianne and the others had followed when they fled from the Pa to the Torere. It was at the foot of the great rock that contained the Torere that the spirits of the dead were to be conjured up at nightfall, and it was that now. The curtains of green were now curtains of ebony and silver-grey, with broken blue lights overhead. The sound of the tumult in the village died away as he went forward and he heard instead the rustle of the night wind in the trees. He had no fears for Tai Haruru, for the man had great power to dominate his surroundings and the Maoris left behind in the village were not those who had been embittered by the deaths of the two young Tuas—those were ahead of him at the foot of the great rock—but he had great fear for himself, that he might not set down the seal upon that statement as he should. The Tohunga had invited him to set the seal "if he had the courage", and he was more physically afraid than he had known it was possible to be. Physical fear had never been one of his disabilities, and he was therefore all the more horrified and shamed by the exhibition he was making of himself as he walked along the path. For the sweat was pouring off him and he was panting like a scared rabbit. His mouth was so dry that he could scarcely swallow and his knees seemed folding up beneath him, as though they were no longer a part of his body. Just fear? Just animal, craven fear, but it brought him at last to a standstill. He stopped dead upon the path, physically unable to go on. He could do no good in this condition, he told himself confusedly. He would bring shame, not honour, upon the cause of his Master. Better turn back, take Tai Haruru's advice and return to Wellington. He owed it to Susanna. And he had useful work to do in Wellington. Far better to continue a useful ministry there than to die in the wilds a death by torture that would do not the slightest good to a single living soul. He turned round, his face to the village again, stumbled a few steps, tripped over a root in the path and fell headlong.

The shock of the fall, coming upon him when his body was so wrenched by fear, stunned him for a few moments. As he came to himself again he unconsciously pulled himself up a little, so that he was crouching forward on his knees. The chance attitude, and the instant mechanical response of his mind to that attitude, saved him. For years he had been kneeling to pray, for years twilight and the murmuring of the night wind in the trees had brought certain words to his mind. He said them out loud now, not of intention but as a mere reflex action of the muscles of throat and tongue. "If this cup may not pass away from me except I drink it, thy will be done."

Yet he heard the words and slowly and inexorably they dragged him to his feet and turned him about on the path again. He went stumbling on as before, in the same despicable condition, incapable of reasoned thought or action, merely blindly obeying an example.

Yet as the path rose steeply towards the great cliff where the Torere was hidden he found that his physical distress was lessening. In spite of the slope of the hill he could breathe more easily and his body felt co-ordinated once again. He had the sensation that he was not alone, that some unknown prayer sustained him, and the sense of companionship brought its corollary of a sense of doubled strength. Presently, as he climbed over the boulders that were beginning to appear in the path, he was smiling. He was thinking to himself that if it were to be his lot to join the company of the martyrs he would have to slink in at the very tail end of the procession, for he would be a martyr not from choice but because he had tripped over the root of a tree. It was a humiliating thought, and made his smile exceedingly rueful. And if nothing untoward happened at the séance to-night, if it were a mere anti-climax, as it very well might be, then he would have to carry with him for the rest of his life the memory of the exhibition he had made of himself. He blushed hotly in the darkness. He was aware that the fanatical fire of his lifelong service of God and man had not been without a certain arrogance. He had been proud of it. But now—whatever happened to-night he would have to walk softly through time and eternity.

2

There was a flat space among the trees to the right of the rock staircase that led up to the Torere, and here a group of dusky figures were gathered about a fire. The men were gravely leaning on their spears, the women a little withdrawn from them in a group together. The Tohunga stood in the full light of the fire. He was still and silent, his eyes hooded, but his tall figure was full of a majestic brooding power that was echoed by the great rock towering up out of sight behind him. The broken blue lights overhead were dimmed now, and outside the circle of the firelight there was darkness, for moonrise was still an hour away. There was no sound except the wind in the trees and the sobbing of the young girl who had been betrothed to Taketu. Awe, not contempt, took hold of Samuel, and it was almost with reverence that he moved forward and joined the group of silent men leaning on their spears. They saw him but made no movement. The women saw him but gave no sign; except that the weeping girl gave one sharp cry of anguish. The Tohunga lifted his heavy eyelids and his dark eyes rested on the white man's face, but his rigid body did not move.

"Have you come to mock at us, oh murderer of Taketu?" he asked him in a low yet clear voice, articulating carefully so that Samuel should understand him.

Samuel lifted his head and spoke out clearly in the Maori language the words that he had carefully prepared. "I have come, but not to mock at you, oh Tohunga. I come in friendship. I grieve for the death of your Tuas and I am not the murderer of Taketu. I loved Taketu and served him to the best of my power, as I have served you all. I have come not to mock but to tell you that this which you are about to do is sin. It is forbidden by the one true God, whose gospel I have preached to you, that men should attempt to call back the spirits of the dead. The spirits of the dead are in the keeping of God, infinitely cared for by His love, and can commune with us only as and when He wills, not as and when we will."

He had expected an outcry but there was none. All the people remained still and the Tohunga continued to speak quietly.

"We will put that to the proof, oh murderer of Taketu," he said. "If I fail to call up the spirits of the dead to speak with us then am I and my gods discredited, if I succeed then you and your God will be cast out from among us. Shall we put it to the proof, all you here who loved Taketu and Te Turi?"

There was a low murmur of assent from the people.

"I declare to you all," cried out Samuel, "that if voices are heard speaking they will not be the voices of the young Tuas."

"Be silent!" cried the Tohunga. "Be silent now, all of you, while in silence I call upon the spirits of Taketu and Te Turi."

He drew back from the circle of firelight into the shadow of the great rock, so that they could no longer see him, and there was at once a silence so heavily laden with emotion, with grief and awe, terror and expectancy, that the weight of it was hardly to be borne. Moving a little to ease the burden of it Samuel suddenly became aware of Tiki standing among the men and regarding him intently and sorrowfully. He and Tiki had been good friends during and after the boy's illness, but since the death of Taketu, who had been Tiki's greatest friend, the boy had avoided him. He realised that Tiki did not know what to believe about the white Tohunga. Tonight would decide that question for him.

"Salutation! Salutation to my family and my friends. I, Te Turi, killed by the wild boar in the forest, salute you. Salutation!"

Samuel felt his knees folding up beneath him again, and the palms of his hands were wet. For the voice crying out in the darkness was Te Turi's voice, a boy's treble cracking suddenly into a man's bass, as Te Turi's had done, not beautiful but infinitely moving. Sighing and movement broke the unnatural stillness and silence of the listeners. They lamented and rocked themselves in their sorrow like reeds with the wind blowing over them, and one woman, Te Turi's mother, held out her arms towards the voice. "Is it well with you, my son?" she asked. "Is it well with you in that far country?" The infinite longing and tenderness in her voice brought the tears pricking behind Samuel's eyelids, and looking about him at the firelit faces he did not see one that was not wet. Never in all his life had he attended a ceremony as moving as this. And he was not conscious of any taint of evil in it. He was not even conscious of any deception. Hypnotised by the voice crying out of the darkness, by the love and sorrow of the Maori people all about him, he was very near to a faith as great as their own.

"It is well with me," cried the boy's voice, a little fainter now, as though he were leaving them. "I fought bravely with the boar and for the brave there is honour in Reinga. Yet it is lonely there. I sigh for my mother's arms and the laughter of my friends. It is lonely in Reinga. Farewell. Farewell. It is lonely in Reinga. Farewell."

The voice was dying away all the time, as though carried by the wind. The last farewell was no more than an echo in the woods. The weeping of the Maoris was held in so low a key by their awe that it too seemed no more than a timeless echo of the weeping of all time, so low that the Tohunga's broken exhausted voice could be heard clearly above it.

"I could hold him no longer. His spirit is not chained to this world by the bands of sin, his own or another's. He is free, laying upon us no duty to perform for him, either of restitution or revenge."

Samuel had not been able to follow these sentences of the Tohunga, spoken so brokenly, but he realised that the last word had fallen upon the overcharged hearts about him like a spark upon stubble. The whole atmosphere was abruptly changed. A man laughed loudly and harshly, in rather horrible reaction from past emotion. The tenderness was lost in a sense of excitement, that mounting excitement that cannot be checked but must spend itself in violent action.

"Taketu! Taketu! Taketu!"

It was the girl who had been betrothed to him who was screaming out his name in that horrible fashion. Looking at her Samuel saw that she was beside herself and that two men were holding her arms to restrain her.

"Be silent!" cried the Tohunga. "Be silent while I call upon the spirit of Taketu."

And the heavy nightmare silence came again, but this time Samuel was conscious of a stirring of evil in its depths. It did not so much press upon him this time as pluck at his nerves so that his limbs jerked as though he were a marionette upon strings. This too was fear but not the same kind of fear as had assailed him down in the valley. He was not panicky this time, but most acutely aware.

"Salutation! Are you there, my friends? Salutation!"

Taketu had been older than Te Turi and the voice was the full clear bass of a young man in the prime of life. It spoke with passion, and a violence that awoke answering violence in the lamentations of the listeners. It seemed a long time to Samuel until the hubbub subsided and the terrible young voice took up the tale in the darkness.

"Are you there, my family and tribe? Are you there, my white blossom, the beloved of my heart? Are you there, Tiki, my friend?"

"We are here," cried out the girl who had been betrothed to Taketu, straining against the hands that held her. "We are here, Taketu. Is it well with you, Taketu?"

"No, it is not well with me in Reinga, my friends, it is not well. I am bereft of my beloved, and Tiki, my friend, has not revenged my blood."

The hubbub rose and fell once again.

"Who killed you, Taketu?" asked Tiki.

"The white Tohunga killed me. The white Tohunga. Kill the white Tohunga, Tiki, and then shall my soul have rest. My tribe, my family, my beloved, kill the white Tohunga!" The voice rose passionately, then quite suddenly broke, becoming the voice of a ventriloquist. "Revenge me and set me free, Tiki. Kill the white Tohunga." Then the voice was Taketu's once more, dying away through the trees. "Farewell! It is lonely in Reinga. There is weeping in Reinga for the unavenged. Farewell. Farewell."

The Tohunga's failure had been only momentary. He had recovered himself so quickly that only Samuel had noticed it. He gave thanks that the latest onslaught of fear had not deadened but increased perception. For now he knew. The whole thing had been a most brilliant imposture. A cold contempt took hold of him and his body was quiet again. . . . He at least took his stand upon the truth.

The séance ended and bedlam broke loose. The Tohunga came forward again into the circle of light, no longer an awe-inspiring figure but a weary man drained of strength by the effort he had made, incapable even had he wished it of controlling the uproar he had aroused. The whole scene became to Samuel simply devilish. The genuine faith and devotion that had made the beginning of the ceremony so moving were submerged now beneath a primitive savagery. These séances almost always ended, he had been told, with the shedding of blood, usually the suicide of near relatives of the dead, but though he could not understand what they said, the demeanour of the yelling mob about him made him quite sure that this time the necessity for revenge was providing them with all that was needed in the way of human sacrifice. Well, if his presence here had saved Te Turi's mother and Taketu's betrothed that was two more lives salvaged by himself and Tai Haruru. He wished they were not making so much noise. Though he had so often spoken to them of the love of God he felt now that he had spoken always with hopeless inadequacy; he would have liked a last chance to speak again, but the uproar was too great. All he could do was to hold out his hands with courtesy to the men who came to bind them, and when they struck him he prayed for them and tried not to flinch.

Tiki stood apart with the Tohunga and a few of the leading Tuas, and it seemed to Samuel that they were arguing as to the way of his death. Tiki's young face was resolved but deeply troubled. His friend Taketu had appointed him the avenger of his death and he would not shrink from the sacred duty, but the white Tohunga had cared for him in his sickness and so his duty was not much to his taste. Just once their eyes met and Samuel smiled. After that Tiki took very good care that their eyes should not meet again.

It was clear that Tiki was not in agreement with the other Maoris as to the most desirable method of revenge. Samuel tried not to let himself think what the alternatives might be. He tried not to think at all beyond the right response to the pain of each moment as it came.

Then Tiki seemed to lose his temper. He jumped on a rock, shouting and gesticulating furiously, the word Taketu coming again and again in his speech, together with an angry questioning note. Samuel guessed what he was saying. If Taketu had appointed him his avenger had he not the right of choice? Quite suddenly he seemed to win his point. He jumped down from his rock, pushed his way through the Maoris, came to Samuel and with averted face took hold of the end of the thong that bound his hands. Immense relief flooded Samuel. Tiki would give him a clean death. He would not be put to a test beyond his power to sustain.

3

He had expected to be put against a tree trunk and shot and it was a surprise to find himself being dragged up a steep rocky path that wound up the cliff face. To the cat-footed Maoris the climb was easy but the lame Samuel found it arduous. "Free my hands," he said to Tiki. "I can climb more easily then. I shall not try to escape."

There was a howl of protest from the other Maoris when Tiki did so, but he shot venomous words at them over his shoulder and they did not protest again.

In halting breathless sentences Samuel tried to talk to Tiki as they climbed. "I did not kill Taketu, Tiki," he said.

"Then whom do you accuse?" asked Tiki savagely.

"I accuse no one," said Samuel gently. "But I tell you again it was not I who killed Taketu. The God whom I serve is not a destroyer of life, like your Tu, but the preserver of it, and His servants do not kill. My God is Creator, Saviour, Comforter and Strengthener. He made men, He loves them, He died for them, He saves those who believe on Him from the power of evil, from the devils, from sin and disease. He comforts them in sorrow and makes them so strong in death that they cannot be held by its bands and pass with gladness into the world beyond." He stopped, breathless, doubtful if Tiki had listened to a word, yet driven to go on by the fact that what he had wanted, that last chance to speak again, had been given to him, even if his audience was only this one inattentive boy. "Our heaven is not as your Reinga," he went on, "a land of exile and loneliness where your gods give you no comfort. We go there not weeping but rejoicing because we shall there be in the presence of a God so glorious that the torture and death of the body are a small price to pay that we may see His face and serve Him for ever in the spirit land."

"Mighty words," said Tiki contemptuously. "Mighty like the wind. And I know that only Tuas show no fear when they die. Men of peace show fear. For all your wind of words you will be afraid."

"Because I die for the God who died for me I shall not be afraid," said Samuel. "Because of my death you will ask yourself, 'Who is this God that men should die thus for Him?' And you will remember what I have taught you about my God, and you will seek out other men who will teach you more. You Maoris do not die for the honour of your gods, Tiki, because your gods have never died for you. Death tests love, and the love that stands the test is the greatest treasure in the world. With such a love does my God love me, and I possess His love, and with such a love do I love Him."

Tiki grunted and Samuel's halting sentences failed him altogether, for they had entered the steep gully in the rock that led directly up to the Torere, and he had no breath. He was not altogether sorry, for what was the use of saying anything when his words were so paltry and his hearer so inattentive? Tiki moved behind him, for they could climb now only in single file. The moon had risen and it was almost as bright as daylight. Some half dozen of the Maoris were climbing in front of Samuel and the rest were behind Tiki. His world narrowed to the chimney of rock where he was and all his energy and thought were concentrated on the effort to get up it.

They reached the ledge of rock before the entrance to the cave and instantly the Maoris began to wail and lament. Samuel guessed that this was the Torere and that the bodies of Te Turi and Taketu were now within it. The Maoris shunned the Toreres, he knew, and he was not surprised when a gust of superstitious fear carried them all past it as though they were a handful of bronzed Autumn leaves before the wind. Then they were climbing again, up the sheer rock face this time, and Samuel was terrified lest he should not be able to get up it, and his physical failure be mistaken by Tiki for the terror shown in the face of death by men of peace. Tiki's eyes scarcely ever left him now, he knew. He could feel the boy's whole consciousness focussed upon him as though he were some midge of a creature pinned down beneath the microscope. And not only Tiki's consciousness. The boy's eyes were like a focal point of vision that widened out into a blaze of light that enveloped the whole of existence. All that ever was, that ever would be, watched through Tiki's eyes. He knew then, if he had not known before, the ultimate importance of one human soul.

Just when he thought that he was beaten, that he could drag himself up the rock for not one inch further, his physical ordeal ended and he stumbled out into what seemed to him, in his dazed condition, the anteroom of heaven. Had he died already? Had he died climbing the rock? No. The pain of wrenched limbs and panting breath told him that he was still in this world, but that mother earth, whose beauty he had delayed to acknowledge and worship almost until his last breath, was being merciful to him.

He was standing in the full moonlight in the centre of that small and beautiful amphitheatre in the rocky hillside where Hine-Moa had made a resting place for her white folk. Now, as then, it was carpeted with grass and flowers, and wind-tossed mountain larches bent over from the forest of them that climbed the hillside above, but now the brightest of bright moons gave to its beauty an un-earthliness that hushed even the Maoris to a motionless silence. Each flower petal was like a sea-shell of mother-of-pearl, each veined leaf a tiny sword of silver. The larch trunks were polished ivory be-neath the weightless, cloud-like canopies of shimmering leaves that they lifted up and up, higher and higher on the hillside, until at last the brightness of them was lost in the brightness of moonlit snow. That mountain that Samuel loved seemed very close now, towering up into the sky with the stars motionless about its head. He looked his last at it, then turned and looked out over the forest far down at the foot of the precipice that they had lately climbed, so far away that it was like a silvery shroud spread upon the floor of the world. Down there beneath it birds nested and animals had their lairs, men hunted, women built hearthfires and little children played. But for him these familiar things were past and over, muffled away beneath a shroud. The stillness was like ice, benumbing him, and there came to him suddenly the feeling that everything was slipping away. Noth-ing moved and yet everything was leaving him. He was on the brink of an awful darkness, the kind that children dread, that unknown darkness that is on the other side of a drawn curtain in a lighted room. He would be in it soon, with everything familiar left behind on the wrong side of the curtain. All in a moment his adoration of earth's beauty was lost in sickening fear, the last fear of all, and the worst.

Then that too passed and he knew that between the moment when he had staggered out into this lovely place, and the moment that the icy fear let go of him, had ticked away not an hour but only a minute of clock time. It had seemed a lifetime but it had only been sixty seconds. He straightened himself and looked round at the Maoris, smiling. They were closing in upon him, very watchful. He was vaguely aware of the Tohunga, not quite satisfied with the turn that things were taking, and vividly aware of Tiki, whose eyes were never off him for a moment. He knew why the Tohunga was not satisfied. . . . . He had not failed yet. . . . He had shown no fear when things went against him at the séance, he had managed to climb up the precipice without assistance, though it had been a hard test of endur-ance for a man weakened by the long strain of the night's uncer-tainty, he could smile as they closed in upon him. But the thoughts of the Tohunga were nothing to him. It was Tiki who mattered.

At a signal from the Tohunga two of the Maoris sprang, lithe as panthers, and dragged him towards the edge of the precipice. He knew now what they were going to do with him. They were going to hurl him over. Tiki had chosen for him a merciful death, as deaths go, yet from the Maori point of view full of poetic justice, for as he hurtled down his body would fall past the opening of the cave where Taketu lay buried.

"Let go!" he cried to the men who were dragging him forward. "You need not throw me over like an animal. For the glory of my God I'll jump without your help."

"Let go of him," commanded Tiki. "Let's see if he will do it."

They let go of him and he swung round to face them, though of the many eyes that watched him he was conscious only of Tiki's.

"The Maori people have given me hospitality, for which I thank them," he said. "And to you, Tiki, I owe my thanks for mercy in my death. You are tino tangata and I will not forget you."

Then with the eagerness of a young man going to his bridal, of a hunter on the trail or a Tua speeding to his first fight, commending his soul to God and his body to the keeping of earth, he ran and leaped and fell.

CHAPTER FIVE

1

Tai Haruru, mounted on his own horse and leading Samuel's, went angrily riding through the fern, facing not eastward but back towards Wellington again, back towards Susanna and the task of telling her what had happened during that hour when he had been labouring to put out the fire in the village. He had never faced a task he dreaded more but it was a duty that could not be avoided. When it was over then he would travel eastward; and in his fury he prayed heaven he might never set eyes on a Maori again. Eastward he would find some community of white folk, he hoped, practising some way of life that would be new to him, and throw in his lot with them. This was the second time in his life that he had abruptly left the Maori people, sickened by their cruelty. Only this time, he thought, he was done with them for good; treacherous, cruel, without ruth; he was done with them. He turned a deaf ear to the voice that said low in his mind that only one man had been truly treacherous and cruel, that the rest had been no worse than a pack of fearful, superstitious children, and that one, Tiki, had shown pity. Nor did he pay any attention to the thought that Samuel had rushed upon his death with a fanaticism that most men would have thought sheer madness. His mind would admit of no extenuating circumstances as it sat in judgment, for it could find no relief for its pain except in contemplation of two clear-cut pictures of black and white. He had loved Samuel Kelly and was at the stage of grief that can endure to admit no blemish in the beloved. The blacker he painted the figures of Samuel's murderers the more outlet had he for his hate and the more love-worthy shone the figure of his friend.

Love. Was he never to be done with it? Apparently not. He had escaped from Marianne only to become entangled with Samuel. Independence was a mirage that for ever eluded him. Marianne was in South Island by this time, Samuel was dead, yet they rode through the fern on either side of him, insistent with their claims. Marianne upon the one side claimed him for herself; he was hers, she insisted, had been, was, would be, even as she was his. Samuel upon the other claimed him for that faith in God which can admit of no finality. To Tai Haruru at this moment of riding through the fern there came a sudden intense awareness of just what Samuel had meant by that "no finality". In that moment he saw everything about him, every frond of green fern and every shaft of sunlight, as a voyager from the eternal creating Spirit, yet not parted from that Spirit because the life within it was as it were a thread of divinity, a gossamer life-line from Creator to creature that nothing in heaven or earth could ever break. Through whatever changes the creature might pass, changes to which man in his ignorance might give the name of death, the life-line still held and brought it back at last to the Creator's heart. He had been right to think that life was divine, wrong to think of it as an end in itself. He saw, as though the power of an unknown prayer had pulled a film from his eyes, and it seemed to him that somewhere walls crumbled and a trumpet sounded. "You've won," he said to the two riding beside him. "Your soul and mine, Marianne, have made a long journey, past many milestones of as many deaths, and the end of it is not yet even in sight. . . . Samuel, I believe in the Lord God Almighty, the Maker of heaven and earth."

He had unconsciously spoken the last words aloud, as though making a vow, and when the words had gone from him, not to be recalled, alive for ever, he swore under his breath. Now he had committed himself. Now he was done for. By what chains do parting and death bind the soul of a man. It was in parting that Marianne had revealed herself to him as the other half of himself, it was by dying that Samuel had dragged him to his knees. Had Samuel been with him in the body at this moment he doubted if he would have made that vow. There would have been no need, for he could have stretched out his hand and touched his friend, he would not have had to seek union with him by feeling through the darkness for the source of their mutual life, dragging himself back up the life-line to the place where their souls could meet. That much, at any rate, Samuel had accomplished by his death.

He had, as far as Tai Haruru had been able to see, captured the soul of not one single Maori. They had taken his death with indifference, and though they had cowered before the raging storm of the anger and pain of Tai Haruru the Sounding Sea they had not been broken by it. The success of their Tohunga in calling up the spirits of the dead had restored his mana. They still had a wholesome awe of Tai Haruru, and would not have molested him in any way, but he was no longer a god to them. . . . The white Tohunga's death had been a bad failure.

Yet an eye for an eye and a tooth for a tooth, and once they felt even with him over Taketu's death they had not been averse to cooperating pleasantly in his funeral. Tiki, in particular, had been definitely helpful. He had himself dug Samuel's grave in the spot chosen by Tai Haruru, the beautiful dell where the old woman's kid had been found, and breaking right away from the Maori tradition he had even touched the body and helped Tai Haruru carry it on a bier to the grave. The other Maoris had followed at a distance, and had not come further than the edge of the dell, but Tiki had stood beside Tai Haruru with bent head while he recited in his deep voice a queer form of burial service of his own concoction. He had found no prayer book among Samuel's possessions, only a worn Bible, and from this he had repeated the ninety-first psalm, directed to it by his remembrance of Samuel with the kid on his shoulder and by the stream running through the flowers and grasses. Then he had repeated the Maori words of dismissal:

"*Be one with the wide light, the Sun!*
With Night and Darkness, O be one, be one,"

followed by other words that he had repeated haltingly from memory, "Then shall the dust return to the earth as it was and the spirit shall return unto God who gave it." Even as he had repeated the two dismissals he had been startled by their likeness. . . . The soul drawn upwards to the Father of Light, the body folded within the dark robe of earth the mother. . . . Then with the Maoris still watching, he and Tiki had filled in the grave and at the head of it he had planted the wooden cross that he had rescued from Samuel's burning church.

Then turning to the Maoris he had delivered the customary speech

THE WORLD'S END

THE WORLD'S END

in praise of the dead. The white Tohunga had been a great and good man, he had told them, a man who had served his God and his fellow men to the death with love and passion. He had not killed Taketu. In a few weeks, when all the excitement had died away and they were once more able to put to use what little intelligence they possessed, they would know quite well who had killed Taketu. He himself would name no names, for the white Tohunga had never in life desired vengeance for the ill done to him, and in death as in life he had desired only to love and serve his enemies. This totem of the white Tohunga's, these two sticks crossed that had kept guard over his church and now kept guard over his body, was the symbol of love, and it must remain here marking the place of his grave for always. If any Maori dared remove it—and here Tai Haruru's eyes had flashed fire and he had bellowed at them even as he had bellowed on the night when he had snatched the cross from the flames—the spirit of the white Tohunga would do them no harm, for his spirit was compounded of love only, but he, Tai Haruru, would know wherever he was what they had done and curse them with all the curses at his command—and the curses at his command were very many.

After this somewhat fiery conclusion he had marched angrily back to the village, the funeral procession trailing meekly at his heels, and next morning had saddled his horse and Samuel's and ridden away. He'd done with the Maori people. He'd never have any dealings with a single one of them again.

There was a low call behind him and he stopped and turned round the saddle. It was the boy Tiki, running towards him through the fern, with his musket and mere poumanu slung over one shoulder and a blanket over the other. His tomahawk and cartridge box were fastened to his belt and there were many feathers in his head. He was, in fact, wearing all his earthly possessions. He was moving house. He ran up to Tai Haruru and laid his hand on his horse's neck. "I come with you," he said.

"No," said Tai Haruru sternly. "The Maori people have killed my friend. I ride with no Maori again."

"I come with you," said Tiki.

"No," said Tai Haruru. "Take your hand from my horse's neck."

Tiki removed his hand, ran round to the other side of Tai Haruru and vaulted lightly into the saddle of Samuel's horse. "I come with you," he said, and grinned.

"Get down off that horse!" thundered Tai Haruru.

"No," said Tiki. "The horse is my horse."

"That is the horse of my friend the white Tohunga, whom you killed," said Tai Haruru. "Get down."

Tiki grinned again. His face had not been tattooed yet. It was smooth and brown as an acorn, with childish contours, and his eyes were bright like a squirrel's. On his bare arm Tai Haruru could see the scar of the wound he had himself made when he extracted the poison, and his doctor's heart softened suddenly towards the life that he had saved. "Tiki! Tiki!" he cried in pain. "Why did you kill my friend?"

Tiki's bright eyes were hooded and he hung his head. "I thought Taketu commanded it," he said. "But if Taketu commanded it was without understanding. The white Tohunga did not kill him. Not so would the white Tohunga have died had he killed Taketu."

"I have not asked if the white Tohunga died with courage," said Tai Haruru. "I had no need to ask."

"Also with joy," said Tiki, "and for love of his God. Just so should I wish to die. Therefore from this day forward I serve the white man's God, and I will follow Tai Haruru the Sounding Sea because he is the friend of the white Tohunga."

"You will do nothing of the sort, Tiki," said Tai Haruru. "I am riding far away to a part of the country that is not your part of the country. Go back to your father's house. Return to your own people and your own gods."

"Entreat me not to leave you," said Tiki, his bright eyes lifted now to the older man's face. "Nor to return from following after you."

Tai Haruru looked into the boy's eyes, startled. Where had this conversation, or one like it, taken place before? Where had he heard it, or read it?

"I cleave to Tai Haruru, who healed my sickness," persisted Tiki. "Where he goes, I will go. His people shall be my people and his God mine. Where he dies I will die, and there will I be buried."

Tai Haruru lifted his hands and let them fall again on his horse's neck in a gesture of resignation. Though he could not place the strangely familiar words yet he recognised in them the authentic cry of love that could not be gainsaid. . . . So Samuel had captured the soul of a Maori after all. . . . Just one.

The boy and the man rode forward together through the fern.

2

It was drawing towards evening when they reached their journey's end. After leaving Wellington they had ridden eastward for days and nights and weeks. Tai Haruru was incredibly weary and the horses were almost foundering. Only Tiki was still fresh, bright-eyed as ever, the feathers in his head lighting up gaily where shafts of sunlight came like arrows through the great trees overhead and fell about them in showers of gold.

Yet though he was weary Tai Haruru was content, for at last he was among kauri trees again. They had traversed strange country on this journey, bare hills and swampy reed-fringed flats, brooded over by immense and lonely mountains. "The wilderness, a land that was not sown, a land that no man passed through and where no man dwelt." He was glad that he had seen it, glad of the vast star-filled skies that he had seen, stretching from horizon to horizon, their terrible splendour unsoftened by the tender veiling of the trees, glad of the strange blue lights of evening and the cold dawns stepping down from the mountain passes, glad of the hot mid-day silences when no bird sang, above all glad of the new meaning these things had for him now that there was no finality. Once, when Tiki had twisted his ankle and the power that was in his hands had healed the pain, he remembered that he had always felt that it was some power outside himself that took possession of his hands. He had looked up then at the sunlit snowdrifts that streaked a fabulous mountain upon the horizon, and smiled in comradeship. The mountain could no more take credit to itself for the glory that filled each hollow and crevice on its storm-riven side than he for his healing power. They flowed from the same source and like the incoming tide on a crescent seabeach brimmed the cupped hands of little children playing on the shore. In this childlike humility, this stricken silence, he had traversed the desert and been glad. As he had said to William, he was not too old for fresh discovery.

But it was good to have the kauri trees about him again. He had taken an immense journey, that authentic journey that lands spirit as well as body in a new country, and to see the kauri trees gave him a shock of enraptured yet almost incredulous surprise, as who should see the faces of familiar friends smiling from an unfamiliar shore. This, then, surely, must be journey's end. There thrilled all through his weary body that sense of relief that comes to a man when he hears the rattling of the hawser before the anchor drops.

But there was nothing to be seen yet except the dark ranks of the kauri trees and the falling arrows of sunlight lighting up Tiki's feathered head. Yet Tiki too was aware of the music of the hawser. He raised his head and sniffed.

"Smoke," he said, "woodsmoke." He sniffed again. "Smoke . . . and . . ." His eyes were suddenly bright with excitement. "Tai Haruru, there is that other smell, that great smell that we smelt at Wellington, like all the winds of heaven sweeping the rain from the sky. And there is a sound like thunder, only not angry like thunder. Tai Haruru, it is the sea again!"

Tai Haruru's woodsman's senses were quick but Tiki's were yet quicker. It was not until they had been riding for another ten minutes that he too smelt the woodsmoke and the salt smell of the sea, and heard through the murmuring of the branches overhead the thunder of surf on the shore. "You're right, Tiki," he said.

They rode on, Tiki's nostrils quivering like a rabbit's, for a whole medley of attractive smells, including roast pig, was now reaching him. "It is a kainga," he said.

Tai Haruru sighed. Had he escaped from one Maori tribe, and shaken the dust of their village from off his feet, and taken this immense journey of escape, only to find himself embroiled with another village and another tribe? Yet what exactly had he expected to find upon this eastern seashore? Some fabulous city built out of the clouds of sunrise by demigods? There were no such cities and no such demigods in this world, only smoke-stained friable habitations of wood and mud and reed, and equally friable human beings viewed from a new angle. That was the only really important change that could happen to a man in this world—the changing of his point of view. His weariness fell from him and he was suddenly as excited as Tiki. When he had left the other Maori village his vow had been unspoken, when he looked upon this new one it would be from the angle of eternity. Not since his boyhood had he felt such a sense of tingling expectancy.

The trees thinned out and the light strengthened. They drew rein and looked through the pillars of the pines at so fair a prospect that Tai Haruru smiled and Tiki caught his breath upon a cry of wonder. This was no longer "the land that was not sown". Here, at what seemed like the world's end, a small oasis of human cultivation had settled itself comfortably between the two wildernesses of earth and sea. Well-cared-for harvest fields were spread like a patchwork quilt upon the slope of the gentle hill whose crest was their halting place. At the foot of the hill, and fringing a rocky bay, a good-sized prosperous-looking little village nestled within a luxuriant sea of fern and a few gay little flower gardens, the smoke of its hearth fires coiling lazily up from the thatched roofs. And beyond was the sea, immense, majestic, still and smooth as a dancing floor where its sapphire met the lighter turquoise blue of the sky, breaking in a thunder of foam along the beach. At this hour, with the sun making haste to leave them, the whole landscape was an unearthly sequence of misty blues; the sea, the sky, the violet haze of the woodsmoke, the indigo of the pine branches, the long dark shadows of evening, the blue-grey rocks on the shore cupping pools the colour of blue-bells, piling themselves up on one side of the bay to form a causeway running out into the sea. What looked like an old Maori stronghold was built at the end of this causeway, where it widened out to form what was almost an island in the sea. It was built of stone, ancient as the rock to which it clung, and above its weathered roof was a belfry, with a bell hanging in it. Tiki's eyes were fixed upon the sea, but Tai Haruru looked from the belfry to those flower gardens in the village, and then back again to the belfry. . . . He had never yet encountered Maoris who indulged in flower plots and belfries. . . . The bell began to ring, tolling out the hour. It was sweet-toned and the word it spoke to the ear was the same as that of the evening star that stabs through the eyes to the soul with a name unutterable. The sea took up the word, rolling it in thunder along the shore, and the hearts of the two men answered as though with a roll of muffled drums.

They rode carefully down the hill, along the winding path that led between the harvest fields, and then, silently yet by mutual consent, they dismounted and parted company, Tiki leading their horses towards the centre of the village and his people, Tai Haruru making his way on foot along the shore towards the headland and the belfry, and whoever it was of his people who had rung that bell.

3

The old stronghold was more like a cairn of piled stones than anything else, so ancient was it, so primitively built. It contrasted oddly with the small lancet windows let into its walls, that might have come from the church in Cumberland where Tai Haruru had yawned his way through Mass when he was a boy, and with the modern belfry and bell and the wooden bench beside the door of kauri wood. The door was ajar, hanging loosely upon broken hinges, and Tai Haruru went inside. Yes, it was a church. There was a rough stone altar with a cross upon it, flanked by candlesticks, and wooden benches, and matting on the floor. And it might have been that church in Cumberland. There was the same smell of candle-grease and damp, the same murmur outside the walls, that in Cumberland had been the rush of a stream down a ravine, and here was the sea.

A fantastic figure of a man stood praying before the altar. He was tall, and the tattered remnants of what might once have been a cassock draped his powerful limbs with the utmost incongruity above the breeches and leggings of a woodsman. But for the evidence of his speech he might have been taken for a Maori, so dark was the skin of his withered neck and of the bald head surrounded by a fringe of grey hair, but he was speaking aloud, as the lonely do, and speaking Latin with the intonation of a cultured Irishman.

Tai Haruru discovered to his surprise that he had not forgotten all his Latin, for he easily recognised the psalm as one he had often yawned through as a boy. "All thy waves and storms are gone over me." For some unknown reason the words reminded him of Marianne, sending a stab of pain through him, and as though he too had felt it the man looked over his shoulder and saw him. He showed no surprise at all. He did not even leave off speaking. "My soul is athirst for God," he said, and turned back to the altar. "Yea, even for the living God. When shall I come to appear before the presence of God."

Tai Haruru went outside to wait until he should have finished his office, and sat down on the bench beside the broken door. The blues of the landscape had deepened and darkened since he had been within, but they were still translucent. The veil of evening had not so much hidden the exquisite details of the scene about him as gathered them up and brought them nearer. He felt as though he could have stretched out his hand and picked them up, the woods and the village and the harvest fields, like toys that had been brought for a child to play with at the evening hour.

A step sounded beside him and he looked up into the face that he had as yet scarcely seen, a rugged weatherbeaten face where the bright penetrating eyes reminded him at first sight uneasily of Samuel, but where the wide humorous mouth and the strong ugly jaw immediately set his unease to rest. For this was not a man likely to be martyred. So serious a thing as martyrdom was not likely to keep company with anything so comical as that wide gargoyle grin, and the fiercest of Tuas would think twice about assaulting a man with a jaw like a steel trap and—Tai Haruru's eyes travelled over the fantastic figure beside him—a fist like a sledge hammer, a breadth of shoulder and chest whose pugilistic strength not even the cassock could disguise, and long lean flanks like a thoroughbred horse. The man was old but age had had about as much effect upon his strength as the beating of the waves had had upon the walls of this stronghold at the world's end out of which he had made his church. Both of them were discoloured and dinted, and totally without beauty, but for the purposes for which they had been created they were still as good as new.

"D'ye know anythin' about carpenterin'?" asked the old man, indicating the broken door, and speaking as casually as though this sudden appearance of Tai Haruru upon the threshold of his church was expected by him.

"All there is to know," said Tai Haruru. "I've been a carpenter in my day."

"That's fortunate, now," said the old man. "My great fists come in handy for fellin' trees, an' they can take the parties to a fight by the scruffs of their necks an' fling 'em twenty yards apart as easy as you please, an' me in my sixty-fifth year, but they're no use for delicate fool jobs like this. There were three of us here once. Brother Jonathan was handy with an awl, an' Brother Elias could mend a broken leg and have it good as new next mornin', but the body of your humble servant is an ass and my brothers in religion rightly named its rider Balaam; though Benedict was the name I took when I shaved my crown and gave my soul to God and the blasted Maoris."

He had sat down beside Tai Haruru and was garrulous, as though it were long since he had spoken to his own kind.

"How long ago was it that Brother Jonathan and Brother Elias died?" asked Tai Haruru.

Brother Balaam hesitated. "Out here in the wilds a man loses track of time," he said at last.

"Years ago," decided Tai Haruru. "Murdered?"

Brother Balaam nodded. "Buried 'em under the flagstones of the church," he said.

"You're mad, you missionaries," ejaculated Tai Haruru angrily. "What good do you think you do, crawling out to the extremities of all the different world's ends and dying there like lizards spiked on sticks?"

Brother Balaam jabbed his thumb over his shoulder at the church behind him. "Ye'll get no civilisation worth havin' in a new country unless ye lay down a few martyrs' bones for a foundation," he said. "They generate. Slow but sure."

"English Evangelical and Irish Catholic, you're all as crazy as each other," growled Tai Haruru. And then, almost before he knew what he was doing, he had told Brother Balaam the whole story of Samuel. To speak of that death to one of his own kind was an unspeakable relief, like receiving the softness of oil upon a sore wound.

Brother Balaam nodded sympathetically when the tale was done but made no immediate comment upon it other than the signing of the cross upon his immense chest. But a few moments later he said, "Ah, well, he's bought ye. An' now ye can stay here an' lend me a hand."

Tai Haruru opened his mouth to protest. Back again yoked in harness with a crazy missionary? Was this to be the end of his long journey in search of independence? His protestations were so violent that they choked his utterance, and Brother Balaam mistook his strangled silence for consent.

"I'll be off," he said, heaving his great bulk up from the bench. "Ye'll need a decent meal an' a bed prepared. Ye can follow me on home in half an hour."

His tall figure went striding off down the causeway and Tai Haruru was left alone. Dumbfounded he took out his old pipe, carved like a bird in flight, and filled it. Well, why not? A man could not remain in flight for ever, permanent independence was apparently impossible of attainment, and this was as good a resting place, and the old priest probably as good company, as any other. . . . And he was getting old. . . . And there was that vow, "I believe in the Lord God Almighty, Maker of heaven and earth." A vow by definition demands fulfilment.

His tense figure relaxed suddenly, as the haze of the tobacco smoke added its own peculiar tincture of blue to the symphony of colour that sang in silence all about him. The sea murmured against the rocks below and that ghost of a wind that follows the sun around the world coaxed the ghost of a chime from the belfry over his head. "Home," the old man had said. Certainly he felt astonishingly at home, more at home than he had ever felt since his boyhood in Cumberland. It was amazingly peaceful. He was half asleep, and a trivial incident of his childhood, forgotten for a lifetime, came back to his dreaming mind. He had played truant from his nurse and gone off on a journey of exploration up into the fells behind his home. It had been the first time that he had gone exploring on his own, and his short fat legs had ached as he climbed all alone into the great hills. But he had not been afraid. He had not even been afraid when he found himself completely lost in a wilderness of rock that looked like the end of the world, with no sound at all but the falling of a stream from the heights above, and nothing to be seen but the rocks, and the dusk falling about him in veils of lilac and grey and blue. He had just sat down on a rock and waited, and listened to that murmur of the water and the far-away sound of sheep bells up in the hills, and soaked up the lovely blueness of the dusk into himself . . . and waited . . . and presently a shepherd had come and taken him home. . . . Perhaps it was of that incident that he had been reminded when Samuel had lifted the kid to his shoulder.

The two dusks merged into one. The stream murmuring down an English hillside and the waves of the Pacific Ocean murmuring against the rocks of New Zealand spoke the same language. The music of the sheep bells and of the belfry was not distinguishable. The end was present in the beginning and the beginning in the end, so that there was neither beginning nor end but only the perfection of the whole. Life had come round full circle and the ageing man that he was admitted it not with weariness but with a welling up within him of refreshment that was like the welling up of youth.

"Then said I, Ah, Lord God! behold, I cannot speak, for I am a child."

CHAPTER SIX

1

The packet from Saint Malo to the Islands had set sail in a stiff southerly breeze and was speeding like a gull before the wind. All the passengers except one were groaning down below, and that one had the deck to herself and was glad of it. A kindly sailor had found her a sheltered corner to sit in but she was forever coming out of it again that she might feel the spindrift on her face and smell the salt and taste it on her lips, and feel the wind blowing right through her cloak and habit into her body, and the lift of the ship as she bounded forward. The sailors eyed her with amusement. In their experience nuns were usually timid creatures, unused to travel, who sat in corners and told their beads with frightened eyes, and shrank from passing the time of day with anything in trousers. But there was nothing timid about this one. She tramped the deck as though she were a man, smiling at them with easy friendliness, and when she spoke to them it was as one sailor to another with knowledge and experience of ships and the sea. Yet they took no liberties with her. Apart from the respect they felt for her habit the shining ecstasy of her pale face awed them. They had not hitherto beheld quite such delight as this. Though it was a grey day, with sudden squalls of rain scudding before the wind, her joy seemed to steep the ship in sunshine whenever she passed.

For how many years, wondered Marguerite, coming to a standstill at last in the bows of the ship, for how many years had she been exiled from the sea? For so many that it was surely waste of time to count them. She would not count them, she would look forward, not back. She was going home. She was so happy that it was worth while to have lived if only for this.

She was lucky, lucky, lucky. Through the love and understanding of her friend Marie Ursule, and the goodness of God, she had been given her heart's desire. It was not given to many of the knights of God after long wandering to turn homeward in this way; for the most part they rode out to the world's end and died there. Notre Dame du Castel must have seemed the world's end to Marie Ursule and to poor old Mère Madeleine. The Island itself must have seemed the world's end to those monks of Mont St. Michel who had rowed across this same stormy sea in their little boats, landed at La Baie des Saints and built that hermitage on the cliff top that was now the convent of which she was Mother Superior. The ship's bell rang out like a call to prayer and she shut her eyes and crossed herself and prayed for their souls. And then she prayed for all those knights of God, still living, who were travelling now not homeward but out into the wilderness to plant the cross of Christ in desert places. Some, now, were in danger on the sea, some facing peril in the desert or in tropical forests. And many were afraid. Before the blackness of her closed eyes she saw a forest path and a man there who was turning back in terror from the appointed task. She could not see his face, for the scene was very dark, but she could see the hesitant figure and the turning back, and with all her heart and soul she prayed for him that he might turn again. To her he was a symbolic figure. She prayed for the many in the one.

When she lifted her head and opened her eyes again it was to see something that transformed her instantly from praying nun to excited child. A dim grey shape was rising up out of the sea. She gave an exclamation of joy and leaned forward over the bulwarks, shading her eyes with her hand. A couple of seamen also turned to look, almost taken aback by what they saw, so swiftly had the ship sped before the wind.

The nun had been the first to sight the Island.

2

Her first few days at the convent passed bewilderingly for the new Reverend Mother. There was so much to see and do, so much to think of. It was not until the evening of her first Sunday, when she went to her study at the day's end and shut the door behind her, that for the first time she felt alone and at peace.

She stood in the centre of the room, her hands linked behind her back, and gazed about her, still incredulous and amazed. For it was all exactly the same. There was the desk, the two old oak chairs, the stool, the bookshelf, the strip of matting, the statue of the Virgin in the niche in the wall and the prie-Dieu with the crucifix of ebony and ivory hanging over it. It was a cold night and a fire of vraic was burning in the grate, lighting the whitewashed walls with a rosy glow, like the inside of a seashell. Beyond the two narrow windows, set in the huge thickness of the wall, the Atlantic was restless in the darkness, lit only by the beam of light that shone from the west window of the tower. She could hear the booming of the waves on the rocks of La

Baie des Petit Fleurs far below, the sound of the wind, the crying of the gulls, The years rolled back full circle and she was a child again, sitting on that stool before the fire with Mère Madeleine combing the tangles out of her hair. In that high-backed chair sat Reverend Mother with her holy face, erect, severe, chaste and tempered like a sword. In this room, she thought, the seed of faith had been sown in her soul. She had been a happy child but she was a happier woman. The child had been happy like a bird singing, trilling the first phrase of a symphony over and over, questioning to what end, subconsciously holding back from the consequences of that first utterance. But the woman had lived through the consequences and come out on the other side. The symphony had reached the last movement. The question had become a statement that was singing its way to the triumphant finale with depth and power.

She knelt at the prie-Dieu and prayed for those without faith. She saw the faithless as a man of stark courage, fighting the evil things without hope of victory, worshipping the lovely things without hope of their endurance, a man whose aristocracy of soul was a thing both to marvel at and weep over, because he knew not whose was the imprint that was being set upon him and yet suffered the chiselling of the image in silence, scorning the vulgarity of complaint. Was he a grander figure without faith, she wondered? Was the peace of his stoicism a finer thing than the serenity of her own happy certainty? The doubt passed so quickly that it scarcely even halted her prayer. Between the marble image with its cold acceptance of finality and the living, breathing, growing flesh and blood, there can be no comparison. She prayed on and on as the night deepened and the flames of the vraic fire sank low. She was conscious at last of the chill of this ancient place gripping her body. She got up, shivering, and put fresh fuel on the fire. The winters could be very cold in these old grey strongholds of the faith. As the flames leaped up again she looked lovingly about her fire-lit room and thought how many of these strongholds there were girdling the earth, and she had a quick warm sense of comradeship with all the other fighters who lived within them and who cried out at the world's end, as she did, "I believe."

BOOK FOUR

THE COUNTRY OF THE
GREEN PASTURES

PART I

ARCADIA

Right against the Eastern gate,
Where the great Sun begins his state,
Rob'd in flames, and Amber light,
The clouds in thousand Liveries dight.
Russet Lawns and Fallows Gray,
Where the nibbling flocks do stray,
Mountains on whose barren brest
The labouring clouds do often rest:
Meadows trim with Daisies pide,
Shallow Brooks and Rivers wide.

JOHN MILTON.

CHAPTER ONE

1

A cock crowed and William woke up. It was still dark but he was a farmer now and as punctual to the crowing of the cock as the ghost of Hamlet's father. Not that there was anything ghostlike about William at this period. In the last ten years he had put on weight to such an extent that the price of a new suit was nearly doubled and his bill for shoe leather would have kept him awake at night had he not been so rich a man.

But these were minor trials. The real difficulty for a man of great weight is how to come and go unobserved by his wife when his foot-fall is one that can be heard half a mile off. William considered himself nowadays a happily married man, but nevertheless there were occasions when he still wished to come or go unobserved by Marianne, and this was one of them. He sat slowly up in bed, yawning, while he wondered how to get out of bed and out of the room without waking her. Everything was against him: his breathing, slightly stertorous nowadays when he moved; the exquisite brocade curtains of the huge four-poster, whose brass rings rattled when they were pulled aside; the little flight of steps leading from four-poster to floor, which creaked when stepped on; the door, which squeaked; and his wife's preternaturally sharp hearing, which functioned even when she was asleep. Nevertheless the problems must be surmounted or his early morning ride up into the mountains to watch the sunrise with Véronique, an expedition planned to greet the first official day of spring, would be discovered by Marianne and she would be jealous. . . . Poor Marianne. Poor girl. . . . She did not nowadays visit her jealousy of her husband's and child's great love for each other upon their heads in temper, as she had done ten years ago, she'd progressed beyond that, but her hurt silences were just as hard to put up with, and William and Véronique avoided them at all costs short of abandoning their mountain rides together. These rides could not be given up for they were the modern equivalent of the old adventures in Green Dolphin Country, and for father and daughter their abandonment would have meant the loss of something that was essential in their relationship. Up in the Arcadia of the mountains they escaped into some timeless place not of this world as completely as they had once done in Green Dolphin Country, and they knew instinctively that for some reason or other it was necessary for the happiness of both of them that they should keep their footing there.

Holding his breath, William edged himself little by little towards his side of the bed, pulled aside the curtain cautiously and lowered himself down the steps to the floor. Here he stood upright, listening intently. But there was no sound from the bed. The curtain rings had refrained from rattling and the steps had not creaked. He grinned. He had been in luck. He had fancied there had been an extra note of triumph in the crowing of the cock.

Reassured he stole rather too quickly across the floor in the darkness and stubbed his bare toe against the corner of the chest of drawers. "Damn!" The exclamation was out before he could stop himself, and a sharp voice spoke suddenly from within the curtains of the bed.

"William!"

"Yes, dear," said William miserably.

"What on earth are you doing, getting up at this hour? It's the middle of the night."

"No, dear," said William gently. "Nearly morning now. I'm anxious about that cow that calved yesterday. She felt bad last night."

"My dear William, Nat understands far more about the cows than you do, and he's sitting up with her. And James and Mack will be about soon. When one considers the number of responsible men we employ on this farm it is merely foolish for you to be perpetually poking your nose into petty details in the way you do. If you were to pay as much attention to the fluctuations of market prices as you do to the fluctuations of the animals' emotions we should be a great deal more prosperous than we are."

"You're a marvel, Marianne," said William admiringly. "The minute you wake up you're as voluble and alert as though it were three o'clock in the afternoon. Right on top of things you are, and you with your head scarcely lifted from the pillow."

"And a good thing too," retorted Marianne. "A poor thing it would be if both of us wandered about all day in a half dream. Come back to bed, William."

"No, dear," said William, "I'm going to see about that cow," and he opened the door and went out. He had left his clothes the night before in the kitchen downstairs, not in the dressing room that led out of their bedroom, so that he could dress without disturbing Marianne. As he lit the candles in the kitchen, and struggled into his clothes, he said to himself suddenly that he was sick of deceiving Marianne, even though it was for her own peace of mind. Their marriage, becoming progressively satisfactory as they accommodated themselves to each other's failings and increasingly admired each other's virtues, was surely now worthy of the truth. . . . But all his lies were the offspring of that first great whopping falsehood that had been the foundation stone of their married life, and he would never be able to tell Marianne the truth about that. . . . Poor girl, it would kill her.

His dressing finished he examined himself critically in the mirror over the mantelpiece, for such was his infatuation for his daughter that whenever he went out with her he was as fussy about his appearance as a young man in love for the first time.

"Oh my!" said a sarcastic voice from the window, where Old Nick hung in his cage.

"Hold your tongue, you old scoundrel!" ejaculated William, and flung his discarded nightshirt over the top of the cage. From beneath its folds Old Nick continued to squawk derisively. He was just the same. He had not changed at all.

The same could not be said of William who at fifty-three, with his great girth and stooping shoulders, looked a good deal older than his actual age. Yet he was still an attractive-looking man with his fresh-coloured genial face, kind blue eyes and handsome grey Dundreary whiskers that made some amends with their luxuriance for his now completely bald head. They might live in the wilds but with the help of the fashion-plates that still came to her from London Marianne kept them all looking as up-to-date as she could. It was she who had insisted on the Dundreary whiskers, and the loose tweed coat and flat cap with a turned-up brim that seemed to William, as he surveyed himself, to look slightly ridiculous above his farmer's corduroys. But his loose blue tie was all right, because Véronique had knitted it for him, and everything Véronique did was always perfection in his eyes. He knotted it with great care, breathing heavily, so absorbed that he did not hear the door open, did not know she was there until she slipped her arms round his neck from behind.

"Papa! Papa!" she cried excitedly.

He swung round. "Why, you little monkey, I was going to wake you with a cup of tea."

"The cock woke me. 'The cock that is the trumpet to the morn.' We'll make a cup of tea for Nat instead. Hurry up, Papa! Light the fire while I lay the table."

She was skimming about the kitchen, laying the table for breakfast, filling the kettle and putting it on the hob, shaking up the cushions on the settle and putting the room to rights with a hundred little deft touches. They had two maids, the daughters of Murray, one of their shepherds, but they lived up the valley and did not come until later in the morning and Véronique did the before breakfast work so that Marianne could lie longer in bed; Marianne was always very tired these days. Véronique did not fall much behind her mother in capability but as she was unaware of her efficiency it did not irritate.

Her father, laying the fire with clumsiness and inattention, watched her out of the corner of his eye. She was grown up now, intellectually mature but emotionally rather undeveloped for her age, like all only children. She was tall and slim, in appearance almost ridiculously like Marguerite at her age, except that she retained that look of fragility that had worried William so much when she was a child. It worried him less now, for she had not had one single serious illness throughout the seventeen years of her short life; he found more reason for anxiety in that look of unearthliness that was her distinguishing characteristic. He did not know quite what it was that gave her this nymph-like air, whether it was her swift movements, the almost luminous pallor of her skin or the silvery fairness of her hair, but anyway it was there; something that his love must reckon with aright at the turning points of life. She belonged in those dream countries where they had wandered in her childhood, and in this exquisite upland valley where they lived now, but he knew instinctively that all would not be well with her in another place, and it was because of this knowledge that he was fighting now tooth and nail, as he had never fought before, to prevent Marianne from inaugurating a complete upheaval in their whole way of life.

As he laid the fire William groaned and sighed over his wife's insatiable, restless ambition. They had now all that she had longed for when ten years ago they had set out almost penniless on the long journey from Nelson to this place. She had wanted to own land, flocks of sheep, a fine farm house, wealth, and she had all these things; only to find them apparently not as satisfactory as she had expected.

For she was very busy nowadays pointing out to him without cessation, and with perfect truth, that the wool trade was not quite what it had been and that they would be wise to sell their land and farm and engage in some more profitable trade before there was any serious fall in the price of wool. To this William replied steadily that fluctuations in the price of wool were only what was to be expected, that things were bound to look up again, that they had capital behind them and could weather a few lean years with ease. Marianne would respond by painting glowing pictures of all that they could do with their capital in another way of life. In the darkness of their four-poster at night she would whisper the two magic words "gold" and "steam" and he would know that her eyes were sparkling with excitement. Gold had been discovered in New Zealand now, as well as in Australia, in the mountains of Central Otago and on the west coast. She did not need to tell him, she would whisper in the darkness, what that meant in terms of prosperity to a man possessed of push and initiative. "I've neither," William would growl, aware even while he growled that that was of no consequence to a man whose wife had both. "I've nothing in common with most of these gold diggers," he would go on. "Jews and upstarts. Not like the good old pioneering stock. I hate 'em."

But it was no good to run down gold, for Marianne only produced steam. The country was being opened up now not only by roads but by railways, and a group of Dunedin merchants had lately formed the Union Steamship Company to cater for the coastal and inter-colonial trade. There was even talk of laying a deep-sea cable to Australia, connecting them with the cable service to Europe and America. Of the two Marianne was perhaps more attracted to steam than to gold. It had always thrilled her, just as it had always repelled William. They sometimes argued about it, as they had done in the old days on the Island, by the hour together. But the present-day arguments were not so enjoyable as the old ones had been. William saw steam as a threat to Véronique's happiness and hated it more than ever, and Marianne was embittered by his stick-in-the-mud attitude to modern discovery. With all these exciting new ventures crying out for development how could William, how could any man, choose to stay incarcerated in a lonely valley at the back of beyond and keep sheep? Oh, if only she were a man!

At this point William would break in upon her reverie to ask what could be given them by greater wealth that they had not got already?

Then she would tell him. . . . A town house in one of the fashionable South Island ports, a carriage and pair, dinner parties, card parties and balls.

"For Véronique," she would say. "She is beautiful and should marry well. She must be given her chance."

"She's young yet," William always temporised. "Wait a little. She's not very strong."

"She's perfectly strong," Marianne would reply. "Has she ever ailed at all?"

"No," William would agree. "Never. But I do not want her to marry just yet."

"You're jealous," Marianne would flash out when especially goaded. "You want to keep her for yourself."

"No," William would reply with a huge patience. "I want only her happiness."

But last night, for the first time, his patience had given out, and he had flashed back at her, "You know, my girl, you want that town house not for Véronique but for yourself."

Marianne had not lost her temper at what she considered the rank injustice of this remark, she had relapsed into one of her hurt silences, and then into sleep, while William had lain awake for hours and cursed himself for wounding her so deeply.

He sighed again, fumbling with the tinder box and pondering the problem of his wife's temperament. Poor girl, it seemed unfair that she should fight so hard for what she wanted and then when she had won the fight it was not she who enjoyed the spoils but himself and Véronique. It was they who loved this place, not she.

William was a just man and gave the credit of his success where it belonged, to Marianne. It was true he had worked hard, deucedly hard, but it had been under her orders and inspired by her creative energy, and with one eye somewhat uneasily closed to her business methods. For they had not attained to their present prosperity by overscrupulousness. When it had been possible for Marianne to grab she had grabbed, and what she had once grabbed she did not let go. Since their adventures at the Pa, and the parting from Tai Haruru, she had been a gentler woman but she had not become a less acquisitive one. He tried not to think that her acquisitiveness had become a little vulgar during these last ten years, and it never even occurred to him to wonder if the loss of Tai Haruru's influence had anything to do with that. He had never realised that Marianne's attitude towards his friend had undergone a change. For she never spoke of Tai Haruru, even as he never spoke of Marguerite.

2

The kindling of the fire upon his hearth warmed the cockles of William's heart and he sat back, hands on knees, smiling at the flames. The house at the settlement, built for Marguerite and never fulfilling its purpose, he had never cared for, but this house, made for Véronique and enshrining her, he most intensely loved. It was a good home, however it had been come by, and now that distance lent enchantment to the view he could smile at the way it had been come by. That Israelitish journey in the wagon piled high with luggage, Old Nick in his cage swearing on the summit! Lord, what a nightmare! It had been the distance they had had to travel that had made it so appalling, for compared with the journey from the Pa it had been quite a civilised progression. South Island, undisturbed by native troubles, had at that date developed far ahead of North Island. The discovery of gold in Australia had set the first struggling colonists well upon their feet. The thousands of Australian gold seekers had had to be fed and the New Zealand farmers had reaped a rich harvest by sending over wheat, potatoes, live-stock and other farm products. There had been good roads and prosperous farms along the way where now and then they could get a good rest and sleep upon a feather bed instead of in the open. They had made friends at these farms with whom they could have thrown in their lot had they wished, but Marianne's ambition had been set upon the even better prospects of the sheep-runs further south, and she had made up her mind to satisfy it or perish in the attempt. So they had gone on and on, traversing at last nearly the whole length of the island. It had seemed an endless journey. He and Nat had been hard put to it to endure sometimes and it had been a marvel to him that Marianne had weathered it at all without collapse. Yet she had neither collapsed nor complained. The odd woman never did complain on journeys, it was only in the days of static comfort that she grew so querulous. It was as though no particular place ever satisfied her, but only the journeying there.

But if arduous the journey had been beautiful, and Véronique, too young at that time to be incommoded by the bumping of the wagon that shook her parents and Nat nearly to pieces, remembered it even now with ecstasy. They had seen the blue rivers and blond grass of the great plains, and later the lagoons he had promised her she should see had been upon the one side of them while upon the other the ramparts of the mountains had risen up to touch the sky. And later still they had turned up into the foothills and there had been flowers in the grass and birds singing, just as he had promised her.

Where was the farmhouse in the valley ringed round with mountains, she had begun to ask at this point? And William had broken out into a cold sweat, cursing the accurate memory of childhood. If that upland valley that he had described to her were not to be found, if the dream were not to become fact, he would be for ever discredited in the eyes of his one and only love.

They had found it. Because the search had been conditioned by the dream, they had found it. It had been because of the dream that one hot afternoon he had resolutely led the wagon up into the foot-hills when Marianne had been for keeping on through the plain. It had been because of the dream that when they had come at sunset to a parting of the ways with upon one side a decent road winding pleasantly away through gentle woods, and on ahead a steep for-bidding rocky ravine, with a mere travesty of a cart track leading apparently abruptly up into nowhere, he had chosen the cart track. "No, William!" Marianne had protested. "For goodness sake, William! Night's coming on and along that decent road we might find bed and lodging, but up here—William, turn round at once!"

But where Véronique's happiness was concerned William could be obstinate as the devil. Gently encouraging the straining horses he and Nat had led them on and up, the wagon bumping wildly over the boulders in the track, oblivious of Marianne's furious protests and Old Nick's squawks, hearing only Véronique's peals of happy laughter at each fresh bump and lurch. Ahead of them, at the top of the gorge, an archway of rock had framed a dazzle of sunset sky bright with promise.

But when they had passed through the archway Marianne's pro-tests had changed to exclamations of astonished wonder, and Véronique's joyful squeaks had died away altogether into the silence of sheer round-eyed ecstasy. The upland valley had looked so ex-quisitely beautiful at that evening hour, a green cup brimming with golden light, and so safe in its setting of opal-coloured mountains. There had been nothing forbidding about these hills. Their lower slopes had been gentle, clothed with short sweet turf where a few sheep had been feeding, luxuriant ferns marking the courses of the streams, and at this hour even the ravines and precipices above, mounting up and up towards the snows, had lost their fierceness and taken to themselves the colour of dreams. Quite close to them they had seen a tumbledown wooden house surrounded by farm build-ings, with a tangled garden sloping to a stream and a fair prospect to the south, while to the north a group of lombardy poplars, planted perhaps by the man who had built the house, for trees were not in-digenous to this country, gave protection from cold winds. There had been no sign of life about the house and nothing to be heard except the tinkle of sheep bells and the voice of a hidden waterfall. The weary horses had dropped their heads to crop the green grass and the two men, the woman and the child had looked round upon each other and smiled.

But William and Marianne had not smiled for long. Leaving Nat with Véronique in the wagon they had gone forward on foot to prospect. The tangled garden had looked enchanting from a distance but on a close view they had found it choked with weeds and they had reached the door of the tumbledown house only circuitously, because of the manure heap that had blocked the way. Their knock on the door had produced no answer, and William's heart had begun to fail him. Not so Marianne's. Though she had protested so fiercely at the appalling cart track up which William had bumped the wagon yet at sight of the valley she had immediately changed her mind. . . . Never in all her life had she set eyes upon such perfect grazing country. A sheep farmer possessed of a clever wife could scarcely fail to make his fortune in this place. . . . Pushing William aside she had lifted the latch of the door and flung it open, revealing a dirty disordered kitchen and a big man with a matted black beard lying unconscious in the middle of the floor in a pool of blood. With an exclamation of horror William had stretched out a hand to pull Marianne back. But she had already stepped over the sill and gone in.

"Only drunk," she had said coolly. "He hit his head against that table as he fell." And then, standing in the centre of the disordered kitchen, looking distastefully down at the man lying at her feet, she had slowly and deliberately removed her bonnet. "Come along, William," she had said. "We must get him to bed before Véronique sees him."

The next year had been a period of existence to which nowadays William's thoughts returned reluctantly, but to which he suspected that Marianne's flew back with self-congratulatory pleasure, so resoundingly successful had been the labours undertaken by that incomparable woman from the moment when she had taken her bonnet off in Alec Magee's kitchen to the moment, twelve months later, when she had outraged Victorian convention by giving herself the satisfaction of attending his funeral.

He had not been a bad man, merely a weak one disintegrated by loneliness, and by the fear of the death that was even then throwing its shadow over him. From the moment when he had regained consciousness in his attic bedroom, to find himself being expertly cared for by Marianne's capability and William's pitiful kindness, he had been like a child in their hands. He had been able to do what he had been longing to do ever since he had known that he was a dying man —let go. He wanted only kindness and care, and that they had given him. For the rest they had been able to do what they liked—with his house, his farm, his land, his sheep, his shepherds, and the little bit of money hoarded in an old calico bag under the mattress of his bed.

And Marianne had done it with an efficiency and speed that had surpassed anything that even she had accomplished before. With Nat's help she had got the house to rights in less than a week, and in less than a fortnight she had goaded William into establishing similar order on the farm. In three weeks she had put the fear of God into the shepherds to such an extent that they had not dared to presume on either her or William's ignorance; and at the end of a month they could not have done so even had they dared, for she had known almost as much about their trade as they did.

Magee's farm was not the only one in the valley. There were a few others, widely scattered, and at the far end of the valley there was even a little village, with a church, a store, and a school-house where Véronique had gone to school. The other farmers were for the most part Scotch gentlefolk and their gently nurtured children had been just the companions she had needed. While she had been still a little girl Nat or William had driven her to school every day in the farm gig, but as she grew older she had trotted thither on her pony, fearless and happy. There had never been anything in the valley to make her afraid, and from the very first moment that she had entered it she had never known fear. Even during the first year, while Alec Magee still lived, she had not been afraid, for he had loved her and always been gentle with her, and when the time had come for him to die she had been sent to stay with the schoolmaster and his wife, that fine and upright couple Andrew and Janet Ogilvie, whose eldest child John was her greatest friend. And they, too, had loved her, and she had loved them with an unswerving devotion that had grown with her growth and was at the present time causing poor Marianne pangs of most painful jealousy. . . . She could not bear those Ogilvies.

William and Marianne had won the friendship of their neighbours less quickly than their little daughter. The homesteads were so far apart, the men and women who lived in them so desperately hard-worked, that they could not foregather very much. And William and Marianne were not Scotch, and so regarded somewhat in the light of foreigners by that clannish race. And then the way in which they had taken possession of Alec Magee had seemed to their neighbours a little odd. Had he really wished to take them into partnership, or to make that will, leaving them everything he died possessed of, or had that sharp-tongued shrewish little woman persuaded him into it? They were without proof that he had, and they were also without proof as to the means by which William Ozanne had so very soon become the wealthiest sheep farmer in the district. Sheep farming demanded large areas of land for its success and Magee had owned very little. Land had to be purchased from the New Zealand company, the price of it was high, and William had obviously had very little capital behind him at the start. Yet as the years went on more and more of the mountain pastures seemed to be his. There were, of course, methods by which a man could become possessed of land without buying all of it outright. He could buy narrow strips of pasture which were so situated as to enclose a large area to which no one else had access and of which he therefore had undisputed use. Or there was "dummying"—shepherds bought land cheaply apparently for themselves, in reality for their masters. Well, they were none of them above reproach, and just as in the early days in North Island it had been a matter of delicacy not to enquire into a man's personal history, so nowadays in South Island one did not ask how he had come by his land. . . . Only none of them had come by their wealth quite as quickly as William. . . . But the men had to make friends with him in the end, he was such a good fellow, such good company, so hugely kind, and so obviously browbeaten by his forceful wife. The women could never really like Marianne; her clothes were too smart for a farmer's wife and she captivated the men with them at the rare local festivities with a thoroughness that was not seemly in a woman of her age; and the brilliance of her talk was a thing that they themselves could not aspire to; nor could they bake cakes like hers. . . . But she was the mother of Véronique, and that was a circumstance that covered a multitude of sins.

3

And, in her husband's eyes, covered them all. For she was not only the mother of Véronique, it was her genius that had created for her child the perfect setting for her life. The original tumble-down wooden farm had now been repaired and enlarged into a house out of a fairytale. Year by year, as their prosperity increased, Marianne had been adding to its attractions, contented while there had been so much still left to do, discontented only now that her creation was finished down to the last shelf in the store cupboard and the last dimity frill in Véronique's bedroom. It had been Véronique's bedroom that she had made first, enduring heaven knew how many jolting wagon journeys to the nearest town to buy pretty furniture and flowered pink hangings, and a little round mirror that should be large enough to show Véronique if her hair was tidy but not large enough to reveal her beauty to her and encourage vanity. Then she had tackled the parlour, with its small upright piano for Véronique to play on, its blue brocade curtains, pretty china ornaments and lovely fragile pieces of furniture. It was not until Véronique's bedroom and the parlour with her piano had been perfect down to the last detail that Marianne had turned her attention to the immense four-poster for herself and William, in place of the rough mattresses on the floor that they had had hitherto, a wardrobe like a mausoleum and a washstand with a marble top. . . . The carting of these articles of furniture up the steep rocky road that led to the valley, and the inserting of them into the farmhouse, a matter of great difficulty requiring the removal of several windows, was now one of the valley sagas and would not cease to be recited while any lived who had beheld the miracle. . . . Then there had been Nat's little room in the roof to be made comfortable and ship-shape, and the pantry and still room and store-cupboards and dairy to be made as up to date as possible, and then, but only then, had she turned her attention to the kitchen.

To be met with a flat refusal, on the part of her husband and daughter, to have it touched. They were prepared to put up with the number and breakability of the parlour ornaments to please her, and William was resigned to the nightly incarceration of himself in the stuffy four-poster, and Véronique never said that the pink of her bedroom curtains was a colour she disliked, but they would not have the kitchen touched. They loved it just as it was, with the great wide fireplace where on winter evenings, with snow falling in the mountains, they sat before the blazing logs and told each other stories, the ingle nook where motherless lambs were sometimes laid to keep warm and where Véronique petted them and fed them with warm milk from a baby's bottle, the smoke-blackened beams where home-cured hams and bunches of herbs hung from the hooks, the rag rugs made by Alec Magee's mother upon the clean scrubbed stone floor, the settle and the copper pans that had belonged to Alec, the old grandfather clock that had been his, and the purple tobacco jar. To Marianne Alec Magee had been merely a means to an end but William and Véronique had been fond of him; and they would not have his mother's rag rugs banished to the attic, nor his tobacco jar placed anywhere except in the place of honour on the mantelpiece. Véronique, always so lovingly amenable to all her mother's wishes, had been curiously obstinate about the kitchen. It was hers, she had cried out in a sudden fit of temper, on that day when Marianne had finished with the rest of the house and was turning her attention to the kitchen, it was hers and Papa's, she had made it for herself and Papa, and Mamma was not to touch it. And Marianne, stabbed to silence by the bitter hurt of her daughter's words, had looked about her and noted with astonishment that Véronique *had* made the kitchen. All her little treasures, that one would have expected her to keep in her bedroom, she kept here. The lacquer desk and the Chinese workbox, which Marguerite had sent to her niece as soon as she had returned to the Island, stood on a table beside the grandfather clock. The absurd little box of shells from La Baie des Petits Fleurs stood on the mantelpiece between the tobacco jar and a particularly blatant tea caddy ornamented with a portrait of Queen Victoria, a present from Nat that Véronique adored. The cross-stitch kettle-holder had been made by Véronique, and the little sampler of a ship in full sail that hung over the mantelpiece. She kept bowls full of flowers in special places. On the wall beside the window where Old Nick hung in his cage, within reach of the deep window-seat where she so often sat, her father had hung the bookshelf he had made for her. It held her few precious books, her Bible and Pilgrim's Progress, Grimm's fairy tales, Shakespeare and Milton, and a fat manuscript book in which she had written out the old tales her father had told her when she was small, the tales of Green Dolphin Country and the Island. She had no taste for scientific study, like her mother at her age, but she had Marianne's clear mind, which combined with her father's imagination had given her a taste for literature which had been encouraged by Mr. Ogilvie, her beloved Scotch schoolmaster. And she had her mother's gift of concentration upon the matter in hand. She could sit curled up on the window-seat reading for an hour at a time, completely oblivious of whatever might be going on in the kitchen around her. Yes, it was Véronique's room. Though Marianne and her maids bustled about it all day long, though lambs bleated in the ingle nook and shepherds came knocking at the door, though Nat came and went with pails of milk and baskets of vegetables and the cat and her kittens thought the place theirs, it remained Véronique's room. After Marianne, always so tired these days, had gone early to bed, Véronique and her father sat together and watched the logs fall from rosy flame to feathery ash, and in the grey dawns it was more often than not they who kindled the fire on the hearth again. That was as it should be, William thought. This room where the fire on the hearth burned all the year round was the centre of life for house and farm, and so it was natural that Véronique should guard the fire and that this should be her special room, for the whole of this place existed solely for Véronique.

It seemed to him that his life, and Marianne's, and Nat's, and the lives of the shepherds, and the lives of all the living things that they owned in field and pasture, even the lives of the very birds and flowers, and the hills themselves, were just so many petals of a flower of love that closed in upon the golden heart that was Véronique.

4

"Quick now," he said. "The kettle's boiling. Make that cup of tea for Nat and come along or we'll be back late and upset your Mother." He was thankful that Véronique had ordained this visit to Nat and the cow, for it turned his lie to Marianne into a truth.

Véronique was already dressed in her habit of warm blue cloth, and her curls were done up tidily on top of her head. She needed no hat in this free wild country. She made Nat's tea, very strong and sweet as he liked it, poured it into a can and put it into a basket with some little cakes, and took her crop from its corner by the grandfather clock. Then they lifted the latch of the door and stole outside.

" 'The still morn went out with sandals grey,' " murmured Véronique, quoting her favourite poem, one that she used as commentary upon the beauty about her so constantly that William had bits of it well by heart.

A mountain mist still shrouded the world but from behind it came the singing of the birds and the sound of running water. "Ye valleys low where the mild whispers use," Véronique said silently to herself, low in her own mind.

> "Of shades and wanton winds, and gushing brooks,
> On whose fresh lap the swart Star sparely looks."

She slipped her hand into her father's as they walked through the garden towards the stables and farm buildings to the right of the house. "Smell my flowers," she commanded him. It was she who under her mother's direction chiefly looked after the garden, and she had green fingers. She could command the Vales, "Throw hither all your quant enameld eyes," and they would do it. The wilderness of weeds of ten years ago had disappeared and a lovely plot of colour and scent had taken its place, and it was always in the Ozannes' garden that the first spring flowers appeared.

William's great frame thrilled to the touch of his daughter's hand and the whisper of her voice. He stopped, took her basket from her and put it down on the path and drew her into his arms, holding her strongly yet with indescribable tenderness, without speaking, his cheek against hers. Her hair was a little wet with the mist, and the scent of her flowers seemed a part of her. The moment was one of a happiness almost too great to be borne. His breath came quickly and his heart thundered.

"Darling Papa!" laughed Véronique. "Poor old Nat's tea will be cold." And then she lifted her face and fluttered her eyelashes to give him a butterfly kiss. There were times, and this was one of them, when her father's love for her frightened her a little. There seemed more in it than just a Papa's love for his child. It was as though Papa looked to her for the satisfaction of all the longings that a man can have, and she knew that no woman has it in her to satisfy a man to that extent. Yet she loved having Papa's strong arms about her, and the feel of his cheek against hers. When he was young he must have been a wonderful lover, she thought, for he seemed created to love. Mamma must have had a glorious time being loved by him when she, too, was young. Lucky Mamma! Véronique thought that she too would like to have a lover one day, a man who was strong and yet gentle, patient and considerate like Papa, and like John Ogilvie their head shepherd, who had been her greatest friend since her childhood, but yet who had dash and fire and gallantry and was gloriously handsome, with dark flashing eyes, like a prince in a fairytale. Neither Papa nor John could be said to have dash and fire, nor to be gloriously handsome, so neither of them exactly fitted the bill. But the ideal lover would turn up one day, and meanwhile she was content to wait, for at present she got a trifle scared by the bigness of the thing that pressed down upon her when Papa held her in his arms a little too closely and too long; she had to hold it off by a laughing word and the lightness of butterfly kisses. And he always seemed to understand and not to be hurt. Mamma was always thinking herself slighted, doubting Veronique's love and being hurt, but Papa never doubted. He laughed now, and released her, giving her back her basket and tucking her free hand through his arm as they went along to the stable.

They pushed open a door and were at once enfolded in the warm lantern-lit enchantment of that place. Véronique gave a little laugh of pleasure. . . . Out there, the scent of the spring flowers and the birds singing behind the grey veil, and in here the smell of clean hay and horses, and in a pool of orange lantern light dear old Nat sitting beside the cow and the new-born calf. Rhoda, the cow, had great dark eyes that just now were pools of mystery as she bent her head and feebly caressed her absurd calf with its creamy skin and long legs straggling out weakly and helplessly in the hay, and Nat's aged wrinkled countenance was twinkling with delight as he contemplated the satisfying results of his expert midwifery.

"How are they, Nat?" asked William.

"Doin' fine," said Nat, with pride, and tipped Véronique's can of tea over his nose and drank long and satisfyingly. William watched him with a smile as Véronique knelt down to caress Rhoda and the calf. Nat had been astonishingly happy these last ten years. His boyhood's skill with animals and his love for them, that had scarcely found sufficient satisfaction during the long years at sea, had come back to him and were now expended to the utmost. His life had come round full circle and it seemed that in the Country of the Green Pastures he had found in old age that childhood's paradise, the right of every child, that had been denied him in his boyhood. Blessings on Marianne, thought William. It was he who had saved Nat's life but it was she who had made it worth living after it had been saved. It was he who had invented the Country of the Green Pastures as a fairy tale for Véronique's entertainment, but she who had translated it into actual satisfying fact. Quite suddenly, he realised what he owed to her. He was a blundering ass of a fellow, capable of good moments but of no sustained direction of purpose, but she had given the direction and guided their lives to this complete and perfect happiness; that might be theirs for years to come if only she would now let them be.

That "if only", the knowledge that life, like a restless woman, lets nothing stay still as it is, was like a sudden cold draught blowing down the back of his neck. He turned abruptly away and went to the far end of the stable to saddle their horses; Véronique's white pony and the stout chestnut cob who supported his master's great weight with such exemplary fortitude and patience.

But cantering through the green meadow beyond the farm with Véronique he forgot that momentary chill in the delight of the moment. He himself was a clumsy rider who would have preferred his own feet to a horse's back any day had not the great distances that he had to cover, if he was to keep his eye upon the whole of his domain, made a horse a necessity, but Véronique rode as though she had been born on horseback and to be with her was to share her joy.

They cantered over a stout wooden bridge that spanned one of those swift clear streams that came down from the mountains to water their delectable valley, across another meadow, and then their sure-footed horses were climbing a steep path up the hillside. Though the sun had not yet lifted above the mountains it was full daylight now, with the mist still opaque but thinning to an opalescent veil of light that would soon be the sunshot blue of infinite space.

The turf was a pure bright green, the bushes misted over with the delicate bright gauze of spiders' webs. They rode in silence, attentive, as the valley music of birdsong died away behind them, to the music of the high hills that almost imperceptibly stole in and took its place, that music of distant sheep bells blended with the murmur of falling streams that can stir some hearts more deeply than any other music in the world. It could so stir Véronique, for it was the music of her own country. Her face had the gravity of utter happiness as quite unconsciously, and riding like a queen, she passed on ahead of her father to lead the way. William smiled as he plodded humbly and doggedly in the rear, delighting inexpressibly in the fact that he was only nominally the owner of this mountain side, pitying from the bottom of his heart all those poor devils who possessed no Véronique at the heart's core of their existence. That she should be queen of this country—that was why he had lived.

Half an hour later they dismounted on a small green plateau high up among the rocks, facing eastward, and leaving their horses to crop the turf stood side by side to behold the wonder they had come to see. They watched for perhaps the fiftieth time in their lives, yet with the same amazement. Down below them the valley where they lived was drowned in shadow, about them the mountains were still wreathed in mist, overhead the sky was clear but cold, its ice-blue mirrored in the mountain tarn beside them. They could no longer hear the sheep bells or the voice of the hidden waterfalls, for though the music was still there it had fallen away from the consciousness of the watchers, that was focussed now upon the music of colour and light.

They knew the opening bars of the symphony, or the opening movements of the brush, choosing what analogy they might in their striving for apprehension, by heart now—the silvery lightening of the sky behind the eastern mountains, the corresponding darkening of the peaks that brought their exquisite silhouette into being—yet the movement into life was never perceptible, never the same, and always there was the shock of surprise at finding in existence a something to whose gradual unfolding one had thought one was raptly attentive, and yet there it was caught in the moment of perfect attainment and one did not know how it had attained. And nature, that unlike man admits not even the thought of finality into any of her processes, did not allow to the moment even that breath of a pause that comes between the movements of a symphony, the strokes of an artist's brush. "And now the Sun has stretched out all the hills." The simplicity of that first statement, the clear-cut contrast of the dark silhouette against the silver sky, was all at once a flood of colour and light that poured over the world as though the eastern mountains were a rampart that had broken, letting in the sea. As if the immensity of sky were a canvas not large enough the colour came streaming down the mountain-side, staining the snows with lilac and rose, brimming the deep ravines with purple and the tarns with gold, down and down until it reached the lower slopes where each rock and tree, each patch of gorse or clump of flowers beside a stream, became a dazzling jewel sown upon the green hem of a garment woven from the height of heaven to the depth of earth without seam or flaw; without even beginning or end except that arbitrary one of height and depth, man-made because of eyes that could penetrate neither the blinding light overhead nor the shadows that would linger in the depth of the valley until mid-day.

Véronique sighed, rubbing her knuckles in her eyes like a child, and William grinned selfconsciously, lowered his bulk to a rock and filled his pipe. They could not take in any more. For a full five minutes they did not even look at the glory round about them.

Véronique spoke first. "Let's go and look at our hoggets."

Leading the horses they climbed a little further and reached the lip of one of those lovely green cups of shelter that were to be found hidden here and there within the folds of these hills. One did not know it was there until one had climbed to the summit of the long ridge of rock that protected it upon this eastern side and looked down upon the wide green lawn below, dotted with the beautiful yearling merinos. There were hundreds of them cropping the spring turf and Véronique laughed for joy at the sight. They had only lately been moved up from the valley below, where they had wintered, and they were in ecstasy at their change of quarters. Their short tails quivered as they ate and their bodies gleamed white in the early sunshine. Yet when they looked round at their owners they had the faces of wise old dowagers. And, in repose, the dignity. They knew their worth, perhaps. Some instinct had made them aware of the price of wool at this period.

"There's something wrong with grass that has not got sheep upon it," said Véronique.

William laughed. "There speaks the true shepherdess."

Véronique looked up at him, flushing with pleasure. "A shepherdess," she said softly. "I like that."

And then her eyes went to the far end of the green lawn where there was a rough hut built of piled stones, and were shadowed with disappointment because there seemed no one there. . . . A shepherdess. Where was the shepherd? . . . Resolutely she turned back to William and plunged into animated talk upon the subject of the hoggets. She had always known a lot about the practical side of her father's trade and just lately, he had noticed, she had been at great pains to inform herself accurately as to statistics.

"Is this fall in the price of wool serious, Papa?" she asked him.

"No, Véronique," he replied, his eyes twinkling with amusement, for he had noticed that quite unconscious search of Amaryllis for Lycidas. "The boom years are over but there will always be a demand for wool. I'm not making the money that I did, but then to my way of thinking I was making a bit too much a few years back. I'm one of those fellows who find a lot of money hanging round my neck burdensome. I want no more than what is sufficient to keep our home exactly as it is."

"Nor I, Papa," she answered fervently. "But Mamma——"

She checked herself, for there was a tacit understanding between these two that they should never criticise their wife and mother to each other. But for her that adored home down in the valley would never have existed at all.

"Grand morning."

John Ogilvie had come up behind them and taken them by surprise. They swung round in greeting, and Véronique, with the sun in her eyes, put up her hand to shield them that she might see John the better. With absolute unselfconsciousness, she looked up at his face, delighting in him with the frankness of a child, laughing a little because he was so good to see. Her father glanced at her intently. No, she did not know yet. Her delight in John was of the same quality as her delight in her home, in the beauty of the morning, in the hoggets. He was just a part of it all, he always had been and she had not woken up yet to the fact that he was the most integral part.

And the man? William's glance went to John's face, and then quickly away again, shamed. Not right to look at a man at quite such a naked moment. But curse the fellow! If Véronique had not had the sun in her eyes surely she would have seen; and John had promised William that she should not see just yet. Four months ago, when John had first spoken to William of his love for Véronique, William had pleaded that she was a child still, and had asked John to wait. He had spoken so not out of selfishness, for his deep love for Véronique desired her eventual marriage with this man more than anything else on earth, but because he believed she was not quite ready yet, either mentally or physically. And John with the insight of a love that was almost as great as William's, had accepted the decision, and was waiting. He was six years older than Véronique, but that was no great age, and like all countrymen he was inured to patience.

But it was damned hard on the poor fellow, William thought, and compassion compelled him to glance at him once more. John had got himself in hand again. That brief flare-up of passion that had set his tanned face burning, widened his eyes and tightened his mouth as though with a sudden tremor of fiery pain, had gone, leaving him becalmed in his usual quietude.

Marianne considered John a lazy stupid fellow. She was deceived by the slow deliberation of his movements and the fact that he did not speak unless he had something to say. She did not like him. She did not like the steady regard of his keen grey eyes that went on looking at the object or person before them until it seemed they knew all there was to know about it or her, when they would blink suddenly, just once, as though the mind behind the eyes had totted up a total and drawn a line. And the great kindness that was always in his eyes did not necessarily leave one with the feeling that his deductions had been other than entirely accurate; any more than the tenderness that was in his slow wide smile could disguise the obstinacy of his mouth and the strength of his jaw. Vaguely Marianne felt this man to be a threat and a portent, a symbol of an unchangeable way of life that would clamp down upon her husband and child for good and all if she was not careful, and in consequence she couldn't abide him. It was William's most desperate and urgent hope, just at present, that the gradual drawing together of Véronique and John should escape her notice until their oneness was a thing that even she could not divide. She had noticed nothing yet, for John, instinctively aware of her dislike and uneasy with her, had up till now been as reticent as a clam in her presence. Moreover she thought of him as a mere common shepherd, of the earth earthy, and her ambitions for her child had soared so high that they had quite lost sight of things down on the earth. . . . Yet it was incredible to William that her sharp sight should have overlooked the fact, so obvious to him, that if this place was Véronique's true home then this man was her true mate, so indigenous was he to the soil of this valley.

He had been born here, and his early brilliance had led his father to expect great things of him and to endure many deprivations to send his son to school at Dunedin. . . . He was not to be a mere country dominie, like his father, but to become headmaster of Dunedin College at the very least. . . . But John had disappointed his father. With a good education behind him, and a fine mind, he had chosen to come back to the valley where he had been born and devote his life to sheep, and among his elders only William had not expressed surprise. For William knew that there are some places, like some mothers, that have more power than others of binding their children to them. And there are some children, natives of certain lovely valleys, certain hill towns or hamlets by the sea, whose roots cannot be dragged out of their native soil without agony. These are those whose birthplace is the physical counterpart of their especial spiritual country. They are doubly at home, doubly blessed if they are left where they belong, doubly wretched if they are uprooted. John was one of these children and Véronique was another, and the echoing in their personalities of the qualities that distinguished their native country was a reiteration that seemed to William to make those qualities trebly remarkable.

For he had been accustomed to think that those without ambition, like himself, are bound to be indolent, and that folk such as Marianne, who exude creative energy at every pore, are bound to be ambitious, but this Country of the Green Pastures, and Véronique and John Ogilvie, had proved to him that with the rarest spirits it is not so. This upland valley was as productive as any country he had known, yet in all the years that he had lived here he had never felt that restlessness that had been his sometimes in other places where life teemed. He guessed it was because there were no far-away horizons to tease the mind with thoughts of men and cities girdling the earth with activities and wonders which one could neither share nor see. The mountains all about this valley led the mind not out and out into an extension of one's own orbit but up and up into an infinity of sky where was no restlessness but only silence and awe. The early pioneers had found good names for some of these South Island peaks—Cloudpiercer, Aspiring, Moonraker, Stargazer. Natives of this country, men and women who did their day's work with these peaks or their fellows standing round about them, were always lifted up in spirit, at peace and content. . . . Yet without indolence. . . . There were never any lazy days in this country. There was always the austerity of the snow lacing the sunshine, always on the hottest day the cool sight and sound of falling water.

And Véronique and John Ogilvie were the children of this country, neither indolent nor ambitious, energetic yet content. Desire for fame would never drive them, as it drove Marianne, "to scorn delights and live laborious days." They delighted in laborious days for their own sake, enjoying them as a tree its growth and a bird its song, and like the tree and the bird lived contentedly in a proscribed space because of their instinctive knowledge that the grain of sand held in the hand is a microcosm of the universe and the voice of the shepherd in the pasture an echo of the voice of God; multiply the grains of sand to a desert, the echoes to a tumult, and you know no more but only lose the essence in confusion. Like one of their own mountain tarns they stayed still and went deep and were altogether creatures of a rarity that William found it impossible to fit into any of the types of humanity he was familiar with. They were more like Marguerite than they were like himself and Marianne, only the touch of the mystic in them was pagan, not Christian. They were nymph and shepherd, Amaryllis and Lycidas, and looking from one to the other in the fresh mountain dawn terror seized William. For the rude winds of the world may be powerless against the flowers of Paradise but they can wither the flowers of Arcadia very easily, and it would be difficult, even for his great love, to keep them from blowing in.

"Time to go home," he said abruptly. Riding back down the steep mountain path, talking with her, laughing with her, having her all to himself within the circle of his protection, which always seemed to him more impregnable when there was no one in it but they two alone, he would forget his fears.

But John elected to come too. "Just as far as the bridge," he said, and it was he who helped Véronique on to her pony, lifting her with a swift easy swing, scrupulously not letting his hands linger on her body or his eyes meet hers, and he who walked beside her, laughing and talking with her, holding her bridle when the path was rough and stony, and William had perforce to fall behind.

He fell a good way behind, of deliberate intent, so that John might have a free field. John, usually so taciturn, always had a good deal to say to Véronique; William could hear the murmur of his gentle low-pitched Scotch voice and Véronique's answering happy laughter. Only when she was with John was there quite that bell-like note in her laughter. Watching them together more lines from that poem that Véronique had quoted came into William's mind.

> "*For we were nursed upon the self-same hill,*
> *Fed the same flock, by fountain, shade and rill.*
> *Together both ere the high lawns appeared*
> *Under the opening eyelids of the morn. . . .*"

He forbore to hurry them, even though time was going on and to be late back might lead to difficulties with Marianne. Watching them he acknowledged to himself that it was not only, though chiefly, for Véronique's sake that he so deeply desired this marriage. It was for his own sake too. If Véronique were to marry a valley man he and she would never be far apart. When he said to himself that there was no price he would not pay for her happiness it was always with a half-unconscious reservation—that he himself should never lose her.

CHAPTER TWO

1

Marianne had restricted the acreage of looking glass in her daughter's room lest vanity be encouraged, but in her own she saw her reflection at every turn. Besides the looking glass on her dressing-table, and the hand mirror that she kept on the table beside the bed, there were two long pier glasses let into the panels of the wardrobe in which it was possible to see the whole of one's person from top to toe. It was very necessary that one should at her age, she considered. When a woman is fifty-six years old and for twenty-four years has endured the rigours of pioneering in a new country she is no longer in any danger of vanity when she looks in the glass, but she needs to see herself from every angle if her façade of dignity is to be equally impressive to the beholder whether he beholds from north, south, east or west.

For that was what she aimed at now, dignity. As a girl, as she could not be beautiful, she had decided to be chic, and had been it, but she had most surprisingly put on weight just lately, and you cannot be chic and stout. But you can be dignified and stout—look at Queen Victoria—and Marianne, though she did not yet equal Her Majesty in the matter of embonpoint, outdid even her great exemplar in the matter of dignity.

The clothes of the period helped. As she stood before the two long pier glasses on this fairest of fair spring mornings, adjusting the dark green folds of her morning gown, she decided that there is nothing like a bustle for dignity. On girls like Véronique she disliked it, for it tended to detract from their natural grace, but for women who were no longer slim it was just the thing. That sixteen-inch projection at the back was in itself a suggestion that extenuation of outline is desirable, and the elegant drapings of the voluminous gown that incorporated it into its being were a further declaration that quantity as well as quality is required for supreme excellence.

Encouraged by this thought, rustling with importance, Marianne moved back to her dressing-table to put on her heavy gold locket, her gold watch and chain and the green-stone earrings that she still wore sometimes in memory of Captain O'Hara. She always put the final touches to her toilette at her dressing-table, for the draped looking glass with its back to the light gave back a more flattering reflection of her face than did the pier glass. There is less to be done about an ageing face than an ageing figure; one cannot, unfortunately, drape it. More's the pity, thought Marianne, looking at hers with grim resignation. Beneath the demurely parted grey hair her face was sallower than ever, and very lined. But there was still something to be said for it, she thought. She had not, like Queen Victoria, been beaten by her mouth, for she could still smilingly frustrate its tendency to droop at the corners, and the glance of her dark eyes was still bright and bird-like. Tai Haruru, were they to meet again, would recognise her.

But she knew they would never meet again, and it was odd, and a little exasperating, that at every dawning she should think of him, and at the first glimmer of star-shine, and during those rare brief moments of her busy day when some shape or sound of beauty made her pause for a moment and look or listen. And peculiar that she who had never been a dreamer should dream now so constantly that she was running home to him through a dark wood, and odder still that in these dreams she should always be a little girl.

For it was William whom she believed to be the one man in her life, whose soul by day she was still seeking up and down the hills and valleys of that arid adventurous country where her spirit lived, that country where the beautiful city on the horizon always turned out to be a desert mirage when one got to it. This turning of the city into a mirage, this pursuit of William's spirit by her spirit, were twin facts that she scarcely acknowledged to herself, but so wearied was the woman by the perpetual escape of the quarry, the perpetual withdrawal of the city, that of late years, though hardly aware of it, she had turned with relief to the peculiar dreams that turned her into a little girl again running home to Tai Haruru. In her dream she never reached the home with the lighted windows that was built in the wood, yet the sense of fear and frustration that tormented her in the daytime pursuit of William was not present in this dream. For the little girl in the dream knew that fairytales always have the right ending, and knew that this was a fairytale because she had been inside one before and knew the feel of it. . . . Marianne Ozanne had stood in Tai Haruru's arms under the stars at Wellington.

But the ageing woman of fifty-six, who was adjusting earrings and watch and chain and locket before her glass, had almost forgotten the sensations of that brief experience; had indeed not tried to remember them, because a full understanding of herself was not a thing that she had ever wanted. . . . Those rare moments of humility when some measure of it had come to her had always proved most disintegrating and uncomfortable. . . . It was only the little girl of the dream who was wise enough to know that there are more sorts of love than one, only the little girl who knew that Marianne Ozanne the woman had mistaken the nature of the city she wanted and had been throughout her life pursuing the wrong man. Had she paid any attention to the life of her spirit the persistent intrusion of Tai Haruru into it might have told Marianne that the right man does not have to be pursued. There had been neither pursuit nor withdrawal upon the deck of the Orion, nor in the garden of the Parsonage at Wellington, only a tacit acknowledgement of oneness.

What was he doing now? wondered Marianne, taking a handkerchief from her drawer. Ringing the bell for Mass in that ridiculous church at the world's end that he had described in that one long letter he had written to her and William about a year after he had left them? Setting out for a day's work in the forest among his precious kauri trees? Sitting on the sea shore in the sun smoking his long curved pipe and waiting for that crazy priest he lived with to come back from a night's fishing? His letter, carried through the wilderness by a Maori to the nearest coast settlement where trading ships put in, had been months in transit, but its many pages had been penned with such vigour and freshness that they had brought his life as vividly before her as though for a while she had lived it with him and were recapturing it in memory. . . . Even now, when she paused in her work, there came sometimes the odd feeling that she not only had lived it with him, but was living it. . . . But this was a sensation that she quickly thrust aside, for she disliked odd feelings and had no wish to become as crazy as he was himself. . . . He and Samuel.

That couple of lunatics! Angrily she banged the drawer of her dressing-table shut and flung open the windows to the sweet morning air. Mad as hatters, both of them. And Samuel had been worse than mad, he had been a monster of selfishness into the bargain. Tai Haruru had at least been without ties but Samuel had been a married man and had had no right whatever to break the heart of her poor Susanna in the way he had. She had no patience with him, and in the story of his death was unable to find anything at all except the pig-headedness and self-will of a man who has never been properly broken in by his wife. . . . William would never have gone adventuring off by himself like that.

Luckily Susanna, judging by her letters, saw it all differently. Tai Haruru, when he visited her in Wellington, had doubtless managed to present the whole crazy business in a favourable light, and once the violence of her first grief had passed she had been able to regard herself with inordinate pride as the wife of a martyr. Well, let her, poor soul, if that comforted her, Marianne had thought, and in the letters that she had written back in answer to Susanna's outpourings she had encouraged the idea, while insisting vehemently that Susanna should leave New Zealand, that she had always disliked, and return to England where the tranquillising effect of a settled government and the gulf stream encouraged a mode of behaviour in men and weather less calculated to undermine a woman's peace.

But Susanna, most surprisingly, had refused to do any such thing. With an obstinacy surprising in one so gentle, and aided and abetted by the bishop and other influential folk who were comparative strangers to her and yet had taken it upon themselves to know better what was for her welfare than Marianne, who had known her for years, she had elected to remain in Wellington and teach in the school there, in the hope of one day becoming a missionary herself.

And when the second Maori war had at last dragged to its conclusion she had had her wish. Two years ago, in 1872, when the last vestiges of rebellion had died away, when there were no more massacres and the white folk could once again draw easy breath, she had been one of a small company of white men and women who established a mission station at the very village in the forest where Samuel had died. They had found his grave with the cross still intact, so terrified had been the Maoris of the curses of Tai Haruru the Sounding Sea. They had built a stout wooden church upon the site of the burnt-out little hut that had been his church, and a dispensary where had been his dispensary, and Marianne would be interested to hear, wrote Susanna in glowing pride, that they had made a few converts already. Marianne, her interest in missions being merely tepid, was not particularly interested. If she was interested in any mission it was a Roman Catholic one at the world's end, about which she had been told only once, and was not likely to be told again.

No, she would not hear from Tai Haruru again. She knew that quite certainly. Her only contact with him now was this strange holding of him in her thoughts and dreams by day and night, that she accomplished without any volition of her own.

She consulted the large important-looking gold watch that was tucked into her waistband, that William had given her when the tide of their fortunes had first turned in this place and he had had a little money to spare for luxuries. She smiled tenderly as she consulted it. It had not been anything for himself that he had bought, nor even for Véronique, but a watch and chain for his wife. It was ridiculous of her to feel sometimes that he was not yet entirely hers. She had made him and saved him and he worshipped her.

It was a pity that there was no one to see her sail down the stairs and into the kitchen. Her exits and entrances had always been memorable but now with her added weight they had become positively majestic. She herself, this morning, expecting to find William,

Véronique and Nat all in the kitchen to greet her, felt her superb entry fall a little flat. Majesty is scarcely majesty without subservient servitors, and Old Nick's raucous, "Oh my, dearie!" was more mocking than subservient. She eyed him coldly. She loved him no better as the years went on, and found his obstinate longevity as irksome as it was astounding. She looked about her. Where in the world were they all? The kettle was singing on the hob and the table was laid, but Véronique should have been frying the bacon and eggs and cutting the bread, William should have been bringing in water from the well and Nat mixing up the food for the chickens. Her mouth set a little grimly as she tied on an apron and prepared to do Véronique's work for her. The child was probably only just outside, weeding her precious garden, but she had found by experience that it is much more efficacious, as well as more dignified, to do other people's neglected jobs yourself, with the air of a martyr, than to shout in a vulgar way for them to come and do them. When they come and find you burning at the stake without a word of complaint they are made so uncomfortable that they do not sin again. Marianne imagined that she had long since practically abandoned anger for subtler weapons. . . . Anger was too exhausting a weapon for a tired woman. . . . But she had done no more than stretch out her hand for the frying pan when that hand was arrested in mid-air. The frying pan hung always on a hook by the grandfather clock, with Véronique's crop on a hook just below it, and the crop was not there. It needed only that tiny fact, combined with William's sheepishness early this morning, to tell her what had happened. Once again, like a couple of naughty children playing truant from their schoolmarm, they had run off to enjoy themselves without her knowledge. Several times before she had caught them doing this, and had said nothing, and they had not known that she had known. But this morning William had actually lied to her. That was too much. White-faced, she held on to the kitchen table fighting an onslaught of the old anger that she had never expected to feel again. She was in truth very tired. Her years of struggle had taxed even her vitality, and she had been short of sleep last night, so long had she and William argued about the relative values of steam and gold and sheep. She was incredibly tired and her fatigue opened the way to her anger. Why must they deceive her in this way? Had she ever begrudged them their pleasures? No, never, and she worked her fingers to the bone for them. She was an old woman, worn out before her time, and all because she had toiled night and day for years and years for a couple of ingrates who had not even sufficient affection for her to admit her to their confidence. She had given her whole life to

William only to have him desert her now for the child she had given him; and that same child preferred the father who had suffered for her not so much as an ache in his little finger to the mother who had borne her in so much pain. Here she was, alone in this beautiful home that she had made for them, expected to fry the bacon and eggs and bring the water from the well without assistance, while they went gallivanting off up the mountains without a single thought for anyone or anything except their own selfish pleasure. Leaving her alone here. Alone. Even Nat, who ought to have been here mixing up the chickens' food, was out in the stable fussing over those wretched animals whom he cared for far more than he cared for Marianne Ozanne, who had opened her home to him when Captain O'Hara died, who had given him such astonishing love and devotion, recking nothing at all of the burden that his increasing years and frailty laid upon her already overburdened strength. Yes, she was near the breaking point now. She had toiled and toiled for years and years, only to be left quite alone at the end of it all without a word of thanks from a single soul for whom she had laboured. It had always been like this. Not a word of thanks had she ever had for all the work she had done for the poor on the Island. And no one really loved her. They might say they did, but they didn't. Tai Haruru had said he loved her, but he had ridden off to the world's end and left her to tackle the new life in South Island quite alone. Her husband and child might say they loved her but they rode off up the mountains to enjoy themselves and left her alone to fry the breakfast and carry the water from the well. Nat might indicate affection by those queer noises he made but he was not here with her now in this misery. She was alone. She always had been and she always would be. She was a changeling who only in dreams could find the way home. She sank down on to the chair behind her, covered her face with her hands and wept.

A hand was laid on her shoulder with a reassuring pressure and a series of loving and distressful noises went off like fireworks in her right ear. She looked up to find Nat beside her, his one eye anxiously searching her face, his ancient monkey countenance puckered into a mask of distress that would have been comical but for the anguish of it, the anguish of love that asks nothing better than to take upon itself all the pain of the beloved but is denied that supreme joy by the insulating nature of pain, that once let loose makes of its victim a lost island in the flood. Your country can be my country, Nat cried out voicelessly to Marianne, and your God mine, where you live I can live and there can I be buried, but your pain cannot be my pain and because it cannot I too am in pain, and so we look at each other across the double flood of it and know the ultimate sorrow of mortality.

Marianne was all at once most deeply touched and most profoundly irritated. To realise for the first time the greatness of Nat's love for her, that was balm, but the knowledge that this terrific scene of emotion had been called forth by such a trivial incident, that she was in fact making an enormous fuss about nothing, was galling to her pride and rubbed her up the wrong way so completely that she flashed out at poor Nat in a perfect fury of self-justification.

"No, I'm not ill," she stormed in answer to his anxious noises of enquiry. "Not ill, only bitterly hurt. Why do they go off like this without telling me?"

"To spare ye, Ma'am," said Nat.

"To *spare* me?" demanded Marianne.

"Ye see, Ma'am," said Nat gently, and speaking the exact truth, as was his habit, "if Mr. Ozanne and Miss Véronique tell ye they are seekin' a bit of pleasure without ye, it bein', maybe, somethin' they can't invite ye to partake in, such as ridin', ye Ma'am never havin' learnt to ride, why then Ma'am ye're that hurt an' jealous that it grieves 'em. An' so, Ma'am, ye see, they keep silent."

Used though she was to Nat's mumbling remarks Marianne in her anger missed most of this. But she caught the word "jealous" and it was like fuel thrown on the fire of her anger.

"Jealous?" she raged. "Jealous? I'm never jealous! And to spare me, you said? Is it to spare me that I am left to carry in the water alone? All my life long, Nat, I have been toiling for those I love without a word of thanks! Have you mixed the chicken food this morning, Nat? I don't see it."

Nat went quietly out of the kitchen and that small portion of her mind that was not occupied with her own troubles noticed that his face looked suddenly grey. It was years since she had lost her temper like this, and it was the very first time that she had lost it with Nat himself. Then her sobs broke out afresh and she forgot all about him.

She took down the frying pan and began to fry the eggs and bacon. If they were cold by the time William and Véronique arrived, that would be their fault, for it was already long past breakfast time. As she turned the fizzling slices over and over she fought down her sobs, for she was not going to be caught crying by her erring husband and child. They should not know how deeply their callous behaviour had hurt her. She had too much pride for that. Jealous! How dared Nat say such a thing? Yet he, at least, loved her still. She would not forget the look of love she had seen on his face. Vaguely she was aware of him coming in and out, first with the chicken food ready mixed to be boiled over the fire later, and then with buckets of water that he had drawn up from the well, and her anger against her husband stirred afresh. For it was not fair that Nat should have to do William's work for him. He was a very old man now, probably nearer ninety than eighty, and sometimes she thought that his heart was not strong. It was too bad of William.

A moment later the door opened to admit William, with Véronique just behind him, both of them smiling those broad yet uneasy smiles with which the erring endeavour to deflect attention from their sins. They opened their mouths wide to utter bright, affectionate remarks, similarly intentioned, but Marianne cut them short.

"You're very late," she said coldly. "How untidy you look, Véronique. Nat is drawing the water for you, William."

"The old scoundrel!" ejaculated William in consternation. "I've told him time and again never to do that. It's too heavy a job. What induced him to do such a thing? I'd have been back in a moment. Where is he?"

"At the well, no doubt," said Marianne.

William went out and Véronique came to Marianne. "Give me the frying pan, Mamma darling," she said gaily. "That's my job, you know."

"I am aware of it," said Marianne. "But I am quite accustomed to doing all the work. I have been doing it all my life. Hadn't you better wash your extremely dirty hands?"

Véronique drew back, biting her lip to keep the tears from coming, and there was a cold hateful silence in the kitchen, while she washed her hands at the sink and Marianne laid the bacon and eggs, perfectly cooked in spite of her emotion, on a pink china dish.

Then the door was kicked open from outside and the two women turned, startled, to see William standing on the threshold with Nat in his arms.

"Found him lying in a faint over the well parapet," said William briefly. "Where's the whisky?"

2

Two days later Nat died in his sleep of heart failure and extreme old age, his death as easy and painless as a death well can be. He never fully recovered consciousness again and throughout the last day of his life he was reliving the last hours of the Green Dolphin, standing beside Captain O'Hara on the poop as the great ship sped to her death. Marianne, performing every service for him herself, sitting beside him when there was nothing active that she could do and watching him in an agony of love, wished that he would say one word to her before he went away. But he spoke only to Captain O'Hara, and that in such confused and broken speech that she could seldom make out what he said, until the last sentence of all, which came out clear and strong, almost in the tones of Captain O'Hara's own voice. "I'm followin' close behind ye. I'll be with ye in a moment." After that he fell asleep and did not wake again.

William and Véronique grieved for Nat, and William reproached himself most humbly for that unpunctuality of his that had been the cause of the old fellow's death, yet they both sorrowed without bitterness, for after all dear old Nat had been incredibly old, and they were glad for him that his death had been so peaceful and so easy. Old Nick, too, though he drooped in his cage and moulted quite a lot of tail feathers, seemed resigned. The sorrow of the three of them, though sincere, had a gentleness that befitted the circumstances, and against its background the violence of Marianne's grief appeared almost ridiculous.

"After all, dearest, it isn't as though you had anything to reproach yourself with," argued William tenderly, leaning over the foot of the great four-poster and regarding his wife's ravaged face upon the pillow with considerable perturbation. . . . The blow of Nat's death, coming upon her when she was overwrought and overtired, had so completely exhausted her that he and Véronique had had to put her to bed, and the sight of Marianne in bed in the daytime, when she was not actually ill, was so astonishing that he felt as perturbed as though this were North Island and there'd been an earthquake. "Not a darned thing with which to reproach yourself," he repeated energetically. "Astonishing, the way you always looked after the old fellow."

"You see, he was—the poor," said Marianne brokenly. "I promised your father."

William gaped at her in consternation. Was she light-headed?

"I'll not be so nice a woman now he's gone, William," she continued. "He called out all that is best in me. He was—the child. I see now why I've always loved the poor. They stood to me for the child."

"What child?" asked the puzzled William.

"There is a child standing alongside us all whom we must love and emulate," said Marianne. "Otherwise it's all no good."

"Upon my word, dearest, I don't quite know what you're talking about," said William, and he came round the bed and laid his great hand on her forehead. "Must have a temperature," he muttered.

"I doubt if I know what I'm talking about either," said Marianne, "but I haven't got a temperature."

And then she began weakly to sob again.

"There! There!" said William. "There's nothing to cry about. You've not got a single thing to reproach yourself with. Not a damn thing."

This parrot cry of his was the least comforting thing he could have said to poor Marianne, for like a thorn stuck in her mind was the unacknowledged knowledge that she had. "It's because you were late for breakfast that he drew the water from the well," she sobbed.

"Yes, yes, yes," said William humbly. "All my fault, dearest. All my fault. I'm damn sorry."

"Don't swear, William," sobbed Marianne.

Véronique's head came round the door. "I've some tea here, Mamma. Could you fancy it?"

"Just a cup. My head's too bad to eat," lamented Marianne. "William, take your hand off my forehead, you're driving me distracted."

William tiptoed on squeaking boots from the room, thankfully leaving the floor to his daughter. Véronique's pretty face was puckered with distress as she set the tray beside the bed and plumped up her mother's pillows. Except for an occasional cold in the head Mamma never ailed, and she was in a regular panic. It couldn't be only the grief for Nat that was making her so bad. What if she was going into a decline? What if she had scarlet fever or diphtheria? What if she were going to die? Tears rose to Véronique's eyes and her heart seemed to be beating in her throat.

"Oh, Mamma, Mamma, I wish I knew what was the matter with you!" she wailed.

Marianne looked up into her daughter's beautiful tear-filled eyes and saw there a love far greater than she had known Véronique felt for her. She had known the child loved her, of course, but she had not known she loved her as much as this. Triumph welled in her at the sight of her daughter's distress; but after it came that cold calculation that had always enabled her to seize upon everything that came to hand, even the suffering or love of those she cared for, to bring her nearer to that new magical city that all her life long had been looming up so enticingly on her horizon.

"There's nothing the matter with me, dear," she said, "but I'm worn out with toiling away year after year in this wretched farm at the back of beyond. It's rest and change I want, Véronique, and if I don't get them I don't see how I can go on."

"But of course you must have them, darling Mamma!"

"It would have been so heavenly to have gone and stayed at Dunedin for a bit," said Marianne, "and smelled the sea again and had a little society. I was born by the sea, you know, and it's the breath of life to me, and in my girlhood I always moved in the best society. I abandoned everything for your dear Papa, and I've never reproached him for the hardships of my life since my marriage, but there are times when one longs for a little ease, a little comfort——"

She wept again and Véronique's mind was too distracted by anxiety to note the comfort of her mother's bedroom, or the pile of exquisite down-filled pillows against which Marianne was taking her ease at this moment.

"But of course, Mamma," she cried. "You must go away for a good long holiday. I'll look after Papa and the house. You need not worry about anything, I'll look after everything."

"I very much doubt if I am fit to go alone, darling," lamented Marianne. "You've no idea how weak and ill I feel."

"Then I'll come with you," said Véronique.

"But I'd be distracted with anxiety if poor Papa was left here all alone without either of us."

"I know what we'll do!" cried Véronique in triumph. "We'll *all* go! John Ogilvie can look after everything for Papa. Dear old John is as reliable as an oak tree. Papa has said so over and over again."

Marianne's broken voice steadied and rose to tones of almost epic tragedy. "There's nothing in the world," she declared, "that would root your father up out of this hateful valley. If only you knew, Véronique, how I've argued and implored, and all to no purpose!"

"There's nothing Papa wouldn't do to get you well, Mamma," said Véronique. "We love you so dearly, he and I. Leave it to me, Mamma. I'll persuade him."

Véronique was happy again now. Her mother's passionate spate of conversation had relieved her mind as to the seriousness of her condition, and she was already planning how she would pack her mother's trunks for her, run her errands, give her her breakfast in bed every single day, do everything in her power to get her rested before they started. Marianne looked at her daughter over the top of her lace-trimmed handkerchief and the brightness of her bird-like glance was not due to fever.

"We'd have such fun, Véronique," she cried. "You'd be able to go to balls and parties and I could buy you some really smart gowns. You're so pretty, dearest, and there's no one here to see you except the silly sheep. You're so patient about it, darling, but you never have any fun here. Even though it is rather too full of strait-laced Scotch people there is plenty of society in Dunedin. Now I come to think of it Mrs. Bennet lives there. She's a sister of that friend of Aunt Susanna's whom we stayed with years ago at Nelson, and I have her address. She's wealthy and moves in the best society. She'd introduce you to the right people. . . . The Union Steamship Company was formed by Dunedin men," she added, "and your father is so interested in steam. If *only* he——"

"Leave Papa to me," interrupted Véronique, her eyes dancing, and flew out of the room. Marianne lay back on her pillows flushed with triumph. She had inserted the thin end of the wedge.

Then into her rosy triumph there intruded a cold little trickle of memory. She was back again in the Le Paradis garden, congratulating herself because Dr. Ozanne's illness had enabled her to strengthen her hold on William. Why should she think of that just now, and why should the memory make her feel so uncomfortable? She thrust the questions away, remembering suddenly that morbid introspection should not be encouraged in illness, poured herself out a second cup of tea and found that she could eat something after all.

3

Véronique entered the kitchen like a whirlwind and precipitated herself into her father's arms. "Papa! Papa! Please will you take Mamma and me for a holiday to Dunedin? Oh Papa, please, please! Mamma will get quite well again if she has a rest and change, and I shall be able to go to balls, Papa, and have some new frocks."

William looked down soberly at his daughter, and his face hardened and a slight bitterness dawned in his eyes. He had always wondered why Marianne had not tried to enlist her daughter as an ally in her fight to leave the Country of the Green Pastures. She had been waiting, no doubt, for the right moment. Marianne was always very clever at choosing the right moment. Véronique would probably have resisted the thought of leaving her lovely valley for ever, but to leave it for a holiday was another thing altogether, and a thrilling idea for a girl who had never had much fun. Yes, Marianne had been very clever, and in sheer humanity he could not refuse to let her and Véronique go. But he was not going too. He must hold on here tenaciously, for if Marianne once got him to Dunedin heaven knew what wiles she might not exert to keep him there.

"Of course you and Mamma shall go," he said. "But you won't need me. I must stay here."

"But, Papa, Mamma won't go unless you go too. She's made up her mind about that, and you know what Mamma is once she makes up her mind. Oh, Papa, you *must* come too. You can trust John to look after everything here. You know you can. Oh, Papa, Papa, please, please! Mamma is grieving so dreadfully over Nat and it will turn her thoughts. I'd like it, too, Papa. You know, Papa, I've never been to a proper ball."

Her face was flushed and sparkling with eagerness, but in the wide blue eyes he saw a dawning of surprise and apprehension, and he knew it was because this was the first time in her life that she had seen him with a hard-set mouth and bitterness in his eyes. If he held out she might find it difficult to forgive him. . . . Weakly he gave in.

"Have it all your own way, darling," he said, his cheek against hers. "I'll do anything that you and Mamma want."

And after all, he thought, what right had he to think that Marianne, overwhelmed with grief as she was, had any ulterior motive behind this suggestion of a holiday? It was detestable of him to think such a thing, with dear old Nat not two days buried, and suddenly he flushed hotly with shame as he clasped the ecstatic Véronique in his arms. And if he went with them he would be able to look after Véronique. Through life and death and beyond he believed he would always be able to save Véronique from all harm.

CHAPTER THREE

1

Véronique sat in the window seat of their parlour looking out across the street to the houses opposite. They had taken extremely expensive rooms in one of the most prosperous quarters of Dunedin and the houses that Véronique looked at were charming and dignified, with flights of steps leading up to front doors flanked by pillars. Trees lined the street, and the smart carriages that drove up and down all day long were chequered by the faintly stirring leaf shadows of high summer. Véronique had pushed the window wide open, so that she might feel the cool breeze upon her hot cheeks; it came from the sea, the cold Pacific that beat against the high cliffs of Dunedin, and the mountain-bred girl welcomed its coolness with delight. She found a town in summer rather stuffy, even Dunedin with its generally rigorous climate, and so did Old Nick, petulantly scratching himself and swearing under his breath in the cage beside her, but whereas Old Nick did not in the least mind expressing his feelings on the subject Véronique refused to own them even to herself. Dunedin was perfect. Life was an ecstatic whirling dream of fun and laughter, and she had never been so deliriously happy in all her life before. Every evening she assured William of this fact, and every evening his gentle answering smile left her vaguely irritated. Why couldn't he be more enthusiastic about this glorious holiday that they were having? Why couldn't he enjoy himself more at the lovely parties they went to? It spoilt things for her to have him not so thrilled over everything as she and Marianne were. She couldn't help being vexed with him because he was not so thrilled. And imperceptibly, during these last two months, she had drawn a little away from her father and nearer to her mother. . . . Marianne liked Frederick. . . . William had never said he didn't like Frederick, and he was always exceedingly polite to him, but Véronique knew in her bones that her father was withholding from Frederick that entire devotion that was Frederick's due.

And she considered it most ungrateful of him because Frederick had done simply everything for them. They had been in quite humble lodgings at first, clean but not very luxurious. William had gone on to Dunedin ahead of his wife and daughter and found them himself, and had got everything ready to receive Marianne when she and Véronique arrived, even to flowers in bowls on the window-sills and books from the circulating library upon the table. Véronique had liked these lodgings, and had enjoyed exploring Dunedin with him, and going shopping with Marianne, and the novelty of everything had at first completely satisfied her. But Marianne had been discontented from the beginning. She had found the lodgings cramped and the cooking too plain and she hadn't got well as quickly as she should have done. William had thought the quiet of the lodgings he had found—they were in a cul-de-sac and so one was spared the noise of passing carriages—would have been just the thing for her in her exhausted condition, but somehow they hadn't seemed to be. Mrs. Bennet had been duly notified of their presence and had called, but had turned out to be a sad sufferer from asthma. She was unable to entertain other than very quietly, she had said with a sigh, she was unequal to the exertion. And when she had asked them to her house there had been no one there under seventy and it had, indeed, been very quiet. "But she would have put herself out a bit more," Marianne had said irritably to William, "if we had been in more stylish lodgings." And William had looked very discouraged and Marianne had gone to bed early with a headache, though she had done nothing at all to bring it on, had scarcely, in fact, except for the dull party, stirred out of her armchair all day.

And then Frederick had come to the rescue, exactly like the prince in a fairytale.

Véronique and Marianne had attended an afternoon concert

dressed in the very smartest of their new gowns, Marianne in purple silk, beribboned and flounced, with a very smart little hat trimmed with violets, and Véronique in pale blue, the overskirt draped in U-shaped folds in front and hitched up at the back to show an underskirt composed of hundreds of cascading frills. Her little white hat had been tipped well forward over her nose so as to show the mass of pale gold ringlets at the back of her head, and had had a blue feather in it. When they had entered the vestibule Frederick had just been entering too, and had stood politely aside, with a most graceful bow, to let them go in first. Marianne had swept past him with a regal inclination of the head but Véronique had paused a moment intending to say thank you, because she thought it was so good of him to bow like that to strangers. . . . The shepherds at home never bowed and she was not accustomed to the courtesy. . . . Nor was she accustomed to young men like Frederick and the glorious spectacle had been so astonishing that instead of saying thank you she had just stopped still and stared. And then, as she had stood there rooted to the ground like the nymph Daphne, a strange glow had thrilled through her, so that even her fingertips tingled. . . . For this was the lover of her dreams. . . . This, without any doubt at all, was the lover she had dreamed of in the valley at home.

Véronique was a romantic child, yet Frederick Ackroyd, newly arrived from England, was enough of an anachronism in this country to make even an experienced matron stand and stare. There were men of wealth in Dunedin but their wealth had been won by gruelling hard work, and they bore the marks of it in a ruggedness of demeanour that did not allow of easy smiles and bows. Not so Frederick, who had never hitherto done a hand's turn in his life. Yet his grace, though exquisite, was like that of a tiger-lily, completely masculine. Véronique, bred to hardness, would not have been attracted by an effeminate man. The lover of her dreams had been a tiger-lily man and Frederick exactly filled the bill. He was tall and dark, with a skin tanned brown by the long sea voyage from England. His face, with its oddly irregular features, was not perhaps strictly beautiful, but the challenging brilliance of his ardent dark eyes and flashing smile made it immensely attractive. His vitality was to most older people as shattering as a couple of days' hard work with no night's rest in between, but to those of his own generation, or to those like Marianne whose vitality nearly matched his own, as exciting as a gale of wind. Guardsman that he was, with a back as straight as a ramrod and strong hands hardened by much holding of the bridle, he yet wore the indolent clothes of the period, the velvet sack coat with a flower in the buttonhole, the soft turned-down collar and loosely knotted tie, with an easy naturalness that made them look exactly right on him. But then everything that Frederick wore always looked exactly right, just as everything he did and said was the right word and action for that particular moment, for he was an experienced man of the world and by birth an aristocrat. Until that afternoon Véronique had not met his like before and Marianne had only seen it in the distance, so that by the time the concert was over and he had escorted them back to their lodgings he had had them both completely captivated. . . . How exactly he had managed to introduce himself to them they could not afterwards remember, but they had assured William it had all been done in the most gentlemanly manner, without a trace of presumption. . . . And before they had had time to turn round he had found them new lodgings and introduced them to the smartest society in Dunedin, and was attending them to all the parties, and Marianne was completely well again and Véronique was living in a fairyland of bliss.

Only William was unhappy. Frederick Ackroyd had not come out to New Zealand merely to visit his maternal uncle, old Tom Anderson the shipping magnate, he had come to stay. His uncle had given him work and he was already slaving like a nigger—so he assured William, though William could see no signs of overwork—in the office of the Union Steamship Company. Why? Why should a young guardsman who—so one gathered from the little remarks that he let fall now and then with the most charming nonchalance—had had the London of the seventies entirely at his feet, throw the whole thing up and come out to the other side of the world to be a quill driver in his uncle's office? Why? William was haunted by the remembrance that the colonies are a convenient dumping ground for unsatisfactory younger sons, but there seemed no one whom he could ask for precise information. Old Tom Anderson was a shrewd hard-headed genial old party who had also emigrated as a young man and had made his pile speculating in gold, but in spite of his geniality, and his obvious liking for William, it was difficult to question him about his nephew. For one thing William knew that Tom Anderson was not incommoded by a conscience and spoke the truth only when he found it to his convenience to do so. And then there was the old unwritten law of pioneer life—never ask questions about a man's past life—and there was the humbling memory that he himself in his youth had not been able to continue living in his native land. So he just blundered on from day to day, trying to think the best of Frederick, trying not to notice, on those rare occasions when his charming irregular face was not irradiated by laughter, the hardness of Frederick's jaw, the fullness of his lips, the ruthless ardour of his eyes when they rested on Véronique; above all trying not to notice the extraordinary cleverness of his handling of Véronique and her mother. For head over ears in love though he was, and obviously passionate by nature, he was going slow with Véronique, evidently aware that so delicate a nymph would have been scared by too blatant a possessiveness. And with Marianne he was also being detestably clever. He had taken her measure at the first glance, apparently, and the subtleness of the flattery with which he fed her, his agreement with her every opinion, his instant yielding to her every whim, while all the while he talked to her there was that faint whip-lash of contempt in his bright glance, made William feel positively ill. For neither Frederick's gentleness with Véronique nor his deference to her mother were in keeping either with his jaw or his mouth; if he were to attain the end for which he was imposing this unnatural restraint upon himself his reaction would most certainly be in proportion to the greatness of the previous restraint.

In only one thing was Frederick's judgment at fault, he regarded William as quite negligible. Love such as William's for his daughter had not hitherto fallen within Frederick's experience; he was un-aware how as regards the beloved it can sharpen the perceptions of even those who are not in most things acute observers, and when the time comes for action can give to a naturally yielding nature an obstinacy as adamant as iron.

But if Frederick was not yet up against that hidden vein of strength in William Marianne was. When at the end of the first month of their holiday his suggestion that they should all return home now had been vigorously resisted by his wife and daughter he had yielded and agreed to stay on for two more months, but nothing would induce him to yield to the suggestion of Mr. Anderson that he should sell his farm and throw in his lot with the Union Steamship Company. Marianne, sensing at once the old man's great liking for her husband, had put in an immense amount of skilful underground labour to induce him to make a very favourable offer to William. . . . Only to have William refuse it point blank. . . . He liked being a sheep farmer, he told Mr. Anderson, and a sheep farmer he would remain, let the price of wool fall as it might. He realised the im-mense prospects held out by steam, but as a sailor of the old days of sail he had always disliked steam, and excessive wealth held no attractions for him. He thanked Mr. Anderson for his generous offer but begged leave to refuse it. His obstinacy was enough to drive one distracted, Marianne lamented to Véronique. Had he no consideration at all for his poor wife, enjoying a little ease and com-fort for the first time since she had married him? She was so happy here, she was so well, she had made such friends with Mrs. Anderson, there was such a beautiful house for sale in the very next street to the Andersons, and Papa was most unfeeling and cruel to propose dragging her back again to the hardships of that detestable mountain valley. After all, she had endured ten years of it just to please him, could he not now endure a spell of city life to please her? And Véronique, to whom in her new mood of hectic excitement her old home had become almost a forgotten dream of childhood, agreed with her mother. She had had an idea that they had originally settled in the Country of the Green Pastures to please Mamma, but evidently she had been mistaken, for according to Mamma it had been to please Papa, in which case Papa certainly ought to let Mamma, this time, choose where they should live. "It will be all right, Mamma," she would say consolingly to the despairing Marianne. "Frederick has spoken to Mr. Anderson and he has promised to keep the offer open indefinitely. We'll bring Papa round, you'll see."

Véronique's confidence quieted Marianne, for the child had always been able to manage her father. If only Véronique and Frederick would become definitely engaged. The prospect of being near his daughter after her marriage would do more than anything else to keep William in Dunedin.

Véronique, too, as she sat in the window-seat looking across the street, wished that she and Frederick could become properly engaged. Unknown to their relatives they had long ago, just a week after their first meeting, declared their undying and unalterable devotion to each other, but Frederick did not want their love to become public property just at present. His affairs in England were not definitely wound up yet, he said, and it was better that they should be before he announced his engagement. Véronique acquiesced without question, though she was aware that Frederick was departing from the usual procedure in speaking to her before he had spoken to her Papa. Such was her faith in him that she was sure his reasons were all they should be. . . . But she did hate keeping their engagement secret. . . . It was the first time in her life that she had kept anything from her father.

The clock on the mantelpiece chimed out the hour and she jumped up. There was a ball at the Andersons' this evening and they were all going, and Frederick was to fetch them. It was time she got dressed. Mamma was already dressing, had been for the last half hour, but then Mamma took so long to dress.

In her room, instead of beginning at once to dress, she lay down for a little on her bed. She had not meant to do so but her bed looked so cool and inviting and her head was aching abominably. This headache was always with her nowadays and it was a most dreadful nuisance. It was the serpent in her paradise, forcing her to the perpetual playing of a part. Pain divided one into two selves, she had discovered, a querulous complaining person who only wanted to go to bed and stay there and not to be made to feel or do anything at all ever again, and another person who was always trying to be extravagantly bright and gay so that no one should notice the existence of the querulous person, and neither of these people seemed to be one's real self. . . . And to lose one's sense of reality made one feel like a lost soul, a feeling that was simply horrid. . . . Now she came to think of it she had not felt like her real self for a very long time, not, surely, since she had met Frederick. And she wanted to be her real self for Frederick's sake. She did not want to give her wonderful lover either the querulous headachy Véronique, nor the excited person whose laugh was too high and whose talk got so out of hand that there were times when the only thing she knew about what she was saying was that she oughtn't to have said it. She wanted to give him the real Véronique who as one whole and happy person had moved so serenely through the peaceful days that now seemed to her as distant as a dream. . . . To her astonishment she found that she was crying.

She got up at once, poured cold water into her basin and angrily bathed away the tears. It was absurd to cry when she was so gloriously happy! The douche of cold water stopped the crying fit, and did her head good too, and as she dressed she found herself thinking quite consecutively and clearly, almost as though the confusion of being two people had vanished and she was made one again, about being in love.

It was not a bit like she had expected it to be. She had expected that the coming together of two people destined to be one person would be a tranquillising, satisfying, energising thing. As a country girl she had knowledge of many matings. She had heard that exquisite, cool, tranquil note that creeps into the song of a bird when the beloved is won, had seen the union of sun and rain proclaim itself in the utterly satisfying circle of the rainbow, and new strong energy spring from the union of shower and sod, flint and tinder, mill-wheel and water. But what she was experiencing now wasn't like that at all. There was nothing tranquil or cool about it—it was hot and scorching. Nor was it satisfying. Frederick's kisses, tender yet given with hot lips, left her not satisfied but hungry for whatever it was that was pent up behind what Marianne called the gentlemanly rectitude of his behaviour like flood water behind a dam; she was hungry for it and yet she was instinctively afraid of it.

She pulled herself up sharply. Whatever was she thinking? To think this way was treason to her love. If this sudden momentary fusion of her two selves into one person again was making a traitor of her then it would be better not to be whole. And if being in love was not what she had expected it to be it was nevertheless glorious. In spite of the headache she was madly happy. When she walked along the street with Frederick the wind sounded like trumpets and the clouds were banners flying in the air. If she drank tea in his presence it turned to champagne, and the bread and butter to peaches and caviare. And as for waltzing with Frederick—there were no words at all that could describe what that was. It was the nearest thing to heaven that she had ever known.

At thought of the ball to-night she suddenly became like a mad thing for excitement. Oh, the ecstasy of the waltz! Although before she had come to Dunedin she had danced only the country dances that her mother had taught her she had picked it up very quickly under Frederick's expert tuition, and now she vowed that she was the most exquisite dancer he had ever known. To-night, once again, they would circle together to the music of Strauss and Waldteufel and she would rise to the topmost heights of ecstasy. . . . If her headache let her.

Profoundly exasperated she paused in the feverish brushing of her curls to fish out from her drawer a little bottle of tablets that she had secretly bought from the chemist. She swallowed two, with one eye on the door lest Mamma should come in, for Mamma disapproved of drug-taking in the very mildest form and had expressly forbidden it, and then returned again to her toilette.

When she had finished it she looked at herself for a long time in the glass and was satisfied. Her frock was a new one, made for her by Mrs. Anderson's own dressmaker, and it was the very latest mode. It was white satin, fitting like a sheath over her breasts and into the curve of her waist, then breaking over the hips into a cascade of frills and flounces. A huge bow was perched upon the bustle at the back and the neck was very low indeed. In her hair and in the front of her dress she fastened some crimson hothouse gardenias that Frederick had sent her. Altogether her toilette was exceedingly smart and she was quite sure that Papa would not approve of it. This thought caused her only the tiniest pang, for Frederick's conviction that William and his opinions were alike negligible, though unexpressed, had nevertheless not been without influence upon Véronique's present attitude towards her father. Yes, the dress was

smart, and she looked lovely in it, with her feverishly flushed cheeks
and sparkling eyes. At home, what with having only such a tiny
mirror in her room and nobody telling her she was beautiful she had
not known that she was. It was nice, now, to know it; exhilarating
to see the reflection of her exquisiteness in Frederick's eyes as well
as in this nice large looking glass. She left her room with head held
high and proudly smiling mouth and swept into the parlour.

William, slumped rather moodily in the armchair reading the
paper with inattention, looked up and from force of habit gave her
the old smile of comradeship that had always been hers only. Then
his smile died out, for her proud mouth, though it went through the
motions of smiling at him, could no longer achieve quite the old
answering sweetness. . . . She no longer considered him her dearest
on earth. . . . And something of her old nymph-like air had deserted
her too; her gait was too self-conscious now for the perfection of
grace. Rare creature though she was she was made of too im-
pressionable stuff, he thought, and he was to blame that he had
brought her to an environment that could stamp her with the wrong
device. His shepherdess had not been made to flaunt the proud airs
and the exotic blossoms of a fashionable woman of the world but to
carry the crook and the wild flowers of those who tend their
thoughts in quiet places.

Yet never had he loved her so deeply as he did now, and he felt no
bitterness that he was no longer first with her; only grief and pain
that she seemed to be passing away from him into unworthy keeping.
Looking at her he thought for the hundredth time that he would
pay any price demanded of him to secure her happiness. . . . Except
separation from her. . . .

Her smile faded abruptly. "Papa!" she cried in exasperation.
"You're not dressed! And Frederick may be here at any moment.
You'll keep us all waiting. Hurry!"

Her usually gentle voice had an edge of sharp nervous exasperation that he had never heard before. Though there was plenty of
time he got up quickly, almost as nervous as she was, and sent an
ornate china vase full of peacocks' feathers, that was balanced pre-
cariously upon a small unnecessary bracket next to his chair,
crashing to the ground.

"Papa!" The shock and crash broke the tension of her strained
nerves altogether, and she stamped her foot and began to sob.

"Allow me," said Frederick's cool voice.

He bent with William to retrieve the scattered pieces while she
stood in the window struggling with her anger and her tears. Her
father, red-faced, stout, breathing stertorously, his collar awry and

the perspiration of his embarrassment standing out on his forehead, looked to her newly critical eyes almost vulgar beside the immaculate Frederick, cool, shining and polished in his evening clothes. How *could* Papa shame her like this before Frederick!

"Don't you trouble, Sir. I'll do it."

The words were suavely polite, but William felt himself dismissed, and went humbly away to the large bedroom where Marianne had just hooked her stay laces to the bedpost. She looked round to rebuke him sharply, for he had forgotten to knock at the door, and she did not like to be intruded upon at these intimate moments without due warning, but something in his aspect checked her. He was looking like a sad mangy old lion, looking, in fact, exactly as his father had done in moments of depression. She untethered herself, flung her wrapper round her, came to him and put her arms round his neck, feeling as she kissed him that her love was enfolding not one man but two, those two who had always been so good to her. "We have each other, William," she consoled him. "Do you remember the day when you first came to the Island and we sat side by side on the packing case? Even then I loved you. There was no Véronique then. Sensible fathers and mothers, when their children marry, go back to the old days and renew their youth."

He kissed her tenderly, but the vision that her words had called up was that of rosy, plump little Marguerite sitting on the stool at his father's knee and smiling at him over the top of a huge slice of bread and treacle. Her smile was so vivid and so real that she might have been with him in the room, a living presence who had flown across time and space to comfort him. To Marianne's intense delight his face shone as she had never yet seen it shining at words of hers. She glowed with triumph. With Véronique married he would be utterly hers.

2

Frederick, meanwhile, was comforting his love. "It is not your father who is late but I who am early, sweetheart," he consoled her. "I am always early when I am to take you anywhere. It's an intolerable infliction to be away from you. You look lovelier than ever, Véronique. It suits you to be a little angry."

He took her in his arms gently, as he always did, but suddenly his calculated restraint snapped and he pulled her so close to him that she could scarcely breathe. It came so suddenly that she was startled and unconsciously lifted her face to give him a butterfly kiss, as she did when William held her tighter than she liked. But Frederick was not accustomed to the delicacy of Arcadian love and mis-understood her movement, and the ardour of his fiery kisses, the almost brutal grip of his arms, now not only startled but frightened her. She struggled to get free, and this time he knew that she was struggling, but his passion was roused and he could not let her go. And with a quick flash of understanding she recognised his refusal for what it was, the action of a selfish lover who puts his own pleasure before that of his beloved. And she was more frightened than ever, feeling within her that sudden terrified recoil of a human spirit faced with a task beyond its power. Was it possible that marriage with Frederick, the prize towards which she had been running with such eagerness all these last weeks, would, when she got there, turn out to be a burden too heavy for her strength to lift? . . . But she was running too fast to be able to stop now.

Somehow, when Marianne and William came in, she managed to summon enough strength not to fall to the ground when Frederick abruptly released her. He had just been going to tell her something, or had already begun to tell her, she was not sure which, when her parents interrupted them. "Later," he had whispered when he heard their bedroom door open. "I'll tell you later. I've got the ring. And to-morrow, if you like, we'll tell 'em all."

Driving through the streets in the Andersons' luxurious carriage, with Frederick his usual decorous self again and chatting quietly and amiably to Marianne and William about politics and the weather, walking across the strip of red carpet that stretched across the pavement to the imposing front door, taking off her shawl in company with other laughing girls and their proud mammas, Véronique managed to push the memory of that moment of recoil right away to the back of her mind. Frederick hadn't really been rough with her, she told herself, she had just thought he was because she was tired and had a headache. She loved him and wanted to be his wife. And she loved this gay town life, and wearing smart clothes, and knowing she was beautiful, and being flattered and admired. That girl who had lived in a mountain valley, and got excited over sunrises and hoggets and the price of wool, had been as absurd as the things she had been interested in, just a ridiculous country bumpkin like her father's shepherds, Murray and James and Mack and—John.

Why should she think of him now, so suddenly, sitting here beside Marianne waiting for the ball to begin? She saw him as she had seen him last, standing at the door of their farmhouse, where he was to live until they got back again, waving good-bye to them. The ball-room was blotted out while she looked long at the strong, slow-moving figure and the tanned face with the penetrating smiling eyes that saw so much yet with such sympathy that those like herself who were fond of John rather welcomed than resented their scrutiny. Besides, she had never wanted to hide anything from John. From her childhood onward she had always been herself with him, never played a part, never prevaricated. But then they had always wanted to do the same things—dig in the garden, care for young animals and children, read the same books, pray the same prayers, love the same people, take the same walks through the green pastures while the dew was still on the grass—

"Véronique!"

She woke up from her reverie to find that the band was playing "The Blue Danube" and that Frederick was bowing before her; and to find also that for the first time since she had known him she did not want to dance with him. Yet she jumped up eagerly, playing her part to perfection, and went into his arms as trustfully as though that horrid moment of terror in the lodgings had not woken in her an instinctive distrust of them.

And in a moment or two the intoxication of the music and of Frederick's exquisite dancing had put the old spell on her and she was happy again. But she wanted to stay among the other dancers, she did not want to be carried off to the conservatory for that love-making behind the potted plants that hitherto she had found so wonderful. For the first dance she managed to evade the conservatory, but Frederick had something to say to her and during their second dance together he inveigled her to the spot where he wanted her, a warm, scented corner entirely hidden by a huge bank of lilies. There was a seat that just held two and sitting beside her, holding her hand tightly, his eyes on hers, he told her what he had to say.

He told her with great skill, with none of that violence of passion that had frightened her before. He had blundered then, he realised, and he did not mean to blunder again. He was genuinely in love with Véronique, the exquisite freshness of her beauty had gone completely to his head, and he wanted her as he had never wanted anything yet.

He had been married before, he told her. He was twenty-six now and since his twenty-second year he had been married to a woman older than himself, a widow with two children, who had made him utterly wretched. He had known more misery, he said, in those four years, than he hoped Véronique would ever know in the whole of her life. His wife had been not only unfaithful but wildly extravagant too, and their unhappiness together had been made worse by their money worries. Then she had died, setting him free, but leaving him

with so many bills to pay that he had got into serious financial
trouble and had had to sell his commission and leave England.
Well, it was all over now. He had heard to-day that his father had
straightened everything out and settled a little income upon him.
All the unhappiness was behind him now. Véronique would never
know how deeply he had suffered, so deeply that he had never
expected to be happy again, though he had thought that in a new
land he might be able to shake off something of the nightmare of the
past and at least recover his self-respect, his old vigour of body and
mind, sapped by misery. But he had done more than that. He had
met Véronique and recovered joy. Loving her had been like a
miracle. Then with Véronique held gently in his arms he pleaded
with her that she should not turn from him because of the money
trouble he had got into in England—it had been none of his fault—
nor because he had been married before. Though she would be his
second wife his first marriage had been so disastrous that it just
simply did not count. With her as his faithfully loving wife he would
be able to make a grand thing of the new life, but if she were to turn
from him now then he would be lost. She had his life in her hands.

By the end of it he was whispering into her curls and neither of
them could see the face of the other. The scent of the lilies had for
Véronique ceased to be intoxicatingly sweet and become so sickly
that for one awful moment she thought she was going to faint.
Then she took a grip upon herself and the sensation passed, but she
felt so weak that she could only lean against Frederick without word
or movement.

His story had given her a shock. Though she took his word for it
that he had not been to blame for his troubles yet she felt, somehow,
betrayed by that first marriage. Child that she was she had imagined
that she was his first love, as he was hers. To find her fairytale lover
a widower seemed to spoil things, and her instinct sensed a sordid-
ness somewhere in his story.

Frederick felt her dismay and pulled her closer. "Véronique, little
love, I knew you'd be loyal," he whispered. "I knew you'd stick to
me. Darling Véronique!"

There was a lot more in the same strain and it did the trick, as he
had known it would. With something of the same mighty effort as
her mother had made on board the Green Dolphin at Wellington
Véronique steadied herself and took her resolve. . . . "Did you say
that you had the ring in your pocket?" she whispered. . . . But she
had not the firm ground beneath her feet that her mother had had.
The man's character was not the same. Even as she spoke she felt the
quicksands quaking, and once again she was afraid.

3

William, meanwhile, had found a refuge in an obscure corner of the garden with old Obadiah Trimble. Sitting on a rustic bench, secured from the observation of their wives by a convenient screen of bushes, comforting drinks beside them on the seat, they puffed at their pipes and knew a momentary respite from the pleasures of society. Only momentary, for William was uneasy about Véronique, and Obadiah, by marrying above his station in life, had condemned himself to the to and fro existence of a fish who has snapped at a bright fly in the upper air and thereafter finds himself with a hook in his gills. No sooner did Obadiah seek the refreshment of the place where he belonged than he was jerked upward again into those upper regions where he was not at home. Even now, quite out of sight though he was behind the bushes, he had one ear cocked for the step of Mrs. Trimble on the flagged path coming to fetch him back again to the card tables.

Obadiah was a crony of old Tom Anderson's. He, too, had made his pile in gold and now was immersed in steam. But William liked him. Of all the men whom he had met in Dunedin Obadiah had come the nearest to being his friend. He was a rough, rugged old fellow of the old pioneer stock and reminded William of Scant and Isaac, who had perished so long ago in the second Maori war. For that reason he had not told Marianne of his friendship with Obadiah; subconsciously he was afraid she would be rude to him. Nor had he spoken much to Obadiah of Véronique, for Obadiah like himself was an old sailor and their talk was all of the sea and ships, and the old pioneering days that in retrospect seemed so much more enchanting than they really had been, and the old fellow, who avoided society as much as he could, was unaware of the friendship between Frederick Ackroyd and Ozanne's pretty daughter. So it was not of Véronique's welfare he was thinking, but of the welfare of the Union Steamship Company, when he remarked casually to William, "Hope Anderson don't take that fellow Ackroyd too much into his confidence. Don't trust 'im."

William paused for a full moment, then asked in a tone of careful nonchalance, "Know anything against him?"

"Plenty," grunted old Obadiah.

"How?" asked William, for it had not even occurred to him that Obadiah might know anything about Frederick.

"Heard it from a pal of mine—Roger Watts, mate on board one of our steamships—his sister was maid to Ackroyd's late wife. Queer how small the world is. The young fellow thought he'd left his past behind him, maybe, when he came out here. Well, I told Watts to keep his mouth shut. Give the boy a chance, I said. But I doubt if he will. The girl, his sister, was attached to Mrs. Ackroyd."

William said nothing at all, and thanked heaven for the gathering darkness that hid the trembling of his hands. He was aware that Obadiah was not usually garrulous. Only the feeling that William was uninterested, and likely to forget what he was told, combined with the mellowing influence of the hour and the comfortable drink, was causing his tongue to run away with him so unexpectedly. So William yawned and made not the slightest comment as bit by bit the story was related to him. It was not uglier than many others; just that of an extravagant young man who had been without scruple as to how he obtained the means to pay his debts. No doubt he had meant to deal faithfully with the rich woman he had married for her money, but meaning's one thing and performing's another, said Obadiah dourly, and he'd treated her very badly. A nice woman she had been, but a widow with two children should have known better than to marry a young scamp like Ackroyd. She'd borne a lot from him before she'd finally left him. She'd died soon after in a carriage accident, poor soul, and by the terms of her will he'd had the hand-ling of her children's money until they came of age. The result had been the final mess that had made his family ship him off to the colonies. Roger Watts had hinted at embezzlement, no less, though he had no proof of that. But it must have been a bad mess for his family to have shipped him off. Bad stock, said Obadiah, bad stock upon the father's side. Good of old Anderson to take him on, for his own sister had had a bad enough time with the boy's father—he'd told him so himself once, before the boy came out here. Good of Anderson. But he was fond of the boy and was doing a lot for him, and keeping the story very dark. Keen to marry him again to some nice girl, they said.

William yawned again and knocked out his pipe. "Shall we go in before we're fetched?" he asked lazily. "How are the shares going now in the steamship business?"

Obadiah rose, his attention instantly diverted from Frederick. "Rising," he said triumphantly. "You'll be a fool, Ozanne, if you don't close with that offer."

"A fool," said William slowly and bitterly, "is exactly what I am."

A fool ever to let Véronique come to this place, Véronique with her beauty whose power over other men besides himself and John he had not gauged sufficiently in the Country of the Green Pastures, and her impressionability that he had not been sufficiently aware of either. . . . A thousand times a fool. . . . Well, there was nothing to do now but to tell her the truth about Frederick and hope that it would not break her heart. As far as he knew Frederick had made no declaration of love. Perhaps he never meant to.

They entered the house and found a dance in progress, and a group of older folk sitting in a flower-decked alcove watching it; Marianne and Mr. and Mrs. Anderson and the three or four most influential people of the town. William and Obadiah joined them and William's eyes instantly went round the ballroom in search of Véronique. There she was, dancing with Frederick. But she was a changed Véronique. Beautiful as ever she yet seemed to him to have aged five years. And she had shed her modesty. Instead of dancing with eyes downcast, as a young girl should, she was dancing with her head up and her eyes gazing into Frederick's, and there was a patch of burning colour upon either of her cheekbones. Then he noticed that she had parted with her gloves as well as her modesty, and that upon the fourth finger of the hand that lay upon Frederick's shoulder there shone a large emerald ring. So Frederick had captured her already, and without that preliminary word to her father without which no gentleman should dare speak his love to a lady. William's rage nearly choked him. The damned scoundrel! And the ring—it looked worth a fortune and to a surety had not been paid for. And how she was flaunting it, the little witch! Several times as he watched her she lifted her hand and turned it from side to side that the jewel might catch the light from the hundreds of wax candles burning round the room, and when her gesture attracted the smiling glances of the other dancers she tilted her chin arrogantly. Could this forward young minx be his shy Arcadian nymph? The beautiful ballroom seemed to turn upside down with poor William. Never in his whole life had he felt more wretched. . . . No, not even on his wedding night. . . . This that had happened to Véronique was worse even than the loss of Marguerite.

And then she saw him in the alcove, smiled and whispered a word to Frederick, who guided her skilfully through the dancers until the two of them stood side by side at the entrance to the alcove, confronting their elders hand in hand like a couple of beautiful children. But with no becoming shame. They stood there smiling, with heads up, and it was Véronique, the hussy, who spoke first.

"Please will you all congratulate us?" she said in a high clear voice that reached well beyond the alcove. "Frederick and I have become engaged to be married."

A chorus of congratulations broke out, expressed chiefly by the gentlemen, for the ladies were all slightly scandalised by the brazen behaviour of Véronique Ozanne. All, that is, except her own mother. Glancing at Marianne William saw her face transfigured with joy and his heart sank. She had been desperately ambitious for her daughter and now her ambition was to be satisfied, and he knew of old that once she was in headlong pursuit of what she wanted she was impervious to reason. Looking at her face he realised that in the days to come he would be unable to get her to hear a single word against Frederick.

Then he looked again at Véronique and her eyes met his, full of misery. Contrasted with her smiling lips and proudly poised head the misery in her eyes was painful to see, yet William's heavy heart suddenly lightened. For a moment he held her eyes with his steady glance, then she quickly veiled them. Not again, he realised, would she let him see her wretchedness, and her mother and her friends would never see it. But he understood her, and it was because he understood that his heart was suddenly light. For this was the old Véronique after all. He realised what had happened. Frederick had first secured her promise to marry him and then, only then, told his story—his own version of it—and flung himself upon her loyalty and compassion. And she was sticking to her promise. She was no quitter— William himself had taught her, as Tai Haruru had long ago taught him, not to quit. She fancied herself in love with the man and she was sticking to him. But she was badly scared, poor child. It was because she was scared that she had acted so brazenly. She had wanted to put it absolutely beyond her own power to retract. . . . And, hang it all, it certainly looked as though she had done so. . . . He'd have the devil of a time getting her out of it now. For it would be her own resolve, as well as Marianne's, that he would have to fight. When she looked at him again the misery had gone from her eyes and there was in them instead a veiled hostility. Yet he was still light-hearted. She was his nymph after all, and that one quick look of misery had been a call for help that he would not fail to answer.

CHAPTER FOUR

1

Easier said than done, thought William in the days that followed. He knew better than straight away to refuse his consent to the marriage—that would have been to increase Marianne's obstinacy tenfold and might not inconceivably have driven Véronique and Frederick to elopement.

He related Obadiah's version of Frederick's story to Marianne, but Tom Anderson had been beforehand with him and on the very night of the ball had enlisted Marianne's pity for a young man more sinned against than sinning, and his wife had from the very beginning poured praise of Frederick into her willing ears. It was not to be expected that Marianne, passionately attached to the Andersons and disliking Obadiah quite intensely, should give more credence to his unsubstantiated story than to theirs. It was true that the discovery that Frederick was a widower had given her a momentary pang of disappointment, but she soon forgot it. Frederick's unhappy past was an old sad story that could be forgotten now that the dear boy was beginning a new life in a new land. As for his financial troubles, the Andersons assured her he had been in no way to blame for those, and though it gave her a further pang to discover that except for the small income settled upon him by his father the apparently rich young man was totally without wealth, yet his further prospects with the Union Steamship Company were good, and the Andersons, a childless couple, were genuinely attached to him and could probably be persuaded to make him their heir.

So Marianne was intensely happy at this time. Having detected the two flies in the ointment, taken them out and thrown them away, she flung herself with whole-hearted enthusiasm into the preparations for the wedding that Véronique was determined should take place as soon as possible. Her beautiful child was to have a great place in the world and would never have to suffer the hardships that her mother had suffered. And better still, she was to marry the man she loved while she was young and lovely; she would never have to endure the frustrations that had been Marianne's in her youth. Not only was Marianne's wordly ambition for her child satisfied, but she was achieving the passionate desire of every mother and saving her daughter from the special miseries which she had herself endured. . . . William was not surprised that his arguments made no headway.

He fared no better with Véronique. He gave her a carefully edited edition of the tale Obadiah had told him, but she naturally refused to believe any version of the story except Frederick's own. He told her straight out that he neither liked nor trusted Frederick, and she looked at him with the eyes of a wounded doe and turned again to the everlasting sewing of her wedding clothes. . . . She was no quitter.

The word "trousseau" dominated their whole life now, and to William they seemed to wade all day long through a sea of silk and satin, muslin and lace, yards and yards of it that seemed to coil about his ankles whenever he moved. And he was choked by the perfume of the little scent sachets that Marianne was making to lie between the folds of Véronique's petticoats, and by the smell of the frangipani and opopanax which the ladies sniffed from cut-glass smelling bottles when they felt too tired to set another stitch. . . . For it continued unusually hot, the dusty heat of continued drought, and in the intervals of shopping and sewing and cutting out and trying on Frederick whirled them from one party to another with the untiring enthusiasm of a young man who has never felt fatigued in his life.

And then Véronique fell ill with a feverish attack. The indisposition seemed slight and Marianne declared that a couple of days in bed would put her to rights, but William was seized by panic and demanded the doctor.

He came, examined Véronique, found no cause for alarm, and wrote out a prescription for a soothing mixture. In the parlour he concurred with Marianne's opinion that prolonged drought often causes feverish attacks, but when William was showing him out at the front door he said, "I did not wish to alarm your wife, but your daughter is by no means strong, Sir. There is no disease, you understand, but there is a slight weakness of the chest, and a general tendency to debility."

Once more the world seemed to turn upside down with William. "She was a seven-months child," he murmured.

"So I should have guessed," said the doctor. "It would be her salvation to live in the country—preferably in mountain air. Town life is not the best possible for a constitution such as hers. Goodmorning."

William did not share the doctor's reluctance to alarm Marianne. He went back up the stairs two steps at a time and repeated the conversation with heavy underlinings.

"Nonsense!" said Marianne. "I am a seven-months child, and look what I've been through since I married you!"

"But in country air," said William. "Marriage with me has meant some pretty stiff experiences for you, my girl, I know that, but always in country air."

"The air of Dunedin is excellent," snapped Marianne. "Straight off the sea."

"One doesn't notice that in crowded ballrooms and stuffy shops," William reminded her.

Marianne came to him and put her hands on his shoulders. "Véronique will be all right, William," she said gently. "Believe me, my dear, she will be all right. And you and I will always be at hand to look after her. For of course, as things are now, you'll accept Mr. Anderson's offer, won't you, darling?"

William looked at her. Her beautiful dark eyes met his with the straight glance of sincerity. He knew her now. When she had seen a new magic city on the horizon, a new way of life that she wanted, she would look at every circumstance in the light of her desire and not realise that by doing so she had changed its natural hue. She could not help this, perhaps, but yet he was angry with her, for this characteristic of hers was a danger to Véronique.

"I shall not accept Anderson's offer," he said coldly.

"You'll surely not want to go back to the valley with Véronique living in Dunedin?"

"I love that valley and I'll never leave it," said William wildly. "As it happens," he went on, "I am going home this very day to see how things are faring without me."

"Leaving me alone with Véronique ill?" asked Marianne, her eyes flashing sparks.

"I'm only in the way in times of illness," said William. "At least, so you always tell me. And I shall be gone for four nights only. I'll borrow a horse off Anderson. Where did you put my riding boots?"

The decision to go back to the Country of the Green Pastures had come to William like a lightning flash. For days he had known that he must write and tell John what had happened, but he had put it off. Now, clinging blindly and unthinkingly to possession of the Green Pastures because he knew Véronique's salvation to lie within them, he knew that John was the man to help him. He was only Véronique's father but he believed John to be her mate. Given the chance he would know how to secure what was his by right from the marauder. . . . Good shepherds always have this instinctive wisdom, William told himself.

"Pack me up what I'll need," he said to his wife. "Just what will go in a saddle-bag. Yes, my dear. Now at once."

Marianne, though she was inwardly raging, was obliged to obey. Intense emotion had once again tapped William's hidden strength. It was Véronique's illness, she supposed, that had let it loose upon her now. When she had been ill, she remembered with a pang of jealousy, he had remained weak and pliable as ever. Yet it was odd of him to go away with the child ill. What was he after, she wondered uneasily, as she packed for him.

William, meanwhile, was saying good-bye to Véronique.

"I'm off home for a couple of nights, darling," he said to her. "Just to see how John is getting on alone. Anything you would like me to bring you?"

He spoke casually, yet he watched her closely, and he did not miss the quick light that came to her eyes at the mention of "home". It was gone in a moment, but he had seen it, and it strengthened his faith in the veracity of the call for help that she had sent him on her engagement night. Just lately, so engrossed in the preparations for her wedding had she been, that he had sometimes wondered if he had imagined it.

He went to her and put his hand on her hot forehead. "No commissions?" he asked. "There's nothing I wouldn't do for you, you know."

"I know, Papa," she said, and there was almost a touch of the old love in her voice.

"Always stood by you, haven't I?" he said irrelevantly. "And always will, whatever you decide to do. Your old father will always back you up. You know that."

"Yes," she said.

"Any messages for John?" he asked, and again he watched her.

But she was lying now with her eyes shut, and only murmured "No."

Yet the monosyllabic reply cheered him. Had John meant nothing to her she would have sent a whole string of polite messages.

2

Yet during the long lonely ride his spirits fell to zero. Véronique's happiness, he told himself, was too delicate a thing to be fought for by such a clumsy ass as himself, and in the fight he had surely so far made every possible mistake; and the first and worst had been his refusal to let John speak his mind to her earlier. Yet he loved Véronique so deeply. Strange that such love should beget such little wisdom. There was no price that he was not ready to pay for her salvation, but this readiness was not the needed wisdom.

Or was it?

His horse was tired after a long trek uphill and he had dismounted to let him drink from a mountain stream that tumbled gaily over the rocks beside the road. They were in the foothills now, and he could look up and see the familiar mountains of home rising in all their glory against the peerless sky. The sight of them refreshed him, both in body and mind, and as he stretched himself on the sweet turf beside the stream the bitterness of his self-reproach turned gradually to a humble hope. Salvation was through sacrifice. Samuel, he remembered, had told him that a hundred times over, told him till he had been sick of hearing it, and had been ready with specific instructions as to how the happiness of Marianne was to be salvaged from the wreck of their marriage at that time. But Samuel was not here now to tell him what sacrifice of his would save Véronique.

"The readiness is all." Who had said that? He did not remember but he believed it came out of one of Véronique's books of poetry from the shelf beside the kitchen window. He believed it had been said by some fellow facing his death. Well, if readiness for self-giving was all the wisdom needed he certainly had it at this moment. He was ready to purchase Véronique's happiness with any price demanded of him, yes, even that impossible one of being parted from her. . . . Yes, he took back that reservation. . . . Lying on the grass with his arms beneath his head, looking at the mountains, he prayed the same sort of prayer that Captain O'Hara had prayed at his death. I am ready for any sort of sacrifice, big or small, sublime or comic, take what you will from me in exchange for Véronique's happiness. All I ask is that when the time comes to pay the price I shall know it and pay promptly. Like Captain O'Hara, he was scarcely aware of forming the words in his mind, his prayer was contained in the creative act of abnegation that he made as he lay with his eyes on the mountains.

After a long time he got up and rode on, with a mind at peace. For if his love was ready to give all for Véronique, then life or God, or whatever one liked to call the mystery that with him was responsible for her being, was surely ready to give all too.

It was evening when he reached the valley. Was it only a few short weeks that he had been away? The joy of seeing the beloved place again was as deep as any he had known. And never had the valley looked more exquisite. The shadows of evening lay deep and tranquil over the Green Pastures, the beautiful homestead and its flower-filled garden, but above the mountain peaks were lit with the colours of sunset. William drew rein and sighed with deep contentment. He loved this place. Even more than the Island of his boyhood he loved this home that had been made for Véronique. Somehow or other he would get her free from this pitiful tangle in which his stupidity had involved her, and she would come back here too to her own country and her own mate, and he would grow peacefully old in this beloved valley and see her happy with her children about her.

And Marianne? The thought of Marianne brought him up short with the realisation that he had been guilty of day-dreaming. He thrust the nostalgic mood from him, conscious that such dreams are enervating things that sap the strength of strong men's vows, and rode on.

John was leaning over the garden gate smoking a pipe in the cool of the evening. He showed no surprise at the sight of William, merely removed his pipe, grinned, and opened the gate. "Come on in," he said. "I've a stew cooking."

Its delicious smell greeted William as he entered the kitchen. He looked quickly round. Everything was spotlessly neat and clean. All Véronique's little treasures were in the right places, and where she had been accustomed to put bowls of flowers John had put them also. One of her aprons, that in the excitement of the departure for Dunedin she must have thrown down and forgotten, had been carefully folded by John and placed upon the settle. A spotless cloth was upon the table and the supper was laid—for two.

William looked at the extra place and gaped. "You weren't expecting me, were you?" he asked.

John was always truthful. He flushed brick red and answered, "No."

William understood. That practical sensible man John Ogilvie had his day dreams too. He was living here with the wraith of his wife Véronique.

William, caught spying on something that was not intended for his eyes, also became brick red. "I'll go and have a wash," he mumbled. "Find some clean clothes."

"The stew will be ready by the time you come down," said John.

He asked no questions while William dealt with the stew, and William, more hungry and tired than he had realised, was grateful to him. John was the perfect host, sensitively considerate, his very presence a welcome as warm as his crackling wood fire. . . . One was glad of a fire even on summer evenings in these mountain pastures.

John's fire? William had fallen so easily into the rôle of guest that it was not until the end of the meal that he realised suddenly that the wood on the hearth was his, the food his, the crockery, the house, all his. Yet he left it to John to push back his chair and rise first, and to reach down the purple tobacco jar from the mantelpiece. "Thanks," said William gratefully, filling his pipe with his own tobacco, and hesitated a moment, waiting for John's invitation to sit down on his own settle. That seemed the right way of it, somehow. Whatever his mind might be saying as to the rights of ownership he realised with a shiver of dismay that his spirit had abdicated. His spirit had made a vow and was already following some path to a goal that the less clear-sighted mind had not as yet perceived, though it shrank from it with an instinctive fear.

"Cold?" asked John in surprise. "Have a whisky?"

"Yes," said William. "Neat. I've a damned unpleasant story to tell you."

John heard it out without a word and when it was finished William at first forbore to look at him. When at last he did look he saw the man beside him with a face blanched beneath his tan, his pipe out and his drink untouched. His hands gripped the arms of his chair with so tense an anger that it looked as though they would never unclench again.

William took the anger to himself. "I'm sorry," he said humbly. "I've been every sort of a fool."

John made a mighty effort, unclenched his hands and put his pipe aside. "No," he said thickly. "But Mrs. Ozanne——" He pulled himself up sharply, picked up his glass and drowned what he would have liked to say about Marianne in good strong fiery Scotch whisky. William made no attempt to justify his wife. It would, he realised, not have been of the slightest use. A peaceful future amalgamation of John and Marianne was a thing no more likely to take place than that of fire and water. But he continued to take the blame to himself.

"I should have let you speak to Véronique long ago," he said.

"No," said John. "You were quite right. She was not ready."

"I should never have given way and let her go to Dunedin."

"Even now it may turn out that you did right," said John. "Would she ever have realised that this place is her place if she had not gone out into the world and felt like a lost soul there? That was how it worked with me. If my father had not sent me to that damn school at Dunedin I might have been eating my heart out for a wider life at this moment."

"She shows no signs of feeling like a lost soul," groaned William. "To the eye she appears to be a wildly excited young woman preparing to play the chief rôle in the wedding of the season. . . . And it's not far off, either."

"No time to lose," agreed John, and got up. "You go and get a good night's rest. I'll see Murray to-night, for the Green Pastures must carry on without either of us for a few days, and be back first thing in the morning with my mother and the light buggy. She's a tough traveller, is my mother. It won't take the three of us long to get back to Dunedin."

William's jaw dropped, for he was slightly scared of that dour, upright Scotswoman Mrs. Ogilvie, though grateful to her for the tender love she had always shown Véronique. Marianne couldn't abide her. There would be the devil and all to pay if she were to turn up at their lodgings. What was John getting at?

"My mother is necessary," said John firmly. "I'm not going to compromise Véronique in any way. She is not yet my wife."

He was gone, banging the door. William finished his drink, smoked out his pipe and dragged himself wearily up the stairs to bed. In the four-poster, with the uncurtained window wide to the stars, he heaved and yawned luxuriously, safe from reprimand by Marianne. He had no idea what plan John had in mind but he realised that he had been right in thinking that the shepherd Lycidas would know best how to rescue Amaryllis from the wolf. With a final luxurious stretching of his great bulk right across the bed he fell asleep and slept better than he had done for months.

3

Véronique lifted her lavender print gown down from the wardrobe and slipped it over her head. She had not worn it since the journey from home. She had thought it extremely smart then but after only a few hours in Dunedin she had realised that it was hopelessly countrified and had put it away in disgrace. But now she felt quite tenderly sentimental towards it, almost as though it had belonged to her great grandmother. . . . The time that had elapsed since she had last worn it, measured not by weeks but by intensity of experience, had been so very great.

She moved quietly, for this getting up and dressing was contrary to orders. The doctor had told her that she might go into the parlour to-morrow, when William was expected home again, but that she must stay in bed to-day. She had meant to obey, but her room was so hot and she felt so restless. Her head would be better, she thought, if she could sit by the window and get a little air. And seated by the window she did feel much better. And how blessed it was to be alone. All her life she had liked to be alone sometimes, and in the Country of the Green Pastures there had been plenty of opportunity for solitude; walks and rides alone, spells of solitary gardening, of reading in the kitchen window; she had not realised how precious they had been, and how necessary to her, until she had lost them in this thronging social life in which one never seemed to be alone for a single instant, and one's head never stopped aching.

How was she going to live this life? It was partly to find the answer to this question that she had got up, for it is difficult to think in bed, and she needed to think. Marianne might say what she would about the prevalence of fever in droughts but Véronique knew quite well that she had only been ill because she had got too tired. She was not strong, it seemed, either in body or in will power. She got tired quickly and her will was not strong enough to keep her from collapsing. Mamma, as far as she remembered, had succumbed to fatigue only twice in ten years, but she had collapsed at its very first serious onslaught. She had always thought of herself as strong—at home in the fresh mountain air she had been able to ride and walk and dance with the best—but here it was all quite different. The late nights exhausted her, the airless rooms, and—Frederick.

"You had better keep quite quiet, darling, and not see Frederick for a few days," Marianne had said to her on the first day of her illness, and an overwhelming relief had flooded her. But the relief had quickly been followed by appalled dismay. Relieved not to see Frederick when she loved him so? *Relieved* not to see Frederick? Why? Through feverish days and nights she had sought for the reason, and found it. As she was not strong enough for his sort of life so she was not strong enough for his sort of love; for it was not a protecting, strengthening thing, like Papa's, a saving sort of love, but a passionate demanding sort of thing that seemed to burn up one's strength and leave one desiccated and exhausted. If only she had known, when at first sight of him that exciting glow had thrilled through her, that it would end not by warming but by burning her. But she had not known. She had lost her heart to a man she knew nothing about just because he had looked so exactly like the lover of her dreams; and in his early considerate gentleness that had combined so wonderfully with his thrill and dash, he had behaved like him too. It was only on the night of the Andersons' ball that he had begun to show her something of the kind of man whom Frederick Ackroyd really was, and she had begun to realise that in a man of flesh and blood thrill and dash do not exist side by side with gentleness and consideration; nor with single-minded attachment to one woman only. There was the rub. If she was not the first woman in Frederick's life instinct told her that she was not at all likely to be the last.

She sighed and shivered, and looked round the empty room as though for help. As yet it had scarcely occurred to her to go back on her bargain; she still fancied herself in love with Frederick, he had vowed a hundred times that without her he was a lost man, and she was no quitter. Her problem was to find the strength to tackle the job she had taken on. For though the thought of saving a man was as deliciously attractive to her as to any woman of her generation she was without the self-confidence that had been Marianne's upon the deck of the Green Dolphin. Marianne had known herself possessed of strength both of body and will, but Véronique at this moment knew herself possessed of neither. For not even the awareness of her beauty that Dunedin had awakened in her had destroyed that fundamental humility that she had inherited from her father.... And so she looked about her for the needed strength, as though she would find it lying like a golden ball upon the floor. . . . But it was not there, and the horrid conviction came to her that people are born with certain fundamentals of personality that are of the very essence of them, and cannot be changed, because without them they would not be themselves. Was that how it was with her weakness? And was that how it was with Frederick's passionate, exhausting possessiveness, his variable love, as well as with her weakness? She sat quite still on her chair and in spite of the heat of the day her body turned slowly to ice.

4

Meanwhile Marianne sat in the parlour in a state of some anxiety. So anxious was she that she actually had a headache. For Véronique was not recovering as she should and she could not escape the feeling that there was something very wrong with the child just now, quite apart from her illness. Well, probably it would all come right when she was married. Girls were often very nervy and queer during the weeks before their wedding. It was perfectly natural and she would not worry any more. Nevertheless, in spite of this sensible decision, she was glad when she heard a man's heavy tread upon the stairs. . . . William, back a day earlier than he had expected. . . . In spite of his having been so tiresome lately she would be glad to have him back.

But it was not William who entered, it was John Ogilvie, and that after a knock that was merely perfunctory.

"Good afternoon, Ma'am." He had taken her hand and was smiling down at her very kindly, but as usual she found the directness of his gaze both disconcerting and exasperating. And what a clodhopper he looked, even though he wore his best coat and had evidently had a good wash and brush-up before coming to see her. Accustomed as she was now to the elegance of Frederick, the thickness of his boots, the rude strength of his hand clasp and the slight scent of naphthaline that came from his best coat (obviously a man is no gentleman if his coat smells of naphthaline, for obviously he wears it but seldom) affected her most unfavourably.

"Do sit down," she said coldly. "Is my husband with you?"

"Yes, we drove from home together; Mr. Ozanne, my mother and I. My mother and I are taking a little holiday. Mr. Ozanne is with her now, helping her to find comfortable lodgings, while I've come to see you. You'll say it should have been the other way round, but he thought she'd like the rooms you had when you first came here, so he went himself. . . . And I was eager to see you and Véronique."

He smiled at her again, and he was still holding her hand in that awful strenuous grip of his, and both from the smile and the hand clasp there came to her the distinct impression that he was sorry for her, that he wanted to arm her with his own strength against some blow. How dared he? To Marianne pity from an inferior was a definite insult. She drew her hand away and motioned him to a chair.

"I'm afraid you won't see Véronique," she said curtly. "She is unwell and in her room. . . . Your mother won't like those lodgings," she added. "They are most uncomfortable."

"It won't be for long," said John. "If all goes well I hope we shall start for home again in a day or two. I can't leave the farm for long."

"I am astonished that you should leave it at all," said Marianne. "I thought you were supposed to be caring for it in our absence. And what a very long journey to take for so short a time. I am surprised your mother thought it worth the exertion."

"Mother and I are fond of Dunedin," said John. "I was at school here, you know."

There was a short silence. John was sitting well back in his chair and looked as though he meant to stay for ever.

"I shall, of course, call upon your mother," said Marianne graciously, but she stifled a small sigh, for she did so dislike Mrs. Ogilvie.

"That will be very kind of you, Ma'am."

John paused, ruminating like a cow. What a heavy, stupid fellow he was. And what a vulgarly loud voice he had. When he spoke again it seemed to Marianne, afflicted with a headache as she was, to be an absolute shout. Oh, these boorish manners! She had become accustomed to such cultured voices lately.

"Are those lodgings really so uncomfortable, Ma'am?" he asked loudly.

"Most uncomfortable," said Marianne. "And deadly dull. At the end of a cul-de-sac."

John looked troubled. "Mother won't like that," he said. "She wanted to see a bit of life. I suppose, Ma'am, you don't know of any others that would suit her better?"

Bother the man! But he was looking at her with the trustfulness of a nice child who knows the grown-up is going to be helpful, and she heard herself answering, "In the next road I believe there are some quite respectable rooms with a far more lively aspect."

He beamed and shifted himself a little forward in his chair. "I'll go at once, Ma'am, if you'll excuse me, and tell her about them." Then just as her hopes were rising he seemed to change his mind, shifted back again and raised his voice even louder. "But I must pay my respects to Véronique first."

"But I have already told you that you cannot," snapped Marianne, lowering her voice in the dim hope that that would cause him to lower his. "She is unwell and confined to her room."

"In bed, Ma'am?"

"Yes. In bed. And I do implore you, Mr. Ogilvie, to remember her condition and speak a little lower. I am most anxious about her."

"In bed!" roared John in considerable consternation. "Is that wise, Ma'am, in this stifling weather? Don't you think that a little fresh air——"

He did not finish his sentence, and Marianne was given no opportunity to express the rage that rose in her at this unwarrantable criticism of her nursing of her own child, for the door opened and in came Véronique, wearing her old lavender gown, her hair tumbled, her cheeks flushed and her eyes shining, so glowing with delight that her appearance gave the complete lie to her mother's description of her delicate condition.

"John!" she cried. "I heard your voice right across the passage in my room. How are you, John? Oh, it's good to see you! How are the hoggets, John, and my pony? And the garden? Have you kept my plants watered, as you promised? Oh John, it is good to see you! How are the dogs? Has Nell had her litter yet?"

He had jumped up at her entrance, and she had gone to him with the most unmaidenly eagerness, and was holding his hand as she poured out her questions in an eager flood, giving him no time to answer. Not that he seemed to want to answer. He just stood there smiling at her, and the look on his face gave Marianne such a shock that it was as though the ground opened at her feet. It was out of a sort of daze that she heard John speaking, and the voice that slipped in between Véronique's eager questions was so low and gentle that it was impossible to think that it belonged to the same man who had bellowed so loudly a moment before. "My mother is with me, Véronique, and your father is helping her to find lodgings. I'm just going to join them. Will you come too? Your mother and I were just saying that you needed some fresh air." He smiled at Marianne over Véronique's head. "Have we your permission, Ma'am?"

Marianne clutched at her scattered wits. "No, Mr. Ogilvie. She is not fit for walking."

"But I have my buggy here, Ma'am. I left it tied to the lamp post. Surely a little carriage exercise——"

"It'll do me all the good in the world, Mamma," interrupted

Véronique. "Back in a moment, John." And like a whirlwind she flew out of the room, and like a whirlwind she returned, her hat askew on her disordered curls and her shawl clutched in her hand. "Good-bye, darling Mamma," she cried, embracing her mother with the exuberance of a little girl of twelve. "I'll be back before you've had time to miss me."

And then they were gone, and Marianne, stunned, sank into a chair. The discovery that John Ogilvie was in love with Véronique had upset her completely. Yet why? Véronique was safely engaged to another man, and even had she not been it was unthinkable that she should marry her father's shepherd. Marianne pulled herself together. She was being ridiculous. That feeling that she had always had, that John was a menace and a portent in her life, was just nonsense. . . . He was such a stupid fellow. . . . She picked up her sewing and tried to stop thinking about him.

Yet as she set her stitches, her thoughts going back over the past interview, the thought kept intruding—was he so stupid?

5

John did not take Véronique to William and Mrs. Ogilvie. He drove her slowly through the streets of Dunedin, answering gently all her eager questions about her flowers and her dogs, the hoggets and the farm, until they reached a quiet, tree-bordered road, where he drew up. The tired horse drooped between the shafts, thankful to stay still.

"Véronique," said John, "I want to talk to you."

"Yes?" said Véronique, lifting her face to the sunlight that fell through the green leaves overhead. It was fresh and cool here, and John's familiar presence was infinitely restful.

"Are you happy, Véronique?" he asked.

She looked at him, startled.

"You see, Véronique, I have a right to know, because I have loved you ever since you were a little girl. I have never loved anyone but you, and I never shall."

He paused, and Véronique bent her head. To be the first woman—the only woman—that was the gift of queenship that every woman wanted, and she had seen enough of life now to know that the gift was seldom granted and that a lover who could give it was a rare phenomenon.

"If you love this man you're betrothed to," went on John, "if you think you will be happy with him, then I'll take myself off and we'll forget we ever had this conversation, but if you're unhappy,

Véronique, then my mother and I will take you straight home to the Green Pastures to-morrow. You need not even see Mr. Ackroyd again if you don't want to. Your father will deal with all that."

"Does Papa know you are saying this to me?" she asked. She had drooped her head so low that he could not see her face beneath the shade of her hat, but he saw that she was gripping her hands together so tightly that the knuckles were white. "Yes," he replied.

"Papa does not like Frederick," she said in a small voice.

"No," said John. "Not that that is particularly important. What matters is—do you like him? You fell in love with him, I know, but do you like him—like the kind of man that he is?"

"I have given my word," replied Véronique to this.

"I know you have," said John. "And you're a woman of your word. But there's another sort of loyalty that has to be considered too—to the kind of life where you belong. Generally speaking, we only make a success of the kind of life that suits us. . . . I found that out when I tried to be a city dominie to please my father, and made such a mess of it that I had to go back to the Green Pastures and be a shepherd after all. . . . Could you make a success of Ackroyd's kind of life, or he of yours? One must make a success of life, you know. That's one's first duty. I don't mean worldly success, I mean —being happy."

"Perhaps I could change the sort of person that I am—grow a stronger sort of woman—so as to belong to Frederick's world," whispered Véronique.

"No, you can't do that. And nor can he. We cannot change the sort of person that we are."

There was a long silence. John had seldom in his life before talked so seriously at such a stretch, and was now crimson and confused. Moreover he was fighting such a longing to fling his arms round the drooping little figure at his side, and kiss her into awareness of his huge love for her, that it needed all his self-control to remain immovable upon the seat. But he thought perhaps it wouldn't do to show passion just at present, for she'd probably had enough of that from Ackroyd. And he was appealing now to her reason, not to her exhausted emotions.

"No need to make up your mind now, Véronique," he said gently. "I'll wait in Dunedin for your answer for as long as you like."

"John," she whispered, still with her face hidden, "why didn't you tell me before that you loved me?"

"Because it did not seem right to tell you. You see, until just lately you weren't grown-up."

"Was it hard to wait?" she asked.

"Yes," he said, "it was hard."

She was silent again, and he wondered agonisedly if she was antagonised by his past control, his present reserve. He need not have worried. She was pondering on the nature of his love, that, like Papa's, put the other person first. That was a thing that Frederick had never done.

Then she asked irrelevantly, "How did you know that Papa and I called our valley 'The Country of the Green Pastures'?"

"Your father told me. But long ago, when I was a little boy, I called it that myself."

"The twenty-third psalm was the first I learned to say by heart," said Véronique. "Uncle Samuel taught it to me."

"The first that I learned too," said John. "And it's still my favourite."

"Mine too," said Véronique. "We think alike about lots of things, don't we?"

"Naturally," mumbled John. "'For we were nurst upon the self-same hill, fed the same flock . . .'"

Suddenly she turned to him, lifting a transfigured face, and slipped her arms round his neck. "Your country is my country," she said.

Regardless of who might be passing by in the street he flung his arms about her, while old familiar words sprang to his lips as the pledge of faith. "'The Lord do so to me, and more also, if aught but death part thee and me.'"

6

It was the evening of the next day and Marianne, alone in their lodgings, wept bitterly. It was almost dark but she had not bothered to light the lamp. She was too wretched. She could not remember when she had been so wretched, or felt so utterly forsaken. She had been deceived and frustrated by her husband and child, and played like a fish on a string by that dreadful man John Ogilvie. . . . Ah, there lay the humiliation of it! Played like a fish on a string by John Ogilvie whom she had always patronised. . . . And deceived by Véronique, who with her poor mother working her fingers to the bone over her trousseau had been planning all the while to throw over poor dear Frederick. . . . And frustrated by William, who knew how she ached to see her darling Véronique safely established in a life of ease, and how for herself also she longed for the hard-won leisure that was surely now her right. . . . And played like a fish on a string by that rough common man who was now to be Véro-nique's husband. . . . *That* man husband to her darling, delicate, beautiful child for whom she had dreamed such soaring dreams and laid such ambitious, glowing plans. . . . *That* man, with his wicked deep-laid schemes dragging them all back to that dreadful valley where they would now live among the bleating sheep, toiling and moiling in the snow and the rain, until they died. . . . And once back in that wretched valley she wouldn't care how soon she did die, either. . . . She was an old woman now, broken and frustrated, utterly forsaken, and she did not care how soon she was dead; dead like dear old Nat, the only creature who had ever really loved her.

And it had all happened with such dreadful speed. . . . Véronique and that man coming back from their drive and telling her they were going to be married. . . . William coming in and taking their part. . . . All of them kissing her, and trying to comfort her, and saying they hadn't deceived her when of course they had, and it only made things worse to say they hadn't. . . . Véronique packing, and sitting up most of the night to write a letter to poor dear Frederick. . . . Breakfast and no one able to eat anything. . . . Véronique driving off with John and Mrs. Ogilvie, driving away out of her mother's life and choosing that hateful woman Mrs. Ogilvie to be her mother instead of her own dear Mamma who adored her so. . . . William going off to see Frederick, to see the lawyer, to countermand the wedding cake, to say they wouldn't want the wedding dress, going off all day long to do this, that and the other and leaving her alone in her misery and pain. . . . William off at this moment doing goodness knew what (drinking probably, with that wicked old man Obadiah Trimble, who had been the cause of all the trouble) and leaving her utterly alone . . .

"Oh my!" said Old Nick.

. . . alone except for that hateful parrot. For the rest of her life now she would have no companion except Old Nick. William would spend all his time riding about in the mountains with Véronique and John, and she would be left all alone in that storm-battered farmhouse with Old Nick.

She was weeping so desperately that she did not hear William's step on the stairs, nor the opening of the door. She did not know he was there until he knelt down beside her and took her in his arms. "There, there, my girl," he said tenderly, "you'll make yourself ill with all this weeping. Stop it, Marianne! We've got each other, my girl, we've got each other."

She tried to push him away from her but he would not let her go. He caressed her as though he were a young and ardent lover, kissing her forehead and her wet eyelids, her lips and her hair. He had never kissed her like this before and in spite of her bitter anger she yielded at last to the sweetness of it, leaning back against him and putting up her hand to hold his face against hers. "Where have you been, William?" she whispered. "You had no right to leave me alone like this. Where have you been all this while?"

"With Tom Anderson," said William.

"Tom Anderson!" ejaculated Marianne. "Oh, poor Mr. Anderson! He must have been furious!"

"No," said William. "He took it well. I think he knew all the while, in his heart, that Frederick was no fit husband for Véronique."

"He *was*," said Marianne passionately. "You all misjudged poor Frederick! He only wanted a wife like Véronique to be the best husband in the world."

"As a matter of fact," said William, "Tom didn't waste much time over Frederick. It's the Union Steamship Company, not Frederick, that is the darling of Tom's heart. And he likes your old husband, Marianne. What's happened seems to have made no difference to his liking. He renewed that offer, my dear, and I accepted it. From henceforth, Mrs. Ozanne, you will live in that fine house in the street next the Andersons' that you want so much, and watch your husband propelled higher and higher up the social ladder by the power of steam. If you're not the leader of society in this city in another three years, my dear, I'll eat my hat."

"William!" She leaned back in his arms, gazing up into his face, and she could scarcely believe it. "William! But the farm?"

He smiled back at her. "It's John's," he said. "My wedding present to him and Véronique. Your daughter won't be the wife of a poor shepherd, Marianne, she'll be the wife of a well-to-do sheep farmer. And she'll be happy. All is well with your child, Marianne. Believe me, Marianne, that all is well with your child."

Shock, delight, incredulity, were all struggling for the mastery in Marianne, so that she scarcely knew what she felt. "But William," she gasped, "how will you bear to live away from her? How will you bear it?"

William met her eyes steadily. "I shall have you, my girl," he said. "Remember what you said to me, not so long ago? 'Sensible fathers and mothers, when their children marry, go back to the old days and renew their youth.' I'll have you, my girl, and you are all I want."

She was in his arms and crying again, but crying now from sheer joy. A moment ago she had seemed to have nothing left, and now, quite suddenly, she had everything. William was hers as he had never been, and the new magic city on the horizon was drawing nearer and nearer. Already, even, she seemed entering the pearly gates and treading the streets of gold.

7

A couple of hours later William lay beside his sleeping wife and stared wide-eyed into the darkness. It was too hot to sleep. He'd not get to sleep this night, of that he was certain. Damn this stifling city heat! He would have liked to have got up and flung the window wide, but if he had he would have wakened Marianne, who did not hold with open windows at night; night air, she said, was injurious to the health. He remembered the lovely cool night at the Green Pastures when with his window wide to the stars he had had the four-poster all to himself, and he swore under his breath. The Green Pastures! Separation both from Véronique and the Green Pastures! What an impossible price to pay! Well, impossible or not, it was done now, and he was condemned to the treadmill of city life, a business man concerned, of all things, with steam, *steam*, that he had always hated. Money-making out of steam—day after day— just money-making that Marianne might have her fine town house, her carriage and servants, her round of social gaieties in over-crowded, overheated rooms, to which no doubt he would be dragged also, hot and perspiring, knocking things over, treading on people's toes, out of place, making a fool of himself, he the sailor, lumberman and farmer who was only happy nowadays in the wilds. What a price! And then there would be married life with Marianne, un-sweetened now by the presence of their child. He loved his wife, oh yes, he loved her, their marriage was on the whole as happy as most, perhaps happier, but he still did not love her as she loved him, and still, after all these years, he shrank from the close intimacy that she still craved for with such desperation. Yes, after all these years, she was as ardent as ever. She still wanted the core of his soul that he could not give her. Well, he must do his best. By that bit of play-acting in the parlour just now he had pledged himself to her all over again. It had been a re-enactment of the scene on the Green Dolphin on the morning of their wedding, and as that had set the standard for their life together before Véronique came, this must set it for their life now that she had left them. What had Kelly said? "Wrest your life into conformity with that one moment." Well, he'd do it. But, God, what a price to pay!

Yet he knew that it was the price that had to be paid for Véronique's happiness, the price demanded of him. He had begun to know it at the farm, when he had felt the beloved home withdrawing itself from his keeping and passing to John's, and he had known it quite certainly as soon as they had told the news of Véronique's broken engagement to Marianne and she had taken it to heart so distressingly. For he and she had had different plans for Véronique's happiness, and they had fought and he had won, and upon the victor there lies always the obligation for the future welfare of the defeated. Véronique, the great love of his life, had passed from his keeping into that of another man. His responsibility now, as at the beginning, was for Marianne alone.

And then, abruptly, he found himself thinking of the Reverend Mother of the Convent of Notre Dame du Castel. Odd, he thought, how in this life our closest physical companionships are not always with those we love the best. . . . Very odd.

Unable to think any longer of the grim hard road that lay before him, equally unable, just yet, to think of Véronique finding her happiness in the keeping of another man, even though it was he himself who had given her to him, he lay in the stuffy darkness and thought of Marguerite. Was she happy upon her grey storm-beaten rock upon the other side of the world? He thought that she was. He imagined that all nuns were happy because they had, in religious parlance, "found God". Well, that was a thing that as far as he knew he had not done, probably would never do, for he was not a religious sort of fellow. He never had been, he thought, remembering with a smile how long ago, while having little use for either of them, he had yet infinitely preferred Captain O'Hara's God, the Creator of wind and earth and water, to the saving suffering God of Samuel Kelly. He was not sure that he felt the same about it now, for he understood now that love is not love at all until it has paid the price.

And when you have paid there comes a sort of peace. William, lying completely wretched in the stuffy darkness, yet felt himself lifted by it as though on the long slow waves of some vast, calm sea. He was lifted up and borne away and set down on a distant shore at the world's end. And he was a boy again, running with the wind and shouting to the sun, and capering beside him was a small sunburned golden-haired girl in a blue frock. . . . Contrary to his expectations William had fallen asleep.

FAIRYLAND

They came out on a lovely pleasance, that dream'd of oasis,
Fortunate isle, the abode o' the blest, their fair Happy Woodland.
VIRGIL.

CHAPTER ONE

1

The slump of the Eighties. That was how the next generation would speak of it, and no doubt it was an exceedingly interesting period of New Zealand history. But Marianne had no opinion of history. Men might like it—they certainly made it with their wars and one thing and another—but for a woman the word history more often than not merely spelled the destruction of something beautiful that she had made. She would spin a web of fine living and then along would come history in the shape of a war or a business slump and like a pair of shears would slit the delicate thing to pieces. Marianne, rolling home from a tea-party in the Autumn dusk in the fine carriage that would soon have to be put down, to the beautiful house that would soon have to be sold because they had lost so much money, meditated upon these things in a curious condition of discouragement for which she could find no adequate reason. It was true that another period of their life together was about to close for herself and William, but there had been other endings in the past and they had not discouraged her. So why was she so discouraged now? She turned her thoughts backwards to the past, for she must find out.

During the earlier part of the last twelve years William, with her expert help, had made a vast amount of money and she had spent it superbly. Their house had been the finest in town, their dinner parties (though always in exquisite taste) the most lavish, while she herself had had the reputation of being the best-dressed woman in Dunedin, the most intelligent, and the most accomplished hostess. To have the entrée to the Ozannes' house was to have "arrived". She had even challenged Mrs. Anderson as the leader of Dunedin society and their friendship had waned considerably in consequence. She had not had many friends. Her chief friends had been among the men who delighted in the brilliance of her talk and the excellence of her cuisine, but the women, though they had never felt their festivities to be complete without the adornment of her presence, had not really liked her. It had been the old story. She had been too successful, and because of her success too arrogant, and so unloved. But she had not, as long ago on the Island, let that upset her, for the sheer overwhelming success of her achievement had been too exhilarating. She had done what she had said she would do. She had begun her life in New Zealand the wife of a poor lumberman and she had made the two of them wealthy, envied and admired. They could climb no higher in this country than they had climbed. They had reached the top.

Her exhilaration had been partly personal, partly the reflection of the exhilaration of money-making that had gripped everyone . . . except William. The boom years, with the demand for raw materials apparently insatiable, the mining of gold, the development of steam, the building of more and more roads and railways, the laying of the deep-sea cable to Australia, the whole wonderful business helped on by the lavish spending of borrowed money, had kept the whole community awhirl with excitement, and Marianne had drunk of that excitement as though it were wine. William had not. He had moved ponderously and obediently through the days, working like a titan to give his wife all she wanted, eating hugely, drinking just a little more than was good for him to get the needed spurt for yet more endeavour, genial, patient, kind, beloved by all who knew him and appearing to the unobservant eye to be enjoying himself. . . . But not deceived. . . . "It won't last," he had said over and over again to Marianne. "My dear, it won't last. I think we ought to go slow. Not entertain quite so much. Put by a little more." This remark of his had always irritated her profoundly. "Nonsense!" she had snapped, invariably ignoring that bit about putting by a little more, "why shouldn't it last? We are living in the age of progress, William. Mankind is progressing." To which remark William had always replied with the irritating question, "What to?"

In their small corner of the world it had been to a slump. Their mad pursuit of wealth had been a flame of desire that had burned too fast; in other words the alluvial surface gold had been mined too fiercely and was worked out. Gold, now, could only be procured by dredging and quartz-mining, methods that were vastly expensive. And there had been an even sharper fall in the price of wool caused by the competition from the newly-opened plains of North America and Russia. And that policy of helping on the good times by the spending of large sums of borrowed money had turned out not to be a very wise one after all.

And William and Marianne were hard hit. The carriage must go and they must move into a smaller house. And the future was not rosy. They had not saved like the Andersons and other more provident folk and were faced with a catastrophic change in their way of life. With no carriage and only a small house it was difficult to see how one would be able to continue to entertain as one had done in the past. . . . There was no doubt about it, the pressure of events was about to force Marianne down from her pedestal.

Force her? Force *her*, Marianne Ozanne? There was the rub. There was the reason for her discouragement. She had put her finger on it. In other years, when one way of life had ended and another had begun, it had been because she had chosen that it should be so. She had chosen to leave the Island and become William's wife. It was she who had decreed that they should give up the lumber trade for sheep-farming, she who had moved herself and William from the Country of the Green Pastures to Dunedin. . . . And now the pressure of events, history, had dared to push Marianne Ozanne down from the high place that was hers after a lifetime of effort, hers by right because it had been won by courage and determination and not by luck alone.

No! She took a sudden decision. She was not going to move into that smaller house. She was not going to yield first place once again to Mrs. Anderson, to find herself the object of pitying glances from all those ladies of Dunedin whom she had hitherto patronised, merely because her husband had been improvident and had not saved sufficiently. No! Old though she was she was once more going to strike out afresh in an entirely new way, an entirely new place. . . . Where, she did not know yet, but time would show. . . . Once more, in the words of that poem Véronique was so fond of, she was going to seek fresh fields and pastures new and rise upon them like the sun. Yes, she was. Her decision became like iron, not to be deflected by anything on earth. Old? She was not old. She was only sixty-eight, and had completely recaptured the vigour that had deserted her a little in the Country of the Green Pastures.

Yet she looked more than sixty-eight as she sat there in her fine carriage, rolling along through the Autumn dusk. The stoutness that had come upon her in her fifties had unaccountably receded of late years in spite of all the good dinners she ate, and her figure was once more tiny, taut, resolute, proud and upright as a ramrod, and this very littleness gave her somehow a look of age, as though time had worn her down to the mere essentials of her being. Her hair was still iron-grey and plentiful, her eyes bright, the corners of her mouth still under control, but her skin had the colour of parchment and was as wrinkled as though she were eighty. Her dainty little hands, sparkling with jewels, were wrinkled too. Her skin betrayed her badly as a woman who had faced rough weather and much hard labour in her time, and accorded a little incongruously with the exquisite close-fitting coat of purple velvet that she wore, her sables, her small plumed velvet hat and the diamonds in her ears. . . . She never wore the greenstone earrings now, for they were too homely, and the servants would have laughed to see her wearing Maori adornments. . . . Delightful though it was to have a large staff of servants it was in some ways a little hampering to one's freedom.

Freedom! There came to her a sudden little vision of a bright stretch of shining sand and three children racing across it. She so seldom thought of the Island nowadays that the memory surprised her. . . . The wind was off the sea to-day, and though it was calm and still, with a beautiful after-glow in the sky, William had said this morning that he thought there was bad weather on the way.

The carriage stopped before the flight of steps that led up to her front door with its imposing brass knocker and its beautiful fanlight through which the light was streaming. As soon as the carriage stopped the front door opened as though automatically and her man-servant came down the steps to open the carriage door for her, his smooth high-nosed face impassive, his movements those of an oiled machine. There were no servants in Dunedin so well-trained as Marianne's, yet this afternoon this clock-work efficiency irritated her slightly, for she had a fancy to pause on the pavement and listen for the crying of the sea birds, who often flew inland over the town when a storm was brewing, and it is impossible to stand still on a pavement listening for bird-voices while a butler with the face of an Egyptian Pharaoh is waiting to attend you up the steps.

In the beautiful hall, warm and fragrant with its blazing fire in the grate and its banks of magnificent potted plants, she paused to speak to her man-servant. "Mr. Ozanne in yet, Parker?"

"No, Madam."

"Then tell cook to put dinner back half-an-hour."

"Very good, Madam."

Half-an-hour. That would give William time to get back from his board meeting and herself time to listen to bird voices in her bed-room before she dressed for dinner. Listen to the birds! How absurd she was being! She had not bothered to listen to them for years and years—not, surely, since the North Island days, when she had worked in that little office at the harbour at Wellington.

In her luxurious bedroom, to her intense annoyance, she found the crimson velvet curtains closely drawn, her fire burning and her

maid waiting for her. She opened her lips to chide Harriet sharply
for drawing the curtains while it was still quite light, then shut them
again, remembering that the curtains were drawn all over the house
at dusk by her orders, no matter how lovely the afterglow, for she
was not usually in the habit of worrying herself about such things.
She did not know what had come over her that she was worrying
about them now.

"No need to wait, Harriet," she said gently. "I will take off my
things myself. I'll ring when I want you."

In spite of the excellent training she had received Harriet's face
registered slight surprise. She had been with Marianne for six years
and throughout the whole of that period her mistress had remained
quite incapable of removing her own hat or unfastening her own
shoes. But with a murmured, "Certainly, Madam," she withdrew.

Marianne was quite unable to explain to herself why at her maid's
exit she immediately locked her bedroom door. Some instinct for
escape, for solitude, perhaps; her spirit was travelling quicker than
her mind to-day and she could not quite follow it. She flung off her
sables as though they were stifling her, moved to the nearest window,
pulled back the curtains, opened it and leaned out. A lovely orange
light suffused the sky, but it was a stormy light, and, yes, over the
roofs of the city the sea birds were circling and crying.

She pulled up a chair to the window and sat down, her elbows on
the sill. It was quite warm and the scent of the sea was strongly in
the air. Once again she remembered that little office at Wellington
and how she had thought as she worked there, with the harbour
sights and sounds all about her, that one day when she was an old
woman she would like to go back to Saint Pierre, sail into the
harbour and let down her anchor for ever.

Suddenly she sat up straight, her hands clasped, her eyes shining
like stars. Why not? That old trouble of William's was so long ago
that it would not be remembered now; and if it was remembered
none of the Islanders would give them away, for Island folk are
always loyal one to the other. They could go back to No. 3 Le
Paradis, the lovely home of her girlhood, for it was not a large
house, and they would surely be able to scrape up enough money to
live there quite elegantly. It was still only let to Marguerite's Order
as an orphanage, for Marguerite, obeying her, had never sold it,
and as far as she remembered the present lease had nearly run out.
She would write at once to Marguerite, still Mother Superior of
Notre Dame du Castel, and tell her not to re-let, for they were
coming home. Home! Yes, that was the solution. The fresh fields
and pastures new should be the old pastures of her childhood. She

remembered saying good-bye to Europe on board the Green Dolphin. . . . Europe, old and lovely, good-bye. Fairyland of childhood, good-bye. I'll not see you again till life comes round full circle and the gate that a child came out of will be the gate where an old woman enters in. . . . Yes, she had always meant to go back. With the passing of the years her mind had forgotten the old wish but her spirit had remembered. Home with William! There, at last, in the old home of their childhood, she would possess him utterly. Marguerite would have no part in him now; Marguerite was not a pretty girl any more but an old nun absorbed in her prayers. Mewed up in her convent as she was they would probably see next to nothing of her, and what they did see would doubtless prove unprepossessing; for nuns, thought Marianne, the wish fathering the thought, age quickly, worn out by their hard life they become incredibly ugly in just no time at all. . . . She was not worn out. . . . With her charm and brilliance and vigour she was likely to make a complete conquest of that homely little Island. She had made no conquest of New Zealand, and looking out into the gathering dusk she owned it. Upon her first sight of this country she had felt they would be a match for each other, and so they had been, but in the end New Zealand had won. She had set no stamp upon the kauri trees, nor upon the mountain pastures, and she was withdrawing beaten from the raw new city life. New Zealand was too vast. But on the Island it would be different. Even as a girl she had made a place for herself in its life, and now, with the garnered wisdom of a lifetime to aid her, she should experience no difficulty in stamping her personality upon it. And upon No. 3 Le Paradis too. No. 3 would be her very own house now. Not her mother's—hers. . . . She let out a deep sigh of happiness. Yes, it was settled. She would tell William to-night.

But at the thought of telling William a slight chill of foreboding invaded her joy. Would she have trouble with William? He had loved the little Island in his youth, but how would that love weigh against his love for his daughter? Would he be willing to leave Véronique? He saw little of her these days, but he did go and stay with her sometimes, on the rare occasions when business could spare him, and on even rarer occasions—for she was one of those infatuated wives who cannot bear to leave their husbands for a single moment—she would bring one or two of the children to stay with them, and Marianne knew that he lived for these visits. The fact was that he just about worshipped that daughter of his. Would he be willing to leave her? In these days of steamships the separation between the new world and the old was not what it had been, and New Zealanders who could afford the journey frequently took holidays in Europe, so that Véronique and her children would be able to visit them. But even so—it would be a big separation.

And it surprised Marianne considerably to find that she was herself willing to face it. . . . For just a moment it even shocked her. . . . Did she, then, love her beautiful child less than she had done? She refused to answer that question point-blank, temporising with the thought that if she and Véronique had drawn apart of late years it was all William's fault; he had separated Véronique from poor dear Frederick and thrown her into the arms of those dreadful Ogilvies. Marianne's mouth set in a bitter line, drooping at the corners. The Ogilvies had always disliked her, she told herself, and after that fatal marriage they had deliberately alienated her child's affection from her. Poor dear Frederick would never have done that, for he had loved and admired her and if only Véronique had married him she would have gained a son without losing a daughter. . . . And poor dear Frederick would not have disappointed his good uncle and aunt in the regrettable way he had. . . . William might say what he liked but Marianne knew quite well that it was because he had lost Véronique that the path subsequently pursued by Frederick had not been altogether the path of honour. Married to Véronique he would have been the soul of virtue and would have welded, not weakened, the bond between mother and child. The Ogilvies, of course, especially John, had made it their business to weaken it. It was only her father, who flattered them, whom they permitted Véronique to love now, not her mother who had borne her, and they had done their utmost, through Véronique, who was weak as water in their hands, and gave credence to all the wicked things they said about her poor mother, to withdraw William's love from the wife of his bosom and centre it entirely upon his daughter and her children. Well, they had not succeeded yet, for William still loved her, and if she were to remove him right away to the other side of the world they would never succeed. . . . No, never. . . . She got up quickly and went to the dressing-table to fetch her eau-de-Cologne, for she was suddenly crying. It had been so cruel of them to take her child's love from her, but the effort to take her husband's love too had been not only cruel but wicked also. What wicked people there were in the world! Well, in this case their wickedness would not succeed. She would tackle William about the Island this very night. . . . Through the open window came the faint crying of the sea birds, and the breath of the sea touched her cheek like a caress. Her bitterness was eased and she smiled a little. . . . On the beloved Island William would be wholly hers.

William, meanwhile, was strolling homeward through the orange dusk in happy ignorance of the bombshell that Marianne was preparing for him at home. As he strolled he hummed a little tune to himself, for he was enjoying an hour of rare felicity. The board meeting had been a gloomy business, but it had been soon over and since then he had been joyously employed in buying birthday presents for Jane Anne, Véronique's eldest. She was just about to go into two figures, was Jane Anne, and in William's mind the slump ranked just nowhere in comparison with this earth-shaking event. Merry little Jane Anne ten years old! Of his four adored grandchildren she was perhaps his favourite. . . . But yet he didn't know. . . . William John with the five freckles on his snub nose and a grin like the Cheshire cat was an engaging young rascal, and little Lettice a creature of astonishing beauty, while the prowess of baby Robin had filled four sheets (crossed and re-crossed) of his last letter from Véronique, reposing in his breast pocket over his heart at this moment. . . . But Jane Anne. . . .

What William felt about Jane Anne was well expressed by the number of parcels that bulged from the pockets of his overcoat. With his cheery red face, the song upon his lips, and the parcels, he reminded passers-by that Christmas was on the way, and they smiled as he passed them. Though even without parcels William's passage through the streets nowadays always gave pleasure. He had developed into something of a "character", with a delightful Pickwickian flavour about him that made every heart feel lighter. He was the best-known and the most popular man in Dunedin. Unknown to Marianne the bulk of the money that she had allowed him for his personal use had been devoted for years past to helping lame dogs over stiles. No-one who came to William in trouble was ever sent away uncomforted, and with a lifetime of experience behind him he could succour wisely. During these last twelve years, with his left hand scarcely aware of what his right was up to, he had saved many souls. And he never saw a weeping child in the street without administering lollipops, or an old woman carrying a heavy burden but he did not turn aside to carry it for her. His huge kindness grew with the years and his wealth, by giving him the means of gratifying it, had enlarged rather than shut up his heart. Though he had continued through all these years to detest the pursuit of money yet its possession had done much for him. Apart from the enlarging of his heart it had given back to him again the old lost elegance of his youth. That something of his mother in him, lost in the roughness of pioneer existence, had reappeared again in his old age, and as he strolled along the street humming his little tune he looked once more a fine gentleman.

His round red rugged face was shaved to a velvety softness, his handsome grey whiskers perfectly groomed. He wore a flower in the button-hole of his overcoat of fine dark blue cloth, his eyeglasses hung from a glossy black satin ribbon and the grey top-hat that hid his bald head was worn at a jaunty angle. But it was not only these outward things that gave William his present air of aristocracy. There was about him a certain air that Tai Haruru would have recognised, that poised dignity that is the corollary of an absence of fuss and strain, that look of peace that is born when a man accepts the burden of life not with railing but with reverence for the mystery behind.

For it seemed to William that whatever else the mystery might do or not do it did not cheat. All that he could do for his child he had done, withholding nothing, and he knew that life too, keeping its share of the bargain, had withheld from Véronique nothing that her spirit needed for salvation. During the last twelve years, as day by day he had lifted the difficult burden of the uncongenial days, he had known with absolute certainty that all was well with the child. She might suffer, she had suffered in toil and childbirth and the daily weariness of life in a fragile body, but she'd accepted that suffering, she'd paid it down willingly and gladly for husband and children, and whenever he saw her and looked deep into her calm and happy eyes he knew that all was well, and that all would be well. Not only had she paid, but the three elements that make for happiness had met in her; not only divine love but human love as unselfish as love can be had been given her, and her own spirit had been strong enough to give love back in full measure. So she was safe for ever. If she were to die to-morrow all would still be well with her. William knew that and was at peace.

He came in sight of the brightly lit windows of his house and his song died abruptly on his lips. The lights should have been so welcoming but yet, somehow, they were not. That place of the fire on the hearth—home—it struck him suddenly that he and Marianne had never really had it. At the settlement there had been so much bitterness, and the Green Pastures, that he still loved better than any spot on earth, he saw now to have been always more Véronique's home than his and Marianne's. And this house, dedicated to dinner parties, had never seemed to him to belong to anyone except the servants. He was glad they were leaving it for a smaller one. He'd always hated the place.

Well, Marianne liked it, and that she should have what she liked had, next to Véronique's happiness, been the object of his labours all these years. This last decade, he rather thought, had been the happiest of her life; or would have been had it not been for her ridiculous dislike of the Ogilvies. Her jealousy of them had been unfounded, her hatred of Véronique's marriage without reason, born of nothing but the thwarting of her own wishes, but it had poisoned the lives of all of them. John had done his absolute best, with unending patience, but nothing he could do or say had seemed able to win over his mother-in-law, and now Marianne never went to the farm and he never came to Dunedin. Véronique came to stay now and then without him with one or two of the children, and bore Marianne's autocratic interference with her manner of dealing with her offspring with exemplary gentleness, but the visits were not very happy, for Marianne's dislike of John was a barrier between mother and daughter that nothing could bridge. William's solitary visits to the Country of the Green Pastures were sheer bliss but they could take place seldom, so busy was he, and so stricken was Marianne that he could like to leave her for them. It was a tragic state of affairs all round, reflected William, tragic for Marianne because she did most truly suffer in her unreason, and tragic for himself because it meant that he could see so little of Véronique. Yet what did that matter, he thought, mounting the steps towards his front door. It was Véronique who mattered, and with her all was well.

Before he had time to insert his latchkey the front door was flung open by the butler and his overcoat peeled off him before he had time to rescue the parcels in the pockets. The man removed them—the flaxen curls of a doll were showing through the paper of one of them and some lollipops fell on the floor from another—with an impassive countenance that yet managed to combine obsequiousness with a veiled contempt in a way that fell little short of genius, and stood holding them, awaiting William's instructions. Confound the fellow! William detested servants shooting up around him like mushrooms at every step he took. One was without privacy. A home was no home when every single thing one did was commented upon at every turn. "Put 'em in the library," he said irritably. "Mrs. Ozanne in?"

"Awaiting you in the parlour, Sir. Dinner has been put back."

The tone of the man's voice implied reproof and William stumped upstairs to change feeling like a chidden child. In the smaller house, thank God, they'd not be able to afford a butler.

Twenty minutes later, clad in his perfectly cut evening clothes, he faced Marianne across the glittering expanse of their dinner table, with its shining damask and silver and bowls of exquisitely arranged flowers. Marianne wore a gown of cherry-coloured velvet to-night with a fichu of exquisite lace, and the diamonds in her ears sparkled when she moved her shapely head. Her detractors vowed that she dressed in a fashion most unsuitable for her years, disdaining the bonnets and sombre colours affected by most old ladies. Yet her bizarre clothes always became her, and she was looking especially fine to-night. William opened his mouth to tell her so, but remembered the presence of the butler just in time.

"Storm before morning," he said. "The wind was getting up as I came home."

Marianne made a suitable reply and they talked upon impersonal topics with great skill throughout the length of the elaborate meal. It had taken Marianne a long time to train William in the art of conversing before servants, but he could do it now to admiration. Her heart swelled with pride as she looked at him sitting there benign and immaculate at the head of the table. Who could believe that this handsome old gentleman was the same being as the rough lumberman who had come to meet her at Wellington? Her fight was won. She'd made a grand thing of William.

They were alone at last in their armchairs one on each side of the parlour fire, Marianne with her knitting, William with a newspaper that he had no intention of reading. With a sigh of relief he slipped his heels out of his too-tight evening shoes, folded his hands across his waistcoat and prepared to doze. Old Nick was already asleep, in a very smart new cage, with a green satin cover on the top. A tendency to sleep more and to limit his vocabulary to the one ejaculation, "Oh my!", uttered with so many shades of meaning that the limitation was scarcely any restriction at all, were the only signs he gave of an age that by this time was surely colossal. His health was still excellent and Marianne had long ago given up all hope of his demise. He would outlive her to a certainty.

"William!" she said, "don't slouch like that. Sit up. I want to talk to you."

William opened his eyes, sighed, and levered himself to an upright position. "Yes, dear?"

"What sort of meeting did you have this afternoon?"

"Deuced unpleasant," said William. "Business is bad. The sooner we get out of this house, dear, the better."

Marianne's needles clicked on sharply, and she did not even raise her head as she said decidedly, "And the sooner we get out of this country the better."

"Eh?" ejaculated William.

"I said," repeated Marianne, "the sooner we get out of this country the better. If we stay on here we shall only lose what little money we have left. You've not much head for business, you know, William, and if it hadn't been for me we'd have been bankrupt long ago. I don't blame you of course, dear, it's the way you're made, but I'm too tired now to continue playing the man's part as well as the woman's. I need rest in my old age, and rest is a thing that one cannot encompass in a new country. We'll go back to Europe, back to the Island, William, and end our days at Le Paradis. No. 3 is a house eminently suitable for dignified retirement and we've enough money, if you're not too extravagant and leave the management of our affairs to me, to contrive quite nicely. That little trouble you got into in China is so long ago that no one will remember it now. And it will be an excellent thing for Véronique and her children to have us settled in Europe. As the children get older she will be able to bring them to visit us. That will broaden their minds, and hers, and give her a rest from John and that dreadful farm life to which you condemned her when you married her to him. But I am not only thinking of Véronique, William, I am thinking a little, too, of Marguerite. For a whole lifetime she has been separated from her nearest and dearest. It will be an unspeakable joy to her to see us once again."

Marianne's voice had flowed on quietly and her needles had not ceased to flash and click. And still she did not look up. So matter-of-fact was she that she might have been suggesting that they should have coffee for breakfast instead of tea.

"Eh?" whispered William hoarsely.

"It would be sweet to go home, William," continued Marianne very softly. "That lovely little Island—no one knows what it cost me to leave it when I came out here to this raw terrible country to marry you. Only your great need of me, William dear, could have induced me to leave it. I was born there, William. I should like to die there."

And now, at last, she looked up and their eyes met. Her eyes were lovelier now in her old age than they had ever been, he thought. Though bright as ever they were not so needle-sharp.

"William?" she pleaded softly.

He gave her no answer. He heaved himself up out of his chair and blundered over to the library door like a blind man, knocking over two flower vases and a small table on his way. He went in, shut the door and locked it. Marianne rang for the butler. "Mop up that water if you please," she said, and continued calmly with her knitting. The thought that her servants were commenting upon the little incidents of her personal life never disturbed her as it did William. Feeling herself the inhabitant of a more exalted world than theirs she was able to retain her sense of privacy within it. William felt his world and theirs to be the same.

But when the butler had gone she dropped her knitting and clasped her hands tightly together on her lap. William had vouchsafed her no glimpse at all into his mind and she was terribly anxious. The wind had risen now and was rattling the casement, just as it had rattled the old schoolroom window at home on the day when she and Marguerite had lain upon their backboards and their mother had read aloud to them from the book of Ruth. "Ton peuple sera mon peuple." Yes, but it was with insight that the young man Keats had written, "She stood in tears amid the alien corn." Quite suddenly all her wily arguments for going home, real or unconsciously fabricated, fell away, leaving her with just the one sincere and aching longing—to be in that old schoolroom again and hear the wind rattling the window.

2

William blundered to the chair before his writing table and sat down. He was confronted by a neat row of presents—the doll, the bag of lollipops, a little workbox, a miniature teaset of painted wood and a tiny dustpan and brush. Jane Anne was a very domesticated child and nothing pleased her so much as to play at being a house-wife like Mamma. He could see her in his mind's eye now, as he had seen her when he was last at the farm, sitting on a wooden stool before the kitchen fire beside Véronique, each of them bathing a baby, Véronique bathing Robin in his tin tub and Jane Anne bathing the smallest of her wooden dolls in the slop-basin. It was stormy weather, and wind whirled round the house, but in the kitchen it was deliciously warm and cosy and they did not care. He could see the beloved room, still the heart of the house, the firelight shining on all the treasures, the copper pans, the purple tobacco jar, the box of shells from La Baie des Petits Fleurs that had once been Véronique's favourite playthings and were now just as beloved by her children. Robin was shouting lustily in his bath, lovely little Lettice was threading a bead necklace and William John of the five freckles, who did not take kindly to intellectual pursuits, was seated at the kitchen table with John, sighing deeply while the mysteries of multiplication and subtraction were explained to him by the most patient father in the world. And Véronique? Her face was so glowing with happiness as she lifted Robin from his tub to her lap that William was reminded of an old picture of the Nativity that he had seen once, where all the light in the stable shines out from the mother's face. It was as it had always been in the Country of the Green Pastures, the lives of all about her were just so many petals of a flower of love that closed in about the golden heart that was Véronique.

And now it was demanded of him that he should tear himself out of that charmed circle and put half the world between himself and that glowing face. No! His hands, lying on the writing table before him, clenched themselves fiercely. There are demands that can be made of a man that are too great to be met, and this was one of them. No! For a long while he sat there, the whole of him taut with negation, defending the citadel of his being with all his strength against the besieging army of Marianne's arguments.

For they were good arguments. He and she were old now to continue in business, struggling against a tide of adverse fortune, yet in a pioneer country, humming like a beehive with restless activity, it was not easy to stand aside in idleness. The tempo was too quick. Restless striving was in the blood. Europe was the place for rest, Europe where the slow swing of tradition and the mellowed serenity of ancient cities dreaming under a tranquil sun were of the very essence of peace. Yes, it would be good for Véronique's children, when they were grown, to experience that peculiar serenity of old Europe, a different sort of peace from the fresh morning quiet of the Green Pastures, the peace of age. It would be good to give them the experience of that dignity. And Véronique herself? But would she ever come? John was not the sort of man who would want to leave his native country and would she leave him alone? She might, but it was not very likely. Though she loved her father he was not her world as she was his. John and her children were now her world. No, if they went it was possible that he might never see Véronique again, and that he could not face. Nor, he realised abruptly, could he face that meeting with the Mother Superior of Notre Dame du Castel, that old woman who had once been the girl he had so deeply loved. His imagination conjured up a horrific picture of a wrinkled, sallow face framed in white linen, gnarled hands thrust into black sleeves, a hushed voice, a sedate and cloistered walk where once there had been colour and laughter and the grace of morning, and his soul rose up in revolt. Just as he could not face the parting with Véronique, so he could not face the meeting with Marguerite. . . . The thing was impossible. . . . Marianne's arguments were good but the thing was impossible.

There was a soft knocking at his locked door and a voice, a little girl's voice, cried, "Let me in, William! Let me in!" He lifted his head, startled. It was years since he had heard that voice. Not, surely, since that evening at the settlement when he had found her weeping in her room and she had cried out to him like a changeling child, "If only you'll love me, William. If only you'll love me." He got up quickly and unlocked the door, and there she was standing like a chidden child, her hands covering her face.

"Marianne!" he ejaculated. "Marianne!"

He pulled her in, locked the door again in case that damned butler should come along, and sat down in his writing chair once more, taking her on his knee. Absurd to see this modish old lady, in her jewels and cherry-red gown, sitting like a child on his knee.

"I want to go home, William," she said weakly. "Oh, William, I do so badly want to go home!"

It was a cry of absolute sincerity. Beneath all her vanity, her pride, her spider-like spinning of intrigue, it seemed that there lived always this sincere little girl. And it was for the welfare of this immortal child that he was in this world responsible.

Home? They'd never really had one, he had been thinking this evening. Yet it was, perhaps, not yet too late. . . . And it came to him suddenly that when he had paid down for Véronique's happiness the price of partial separation from her perhaps he had not paid the whole price. This deeper separation would cancel the debt.

"Very well, Marianne," he said. "We'll go home."

CHAPTER TWO

1

"We shall be in in an hour, Madam."

Marianne opened her eyes and blinked at the stewardess, astonished to find that she had been deeply asleep. Worn out by the long railway journey from Liverpool, where the steamship from New Zealand had docked, to Weymouth, where they had come aboard the steam packet for the Channel Islands, she and William had gone to the private cabin they had engaged for just forty winks. But they had been so tired that the little nap had become deep sleep. Glancing across the tiny cabin Marianne could see that William had not yet awakened, and that Old Nick in his cage was still immobile.

"Already?" she ejaculated in astonishment.

"It's such lovely weather, Madam," said the stewardess. "It's been a calm quick voyage." Then she smiled at the little old lady sitting up in her berth, bright-eyed and excited as a child of twelve. "Your first visit to the Islands, Madam?"

"Oh, no, no!" cried Marianne. "I was born there. My husband

and I are going home after thirty-six years' exile on the other side of the world."

"Thirty-six years!" ejaculated the stewardess. "Why, Madam, it must have been sailing ships in those days!"

"It was," said Marianne. "The journey out seemed to take a lifetime, and the journey home just five minutes. Unbelievable, the speed. Absolutely unbelievable! In an hour, did you say? Good gracious me! William! William!"

The handsome old gentleman lying flat on his back in the other berth, with his mouth open, snoring cheerfully, opened one eye. "Eh?" he enquired.

"William! We shall be in in an hour!"

"Forty minutes, now, Madam," said the stewardess, and withdrew smiling, to spread the news that the lovable old couple in No. 1 cabin were returning home after thirty-six years.

Marianne, who seemed to be shedding years as fast as the speeding hour was shedding minutes, flew across the cabin like a ten-year-old and shook her husband vigorously awake. "William! William! In in forty minutes." Then she turned from him to the birdcage on the floor and whisked away its green satin cover. "Wake up, you wicked old bird! In in forty minutes!"

Never in all her life had she spoken to Old Nick so companionably. Opening his eyes he blinked in astonishment. Then squawked. "Oh, my!" he ejaculated. "Back the mainyard, mates."

"You silly old bird, there is no mainyard," Marianne informed him. "This is a steamship. You've come speeding from the other side of the world, my dear, in a steamship."

"And the most damned uncomfortable voyage too," growled William, who was now on his feet, trying to button his waistcoat with fingers that trembled. "Hustle—that's what it's been—hustle, hustle the whole way over. And the smell of the engines enough to upset a man's liver for life."

They had been arguing about the relative merits of sail and steam ever since they had left New Zealand, and Marianne opened her mouth to make a sharp retort. Then she closed it again, realising that William had taken refuge in the old controversy merely to cover up an almost unbearable emotion. . . . He had buttoned his waistcoat all crooked and was making a very poor job of finding the hat that was staring him in the face as large as life. . . . With her efficiency not in the least impaired by her excitement she came to him, re-buttoned his waistcoat, handed him his hat and Old Nick in his cage, adjusted his plaid inverness over his shoulders and sent him to see the steward about the luggage. Then, alone in the cabin, she smoothed the folds of her elegant green travelling dress and poised the smart but absurd green hat with the tall crown, that was the very latest fashion, upon her piled-up hair. Then she took the diamonds out of her ears, put them away in the green leather jewel case that was fastened to her wrist by a thin gold chain, and hung in their place the greenstone earrings which she had worn when she left the Island. Then she stood for a moment looking out of the porthole and through a sudden mist of tears it seemed that she saw a white-winged sailing ship, a superb and graceful clipper, speeding over the smooth summer sea. "Captain O'Hara," she said aloud. "Nat. I don't forget you. Green Dolphin, lovely Green Dolphin, they may build smelly, noisy steamships ten times your size but they'll never build a ship like you. I hope I'll not be alive, Green Dolphin, when the last clipper goes home from the sea."

This was treason to the pulsing engines that had borne her so swiftly and luxuriously home, and in William's hearing nothing would have induced her to utter it, but to the ghost of the Green Dolphin she could say what she liked, for to the dead our hearts are known.

Resolutely she swung her green mantle round her shoulders, picked up her green umbrella, jewel case and reticule and went on deck to join William.

Hand in hand, with Old Nick beside them, they stood by the rail. It was late afternoon and the slight heat mist that had veiled the world when they left Weymouth had drawn away, and sea and sky held an intensity of deep tranquil colour that probed not only height and depth but hearts too. The wind was cool and fresh and the sun so gentle that its light was a benediction and its warmth a feather-soft caress. Small rocky islands, the fringe of what Marianne had long ago so proudly called the archipelago, that were as the first sight of home to returning islanders, were slipping swiftly by, each with its garland of white foam worn with the old proud air.

"Will she be at the harbour to meet us?" asked William hoarsely.

"Who? Marguerite? No, of course not," said Marianne a little tartly. "Nuns are not allowed to go gadding about the place meeting people off boats. There'll be no one at the harbour, William, but dear Charlotte will be at Le Paradis. It was good of Marguerite to arrange for us to have Charlotte."

They were silent again, blessing Marguerite in their hearts. For she had done great things for them. She had found another house for the orphanage in double-quick time and had had Le Paradis re-painted and had put in it the furniture and china that Marianne had long ago told her to put into store. And best of all she had installed Charlotte Marquand as housekeeper, with one of her daughters to help her, because Charlotte too was getting old. Their home was ready for them. They had only to open the door and walk in.

The Island came into view, just the same, not changed at all, with the stretches of wind-swept sand and golden common misted with the lilac of sea-holly and sea-lavender just as they used to be, and the white-washed cottages peeping from behind the shelter of grey-green hillocks just as they used to do. And then the long sea wall and the first sight of Saint Pierre with its grey granite houses piling up and up upon the rock. And now the steamer was slackening speed as the harbour held out its arms to gather them in, the pier upon one side, the fort upon the other. They could see the flights of stone steps leading down to the water from the harbour wall, and the masts of the fishing boats, and the tower of the Town Church. The noise of the engines died away as they glided in and they could hear the familiar harbour sounds that are the same all the world over: the small ripples slapping against the hulls of quiet ships, the ringing of a church bell on land, the crying of the gulls whose silver wings were wheeling overhead. They were alongside now, the ship's bell clanged and the gang-plank was rattling out, and all was bustle and confusion, for as usual half the Island had come down to the pier to meet the steamer. Bronzed blue-jerseyed sailormen, the sons and grandsons of the men they had known in their youth, were surging all about them and the familiar Island patois was ringing in their ears. The old smells assailed them: the scent of the squelching green seaweed that carpeted the harbour steps, the smell of fish, of tar, of wet wood, of the old-fashioned carriages with their patient horses drawn up in a row along the pier, the smell of flowers and the salt smell of the sea. . . . They were home.

They found themselves in a carriage, rattling along over the cobbles, their heavy boxes on the roof and Old Nick and their hand luggage piled up around them. They had no very clear idea as to how they had got there but they seemed to remember that an immense welcome had enfolded them as soon as they had crossed the gang-plank. Word had passed from the ship to the pier, perhaps, that they were returned islanders, for not only the sailors who had handled their luggage and the driver who every now and then bent down from his box to nod to them through the little window of the carriage, had given them a great welcome, but the very gulls had cried aloud in delight, and everyone had seemed to smile at them. That knowledge that comes only once or twice in a lifetime, that conviction of having done the right thing, the thing that was planned, that was meant from the beginning, came to them in full flood. . . . They had done right to come home.

As the coach climbed slowly up the steep old twisting streets the air seemed all gold. They could not see very well, because their eyes were misted, but they knew when they had come to the street of Le Paradis because they could smell the hydrangeas and the jessamine. And then the carriage stopped with a jolt, and there was the familiar flight of shallow steps, scrubbed to a snowy whiteness, flanked by the fluted columns and the lantern holders. The front door was flung open and there stood Charlotte, not changed very much in spite of her white hair. Her face was shining with welcome as she came down the steps to greet them, but so serene that it might have been only yesterday that she had seen them last.

2

Changed, bathed, rested, they sat together in the parlour after dinner, with Old Nick in his cage in the window near them. William had a book in his hands and his eyeglasses on his nose, but was still too stupefied by emotion to take in a single word of what he was reading. Marianne, however, had entirely recovered from it and was busy as she knitted with plans for the embellishment of No. 3 Le Paradis. She was one of those competent women who do not have to watch their stitches as they knit, and as her needles flew her eyes, bright with their scheming, roamed round the room.

Marguerite had evidently been busy with it, for there were many little touches that only she could have given. The beautiful sampler that Marianne herself had worked in her childhood had been framed and hung upon the wall, and the petit point chair seat, representing a ship in full sail, that she had worked long ago, and that Sophie had used in an unworthy chair, had been transferred to the beautiful Chippendale one that she was sitting upon at this moment. All over the house she had been aware of Marguerite's touches, and the whole of it had been made completely habitable, with not a single thing in it that was not beautiful. But the weeding out of the least valuable furniture for the sale that had been held after Octavius' death had left it looking singularly austere. And somehow, Marianne felt, you could tell that a religious order had had the running of this house for many years. There was a feeling as though the fires that had been lit here had been sufficient for health but not for luxury, and one got the impression that rather too much sunlight and fresh air had been allowed to stream through inadequately curtained windows over uncarpeted floors that could not fade into well-scrubbed corners where nothing was ever hidden. In short, there was over the whole place an atmosphere of doing-without and non-concealment that was entirely uncongenial to Marianne's temperament; as uncongenial as the gentle flavour of feminine resignation that seemed to hang about her mother's fragile escritoire, over there in the corner, and the elegant and valuable but rather wishy-washy china ornaments on the mantelpiece that had been Sophie's choice. Sophie's wifely subservience to Octavius had always annoyed Marianne, and it annoyed her now, as did this newer nunnery flavour. Well, she'd soon get rid of them both. In a month's time the atmosphere of this house would be that neither of self-immolation nor self-denial but self-fulfilment; it would be her own atmosphere. As regarded the re-creation of No. 3 Le Paradis she was going to succeed in getting what she wanted as she had never succeeded yet.

So much noise were her triumphant needles making, so absorbed was she in the turning of the heel, that she failed to hear the door open and was unaware that anyone had come in until William, his eyeglasses falling from his nose and his book crashing to the floor, lumbered to his feet with a queer strangled cry; a very odd cry indeed, such as Marianne never remembered to have heard before from his lips, compounded of love and heartbreak, surprise and incredulity, and a sheer childlike joy that tore her soul in two.

She was on her feet in an instant, rigid with the pain that cry had caused her, looking with a direct and yet panic-stricken gaze straight into the eyes of her sister Marguerite. . . . And Marguerite was beautiful in age, beautiful as she had never been even in the hey-day of youth. . . . Marianne had time for just one thought, and for the astonished dismay it caused her, before her sister's arms were about her and she was being pressed to Marguerite's bosom and kissed upon both cheeks with a passionate warmth of affection that would surely have been more becoming in a little child than in a staid and elderly nun. Staid? But she wasn't staid at all. She was kissing William now, also upon both cheeks, and laughing and crying and talking all at the same time in that abandoned Gallic fashion that had become distasteful to Marianne during her long sojourn among the undemonstrative Scotch folk of Dunedin. Obviously Marguerite's years in France had done her no good. And she was making a complete fool of William. The tears were running down his rugged old cheeks and he too was laughing and talking both together in a way that a man of his age should have been ashamed of. Marianne's legs gave way beneath her and she sat down rather suddenly, though with no fraction of a loss of dignity, upon the chair that was mercifully just behind her. Upright and impassive, regal in her evening finery of satin and old lace, she waited until the other two should come to their senses.

Marguerite recovered first, sat down beside Marianne and laid her hand upon her sister's. She was speaking quite calmly and collectedly now, though Marianne had no idea what she was saying; she was aware only of the beauty of the low-pitched voice and of the slender white hand that lay upon her own. It was a bad shock to find Marguerite still so lovely when she had hopefully pictured her aged and ugly. These nuns, of course, did no work at all. They led disgracefully lazy lives—just praying. Marguerite had not been worn with toil and hardship like her poor sister. Marianne's rigid back became straighter than ever with resentment as she looked up steadily into Marguerite's face, courageously intent upon knowing the worst.

And from the point of view of a jealous wife the worst was very bad indeed, for Marguerite, like many women who lose their beauty when their first youth is past, had regained it again in age and at sixty-three was strikingly lovely. If her face was worn the faint hollowing of cheeks and temples was not unbecoming, for she had made such friends with time the sculptor that he had touched her face only with loving fingers. The fine bone-structure of her face was more noticeable now than it had been in her girlhood and the delicacy of line and plane, the clear pallor, were that of a perfectly cut cameo. The good health that was still hers showed itself in the fine texture of her skin and the easy strong carriage of head and shoulders. Her eyes, if they were a little sunken, had lost none of their lovely colour; they were the deep blue of gentians beneath the perfectly arched eyebrows. Her mouth was merry and tender as ever and Marianne noticed with a pang of envy that if she had lost any teeth the loss was not noticeable. And if all this were not enough, thought poor Marianne, her face bore the indefinable stamp of spiritual power. She was young as only the re-born are young, wearing the serenity of her spiritual acceptance like a light about her. With an aching sense of exile Marianne realised that she and her sister lived upon different sides of a closed door. Marguerite turned to say something to William and Marianne too turned to look at her husband, whose round red face was beaming like the rising sun in a most ridiculous way, his hazel eyes brimming with light like a boy's. She saw the comradeship of their easy meeting glances and knew with a flash of insight that William too was on the other side of the door.

Marianne did not know quite how she got through the rest of the visit, though she heard her voice making precise and appropriate answers in the right places. Mercifully Marguerite did not stay long, and Marianne gathered to her intense relief that this visit of welcome was a special dispensation and that hereafter they would see her only when they visited her at stated intervals at the convent. "Yet I shall feel you so near," said Marguerite. "The three of us here together on the Island—it's as though we were children again."

"Even upon the other side of the world you always felt near," said William suddenly.

"Of course," asserted Marguerite matter-of-factly, and turned to bid Marianne good-bye. "Nothing could separate us three," she said with her cheek against her sister's.

Marianne, aware of the closed door, found that her lips were so stiff that she could scarcely return Marguerite's kiss. William, she noticed, when his turn came, seemed to experience no difficulty, and it seemed to her that it took him a full half hour to conduct Marguerite out to her waiting carriage. . . . Though the French clock on the mantelpiece said two minutes.

"Holy Moses!" he exclaimed, returning quite unconsciously to the favourite ejaculation of his boyhood as he came back to her again, rubbing his hands with delight, "whoever would have expected to find her so little changed?"

"Her appearance was a great shock to me," said Marianne with truth.

CHAPTER THREE

1

In the weeks that followed William continued to find everything unchanged while Marianne continued to suffer from shock. William found himself happy when he had expected to be unhappy and Marianne was unhappy when she had expected to be happy. They were alike only in their mutual realisation that whatever one expects to feel in this life one will probably feel the opposite.

Certainly, meditated William, he had never expected that in old age a man could re-enter the fairyland of his boyhood and experience its delights all over again. Holy Moses, but he'd not known the thing was possible. He honestly believed that he was happier now than he'd ever been in all his life before. Damned if he wasn't.

These pleasing reflections occurred to William upon the cliff top above La Baie des Saints, where he sat upon a seat basking in the September sunlight, his hat on the back of his head and his hands folded upon the gold knob of the handsome new walking stick

Marianne had given him to assist his peregrinations about the unchanged Island.

Holy Moses, but how he enjoyed these walks! The perfect summer weather, the rest, the leisure, the freedom from business worries, had made a new man of him. Vigour he had thought lost for ever had come back with astonishing speed, and sixty-five years old though he was he had never felt so fit. It was positively good to be alive these days. Of course, one couldn't expect things to go on for ever in this blissful fashion. Life being life there were bound to be a few ups and downs sooner or later, but meanwhile it was worth while to have lived if only for the enjoyment of this Indian summer.

La Baie des Saints was not changed at all. The grey granite cliffs fell away beneath him just as they had always done, clothed now with the purple of the heather, and down below was the little bay with its crescent of golden sand now veiled and now revealed by the outgoing tide. The village of Notre Dame was just the same. It seemed that the same smoke curled up from its chimneys and the same fishing nets were spread to dry over the low stone walls that enclosed the small sweet gardens full of tamarisk and fuchsia. And upon the other side of the bay the convent towered up upon the cliff top. He could see the tower of the church, where by night the light still burned to guide mariners home, and he remembered that just below the window where it shone the Madonna stood in her niche looking out to sea. He had walked all the way out from Saint Pierre, strolling along the unchanged sandy lanes sniffing the scent of the bracken and the escallonia flowers, pausing to get his breath on the hilltop where Octavius had halted the chariot so many years ago and looking at the islands flung like a handful of flowers upon the radiant sea. . . . There was dear Marie Tape-Tout and Le Petit Aiguillon, he had said to himself, identifying them, and there was the island shaped like a floating fairy castle, and the green one with a grey bowed head, like an old man in an emerald cloak praising God, and the exquisite amethyst-coloured one shaped like a bird just poised for flight. . . . Those last three islands had reminded him suddenly of Marianne and Marguerite and himself, though he could not imagine why. Yes, it was all the same. He could find no change except this arrival upon the cliff top of the comfortable seat he was sitting on. There were quite a number of these convenient seats scattered about the cliffs nowadays. Most thoughtful of the islanders to have provided them just in time for his home-coming in old age.

He took out his huge turnip of a gold watch, poised his eyeglasses on his nose and consulted it. He was on his way to visit the

Mother Superior of Notre Dame du Castel and he must be neither too early nor too late, for it seemed that the laws of the Medes and Persians were as nothing for strictness in comparison with those governing the visiting hours at convents. He had seen Marguerite only once since the visit of welcome she had paid them at Le Paradis, and upon that occasion Marianne had been with him. They had driven out together in one of the little Island carriages that were used when there was no luggage, odd attractive horse-drawn conveyances like a bath chair for two, for they could not afford a carriage of their own, and had sat upon the hardest chairs in the world and conversed with Marguerite in the convent visitors' room for the allotted forty minutes, timed by the clock on the mantelpiece. Marianne had been oppressed by the timing of the visit, by the gloom of the visitors' room, which smelled of mice and faced landward into a shrubbery of ancient mouldering laurel bushes, and boasted no decoration whatsoever except a particularly alarming picture of the Last Judgement suspended upon a wall covered with the most hideous wallpaper ever seen, most distressingly stained with damp. So oppressed had she been that this morning, just as all their plans had been made to drive out together again, she had said she wasn't going. She had the kind of headache that would not be improved by sitting on a hard kitchen chair in an aroma of mice, getting rheumatics from the damp and meditating upon her latter end, she had said. If that was William's idea of the best way to spend a summer afternoon he could go alone.

So he had countermanded the little carriage and had come alone, and now as he waited for the appointed hour his heart was carrying on inside him like a singing bird on a spring morning. For on that previous visit he had not been oppressed by the gloom and damp of the visitors' room. He hadn't even noticed them. He had seen nothing but the face of the woman he loved, felt nothing but the utter happiness of being with her. He chuckled as he remembered how he had dreaded seeing Marguerite again. Changed? He had not realised to what extent bodies can be moulded by the soul's impact upon them, so that the recognition of comradely spirits by each other becomes easier with age.

Time to go. Humming a tune, swinging his gold-headed stick, he strolled along the cliff towards the sandy lane that wound through the laurel bushes to the convent door.

After he had been inspected through the grille the door was opened to him by a lay sister, an immense and very aged peasant woman with large flat feet and little black eyes that twinkled with kindliness in her round red foolish good-humoured face. Her bosom was like a large black sofa cushion and had an astonishing number of safety pins skewered into it.

"Bonjour, ma soeur," said William, smiling at her. He loved the comical old porteress. He loved the massive old door with its iron grille, like the door of a dungeon in a fairytale. He loved the faint scent of incense that drifted to him from the interior of the convent. He loved the September sunshine hot on his back and the sound of the sea, and the feel of the gold knob of the stick Marianne had given him smooth and warm in the palm of his hand. He savoured every sight and sound that his senses gave him with the eager enjoyment of a boy. . . . Only in the fairyland of boyhood one had enjoyed unconsciously, while in the return to it one knew that one was blessed and bowed one's head and praised God. . . . He took off his hat and with bent head followed Soeur Angélique down the stone-floored passage.

But instead of conducting him to the visitors' room she turned aside at the end of the passage towards a spiral stone staircase. "Reverend Mother will receive you in her study to-day, M'sieur," she said in an impressive whisper, pausing at the foot of the stairs to hitch up her black skirts. "There are workmen in the visitors' room. There has been an accident there. All the wallpaper fell off the walls quite suddenly. It was the damp, you understand, M'sieur."

"I understand, ma soeur," said William gravely, and followed her up the spiral staircase. Round and round the two old people laboured, panting and blowing, Soeur Angélique lifting her black skirts higher and higher above her black button boots as though to aid her ascent, William clutching hat and stick and hard put to it to control the loud schoolboyish guffaw that was always bursting from him nowadays for no adequate reason.

But all desire to laugh left him at the door of Marguerite's study. This was where the woman he loved lived and prayed and a rush of glorious sentimentality broke right over him like a rainbow wave. He was announced, and entered with sight obscured by its blissful mist.

"Good afternoon, William. Put your hat down. Where's Marianne?"

Marguerite's gay matter-of-fact voice dispelled the mist and while he explained about Marianne's headache he looked about him delightedly. Nothing gloomy about this room. There was no vraic fire to-day to colour the whitewashed walls, but the warm sunlight coloured them, and the reflection of the blue summer sea beyond the windows rippled over the ceiling in waves of light.

"It's like the inside of a sea-shell," he said.

"That's what I've always thought," said Marguerite. "I love this room. I'm glad to show it to you. Sit down, William. Put your watch on the window ledge, for my clock has stopped."

He sat in one of the straight-backed chairs of old oak, Marguerite in the other, both of them looking out through the open window to the sea. His watch ticked inexorably and he was conscious of a slight sensation of panic. . . . So much to say and so short a time in which to say it. . . . But Marguerite, going straight to the point as she had learned to do in a life where words had to be used so sparingly that they must be used with skill, set him at ease again. She knew how to use these forty minutes. He only had to follow where she led.

"Véronique," she said. "Tell me all you can about her. And tell me how it came about that you could bear to leave her."

Véronique. Yes, Véronique was the central point. Not only had his life always revolved about her but his love for Marguerite had been caught up into his love for Véronique and had revolved about her too, giving her a nimbus of glory that she might have lacked had Marguerite never lived and been loved by him. But how could he explain this to Marguerite? He could not even tell her he had wanted to marry her. Loyalty to Marianne forbade it. . . . Besides, one did not say these things to nuns.

He told her all he could about Véronique, and then said simply, "I came home because Marianne wished it. Véronique was safe. For her I had done all I could. But I had not done all I could for Marianne."

"You've not quite saved her yet?" asked Marguerite.

He looked at her, startled.

"I was thinking, William," she said, "of the bitter frustrated woman Marianne was when your letter came asking her to marry you. That began her salvation, you know, for she'd always loved you. But marriage is a very long process, William, isn't it? You've not finished with each other yet." Her eyes were shining with amusement and William had the sense that she knew more than had ever been told her of the ups and downs of his life with Marianne. . . . But she had gone back again to the central point.

"That was the most unselfish act of your life, perhaps—leaving Véronique. But you'll not really be separated, William. 'My soul, there is a country.' A door opens into it from the Country of the Green Pastures and a door opens into it from the Island Country."

William, hands on knees, was silent. There were so many things that he wanted to say, without knowledge of how to say them, that he felt himself gaping for words like a landed fish for water. "When

Véronique was only a little thing," he said at last, making an effort, "she said to me, 'Maybe lots of different countries make up Paradise like lots of different countries make up the world. Maybe it's just the place where your spirit can go without your body.' "

"Did she?" said Marguerite. "She was a wise child, but she hadn't found her way then to the central country of all, the inner Paradise. But if she's just such another lover as her father's found it now. She's turned the key and gone in."

"And the key?" asked William.

"You know what it is as well as I do, William."

He nodded. It was a special kind of love. He'd made a blundering attempt to practise it when he'd paid the price for Marianne's happiness. He'd practised it as perfectly as a man can when he'd paid the price for Véronique's. He saw now that the man he'd been after that had not been quite the same fellow as before.

"Yes, she's paid," he said. "And—you're right—somehow or other we're together here. I don't miss her as I thought I would. I don't mind telling you, Marguerite, I thought life would be intolerable on this island without Véronique, and instead of that I'm enjoying myself to the top of my bent—feel like a boy again——"

He paused, scarlet in the face, breathing heavily, without the ghost of an idea as to how to say what he must say.

Marguerite said it for him. "And sometimes does she seem like a little girl again? The same little girl that I was once? That I still am? The child in us is always there, you know, and it's the best part of us, the winged part that travels furthest."

His jaw dropped and Marguerite laughed. "I've always felt very close to Véronique," she explained. "Almost, sometimes, as though we were the same child. You've been a good brother to me, William. There's always been a special bond between us, and of late years I've called the bond Marguerite-Véronique. Have you called it that too? You look startled, William. Have I said anything very odd?"

"No," said William. "You've only said it—all."

"The all is never said, William."

William looked at her out of the corner of his eye, thinking of the proposal of marriage in that letter of his that she had spoken of, and of the slip of the pen in it. No, it certainly was not. Would that it could be.

She got up abruptly. She had found out what she had longed to know—he was happy—all was well with Véronique—he was aware of the bond between them—when she had tried to reach him through the child she had been successful. Legitimate curiosity being now satisfied it was not fitting that a conversation of such extreme sensibility should be allowed to continue in the study of a nun. "I'm going to show you all that I can of the convent, William," she said. "It is of great historical interest and the Chapel is very lovely. Bring your watch. We must be careful of the time."

Damn the time, thought William, damn the historical interest of the convent, but he followed her obediently down the winding staircase to gaze benevolently at the Norman vaulting of the refectory and the beautiful carved corbels of the library. And the Chapel really impressed him. Its rare brave colours burning in the gloom expressed so very perfectly its atmosphere of worship and mystery and touched him deeply. This place, he realised, was at the heart of Marguerite's life. And it was a brave life. Standing in the Chapel he realised for the first time just how brave it was. Not easy, surely, to renounce all worldly certainty just to worship something which, when all was said and done, must remain until the end of life an impenetrable mystery.

"Has it been worth while?" he asked Marguerite in a hoarse whisper.

"Yes," she answered. "I doubt if we nuns are really as self-sacrificing as we must seem to be to you who live in the world. We don't give everything for nothing, you know. The mystery plays fair."

"Yes," said William. "I've found that out. It plays fair."

Marguerite opened the heavy west door and they stepped out into the sunshine on the rocky ledge outside. "This is where I climbed up when I was a child," she said.

"Bless my soul!" gasped William, and then gazed around him stunned by the beauty of what he saw. Over his head was the glorious statue of the Madonna, her tall figure battered but undaunted by centuries of storm, her hood pulled over her watching eyes to shield them from the sun, her strong arm carrying with superb ease the bare-headed unprotected child with hand raised in blessing for those who travelled homeward over the sea. And over her head was the window where at night shone the light that guided them, and from her feet the granite cliff fell away to La Baie des Petits Fleurs far down below, where Marguerite had gathered the shells that were now the playthings of Véronique's children. They could see the floor of the bay covered with silver sand, and the rocks draped with purple brown weed, and the anemone pools.

"It seemed to me a fairy place when I was a child," said Marguerite. "I saw the pebbles with fat smiling faces and the anemones with mad bright eyes. I wish I could see them that way now."

"You will," said William with conviction.

Then he looked far out across the sparkling sea, and there again were the three islands, the fairy castle, the old man who praised God and the bird poised for flight. He pointed them out to Marguerite. "I don't know why," he said, "but as I came along to-day they reminded me of the three of us, you and myself and Marianne."

"That was natural," said Marguerite. "The restless traveller, always journeying on to the fairy city on the horizon. And the lover in his gay green cloak who loves so many and comes in the end to worship God alone. And the one who has sought detachment from place and person for love of the winged state of prayer. Not long before I took my vows, William, I came out here to this ledge and thought of that trinity of search that is the same search, and I thought of the three of us, and I repeated to myself what you had said in your letter to me—'A three-fold cord shall not be broken.' You remember that letter you wrote me? I have it still, and I obeyed it."

"I know you did," said William. "I know, because taking everything by and large Marianne and I have had a good life together. We've been happy."

Thankfulness surged over Marguerite, followed by a quick painful humility. For she could not know what part she had had in that good life, and she acknowledged herself unworthy to have had any— but they had had it. "What's the time, William?" she ejaculated suddenly.

Oh, damn the time, thought William. He pulled out his turnip watch and looked at it. "It's up," he said hoarsely. "Forty minutes is just no time at all."

"It's been long enough for the re-twisting of the cord," said Marguerite. "Next time it must be Marianne who comes alone. Tell her that, please, William. Things don't seem quite right between us and they *must* be right. Give her my love and tell her to come and see me without you."

2

Meanwhile, at home at Le Paradis, Marianne was rearranging the parlour furniture for the fiftieth time and wishing to goodness she had not let William go to the convent without her. The fact of the matter was that just two days ago she had made a discovery that had filled her with such jealousy of Marguerite that she simply had not felt to-day that she could face her sister and be civil to her. And so, on an impulse, she had sent William off alone. But it had been a crazy impulse, for heaven only knew what those two were saying to each other in her absence. She did not trust these nuns. They were as sentimental as women are made. . . . And Marguerite had loved William.

That she had always known, but what she did not know, and what she felt now that she must discover, or have no peace of mind until the end of her days, was the exact truth about William's feelings for Marguerite. Long ago he had had a boy's love for Marguerite, yet he had chosen Marianne for his wife, and she had always told herself that she was secure in the possession of the love of his manhood. Had it been a false security? Certainly it was odd that she had had to assure herself of it so persistently. Was it the awful truth that something in William that she had been pursuing all her life long could never be hers because he had given it to another woman? To Marguerite?

She would not have been asking herself these tormenting questions if she had not found that letter in William's desk.

Two days ago she had sent William off for a walk that she might be alone to deal with some business correspondence regarding their investments, that she had refused to let him cope with himself lest he make a mess of it, and she had not been able to find a certain paper that she wanted. It might be in William's desk, she had thought, for he did sometimes carry off business papers to his own domain, even though he knew perfectly well that he lacked the intelligence to deal with them satisfactorily. No good waiting till he came back from his walk, she had said to herself, for the post would be gone by then. To-morrow's post would perhaps be in time but she hated delay in business matters. She must search his desk.

Yet even though the necessity for the search had been quite clear to her she had felt a little uncomfortable when she had rustled into the room that had once been Octavius's library and was now William's smoking room and private sanctum, and had sat down before the big old mahogany desk to rifle his papers. . . . He never opened a single drawer in her bedroom without her permission. . . . Well, she had said to herself, he shouldn't have gone off enjoying himself and left her alone to do all the work as usual. And how disgracefully untidy he was! They had only been in the house a few months and yet already his pigeon-holes were a welter of tangled string and crumpled envelopes and tobacco ash and absurd bits of pebbles picked up on the beach.

The paper she wanted had not been in the pigeon-holes but there had been a small locked cupboard in the centre of the desk and she had thought it might be there. William's keys, of course, had not been in his pocket, where they should have been, but dropped carelessly on the floor beside the desk, so she had had no difficulty in opening the cupboard.

But there had been no business papers in the little cupboard, only a collection of treasures such as a child would have made. What a sentimental old thing her husband was, she had thought. Would he never grow up? With a beating heart she had looked through his little hoard, wondering if it would contain anything to remind him of his wife and their love.

Her bitter disappointment, as she pulled out first the Maori knife that Captain O'Hara had given William, and then a huge packet of Véronique's letters, and then one of Véronique's baby curls folded in silver paper, and the curls of all the grandchildren, and then some absurd little oddments made for him by Jane Anne, and still nothing connected with herself, had been only a little eased by the recollection that she had never been the kind of woman who gave ridiculous little gifts for no reason whatever. Her gifts to William had always been sensible things—nightshirts and socks that she had made for him, and books of the type that she had hoped would give a higher tone to his mind. But still, she had been wounded. Surely he had kept one or two of her letters? They had been parted so seldom that she had written him very few, but he had been away from her sometimes on business trips, and then she had never failed to write him sheet upon sheet of instructions. Surely he had kept a few of them? And surely he had kept the little love letter she had sent him before their marriage, enclosing the bunch of primroses? Yes! Her exploring fingers had met the crackle of thin paper, and her eyes had been so dimmed by tears of delight that it had been quite a moment or two before she had realised that it was in Marguerite's handwriting.

She had wiped away her tears, controlled herself, and read it through with icy calm. It was nothing that she had not seen before—only that old letter that Marguerite had written to the two of them, announcing her decision to become a Roman Catholic and a nun. . . . But William had distinctly told her, long ago at the settlement, that he had lost it in the forest. She remembered the circumstance perfectly. But he hadn't lost it. He had lied to her, for he had treasured the letter all these years. . . . She had read it again and this time the last words of it had seemed to stand out from the paper as though the faded ink were not yet dry. "I picture you in every detail of your daily living and think of you surrounded by strange birds and beasts and butterflies that make a necklace of beauty about your day. I shall pray fervently for your happiness. Though you are so far away the bond between us is very strong and a threefold cord shall not be broken. You have my love and devotion always. I think of you day and night. Marguerite."

Those last words, Marianne had thought, as they burned them-selves deeply into her memory, had been addressed to William only.

And so now, two days later, as she re-arranged the parlour for the fiftieth time, she was beside herself. For she could see no way of arriving at the truth, and yet arrive at it she must, for uncertainty was a thing that she had never been able to endure—above all in this vital matter of her possession of William. Beside it her other intense pre-occupation, the remodelling of No. 3 Le Paradis, seemed now of little importance. Yet she would bend all her will to it this afternoon, she decided, just to keep herself upon an even keel.

For weeks now she had been labouring at the transformation of No. 3 into a home that from attic to cellar should have upon it the stamp of Marianne Ozanne, and it was an extraordinary thing, but she could not do it. In old days she had succeeded in making her bedroom the mirror of her personality, but that had been only one room, the whole house was another matter. And almost she felt that it was alive and fighting her. She imagined that she had done what she wanted with the farmhouse at the Green Pastures, and the house at the settlement, but they had been new houses. This one was very old—far older than its eighteenth-century columns and stucco front —as old as any house in Saint Pierre. At what age did old houses come alive and take to themselves this fighting power? It was not that the house could not take impressions, for the stamp of the convent had been strong upon it, and below that had been Sophie's gentle image, and below that, when she was trying to eradicate it, she had distinctly found the old sea captain from whom Octavius had bought the house upon his marriage, and beyond him again there were ghosts in the shadows of the house whose presence she resented quite intensely, but it took them as though they were the petals of a flower and incorporated them into the living whole that was itself. That was all she could hope to be, she was beginning to realise, one small and unimportant petal. Struggling with the obstinate house she was reminded of a remark of Captain O'Hara's, "There's much that goes to the makin' of a man or woman into somethin' better than a brute beast, but there's three things in chief, an' they're the places where life sets us down, an' the folk life knocks us up against, an'—not the things ye get but the things ye *don't* get." As regarded herself and places she had always imagined that it was she who did the making. But perhaps she had been wrong. Certainly this old house of Le Paradis was doing the making this time—it was turning her into a defeated woman. And fighting it was taking up so much of her time that she had not even begun yet to see about establishing social ascendancy in Island society. People had called and given her and William a warm welcome, and William had embarked already upon the beginnings of several pleasant friendships, but so absorbed with the house had she been that she had, she realised suddenly, taken a back seat.

It would not do. It simply would not do. She was not going to be beaten like this in her old age. She stood in the centre of the parlour and glared about her. What had induced her to buy those curtains? This wretched convent influence must have been upon her when she did it, for they were Madonna blue and far too plain. Blue was not her colour. It was Marguerite's. She would do away with them and get some others—green or cherry red. Sophie's escritoire hit her in the eye and she could almost see her mother's lovely fair head bent over her correspondence. The escritoire was in too prominent a position and she pushed it to a shadowed corner. It was not that she had not loved her mother, she said to herself defensively, but this was *her* house now, not Sophie's. Where had that old Dutch plate, hung below her sampler, come from? She remembered now. Several things that had belonged to the old sea captain had been bought by Octavius when he bought the house, and that was one of them. It was a thing of value, and she would find a place for it somewhere, but it must not hang there below her sampler, for it detracted attention from her exquisite embroidery. She lifted it down. For the time being she would put it in the cupboard where Sophie had been used to store surplus china—the one beside the fireplace.

But the cupboard was locked.

She rang the bell for Charlotte, who appeared instantly, her hands still floury from her cake-making, for she had learned years ago to answer Marianne's bells at once, lest worse befall.

"Charlotte, where is the key of this cupboard? And how did it come to be locked? I don't like locked cupboards in my house."

Charlotte looked vague. This vagueness was the only indication of old age that she gave but Marianne found it a most annoying one.

"I believe, M'dame, that I locked that cupboard when the orphans moved in. There was a cedarwood box of your mother's inside that I did not want the children to meddle with. Now what could I have done with the key?"

"Fetch me that box of keys from the hall drawer," commanded Marianne. "I expect we'll find another that fits."

They found one quite easily and the inside of the cupboard was revealed—quite empty except for the cedarwood box. Marianne pulled it out and opened it.

"There it is!" ejaculated Charlotte.

"Where is what?" demanded Marianne.

"Miss Marguerite's sampler. When she was having your sampler framed, M'dame, she said she wished she could find her own. But she could not remember what she had done with it when she left Le Paradis for the convent."

"It was not worth framing," snapped Marianne, and then, ashamed of having spoken so bitterly before a servant, she said gently, "Thank you, Charlotte. That will do. Now go back to your cake-making."

Alone again she sat down on the sofa, bright with its new honey-suckle chintz, and took out the contents of the cedarwood box. . . . Marguerite's absurd little sampler, with its stiff little potted trees hung with golden fruit, the border of the stars of Paradise and "Au nom de Dieu soit" worked in crooked scarlet cross-stitch, the wooden mouse with the sticking-plaster ears and the ribald expression that William had given Marguerite upon her twelfth birthday, and an exquisite carved Chinese necklace that she had never seen before. . . . Obviously three treasures of Marguerite's that she had not been able to bring herself to destroy when she left her home for the convent. How like Marguerite's sentimentality to cherish such rubbish, and how like her unpracticality to have no better idea as to what to do with it than shoving it away at the back of a dark cupboard! Marianne folded up the sampler again and dropped the silly little mouse on her lap as though it were burning her fingers. She had always hated that mouse, and the thought that even in her middle age Marguerite had cared so much for the creature that she had not been able to consign it to the flames was not pleasant. It was confirmation of the unwelcome idea that Marguerite had never got over her love for William.

Remained the necklace. Had that, too, been a present from William? She examined it carefully. It was a lovely thing, like a rosary, each separate bead an exquisite carving of some bird or beast or butterfly. "I picture you in every detail of your daily living and think of you surrounded by strange birds and beasts and butterflies that make a necklace of beauty about your day. You have my love and devotion always. I think of you day and night." Yes, he had sent this exquisite thing to Marguerite, and in that wicked deceitful letter of hers, pretending to be for the two of them but in reality addressed only to William, she had thanked him for it. All their lives, evidently, these two had been carrying on some sort of clandestine love affair behind her back. And Marguerite a nun! Her lifelong jealousy of that wicked woman had evidently not been unreasonable. But why had William married her? Why? Why? Why? Her small jewelled hands clutching the necklace and the mouse, she sat there rigid on the sofa, suffering as surely not even she had suffered yet. Her sampler hung there on the wall looking at her. "Au bruit de tes torrents, un abîme appelait un autre abîme: tous tes flots, toutes tes vagues ont passé sur moi." The noise of a great flood was in her ears, drawing nearer and nearer, and her soul shrank within her with fear, knowing that very soon she would be overwhelmed.

Not even a glimmering of self-control or common sense had returned to her when a happy stumping and a cheery carolling of song in the hall told her that William had returned—from Marguerite. Sentimental ballads were very popular just now, and William was very partial to them. The sea chanties he had carolled in his youth, "What shall we do with the Drunken Sailor?" and "Blow the Man Down", had been superseded in his affections by "Oft in the Stilly Night" and "O Red, Red Rose". There were times when Marianne felt that if she was given any more information (a semitone flat) about the cheerful hearts now broken, or alternatively (two semitones flat) about the melody that's sweetly played in tune, she would surely go demented. And the happier William was the louder and flatter he sang.

"As fair art thou, my bonnie lass," he boomed now, banging the front door shut,

> "So deep in luve am I;
> And I will luve thee still, my dear,
> Till a' the seas gang dry."

There was a pause while he flung his walking stick clattering into the hall stand.

> "Till a' the seas gang dry, my dear,
> And the rocks melt wi' the sun;
> I will luve thee still, my dear,
> While the sands o' life shall run."

He wiped his feet on the hall mat.

> "And fare thee well, my only luve,
> And fare thee well awhile!
> And I will come again, my luve,
> Though it were ten thousand mile."

And so he had. And Marianne herself had assisted him upon the journey.

Upon the last triumphant note the parlour door flew open and William entered upon his wife, his round red face beaming with the deep and satisfying happiness that his interview with Marguerite had brought him. Had it not been for the joy in his face perhaps Marianne might have been able to regain possession of her senses, but the joy finished her. She could scarcely breathe as William came stumping cheerily over to her, his attention caught by the treasures on her lap.

"Eh?" he ejaculated, fumbling for his glasses on their black satin ribbon. "What's that, Marianne? What have you found? Eh?"

He perched his glasses on his nose and verified them. "Bless my soul!" he ejaculated, completely off his guard. "Bless my soul, if it's not that mouse I made for Marguerite! And the necklace I sent her! And her funny little sampler, bless her! Where'd you find 'em, Marianne?"

She flung them on the sofa and got up and faced him. "Hidden away," she said. "Hidden—like all that has been between you and my sister all these years. Why did you marry me, William, when you loved her best all the while? Why? Why?"

She had come close to him and she was holding his arms, shaking him, watching his face with an agonised intentness. Caught in a relaxed mood, completely bemused by the summer sunshine, his long walk and the bliss of his afternoon, William's common sense also was at a low ebb. "Eh?" he ejaculated stupidly, and his red face went beetroot and his jaw dropped. Looking at him Marianne thought she had never seen such a picture of guilt.

"You've never loved me," she whispered. "You've been a liar always. You expressed such devotion to me in the letter you wrote to my father—that letter——" She paused, gasping. "That letter to my father—you lied—I know now——"

William too was gasping. "No lie," he said, "just a slip of the pen, my dear. And how the dickens did you find out, Marianne? Did I blab in my sleep? Must have. Always thought I should. For I never told a soul. I never told a living soul."

"What did you never tell a living soul?"

Her fingers were nipping into his arms like pincers and her little disfigured face, so near his own, terrified him by its fury. There was not a single grain of sense left in his head. He did not know what he was saying.

"That I mixed up your name and Marguerite's. That I asked your father for the wrong girl."

3

Marianne was alone in her four-poster, in the big bedroom looking towards the sea that had once been occupied by Sophie and Octavius. She was secure in her loneliness, for she had locked both the bedroom door and William's dressing-room door. The bed was made up in his dressing-room and he could sleep there if he came upstairs. He had not come upstairs yet though it was long after midnight. She supposed he was still in his little smoking room, to which he had gone when that long ghastly after-dinner explanation was at last over. That dinner! She did not know how they had got through it, keeping up a conversation before Charlotte's daughter, their parlourmaid, forcing food down their throats that they could not taste. She suspected that William had managed better than she had. But then he was used to deception. His performance at dinner had been just one more lie in the lifetime of deception that he had lived at her side. Had ever any woman in the whole course of the world been so shamefully deceived?

Oh, the shame of it! The shame of it! She could get no further than that. In this abysmal hour she seemed lying at the bottom of a great pit and the waters were closing over her head. "All thy waves and storms are gone over me." She was drowned in the depth of her shame. There was nothing left in her life at all—only her shame. Her faith that William had loved her and desired her, that she had been, was, always would be, first in his life, a faith that she saw now had existed always with an undercurrent of unacknowledged suspicion, was shattered, and because it had been the most important thing in her life it seemed that everything else had gone too. Everything had hinged upon her pride in having been loved and chosen by William. That pride had justified her self-confidence and been the mainspring of every effort that she had made, and now the breaking of it had turned every achievement of her life to dust and ashes. There was nothing left at all. It was useless for William to tell her, as he had told her over and over again during the long hours of their dreadful evening together, that he loved her, that she had been the making of him, that without her heaven knew what might have become of him out there in New Zealand, that he owed everything to her—success, the respect of friends and neighbours, his child, his grandchildren, everything—that she was his loving and beloved wife and that he shared with her the closest tie on earth. It was all no good. He had neither desired nor chosen her. Whatever love he might now feel for her had not been spontaneously given but deliberately manufactured. When she had thrown this at his head he had not denied it but had said—what that strange little girl of her dreams had also said to her inattentive ear—that there are more sorts of love than one, and that the love he had given to her was just as worth having as the love he had given to Marguerite. This she had denied, and was still denying, as she lay alone in the darkness, with passion. The sort of love that he had given her, deliberately created, not drawn irresistibly forth by the loveliness of the beloved, implied no merit in the object of it and was not worth having. No, she had nothing—nothing.

Another hour passed and she heard William come up to bed. He tried the door, with a gentleness that implied that he was wanting to comfort her, but when he found it locked he made no further effort to come to her, and presently she heard the bed in his dressing-room creaking. But the creaks were not followed by his usual cheerful snoring. . . . He was not sleeping. . . . At first she rejoiced cruelly in his sleeplessness. Then she forgot about him. The adoring husband of her imagination had never had any existence in actual fact. He did not exist. Nothing existed. Nothing . . . except the dark night.

But there *was* the dark night. Very slowly she became conscious of it, and then she found that she was hugging it to her in her misery, rejoicing in it as something given back to her out of the nothingness, a cloak to hide her in this hour of her humiliation. . . . Something. . . . For a long while the night was all that she had, and then suddenly she was aware of a bright beam of light that pierced through the drawn curtains of her four-poster and lay like a sword across the foot of her bed. . . . Moonlight. . . . She put out a hand and drew the curtains aside, and with a stunning sense of shock saw all the stars of heaven blazing in the night sky. Charlotte had forgotten to draw her window curtains that evening and when she undressed she had been too much absorbed in her misery to notice the omission. Now she lay and looked at the stars. They were unusually bright. The warm still day had ended with wind, and it was as though the wind had burnished the stars to flame. They were like New Zealand stars, like the stars that had shone down upon the parsonage garden at Wellington when Tai Haruru had taken her in his arms and told her that he loved her. . . . That he loved her. . . . That he loved the child in her, the lost, lonely, passionate changeling child. He had not wanted to love her, he had not tried to do it, his love had been called forth without his volition simply by the fact of what she was. As benignant as the moonlight, like a salve pouring over a wound, came the knowledge that Tai Haruru had loved her exactly as William had loved Marguerite. Unloved? Possessing nothing? She had been loved by two men, who had loved her quite differently but with equal selflessness; Tai Haruru just for the fact of what she was and William for what he could give her. She was rich. She was rich beyond measure, yet aware now that it was through no merit of her own. Something that Tai Haruru had said to her that night under the stars came back to her now. He had said that the breaking of her conviction that William utterly belonged to her would be the only thing that would ever really humble her. Perhaps he was right. She didn't know. She was too humiliated just at present to dare to think that the virtue of humility might one day be her own.

The next day she was speechless with exhaustion and seemed to have aged ten years in the night. William, also weary with heavily sagging shoulders, had the wisdom to leave her alone. After breakfast, a farce of a meal at which neither of them could eat anything, he went off for a walk, leaving the house silently, with no romantic burst of song, no cheery banging of the door, and she sat all the morning on the sofa, listless, her hands folded idly in her lap. She sat as once she had sat on the deck of the Orion, like a lost child. She had taken her hand off the tiller and was waiting patiently for something beyond herself to take her in charge.

But she was thinking none the less, thinking slowly, wearily, fumblingly, of the nature of William's love. She did not think about Tai Haruru's, for that had been quite simple—just the spontaneous turning of a creature to its mate. She saw that at last. They were the two halves of a whole, he and she, and one day they would come together again. "You'll not forget me though you live to be a hundred," he had said. Certainly she would not. The movement of her old woman's body through the years to its appointed end would now always consciously be accompanied by the running of the little child home through the dark wood. That was simple. It was William's love that she thought about, the slow difficult thing that he had built up through the years to save her.

Yes, he had saved her, and she acknowledged it. Perhaps he was right in saying that in material ways she had saved him, but spiritually it had been the other way round. What sort of woman would she have become if he had not made the mistake in that letter, if it had been Marguerite who had sailed out to New Zealand to marry him and she who had been left behind on the Island? She had a good look at the bitter woman she had been at the time when his letter came, and trembled. And what sort of woman would she have become if he had told her the truth at Wellington and packed her off home again? She dared not even take a look at that woman.

And yet last night she had been furious with William because he had deceived her. "William! William!" she cried, and the tears rolled down her cheeks. How desperately hard it must have been for him. What a price he must have paid for her salvation! That was what love was—a paying of the price. That was the key that she had always been feeling after and had never found, the key that would admit her to the new state of being that she had always longed for. Just paying the price. As simple as that, and yet supremely difficult, because though there might and must be symbolic action it was the state of mind that mattered. There had to be a childlike humble abandonment that was the most difficult thing to achieve in all the world. She had always wanted to set her own stamp upon life— heaven knew what it would cost her to give herself up to being the wax and not the seal. Yet how she had always unconsciously loved that great principle of childlikeness, dimly aware of it often as a presence standing by her. She had loved it in the poor, loved it above all in Nat, loved it in William. William! William! "Ton peuple sera mon peuple, et ton Dieu sera mon Dieu." From henceforth it would not be only to some earthly country that she would follow him but she would try to follow him into his spiritual country too, to that country where great kindness reigned, where the fire blazed on the hearth, the doors were flung wide open and men and women gave to each other all that they could. It would not be too difficult, surely. On that day when Dr. Ozanne and William had come to the Island she had quite easily run in through their open door, beside the swinging sign of the merry Green Dolphin, and found William standing before the fire. . . . How long the hours seemed now, with him out of the house. . . . She longed for him to come back from his walk that she might try and tell him something of what was in her heart, yet she knew that when he did come she would still be too shaken to say anything. They would struggle with their lunch in silence, as they had struggled with their breakfast.

She wondered where he was. Could he be with Marguerite? She had no bitter feelings towards Marguerite now, only an immense respect. For Marguerite, loving William, and believing her sister to have been chosen instead of herself, had not become the kind of woman Marianne would have become if left behind upon the Island. She had become—what she was. And not even now did she know that she had really been William's chosen. Marianne had assured herself of that fact yesterday. Over and over again yesterday William had assured her that he had never told Marguerite of the mistake that he had made. That he never would tell her. Marianne could rest assured of that, he had said over and over again—he would never tell Marguerite—he would never subject his wife to such a humiliation. He had never told a living soul.

But this morning, at breakfast, he had corrected that statement, flushing all over his bald head.

"I had forgotten, Marianne, that I told Tai Haruru. I must tell you that I told Tai Haruru."

Yesterday she would have been angry at this. To-day she did not mind. She was glad that there should be nothing at all about her that Tai Haruru did not know.

William came home to lunch and told her that he had been rambling over the common beyond the harbour, that lay in the opposite direction from the convent, and in proof of his statement he had brought her a comic little posy of sea-lavender and sea-holly. She thanked him and set it in water on the parlour mantelpiece, but as she had expected she was still too shaken to dare to begin to say anything. But William was immensely comforted by her gentleness. It gave him hope that when once she had recovered from the shock things would be normal between them again. How he had ever come to let the cat out of the bag he had not now the slightest idea. It had just somehow seemed to happen. The cat had taken sudden life to itself and simply jumped. That was the worst of hidden things. They always seemed to pop out in the end. He had spent a night of self-reproachful misery but now, with Marianne so gentle, he began to hope again. He remembered how, far away in the Country of the Green Pastures, he had wished that there might be truth between them at last. It would be a grand thing if it were to turn out that their love was now so strong and stout that it could stand it.

They spent a strange, silent, yet somehow not unhappy evening, William holding an open book before his nose and not reading a word, Marianne dropping knitting stitches for the first time in her life. She went to bed very early but this time she did not lock the doors for she knew that William had grasped the fact that she must be alone.

But desperately tired though she was she still could not sleep, for she was torn two ways by the thought of her sister. Marguerite did not know, she had never known, she would never know. Was it fair? asked one half of Marianne, the half that had taken its hand off the tiller and was waiting to be taken in charge, and the other half replied—what did it matter after all these years? Marguerite was happy. No need to tell her now. No need to face the humiliation of telling her. It would do no good to either of them. Marguerite, after all these years, would only be distressed, and Marianne shamed as it was not right a woman should be shamed. No. Ridiculous to tell her after all these years. William had not told her. If William had not told her why should she?

Because only she could tell her, said the other half of Marianne. William could not—he was bound by loyalty to his wife. She was bound by nothing but her own pride. If she could break her pride, if she could do this thing, paying this price for Marguerite's sake, would not this be love? The small symbolic action might be the first step, the fitting of the key into the lock of a door that should admit her to another country. Had she not always been seeking another country, a magic city on the horizon just out of her reach? Would she find that it had been close to her all the time—just a state of being? Had she been to the other side of the world and come back again only to find it in the place where she had started from?

But, no, she *could* not do it. How *could* she do it?

The argument went on all night, but six o'clock found her up and dressing herself, very quietly so as not to disturb William, with the astonished Charlotte already roused and sent out to fetch a carriage to take her out to the convent of Notre Dame du Castel. Seated before her mirror, removing her curl papers, she was astonished beyond measure to find herself embarked upon this madness. And how she was to arrange an interview with the busy Mother Superior of a convent at this hour of the morning she had no idea. She supposed matters would arrange themselves somehow. The fact was that she had been taken in charge and seemed to have got out of bed and roused Charlotte at this ridiculous hour without any volition of her own.

There was the carriage. Too late to turn back now.

She was the old Marianne as she put the finishing touches to her toilet with grim determination, arranging her hair becomingly beneath her fashionable high-crowned hat, disposing the folds of her green gown carefully and not forgetting her rings or her ear-rings or the cameo brooch at her throat. With just the same meticulous care had she dressed when the Maoris were sounding their war trumpet outside the settlement house, and in the same spirit had she demanded her corsets when death threatened her at the Pa. She had always taken a pride in dressing up for a fight. And fighting, she had realised long ago in Dr. Ozanne's waiting-room, is never over; only when you are old it narrows to the battlefield of your own body and soul. This, she realised, was probably only the first of a long series of skirmishes with her pride, a series that would end only with the humiliation of her death-bed. She took a clean handkerchief from her drawer, sprinkled eau-de-cologne upon it, shut her reticule with a determined snap and sallied forth.

4

Marguerite shut the door of the cottage behind her and stood for a moment thankfully drinking in the fresh morning air. There had been an epidemic of sickness in the village of Notre Dame and those nuns who were experienced in nursing had been busy this last week dealing with it. But yesterday two of them had themselves fallen ill, and Marguerite had taken the place of one in an all-night vigil at the bedside of a dying old woman. It had been a trying night in the stuffy cottage, and there was still a part of Marguerite, not yet subdued, that shrank from illness. She had been glad when she had been relieved. She was glad now to step out into the sunshine of the new day. Say what one would, death was a horrid discipline, and the abandonment of life seldom easy, even for the saints.

She glanced at her watch. She had twenty minutes before she must be in her place in the refectory for the nuns' silent frugal breakfast of brioches and coffee, that would be followed for her by a short sleep before the work and prayer of the day. The tide was out and she would take a turn across the sands in the hope that the fresh air would banish her headache.

Tall in her black draperies, walking not with the cloistered walk that William had dreaded to see but with the swinging easy grace that she had never lost, she crossed the shining sands towards Le Petit Aiguillon. The beloved old rock towered up there ahead of her. She would walk as far as her old friend and then turn again. It was a heavenly morning, bright and blue and clear, and the familiar feel of the firm rippled sand beneath her feet, the salt tang of the wind in her face, brought happiness flooding back to her again. For the poor woman in the cottage it would soon be over now. The bad things of life were very transitory. It was the good things, the ribbed sand, the wind blowing over the white-capped waves, the sunshine and the stars, that were so tough and durable.

She reached the rock and went round to the far side, where it was easiest to climb. Not that the Mother Superior of Notre Dame du Castel had any intention of climbing Le Petit Aiguillon, not at her age, but she was living again in memory that day of her childhood when three children had climbed to the top of it and a boy and a girl had kissed each other there. She had stood, she remembered, with her small feet in the footprints of the Abbess who had come from Notre Dame du Castel to meet and forgive her sister the Abbess of Marie Tape-Tout. What an absurd legend that was about the two Abbesses! It must have got confused with some fairy story or other, for the footprints on top of the rock were not those of grown women but of fairy creatures. If the two Abbesses were to appear before her now they would not be wearing black habits but garments of elfin green.

Well, it was time for the present Abbess of Notre Dame du Castel to be going home again. She was no fairy and she was uncommonly hungry. She rounded the rock at a brisk pace, eager for brioches and coffee, and came once more in sight of the bay.

And then she stood stock still, her heart missing a beat. Was she light-headed after her sleepless night? Was she dreaming?

For advancing towards her over the shining sand was a strange little figure clad all in elfin green. She held up her full green skirts in either hand, and she wore green shoes, and on her head was an absurd high-crowned green hat. Marguerite stood there watching in incredulous amazement, blinking in the dazzling early-morning sunshine, while before her astonished eyes the fairy creature turned to a somewhat fantastically dressed old lady, and the old lady to her sister Marianne.

"Well!" was all she could say, when the two of them stood together beneath Le Petit Aiguillon. "Well!" And then she burst into a peal of laughter.

Marianne faced her, clasping her reticule, very taut, very upright, very vexed with her sister. If it wasn't just like Marguerite to laugh! At this solemn hour—she laughed. She had always been a flippant creature but one would have expected the holy habit of religion to have modified her flippancy just a little. Hopeless. She was unchanged.

"I am sorry, Marianne," said Marguerite, and her lips were grave again, though her eyes still danced. "I was so astonished—you looked like a fairy."

"A *fairy*?" ejaculated Marianne indignantly. "I'd have you to know, Marguerite, that I am sixty-eight years of age."

"You don't look it, mon petit chou," said Marguerite. "Not in that hat." And then the laughter went out of her eyes as well, and her voice took on a sudden sharp edge of anxiety. "What is it, my dear? Are you in trouble? William? Is William ill?"

"In excellent health, thank you," said Marianne, and changed creature though she had thought she was for the life of her she could not keep her heart from twisting with jealousy in the same old way, or her voice from snapping with exactly the same old snap. "But there is something I wish to say to you, Marguerite. I had meant to call upon you at the convent but from the cliff I saw you down here in the bay and so I left the carriage and came to join you."

"Shall we go back to the convent, my dear?" asked Marguerite gently. She was all gravity now for she had recognised in the face of the woman before her the signs of mortal conflict.

"No," said Marianne firmly. "What I have to tell you is not easy to tell and I should like to get it over. We can sit down together on this rock."

They sat down and Marguerite thrust away her fatigue, her headache, her longing for food and sleep, and became utterly and prayerfully concentrated upon the woman at her side. "I am listening," she said, and she neither moved nor spoke while Marianne told her story.

Marianne did not spare the girl whom she had been. She began at the beginning and told Marguerite how she had fought her for William, and how she had deliberately separated them on board the Orion. She painted that old Marianne in black and truthful colours before she went on to speak of William, of their meeting at Wellington, the misery of the early days of their married life and of his subsequent goodness to her that had turned disaster into happiness. She did not spare the New Zealand Marianne either, neither the woman whose self-will at the settlement had nearly brought a horrible death upon them all, nor the woman whose ambition had nearly wrecked her daughter's happiness, nor the woman who only a few months ago had not scrupled to separate William and Véronique in order that her pride might not be humbled. During the last two days and nights all her rags of self-deception had been stripped from her and she had seen herself exactly as she was, and this woman she now showed pitilessly to Marguerite. Then she came to what had happened two days ago and slowly and deliberately told Marguerite of William's slip of the pen in his letter to their father. "It was you he wanted," she said. "You were his love, his chosen mate. And you still are. I am only the woman he married because he had to. To marry me was the only way to save me from disaster and he knew that. It was you he wanted. You are his love."

She said this over and over again, impressing it upon herself as well as upon Marguerite, in a quite expressionless voice. Only the stony rigidity of her upright little figure upon the rock, her hands locked together so tightly on her lap that they seemed all bone, betrayed her to the woman who sat beside her as a creature all but drowned in the depths of her humiliation.

"It was odd," said Marianne, "that William should have let it out by chance in that casual sort of way. He reproaches himself terribly that he did so. . . . Yet perhaps, Marguerite, of all the things that he has ever done for me that little bit of chance carelessness will turn out to have been of the most benefit."

"Perhaps there is less chance in life than we realise," said Marguerite softly. She was holding on with both hands to the rock, for the singing joy that was seeping through every part of her was making her body feel light and airy as blown sea spray, light as the body of a young girl running to her lover's arms in the morning of the world. Her soul too was running, faster and faster, across a blue meadow where the stars grew like flowers upon either side, to some unimaginable meeting place beyond the sun and moon. With a great effort she steadied herself and stopped running. Not yet could this young girl give way to her joy, for she had to rescue this poor old lady beside her from the depths of a too great shame. Old lady? But she, Marguerite, was an old lady too, an old nun in a black habit. "I'm old," she said to herself incredulously, "I'm nearly as old as Marianne. And a comic spectacle we must be, too, sitting side by side on this rock, Marianne in that absurd green fairy hat and me in this ridiculous white wimple, having all this to-do about a portly old gentleman we were both in love with forty-six years ago. . . ." And she began to laugh again.

"Really, Marguerite," said Marianne severely, "you are the most astonishing woman I ever met. I expected your reproaches—I deserve them—but what you can find to laugh at in our situation I do *not* know."

Marguerite stopped laughing and put her hand on her sister's. "Forgive me," she said. "I always thought the phrase 'drunk with joy' such a silly one. But that's how I feel, Marianne—just drunk. And not only with joy. With admiration too."

"For William?"

"For you."

"Don't be ridiculous, Marguerite!" said Marianne testily.

"I'm not being ridiculous. When a humble soul humbles herself she has not got far to fall but when a proud soul humbles herself it's like jumping off the top of a Cathedral tower. I don't know how you had the courage to do it, Marianne. But you were always brave. And always a traveller. We've all come a long way, you and William and I, but you've made the longest journey of the three. It's my belief, Marianne, that of the three of us you are the strongest and the best."

"Don't be ridiculous, Marguerite!" repeated Marianne. And then she turned to her sister, her resolute old face crumpling beneath the absurd green hat like that of a child who is going to cry. "I can never forgive myself," she said, "but if you can forgive me it will be very sweet."

"There isn't any question of forgiveness," said Marguerite. "If I

once was unhappy because of what you did the joy of to-day out-
weighs it a hundredfold."

Beneath the shadow of Le Petit Aiguillon they kissed.

5

Half an hour later Marguerite stood watching the tiny green fairylike figure of her sister bobbing away into the distance. They had
talked of many things after that kiss, of William and Véronique and
their parents, and of the childhood's years that now in old age
seemed more vivid to both of them than any of the years that lay
between. And Marguerite too had asked for forgiveness for that
bitterness that had tinged her thoughts of her sister for years past,
and for perhaps a too great intimacy in her talk with William the
other day, for which she now reproached herself. "Then reproach
yourself no longer," Marianne had retorted to this. "Surely, now,
between the three of us, there cannot be too great an intimacy. I am
going home at once to tell William that you know you have always
been his love."

"One of them," had corrected Marguerite.

"Yes, one of them," Marianne had agreed. "He loves me. He is
quite crazy about Véronique. He is an idiotically doting grandfather.
Never was there such a lover as William. Good-bye, Marguerite. I
have never loved you so well. You'd better go straight home and get
breakfast and go to sleep."

And now she was disappearing into the distance and Marguerite
was watching her. Now the little green figure had disappeared
altogether among the tamarisk trees of the village.

Go straight home? It was good advice, as well as her duty. Yet
when she left Le Petit Aiguillon it was towards La Baie des Petits
Fleurs that her feet took her, for this singing happiness that possessed her was the happiness that children feel, and she was back
again in her childhood. Quickly she crossed the golden sand and
went in between the two great rocks that guarded the entrance to the
little bay. She had visited it many times since her childhood but
always burdened with adult preoccupations, never in this child-like
mood. What had happened to the little bay this morning? It was
peopled with fairy creatures whom she could not see but of whom
she was as vividly aware as she was aware of the sunshine and the
fresh air. She stood entranced, listening and watching. The sand
was silver here, not golden as it was in the larger bay, and was
studded with opal-tinted jewel-like pebbles and rock-pools full of
frilly anemones. And all the pebbles had fat smiling faces and the

anemones had mad bright eyes above their frills. And the little
shell-beach beyond was carpeted with shells as a wood is carpeted
with flowers in springtime, and all the shells had mouths and all of
them were singing, their myriad tiny voices making a music that one
could hear and not hear, like the sound of bells that the wind is
always catching away. She caught her breath in delight. When the
gates of fairyland had clanged shut behind her in her childhood she
did not know that they would open again when she was old. She
looked up and a seagull was flying slowly backwards and forwards,
seeming to gather all the light of the place with his shining wings and
to trail it in long threads of silver after him, as though weaving a
pattern in the air over her head, like one of those canopies powdered
with stars that one sees in old pictures over the heads of Queens.
She looked up at him, loving him. He was a symbol of prayer, of
the prayer that went on day and night in the great convent that was
towering up above her, the convent that was home.

6

Marianne, too, as she drove home through the perfect summer
morning, was absurdly happy. The catharsis of the last few days had
left her feeling dead tired, yet it was a pleasant, tranquil sort of
fatigue, the kind of tiredness that a traveller feels who is home at last
after a long and wearisome journey. And deep inside her she was
not tired at all but younger and stronger than she had ever been,
nourished as never before. "Comme le cerf soupire après l'eau des
fontaines, ainsi mon âme soupire après toi O mon Dieu," she had
embroidered on her sampler long ago. "Mon âme a soif de Dieu,
du Dieu vivant: quand entrerai-je et me présenterai-je devant
la face de Dieu?" In those days she had not been able to understand
her own insatiable hunger for experience. She understood it now.
It had just been the old age-long hunger for le Dieu vivant. In her
childhood she had pictured le Dieu vivant as an old man with a long
white beard so distantly removed from her that it was really not
possible to take an overwhelming interest in him, but now she took
the phrase as being descriptive of an indescribable something from
which the soul breathed in her life when she was home at last, home
in that country on the other side of the locked door. She gave no
name to that country. Others might call it what they liked but for
herself she preferred to leave nameless a thing so far beyond her
power to comprehend. Yet the analogy of the thirsty hart was
precious to her. She saw the trembling creature, exhausted by the
storms of the long day of travel, coming at last in the cool of the

evening to the waterbrook flowing beneath the green fern. Standing in the lush green grass of that country, sucking in the life-giving water, he was herself.

Yet he was not at the source of the water, and perhaps it was like her arrogance to dare to call this happiness of hers a coming home. Humbly she acknowledged that there was no permanence about it. By this time next week, such was her selfishness and pride, she might find herself once more a changeling, strayed again from home, with the door to unlock all over again. Yet once you had been home, surely it was easier to get home again, and each fresh fight to get back to the waterbrook would bring one nearer to its source, and that final coming home that would be the satisfaction of every longing and the healing of every pain.

Meanwhile the small recurrent shadow home-comings of this life were the best things in it, the physical returns as well as the spiritual ones. Would she ever forget the delight of coming back to the Island with William? Later she had shadowed their joy with her jealousy and striving but for a few hours it had been perfect happiness. And so it would be again.

"I'll keep those blue curtains," she thought, falling suddenly to mundane affairs again. Yes, she'd keep them, and the old Dutch plate too. What an idiot she had been to try and make Le Paradis wholly her own. It was of the essence of home that it should hold out its arms to diverse personalities and gather them together into a harmonious whole. A house stamped with one personality only was surely more like the cell of a prisoner condemned to solitary confinement than a home. Yes, they should all live together at Le Paradis now, herself and William, Marguerite and Charlotte, the little convent orphans, Sophie and Octavius, the old sea captain, and all the other happy ghosts whose presence in the shadows of her home she had so much resented.

She leaned back against the cushions of the little carriage and looked about her. How lovely the Island was. For years she had been too busy to have much attention to spare for beauty, but now she felt carefree as a child again and had a child's clear sight. The islands lying on the blue sea stabbed her with their beauty, and the scent of the escallonia flowers, drifting to her now and again on the wind, moved her to just the same sudden ecstatic surprise that she had known in her childhood when her "moments" had fallen upon her like snowflakes out of a clear sky. The whole drive seemed to her heightened awareness a succession of these lovely moments. She could have cried aloud with delight at the sight of the windmills on their green knolls and the old church towers showing above the green trees, at the sight of the dun-coloured cattle browsing in the fresh green grass and the small streams flowing swiftly through the water-lanes down to the sea. And then they reached Saint Pierre and were driving through sunlit streets whose familiarity was so veiled by a new enchantment that the cobbles might all have turned to gold and the walls to mother of pearl. And then they had reached Le Paradis and the front door stood wide open between the hydrangeas, with the panelled hall cool and welcoming beyond, and she was running up the steps to find William.

He was in the parlour, striding up and down in a great state of agitation, and she went straight into his arms like a child.

"I am sorry I am so late for breakfast," she said. "I went out to the convent to see Marguerite and to tell her about the mistake you made in your letter."

"Eh?" asked William stupidly.

"I have been with Marguerite, William. I told her it was she whom you had really wanted to marry. I told her the whole story."

"You—told—Marguerite?" ejaculated William.

"Yes. You don't mind, William, do you?"

"*Mind?*"

She was a little scared, for he was holding her so tightly and bellowing so loudly over her head. She peeped up at him under the brim of her absurd tall green hat. No, he was not angry. His face was shining like the rising sun.

"Now there's absolute truth between the three of us, William. And as perfect love as there can be on this earth. And forgiveness. For you have forgiven me, haven't you, William?"

"Forgiven you?" bellowed William.

Again she peeped up at him and saw his tawny eyes blazing with love . . . for her.

She had got him at last. The triumph of it! Oh, the triumph of it! Now at last they were going to experience together the fairyland of mutual love that she had always longed for. Oh, the triumph of it!

"And I'll never be proud again, William," she whispered brokenly yet proudly in his arms. "Never, never again."

There was a derisive squawk from the birdcage hanging in the window.

"Oh my!" ejaculated Old Nick in mocking tones. And then, very doubtfully indeed, "Oh my?"

OTHER BESTSELLING NOVELS BY ELIZABETH GOUDGE

All these books are available at your bookshop or newsagent, or can be ordered direct from the publisher. Just tick the titles you want and fill in the form below. It should be appreciated that from time to time titles do go temporarily out of print—but this *is* only temporary.

....

CORONET BOOKS, Cash Sales Department, Kernick Industrial Estate, Penryn, Cornwall.

Please send cheque or postal order, no currency, and allow 5p per book (4p per book on orders of five copies and over) to cover the cost of postage and packing in U.K., 5p per copy overseas.

Name ....

Address ....

....

....